MUST LOVE MURDER: COZY MYSTERY COLLECTION WITH RECIPES

By

LEENA CLOVER

Copyright © Leena Clover, Author 2020

All rights reserved. No part of this publication may be reproduced, stored in a retrieval system, or transmitted, in any form, or by any means (electronic, mechanical, photocopying, recording or otherwise) without the prior written permission of the author.

This book is a work of fiction. Names, characters, places, organizations and incidents are either products of the author's imagination or used fictitiously. Any resemblance to actual events, places, organizations or persons, living or dead, is entirely coincidental.

First Published December 30, 2020

Author's Note

Cupcakes and Celebrities – Pelican Cove Cozy Mystery Series Book 2

By Leena Clover

- Chapter 1
- Chapter 2
- Chapter 3
- Chapter 4
- Chapter 5
- Chapter 6
- Chapter 7
- Chapter 8
- Chapter 9
- Chapter 10
- Chapter 11
- Chapter 12
- Chapter 13
- Chapter 14
- Chapter 15
- Chapter 16
- Chapter 17
- Chapter 18
- Chapter 19
- Chapter 20
- Chapter 21
- Chapter 22
- Epilogue

Sprinkles and Skeletons – Pelican Cove Cozy Mystery Series Book 4

By Leena Clover

- Chapter 1
- Chapter 2
- Chapter 3
- Chapter 4
- Chapter 5
- Chapter 6
- Chapter 7
- Chapter 8
- Chapter 9
- Chapter 10
- Chapter 11
- Chapter 12
- Chapter 13
- Chapter 14
- Chapter 15
- Chapter 16
- Chapter 17
- Chapter 18
- Chapter 19
- Chapter 20
- Chapter 21
- Chapter 22
- Epilogue

Waffles and Weekends – Pelican Cove Cozy Mystery Series Book 5

By Leena Clover

- Chapter 1
- Chapter 2
- Chapter 3

- Chapter 4
- Chapter 5
- Chapter 6
- Chapter 7
- Chapter 8
- Chapter 9
- Chapter 10
- Chapter 11
- Chapter 12
- Chapter 13
- Chapter 14
- Chapter 15
- Chapter 16
- Chapter 17
- Chapter 18
- Chapter 19
- Chapter 20
- Epilogue

Raspberry Chocolate Murder – Dolphin Bay Cozy Mystery Series Book 1

By Leena Clover

- Chapter 1
- Chapter 2
- Chapter 3
- Chapter 4
- Chapter 5
- Chapter 6
- Chapter 7
- Chapter 8
- Chapter 9

Chapter 10

Chapter 11

Chapter 12

Chapter 13

Chapter 14

Chapter 15

Chapter 16

Chapter 17

Chapter 18

Chapter 19

Chapter 20

Chapter 21

Chapter 22

Chapter 23

Chapter 24

Chapter 25

Chapter 26

Chapter 27

Epilogue

A Pocket Full of Pie - A Meera Patel Mystery

By Leena Clover

Cast of Characters

Chapter 1

Chapter 2

Chapter 3

Chapter 4

Chapter 5

Chapter 6

Chapter 7

Chapter 8

Chapter 9
Chapter 10
Chapter 11
Chapter 12
Chapter 13
Chapter 14
Chapter 15
Chapter 16
Chapter 17
Chapter 18
Chapter 19
Chapter 20
Chapter 21
Chapter 22
Chapter 23
Chapter 24
Chapter 25
Chapter 26
Chapter 27
Chapter 28
Chapter 29
Glossary
RECIPE - Black Bean Burger
RECIPE - Mutton Rogan Josh Curry
RECIPE – Cheesy Jalapeno eggs
RECIPE – Orange Tequila Grilled Chicken
RECIPE - Cheese Pakora Fritters
RECIPE - Anna's Avocado Toast
RECIPE – Naughty Mama Cocktail
RECIPE – Strawberry Grilled Cheese Recipe
Join my Newsletter

Author's Note

Thank you for picking up this special five book anthology. It's finally time to say goodbye to 2020. As we usher in 2021, let us hope that lockdowns, quarantines and social distancing become a thing of the past.

What a year it has been, fraught with unforeseen challenges that tested each of us. Those of us that were fortunate enough to survive definitely emerged stronger. Times like these remind us of what matters most. I could not have endured the past year without the love and support of family, friends and my dear readers.

Love makes us laugh and cry and jump through hoops. And it certainly makes the world go around.

I have handpicked some of my favorite stories that are set against a backdrop of love. Hope you enjoy this cozy collection and tell your friends about it.

Happy New Year!

To a new decade – may it bring us closer

Cupcakes and Celebrities – Pelican Cove Cozy Mystery Series Book 2

By Leena Clover

Chapter 1

Jenny King fidgeted with her organza dress, trying to ignore the stream of sweat trickling down her back. Why had she ever agreed to be a bridesmaid, she moaned to herself. Could you technically be a bridesmaid if you were in your forties? The peach dress she was wearing was supposed to be pretty, but Jenny looked and felt like a giant pumpkin. The May morning was unseasonably hot, the temperatures already soaring above 95 degrees.

"Stop that," Heather muttered, jabbing an elbow in her side.

Heather Morse was one of Jenny's new friends, a young woman she had met when she came to live in the town of Pelican Cove a few months ago. Jenny was at a loose end after her twenty year old marriage ended suddenly. Her aunt Star had summoned her to the remote Virginia island where she lived.

The past few months had been a blur. Jenny had fallen in love with Pelican Cove and the diverse group of women she befriended had made her feel right at home.

"This dress is too tight for me," Jenny complained, giving Heather a nasty look. "I should never have agreed to do this."

"I owe you one," Heather sighed. "Let's just get through the ceremony. You can change into something more comfortable as soon as they say 'I do'."

Jenny looked around at her luxurious surroundings. Normally, she wouldn't have been able to set foot in the Pelican Cove Country Club. You either needed plenty of money to get in, or a certain bloodline. Jenny had neither. The Country Club catered to the Eastern Shore elite and only the top families of Virginia's Eastern Shore were members.

"She does look gorgeous," Jenny said, spying the radiant bride who stood a few feet away from her.

Crystal Mars was the most sought after star in Hollywood since she had signed a popular reality TV show. She had a couple of movie deals on the table too. The wedding was supposed to be hush-hush and on the QT, as they said in the business. Crystal was adamant about having a beach wedding with at least five bridesmaids. She had remembered her distant cousin Heather lived on some remote island on the Eastern Shore of Virginia. One look at the Pelican Cove Country Club had sealed the deal for her. A lavish wedding weekend had been planned, with most wedding related activities squeezed into four days.

"That dress!" Heather said enviously. "It's Vera Wang, you know."

Jenny admitted Crystal had been more than generous with her bridesmaids. The dress

Jenny wore was a simple sheath of the finest silk, made by some pricey designer. Jenny couldn't find fault with it, other than the fact that it wasn't her size. But that wasn't Crystal's fault. Jenny was filling in for a girl at the last moment. She was just happy to be part of the wedding party.

"Everything looks beautiful," Jenny nodded, looking around her.

Crystal had chosen white and peach roses for her wedding. The lush green grounds of the country club gently sloped toward a white sandy beach. The turquoise blue waves of the Atlantic Ocean pounded against the shore. A wedding arch covered with dozens of tiny roses in white and peach provided a stunning backdrop for the impending ceremony. The path leading up to the arch was laid with a carpet strewn with petals.

"Shouldn't he be here by now?" Heather spoke loudly.

Crystal turned to glare at her.

A shout went up in the small group just then and someone pointed to the sky. Jenny shaded her eyes with her hands and squinted up.

"What's going on, Heather?"

She could barely make out a small plane in the bright blue sky.

"You don't know?" Heather panted. "That's the groom."

"What?" Jenny asked in confusion.

She had been trying hard to hold her tongue. The bride had walked down the aisle five minutes ago but the groom was nowhere in sight. Jenny had attributed it to some kind of Hollywood quirk.

There was a smattering of applause as something dropped from the plane. The small speck grew in size as it hurtled toward the ground. A cheer went up as a parachute unfurled over the figure.

"That's the groom?" Jenny asked, her jaw hanging open.

"That's the groom alright," Heather said dreamily. "That's Wayne Newman."

She grabbed Jenny's arm and forced her to look up at the sky.

The next few seconds were a blur. A second body dropped out of the plane and plunged toward the ground. It struck the first body and continued racing down. With bated breath, the crowd watched for the second parachute to open. Something shot up in the sky but no canopy opened. Before anyone realized what was happening, the figure crashed into the four tier wedding cake.

Hardly anyone paid attention to the second big thump. Jenny looked up to see a man dressed in a tuxedo rolling on the ground, trying to untangle himself from a colorful parachute.

A scream pierced the air jarring Jenny's senses. It wasn't the only one. A buzz went up as people swore around her.

"She's dead!" someone said unnecessarily, pointing at the body sprawled across the remains of the lavish wedding cake.

It had cost five figures, Jenny remembered Heather telling her. She leaned closer to peer at the unfortunate soul who had just got a free ride to the other world. The girl looked beautiful even in death. Golden blond hair covered her head like a halo. Her deep blue eyes, now lifeless, stared up at the sky. Her svelte body and long limbs indicated she was well over six feet tall. Jenny's eyes popped out when she noticed a large sapphire nestled between the girl's breasts. Her eyes grew larger when she noticed what the girl was wearing.

"Isn't that…" Heather mumbled next to her.

"It's a wedding dress alright," Jenny said grimly. "The exact same dress Crystal Mars is wearing."

"But isn't that couture? I thought they didn't make two of anything?"

Sirens sounded in the distance, and reality set in slowly as people came out of shock. The groom raced up to the body on the ground, still attached to his parachute. His arm hung at an awkward angle and one side of his face was caked with a mixture of grass and blood.

"Bella!" he exclaimed, running a hand through the girl's hair.

"Don't touch her," Jenny sprang forward to caution him. "The police are on their way."

"What was Bella doing on the plane with you?" Crystal Mars asked.

She held the groom's other arm and her face was white with shock.

"I didn't know she was on the plane," the groom wailed.

People around them looked up then, probably trying to spot the plane. It was nowhere to be seen.

"Make way, please," a familiar voice called out and Jenny felt a surge of relief.

Adam Hopkins, the sheriff of Pelican Cove, emerged through the crowd, followed by a bunch of deputies and law enforcement types. He took one look at the prone body and started clearing a perimeter around it. Crime scene tape went up and a couple of policemen stood on guard.

"Why don't you folks head over to the club house?" Adam ordered. "We will want to take a statement from each of you."

The crowd slowly made way to a pavilion at the end of the grounds. Finally, Adam spared a glance at Jenny.

"Hello Jenny," he said softly. "I didn't expect to see you here."

"Crystal's my cousin," Heather spoke up. "A distant cousin."

"I heard about that," Adam told her.

"One of the bridesmaids pulled out due to a last minute gig," Heather explained. "There was a spot in the wedding party. Crystal wanted Jenny to be part of it."

"Another one of your fans?" Adam asked Jenny, cracking a smile.

"Jenny made cupcakes for the wedding shower," Heather nodded vigorously. "Crystal can't stop raving about them."

"So what happened here? Did you ladies see anything?"

"It was all a blur," Jenny spoke up. "Literally. It all went down in a couple of minutes. One minute we were watching the groom arrive in his parachute, and the next we were staring at that poor girl."

"Do you know who she is?" Adam asked Heather. "Is she one of your relations?"

"Oh no," Heather shook her head. "She wasn't in the wedding party. And I don't think she was on the guest list either."

"Looks like someone decided to crash the wedding," Adam said, scratching his head. "I wonder why."

"Crystal and the groom both seemed to know her," Jenny supplied. "They called her Bella."

"Bella Darling was the girl Crystal replaced on the show," Heather said, snapping her fingers. "She had the lead role first but then they pulled her out and Crystal got the part."

"Bella Darling?" Adam said doubtfully. "That's actually a name?"

"It could be her professional name," Heather explained, "but it's a name nevertheless."

"Just like Crystal Mars, I guess," Jenny shrugged.

"I need to go talk to all the guests," Adam said. "I'll see you ladies later."

He barely leaned on his cane as he walked away.

"Is Adam getting better?" Heather asked Jenny. "He's hardly using his cane now."

"It depends," Jenny said, not wanting to speak on Adam's behalf.

Adam was dealing with a war wound which hadn't quite healed yet. He was in extensive physical therapy and Jenny had seen him popping pain pills quite often. He hobbled around with a stick but lately his condition seemed to be improving.

"Has he asked you out yet?" Heather giggled.

Adam Hopkins and Jenny King had been at odds with each other since they met. But neither could deny the spark between them. Jenny's inquisitive nature did not help. When her aunt had been unjustly accused of a tourist's murder earlier that spring, Jenny had done all she could to help her out. Adam saw it as interfering in police work and he made his opinion clear.

"He doesn't see me that way."

"Are you kidding? Adam Hopkins has the hots for you. We can all see it clearly."

"I don't," Jenny said stoutly.

She secretly had a big crush on Adam but she wasn't ready to admit it yet, not even to the Magnolias, the group of friends who met for tea everyday at the Boardwalk Café.

"I guess we won't be able to sample the wedding brunch now," Heather grumbled. "It's been ages since I had the Eggs Benedict at the Country Club."

"For shame, Heather," Jenny said. "Show some respect."

"We didn't know her," Heather objected. "Why do all these people drop dead in our town?"

Jenny had no answer for that.

Chapter 2

Jenny walked to the café the next morning, taking deep breaths of the fresh morning air. The sun was rising over the Atlantic, painting the sky in tones of pink and orange. She sat on her favorite bench overlooking the ocean and watched the sun come up. This was her special time of the day, a few moments to herself before the day caught up with her. The Boardwalk Café was getting busier as the tourist season ramped up.

"Good Morning!" Petunia Clark greeted her with a fresh cup of coffee. "How are you, Jenny?"

Petunia's double chins wobbled as she spoke. She had been running the Boardwalk Café for the past twenty five years.

Jenny barely had time to gobble a blueberry muffin before the breakfast rush started. Her favorite customer was first in line.

"Blueberry muffin for you, Captain Charlie?" she asked an old sailor who came to the café for breakfast and lunch.

"What's the world coming to?" Captain Charlie clucked. "I heard a young girl died at that fancy club yesterday."

Jenny spent some time telling Captain Charlie about the poor dead girl.

"Sounds like some funny business," Captain Charlie said, narrowing his eyes at Jenny. "Are you going to look into it?"

"Oh no! I have enough to do here. See you at lunch, Captain Charlie. I'm making crab salad again."

Jenny flipped her special pancakes, baked trays of muffins and poured endless cups of coffee for the next few hours.

She glanced up at a wall clock when she heard Heather's voice. Heather peeped into the kitchen just then, looking for Jenny.

"Ready for a break?" she smiled.

Jenny had begun to look forward to these mid-morning breaks with her friends. The group of ladies got together at the Boardwalk Café and exchanged gossip and pleasantries over coffee and muffins. Jenny heard the clacking of knitting needles and knew Heather's grandma Betty Sue had accompanied her as usual.

Heather and Betty Sue Morse ran the Bayview Inn on the island. Betty Sue was the fourth generation descendant of James Morse, the first owner and inhabitant of the island. It had been called Morse Isle then.

James Morse of New England travelled south with his wife Caroline and his three children in 1837. He bought the island for $125 and named it Morse Isle. He built a house for his family on a large tract of land. Fishing provided him with a livelihood, so did floating wrecks. He sent for a friend or two from up north. They came and settled on the island with their families. They in turn invited their friends. Morse Isle soon became a thriving community.

Being a barrier island, it took a battering in the great storm of 1962. Half the island was submerged forever. Most of that land had belonged to the Morse family. A new town emerged in the aftermath of the storm and it was named Pelican Cove.

Betty Sue was a formidable woman in her seventies and her word was law.

"Take a break now, Jenny dear," Petunia ordered.

The ladies sat at their usual table out on the deck overlooking the Atlantic Ocean.

"Where is your aunt today?" Betty Sue asked, pulling some lavender wool over her needles.

Rebecca King or Star, Jenny's aunt, was an artist. Now that the days were warmer, Star spent most of her time painting outdoors, her easel set up on one of the numerous beaches or bluffs across the town.

"I'm coming, Betty Sue," a voice sounded as Star came up the stairs from the beach.

She was dressed in a loose, bright colored kaftan that had been hacked off mid thigh. A couple of paintbrushes poked out of her pockets.

"Stop harassing my niece."

"Who said I was harassing her?" Betty Sue took the bait.

"Where's Molly?" Jenny asked, pulling out a chair for her aunt.

Molly Henderson worked at the local library and was Heather's age. She was another of Jenny's new friends.

Petunia came out with a tray loaded with a fresh pot of coffee and a plate piled high with muffins.

Jenny sniffed at her sweaty armpits and longed for a cold shower.

"I never knew it could get so hot in Virginia."

"Wait till July," Star said, "or August. You'll have sweat pouring down your eyes."

"Settle down, girls," Petunia twittered. "I want to hear about what happened at the club."

"Me too," Molly, a tall lanky girl with thick Coke-bottle glasses said as she came out on the deck through the café, slightly out of breath. "You've done it again, Jenny."

"What have I done?" Jenny asked, stuffing a piece of muffin in her mouth.

She savored the flavor of the organic vanilla extract she used. She liked to use plenty of berries so they just burst forth in every bite.

"You have all the fun," Molly said petulantly. "I hear you were present when that girl fell from the sky."

"Are you out of your mind, Molly?" Jenny growled. "A poor young girl lost her life. Where's the fun in that?"

"I guess it wasn't fun for the girl," Molly agreed. "So does anyone know what happened?"

"It looked like she jumped down," Heather told the girls. "Now why should she do that? Do you think it was suicide?"

"She was dressed in a wedding gown, wasn't she?" Betty Sue Morse said, pausing her knitting for a moment. "I say she wanted to ruin the wedding."

"Oh yes," Star said, sipping her coffee. "What about the wedding? I suppose those two didn't get married after all."

"Crystal was too worked up," Heather pronounced. "They could have been married inside privately, but she said she wanted to hold off on the wedding."

"What a colossal waste," Petunia declared. "I can't imagine spending an arm and a leg on something and not going ahead with it. Why! I would have fainted from the shock."

"This is just chump change for those people," Heather said. "Crystal makes a lot of money. A lot…"

Adam Hopkins walked up to the café, looking formidable in his uniform.

"Ladies!" he greeted them.

Jenny got up to see what he wanted.

"I have to go the mainland," he told her. "I thought I might get some lunch to go. I will stop at some rest area on the way and eat in my car."

"How about some grilled chicken salad? It's a new recipe I am trying out for the summer. I would like to get your opinion on it."

"Why not?" Adam shrugged. "Anything you make is delicious, Jenny."

"It's on the house," Jenny smiled up at him. "But you will have to give me your honest feedback."

"When do I not do that?" Adam laughed.

"So you'll tell me tonight?"

"I might not be able to make it to the beach."

Jenny lived with Star in a beach facing house. It was one of the few beaches in Pelican Cove offering a flat stretch of land without any rocks or dunes. Adam Hopkins had a habit of going there for a walk. He had run into Jenny there a few times. She had been out to stretch her legs after dinner. It had become a habit and now they met on the beach by an unspoken arrangement.

"You have a doctor's appointment in the city?" Jenny asked with concern.

"Not this time. I'm going there on official business."

Jenny nodded in understanding.

"This is about that poor girl, isn't it? Has anyone come asking for her? Does she have any family?"

"I can't tell you that, Jenny. Wait till the grapevine catches up though. You'll know soon enough."

"We were talking about her just now. Do you think it was suicide? Or an accident?"

Adam gave her a withering look.

"You're not going to be mixed up in any funny business again, are you?"

Jenny shook her head.

"I've learned my lesson, Adam."

She had narrowly escaped an attempt on her life earlier that year when a killer tried to get rid of her.

"I want to believe you," Adam said, his blue eyes twinkling with mischief. "But something tells me you'll find a way to butt in."

"Are you saying I butt in on purpose?" Jenny asked, her hands on her hips. "I don't even know these people. And we are getting too busy here at the café. I think I will have to give up my mid-morning break soon."

"What about the extra help Petunia was going to hire?"

"We signed a couple of kids on. They start after Memorial Day."

"Is Nick going to be here for the summer?" Adam asked after Jenny's son.

"I haven't talked to him all week," Jenny wailed. "The twins might know more than me."

Adam's twin girls had met Jenny's son and they had hit it off.

"You think the twins call me every day?" Adam sighed. "Sometimes I feel like they barely tolerate me."

"You are pretty cool as a Dad," Jenny consoled him. "They are just busy, I guess."

"I hope at least some of that time is devoted to studying," Adam snorted. "They might look all cherubic but they are a handful."

"You don't suspect foul play, do you?" Jenny burst out.

"There you go again," Adam sighed. "Stay out of this one, Jenny. Please."

His voice softened as he leaned toward her.

"I don't want to be mad at you."

"Then don't be," Jenny said, suddenly feeling out of breath.

"I have a job to do. Calling out people who interfere is part of it."

"Alright, alright. Message received. Drive safely, okay?"

Adam Hopkins took the bag Jenny handed him. It felt suitably heavy and Adam felt his mouth water as he thought about any extra treats Jenny may have packed for him.

Jenny went out to the deck after Adam left, unaware of the smile that lit up her face.

"When are you going out with him?" Molly asked.

"Come on, Molly," Jenny sighed. "Not that again."

"Adam Hopkins needs a kick in his pants," Molly Sue declared.

Star and Petunia agreed with her.

"I don't see what he's waiting for," Star said. "Jason's going to whisk you away one of these days."

"Speaking of…" Petunia said, tipping her head toward the boardwalk.

An attractive black haired man dressed in a suit walked up the steps of the café.

"Hey Jenny!" he called out. "Good Morning, ladies! What's the latest in Pelican Cove today?"

"What do you think this is, boy?" Betty Sue scowled. "Gossip Central?"

Jason gave her a cheeky smile indicating what he thought. Jason Stone was a lawyer, the only lawyer in Pelican Cove. He was one of the Pioneers, the oldest families on the island. He had moved back to the small town after getting tired of the rat race in the city. He had known Jenny years ago when she spent summers on the island as a teenager. He was as impressed with her now as he had been then. Unlike Adam, he made it very clear how much he liked Jenny.

"Aren't you in court today?" Jenny asked with surprise.

"Just getting back from the mainland," Jason told them. "One of my cases got pushed. I thought I might have an early lunch before I go back to the office. I've got plenty of work piled up on my desk."

"Jenny will take care of you, dear," Petunia said meekly.

Jason pulled Jenny up to her feet and put an arm around her shoulders. He whispered something in her ear and almost dragged her back toward the kitchen.

"That's a man who means business," Molly said dreamily. "He just takes charge of the situation, doesn't he?"

"Chris should take a page out of his book," Heather said cattily.

Heather had been dating Chris Williams since a long time. Their families approved of the match and were waiting for Chris to pop the question.

"Summer is going to be interesting this year," Betty Sue cackled, gathering her skeins of yarn. "Time to go, Heather."

The little group broke up, everyone going back to their jobs. Petunia walked into the kitchen to find Jason curling a strand of Jenny's hair in his fingers.

"But why not?" Jason was saying. "You gotta eat."

"Only if you let me pay," Jenny said.

"No way, Jenny. I asked you first. And why do you get so hung up on who's paying?"

Jenny liked Jason Stone a lot. He was smart, good looking, gentle and considerate. He wasn't given to sudden bursts of temper like Adam. But unlike Adam, he didn't make her blood boil.

Chapter 3

Jenny hummed a tune to herself as she chopped celery for her crab salad. Chris Williams had come over with five pounds of jumbo lump crab meat from freshly caught Chesapeake crabs.

"People are loving the chocolate cupcakes," Petunia chortled as she came in with an empty tray.

"Should we make a double batch?"

"Not yet," Petunia said. "Let's keep the supply shorter than the demand. That's a great way to spread the word without spending anything extra."

"That's smart, Petunia," Jenny said, her admiration clear in her voice.

"I've been running this café for twenty five years, girl. I picked up a trick or two."

Jenny added chopped celery and sweet peppers to the crab meat. A generous helping of Old Bay seasoning went in along with fresh lemon juice.

"What's happening out there?" she asked curiously as she started mixing the salad gently.

A faint buzz was coming from the café. Heather came in, followed by another girl. Jenny and Petunia couldn't hide their surprise.

"Hello Heather."

"You remember Crystal?"

Jenny gazed a bit enviously at the tall, slim girl who had come in with Heather. Blonde and blue eyed, she was a real life Barbie doll. Almost six feet tall, her gentle curves were outlined in the perfectly cut summer dress she was wearing. Must be a pricey designer label, Jenny guessed correctly. Crystal Mars glowed like a bright star shining in a midnight blue sky.

"What brings you here?" Jenny asked.

She had never imagined a celebrity like Crystal would actually come to the Boardwalk Café.

"Can we talk?" Crystal asked, looking around her.

The expression in her eyes warred with the smile on her lips. Crystal Mars was clearly out of her element.

Jenny looked at Petunia, silently asking her permission. The lunch rush was about to begin.

"Can you fill orders while you talk?"

Jenny quirked her eyebrow at Crystal.

"Do you mind if I make sandwiches while you talk?"

Crystal shrugged.

"This is a busy time for us," Jenny explained.

"That should be fine," Heather said hurriedly.

She pulled out a couple of chairs and pushed Crystal down in one.

"So tell me," Jenny said, scooping crab salad onto a slice of bread. "What brings you here?"

She added sliced tomato and lettuce and pressed it down with another slice. Placing a toothpick through the center, Jenny placed the sandwich on a tray. They would be flying off the shelves in the next half hour.

"You know what happened yesterday," Crystal said, rubbing the bridge of her nose.

Jenny realized Crystal was barely holding it together. There was a hint of green below her eyes indicating she hadn't slept well.

"You mean the girl?" Jenny asked, trying to be delicate.

"The dead girl," Crystal nodded, not wasting any effort on being subtle. "Bella Darling. I want you to find out what happened to her."

"We have a good police force here in Pelican Cove," Jenny said. "They will get to the bottom of this soon."

"The police don't work for me," Crystal dismissed. "I want my own man on the job."

Jenny let the sexist remark slide.

"I'm not a qualified investigator or anything. You can hire a skilled person for this. You are not short on resources."

"I can pay you double your usual fees."

Jenny opened her mouth to protest.

"Triple. Okay, I will give you a ten thousand dollar bonus on top of your expenses."

Jenny rubbed the charm hanging around her neck on a chain. Her son had given her a gold charm for her birthday every year since he turned eight. She had worn them on a bracelet for several years. She had lately strung them on a gold chain that hung around her neck. The charms lay close to her heart and made her feel closer to her son. She had fallen into the habit of rubbing the charms when she was nervous or disturbed.

"It's not about money, Crystal. Tourist season is coming up. Petunia needs me here at the café."

Jenny belatedly remembered her promise to Adam. He would not be happy to see her meddling in the investigation.

"Do it at your convenience," Crystal pleaded. "I won't be keeping tabs on you."

"Why come to me at all?" Jenny argued.

"Heather told me about that killer you caught last month."

"I was just trying to help my aunt out. She was the prime suspect."

"So help me out this time. Please…"

"What exactly do you expect from me?" Jenny asked.

Petunia came in and Jenny passed the tray full of crab salad sandwiches over to her.

"Wayne is going to be in trouble. I want you to help him, just like you helped your aunt."

Jenny tried to frame a diplomatic reply.

"My aunt was innocent. I knew that 100%. I can't say the same about your husband. I barely know him."

"He's not my husband yet," Crystal hastened to correct her. "We could have been married yesterday. The judge offered to do it after the police finished taking everyone's statement. But I called it off."

"You don't trust him?"

Crystal gave her a pained look.

"I don't know what came over me yesterday. I made a mistake. I should have gone ahead with the ceremony."

"Can't you do it now?"

Crystal massaged her forehead with her fingers. She looked at Heather and sighed dramatically.

"Wayne won't do it now," Heather explained.

"He's sulking!" Crystal cried.

She probably thought she had dibs on being drama queen, Jenny thought to herself.

"He's acting up!" Crystal wailed again. "He's mad at me because I called off the wedding."

"So you're doing this to appease him?"

"I want to show him I care. Hiring you will help me prove that."

"So you want me to fake this?" Jenny asked, outraged.

"I don't care what you do," Crystal dismissed. "Meet a few people, ask a few questions, do your thing."

"What about the truth though?" Jenny asked.

"I don't care. I just want Wayne to stop whining and say yes so we can tie the knot."

"I don't think I can help you," Jenny said.

She was seething inside. She burst out again, unable to stay quiet.

"So you don't care if your husband had a hand in killing that poor girl?"

"Don't be silly," Crystal said, standing up. "Bella Darling was a two bit actress trying to make it big. Wayne wouldn't give her time of day. He hardly knew her."

"But what if he is tied up in all this?" Jenny asked.

"Then he is. Just get him to sign on the dotted line."

"That's up to him. I can't convince him to marry you."

"You just play Nancy Drew. Leave the rest to me."

"There won't be any play acting, Crystal. If I do this, it's going to be as real as it gets. I am going to ask tough questions. Any new information I learn will be shared with the police. I'm going to be looking for the truth. So if either you or Wayne or anyone close to you is involved, I won't be able to help you."

"I'm getting a migraine," Crystal moaned. "Why are you making this so difficult?"

Jenny poured a fresh cup of coffee and handed it to Crystal.

"Can I have one of those cupcakes?" Crystal asked hopefully. "It's not like I have to fit into a wedding dress now."

"I think she just fell off the plane," Heather said, taking pity on Crystal.

Crystal began to nod but Heather cut her off.

"But what was she doing there in the first place? You say Wayne doesn't know her?"

"He knew her name," Jenny said, remembering what the groom had said as he stared at the dead girl.

"That could be from a photo," Crystal said lightly.

She stood up and stared into Jenny's eyes.

"Will you do it?"

"As long as you're ready for the truth, Crystal."

"Whatever. It was probably just a publicity stunt gone wrong."

Crystal snapped her fingers at Heather and walked out, tottering on her four inch heels.

"Of course she wears Louboutins," Jenny muttered to herself.

She didn't get a spare minute for the next couple of hours. Petunia waddled in after the last customer had been served.

"We made record business today. We are going to need a lot more food during the season."

"That's great news for everyone, right?" Jenny asked.

More sandwiches meant more seafood and produce ordered from the local markets and more bread from the bakery. A rising tide lifted all boats, Jenny realized as she noticed the peeling paint in the kitchen. They all needed the boost the tourist season would bring them.

"What was Miss Hollywood doing here?" Petunia asked.

"She wants me to find out what happened to that girl," Jenny explained. "Actually, she just wanted me to pretend to find out what happened. But I told her that's not how I worked."

"Good for you," Petunia cheered. "So are you going to be working on a new mystery?"

"It may be nothing. We don't know how the girl died."

"You will have to talk to the police, huh?"

"I guess so."

Jenny walked to the police station on her way back home. The woman at the desk perked up when she spotted the plate of cupcakes Jenny was carrying.

"You can go right in," she waved, nodding toward a small office.

Adam Hopkins was fiddling with a pill bottle when Jenny went in. She took the bottle from his hand, unscrewed the cap and handed it over.

"Feeling poorly?"

Adam shrugged.

"Nothing new," he said, popping a couple of pills in his mouth.

He took a long sip of water and gave Jenny a questioning glance.

"Dare I ask what brings you here?"

Jenny winced. She could guess what Adam's reaction was going to be.

"Crystal Mars came over. She asked for my help."

"What kind of help?" Adam snapped.

"She wants me to find out what happened to the girl."

"You are doing it again, aren't you?" Adam said, incensed. "I thought we talked about this. Stay out of police business, Jenny."

"I am just going to talk to people, ask a few questions."

"Your few questions almost got you killed. Do you remember that?"

"We don't even know how that poor girl died. Maybe she committed suicide or fell off."

"What interest does Crystal Mars have in all this?"

"Maybe she's just being nice," Jenny said evasively.

She didn't want to tell Adam about the Crystal – Wayne tiff. He would probably laugh at that.

"I don't think this is a good idea."

"I'm not asking your permission," Jenny bristled. She could lose her temper too. "I want to know what you have found out so far."

"How many times have I told you this, Jenny? I can't reveal anything about an ongoing investigation."

"Come on Adam, tell me something. Did she have a heart attack or something? What happened to Bella Darling?"

Adam slammed a fist on his desk.

"Go away, Jenny."

Someone came in with a file and handed it to Adam.

"The autopsy report just came in. You'll want to see this."

Adam opened the file and flipped through it rapidly. His eyes widened as he read something. He looked up at Jenny and shook his head.

"God help you, Jenny. You have stepped into a big pile of crap."

Chapter 4

"Have you talked to Wayne yet?" Heather asked Jenny the next morning. "Crystal called a few minutes ago."

The Magnolias were assembled on the deck of the Boardwalk Café, enjoying a quick break. Jenny held up her hand as she chewed on her muffin.

"I skipped breakfast today, we are that busy. I'm going to faint if I don't eat anything first."

"I'm going to hold you responsible if anything happens to my Jenny," Star warned Heather. "Why are you sucking up to that Crystal anyway? I thought she was just a distant cousin."

"Barely one," Betty Sue agreed, pulling out a ball of turquoise wool from her knitting bag. "On her mother's side," she said meaningfully, eager to establish Crystal Mars was not related to the Morse family.

"Is she keeping tabs on me already?" Jenny asked spitefully. "I thought she was going to give me a free hand."

"Wayne's talking about leaving. He has a gig in Nashville tomorrow."

Wayne Newman was a country music star. He had met Crystal at some awards function and they had hit it off. They had managed to keep their affair secret from the press.

"He'll have to come back," Jenny shrugged.

"Yooo-hooo…" a familiar voice trilled from the boardwalk.

A collective groan went up among the girls as a familiar figure bustled up the stairs, dragging someone along with her.

"How are you, Barb?" Star asked, trying to be polite.

Betty Sue was rolling her eyes in disdain. She didn't get along with Barb Norton.

"It's a beautiful day, isn't it?" Barb panted. "I have news. Big news."

She tipped her head at the young woman accompanying her. A short, brown haired woman dressed in a formal suit stood next to her. She gave the girls a finger wave and her lips stretched into a smile.

"This is Mandy James, our new consultant. She's going to help us win that Prettiest Town tag."

"Huh?" Betty Sue Morse asked, putting her knitting needles down.

There was very little that made her stop knitting. Heather looked at her grandma in surprise.

"I'm the Chairman of the Prettiest Town Contest Committee," Barb Norton explained. "Don't you remember? We discussed this in the town hall meeting last November."

Star, Petunia and Betty Sue looked at each other.

"That's still happening?" Star asked.

"What do you mean?" Barb sighed. "Of course it is! We filed our application in December. We made the first cut. I corresponded with them while I was in Florida."

Barb Norton spent her winters in Florida with her daughter. She never gave up an opportunity to bring it up.

"What's the first cut?" Heather asked.

"We are small enough," Barb explained. "The contest is for the Prettiest Small Town. Many of the applicants were disqualified because of population density."

"Go on…" Petunia said impatiently.

"Round 2 was a questionnaire," Barb continued. "They wanted to know about our layout, the kind of businesses we had etc. I filled that out."

"Where did you get the information?" Betty Sue asked.

"I keep a lot of records," Barb told her. "I managed. Anyhow, we cleared that step too and Pelican Cove is a finalist in the contest."

"Sounds good, Barb," Jenny said eagerly.

Barb put a hand on her hip and glared at Betty Sue.

"You might show a bit more enthusiasm. Pelican Cove could be the Prettiest Small Town in the country. It's a big honor."

"We are all ecstatic, dear," Petunia consoled. "What happens now? How do we win this prize?"

"The judging committee will visit all the finalists. They will be here, in Pelican Cove, for the final inspection. We have a month to get ready."

"Get ready for what?"

"For the judging of course. We need to put our best foot forward, look our best. That's where Mandy comes in."

"What's she going to do?" Betty Sue asked imperiously.

"Mandy's going to make sure we look our best," Barb explained. "The town hired her as an image consultant. She's going to spruce up Main Street."

"We don't need to pay big bucks for that," Betty Sue spat.

"Mandy has hands-on experience," Barb explained. "She helped a small Kentucky town win Greenest Town. And she helped another town in Colorado win Most Pet

Friendly Town."

"Is that true?" Betty Sue asked.

Mandy nodded and preened a bit. "It's what I do."

"So what, you're going to tell us which building needs a lick of paint?" Star asked.

"At the very least," Mandy nodded. "I make a basic study of the conditions, do a gap analysis and come up with an action plan for what needs to be done. Then I coordinate and make it happen."

"Is a month going to be enough time?" Heather asked.

"It's a challenge alright," Mandy James told them. "Most towns hire me well in advance. I need at least three months to execute a systematic overhaul. I will have to put you on fast track."

"Sounds like a lot of mumbo jumbo to me," Betty Sue growled.

"I will make Pelican Cove sparkle like new. You will hardly recognize it."

"We like our town just the way it is, thank you very much," Star said.

"No one's asking your opinion," Barb snapped. "As the committee chairman, I make all the decisions. And I am giving Mandy carte blanche."

"Where is she going to stay?" Heather asked a practical question.

"At your inn, of course," Barb shot back. "You already have her reservation."

"We do?"

"It's under E. James," Mandy spoke up. "Edith is my middle name."

"Do you use it often?" Jenny piped up.

"I'm flying under the radar, you see," Mandy explained. "There's a town in New Hampshire and another in Idaho who want to sign me on. But Pelican Cove looks the best on paper. I think you guys are the strongest contender."

"We are not the richest town though," Betty Sue said, narrowing her eyes.

"I found that out myself," Mandy laughed. "Money isn't everything. I like to win."

"You're pretty confident," Star muttered.

"I have a proven track record," Mandy nodded. "I'm pretty sure I can help you win. Plus, I have never lived on an island."

"Hardly that," Star shot her down. "The new bridge takes you across in ten minutes."

The new bridge Star mentioned had been built in 1970. Star had crossed that bridge to come to Pelican Cove. She had never left.

"Aren't you going to welcome Mandy?" Barb said, widening her eyes meaningfully.

The girls hesitated for a second and then chorused together.

"Can I get you anything, dear?" Petunia asked finally.

"I hope you are as excited about this contest as Barb. She has assured me everyone in Pelican Cove will pitch in and do their bit. It's a group effort, you see. We are only as strong as our weakest link. You don't want to be that link."

Mandy went on like that for five minutes. The women on the deck began losing their patience. Barb pulled Mandy's arm and gave her a silent nod.

"Let's go. The seafood market is next."

"What's Barb got us into this time?" Betty Sue complained as soon as the women went out of sight. "Prettiest Town indeed."

"Do you deny Pelican Cove is pretty?" Jenny asked her.

"I know that, Jenny, but that's not the kind of pretty Miss Main Street is talking about. You'll see."

"It's all going to be a big waste of time," Star agreed, getting up to leave. "I gotta go now. Have a painting due tomorrow."

That set the others off.

"Where's Molly today?" Jenny wondered.

"One of her coworkers is home sick," Heather explained. "She had to pitch in and watch the front desk."

"What did that Hopkins boy say about the girl?" Betty Sue asked.

"The same thing he always says. He can't tell me anything about an ongoing case."

"Did he tell you how Bella died?"

"She died from the fall," Jenny said. "The question is, how or why did she fall. And what was she doing up there in that plane anyway."

"Is that all you have to find out?"

"That's just the beginning, Heather. You remember what she was wearing? I have a strong hunch Crystal is going to be involved in some way."

"You're being biased," Heather protested. "You haven't even talked to her yet."

"The way I see it," Jenny said, "the girl Bella either jumped herself or she was pushed. If she jumped herself, why didn't her chute open? You remember she had one attached to her back. So she either didn't open it or couldn't open it. Or she opened it and something went wrong."

"Stop!" Betty Sue cried. "You're making my head spin."

"Do you think she sneaked onto that plane?" Heather asked.

"I'm going to find out," Jenny said grimly. "What about you, Heather? Are you going to be my wing woman like last time? Or are you going to stick by Crystal?"

"I'm not taking any sides," Heather rushed to clarify. "I can go along with you if you need me, Jenny."

"What about Chris?" Jenny asked. "What does he feel about all this?"

Chris had been Heather's date for the wedding. Although he hadn't had a front row seat to the tragedy, he had been present in the crowd when the girl dropped from the sky.

"Chris is not too crazy about these Hollywood types. He thinks it's all a big publicity stunt."

Jenny shuddered at the thought.

"That's a possible motive, I guess."

"He wants me to stay away from Crystal."

"You might want to listen to that boy, Heather," Betty Sue ordained. "He's saying something smart for a change."

Betty Sue Morse had grown old waiting for Heather to tie the knot with Chris. She was losing her patience with them. Chris had been experiencing her disapproval quite a lot lately.

"Crystal doesn't know anyone here," Heather said stoutly. "I'm just trying to show some support."

"Be careful about that, Heather," Jenny warned. "You don't want to be aiding a criminal."

"You were right there when Bella dropped from the sky," Heather objected. "Crystal was standing four feet away from us. She's innocent."

"Surely you're not that naïve?" Jenny asked. "She could have hired someone for the job."

"Prove it," Heather said. "If Crystal had a hand in this, I will be the first to call the police."

Jenny felt relieved. Heather was so dazzled by the glamour surrounding Crystal Mars, Jenny wondered if she had gone over to the dark side.

Jenny went into the kitchen and started grilling chicken for her salad. Adam had given her two thumbs up for her new salad recipe. Now she hoped the residents of Pelican Cove felt the same. She was trying to come up with a lighter menu for the summer, one that didn't use mayo so it wouldn't spoil in the sun.

"You are wanted outside," Petunia told her.

Adam was standing at the counter, trying to choose between a cookie and a chocolate cupcake.

"How are you, Jenny?" he asked. "Got any more of that new chicken salad?"

"I'm mixing a fresh batch," Jenny told him. "Any more news on Bella?"

"Some, but nothing I can tell you yet."

"Did she have any family?"

Adam gave in.

"Her next of kin will be arriving tomorrow."

"See, that wasn't so difficult."

"Did you meet Mandy James?" he asked.

"Barb Norton brought her around earlier. How do you know her?"

"The police station is situated in a heritage building. I guess we lend a hand in making Pelican Cove pretty."

"She's going to have some pointers for you too then? This will be fun."

Adam rolled his eyes.

"We are too busy already. We don't have time for this frippery."

"Try telling that to Barb. She's in it to win it."

They giggled like naughty high school kids. Jenny felt right at home, trading town gossip with Adam. She liked this fun side of him. It wouldn't be too long before he was back breathing fire at her though.

Chapter 5

Jenny put her feet up on a chair after another tiring day at the café. She couldn't wait to get some extra help. She just hoped the kids Petunia had hired would have good work ethics and a strong back.

"You can go on home if you want, Jenny," Petunia said. "I can clean up around here."

Jenny swallowed the crab salad sandwich she was eating. She was so tired she could barely taste anything.

"I have to go to the country club to meet Crystal's mother."

"Why didn't you ask her to come here?"

"I have been summoned, Petunia. The queen wants me to go to her castle."

"Hmmm…"

"I should be happy I get to go to the country club I guess."

"Is it really that fancy?" Petunia asked.

Jenny nodded.

Heather stuck her head in through the kitchen door.

"Ready to go, Jenny?" she chirped.

"What is Crystal's mother like?" Jenny asked Heather as they drove to the club.

"I haven't talked to her much. She's a bit intimidating."

"How do you know Crystal so well but don't know her mother much?"

"I barely knew Crystal," Heather began. "I met her at college in my senior year. That's when we found out we were cousins. She dropped out after her first semester though."

"So she's your age?"

"Oh no! She's three or four years younger than me."

"So she's in her thirties too?"

"It's a big secret. She's supposed to be 25."

Jenny thought of the ravishing Crystal Mars, her unlined face and toned body.

"She can carry it off easily."

"It means a lot to these Hollywood types, I guess," Heather mused. "Crystal's flipping out because she turned thirty last month."

"Is that why she's so eager to get hitched to this Wayne guy?"

"Crystal says she was supposed to have at least one marriage under her belt by thirty."

Jenny shook her head, marveling at how people in certain walks of life functioned.

"It's a different life, huh?"

They reached the club soon after and Heather directed her to a small bungalow at one end. A maid wearing the club's uniform ushered them inside to a sun room.

Jenny spotted the resemblance as soon as she spied the woman seated in an armchair. She didn't have Crystal's height but Jenny felt the same blue eyes trained on her.

"Thank you for coming," the woman said primly. "You are the girl my Crystal has been talking about?"

"I was in the wedding party, Mrs. Mars," Jenny reminded her. "I catered your daughter's wedding shower a few days ago."

"Ah, yes, that was you."

Heather had been cowering behind Jenny all this time. The woman ignored her.

"I'm glad you got in touch, Mrs. Mars," Jenny said. "I wanted to talk to you anyway."

"You can call me Kathy," the woman said. "Now tell me when you are going to wrap up all this nonsense?"

Jenny was speechless.

"Err, may I ask what you are referring to?"

"This nonsense about Bella Darling, of course. Just do whatever Crystal wants you to do so we can head home to L.A."

"You live in Los Angeles too?"

"Of course I do. I am Crystal's manager. She has a very tight schedule. I have to make sure she gets her workouts in, eats according to her diet plan, sleeps on time. Hell, I even make sure she poops on time."

"You must know most of the people she meets then?"

Kathy shrugged. Her expression told Jenny she was stating the obvious.

"Did you know Bella Darling?"

"I did not. Neither did Crystal."

"But she recognized Bella right away when she dropped down on the wedding cake."

"She must have seen her in a magazine or something."

"Bella was quite famous then?"

"She was in some big scandal a few months ago. That's a different kind of famous."

Kathy's mouth had twisted in a sneer as she spoke about Bella.

"So you didn't know her personally but you knew of her?"

"Well, if you want to nitpick…"

"I'm just trying to get a clear picture here."

"What was she doing here, ruining my daughter's wedding? That's what I want to know."

"We'll find that out eventually," Jenny assured her. "What about Wayne, your son-in-law?"

Kathy looked triumphant when she heard Wayne's name.

"Isn't he hot? Crystal couldn't have picked a better man."

"Wayne Newman is hot alright," Heather spoke up.

Kathy ignored her again.

"Did Wayne know Bella?" Jenny asked.

"I'm sure he didn't."

"But she was on the plane with him. Surely he must have known that."

"I think she was a stowaway," Kathy declared. "Wayne had no idea she was up there with him."

"Did he tell you that?"

"He didn't have to. I trust him."

"So what do you think happened?" Jenny pressed.

"She tried to pull a stunt and it failed. Sounds like the work of a deranged fan."

"You are saying there was a third person up there with them?"

"Someone had to have pushed her."

"You really believe that, Mrs. Mars?"

Kathy folded her hands and stared back at Jenny.

"Yes. Now when are you going to wrap this up? You can tell Crystal some fan pushed the girl. End of story."

"That's not how this works," Jenny said, rubbing a gold horseshoe that hung on her chain. "I will talk to all the people involved, try to match their stories. Then I will try to find out what really happened."

"That's what the police do."

"Right…"

"I thought you were playing along for the fat check Crystal promised you."

"Jenny's not like that," Heather said indignantly. "Why would you think that?"

"Is there anything you want to add, Kathy?" Jenny asked. "Do you suspect anyone?"

"Not really," Kathy said. "Like I said, I barely knew the girl."

"You said you didn't know her at all before," Jenny pointed out. "Which is it really?"

"I didn't know her, okay?" Kathy snapped suddenly. "You are such a pest."

She clapped her hands and called out to the maid.

"Show these people out," she commanded.

Jenny turned back to look at the older woman as they left the room. She was staring back at them, her eyes narrowed and full of fury.

"That was weird," Heather said as they got into the car.

"What's she have against you?" Jenny asked her. "I'm sorry, Heather. I didn't know she was going to act like this."

"She's just throwing her weight around. She never gets to be in the limelight, you know. She's backstage all the time."

"That doesn't excuse her rude behavior."

"She wanted a big Hollywood wedding for Crystal. She hates that she had to come to Pelican Cove. She holds me responsible."

"Surely that was Crystal's decision?"

Heather nodded.

"The wedding is hush-hush, or it was supposed to be. I doubt they will be able to stay below the radar once the news of Bella's death gets out though."

"Crystal looks hungry for publicity," Jenny mused. "Why did she want a quiet wedding?"

"It had to do with their show. Crystal's the star of this new reality show, see? It's like a mashup of a few popular shows. A bunch of girls tackle an obstacle course through an Amazon jungle during the day and the winner gets a date with the guy. The guy chooses a bride out of the finalists."

"And Crystal is one of those girls?"

"She is. And she's going to win."

"Wait a minute. How do you know she will win?"

"That's the way these shows work. They already decide who the winner is going to be. Everything is scripted."

"And Crystal marries this guy on screen? Is it a fake marriage?"

"That's the funny thing. The guy is Wayne Newman. He has to look like the most eligible bachelor."

"Hence the secret wedding!" Jenny connected the dots.

"That's what I gathered from bits and pieces I overheard."

"What's the rush? Couldn't they get married on the show?"

"That's a question for Crystal."

Jenny dropped Heather off at the inn and went home. Star was sitting on the porch, sipping a glass of iced tea.

"It's getting too hot," she observed. "I made dinner."

"Do I have time for a shower?" Jenny asked her.

She put on an old tank top and a fresh pair of shorts. Star had grilled some sea bass and made a green salad.

"Any news on that poor girl?" Star asked as they began eating.

Jenny shook her head.

"Adam hasn't given up anything yet. I met Crystal's mom today. She's a cold fish."

"What else do you expect from these Hollywood types?" Star snorted.

"She's lying through her teeth, Aunt."

"Oh?"

"First she said she didn't know Bella at all. Then she said she barely knew her. She's definitely hiding something."

"Where was she when all this happened?"

"She was standing right there, a few feet away from me."

"She couldn't be involved, in that case."

"At least not directly," Jenny conceded. "That's going to be a big problem actually. Everyone other than Wayne, the groom, was standing right there. Plenty of people will vouch for them. Unless they paid someone else to do the deed, they didn't have any opportunity to commit this crime."

"Did the poor girl have any family?"

"Don't know," Jenny said, trying to remember something Adam had said.

"This looks like a tough one. Make sure you watch over your shoulder, Jenny. I don't want you putting yourself in danger."

"Do you think I should drop the whole thing?"

"Why are you doing it, sweetie? Do you feel any obligation to Crystal?"

Jenny laughed nervously.

"Just because she made me a bridesmaid?"

Star didn't say anything.

"Last time, I was trying to pull you out of trouble. I would have done it whatever the cost."

"I know that, and I'm grateful."

"Now I'm doing it because it seems like the right thing to do. And I don't see anyone else standing up for that poor girl."

"You're smarter than most people. I have no doubt you are going to crack this wide open."

"I wish I was that confident," Jenny muttered.

She watched TV with her aunt for a while and stepped out for her walk. The air was perfumed with a familiar scent of roses and gardenias. The house next to her lit up like a Christmas tree after she walked a few steps, set off by the motion detectors. Jenny looked up longingly at the three storey house that sat empty next to her aunt's little cottage. Seaview was the stuff of dreams. She imagined herself standing on the little balcony overlooking the ocean, wrapped in a pair of strong arms. She just wasn't sure who those arms belonged to.

A bark sounded in the distance and a large hairy body leaped through the air and almost struck her down.

"Tank! You little beast!"

She kissed the yellow Labrador on his head and scratched him under his ears. His tongue wagged as he ran in circles around Jenny.

"Where is he?" Jenny whispered in Tank's ear.

"Stop bothering her, Tank!" Adam's voice boomed as he came up to Jenny.

"You know I don't mind him," Jenny said, holding Tank's collar in her hand. "Long day?"

Adam rubbed his eyes and sighed.

"I'm trying to go easy on the pain pills."

His distressed expression told Jenny it was taking a toll.

"You're hardly leaning on the cane now."

"You noticed that," Adam stuttered.

"Of course I did. You'll be walking without it soon. Not that I care. I don't mind either way. It's just…"

Jenny realized she was bumbling like an idiot. She stopped and looked at Adam. He was looking at her with an intense expression.

They both laughed nervously.

"I used crutches for a long time," Adam told her. "Then this cane."

"Will it be odd to walk without it?" Jenny asked.

"Yes," Adam nodded. A hopeful smile spread across his face. "I can't wait."

Chapter 6

A group of nubile young girls trooped into the Boardwalk Café. The sun had barely risen a foot over the horizon. Jenny had just finished serving Captain Charlie. He was usually one of their first customers of the day.

The girls wanted to sit out on the deck. They waved at Jenny as they went out. She recognized them from the wedding party. They were Crystal's bridesmaids.

"We stayed up all night drinking champagne and watching movies," one girl tittered. "We are so hungry! We thought we'd come check out your place."

"I'm starving!" another one of them added. "What can you get us for breakfast?"

They all looked like clones of each other, tall, perfectly sculpted and tow headed. Jenny got to work in the kitchen making crab omelets. It was another summer recipe she was trying to perfect.

"Can we get mimosas?" one girl piped up.

"Sorry, we don't serve alcohol," Jenny said with a grimace. "I can get you fresh coffee."

Petunia brought over a basket of warm muffins and the girls shifted their attention to the food. One of the girls got up after a few minutes and walked to the kitchen.

Jenny looked up as she flipped an omelet on the café's grill.

"These muffins are delish," the girl said, picking tiny pieces from one she held in her hand. "Do you make them from scratch?"

"Of course," Jenny smiled. "Everything we cook here is made from scratch. It's my own recipe."

"You're a great cook."

Jenny was trying hard to remember the girl's name. It was something exotic.

"I'm Rainbow," the girl offered.

"Oh yeah…" Jenny's face cleared. "I'm glad ya'll came here today."

She didn't know what else to say.

"I heard you're going to find out who killed Bella?"

"I'm not sure someone killed her," Jenny said nervously. "Maybe she just fell off the plane."

"Not Bella."

"Did you know her?"

"I guess."

"Were you surprised to see her?"

"It was a shock! Who would've thunk, huh?"

"She seemed quite young."

"She was. We are all about the same age. In our twenties, you know…"

The girl paused when she said that.

"Bella was the youngest, barely twenty two."

Jenny thought of her college going son.

"That's awfully young."

Rainbow's eyes filled up.

"She deserves justice, you know."

"I agree. I am going to try and get to the bottom of it."

Another girl came up and dragged Rainbow back to their table. Jenny could hear their noisy talk as she plated their food. Bella Darling would never have breakfast with her friends again.

The girls lingered over their meal, chatting nonstop. They were still there when the Magnolias began to trickle in one by one.

"Who's hogging our table?" Betty Sue Morse grumbled, pulling her knitting needles out of her bag.

Heather emitted a cry as she recognized them.

"They're from the bridal party," she squealed and went out to greet them.

Rainbow turned around and looked at Jenny. There was a question in her eyes but she didn't say anything. Jenny wondered what the girl wanted from her.

Jenny was worked off her feet for the rest of the day. She walked over to the police station on her way home, hoping to pick Adam's brain again.

Adam Hopkins sat in his office with his bum leg propped up on a chair. Experience told Jenny he was going to be in a bad mood.

"Howdy!" she greeted him cheerfully.

"What do you want?" he snapped.

"What's the latest on Bella Darling?" Jenny thought it best to cut to the chase.

Adam's expression told her she was being a pain in the neck.

"We are getting ready to release a statement. That is the only reason I am going to tell you this."

Jenny sat down with a thump, eager to hear what was coming.

"The victim, Bella Darling, died from the impact. She was carrying two parachutes. Both of them had been messed with."

"What?" Jenny cried out. "That means…"

"This is a murder investigation."

"What do you mean, messed with?"

"Her main parachute had been slashed. The backup parachute she was carrying had been turned off."

"Why would someone do that?"

"That's what we have to find out."

"What about her family? Has anyone come to claim her?"

"She was married. Her husband should be arriving soon."

"She was barely 22," Jenny whispered.

"How do you know that?" Adam asked sharply.

"One of the bridesmaids mentioned it."

Jenny spent a few minutes processing what Adam had told her.

"Why was she wearing a wedding dress?" Jenny asked Adam. "And what about that giant sapphire around her neck? Was it real?"

"It was real alright. It's valued at some ridiculous price, over a hundred thousand dollars."

Jenny let out a gasp.

"That much?"

"The wedding dress, the sapphire, it's all part of the puzzle. I guess it's safe to say she wanted to disrupt Crystal's wedding."

"So it was a publicity stunt after all."

"Whatever it was, it went horribly wrong," Adam sighed. "It was the last thing the poor girl did in her life."

"Who's your main suspect?"

"I'm not going to tell you that, Jenny."

"Isn't the spouse the most obvious pick?"

"We will have to establish his whereabouts at the time the crime occurred. We don't know anything about him at this point."

"What about Wayne Newman? He was on that plane too."

"I think everyone knows that, Jenny."

"That makes him the most obvious suspect. Surely he's not that foolish."

"We are still questioning him."

"What about Crystal and the other guests?"

"We will be talking to everyone. That includes you since you were present at the scene of the crime."

"Just say when, Adam. I hope you solve this case as soon as possible. That poor girl needs justice."

"We'll do fine if people stop meddling and let us do our job."

"Some people welcome extra help."

Adam refused to take the bait.

"I hear Mandy James is hard at it. She's going to put you to work soon. Why not leave the detecting to the police?"

"Don't worry about me, Adam. I can multitask."

"You're a stubborn woman, Jenny."

"I've been called worse," Jenny laughed.

She pushed her chair back although she was reluctant to leave. Adam looked up at her.

"How about grabbing a bite at Ethan's? The catch must be coming in now."

Ethan Hopkins was Adam's brother. He had a fish shack in town, famous for serving the best fried seafood on the coast.

"Sorry, can't," Jenny said. "Jason's taking me to dinner."

"Of course he is," Adam mumbled, curling his fists under the table.

"Can I take a rain check?" Jenny asked. "We can go to Ethan's later this week."

"We'll see," Adam said evasively. "I'm pretty tied up for the next few days. I do have a murder to solve."

Jenny's face fell. Adam realized he had been nasty on purpose. He almost apologized but something held him back. He didn't want to force Jenny's hand.

Jenny walked home with an empty feeling in her heart. Had Adam been trying to say something?

Jason Stone arrived at Jenny's house in his luxury sedan an hour later. Jenny was ready, wearing a new summer dress she had ordered online.

"Hello, pretty lady!" Jason whistled, offering his arm.

Jenny grabbed it and waved goodbye to her aunt. Jason always made her smile. Unlike Adam, he wasn't the brooding type. Jenny told herself to forget about Adam Hopkins for the rest of the evening.

"Where are we going tonight?" she asked.

Jason knew a lot of good restaurants up and down the coast of the Eastern Shore. He took Jenny to a new place every time.

"You like Mexican, don't you?"

Jenny fiddled with the radio, trying to tune in to a jazz station.

Jason regaled her with something funny he had read on the Internet. The sun was setting as they reached the restaurant, an unassuming place in a strip mall.

"Wait till you taste their fish tacos," Jason crowed.

The server brought over a basket of fresh fried tortilla chips with red and green salsa.

"So you're serious about this girl, huh?" Jason asked.

Jenny guessed he was referring to Bella.

"I just spoke with Adam. They have confirmed it was foul play."

"Be careful, Jenny," Jason said, taking her hand in his. "I don't want you to get hurt."

"Star's already warned me to watch my back," she muttered. "Adam thinks I am crazy to do this. And now you…"

"We care about you," Jason said with emotion. "I don't know how I got along without you."

"Aren't you exaggerating?" she asked in surprise.

"Of course I am," Jason said with a laugh. "But honestly, I am glad you came to Pelican Cove."

"I didn't have much of a choice, Jason. You know my husband kicked me out of my home."

"You have a choice now," Jason said.

Jenny's divorce settlement had come through a few days ago. She had the means to live wherever she wanted now. Jason was one of the few people who knew that.

"Pelican Cove feels like home now. I don't want to go anywhere else."

"Not even to some exotic tropical island?" Jason teased.

"I have my exotic island right here."

The tacos came and Jenny gorged on them with relish.

"This red cabbage slaw is so yummy. I should try making this at the café."

"I may need to have a powwow with you," Jason confided after they ordered dessert. "I have been approached by someone connected to Bella Darling."

"Did Crystal or Wayne hire you?"

"I can't say, yet."

"I would love to pool our resources. You can probably get more out of the cops because of your legal status."

"You can count on my assistance, Jenny."

Jenny shared Adam's information with Jason.

"So that's why her chute didn't open!" Jason shuddered.

"Have you ever been sky diving?"

"Once, and that was enough for me. I can't imagine people pay to have that experience."

"Do you think Bella was a good person?" Jenny mused. "Why did she want to disrupt Crystal's wedding?"

"Professional rivalry?"

"Crystal says she didn't know Bella."

"Doesn't everyone know everyone nowadays?" Jason questioned. "They talk to each other on social media."

"Is that the same as knowing a person?"

"Nick might have a better answer for that, Jenny. We are the wrong generation."

"Crystal's mother lied about knowing Bella. So I guess Crystal could be lying too."

"I missed seeing you in your bridesmaid's dress. Rumor has it you looked prettier than those twenty year olds."

Jenny whooped with laughter.

"Jason Stone, are you trying to flirt with me?"

"Who says I am just trying?"

They stopped in another seaside town and went for a walk on the beach.

"I might have some good news for you soon," Jason said, taking her arm.

"You mean…?"

Jason nodded. Jenny had put in an offer for Seaview, the property adjoining her aunt's house. It had passed over to some distant heir who had shown no interest in it for years. Jenny was confident they could complete the transaction without any problems.

"Your offer is very generous, against my particular advice. That old house is crumbling. You will have to spend a packet on fixing it up."

"Don't be a naysayer. It's going to be fine."

"I hope you're right, Jenny."

Jason dropped her home after that. Jenny sat outside on the porch, watching the waves batter the shore. The whitecaps gleamed in the dark and a gibbous moon rose over the water.

Jenny tried to picture the last few moments of Bella Darling's life. Did she have time to panic before she hit the ground?

Chapter 7

Jenny was dragging her feet at the café the next day. She had stayed out on the porch until midnight, questioning some recent choices she had made in life. She had tossed and turned for hours after she went to bed. When her alarm went off at 5 AM, she was just falling asleep.

The phone in the kitchen rang insistently. Petunia finally answered it when she went in with an empty tray.

"It's for you," she told Jenny.

"Who could it be?"

"Heather!" Petunia mouthed as she handed over the old fashioned handset to Jenny.

"Hi Heather! Aren't you coming over for coffee today?"

"Jenny, can you spare some time?"

"We are rushed off our feet, Heather. You know things are getting insane here as the season ramps up."

"Wayne's here," Heather whispered. "He's asking for you."

"What does he want?"

"He won't say. He says he will only talk to you."

"Why didn't he come here then?"

"It's the crowd at the café. He doesn't want to be recognized."

"He'll have to wait."

Heather giggled and hung up. Jenny felt pulled in many directions. She decided to curb her irritation and start preparing lunch.

"Do you want to go over to Heather's?" Petunia asked. "Why don't you go there and send her over? I am fine as long as I have someone watching the cash register."

"He can wait," Jenny said firmly. "I'm going to start on the salad."

Jenny tossed the salad, made a platter of sandwiches and frosted her special cupcakes. Only then did she allow herself a break. She gulped some tepid coffee and sat down with a thud.

"I guess you should go over now," Petunia said.

"Okay, okay, I'm leaving!"

Betty Sue, Star and Molly were on the deck out back, catching up on the town gossip. Heather had stayed back at her inn to keep Wayne company.

A salty breeze coming off the ocean ruffled Jenny's hair as she walked to Heather's inn. It was a bright and sunny day in May and summer had definitely arrived in Pelican Cove.

"Finally!" Heather rolled her eyes when she saw Jenny. "I've been wracking my brains trying to make small talk."

Wayne Newman sat sprawled on Betty Sue's Victorian sofa, tapping his foot impatiently. He wore a cowboy hat and a plaid shirt with jeans that appeared plastered to his body. He was shorter than Crystal but his V shaped torso and washboard abs meant he paid equal attention to his appearance.

Jenny noticed a bandage on his left arm. He must have injured himself during his landing.

"Howdy Ma'am!" he said, standing up. "Can you spare a few minutes for me?"

"What can I do for you, Mr. Newman?"

"Call me Wayne. Crystal said she hired a detective."

Jenny instantly disliked his wheedling tone.

"I'm no detective. I already told your wife that."

"She's not my wife yet," Wayne whined. "She won't marry me."

Jenny thought back to what Crystal had said. What was wrong with these Hollywood people? The lies came easily to them.

"I heard you were leaving us for a concert."

Wayne Newman's eyes darkened.

"Cops held me back. The sponsors are suing me."

"Surely it's not your fault?"

"Tell them that. You know how much money I lost?"

Jenny tried to bring the conversation back on track.

"How can I help you, Wayne?"

"Solve this whole mess as soon as possible. I can't afford to lose any more gigs."

"Didn't you get a role on TV?"

"Sure did," Wayne gloated. "But I'm a musician at heart. I'll stop breathing if I don't make music."

"Has being a TV star helped you get on tour?"

"I suppose it has. Why?"

"Being a TV star is important to you then?"

"What kind of question is that? They are calling me the hottest reality TV star of the decade."

"Wow! That's big."

Wayne glanced around the room, bobbing his head. Jenny wondered if he was nodding at an imaginary audience.

"I'm glad you came here, Wayne. I need to ask you some questions."

"Hey! I got nothing to hide."

"Shall we begin then?"

Wayne sat up straighter and winked at Jenny. She took it as a sign to carry on.

"What happened to your arm?"

"Faulty landing," he griped. "That girl hit me as she fell to her death. I'm lucky I got away with some bruises."

"But your jump was successful?"

"I wouldn't say that!"

"Whose idea was it? This whole skydiving thing?"

"I wanted to make a big splash. A big statement, you know. I agreed to having a small wedding in the boondocks – no offense…"

"None taken."

"I thought arriving for my wedding in a parachute would be spectacular enough for my fans. I have to keep them happy."

"I thought it was a secret wedding."

"Something always leaks to the press. I am sure there must have been some paparazzi present there."

Jenny figured he had given an anonymous tip to some reporters. Clearly, Wayne Newman didn't want to lose this opportunity to make a splash in the tabloids.

"Crystal was fine with that?"

Wayne gave a sneaky smile.

"She had no choice. I didn't tell her until the last minute."

"I'm guessing you didn't tell her at all."

"I called her from the airport," Wayne admitted. "She didn't have a choice at that point."

"Why didn't you both do it? That would have been even more spectacular."

"Crystal won't go near a small plane. And sky diving is so not her thing. We argued about it."

Jenny quirked one eyebrow, encouraging Wayne to go on.

"What if the show wants her to do it, huh? She can't say no to them. She'll be under contract. I told her this would be good practice. But she wouldn't hear a word."

"But I thought you didn't tell her until the last minute."

"We talked about it," Wayne pursed his lips. "She forbid me to do it. I went ahead and called her from the airport."

Crystal Mars was marrying a douche bag. Jenny admitted he was a very attractive douche bag. He was probably loaded too.

"Did you know Bella Darling?"

"Not really. I might have met her at some event or other."

"What did she have against you?"

"You'll have to ask her that."

He laughed out at his own humor and stopped when he saw neither Jenny nor Heather were joining in.

"Did she have anything against Crystal?"

"Crystal's a sweet girl. She's got her head in the right place."

"What does that mean?"

"These young girls are pitted against each other by the media. There's a lot of competition. Everyone tries to be one up on the other."

"So you are saying Crystal and Bella were rivals."

Wayne shrugged. Jenny assumed that meant yes.

"Did you see her when you climbed up in that plane? What exactly did you do that day?"

"I've done this whole sky diving thing before," Wayne began. "So I know the drill. Once the pilot knew I was licensed for a solo dive, I was pretty much on my own."

"It must be a small plane. Was there room for anyone to hide?"

"I don't know. I was so excited I wasn't paying attention to anything else."

"So you didn't see Bella at all that day?"

"Not until she dashed into me and fell into that cake."

"It must have been a shock."

"Shock? It's surreal. Even the best reality show writers couldn't have scripted this scene."

"Bella was wearing a dress exactly like Crystal's. What's that all about?"

"I don't know. They got it on sale?"

"You know better than that, Wayne. Crystal's dress was couture. They don't make too many of those."

"I don't know much about women's fashion."

"It appears that Bella Darling wanted to cause some kind of disruption at your wedding. Any idea why she would do that?"

"Must have been a publicity stunt, or a spoof of some kind."

"Crystal says she didn't know Bella either."

"Maybe it was supposed to be a big joke. Bella would arrive next to me, say ta-da or something and we would all laugh it off."

"Nobody is laughing right now, Wayne."

"Do you think the TV people arranged it?"

"Why would they do that?"

"They might have wanted to use the segment for the show, or for promos or something."

"Why haven't they come forward then?"

Wayne shrugged.

"Look, I have no idea why this broad was doing this crazy thing. All I know is it put a damper on my wedding. And now Crystal won't marry me."

"But Crystal said you're the one who's refusing to tie the knot."

"You have it wrong. Crystal says she won't go ahead with the wedding until they find out who killed Bella. That's why she hired you."

Jenny decided Crystal and Wayne were definitely not on the same page.

"Why do you say someone killed Bella? She could have jumped on her own."

"I know her chute was messed with. I have my sources."

Had the police already released a statement about the circumstances surrounding Bella's death? Jenny reminded herself to check on that.

"What if I was the real target?" Wayne asked. "Maybe I was supposed to wear the damaged chute."

"Do you have any enemies?"

"Plenty!"

"I'm not talking about petty rivalry. Is there someone who might want to kill you?"

Wayne turned pale.

"I never gave it much thought."

"Maybe you should, Wayne. And I suggest you talk to the cops about it. Give them a list. If you were the real target, you might need protection."

"Crystal could have been the target too," Wayne said. "When I booked the dive, I booked it for a couple."

"But you said Crystal is scared of sky diving."

"A man can hope, can't he? I thought she would make an exception for our wedding day."

"You have given me a lot to think about, Wayne. I am glad we had a chance to talk."

"I'm at your disposal, lady. Just do whatever it takes to sort out this mess. We start shooting the reality show next month. I want to take Crystal on our honeymoon before that. And we need to get married first for that to happen."

"I am going to try," Jenny promised. "Will you let me know if you think of something else? You know where to find me."

"Sure will!" Wayne drawled.

Jenny stood up to leave, then remembered something Jason had said.

"Have you hired a lawyer, Wayne?"

"Why do I need a lawyer?"

If Wayne hadn't hired Jason, who had? Jenny thought about it as she walked back to the café. Her stomach rumbled with hunger and she realized she had spent almost a couple of hours talking to Wayne Newman.

"We sold out of everything," Petunia told her as soon as she walked in. "I hope Heather gave you lunch."

"She didn't."

"I haven't eaten either," Petunia told her. "We'll have to fix something quickly."

"I can make some omelets."

Jenny pulled leftovers from the refrigerator. She chopped down grilled veggies and chicken and shredded a leftover block of cheese. Golden omelets were sizzling on the grill soon after.

"Do you have enough for me?" a voice called from the door.

Heather Morse came in and joined them.

"I thought he would never leave. I missed lunch too, Jenny. Please, please give me something to eat."

"There's enough for everyone," Jenny said with a smile.

"So what do you think of Wayne Newman?" Heather asked, chewing a big bite of her omelet. "Country music icon turned TV star?"

"He's lying."

Chapter 8

"Crystal is hiring a bodyguard," Heather told the Magnolias the next morning.

It was yet another bright and sunny day in Pelican Cove. The women were enjoying their daily coffee break on the deck outside the café.

"She really thinks she is in danger?" Jenny asked.

"She's not sure. But it's good for her image. One of the tabloids is doing a story on it."

Betty Sue stopped knitting for a moment and scowled at Heather.

"You've wasted enough time on those Hollywood people, Heather. All your chores are piling up."

"Like what, Grandma?" Heather asked.

Her brow had set in a frown. Jenny had never seen her argue with Betty Sue.

"Tourist season's here. We need to clean the whole house, do our usual spruce up, check on the towels and sheets…you know the list!"

"I'm taking care of all that."

"When?" Betty Sue demanded.

"Heather's always done her job, Betty Sue," Petunia said, trying to calm them down. "What do you think of that box Mandy has put up?"

"What box?" Jenny asked.

"There's a big suggestion box at the town office. Mandy wants people to come up with ideas about how we can beautify Main Street. She's going to discuss them at the town hall meeting tonight."

"She could've come to me," Betty Sue frowned.

Betty Sue Morse was a force to reckon with in Pelican Cove. She was used to people coming to her for advice. When it came to town matters, she called the shots. Mayors came and went, but everyone knew Betty Sue was the real power center.

"Your mind is full of ideas for the town. Right, Betty Sue?" Star asked mischievously.

Betty Sue took the bait.

"Being a Morse used to mean something. What does this girl know, eh? She hasn't even been here a week."

"The Welcome sign has been broken for ten years," Petunia said. "I'm going to suggest they make a new one."

"Do you have concerts on the beach?" Jenny asked. "We used to have concerts by the river where I lived. It's a great way to draw people out."

"We have the summer festival," Star told Jenny, "and we have a barbecue or two. The local band always strikes up a tune at these times."

"I'm talking about doing something on a larger scale," Jenny explained. "With a proper stage and professional bands. There can be a different band every weekend. We can advertise about it in advance so that people can plan ahead."

"Why don't you put that idea in the box?" Petunia asked eagerly.

"You can hire that Crystal's husband," Betty Sue quipped. "He's loitering here anyway. Maybe he will come to the show in a parachute."

Jenny thought of Bella Darling as soon as Betty Sue mentioned the parachute. Her eyes hardened and she frowned.

"You're thinking of Bella, aren't you?" Heather asked. "Have you made any progress?"

"I'm going to talk to Adam again."

The older women exchanged meaningful glances as soon as Jenny mentioned Adam.

"Have you gone out with him yet?" Molly asked.

"He said something about grabbing dinner at Ethan's shack."

"Ethan's place is like the café," Petunia snorted. "That's not a date."

"If he's not ready…" Star said softly. "The time isn't right, girls."

"Don't you ladies have anything better to do than planning my dates?" Jenny grumbled. "I'm going in to start lunch."

The group broke up after that.

Jenny wrote down her idea about concerts on the beach on a piece of paper. She thought of special discounts the local shops could offer for the concerts. It could be a big boost to business.

She whipped butter and sugar for frosting, thinking about Adam. She wanted to know what Wayne had shared with him.

"Why don't you eat something?" Petunia asked a few hours later.

The lunch crowd had dwindled and they finally had some time to themselves. Jenny placed two plates loaded with sandwiches and chips on the small table and poured sweet tea for the both of them.

"I'm going to drop these off for Mandy," she said shyly. "I know I'm not really a resident but I want us to win that contest."

"What are you saying, dear? You are one of us now."

Jenny walked over to the town office and asked someone for the suggestion box.

Mandy waved at her from a conference room.

"Got some ideas for me?" she asked cheerfully.

Jenny explained her concept.

"I like that. I really like that. But I'm not sure it falls under beautification. It's more like cultural enrichment."

"Isn't that a kind of beauty too?" Jenny asked uncertainly.

"I'm not rejecting your suggestion, Jenny. We can discuss it during the meeting."

"I was thinking a bit higher than fresh paint."

"Fresh paint is important," Mandy said. "Have you looked at the places on Main Street? Really looked? Most of the places are crumbling. They haven't seen a coat of paint in years."

Jenny opened her mouth to object.

"Your café is one of them," Mandy went on. "It's an eyesore."

"The Boardwalk Café is the most popular spot on Main Street. Locals and tourists both flock to the place. We are already rushed off our feet and it's not even Memorial Day."

"That's because they don't have a choice," Mandy said glibly. "If a spanking new place opened next door, no one would step into that derelict café."

"Now you're insulting us."

"I'm just saying it like it is. It's my job."

"Being rude to people and attacking their livelihood is what you do for a living?"

"Come on, Jenny! That's not what I meant. Offering suggestions for improvement is why the town hired me."

"You won't find many takers for your suggestions with that attitude," Jenny fumed.

She stormed out and walked to the police station. Adam Hopkins was next on her list.

"How are you, Jenny?" Adam asked her with a smile.

Jenny was taken aback. In the few months she had visited him at work, Adam Hopkins had rarely greeted her pleasantly.

"I guess you are here to volunteer some information about the crime."

"Are you feeling alright?" Jenny asked. "You don't sound like Adam at all."

"Ha ha!"

"I did want to share something with you."

"Fire away."

"Wayne Newman came to talk to me yesterday. Have you questioned him yet?"

"We talked to him once," Adam admitted. "Twice actually. The first was on the day of the wedding, or murder."

"Wayne thinks the tampered parachute may have been meant for him or Crystal. The earlier plan was for both of them to dive off that plane. Crystal refused because she is afraid of heights or something."

"We thought of that. I have asked both of them to give us a list of anyone they suspect. But I don't think anything will come of it."

"But why?"

"You develop a gut feel about these things. I am convinced Bella was the intended target."

"She's not even famous. Both Crystal and Wayne are more popular than Bella. They must have more enemies."

"We will follow all leads. I'm going to check the list they give me, Jenny."

"Anything new about Bella?"

"Nothing I can tell you."

Jenny hesitated. She wanted to stay and talk to Adam some more.

"That Mandy James is something else. She says the café is an eyesore."

"How dare she!"

"You can laugh all you want. I am worried she's out to get me."

"Don't be paranoid, Jenny. She barely knows you."

Jenny shot herself in the foot before she could stop herself.

"What about grabbing dinner at Ethan's tonight? I fancy some fried fish."

"Sorry, can't."

Jenny wished a sinkhole would appear next to her so she could disappear forever.

"I was just kidding," she giggled nervously.

Adam leaned forward and took her hand in his. His eyes softened as he looked at her.

"Jenny, I would love to go to Ethan's with you. But I can't tonight. I have to work."

"Okay."

"There's a town hall meeting tonight. Aren't you going with Star?"

"I'm not sure I am allowed to go."

"Why would anyone stop you? Almost everyone in town turns up for the meetings. They can be quite entertaining."

"Somehow I can't picture you enjoying a meeting of that kind."

"I don't! But I'm working tonight. They have a couple of cops on duty at these meetings. It's my turn."

"I see."

Jenny made some more small talk with Adam. She asked about his leg, asked about his twin daughters and talked about the weather. Finally, she could think of nothing else.

Adam looked at his watch and sighed.

"I hate to break this up, but I'm expecting someone."

"It's high time I left. I have to go to the seafood market before I go home."

Jenny almost collided with someone on her way out.

"Jenny!" a pair of arms grabbed her.

"Hey Jason!" she smiled back.

"I'm glad I ran into you. Are you going to the town hall meeting? Why don't we go together?"

"Do you want to have dinner with us? I'm going to the market to get some fish."

"That sounds lovely! I'll see you then."

Jenny wondered what Jason was doing there.

"Got a meeting with Adam," he told her himself.

A young man stood next to Jason, scratching his head with a pen. Jenny rightly guessed he was a new client.

Dinner was light hearted with Jason regaling them with gossip from the city courts. They decided to walk to town.

"Who's your new client?" Jenny asked.

"You'll find out soon enough."

Jason bought some ice cream for them from the Pelican Cove Creamery. He handed over the plastic cups loaded with three large scoops of ice cream.

"Raspberry and chocolate!" Jenny exclaimed. "Yum!"

"Wait till you try their peach."

The room where the meeting was being held was packed when they went in. Petunia had saved seats for them. Heather and Molly sat next to her. Jenny spied Betty Sue sitting on a small raised platform, next to Barb Norton and a few other people. One of them was Ada Newbury, the richest woman in town. There was an old man Jenny recognized as Heather's grandpa. He and Betty Sue had been separated for several years.

"They are life members," Heather whispered to Jenny. "Barb may be the chairman of this particular committee but she can't totally ignore the rest of them. According to the guidelines, they have a vote anyway."

"And your grandma has veto power?"

"She kind of does," Heather said seriously, "although she hasn't exercised it in decades."

"Let's hope she doesn't have to make an exception this time."

Jenny told Heather and Petunia about her run in with Mandy James.

"How dare she!" Heather fumed. "She'll be attacking our inn next."

"I wouldn't put it past her," Jenny nodded.

According to her, Heather's inn was more vintage than the café.

An old man seated in the first row started grumbling about the time.

"That's Asher Cohen," Heather told Jenny. "He's a hundred years old."

Mandy James opened the suggestion box with great pomp and began reading the chits of paper one by one. People argued about every idea like their life depended on it. Jenny had never been to a meeting of this kind.

"Repaint the light house," Mandy read the next one. "The light house is not on Main Street, is it? Why are we even talking about it?"

A man in the front row struggled to his feet. He swayed on his feet, trying to maintain balance. Jenny guessed he had imbibed a bit too much as usual.

"Jimmy's here too?" Molly asked.

Jimmy Parsons was the town drunk. He lived in a small cottage next to the light house. Funnily enough, he owned the light house and the land it sat on.

"The light house is a Pelican Cove landmark, missy. It's what makes the town pretty."

Almost everyone present agreed to that. Mandy wasn't ready to consider it though.

"We'll table this for the moment. There are other places that need immediate attention, like the Boardwalk Café. It will have to go."

Chapter 9

The girl called Rainbow paced the verandah of the Pelican Cove Country Club. The meticulously maintained emerald greens of the golf course stretched before her. An inland creek meandered its way through the grounds. Birds twittered, roses bloomed and a cool breeze softened the glare of the bright sun. None of this made an impression on the girl.

Rainbow's career was finally looking up after she had spent months sucking up to Crystal Mars. One word from Crystal and Rainbow had bagged a cameo in the new reality show Crystal was a star in. Was it worth giving it all up for the sake of doing the right thing?

Raised in a devout Catholic family, Rainbow had flouted many tenets of her faith since she reached Hollywood. She had lied and cheated to get ahead. She had coveted what someone else had and she had frequently refused help to those in need. But she had never actually harmed anyone.

Bella Darling's face swam before her eyes. The poor girl had barely known life. She was like a younger sister to Rainbow. At least she had been until Rainbow jumped ship and joined the Crystal Mars camp. She had braved Crystal's ire and met Bella once. Tried hard to talk some sense into her. Blinded by love, Bella had turned her back on Rainbow.

A couple of restless hours later, Rainbow came to a decision.

Jenny slammed a plate of soup on the counter and got some change from the cash register. She avoided looking up at the café's latest customer.

"Don't take it personally, Jenny. I'm just doing my job."

Jenny placed her hands on her hips and glared at Mandy James.

"This café has been around longer than you have, missy. Think twice before you make plans to tear it down."

"Who's talking about tearing it down? You have it all wrong."

"I was there at the town hall meeting last night. I know what you said."

"All I meant is you need to fix up this place."

"Look around you. We are bursting at the seams. Most locals eat here twice a day. Tourists visiting town come and eat at our café year after year. Surely that means something."

"The town wants to win this contest. That's why they hired me. This particular contest calls for a pretty town. Face it, your café isn't pretty."

"Enjoy your lunch," Jenny spat and went into the kitchen.

Jenny had been smoldering since the town hall meeting. Mandy James and her vendetta against the Boardwalk Café had been the main topic of discussion among the Magnolias that morning. They had banded together and vowed to do anything they could to protect their café.

"I'm glad you're standing up for me, Jenny," Petunia said emotionally.

"I don't understand why she is picking on us."

"That Mandy James has come up with a long list. We are not the only ones on her radar."

"She's being too literal, don't you think? I love the idea of repainting the light house. It will give the whole town a face lift."

"She's got a bunch of ideas for Main Street. Fresh flower beds at every corner, murals on building walls, Victorian lamp posts…she wants to color code the trash cans and benches and provide free bicycles for everyone."

"Bicycles?"

"She wants to keep the cars off Main Street. People can either walk or borrow one of these bikes."

Jenny rolled her eyes, making her disdain clear.

There was a knock on the kitchen door and a blonde face peeped in.

"Can I come in?"

"You are from Crystal's wedding party, aren't you?" Petunia asked the girl.

"I'm Rainbow," she said, looking at Jenny. "We met the other day."

"Of course! Come on in. Do you want a table on the deck out back?"

"I'm here by myself," Rainbow said hesitantly. "Can I talk to you?"

"Have you had lunch, dear?" Petunia asked, ladling thick tomato soup into a bowl. "Jenny and I were just sitting down to eat."

Rainbow admitted she had missed lunch.

"Can we eat first?" Jenny asked.

Rainbow nodded and began slurping the tomato soup. Petunia served them hot grilled cheese sandwiches off the grill.

"I never get to eat carbs," Rainbow exclaimed. "Crystal would kill me for this."

"How does it matter to her?" Jenny asked. "You can eat anything if you are blessed with a good metabolism."

"Which I am, thankfully," the girl said, bringing her palms together and closing her eyes for a second. "It's all about image. Appearances mean a lot in Hollywood."

"I've heard. But where does Crystal come in?"

"Crystal has allowed me in her inner circle. I have to toe the line if I want to stay there."

"You mean you're part of some elite posse which Crystal rules over?"

"The entire wedding party is," the girl explained. "Other than you and Heather, we are all 'her girls'. We dress a certain way, and eat according to a diet plan her nutritionist comes up with. Her stylist tells us what to wear."

"That's great. So you get free fashion advice from a pro."

"It's not fashion advice exactly. We can only wear certain colors, or certain styles on a given day. It's all coordinated to make Crystal stand out."

"She's a star. Isn't she supposed to be a notch above the rest anyway?"

"That takes work," Rainbow said.

She clammed up after that, realizing she had spoken too much.

"You are so beautiful," Jenny praised. "I'm sure you have great things in store for you."

Rainbow blushed like the young girl she was. She looked longingly at the cupcakes Jenny offered her but refused to taste them.

"What brings you here, Rainbow?"

"You were going to find out what happened to Bella."

"That's right."

"What if it's someone connected to Crystal?"

Jenny's face clouded as she looked at Rainbow.

"Is there something I should know?"

"I'm not sure how much you have found out."

"I'm just starting out, Rainbow. If you know something about Bella, I suggest you come clean. You can talk to the cops directly. Or I can go with you."

"No cops," Rainbow said immediately. "I need to keep this quiet."

"Why don't you tell me what it is first?"

"Wayne was having an affair with Bella," Rainbow blurted out.

"What? But he said he didn't know her."

"He knew her very well. A bit too well."

"How long have you known about this?"

"Three months or so."

"Does Crystal know this?"

"I don't know."

"Does anyone else know?"

"I'm not sure, Jenny."

"Was this after Crystal and Wayne were engaged?"

"Oh yes."

"How did you find out? Did you come upon them somewhere?"

"Bella used to be my roommate. I moved out when Crystal picked me but I continued to meet Bella."

"She told you about Wayne?"

"Wayne has a reputation with the ladies. I warned her about him but she ignored me."

"Did she know about Wayne and Crystal? I understand their engagement has been hush-hush."

"She did later. But she refused to stop seeing Wayne."

"What was she doing up there on that plane?"

"I've been trying to figure that out. Maybe she wanted to talk Wayne out of it."

"Do you know her parachute had been slashed? Who would do that to her?"

Rainbow suddenly looked frightened.

"I just wanted to tell you about Bella and Wayne. Can you promise you'll keep this between us?"

"You need to tell the police about this. According to Wayne's statement, he did not know Bella at all."

"That's a lie!"

"Do you have any proof about this?"

"We went out to dinner once," Rainbow remembered. "We took some selfies but Wayne made us delete them."

"He knows you knew about him and Bella?"

Rainbow nodded fearfully.

"We never talk about it, especially around Crystal."

"Does Wayne love Crystal? Why are they getting married?"

"Wayne Newman will do anything to further his career. So will Crystal. They are made for each other."

"So neither of them actually loves the other?"

"I've said too much," Rainbow said, picking up her bag. "I just wanted to tell you about Bella."

"Thanks for coming here," Jenny nodded, giving her a hug. "And don't worry. I won't go telling tales to Crystal."

Petunia had been cleaning up outside while Rainbow talked with Jenny. She came in after Rainbow left.

"What did she want with you?"

"Nothing much," Jenny said diplomatically.

She began slicing strawberries for the shortcake she planned to make the next morning. A couple of hours later, she walked to the police station.

Adam Hopkins was out and she decided to head on home. It had been a busy day at the café and her feet were killing her.

Jenny and Star ate dinner in front of the TV, watching Gilmore Girls reruns.

"Skipping your walk today?" Star asked her after the sun went down.

"I would love to but I don't have that luxury. My pants are getting tighter by the day."

Star gave her a knowing smile.

"Honey, we both know what your motivation is behind these evening walks."

Jenny took the high road and said nothing.

Jenny laced up her sneakers and stepped out of her aunt's house. She gazed up at the neighboring house and crossed her fingers. Bending down to sniff at a climbing rose, she inhaled deeply and closed her eyes for a moment. Could it all really be hers?

Jenny had never imagined she would be so happy in Pelican Cove.

A bark sounded in the distance and Tank came running up to her. Jenny laughed as he placed his paws on her shoulders, his tail wagging furiously.

"How are you, handsome?"

"Are you talking to me?" a deep voice she had been yearning for all day spoke.

"Of course not!"

Adam grinned and surprised her by taking her arm in his.

"How are you, Jenny? Done any sleuthing today?"

"I do have something to tell you."

Adam looked astonished when Jenny finished talking.

"I'm not surprised Wayne Newman lied to us. I had him pegged as a fraud."

"It's hard to say who the villain is here. Could she have been blackmailing him?"

"That's possible. But we won't know that now."

"At least not until Wayne tells us that."

"The girl was barely 22, Jenny. She doesn't seem like she would hold out for money."

"Maybe she wanted something more. She could have real feelings for Wayne."

"Is that your woman's intuition, Jenny?"

Jenny pursed her lips, her uncertainty clear on her face.

"You never know with these Hollywood types. They will do anything to get ahead in their careers."

"What could Wayne Newman offer her?"

"Name? Fame? A role in his latest TV series?"

"That's the same one Crystal Mars is in?"

Jenny shrugged.

"I can understand why Wayne didn't tell us about Bella. He's about to get married and she's gone anyway. Why dredge up the past?"

"What if the past had everything to do with Bella's murder?"

"So Bella tried to blackmail Wayne and he silenced her?"

Adam was quiet.

"It's not farfetched," Jenny admitted. "People have lost their lives for less."

"There's something you don't know yet. It could change the whole equation."

Chapter 10

"Mandy James has commissioned someone from Virginia Beach to paint the welcome sign," Molly told the Magnolias one morning.

"What a disgrace!" Betty Sue roared. "Why do we need an out-of-towner when we have our own resident artist?"

Star tried to calm them down.

"She must have a reason. I have never painted a welcome sign."

"You know how to paint, don't you?" Jenny asked her aunt. "Are you saying you can't paint 'Welcome to Pelican Cove' on a piece of wood?"

"What about the murals?" Heather demanded. "Has she commissioned you for them yet, Star?"

Star shook her head.

"She is going to have the school kids do that."

"Nonsense!" Betty Sue fumed. "We want art, not graffiti."

"This guy she hired in Virginia Beach is an award winning artist," Petunia informed them. "He's done welcome signs for many towns and these towns then went on to win some kind of award."

"Oh please!" Jenny snorted.

"Think of the devil…" Heather muttered and tipped her head toward the boardwalk.

Barb Norton was walking purposefully toward the café. Mandy James tagged along. The ladies climbed up the stairs to the deck and sat down.

Mandy James handed over an envelope to Petunia.

"What's this?"

"Just some work you need to get done in the next few weeks."

Petunia tore open the envelope and pulled out a sheet of paper.

"New shingles? I just replaced them five years ago."

"Every building on Main Street needs new shingles. You don't want to be the odd one out, do you?"

"Has everyone else agreed?" Jenny asked.

"They don't have much choice," Barb spoke up. "This is a town decree."

"What if we refuse?" Petunia asked.

"You will have to pay a hefty fine. Trust me, you don't want to go that route."

"Who signed off on that?" Betty Sue asked, holding her hand out for the paper.

Barb gave some lengthy explanation.

"That means nothing. I may have to use my veto power."

"Don't you want Pelican Cove to win the competition?" Mandy James asked.

"Of course we do," Petunia wailed. "But at what cost?"

"I know the people who judge these contests," Mandy said. "I know what they are looking for. You're not even close. Pelican Cove needs a complete makeover."

"So you want us to lose our identity?" Heather scowled. "What good is a prize if we have to mutate into something else to win it?"

"We are just going to gussy up the town, Heather," Barb Norton spoke. "Surely no one can object to that."

"Are you done yet?" Betty Sue railed. "I think you should leave now."

Barb Norton stood up with a huff and dragged Mandy to her feet. She stomped down the stairs to the beach but turned back for a parting shot.

"I am the chair of this committee, Betty Sue Morse. I am going to do whatever it takes to win this contest."

"What's going on here?" Star moaned, rubbing her temples. "Barb's like a dog with a bone. Just give her what she wants."

Petunia handed over the paper she had been reading from.

"This is ridiculous!" Star agreed after she read a few items on the list. "It's going to cost a fortune."

"And I don't have that kind of money," Petunia said, looking worried.

"We'll take a look at it later today," Jenny consoled her. "We can prioritize some things. We'll all pitch in, Petunia."

The group broke up after that and Jenny went out to the cash register. A man sitting at a window table got up when he saw her.

"Are you Jenny King?" he asked timidly. "I have been looking for you."

The man seemed vaguely familiar to Jenny. He was just a few inches taller than her own five feet four inches and very ordinary in appearance.

"Have we met before?"

"I don't think so." He raised his eyebrows questioningly. "Can we talk somewhere?"

Jenny ushered him out to the deck and sat down at a small table.

"How do you know me?" she began.

"My lawyer told me about you."

Jenny immediately connected the dots.

"You were with Jason that day…"

"That's right. I'm Ray Fox. Bella's husband."

"Husband?" Jenny asked incredulously. "Bella Darling was married?"

"She sure was. We were coming up on our one year anniversary."

"Why didn't anyone mention it?"

"Nobody knew," Ray Fox said. "Bella wanted it that way."

Jenny could think of a few reasons why.

Ray hastened to explain.

"Hollywood has certain expectations. They want their girls young and single. A struggling actress loses value as soon as she ties the knot."

Jenny wasn't sure she believed that. She tried to keep the sarcasm out of her voice.

"Lots of Hollywood stars are married. Some even have kids."

"I guess you can call the shots when you become a star."

His face fell suddenly and he looked away. Bella Darling was never going to be a star now.

"What am I thinking?" Jenny exclaimed. "I'm sorry for your loss, Mr. Fox. I didn't know your wife but I am sure she was a good person."

"Please call me Ray," he said softly. "Bella was the best. She was so young."

"Was she really just twenty two?"

"She was, unlike some of the gals who just pretend to be so."

"How can I help you, Ray?"

"Jason told me you are working for Crystal Mars?"

"Crystal has asked me to look into what happened," Jenny agreed. "I am going to do just that. I will report whatever I find to the police. The truth will come out, Ray, whatever it is."

"Even if Crystal Mars is to blame?"

Jenny nodded.

"Jason told me you couldn't be bought."

"I'm not a professional detective, Ray. I'm just a middle aged divorced woman who is talking to people and asking a few questions. I can't guarantee what I will find."

"I am thankful for your efforts, Jenny," Ray Fox said.

His eyes filled up as he spoke.

"Why would anyone want to kill my sweet Bella?"

Jenny patted Ray on the shoulder and tried to console him.

"Can you tell me something about her?"

"She was the best of friends," he began. "We were friends first, lovers later."

"How did you two meet?"

"Sky diving," Ray said with a smile. "We were both mad about it."

"So Bella had been sky diving before?"

"She had hundreds of solo jumps under her belt. She went up almost every weekend."

"And you met her at one of these places?"

"We both got our certifications around the same time. I'm a producer for a sitcom. We connected instantly, being from the industry."

"Does she have any family?"

"She dropped out of school and ran away from home when she was a teen. Her family wrote her off, I guess. She planned to go back home when she made it big."

"Surely they tried to contact her?"

"They might have. But Bella never talked about it. I saw her looking at some photos once on Facebook. She shut it down when I asked her about it."

"I don't care that they had a falling out. I would want to know if anything happened to my kid."

"I agree," Ray Fox said. "But Darling was a stage name. I am not sure what her real name was. She was Bella Darling when I met her. She got her driver's license changed too."

"Why did you decide to get married?"

"I fell for her hook, line and sinker. Bella didn't want to get tied down though. She signed a contract that forbid her from marrying while the show ran. Something went wrong and they dropped her at the last minute."

"Did it have anything to do with Crystal?"

"I can't confirm that. But Crystal did replace her."

"Did they know each other personally?"

"I doubt it."

"What happened then?"

"Bella went into a funk after that. She was barely making ends meet. I proposed again, told her it could be temporary until she got back on her feet."

"So she agreed to marry you."

"I would like to think she was in love with me at least a little. But maybe she just got tired of starving."

"Don't be too hard on yourself, Ray," Jenny soothed.

"We weren't destined to be together after all."

"Did Bella have any enemies?"

"Bella was friends with everyone. She could be too nice sometimes. That's not how you get ahead in the entertainment industry."

"You can't think of anyone who might have wanted to harm her?"

Ray shook his head.

"You know this new reality show Crystal is doing? Bella got the short end of the stick. She's the one who should have had a grudge against Crystal."

"Is that why she wanted to ruin Crystal's wedding?"

"I have no idea. I was shooting on location with my unit. I didn't even know Bella had come to Virginia."

"Did they tell you about the wedding dress she was wearing?"

"Vera Wang was her favorite designer."

"Where did she get hold of that dress?"

"She knew a lot of people who worked in the fashion industry. She must have traded in a favor."

"Crystal Mars was wearing the exact same dress."

"She was? Bella must have been wearing a copy then."

"What about the sapphire around her neck?"

"I have never seen it before. It must have cost a fortune."

"Do you think she stole it?"

Ray looked indignant.

"Bella wouldn't do that. She must have borrowed it from someone."

"Did she know people who owned that kind of jewelry?"

"She was friendly with a lot of famous people. She had a few irons in the fire. She would have landed a big role pretty soon. I don't think she really cared about Crystal Mars one way or the other."

"What would have happened if Bella had landed successfully at the wedding? Was it some kind of publicity stunt?"

"Bella wasn't like that. I really don't understand why she was there."

Jenny thought over her next words before she spoke.

"Bella was having an affair with Wayne Newman."

Ray Fox exploded.

"That's a load of crap! Bella would never cheat on me."

Jenny said nothing.

Ray Fox got up and paced on the deck, muttering to himself. Jenny let him fume. He came and sat down after a while.

"Are you sure about this?" he begged.

"Only two people can confirm this. Bella's gone. Wayne Newman said he didn't know her."

"That's a lie," Ray burst out. "Wayne knew Bella."

"Did they date each other?"

"Bella went out with him a couple of times. This was before we got married."

"So you knew about it and you still married her?"

"It wasn't like that. Wayne was trying to woo her. This was back when she was supposed to star in that TV series. When the network dropped her, Wayne followed suit. She was glad. She said he was a jerk."

"So why did she cheat on you, Ray?"

"There's only one reason Bella would have done it," Ray said. "He must have offered her something I can't."

"Didn't you say she hated him?"

Ray shrugged. He leaned forward and stared into Jenny's eyes.

"You don't have to look any further. Wayne Newman killed my wife."

"That's quite an allegation, Ray."

"It's the truth though."

"Where were you on the day of Crystal's wedding?"

"Back home in L.A."

"Can someone vouch for that?"

"I was home alone, wondering where my wife was," Ray said grimly. "I had no idea my wife was thousands of miles away, jumping to her death."

Chapter 11

Jenny and Heather were driving to the Pelican Cove Country Club again. Jenny wanted to talk to Crystal. A lot of new facts had come to light since she last spoke to her. Spooked by the alleged threat against her life, Crystal had gone to ground at the club.

A maid led them to a verandah overlooking the golf course. Crystal sat at a table, drinking iced tea. A tall, hefty man stood at attention a few feet away. Jenny rightly guessed he was the bodyguard Crystal had hired.

"How are you holding up, Crystal?"

Crystal gave an exaggerated sigh.

"Why do these things happen to me? This was supposed to be my honeymoon. Here I am, watching over my shoulder, running for my life."

"Be thankful you have a life," Heather told her.

Crystal motioned toward the man standing nearby.

"I'm taking this very seriously. Wayne told me what happened to Bella's parachute. I am convinced someone wanted to kill me."

"Why would they do that?" Jenny asked. "Do you have a lot of enemies?"

"People are jealous," Crystal pouted. "A star's life is not easy. You're under the radar all the time and people are waiting for you to slip up."

"I can understand that," Jenny agreed. "There's a lot of competition. That doesn't mean people go around killing each other."

"The parachute is proof, isn't it?"

"How many people knew you were going to jump from the plane, Crystal?"

"I would never have done that. I'm afraid of heights."

"What if someone paid you a big amount of money to do it?"

"They wanted me to do it for the show. I refused. I got my lawyer to add a clause. Sky diving, bungee jumping, zip lining – none of that crazy stuff."

Jenny wondered why the network had hired Crystal.

"So someone who knows you well would know you would never go up in that plane."

Crystal nodded emphatically.

"The whole unit knew it, right from the producers to the camera guys."

Jenny lapsed into thought. If anyone had wanted to hurt Crystal, they would have chosen a different method.

"Have you remembered anything about Bella?"

"I told you, Jenny. I didn't know the girl."

"She was having an affair with Wayne Newman."

"I'm not naïve. I know Wayne's been around the block. We both have. So what?"

"You were okay with him cheating on you?"

"Who said anything about cheating?"

"He was engaged to you, wasn't he?"

"Wait a minute. Are you suggesting he was seeing Bella after we were engaged?"

Jenny nodded.

"Who told you that?"

"Never mind who told me. Did you know anything about it?"

Crystal's eyes hardened.

"I didn't."

"Would you have broken off the engagement if you knew?"

"Probably not."

Jenny was taken aback. She was surprised Crystal was being so upfront. But she didn't understand why Crystal was so desperate to get married."

Crystal leaned forward and whispered in Jenny's ear.

"I turned thirty this year."

Jenny reacted appropriately.

"I thought you were in your early twenties."

Crystal gloated a bit.

"I work very hard to look that way, Jenny. What I mean is, I have an expiry date. Turning thirty is like a death sentence in the industry. I can pull it off for some time, maybe. But the roles will start drying up in a couple of years. I need to make my fortune before that."

"Sounds harsh."

"That's just the way it is."

"What does this have to do with Wayne cheating on you?"

"Wayne's very popular right now. Being his wife will elevate my status instantly. I need that, Jenny."

"So you are willing to overlook a few transgressions like an affair or two."

"Neither of us are kids. Our rose colored glasses have been ripped off long ago."

"Why is Wayne marrying you? Does he love you even a little bit?"

"He says he does," Crystal laughed shrilly. "We both have something to offer each other."

"How far will you go? We already know Wayne's a womanizer. What if he does drugs? What if he is abusive?"

"I can deal with all that once we are married. It will make great news copy. The tragic wife! I can earn a lot of sympathy from the fans."

Jenny stole a glance at Heather. Heather's shock was evident in her expression.

"You mean you're marrying Wayne even after knowing all this bad stuff?"

"Heather, you're such a sweetie. I'm marrying him because I know these things."

Jenny wondered what kind of twisted world Crystal Mars lived in.

"Where do you draw the line?" she exploded. "What if Wayne wanted you out of the way?"

"He wouldn't do that! We have an understanding."

"What if he got rid of Bella?"

"He could have dumped her any time. No one gave a damn about Bella Darling."

Jenny slapped her hand on the table.

"Are you being stupid on purpose? What if Wayne tampered with that parachute, Crystal? Would you still want to marry him?"

"Wayne had no reason to do that. Don't you have any other suspects?"

"Wayne's the only one who had an opportunity to harm Bella. He was up there with her on that plane."

"Why would he do it on our wedding day?"

"I don't have an answer for that. Have you come up with any other names?"

"Maybe someone wanted to hold up my wedding."

"That's a stretch."

"Bella might have gotten away with a broken arm or leg. Why did she have to die?"

"It's hard to predict what will happen when a person drops from ten thousand feet. Only a fool could have thought that."

"Have you met the girls? They are not really bright, Jenny."

"Are you saying one of your bridesmaids did it?"

Crystal shrugged.

"They could have."

"Do you really believe that?"

Crystal settled back in her chair and looked around. She stifled a yawn and looked at Jenny.

"This is all a big waste of time. I am sure this was an accident. Bella was just unlucky."

"Didn't we just talk about the slashed parachute?" Jenny asked her. "Pay attention, Crystal. This was no accident. Someone very definitely wanted Bella out of the way. This is a murder investigation."

"The police said that. I thought they were bluffing to get some reaction out of me."

Jenny wanted to tell Crystal the police didn't bluff about such things.

"Did any of your bridesmaids know Bella?" Heather asked.

She didn't know about Jenny's talk with the girl called Rainbow.

"Rainbow did."

"Were they friends?" Heather went on.

"Anything but," Crystal snorted.

"What was that?" Jenny asked sharply.

"Rainbow hated Bella. They got into a big fight. She got Bella banned from the set."

"But I thought Bella wasn't part of your show?"

"This was before they signed me on. There was some scandal and Bella got fired."

Jenny's head was spinning with possibilities.

Crystal clutched the bridge of her nose suddenly. She closed her eyes and started massaging her temples.

"Are we done here? I think I'm getting a migraine."

Jenny and Heather expressed their sympathy. They took a circuitous route back to the car.

"She could've offered us a drink," Heather complained. "I'm dying from thirst."

"I'll make you a smoothie when we get back to the café," Jenny promised.

She was deep in thought. She couldn't figure out who was lying, Rainbow or Crystal? Rainbow had claimed to be friends with Bella.

"Did you feel we were going around in circles?" Heather asked.

"Led by Crystal," Jenny nodded. "Is she always like this?"

"Like what?"

"A bit dumb."

"I don't know her that well, Jenny."

"She is either completely hare brained or very clever. Wanna bet it's the latter?"

"Did you believe all that stuff about marrying Wayne inspite of knowing bad things about him?"

"Exactly! How do we know she wasn't on to the affair? She could have wanted revenge on Bella."

"Why would she want to ruin her own wedding?"

"That's exactly why. No one would suspect her of doing it."

They spotted a bunch of girls seated in a gazebo overlooking the ocean. One of the girls waved at them and walked over.

"Hello," Rainbow said, smiling sweetly at Jenny. "Were you here to meet Crystal?"

Jenny nodded.

"Can you walk with us? I would like to ask you a few questions."

Rainbow fell in step with them. Jenny waited until they were a good distance away from the gazebo.

"You told me you were friends with Bella."

"Of course! We shared an apartment for some time."

"According to Crystal, you didn't get along at all. She says you got Bella fired."

Rainbow froze, looking like a deer in the headlights. Jenny placed her hands on her hips and quirked an eyebrow questioningly.

"I may not have told you everything," Rainbow mumbled.

"You hated Bella, didn't you?"

"We had a falling out," Rainbow agreed. "But we weren't always like that. I treated her like a younger sister."

"What went wrong?"

"She stabbed me in the back," Rainbow said bitterly. "I didn't see it coming. She acted all innocent, you know. But it was all fake."

"What did she do?"

"I'd rather not talk about it."

"Were you angry with her?"

"She made me so mad!"

"Mad enough to kill?"

Rainbow gasped.

"What? Of course not. This kind of thing is very common. That doesn't mean we go around killing people."

"But someone did kill Bella. Or have you forgotten that?"

"Look, I thought about what you said. Maybe Crystal was the target here."

"Crystal said she's afraid of heights."

"She is. But she'll do anything for a bit of attention."

"Any update on the wedding?"

"Wayne is still holding out. Crystal's trying to convince him."

"How long are you going to stick around?"

Rainbow shrugged.

"We haven't been cleared to leave yet. We don't mind though. This place is so beautiful. It's like an impromptu vacation."

"You didn't tell me Bella was married."

Rainbow looked away, refusing to say anything.

"Why did Bella have an affair with Wayne? Did he promise her something?"

"I don't know. Bella wasn't sharing stuff with me by that time."

"Was Wayne forcing her, do you think?"

"Have you seen Wayne Newman?" Rainbow exhaled. "He doesn't force women. They fall at his feet, begging to be noticed."

Jenny wondered if there was a note of bitterness in Rainbow's voice.

"That dinner you had with Bella and Wayne? Did that really happen?"

"It did," Rainbow said.

"Let me know if you think of anything else, Rainbow."

Jenny and Heather waved goodbye and walked to their car. It was a considerable distance away.

"Shouldn't they offer us those golf cart things?" Heather complained.

Jenny pulled a tissue out of her bag and mopped her brow. The car had been toasting out in the sun. Jenny turned the air conditioner on full blast and stuck her face in front of the vents.

"I could use a cold shower right about now," she groaned.

"I'm getting a headache," Heather said.

She pointed back toward the club.

"Crystal doesn't seem like a good person, does she?"

"She's single minded. I'll say that for her."

"Sometimes I feel I lead a very sheltered life," Heather confessed.

"There's a big bad world out there, kiddo. Pelican Cove is like our own bit of paradise."

"I'm glad you came here, Jenny. I know you're a bit older than me but I like having you for a friend."

"Anymore of that and you'll make Chris jealous," Jenny joked.

"Chris has forgotten I exist."

"Weren't you complaining he was getting too close?" Jenny teased.

"I guess I spoke too soon."

Chapter 12

Mandy James walked along Main Street, waving her phone in the air.

"What is she doing now?" Petunia asked Jenny.

"I think she's taking pictures."

"She couldn't use the ones we have in the town archives?"

The ladies at the Boardwalk Café were enjoying a respite after the breakfast rush. Mandy walked in a few minutes later with Barb Norton in tow.

"Can I have one of your famous chocolate cupcakes? The ones with the raspberry frosting?"

"Sure," Jenny drawled. "Can I get you anything else?"

Mandy took the cupcake out on the deck. She fiddled around with it, putting it on different spots on a table. She took pictures from different angles, climbing up on a chair once to take a top shot. She finally cried in triumph and sat down in one of the chairs.

"What are the photos for?" Jenny asked.

"Pelican Cove is now on Instagram. I'm taking pictures of the best things the town has to offer. The beaches, sand dunes, the flowering trees, anything that will make people flock to Pelican Cove."

"I thought your focus was on Main Street."

"It is. But Main Street is not up to snuff yet. I will start taking photos after the refurbishment."

"So you want to take before and after photos?"

"Not really. Some things don't need a makeover, like the ocean and your delicious cupcakes."

Jenny looked at Mandy suspiciously.

"What do you want, Mandy?"

Mandy dropped all pretense.

"You have Petunia's ear. Please get her to go through the list I sent. You guys need to start on those improvements right away."

"I'm not sure she can afford them."

"That's a problem, Jenny."

"Are you going to force us to shut down?"

"A defunct business will look worse. The café is just too prominent."

"What would you have us do?"

"Get a facelift. Get with the program. Don't you want your town to win? You win once but you can carry the tag forever."

"Is that your usual spiel?"

"You're from the city, aren't you? I thought we'd be on the same page. What can you do to make these hicks see the light? I'll make it worth your while."

Jenny bristled at the suggestion. Her hands went to her hips and she glared at Mandy James.

"Get out. Now."

"Don't get me wrong, Jenny. At least read the list. Please?"

"Alright. I'll give it a look."

Mandy James walked down the steps to the beach.

"What did she want, dear?" Petunia asked, coming out of the kitchen.

"Nothing in particular. Forget about it."

Heather arrived some time later with Betty Sue. Molly wasn't far behind. Petunia told them about Mandy.

"That Mandy James was walking around clicking pictures."

"Does Barb know that?" Betty Sue asked, pulling a ball of blue wool from her bag.

"Barb was following her around. Jenny knows all about it."

Jenny told them about the Instagram.

"What is that?" Betty Sue thundered.

"It's like Facebook, grandma, but it's different."

"How is that going to help us win?"

"Why don't we go over the list you have, Petunia? Maybe we should ask a contractor for an estimate."

"We may not need a contractor," Heather told them. "We can get the guys to pitch in, have a potluck. Everyone will help."

Jenny didn't look convinced.

"What if there's some structural work to be done?"

"The list is not going to tell you that," Petunia argued. "We will need to get an inspector here to check on everything."

"I say let's do that," Jenny urged. "Let's get an estimate for a complete makeover."

"Are you out of your mind?" Petunia asked. "I don't have that kind of money."

"What's the harm in getting an estimate?"

Jenny widened her eyes at Heather. She caught on immediately.

"Bring that list out. We can check off the easy things."

"That's it then. We know what we can do ourselves. We'll get an estimate for the rest."

"Can you imagine Mandy's face if we do all of this?" Heather squealed.

"Don't get ahead of yourself, girls. There's no way I can get all this done."

"Any update on that poor girl?" Betty Sue asked.

"I learn something new every day. She was married, for instance. She had an affair with Crystal's fiancé."

"Maybe she wasn't as innocent as she looks," Molly said.

"She is the victim here, Molls," Jenny reminded her.

She looked at the rest of them.

"Everyone I talk to is lying about something. I am not sure I can trust anyone."

"You should take some advice from Adam," Betty Sue hinted. "See what he thinks."

"Adam keeps things close to his chest," Jenny complained. "He's not going to help."

"So what's the plan?" Molly asked her.

"I'm not sure," Jenny admitted reluctantly. "I'm still thinking."

She took Betty Sue's advice to heart later that day and decided to go meet Adam. Adam was having a bad day.

"What is it, Jenny?" he scowled. "I'm busy."

Jenny sat down and smiled at him. She had brought over a plate of cupcakes for the staff. She was sure no one would disturb them.

"How's the leg?"

"As usual…what do you want?"

"How are the twins? Are they coming home soon?"

Adam banged a fist on the desk.

"Jenny, I don't have time for small talk. What do you want?"

"Can't I just come in to say hello?"

"Of course you can," Adam sighed. "But I really don't have time to take a break."

"Are you working on Bella's case?"

Adam rolled his eyes and tried not to grin.

"So you're on a hunting expedition."

Jenny shrugged.

"I talked to Wayne and Crystal. And Bella's husband came to talk to me."

"Good for you. If it were up to me, none of them would have told you anything."

"Did you know Bella was having an affair with Wayne?"

Adam sat up with a start.

"What?"

"Bella and Wayne had an affair."

"Where do you learn these things?"

"I can be useful to you, Adam. We should work together."

"Be serious, Jenny. How sure are you about this?"

"They definitely had an affair before Bella got married. And they were still seeing each other."

"Even though that Wayne guy was engaged?"

Jenny nodded.

"That changes everything."

It was Jenny's turn to be surprised.

"You are hiding something from me."

"I am not," Adam argued. "That's because I am not required to tell you anything."

"We can agree on that. Now can you please tell me?"

Adam was quiet for a minute.

"Bella was pregnant."

Jenny let out a cry.

"Oh! That poor girl. How far along was she?"

Jenny tried to remember if Bella Darling had been showing her baby bump on that fateful day. She realized she hadn't really looked closely.

"A couple of months, according to the autopsy report."

"It could be Wayne's."

"You realize what this means, don't you?" Adam asked. "This is a double murder."

"You're right," Jenny said softly.

She sat stunned for a few minutes, saying nothing. Then she remembered something

Ray Fox had said.

"What about the sapphire?"

"She was supposed to wear it for a photo shoot," Adam explained. "That's how she got her hands on such an expensive piece."

"Have you cleared Ray Fox?"

"He doesn't have an alibi so he's still under suspicion."

"What about the pilot of the plane?"

"What about him, Jenny?"

"I should go talk to him."

"You are meddling in an ongoing investigation again."

"I'm just trying to find out what happened, Adam. I want to help."

"You are neither trained nor qualified for this," Adam fumed. "Stop putting yourself in danger."

"Nothing's happening to me!" Jenny brushed Adam off.

"Are you done now?"

"Do you know our town is now on Instagram?"

"I don't want to know. I'll see you later, Jenny."

Jenny decided Adam was about to flip. She got up and said goodbye.

"Just one more thing…"

"Now what?"

"Can you recommend a good contractor?"

Adam scribbled something on a notepad and tore the paper off. He handed it to Jenny.

"Now don't bother me for a couple of weeks."

Jenny laughed on her way out. She saw Adam's face break into a smile through the corner of her eye. So he wasn't completely immune to her. She hoped he would hurry up and ask her out on a proper date.

Jenny walked to the seafood market. Chris Williams greeted her with a smile and a hug.

"Where have you been hiding, Chris? You haven't come to the café in a long time."

"We did our annual inventory," he explained. "Restocked everything. Getting ready for tourist season, you know."

"I'm not the only one who's feeling neglected."

Chris blushed.

"Did Heather say something? I thought she was busy at the country club."

"Not really. She misses you, Chris."

'You want to go on a double date? We can take the boat out one evening. You, me, Heather and Jason…"

"Sounds great," Jenny nodded. "Now how about some trout?"

Jenny remembered she was out of Old Bay seasoning. It was an absolutely essential ingredient on the Eastern Shore. Star wouldn't eat fish unless it was liberally sprinkled with the signature spice.

She almost collided with someone in the spice aisle.

"Jenny!" Ray Fox stared back at her.

His eyes were bloodshot and his clothes looked like he had slept in them. Jenny wondered if he knew what Adam had told her.

"What are you doing here, Ray?"

"I don't know. Just walking around."

Jenny picked up a bottle of seasoning, trying to think of what to say next.

There was a haunted look in his eyes.

"We talked about giving it all up, Bella and I. We dreamed of moving to a small town by the sea, just like this one. Somewhere we could raise our kids, far away from the shadow of Hollywood."

"Any luck with Bella's family?"

Ray shook his head.

"I'm trying to reach out to some of her friends, girls she knew when she first moved to Los Angeles. They might know something."

"Why don't you come over to the café tomorrow? Breakfast is on me. Or lunch. Whatever you need, Ray."

"I need my wife," Ray said bitterly. "But she's not coming back."

He turned around and walked away from Jenny, stumbling into another aisle. Chris had been watching from a distance.

"Who's that guy? He looks kind of suspicious."

Jenny told him about Bella.

"You girls will be careful, won't you? You had a narrow escape last time, Jenny."

"Don't worry, Chris. I'm not going up in a plane anytime soon."

"How can you joke about it?" Chris groaned.

"Did you hear about the Main Street project Barb Norton's undertaken?"

"We are at the far end so she hasn't given us much grief."

"Don't count on it," Jenny warned. "She came up with a big list for the café. I think she secretly wants to tear the place down."

"No way! The town can't function without the Boardwalk Café!"

"Shouldn't Barb know that? Wait till you meet her sidekick."

"You mean that girl who is going around snapping pictures?"

"She's put us on Instagram."

Chris whipped out his phone from his pocket.

"This I have to see."

"So we're giving the café a complete makeover. Can I count on you for some sweat equity?"

"As long as you pay me in donuts and cupcakes…"

"Heather said we can have a potluck, gather everyone."

"Now you're talking!" Chris grinned. "Better than risking your life playing detective."

"Bella Darling was barely twenty two, Chris. She didn't deserve such a gruesome end. I won't stop until I find out who did this to her."

Chapter 13

"I looked it up," Heather told Jenny on the phone. "It's in Baltimore."

Jenny had decided she needed to talk to the plane company Wayne had hired. Heather had managed to get the name from Crystal.

"You ready for a road trip?" Jenny asked.

"Oh yeah! Let's ask Molly. We can go shopping and have dinner at a city restaurant. It's been ages since I had some Thai food."

Plans were made and Saturday arrived soon enough. Jenny had secured an appointment at Eagle Aviation, a company that offered sky diving in the area. They also took special assignments like Wayne's where they arranged to fly people out to specific locations. The man Jenny spoke to thought she was booking a dive. She didn't want to tip him off prematurely.

"Do you have a list of questions ready?" Heather asked as they set off in Jenny's car.

Star was pitching in at the café so Jenny could take some time off.

"I mostly want to know if he saw Bella."

"Remember how she was dressed? Would be hard to miss."

Molly spoke up from the back seat.

"If the pilot saw her, surely Wayne saw her too?"

"We'll see," Jenny said grimly.

Jenny followed the directions to a facility outside city limits. There was a big hangar at one end. A bunch of people dressed in colorful flying suits were avidly listening to an instructor.

"We are looking for Captain Jorge," Jenny told a man dressed in overalls.

He pointed her to a small trailer a few feet away.

Jenny, Heather and Molly trooped toward the tiny structure. Jenny knocked on the door and went in.

"Captain Jorge? I'm Jenny King. We just talked on the phone."

"Hello ladies!"

An attractive older man greeted them cheerfully. His angular face was weather beaten. His close cropped hair had plenty of gray in it. Jenny thought of Tom Cruise in Top Gun and figured this is how he would have looked when he aged.

"Is this your first dive? We have some specials for first timers."

Jenny looked apologetic.

"Actually, we are not here for sky diving."

The man frowned and waited for an explanation.

"We live in Pelican Cove. It's a small island off the coast of the Eastern Shore."

"Wait a minute. Isn't that where that country singer jumped?"

Jenny nodded. She was glad he had caught on quickly.

"We were sorry to hear about the girl. Are you related to her?"

"Not really," Jenny admitted. "But I am trying to find out what happened."

"Are you with the police?"

"No. I am doing this on my own."

"The police came here already. I talked to them."

"Can you spare some time for me, please? I just have a few questions."

Captain Jorge looked at his watch.

"I can give you half an hour. I have to take a group of ten up after that."

"You can take ten people up at a time?" Heather burst out. "I thought sky diving planes were really tiny."

"Some of them are," Captain Jorge said with a smile. "We have a larger aircraft here. I can take 20 people up at once."

"Did you have any other people on the plane with Wayne Newman?" Jenny asked.

Jorge shook his head.

"They booked the whole plane. That's generally what they do for special events."

"You mean people sky dive to their wedding a lot?" Molly asked.

"You'd be surprised. Some people propose to their girl friends in the air." He shrugged. "More business for us."

"So you weren't surprised when Wayne Newman booked out your plane?" Jenny asked again.

"It's not that common," Captain Jorge conceded. "It costs a small fortune."

"Wayne isn't hurting for money I guess."

"No ma'am."

"What's the usual process you follow for sky diving? Can you walk me through it please?"

"Most people go for a tandem dive. That's where we provide one of our own people to accompany you."

"Do they have a choice?"

"You need to be licensed if you want to do a solo dive. We make sure you have the right credentials."

"And Wayne Newman produced them?"

"He sure did. He said he was going to do a tandem dive with his wife to be. He was going to take her down himself."

"Did he have his own parachute?"

"I guess. He was already rigged up when I saw him that day."

"Do you inspect the gear before the jump?"

"Of course," Captain Jorge said quickly. "We follow the necessary guidelines. If he rented one of our rigs, it must have gone through a quality check."

"Who was flying the plane that day?"

"I was. I'm the only pilot around here."

"Can you describe what happened?"

"The girl arrived when I was doing my flight checks. She was wearing a fancy wedding dress so I thought she must be the bride."

"Did she say who she was?"

Captain Jorge blinked, then shook his head.

"She told me she wanted to surprise her husband. Would I play along?"

"Then?"

"The way the plane is outfitted, there's hardly any room to hide. I put some stuff up there so she could crouch behind it and stay out of sight."

"What happened after that?"

"This guy arrived wearing a tux. He said his wife was afraid of heights. She wasn't coming after all."

"Go on."

"I played along. I figured the guy's going to get a nice surprise from his missus once we go up."

"When did he realize Bella was on the plane?"

"I don't know. I'm not sure."

"You must have heard them talk."

"We hit some unexpected turbulence. I wasn't really paying attention to them."

"What did you do after they jumped?"

"I realized the second chute didn't open. But there wasn't anything I could do at that point."

"Where do you keep the parachutes? Could someone have tampered with them?"

He waved his hand toward the hangar.

"There's plenty of people underfoot here all the time. I guess anyone could have done it."

"Do you have any security cameras?"

"Just one. The cops are going through the tapes."

"Could it have been an accident?"

"What do you mean?"

"Surely the parachutes have some wear and tear? Could it get ripped on its own?"

"Unlikely. If the chute is not packed properly, it can get stuck. But there's always the reserve."

"What's that?"

"It's a backup parachute," Captain Jorge explained. "If the main parachute is not open at a certain altitude, the backup opens. It's a lifesaver."

"But that didn't happen in this case," Jenny sighed.

"I heard it was turned off."

"Could that have happened accidentally?"

Captain Jorge shook his head.

"Anyone who values his life would never turn the reserve off. So no. And it doesn't get turned off on its own."

"So someone made very sure neither chute would open," Jenny pressed.

"Sure looks that way."

"Could Wayne have caught hold of her mid-air?"

"It depends on a lot of things," Captain Jorge said. "It's possible theoretically but it's not easy."

"Are you a sky diver too?" Jenny asked. "Just curious."

"I am. But I'm also an overworked pilot. I hardly ever get to jump."

"Did you notice anything out of the ordinary that day?"

"That singer guy was sweating like a pig. Wedding jitters, I guess."

Wedding jitters, or a guilty conscience, Jenny wondered.

"Look, I have to go now," Captain Jorge said, glancing at his watch again. "Here's my card. Why don't you give me a call if you have any more questions."

The girls thanked the suave pilot and loitered around for a while.

"We should go sky diving some time," Molly said enthusiastically. "Looks like fun."

"Count me out," Jenny shuddered. "I'm twenty years too old for it."

One of the instructors looked up when he heard that.

"Age has nothing to do with it, lady. You need a strong will. Ain't nothing like that feeling, when you spread your arms up in the sky and feel the wind in your face."

"Sorry, but it's not my thing," Jenny said, thanking the man.

They piled into the car and drove into the city.

"Do you miss it?" Heather asked, as Jenny peered at the tall buildings and big shops.

"Not one bit," she smiled, honking her horn as a semi cut her off. "See that? Who needs that in life?"

Heather had looked up a Thai restaurant she wanted to visit. They ordered the largest mai tais and toasted their friendship.

"Ooooh, spicy!" Heather exclaimed, fanning her mouth as she dunked curry puffs into a sweet chili sauce.

"What did you think of Captain Jorge?" Molly teased. "Was he a hunk or what?"

"Molly Henderson! I saw how you were staring at him."

"I'm single and unattached. I can look. Unlike you two."

"My divorce is final now," Jenny declared tipsily. "I'm as single as they come."

"What about the two men you've wrapped around your finger?"

"There's no such thing," Jenny muttered, sipping her cocktail through a straw.

"And Heather's with Chris. Let's not say any more."

"Until Chris pops the question, I am free to flirt with whoever I want to."

"Why don't you propose to him?" Jenny suggested. "It would be the scandal of the century in Pelican Cove."

"I know what you should do," Molly laughed. "Go sky diving with Chris and propose to him in the air."

There was a moment of silence and they all turned serious.

"What do you think Bella planned to do?" Jenny asked the girls.

"I think she wanted to ruin Crystal's wedding but it went horribly wrong."

"What if Bella messed with the parachutes? The bad chute could have been meant for Wayne but she wore it by mistake."

Jenny looked at Molly in shock.

"So you're saying she was the actual killer. But she ended up killing herself."

"It's possible," Molly protested. "Why wear a wedding dress at all? I think it was a ruse."

"How so?"

"She wanted to pass herself off as Wayne's bride. No one was going to stop a woman dressed like that. The sapphire must have been part of her disguise."

"I guess that makes sense," Jenny agreed.

"What if Wayne wanted Crystal out of the way? He booked the flight for the both of them, right? He could have messed with the parachute beforehand. But Bella wore it and jumped to her death."

"Who do you think Wayne was actually interested in?" Heather asked. "Crystal or Bella?"

"Maybe he was sick of them both," Jenny mused. "But chances are, he didn't want the baby."

"What baby?" Heather and Molly chorused.

Jenny told them about Bella's condition.

"Only a monster would kill his unborn child," Molly spat.

"We don't know who the father is," Jenny said.

"Do you think Crystal found out about the baby?" Heather asked. "She could have decided to get rid of Bella."

"But how did Crystal know Bella was going to be on the plane?" Jenny shot back.

"You're right," Heather sighed. "That doesn't make sense."

"What about that girl who talks to you?" Molly asked Jenny. "She knew Bella, didn't she?"

"Rainbow?" Jenny asked. "Are you saying Rainbow sent Bella up on that plane? But why?"

"It could have been a gag of some kind."

"Everyone I talked to said Bella was a sweet girl. I find it hard to believe she wanted to ruin Crystal's wedding."

"Nice girls don't have affairs," Molly argued.

"Surely Wayne must have noticed her on that plane?" Jenny asked. "What do you think?"

The girls had peeked into the airplane while Captain Jorge was doing some pre-flight checks.

"There's no way anyone could stay hidden in that space," Heather nodded.

"So Wayne Newman is definitely lying about something."

Chapter 14

"How was your trip?" Star asked Heather on Sunday morning. "Did you find out anything useful?"

"I am more confused than I was before," Jenny admitted, taking a big sip of her coffee.

"Why don't you write it down? It must be hard to keep it all straight in your head."

"You spoke my mind," Jenny told her aunt. "I made a rough sketch in a notebook last night. I couldn't sleep."

"Sketch?"

"Sketch may be the wrong word. I just wrote down the names of all the people and who they are connected with. You'd be surprised what the common thread is."

"Don't make me guess."

"Rainbow! She knew all of the players, except maybe Ray Fox. But I am thinking she might have known him too."

"Are you going to talk to her again?"

Jenny nodded.

"Be careful, okay?" Star cautioned. "I don't want you getting hurt."

"Relax! Rainbow's harmless."

"Not if she was mixed up in hurting that poor girl."

Jenny went to the café later than usual. Many people preferred to come for brunch on Sunday. Jenny made a batch of muffins and chopped fresh herbs for her scrambled eggs.

"You could plant herbs in your own patch out back."

Jenny recognized Mandy's voice but ignored her.

"Have you and Petunia gone through my list?"

"Don't you have someone else to pick on?" Jenny grumbled. "I'm busy."

"Some people have already started with their renovations," Mandy proclaimed. "We are painting park benches today. The curbs will be the last."

"We have a contractor coming in to give us an estimate," Jenny told her reluctantly.

"That's a step in the right direction," Mandy said approvingly.

Jenny called Heather at the inn.

"Fancy a trip to the country club?"

Heather had a headache.

"That's what too many mai tais will do to you," Jenny teased. "You need some solid food inside you."

"Don't mention food, please," Heather begged.

They drove to the club a couple of hours later. The first person they ran into was Wayne Newman.

"Ladies!" he greeted, tipping his hat at them. "Here to see Crystal?"

Jenny nodded vaguely. She didn't want to reveal the purpose of her visit.

"She's at the pool with her girls."

"What are they doing?"

"What they always do," Wayne shrugged. "I have no idea."

Jenny had a thought.

"We went to Eagle Aviation," she told Wayne. "Got a tour of the place. We saw the plane you jumped from."

"It's one of the bigger ones," Wayne told them. "That's what I liked about the place."

"I thought the plane was really small," Jenny persisted. "It didn't even have a toilet."

Wayne looked uncomfortable.

"Most of the planes they use for sky diving don't."

"So here's my question," Jenny rushed ahead. "How is it possible you didn't see Bella before you jumped?"

Wayne turned red.

"I was excited. I didn't look around."

"You didn't see that big old white dress she was wearing?"

"Hey! It was my wedding day. I just wanted to get the dive over with so I could stand with my wife."

"You sound like you were doing it against your will."

Wayne clammed up after that.

"I got to go."

"Why did you challenge him like that?" Heather exclaimed as soon as Wayne was out of sight.

"I couldn't help it," Jenny said, shaking with anger.

"It changes nothing, except now he knows what we are thinking."

"Good. Maybe he'll slip up."

They went looking for Rainbow after that. One of the maids at the country club told them where her room was.

Rainbow looked a bit disheveled when she opened the door. She was wearing a silky robe and her hair was mussed. Jenny's nose twitched as she tried to smell something.

"Do you have a hangover too?" Heather laughed as they went in.

Rainbow stifled a yawn.

"There's not much to do here. I decided to sleep in."

"It's a beautiful day," Jenny said. "Don't they have a pool here?"

"Crystal and the girls are hanging out there," Rainbow said. "I couldn't take it anymore. I just want to go home."

"Do you know Ray Fox?" Jenny asked.

"Bella's husband? Sure."

"Do you know he's here in Pelican Cove?"

"I saw him in town."

"He seems lost without Bella."

"He loved her a lot."

"You know what I am thinking, Rainbow?" Jenny asked. "You seem to be the common thread here. You knew Bella, you know Wayne and Crystal, you even know Ray Fox."

"What are you implying?"

"How do we know you didn't carry messages between these people?"

"You think I was spying on someone?"

"You could have. For example, you could have told Crystal about Wayne and Bella. Or you could have told Ray Fox about them."

"Why would I do that? Bella was my friend."

"That's what you told us before. But we heard that you were sworn enemies."

Rainbow rubbed her hands, pacing across the room.

"Who's feeding you this stuff?"

"Do you deny it?"

"There's someone else who knew Bella…"

Jenny's eyebrows shot up.

"Keep talking!"

"Crystal's mother. Why don't you go talk to her?"

"Don't worry, I will."

Jenny grabbed Heather's arm and they swept out of the room.

"Didn't you smell something familiar in there?" she asked Heather.

Heather shook her head.

"Do you believe that girl?"

"She just wanted to get rid of us. But I know Crystal's mother lied to me. I want to talk to her again."

Kathy Mars was seated on the patio, sipping a frosty glass of lemonade. Her summer dress made her look ten years younger. She looked up at them with sparkling blue eyes the exact shade of the sunny skies.

"What brings you here, girls?" she asked. "Do you have any news for us?"

"Some," Jenny answered, choosing a chair opposite her.

Kathy poured some lemonade for them. She settled back in her chair and gave her a speculative look.

"Something's been bothering me since our last meeting," Jenny began. "You knew Bella Darling, didn't you?"

Kathy sighed, looking beaten.

"I met her a few times."

"Why did you keep that from me?"

"Bella and I didn't meet under the best of circumstances."

"Did you have a fight with her?" Jenny asked, sitting up.

"Nothing of that sort."

Kathy Mars gazed over the grassy dunes.

"Crystal is so beautiful. I knew she was special right from the moment I held her for the first time."

Jenny didn't know if Kathy was going somewhere with her reminiscences but she didn't interrupt.

"I gave her the best of everything. When Crystal won a talent contest in junior high, I knew her future was in Hollywood."

"So you were a supportive mother."

"I planned her whole career. We had big plans, you know. Then we went to Hollywood."

"Wasn't it like you imagined?"

"It was everything we imagined and more. There was just one tiny problem. Everyone was beautiful and talented. Crystal needed something extra to stand out. I'm afraid she didn't have it."

"She didn't find any work?" Heather asked.

Kathy Mars snorted rudely.

"She got small roles. A cameo here, a music video there. We managed to get by but none of them were enough to launch her career."

"Until she landed the reality show," Jenny said flatly. "But she wasn't the first choice there too."

"Bella was the star of the show," Kathy said bitterly. "Crystal was one of the minor contestants. They wouldn't have kept her for more than one episode."

"What did you do?"

"I pulled in some favors. There was a scandal. Bella was off the show and Crystal was in."

"You managed that by yourself?"

"I had help. Money talks, Miss King. There are plenty of starving girls out there, ready to do anything for a bit of cash."

"Did you know Wayne Newman at that time?"

Kathy looked triumphant.

"That's where I scored a home run. Bella was having an affair with Wayne Newman at the time. He seemed like a good fit for my Crystal."

"Did you pay him to go out with your daughter?"

"Give me some credit," Kathy Mars bristled. "I just arranged for them to meet accidentally a couple of times. I knew Wayne is a ladies' man. He fell under Crystal's spell."

"It didn't bother you that he might be cheating on your daughter?"

"My Crystal turned thirty this year. Her time's running out. She needed to tie the knot with someone influential and soon."

"I thought Crystal was the bigger star," Heather said.

"She is now," Kathy Mars said proudly. "Her star's been on the rise since she met Wayne. They are good for each other."

"What happened to Bella after you got rid of her?"

Kathy shrugged.

"I heard she had a husband. I figured she would be fine."

"Who helped you get rid of Bella?" Jenny asked.

"It doesn't matter now. Bella's gone."

"Was it Rainbow? Did she tell you some deep dark secret about Bella Darling?"

Kathy Mars changed the subject and refused to divulge any more information.

Jenny stood up and stomped to Rainbow's room. Rainbow had showered in their absence. She was dressed in a pair of shorts and a bikini top.

"What do you want now?" she asked, rolling her eyes.

"You're a two faced liar, Rainbow!"

"What have I done?"

"You threw Bella under the bus, didn't you? Kathy Mars paid you off."

"I don't know what you're talking about."

"It's like I said, Rainbow," Jenny fumed. "You are the connection between all these people. Did you spy on Bella for Ray Fox? Did you tell him about the affair?"

"Look! I didn't ask him to come here, okay? I just saw him in town the night of the rehearsal dinner."

"What?" Heather and Jenny exclaimed.

"Are you sure you saw him the night before the wedding?"

Rainbow nodded.

"Crystal had sent me on an errand. I saw him go into that pub, what's it called?"

"The Rusty Anchor?"

"I guess. How many pubs do you have here anyway?"

"According to Ray Fox, he was back in L.A. when Bella fell to her death."

"No he wasn't," Rainbow shook her head. "He was right here in Pelican Cove."

"This doesn't let you off, Rainbow. You're up to something."

"Have you ever thought I might be a victim too?" she cried.

"Can you elaborate on that?"

Rainbow shut up after that.

"I'm going to the pool," she said, picking up a towel.

"Do you really suspect Rainbow?" Heather asked Jenny that afternoon.

They were watching the sunset from Star's porch, their feet up on the railing.

Jenny smacked her lips as she enjoyed the sundowners she had mixed for them.

"I didn't until now but I'm not sure any longer. She is definitely involved somehow."

"She could have told Ray Fox about Bella's affair. So he came here to confront her."

"Who told him Bella was here?" Jenny mused. "Speaking of which, how many people knew Bella was in town?"

"How did we not know?" Molly asked, coming out with a plate of crab dip and crudités. "Crystal had booked out the entire country club for her wedding. And Bella wasn't staying at Heather's inn."

"She must have been staying out of town," Jenny said. "Someone would have noticed her otherwise."

"You think Kathy Mars stopped after paying Bella off?" Heather mused. "She seems awfully concerned about Crystal turning thirty."

"Turning thirty is a big deal," Molly stressed. "I remember how depressed I was on my thirtieth birthday."

"Rainbow turned out to be something else, didn't she?" Heather said, taking a sip of her drink.

"Each one of them is wearing a mask," Jenny said coldly. "I need to rip it off if I want to find out the truth."

Chapter 15

Jenny's room looked like a tornado had torn through it. The bed was strewn with discarded clothes, so was every available surface. Jenny had spent the past hour trying to find the perfect outfit for the annual Pelican Cove BBQ.

"Is this a big thing?" she had asked Star the previous evening.

"It happens once a year, so yes. The town goes all out. The men set up a smoker and start smoking the meat in the morning. The ladies make a ton of side dishes. And there's ice cream, of course."

"How many people go to this thing?"

"The whole town goes, Jenny. It's one of the highlights of the year."

"What about tourists?"

"We didn't allow tourists until recently. You know how the islanders are, but this year's going to be different."

"How so?"

"Barb Norton and her minion have butted in here too. They are going to charge admission and use the money for the town beautification."

Jenny was getting sick of Mandy James and her brilliant ideas.

Star peeped into Jenny's room and started laughing.

"How old are you, girl? Sixteen?"

Jenny ignored her and held out two outfits. Star shook her head at either one of them.

"It's going to be hot as hell. I suggest you wear a swimsuit and a pair of shorts. You might want to take a dip in the ocean to cool off."

"Good idea!" Jenny said brightly.

The Boardwalk Café was closed for the day. Jenny was going to take advantage of it and enjoy her day. She wondered if she could spend some time with Adam.

"Adam will be there," Star told her, "but he might be on duty."

The two women set off for Main Street some time later. The aroma of smoking meat hit them as they made their way toward the drinks stand. Jenny picked up a paper cup of sweet tea and gulped it down. She was already feeling parched.

"There's Heather and Molly!"

She waved at her friends and hurried over.

A marquee had been set up in the middle of the street. People had brought their own trestle tables and camp chairs and set up wherever they found a spot. Betty Sue and Petunia sat on two plastic Adirondack chairs flanking a long metal table. A red checked table cloth barely covered it. Betty Sue had kept her knitting at home for a change. But her fingers twirled in a familiar rhythm.

Star sat on the chair Petunia had saved for her.

"Don't worry, I have a camp chair here for you too," Heather told Jenny.

The ladies caught up on the gossip for a while. The girls were dispatched to get some food.

"Isn't it too early?" Jenny asked.

"We have to pace ourselves," Heather explained. "I'm guessing you at least want to taste everything."

They were back with plates loaded with barbecued chicken, coleslaw and corn bread.

"The pork needs some more time," Molly told the older ladies. "We'll get baked beans and potato salad when we get the ribs."

"Hello beautiful!" a voice called out.

Heather and Jenny whipped their heads around making the others laugh. Jason and Chris were walking toward them.

"How's the barbecue?" Jason asked.

Chris and Jason were both wearing aprons proclaiming them to be pit masters. Sweat was pouring down their faces.

"You know how to operate a smoker?" Jenny asked Jason. "You are a man of many talents, Jason Stone."

He winked and whispered something in her ear, making her blush.

"What was that?" Betty Sue thundered.

Jason picked up a fork and started eating from Jenny's plate. Chris was eating a drumstick he had lifted off Heather's.

"Have you seen Adam?" Star asked Chris.

"He's on duty," Chris said. "He should be getting off soon though."

"This is not his kind of thing," Jason dismissed. "He'll probably pack a plate of food and go home."

"He's going to meet me here at 1," Jenny said sweetly.

Jason's face fell.

"Time to go back to the pit, buddy," Chris said to him.

"How much longer for the pork, boys?" Molly asked.

"We'll bring a plate for you when it's ready," Jason promised.

"Did you see his face?" Heather laughed when Jason was out of earshot. "There's going to be a battle here, Jenny, and you're the prize."

"Don't be silly," Jenny brushed her off. "Jason is just a friend."

"A friend who takes you out on dates?" Molly teased.

"I see a lot of strangers around," Betty Sue commented. "I'm not sure I like that."

"You have to change with the times, Grandma," Heather consoled her.

"We cater to plenty of tourists year round," Betty Sue grumbled. "Isn't our whole business centered around tourists? The barbecue is supposed to be just for the town."

"Yoo-hoo…"

"Here's who you can thank, Betty Sue," Star said and Barb Norton came up to them, beaming from ear to ear.

Mandy tagged along a few steps behind.

"We're doing great," Barb told them enthusiastically. "Our take has already crossed five hundred bucks. You have Mandy to thank for this."

She paused and widened her eyes meaningfully.

"I'm sorry for taking over your town festival," Mandy James said cheerfully, sounding anything but sorry. "But we need funds, ladies. The town of Pelican Cove desperately needs some TLC."

"TLC?" Betty Sue asked. "Speak English, girl!"

"I mean, it needs a lot of repair."

"We were doing fine until you came along," Petunia snapped.

"I'm just doing my job, ladies," Mandy sighed.

"You better start looking for a new one soon," Betty Sue railed.

"We don't need a prize to tell us our town is pretty," Star added.

"You don't get it, do you?" Barb said, shaking her head. "That contest is going to boost business. It's going to bring in money. You can't stop progress, Betty Sue! Why don't you retire? Give your seat on the town board to Heather?"

Barb Norton stalked off with Mandy in tow.

"What does she care?" Petunia cried. "She doesn't even live here all year."

"How about a walk?" Heather asked Jenny.

There was a desperate look in her eyes. The girls knew where the conversation at the table was headed and they wanted no part of it.

They heard a buzz coming from one end of the street. A group of people was clustered together, pointing at something in the distance. The younger people had goofy looks on their faces. Some people were standing with their mouths hanging open.

"What's going on there?" Molly asked, putting on speed.

Crystal Mars and a bunch of her friends lay sunning themselves on the beach. The skimpiest of bikinis barely covered their honey colored bodies. Sunglasses larger than the bikinis covered their eyes.

"It's the invasion of the Barbies," someone in the crowd said.

"Look," a young acne faced boy chortled as one of the girls pulled off her bikini top.

An older woman, probably his mother, shielded his eyes with her palm.

"We thought this was a family friendly place," she said angrily.

Jenny and the girls walked down to the beach purposefully. Picking up some sarongs that lay in the sand, she flung them over the girls.

"What are you doing here, Crystal?"

"We thought we would get some barbecue."

"You need to cover up," Heather ordered. "There's a lot of kids around."

"But we're on the beach," one of the posse grumbled.

Jenny spotted Rainbow trying to smother a smile.

"Let me guess," Jenny said. "This was your idea."

"What's wrong with getting some sun?"

"Are you trying to create a scandal?"

"Relax," Crystal said lightly. "We get it."

She stood up and tied a sarong around her waist. She pulled the other one around her upper body and tied it around her neck. The other girls got up and copied her actions.

"Good enough?" Crystal asked. "Now where's this food everyone's talking about?"

"Ladies!" an authoritative voice called.

Jenny's heart skipped a beat as she recognized Adam's voice.

"There have been some complaints. This is not a topless beach."

"We're covered head to toe, Officer," Crystal said flirtatiously.

"So you are," Adam nodded.

"Jenny's been looking for you," Heather spoke as Crystal and her posse walked up to the barbecue tent.

"No I haven't," Jenny protested.

"Can we go to your inn?" Molly asked Heather. "I need to freshen up."

Heather and Molly started walking away, arm in arm.

"Molly? Heather?" Jenny called out. "I'm coming too."

They ignored her and broke into a jog.

"I can hear them giggle, you know," Adam said.

Jenny was feeling embarrassed. She wondered if Adam might lose his temper.

"Here we are!" he said softly.

"Are you still on duty?" she asked.

Adam looked at his watch.

"Only for the next five minutes."

"Do you want to get something to eat?"

Adam bobbed his head.

"I'm starving, Jenny. Let's go get some barbecue."

"We have a table somewhere in that big tent," Jenny told him as they stood in line. "The older Magnolias are over there."

"I was hoping we could sit somewhere else," Adam said. "Away from the crowd?"

"Hard to find an empty table," Jenny mumbled.

"I brought a mat," Adam told her. "We can sit on the beach."

They loaded their plates with the smoky meat. Jenny went for some baked beans and macaroni and cheese. Adam took a little bit of everything. They took their food out to the beach.

"We went to the sky diving company," Jenny told Adam. "The pilot mistook Bella for Crystal. That's why she was dressed in that bridal dress. It must have been her plan all along."

"I thought so too," Adam admitted. "Look, can we not talk about work?"

"Sure. What do you want to talk about?"

"Something more interesting," Adam grinned. "You."

"I don't have much to say," Jenny said, feeling a blush steal over her face.

"What's new with you, Jenny King?" Adam asked.

He picked an errant strand of Jenny's hair and tucked it behind her ear.

"How are the twins?"

"They are good. They were asking about you."

"We might have to do some renovations at the café."

"Good," Adam said, looking into her eyes.

Jenny gulped and rubbed the heart shaped charm on her necklace.

"Adam," she said, struggling to find the right words. She didn't want to offend him. "Are we on a date?"

Adam didn't blink.

"When we go on a date, Jenny, you'll know."

"I didn't mean to…I wasn't…"

"I know you weren't," Adam assured her. "Thank you for being so patient."

Jenny knew Adam had loved his wife a lot.

"Do you still miss her?"

"Sometimes I do," Adam said honestly. "I know it's been ten years. The girls are grown. What can I say, Jenny? She was my first love."

Jenny didn't have the same feelings where her ex-husband was concerned. He had dumped her for a younger model less than a year ago. The only thing Jenny felt when she thought of him was rage.

"You're too good, Adam."

"Are you sure you're talking about me?" Adam joked. "I'm cranky and ill tempered most of the time. The younger guys at the station quake in fear when I walk by."

"You're kidding," Jenny laughed.

She picked up his hand and threaded her fingers through his.

"You've been through a lot, Adam. I can understand your frustration."

"One of these days, we will go out on a proper date," Adam promised. "How about taking a kayak out on the water?"

Jenny was deathly afraid of the water. But she didn't want to spoil the mood.

A hearty voice called out just then.

"Ahoy there!"

Jenny looked up to see Jason walking toward them with a tray loaded with food. Chris, Heather and Molly followed close behind.

"This is so not a date," Adam muttered, waving a hand at the new arrivals.

Chapter 16

Mandy James posted pictures of the town barbecue on Instagram. There was a sudden influx of tourists wanting to taste barbecue.

"We don't serve barbecue here," Jenny told a customer for the umpteenth time. "Can I get you a crab salad sandwich? We have Chesapeake Bay crabs, caught this morning."

Four hours later, she was finally ready to call it a day. Jenny thought of Adam on her way back home. She hadn't run into him since the barbecue.

Jason turned up for dinner with Chinese food.

"This is from my favorite restaurant on the mainland," he told them. "Just taste this Moo Shu Pork, Jenny. You'll love it."

"I don't mind some Lo Mein," Star said, dishing out a hefty serving with a pair of chopsticks.

"This is good," Jenny spoke between bites. "I'm so exhausted I can barely taste it though."

She massaged her feet with one hand while she spoke.

"Let me do that."

Jason gently picked up her foot and placed it in his lap. He began giving her a foot massage. Star looked on approvingly.

"Stop it, Jason," Jenny groaned. "You're spoiling me."

"What are you doing Saturday night?"

"Soaking my feet in a big tub of water," Jenny sighed.

The heat and humidity were already getting to her.

"You need to hydrate more," Jason advised. "We should take a canoe out on the water one of these days. It will relax you."

"Err, I think not!"

"Jenny's scared of the water," Star spoke up. "Don't you remember that summer, Jason? All the kids decided to have an impromptu canoe race. Jenny stayed back on land to flag you off."

"Oh yeah!" Jason said, popping a dumpling in his mouth. "But that was years ago."

"Water's not my thing, Jason."

"So we'll do something else. Let's go to Virginia Beach Saturday night. There's a new club everyone's raving about."

"We'll see."

Jason agreed good naturedly. He was so amicable Jenny found it hard to deny him anything. He never lost his temper.

"Don't over think it," Star told her as they watched TV.

Jason had left long ago. He had to be in court first thing in the morning.

"He's nice, but I can't be serious about a lawyer. Not again."

"That's ridiculous. Just because one lawyer dumped you doesn't mean another will."

"I'm out of here," Jenny scowled.

She stepped out and started walking at a clip, barely stopping to look at the roses blooming at Seaview. She almost bumped into a body a while later.

"Jenny?" Adam's deep voice cut through the fog in her mind. "What's the matter?"

Tank put his paws on Jenny's shoulders and gave her a wet welcome.

"Hello sweetie," Jenny said, fondling the big yellow Lab. "I've missed you."

"He's missed you too," Adam said, leaning on his cane. "We've been busy."

"Find anything new?"

Adam shook his head.

"I'm not supposed to talk about this. We haven't confirmed the husband's alibi yet."

Jenny slapped her head and let out a tiny cry.

"I was going to tell you … he was here the day before the wedding."

"How do you know that?" Adam asked, grabbing her arm. "Are you sure about this?"

"Not really," Jenny said. "One of the bridesmaids told me. She said he went into the Rusty Anchor."

"We can easily verify that."

"How come no one at the pub came forward with this?"

Adam shrugged.

"Lots of tourists around these days. A stranger doesn't stand out so much."

"Have you interviewed this girl? She's beginning to look fishy."

Jenny told Adam about Rainbow.

"You say she's accusing Wayne Newman?"

"Not directly, no. But she's connected to everyone one way or the other."

"Maybe she's angling for something."

"All these girls care about is getting ahead in their careers."

"I'm going to talk to her again," Adam promised.

"Ask her about the money she took from Crystal's mother."

"You're amazing. Every time I see you, I learn something the police don't know."

"People don't like to talk to cops, I guess."

"We are stalled. We don't have a single strong lead."

"What if Rainbow planned it all along, huh? Bella jumps from the plane and Crystal is ruined by scandal."

"What happens to Wayne Newman?"

"He gets a new leading lady."

"You think they are in cahoots?"

"It's worth finding out," Jenny said thoughtfully. "I'll go talk to her tomorrow."

Neither of them could have guessed what would happen the next day.

Jenny was worked off her feet all morning. When the phone rang in the kitchen, she continued frosting a cupcake with one hand while she stuck the receiver in the crook of her neck.

Her mouth dropped open in shock when she heard the voice at the other end. The piping bag slipped from her hand and struck the floor, splattering frosting everywhere.

"How did this happen? I'm coming over."

Jenny hit the speed dial and called Heather.

"We need to go. Now!"

She was honking her horn in front of the inn ten minutes later. Heather came running out.

"Rainbow's dead."

"What?" Heather asked, getting in.

Jenny floored the gas pedal and the car took off with a screech of tires.

"Crystal just called the café. Rainbow didn't turn up for breakfast. They didn't think too much of it – she likes to sleep in sometimes. One of the girls knocked on her door when she didn't come out for lunch."

"What happened to her?"

"Some kind of overdose," Jenny spoke. "Sleeping pills, most probably."

They reached the country club soon after. Jenny remembered the building where Rainbow's room was situated. A bunch of police and emergency vehicles were parked outside.

Adam Hopkins frowned when he spotted Jenny.

"You can't be here, Jenny. This is a crime scene."

"What happened to her?"

"We don't know for sure yet. How did you find out about this?"

"Crystal called me."

Adam pointed toward the club house building.

"They are all over there. I think they were just about to have lunch. We are going to question all of them one by one."

"Can I sit in?"

"Of course not!"

"Did you talk to her since last night?"

"She was supposed to come in and meet me at 11."

They both knew Rainbow hadn't made it to the police station. Jenny had a hunch someone made sure about that.

She walked over to the dining room with Heather. Crystal sat on a chintz couch, clutching her mother's hand. Her eyes were red and her mascara had run down one cheek. A couple of girls sat squashed together in a big chair. One girl was pacing the room, burning a hole in the carpet.

"Jenny? Heather? Thank God you're here." Crystal sprang up and hugged Heather. "What's going on? Why is someone killing us off one by one?"

"We don't know what happened to Rainbow yet," Jenny said softly.

"She was such a sweet girl," Kathy Mars said in a sugary voice.

Kathy's expression didn't match her voice.

"We need to leave this place as soon as possible, honey."

Wayne Newman entered the room, holding his hat in his hand.

"Is it true?" he asked Crystal, looking crestfallen. "Is Rainbow gone?"

Crystal nodded, and a tear rolled down her eye.

Jenny wondered how much of it was authentic. If it was a performance, Crystal deserved the tag of reality star.

"Which one of you found her?" Jenny asked.

The girl who was pacing the floor spoke up.

"It was me. Rainbow liked to sleep in when she took one of her pills. I warned her not to take too many. Maybe she took a double dose."

"You think this was an accident?" Jenny asked.

"She was so full of life," Crystal wailed. "And she had a good role in our new series. But her personal life was a disaster."

Jenny and Heather exchanged glances. They stayed quiet as if by an unspoken agreement.

"Wait a minute," Wayne Newman said. "What are you implying?"

Crystal let out another sob but said nothing.

"Let's not jump to conclusions," Jenny said quickly. "The police will tell us more."

Kathy Mars ordered some sandwiches and sweet tea and forced the girls to eat something. A couple of hours passed. Wayne Newman was sitting on the sofa next to Crystal. He caught Jenny's eye and motioned her to go outside.

Jenny stepped out on the long verandah facing the golf course.

"Have you made any progress?" he asked. "First Bella, now Rainbow. I'm beginning to think someone is targeting me."

Jenny stifled a laugh.

"You're alive and well, Wayne. How are you the victim here?"

"They were both my ladies," he said. "Crystal might be next."

"What does that mean?" Jenny asked. "Your 'ladies'?"

Wayne said nothing.

"You know Rainbow was sharing stuff with me?" Jenny asked.

"She was a bit greedy, but she had a good heart. She was feeling guilty about some things. I suggested she go talk to you."

"How long have you known Rainbow?" Jenny asked suspiciously.

"Long enough."

"Can you give me a straight answer?"

"I met Rainbow in Hollywood. We were both struggling at the time."

"I thought you knew her through Crystal?"

"Crystal wasn't on the scene at that time. At least, I didn't know her. Rainbow and I were an item."

Jenny let out a gasp. She hadn't seen it coming.

"Go on!"

"Bella became Rainbow's roommate later. I was famous on the music circuit by then. Bella fawned over me. What can I say, I fell for her."

"So you dumped Rainbow and went out with Bella?"

"I started going out with Bella, okay?"

"What went wrong?"

"They threw her off the set, I don't know how or why. Crystal came into the picture. Before I knew it, we were going out."

"But you continued seeing Bella behind Crystal's back?"

"Bella and I were friends."

"Friends with benefits, you mean."

Wayne shrugged.

"I hate conflict. I like to live in harmony with everyone."

"Do you mean you never break it off with your ex-girlfriends?"

"I don't see the need. Who knows when they might come in handy?"

Jenny struggled to stay calm.

"If you have any information about Rainbow, I suggest you give it to the police."

"She has a four year old son. He lives with her sister in Wisconsin."

"Rainbow had a son?" Heather cried. "Wasn't she too young?"

"None of these girls are as young as they say," Wayne said maliciously. "Bella was the real youngster among them. She was barely 22."

He looked genuinely sad when he said that.

"Do you know how to contact Rainbow's sister?"

Wayne nodded. He promised to give her contact information to the police.

He shook hands with Jenny and patted her on the shoulder. Jenny sprang back with a jerk. She had remembered something.

"What's that smell?" she asked. "Is it some kind of perfume?"

"I don't wear perfume," Wayne said, bewildered. "Just aftershave."

"You scumbag! You were still getting it on with her, weren't you?"

Wayne was quiet.

"You were in Rainbow's room the other day," Jenny accused. "Don't try to deny it."

"Like I said … we go way back."

"You were carrying on with her right under Crystal's nose?" Heather gasped. "Weren't you afraid of getting caught?"

"What's Crystal gonna do? She's so desperate to get married, she'll look the other way no matter what I do."

"Why are you marrying Crystal?" Jenny asked. "Do you love her at all?"

"I loved Bella for a while, and I loved Rainbow. Crystal is just good for the ratings."

Kathy Mars stood in the doorway with a vicious look in her eyes. Jenny was sure she had heard the last bit. Kathy's lips stretched into a horrible smile.

"Why don't you come in? I just called for lemonade."

Chapter 17

Jenny, Heather and Molly walked to the Rusty Anchor one evening.

"Is Chris meeting us there?" Molly asked Heather.

Memorial Day had come and gone. The café had been flooded with tourists eager to taste the cupcakes and crab salad they had seen on Instagram. Mandy James had done them a favor after all.

A team of contractors and volunteers was busy making small changes on Main Street. The town was beginning to look spiffy.

"Don't these look pretty?" Heather asked, pointing toward some new flower beds that had sprung up by the side of the road. "I don't know, Molly," she pouted. "I don't keep tabs on him."

"Trouble in paradise?" Jenny asked.

They found a lot of familiar faces at the Rusty Anchor. Jimmy Parsons waved at them from the bar. Jenny got up to say hello to him. Jimmy had apparently been at it for some time.

"How's your aunt, little lady?" he asked.

Jenny had guessed Jimmy had a thing for her aunt.

"Why don't you come over for dinner sometime, Jimmy?"

Jimmy nodded happily. "I could use a home cooked meal. You're a good girl, Jenny."

Jenny spotted a familiar figure seated at the other end of the bar.

"What is Ray Fox still doing here?" she asked the girls when she went back to their table.

Jason Stone had joined them in her absence.

"You remember he's my client, Jenny? I can't talk about him."

"Haven't the police cleared him yet? Why is he still hanging out in Pelican Cove?"

"My lips are sealed," Jason stressed.

"What if he wants to talk to me?"

Jenny walked over to where Ray was seated. She pulled up a stool and climbed up on it.

"Hello Ray. Remember me?"

Ray Fox looked at her with bloodshot eyes. He nodded and took another sip of his drink.

"How long have you been in town really?"

"Am I busted?" he asked.

"Yes, you are. You were seen here the day before Crystal's wedding."

"Did that old roommate of Bella tell you this?"

"She may have."

"What's it matter to her? She's got to stop meddling in my business."

"You don't have to worry about her."

"Why not? She always had it in for Bella. Did you know she got Bella thrown off the set? My Bella lost the role of a lifetime because of that girl."

"You must have been mad at her."

"You bet I was. We both were."

"Is that why you killed her?"

Ray straightened and blinked at Jenny in confusion.

"What are you talking about?"

"That girl – Rainbow – she was found dead a few days ago."

"You've got to be kidding me."

"I'm not. How did you not hear about this?"

"Nobody told me…"

So Ray Fox had a possible grudge against Rainbow. Jenny decided to talk to Adam about it later.

"Why did you come here, Ray? Did you know Bella was planning something for Crystal's wedding?"

"Look, I don't care one bit about Crystal Mars, okay?"

Jenny folded her hands and waited for him to continue.

"I found out Bella was seeing Wayne Newman again."

"Who told you that?"

"I had my sources…never mind how I found out…people talk."

"So you came here to confront Bella and kill her?"

"Why would I kill her? Bella was the love of my life."

Ray's eyes filled up as he spoke. Jenny wondered if she was witnessing another stellar performance. It was hard to tell.

"Sure! You loved Bella even though she was cheating on you."

"Bella was beautiful and she had a heart to match. She had a string of admirers wherever she went. But she never slipped. Until she ran into Wayne Newman again …"

"What was special about Wayne? From all accounts, he's a womanizer."

"She never got over him."

"You knew about Bella and Wayne before you got married?"

Ray Fox took a big gulp of his drink.

"Bella promised me it was all over. We were very happy for a while. Then I had to go on location for a few months."

"She ran back to Wayne?"

"It wasn't like that. She met him at some awards function. He was engaged to Crystal. Bella hated Crystal. I think she went out with Wayne just to spite Crystal."

"Looks like that backfired."

Ray smiled mirthlessly.

"She got caught up in him again."

He looked at Jenny, struggling with what to say next.

"I know about the baby," Jenny said gently.

Ray wiped his eyes with the back of his hand.

"She thought it was the end. She rushed over here to confront Wayne. She wanted to beg him to marry her."

"What about you?"

"She thought I would dump her."

"So she didn't trust you, huh?"

"Bella was so young," Ray sobbed. "She ran away from home at sixteen. People only took from her. She had been treated like crap by most people in her life."

"She assumed you would do the same."

"That's my fault, I guess. She didn't trust me. I failed to make her believe."

"She was just insecure."

"She shouldn't have been. She was my wife. It was my job to look after her no matter what."

"How did you know she was coming here?"

"I was out of town when Bella got on the plane. I came in to Los Angeles the same evening. She had left a print of her ticket on the coffee table."

"Was that her way of letting you know where she was?"

"I think it was a cry for help."

"What did you do then, Ray?"

"I got the next flight out and came here."

"Bella wanted to break it off with you so you messed with her parachute. Is that right?"

"That's a lie!"

Jenny wondered if she had pushed him a bit too far.

"Bella and I met. We talked about everything. She told me about the child. I didn't mind who the father was. We could raise it as our own."

"Really? You are that noble?"

"I had an accident years ago," Ray confessed. "I can't have kids. We had talked about adoption or sperm donation. This felt like a blessing to me."

"What about Wayne?"

"He could do as he pleased. If he wanted to be a part of the child's life, we would have come to some agreement."

"But didn't Bella come here to disrupt the wedding?"

"She just wanted to talk to Wayne. She had high hopes from him."

"But you decided to raise the child together. Why did she go up on that plane then?"

"That's what I can't figure out," Ray blubbered.

Jenny gave him some time to collect himself.

"You really don't know why she went up in that plane?"

"I had no idea she was going to do that. We were flying back home later that day."

Ray Fox didn't meet Jenny's eyes while he said it.

"You're hiding something, Ray. What is it? Maybe I can help you if you are honest with me."

Ray hesitated.

"She said she had one last thing she needed to take care of."

"So she was going to confront Wayne after all."

"I don't know," Ray said, sounding helpless. "Maybe I should have guessed she would do something silly."

"Could she have wanted to cause a stir at the wedding?"

"Bella wasn't vindictive," Ray said firmly. "And it was Wayne's wedding too. She wouldn't do that to him."

"Something or someone made her go up there," Jenny said, "with a faulty parachute."

"Bella's a pro at sky diving. She would never go up there without checking her rig."

"She must have trusted whoever handed it to her."

"She trusted Wayne Newman," Ray pointed out.

"Do you believe Wayne had something to do with your wife's death?"

"He was right there, wasn't he? And he had a pretty strong motive."

"Surely Bella must have told him you agreed to raise the child?"

"Have you thought about the scandal? Appearances mean more to these people than anything else."

"You realize this is just a theory?"

"I know that," Ray Fox sighed. "That's what the police said when I proposed it."

"I'm sure they will check it out though. Did anyone else know about the baby?"

Ray shrugged.

"She talked to Rainbow a lot. I don't know why though. I never trusted her."

Jenny thought of what Rainbow had done to destroy Bella's career and the money she had taken from Kathy Mars. Ray had been right about Rainbow.

"I never met Bella but it sounds like she was a good person."

"She was the best."

Jenny couldn't believe how Ray could still feel that after Bella cheated on him. Had Bella's murder made a martyr out of her? Jenny examined her own feelings about her cheating ex-husband. She didn't have a single kind thought about him in her mind. Was Ray Fox for real, she wondered. Or was he putting on a big act.

"Let's hope the police solve this case soon."

"Weren't you going to find out what happened?"

"I can't promise anything," Jenny said honestly. "I'm not a trained investigator. I just talk to people and stumble on the truth."

"Don't be so modest. I heard how you solved a stranger's murder a few months ago."

"Is there anything else about Bella that you can tell me? Did you find out anything about her family, for instance?"

"I told you, they disowned her long ago," Ray told her. "I'm all she had."

"Let me know if you remember anything," Jenny stressed. "You can find me at the Boardwalk Café."

Jenny went back to her table after that. Chris had joined them in her absence, along with an unwelcome guest.

"What do you want, Mandy?" Jenny snapped.

Mandy James looked hurt.

"I'm just having a drink with my new friends."

The town had issued an ordinance against the Boardwalk Café that day, ordering them to undertake all the repairs suggested by the beautification committee.

"Friends don't throw each other under the bus."

"You're talking about the letter."

"How'd you guess?"

"Relax, Jenny," Jason said, placing an arm around her shoulders and making her sit. "You're breathing fire. She's just doing her job."

"Exactly!" Mandy exclaimed. "How can you not understand that, Jenny? It's not personal."

"Petunia's blood pressure is up from the stress. That's how personal it is to me."

Mandy stood up and bid goodbye to everyone.

"I know where I am not wanted."

"What was that?" Molly asked. "You could at least have been polite."

"We got the contractor's estimate today," Jenny told her friends. "It's five figures. Five figures!"

"I thought we were pitching in to help?" Chris asked.

"That's just the contractor's work. We will still need you all to help, and we'll need to spend more on paint and other supplies."

"Stop worrying about that for a moment," Jason soothed. "Did you make Ray talk?"

"He's either a very good actor or he's innocent."

"We are here to relax," Heather reminded her. "No more talk of the café or anything unpleasant."

Chris and Jason called for a fresh round of beer. Eddie Cotton brought over their pints on a tray, along with a bowl of potato chips.

"There's one extra," Jenny laughed as she picked up her mug.

Eddie pointed toward the door. Adam Hopkins had just walked in.

"Hello, slacker!" Jason greeted him. "Is the police department going to survive without you tonight?"

Heather whispered something to Molly and they both started to giggle. Jenny guessed it was something about her. She ignored them and pulled up another chair for Adam.

Wedged between Jason on one side and Adam on another, Jenny rubbed the small gold heart hanging on a chain around her neck. She liked them both for different reasons. She might have to choose between them one day but she was in no hurry to do so.

Chapter 18

The high school students Petunia had hired started working at the café. Jenny spent a couple of days showing them the ropes. She hoped they would be more help than hindrance.

There was a tinkling laugh and Jenny looked up to see Crystal and her posse enter the café. They wanted to sit out on the deck.

"Hello Jenny." Crystal hung back to talk to her. "Found anything new?"

Jenny shook her head.

"I'm trying. What are you gals doing out here in town?"

"We got cabin fever," she replied, making a face. "And I was craving your cupcakes. Got anything new?"

"I just finished frosting a new batch of cupcakes with raspberry and Grand Marnier frosting. I'll bring them out."

Jenny put a pitcher of icy lemonade and her cupcakes on a tray. She remembered how Rainbow had talked to her the last time the girls visited the café.

"Anything new on Rainbow?" she asked Crystal.

"The police confirmed she died of an overdose."

According to Jenny, it had either been intentional or an accident. She couldn't imagine Rainbow taking her own life. She was too much in love with herself.

The girls started talking about Rainbow, saving Jenny the need to ask any probing questions.

"She was so happy about her new role," one of the girls said. "It was all thanks to Crystal."

Crystal blew an air kiss at the girl.

"We're going to need someone else to fill that spot now."

"First Bella, now Rainbow," another girl spoke up. "I think the show's jinxed. Who knows, any one of us could be next."

"You remember what happened on the third season of that show we were on?"

The girls plunged into a discussion about the different times they had encountered bad luck.

Jenny went in, tired of listening to their chatter.

"They are a bunch of idiots," Crystal said, following her into the kitchen. "All that matters is the ratings."

"Have your ratings suffered?"

"They are at an all time high," Crystal beamed. "That's the thing about them, Jenny. They shoot up in good times and bad. They are based on the amount of interest the show generates, you know? The company is playing up Rainbow's death. Fans are lining up to place flowers and teddy bears outside the studio back home."

"I didn't know Rainbow was that popular," Jenny remarked. "Wasn't she like a supporting actress?"

"Not even that," Crystal sighed. "But she's got a big following now. It's like the authors who become famous posthumously."

"That's good for your show. You must be happy."

Crystal rolled her eyes.

"It might be good for the show in the short term. But it's not good for me. I am the star of this show, not Rainbow."

Jenny decided that ruled Crystal out as a suspect. She would never do anything to endanger her position as queen bee.

"How was she when you talked to her last?"

"I don't remember. She was her usual self, I guess. She was closer to my mother than me."

"She was friendly with Wayne too, I hear."

"What are you implying, Jenny?"

"Nothing! I'm saying Rainbow was a friendly soul. She was quite chatty."

"Really? What did you talk about?"

"Nothing in particular."

Crystal stifled a yawn and went back to her table. The girls lingered for a couple of hours and ordered lunch.

One of the starlets stepped into the kitchen with a list of special instructions.

"One crab salad sandwich without tomato, one crab salad without mayo and one crab salad sandwich without bread, please."

"The crab salad without mayo will take time," Jenny told her. "You want to wait here while I mix a new batch?"

The girl sat down at the kitchen table.

"How well did you know Rainbow?" Jenny asked her.

"Not very well," the girl admitted. "She didn't hang around with us much."

"Oh? But I thought she was part of Crystal and her group of friends."

"She was a bit older than us, and more experienced."

"You mean she was a senior actress?"

The girl looked over her shoulder and leaned forward.

"Don't tell anyone I said this, but she was a better actor than Crystal."

"Why didn't she get the lead role then?"

The girl shrugged.

"Talent is not the only requirement…"

"Did she get along with everyone?"

"She was nice to everyone but she kept her distance."

Jenny pursed her lips as she asked the next question.

"You don't think anyone had a grudge against her?"

The girl grew uncomfortable.

"Some of the girls were a bit jealous," she finally admitted. "Other than Crystal, Rainbow was the only one who had her own room, see? The rest of us have to share a room."

"How did she manage that?"

The girls shrugged.

"She was pretty friendly with Kathy. Crystal's Mom, you know."

The girl's voice dropped to a whisper.

"And she was friendly with Wayne."

Jenny knew the nature of Rainbow's friendship with Wayne very well. She didn't contradict the girl.

"Did she come to dinner the previous night? When was the last time you saw her?"

"Rainbow didn't join us for dinner. She said she had some personal business to take care of."

"Yeah? Like what?"

"She didn't say. But I saw her drive out of the club around six."

Jenny whirled around to look at the girl. So Rainbow had probably visited someone in town.

"Was that the last time you saw her?"

"Kind of. I saw Wayne coming out of her room later that night. He was saying something. He must have been talking to her, right?"

"What time was this?"

"I don't remember. But it was late."

Jenny thought of the void Rainbow's death had created.

"Was there anyone who was angling for Rainbow's role?"

"Almost everyone was," the girl laughed. "Our roles are scripted beforehand but anything is possible on a reality show. If someone works up a fan following, the producers can keep them on longer, fire someone else."

"So you're trying to be one up on each other all the time?"

"I guess." The girl shrugged.

Jenny decided she would never be able to handle that kind of tension.

"Must be hard on you. Aren't you all friends?"

"We are friends up to a point. But we also need to look out for ourselves. Everyone knows that. There are no hard feelings."

Jenny thanked the girl and promised she would bring over the special orders to their table. She spent the rest of the day thinking over what the girl had said. She needed to talk to Wayne Newman again.

Petunia came in to clean up an hour later.

"Are you going home to change?"

"Change for what, Petunia?"

"Have you forgotten? They are unveiling the new welcome sign. There's going to be a ribbon cutting and a special guest."

"Let me guess. Mandy James is behind all that."

Petunia nodded.

"And you still want to go?"

Petunia sat down with a sigh.

"I know Mandy's been hard on us. But this is about the town. We have been talking about getting a new welcome sign for years."

"In that case, lead me on…"

"Aren't you going to change? The whole town will be there."

Petunia widened her eyes when she said 'whole town'.

"Do we have enough time?"

"It's at five. You will have to hurry."

"Do you want me to pick you up?"

"Thanks dear, but I am riding with Heather and Betty Sue."

Jenny and her aunt drove to the venue in time for the event. The sign was erected a quarter mile before the bridge that led to the island of Pelican Cove. Jenny was surprised to see Wayne Newman standing next to Barb Norton and Mandy James. There were a bunch of reporters clicking pictures like crazy.

It turned out Wayne Newman was going to cut the ribbon and unveil the new sign. He did that with a grin and pulled off the white cloth covering the sign. Then he gave a small speech.

Mandy James thanked everyone for coming and thanked the artist who had created the sign. Star looked stoic while she took it all in.

Wayne caught Jenny's eye and pulled her to a side.

"I couldn't say no," he explained. "That Mandy chick is pretty persuasive."

"I know," Jenny agreed.

She nodded toward the reporters.

"Looks like the paparazzi know where you are now."

Wayne shrugged.

"I've been below the radar long enough. It's time to go home. Maybe the media will put some pressure on the police."

"You lost two friends in a short period of time, Wayne. I am sorry for your loss."

Wayne curled his fingers.

"They were both good people. I know I was seeing all of them at once. But I really cared for Bella and Rainbow."

Once again, Jenny wondered if someone was killing off Wayne's lady loves one by one. Was Crystal in danger too?

"When was the last time you saw Rainbow?"

"I spent some time with her that afternoon."

"Did you arrange to meet her away from the club?"

"Why would I do that, Jenny? I could meet her there any time I wanted to."

So Rainbow hadn't left the club to meet Wayne. Had she just gone out for a drive?

"Someone saw you coming out of Rainbow's room that night."

Wayne looked guilty.

"I looked in on her later that night," he admitted reluctantly. "I liked to spend some time with her before turning in."

He gave Jenny a meaningful look making her blush.

"You didn't go to Crystal before turning in?"

"I did. I went to Rainbow first."

Jenny tried to hide her disgust. Then she told herself she wasn't the moral police.

"Was she in her room?"

Wayne looked flustered again.

"She was fast asleep. I shook her but she wouldn't wake up. I thought she might have taken one of her pills."

Wayne could have given her the pills himself. Why would he do that though, Jenny asked herself.

"Were you talking to yourself when you left her room?"

"I was talking to her," Wayne said sheepishly. "I thought she might be play acting."

"And why would she do that?"

"We had a fight earlier that day," Wayne confessed. "She told me she didn't want to see me again."

Jenny put her hands on her hips and glared at Wayne.

"When were you going to tell me that?"

Wayne ran a hand through his hair.

"Rainbow's dead. How would it look if I admitted we argued on the day she died?"

"It looks bad," Jenny nodded. "But hiding it looks worse."

"I could've done something, Jenny," Wayne cried suddenly. "I could have saved her."

"You didn't know what was wrong with her."

"So what? If I had raised an alarm, got a doctor to look at her, maybe she would be with us right now."

Wayne's distress seemed genuine enough. But Jenny had her doubts.

"What time did you go to her room, Wayne?"

"Around nine? It was a little past that, I think."

"Did you visit her at the same time every night?"

"Not exactly. We would meet at dinner and then decide if we were going to see each other later that night."

"Where did you go after you came out of Rainbow's room?"

"I went to see Crystal."

"Did you tell her about Rainbow?"

Wayne shook his head.

"I think you should tell all this to the police."

Wayne didn't look too happy about the suggestion.

"Do I have to? I think they already suspect me."

Jenny didn't want to comment on that.

"If you're innocent, you should volunteer any information you have, Wayne. Hiding anything, even the smallest detail, makes you look suspicious."

"I'll think about it," Wayne promised.

Mandy came and took Wayne away for a photo session. Jenny saw her coax people into standing on either side of the new sign. She turned around at a familiar voice.

Adam Hopkins stood a few feet away, holding Tank's leash. Tank barked a welcome as soon as he saw Jenny.

"Meddling in police business?" Adam asked with an inscrutable expression.

Chapter 19

The Magnolias were enjoying their usual mid-morning break at the Boardwalk Café. Jenny had been busy getting their new hires up to speed. Petunia had convinced Jenny to let the kids manage the front desk. Jenny was taking a much deserved break.

"What's on your mind, girl?" Betty Sue asked, her hands busy knitting a lime green scarf. "You look like someone stole your candy."

That produced a laugh out of everyone.

"She's been like that for a while," Star told them. "I can't get a smile out of her."

"Are you still thinking about Bella?" Heather asked.

Jenny gave a slight nod.

"What do the police say?" Betty Sue asked. "Haven't you talked to that Hopkins boy recently?"

"The police haven't made any arrests," Jenny told them. "And they are not holding anyone."

"So they are clueless," Molly stated. "What does Adam say?"

Jenny flared up when she heard Adam's name.

"Why would Adam say anything?" Her chest heaved with emotion. "You know he never tells me anything. He hasn't given me a single update on what's happening."

"Are those film people still in town?" Molly asked.

"They are here till the end of the week," Heather informed them. "I spoke to Crystal yesterday."

"And they won't be coming back!" Jenny exclaimed. "How can the cops let them leave?"

"They stuck around long enough," Heather argued. "They all have deadlines. The show has lost a lot of money, it seems. The studio's lawyers are putting a lot of pressure on the authorities here."

"I'm surprised the police haven't charged anyone yet,' Jenny said nastily. "It's not as if they need proof."

An old incident still rankled. Her aunt had been found guilty of murder by the local police earlier that year. The police had latched on to her without any evidence. Jenny had stood by her aunt and worked hard to find the real killer.

"This is a high profile case," Molly said. "They will think twice before pointing the finger at anyone."

"How do you know so much about this?" Petunia asked Molly.

"Jason told me that," she admitted.

"Jason," a trio of voices chorused. "When did you meet Jason?"

"I ran into him at the bakery," Molly snorted. "It's not like we went on a date or anything, Jenny."

"I don't mind," Jenny shrugged. "You can go out with Jason if you want to."

"We all know Jason's sweet on you," Molly laughed.

"Forget about Jason," Star said. "What are you thinking about, Jenny? Do you have any ideas about who might have done this?"

"Is it one person or two?" Heather asked.

"I think the two deaths are related," Molly said. "Both the girls knew each other, didn't they?"

"What do you think, Jenny?" Betty Sue thundered, pausing her hands for a second.

"I don't know. I keep going around in circles."

"I told you, Jenny," Star said. "You need to write it all down."

"I think Wayne's our guy," Molly said. "He's too good looking."

"That's not a crime, honey," Star said.

"Being a womanizer is, isn't it?" Molly asked.

"I don't think so," Jenny said, scrunching up her face in thought. "He's not married yet."

"It's immoral for sure," Molly said stoutly.

"I agree with that," Petunia supported her. "So this Wayne guy is engaged to one girl, and he was carrying around with two other girls."

"He's so nice about it," Heather sighed.

"Of course he's nice!" Molly snapped. "He gets to have his cake and eat it too."

"Not any longer," Jenny reminded them.

"What do you think about Wayne?" Star asked her.

"He's a bit of a bad boy," Jenny admitted. "But he seems nice."

"That's exactly how he gets all the girls to fall for him," Molly laughed. "You too, Jenny?"

"I can't forget he was up there with Bella," Jenny spoke up. "How could he not have seen her?"

"How many people knew that poor girl took sleeping pills?" Petunia asked.

"Almost everyone, it seems," Jenny said, flinging her hands in despair.

"Why would she take an overdose?" Heather asked. "Surely someone must have forced her?"

"Why didn't she make any noise or something?" Molly asked.

"It's no use," Jenny grumbled. "I've asked myself these same questions plenty of times."

"Is Wayne the only one you suspect?" Star asked.

"We can't forget Ray Fox was in town too," Jenny said.

"That's Bella's husband?" Betty Sue asked.

Molly spoke up.

"You think Ray would want to kill her because of the child?"

"He gave me a pretty tall story about wanting a child," Jenny mused. "But it's possible it was a bluff. Maybe he wanted revenge."

"Why would he come all the way to the east coast for that?" Heather asked. "Surely he could have done it when Bella got back home?"

"What if Bella managed to convince Wayne to marry her?"

"That doesn't make sense, Jenny. Bella was married to Ray. She would have gone back home no matter what Wayne said to her. Ray Fox had plenty of opportunity to get even with her once she went to L.A."

"Doing the deed here is like pointing the finger at himself," Molly added. "Surely he's not that stupid?"

"Ray might have been angry at his wife," Star said. "What did he have against Rainbow?"

"Rainbow was the one who introduced Wayne and Bella," Jenny explained. "He could have had a grudge against her for that."

"So he killed her for an old grudge?" Star asked. "That doesn't make sense."

"Why would Wayne kill Rainbow then?" Jenny asked. "He actually liked her. And she was his girl friend."

"What if Rainbow knew what Wayne did to Bella? She decided to spill the beans?" Molly was very happy with her idea.

"She could have threatened to tell Crystal about Bella," Heather suggested.

"After Bella was gone?" Jenny asked. "I am sure Crystal already knew about Bella and Wayne. She said she didn't care about Wayne's character."

"Saying it is one thing, dear," Petunia spoke up. "No woman is going to like the fact that her man is carrying around with someone else."

Jenny thought of Wayne's final visit to Rainbow. She hadn't mentioned it to anyone.

"I'm going to talk to Adam," she declared, standing up suddenly. "I just thought of something."

"Go on then…" Betty Sue cackled.

The older ladies exchanged knowing glances as Jenny sped down the café steps to the boardwalk. She hurried toward the police station which was a couple of blocks down the road.

A few minutes later, she was standing in front of Adam Hopkins with her hands on her hips.

"We need to talk, Adam!"

"What is it, Jenny? I am busy."

"I have some questions about Rainbow."

"That's an ongoing investigation. You know I can't tell you anything about it."

"Even if it might help you solve the case?"

Adam folded his arms and leaned back in his chair.

"One question."

"When did Rainbow die?"

"Any time after 8 PM. Between 8 and midnight is the best guess."

"So she was already dead…" Jenny mumbled to herself.

"What's that?" Adam asked. "Are we done here?"

"She must have been gone when Wayne visited her that night."

"Wayne Newman went to see Rainbow the night she died?" Adam asked incredulously. "How do I not know that?"

"One of the bridesmaids told me," Jenny revealed. "I asked Wayne about it."

"He could have given her the pills," Adam said, incensed.

"Why would she willingly take an overdose?"

"She was in love with this Wayne guy, wasn't she?" Adam asked.

"Wayne's taking it hard."

"It could be an act. I need to talk to Wayne Newman about this."

"He'll probably come to you himself," Jenny told him.

She sat down and pulled at the chain around her neck.

"Did you find out where Rainbow went that day?"

It was yet another fact Adam was not aware of.

"Someone must have seen her in town," Adam said hopefully. "We will start questioning people."

"She could have just gone to the Rusty Anchor for a drink."

"It's all speculation at this point," Adam sighed.

"Did you find any other clues in her room?"

"Yes, Jenny. We found a note telling us who killed her."

"You don't have to be nasty, Adam!"

Adam hid a smile and leaned forward. He clasped Jenny's hand in his.

"You're so cute, Jenny," he said hoarsely.

Jenny wasn't sure she liked being referred to as cute.

"Do you mean stupid?"

"No, I mean cute," Adam insisted, still holding her hand.

Jenny wriggled out of his grip and stood up.

"I have to get back to the café."

Jenny felt flustered as she walked back to the café. Adam had never held her hand before. Spotting an empty bench on the boardwalk, she sat down and stared at the sea. Was Adam beginning to respect her sleuthing abilities or was he just humoring her. Whatever the reason, Jenny decided she liked holding hands with him.

Chaos reigned back at the café. The two new kids had managed to mix up the orders. Jenny redid a dozen orders while Petunia went around pacifying their regular customers.

"Are you ready for lunch?" Petunia asked her a couple of hours later. "Better eat something before we prep for tomorrow."

"Let's make scones for breakfast," Jenny suggested as she speared some grilled chicken on her fork.

It was the special of the day, made with dried cranberries, strawberries and almonds. Jenny added an orange thyme dressing that was very popular with locals and tourists alike.

"We haven't baked any in a while," Petunia agreed. "Let me ask Betty Sue if she wants a batch at the inn."

The phone rang just as Petunia stood up to call Betty Sue.

"It's for you," she told Jenny, handing her the receiver.

The old fashioned wall phone in the kitchen had a long cord so Jenny could stay seated while she grabbed the handset.

"Hello?" she said tentatively, raising her eyebrows at Petunia.

"Hello, Ms. King," a vaguely familiar voice crackled on the line. "This is Jorge, from

Eagle Aviation? You were here a few days ago…"

"Captain Jorge!"

"I hope you don't mind the intrusion."

Jenny felt a burst of excitement as the handsome old pilot's face swam before her eyes. Had Captain Jorge remembered something about Bella?

"Not at all," she hastened to assure him. "How can I help you, Captain?"

"I wonder if you can pass on a message?" he asked hesitantly.

"Of course. What is it?"

"A young girl came to meet me here a couple of days ago. She was staying at the Pelican Cove Country Club. She mentioned knowing you."

"Who was it?"

"I can't recollect the name," Captain Jorge apologized. "It was something exotic. She was tall and blond with violet eyes, quite attractive if you don't mind my saying so."

Jenny's chair toppled to the floor as she stood up suddenly.

"Was it Rainbow? Was that the girl's name?"

"That's it!" Captain Jorge's relief was palpable. "She came here just as we were winding down for the day."

"What did she want?" Jenny asked, holding her breath.

"She wanted to book a dive," Captain Jorge explained. "She had a lot of questions. I handed over the FAQs we print out for first timers. Then she said she had safety concerns."

"What kind of concerns?"

"She wanted to know what happened if she brought her own rig. That's the parachute…would someone still check it out before she went up?"

"And what was your answer?"

"We don't check personal rigs," Captain Jorge said immediately.

"But I thought you said you had strict quality checks?" Jenny probed. "Didn't you mention some kind of guidelines?"

"We do that for our own gear," Captain Jorge explained. "We don't touch your gear. People who bring their own parachutes sign a waiver. We are very meticulous with our paperwork, Ms. King."

Jenny figured the company was just making sure they were not liable.

"I understand," Jenny said. "What was the message, Captain Jorge?"

"She booked a dive for tomorrow evening but she didn't leave any contact information. I just wanted to confirm she's still coming as scheduled?"

Jenny swallowed a lump as her fingers tightened around the telephone cord.

"You should cancel that appointment, Captain Jorge. Something's come up. Rainbow is not available tomorrow."

Jenny plunged into thought as she thanked the pilot and hung up the phone. Why had Rainbow visited the sky diving company? Had she discovered something about Bella's death?

Chapter 20

"You have to come," Heather pleaded with Jenny. "Crystal especially wants you there."

"Look around, Heather," Jenny waved a hand at the crowded café. "People are lining up here thanks to Mandy and her Instagram. They want to book tables. There's no way I can get away."

Heather turned to Petunia.

"It's just a couple of hours. And it's at sunset. The café is closed by then."

"I don't mind," Petunia told her. "I can take care of the prep for one day. Maybe Star can come and keep me company."

Heather went for the jugular.

"It's a chance to say goodbye to Rainbow."

Jenny couldn't say no to that.

A small group of people assembled at the Pelican Cove Country Club later that evening. The gazebo was covered in small bouquets of tulips and roses. Someone whispered they were Rainbow's favorite flowers. A priest had arrived from the mainland. In deference to Rainbow's wishes, no one wore black.

Crystal sniffled and Wayne looked solemn. Kathy Mars dabbed at her eyes with a lace handkerchief. One of the girls gave a violin recital. Wayne asked if anyone wanted to say something. Almost all the girls had something nice to say about Rainbow.

"She's going to be missed," Heather whispered to Jenny.

Jenny's eyes misted over. She felt helpless. All her efforts had been futile. She wasn't any closer to finding out what happened, either to Bella or Rainbow.

"One of these people is a killer," she hissed at Heather. "Maybe it's one of these girls…just waiting to step into her role on the show."

"You think so?" Heather was skeptical.

"She was on to something," Jenny mumbled. "I'm sure about it."

The sun set over the ocean, painting the sky orange and mauve. Rainbow wasn't around to see it, but Jenny admitted she had been given a good farewell. Ray Fox caught her eye as they walked back to the club house.

"I didn't know you were coming."

"Rainbow and Bella were like sisters," he said. "Bella would have wanted me here."

"Do you think she would take her own life?"

"Never," Ray said, shaking his head. "She was ambitious. She had her kid to think about."

"So you believe she was murdered?"

Ray said nothing but his grim expression was answer enough.

Someone had ordered a sumptuous buffet of Rainbow's favorite dishes. Jenny guessed Wayne had something to do with it. He wasn't hiding his grief from anyone.

Jenny overheard the girls talking about the show. Everyone wanted to know who was going to replace Rainbow. The girls seemed excited but Jenny assumed that was natural. She peered at each of their faces as she bit into a slider. Had one of them deliberately poisoned Rainbow?

"Stop staring, Jenny!" Heather hissed in her ear. "Wayne wants to talk to you."

Wayne stood at one end of the long passage, gazing out at the dunes.

"I miss her," he told Jenny. "We were really close."

Wasn't he close to all the women in his life, Jenny mused. A sudden giggle erupted, making her feel mortified.

"I don't mean that way," Wayne clucked. "Rainbow was my best friend. We could talk for hours. She really knew me, you know. Knew Wayne Newman the person, not Wayne Newman the country music star."

"Shouldn't you have that with Crystal?"

Wayne shrugged.

"Crystal and I have an understanding. Getting married now will give a big boost to our careers, and we both understand that."

"What if Crystal wasn't in the picture?" Jenny asked. "Would you have married Rainbow?"

Wayne hesitated. Then he shook his head.

"Rainbow didn't have that kind of fan base."

"But you did. Surely you could have elevated her career if you wanted to."

"It's too late now," Wayne shrugged.

"What's next for you, Wayne?"

"We are going back to Los Angeles in a couple of days. We are shooting the pilot episode next week. We are all going to be pretty busy, I guess."

Kathy Mars spotted them from a distance and walked over.

"Thank you for coming," she told Jenny. "Rainbow would have wanted you here."

"When did you talk to her last?"

"Crystal and I were having tea out here. She seemed to be in a hurry."

"Was she going out?"

"She must be. She was twirling a set of car keys in her hand."

"Do you know when she got back?"

Kathy thought for a moment.

"She didn't turn up for dinner. I figured she must have met someone."

"But she didn't know anyone in town, did she?"

"Just Bella's husband," Kathy quipped.

Jenny tried to read Kathy's expression. Was she implying Ray Fox had harmed Rainbow?

"You must be looking forward to getting back home."

Kathy's handbag buzzed just as she opened her mouth to answer Jenny.

"Who's calling me now?" she muttered, struggling with the clasp.

"Let me help," Wayne said just then.

Kathy and Wayne both pulled at the bag at the same instant. The bag sprang open and its contents scattered on the floor.

"Look what you've done now!" Kathy exclaimed angrily.

Wayne bent down to pick everything up off the floor. A bottle of pills rolled down and came to rest by Jenny's foot.

She picked it up and quickly read the label before handing it back to Kathy.

"You're not sick, are you?" Heather asked solicitously.

"Oh no!" Kathy said, looking flustered. "Those are just my anxiety pills. Almost everyone in the business takes them. Right Wayne?"

"Huh?" Wayne asked.

Jenny couldn't wait to get away. She said goodbye and grabbed Heather's arm.

"What's the rush, Jenny?" Heather scowled, jerking her arm away.

"Did you see those pills?" Jenny asked as she backed out of the parking lot.

"Kathy's anxiety pills?"

"They can double as sleeping pills. I need to talk to Adam right now."

They rushed into the police station. Adam Hopkins stood at the front desk, ready to go home for the day.

"What's the matter now, Jenny?" he asked, correctly reading her expression. "Let's go into my office."

"What's the drug Rainbow took? Quick, tell me."

"We are waiting for a full tox screen," Adam told her patiently. "But if you must know, it was a cocktail of a popular anxiety drug mixed with something else."

"Aha!" Jenny banged her fist on the table.

She quickly told Adam about Kathy's pill bottle.

"It's a very common medicine, Jenny," Adam sighed. "Anybody could have a prescription for it."

"But get this," Jenny said with relish. "The bottle was almost empty."

"We don't know when the prescription was filled."

"But you can find out?"

"I'll look into it," Adam promised. "But it may not be that easy," he warned. "We will probably need a warrant."

"Do what you think is best."

Heather and Jenny lingered outside while Adam made a few calls. He came out just as they were saying goodbye to the desk clerk.

"How about going to Ethan's?" Adam asked. "I could use a bite to eat. I skipped lunch today."

Jenny looked at her watch reluctantly.

"Sorry. I'm meeting Jason in five minutes."

Adam turned around and walked to his car without a word.

"Did you have to blow him off?" Heather grumbled.

"I really have an appointment with Jason," Jenny stressed. "It's important."

"Are you just playing hard to get?"

"No, Heather! I need to talk to Jason about a business matter."

Jenny crossed the street and walked two doors down to Jason's office.

"Come on in," he called out to her.

Jenny grabbed a soda from the small refrigerator in Jason's office. She sat down heavily and took a few sips of the cold drink.

"What do you have for me?"

"It looks tough."

"Do I have enough funds in my account? That's all I want to know."

"You do, Jenny. But if you spend this, you won't have a cushion until next year. You'll have barely enough for any incidental expenses."

"I don't need much," she shrugged. "Living in Pelican Cove is really cheap."

"What about Nick's college fees?"

"His father is paying those. They don't come out of my account."

"I still wouldn't advise it, Jenny."

"Is it going to solve our problems?"

"You know there will always be something else."

"Of course, but I am just talking about the contest. I love this town, Jason. And if there's even a slight chance we could be the Prettiest Town in America, I don't want to stand in the way."

"How do you know Petunia wants this?"

"Are you kidding? She's lived here almost all her life. She wants to win too."

"So when are you giving her the good news?"

"I'm not," Jenny said. "You are."

"How do you mean?"

"The Boardwalk Café is going to get a silent partner. It will be just enough to cover the cost of refurbishment."

"Jenny, you're investing almost a year's income in this. Are you sure you don't want credit for it?"

"I'm sure, Jason. I have to work side by side with Petunia every day. I don't want her to feel beholden to me."

"Jenny King," Jason said, his eyes shining with admiration. "You're something else."

"Stop flattering me," Jenny blushed, slapping Jason on the arm. "Now what about that other matter?"

"I have good news," Jason exulted. "Our offer has been accepted."

Jenny felt her heart speed up.

"What does that mean?" she asked, leaning forward in her seat.

"We are in escrow, Jenny!"

"We are?"

"You are now the owner of a charming sea facing three storied Victorian."

"Seaview," Jenny whispered lovingly. "Is it really mine?"

"Congratulations, Jenny! This is a big leap for you. You are a home owner in Pelican Cove."

"It's like a dream come true."

"Who do you want to tell first?"

"I'm calling Nick," Jenny said, laughing and crying at the same time.

She fished her cell phone out of her purse and waved it around for a signal. Jason picked up his desk phone and placed it in front of Jenny.

"Call him from this. I can add it to your bill."

They both laughed at that.

Jenny spent the next few minutes talking to her son while Jason looked on indulgently.

"What about fixing up Seaview?" Jenny asked after she hung up. "Do I have to wait until next year?"

"I already factored it in," Jason told her. "You have a nice chunk of money set aside for repairs at Seaview."

"Oh Jason, I am so happy!"

"Ready to share the news with everyone?"

"You remember our promise?" she asked Jason. "No one can know about my involvement in the café. No one."

"I'm your lawyer, Jenny. You can trust me with your life."

He took her hand and kissed it gently.

"You can trust me, period."

Jenny sprang up and danced a little jig. She couldn't have imagined this outcome in her wildest dreams. Just a few months ago, she had come to Pelican Cove with just the clothes on her back. A good divorce lawyer had made sure her cheating husband treated her fairly. It was the least she deserved after twenty years of marriage.

"Let's go out and celebrate," Jason said. "There's this great seafood place on the boardwalk at Virginia Beach. They have oysters on the half shell and wood fire grilled fish."

"Can I change first?" Jenny asked. "We can take Star with us, can't we?"

"Of course we can," Jason smiled. "What's a celebration without family?"

Chapter 21

Jenny chatted with Captain Charlie early the next morning. The old salt had appeared on the steps of the Boardwalk Café at 6 AM sharp.

"How about a hot scone?" he asked. "Petunia's been talking them up a lot."

"Coming right up," Jenny smiled. "I made strawberry jam to go with them."

The phone rang at 8 AM. Petunia's face broke into a big smile after she answered it. Jenny acted surprised.

"Someone wants to invest in the café," Petunia said, her eyes saucer like in wonder. "He's ready to pay for all the repairs the town committee wants us to do."

"That's great news," Jenny said, giving her a hug. "You said yes, right?"

"Of course I did. Beggars can't be choosers."

"You're not a beggar, Petunia. The Boardwalk Café is a landmark. Any investor should be proud to invest in such a well loved place."

"All that is fine, dear, but anyone who's putting up a big chunk of money is entitled to think what they want."

"When do we meet this Santa Claus?"

Petunia's expression said she wasn't too happy with Jenny's flippant tone.

"We don't. That's the condition."

"Doesn't matter to us," Jenny shrugged. "Why don't you call Barb and Mandy and rub it in their face?"

"What's got into you, Jenny?" Petunia groaned but she giggled like a naughty girl.

"Call the contractor too while you're at it."

"One thing at a time," Petunia said, pressing the buttons on the phone.

"Hola!" a deep voice came from the counter.

Jenny spotted Ray Fox standing there with a duffel bag slung over his shoulder.

"Good Morning, Ray. You're out early today."

"I came to say bye," he said. "I want to thank you for all your help."

"I didn't really do anything," Jenny said bitterly.

Her failure to find Bella's killer still rankled.

"You did your best," Ray Fox said with a shrug. "I guess we will never know what happened to my Bella."

"Where are you off to?"

"Back home. I'm taking Bella with me."

"So the police cleared you, I guess."

"I can't stay here indefinitely. Jason talked to them. They don't have any evidence against me so they have to let me go."

"When's your flight?"

"I'm flying out from Norfolk later today. But I want to get a head start. I can't wait to get out of here."

"I can understand," Jenny nodded gloomily.

She wrapped a hot scone for him and poured coffee into a travel container.

"It's on the house."

Ray gave her an awkward hug. He was gone soon after that.

Petunia came out looking relieved.

"The contractor can start work today. We should be able to meet the town's deadline by a whisker."

The kitchen phone rang again and Jenny rushed inside to answer it.

"We're going shopping!" Heather screamed over the phone. "I'm picking you up in five minutes, Jenny. Get ready."

"You know I can't leave the café…" Jenny objected. "What's the rush?"

"Just be there, Jenny. We can talk on the way."

A black stretch limo pulled up outside the café five minutes later. Heather's head sprang up through the sun roof. She waved madly at Jenny, urging her to hurry.

"I think you better go, dear," Petunia laughed. "Don't worry about the café."

A uniformed chauffer stepped out of the car and came around to the passenger side. He held the door open for Jenny. Jenny snatched her bag and ran down the stairs, unable to curb her excitement.

Crystal and Heather reclined against the plush seats, sipping glasses of champagne.

"What's going on?"

"Just get in," Heather urged. "We are shopping for Crystal's wedding dress."

"I'm getting married tomorrow," Crystal preened, looking as cool as a cucumber.

"But I thought you were all leaving this weekend."

"Tomorrow is our last day in town," Crystal explained. "What better way to end this horrible trip?"

"Wayne's going along with it then?"

"Of course he is," Crystal told Jenny. "He proposed to me again last night. The studio's thrilled. They are going to film everything this time and use it for the show."

"Wow!" Jenny exclaimed, giving Heather a questioning look.

"Only bummer is, we just have one day to shop for the wedding."

"Aren't you wearing your Vera Wang?"

Crystal's body quivered.

"That dress is jinxed. I'm getting something new from a local designer."

Jenny was honest.

"I don't think you can have a custom-made dress in a day, Crystal."

"Throw enough money and you can get anything," Crystal dismissed. "Mom's already booked appointments for us with the area's top designers. We can give them credit on the show. None of them is going to pass up this opportunity."

"Crystal changed her wedding colors," Heather enthused. "All the bridesmaids get new dresses too. I've got everyone's measurements right here."

"Where are all the other girls?" Jenny asked, noticing their absence.

"They are at the spa," Crystal told them. "Everyone's panicking because they are going on camera tomorrow."

Jenny wondered why Crystal wasn't at the spa too. But she kept her thoughts to herself.

"So I can get a dress that fits this time," she joked.

"Why don't you relax?" Crystal invited. "Sip some champagne. It's Moe Chandon, compliments of the studio."

"Don't mind if I do," Jenny giggled nervously.

Jenny had spent her life attending parties where the finest French champagnes flowed like water. But she had missed them since coming to Pelican Cove.

"What's our first stop?"

"Williamsburg," Heather supplied. "Crystal wanted to go to Richmond but I talked her out of it. It's too far."

"Are we going to the outlets?" Jenny asked eagerly, already planning to squeeze in some discount shopping.

"Outlets?" Crystal asked, looking horrified. "We are not shopping retail, Jenny. Surely you know that."

Jenny began feeling light-headed after an hour of sipping champagne. Heather pulled out some cheese and crackers from a picnic hamper. There was a jar of olive tapenade and a loaf of crusty bread. The girls feasted on them. Crystal refused to eat anything.

They spent a couple of hours in Williamsburg, visiting four different designers. Crystal tried on exactly one wedding gown at each place. Jenny thought she looked gorgeous in every one of them, but Crystal rejected them all.

"Can we stop for lunch?" Heather asked.

"We can eat in the car," Crystal told them. "I ordered Chinese food."

The car sped north toward Hampton Roads while the girls feasted on the greasy salty food.

Crystal tried on two more wedding gowns. She fumed when a designer showed her a mermaid design.

"This is so last year!"

Their next stop was on the outskirts of Virginia Beach. Thankfully, Crystal fell in love with the gown. It came with black gloves and a big bow at the back. Crystal announced it was suitably 'au courant'.

The bridesmaids got dresses in pale blue.

"Wayne's meeting us for dinner in Virginia Beach," Crystal announced, reading a text from her phone. "We are going to this fancy seafood place on the boardwalk."

"I've been there with Jason," Jenny told them. "It's really fancy."

"As fancy as this place can get, I suppose," Crystal quipped.

Wayne was already at their table when they reached the restaurant. They ordered a tower of seafood, with oysters, crab legs and jumbo shrimp. Crab cakes followed, with grilled fish and seared scallops.

"Have you ordered the whole menu, Wayne?" Jenny asked him.

She dipped a giant shrimp into cocktail sauce and exclaimed as she was about to bite into it.

"What's he doing here?"

Jenny had spotted someone who looked like Ray Fox. She stood up and walked over to the table. She had guessed right.

"You're still here?" she burst out.

"My flight was delayed," he told her. "Someone recommended this restaurant so I took a cab and came here."

Jenny thought it was a long way to travel just for some seafood.

"All the way from Norfolk?"

"I have nothing else to do," Ray shrugged. "I'm glad I came. This place is really something, huh?"

Jenny went back to her table after that. Crystal and Wayne were arguing about Jordan almonds. Crystal wanted a mix of white and pale blue nuts to match her wedding colors. Wayne didn't know what the fuss was about.

"I know a shop here that sells them," Heather said eagerly. "Why don't we go check it out, Crystal? They do bulk orders. You can get a few pounds for tomorrow."

Crystal agreed immediately. They decided to walk to the store to work off their meal.

Atlantic Avenue was crowded, with tourists jostling each other for space. Jenny and Heather walked arm in arm, followed by Wayne and Crystal. Wayne was talking about how he had liked the multicolored Jordan almonds as a kid. They stopped to cross the street as the light turned red.

Jenny suddenly felt her knees buckle as she fell into the oncoming traffic. She landed on her side as horns blared and a large SUV screeched to a stop barely inches from her face. Jenny felt the ground spin as she blacked out momentarily.

The next thing she knew, she was sitting on a small stool on the sidewalk. Heather and Wayne were fawning over her, asking if she was hurt. Crystal stood a few feet away, looking at her in disgust.

"You're bleeding!" Heather exclaimed as she noticed Jenny's dress. The right side of her body was soaked in blood.

Wayne pulled out a handkerchief and started dabbing her arm with it. One of the onlookers handed over a bottle of water. Wayne washed her hand and gently wiped the blood off.

"I think it's just a flesh wound," he said. "You must have cut your arm on something."

Jenny felt a searing pain in her shoulder. Her arm didn't respond when she tried to raise it.

"Looks like you dislocated your shoulder," another guy on the sidewalk offered. "There's an urgent care place a couple of miles out. You should get yourself checked out."

"Let's just go home," Jenny pleaded.

Wayne would have none of it. They took her to the 24 hour clinic. The man on the street had been right about Jenny's shoulder. The doctor popped it back in place and gave her a sling to wear. She had a few more scratches and one big cut on her arm. She had to get a tetanus shot because she didn't remember when she had her last one.

The limo sped home over the Chesapeake Bay and crossed the bridge leading to Pelican Cove.

"I'm so sorry about all this," Wayne apologized as he helped Jenny out of the car.

Crystal had dozed off, probably piqued by all the attention Jenny was getting.

There were a few figures sitting out on Star's porch.

"Jenny!"

Three different voices cried out in the night.

Jenny looked up to see Adam and Jason standing on either side of her aunt.

"What are you doing here?"

"Adam wanted to ask you out for a walk," Star explained. "Jason brought dinner."

"What happened, Jenny?" Adam demanded curtly. "Are you hurt?"

"How did this happen?" Jason asked sharply.

Jenny gave them the Cliff Notes version.

"It's getting late," she said meaningfully, tipping her head at Wayne.

Jason thanked Wayne and accepted his impromptu wedding invitation.

Adam opened his mouth as soon as the limo went out of sight. Jason stopped him.

"Let's get her settled in."

"I'm fine," Jenny stressed. "It's just a few cuts and bruises…"

"And a dislocated shoulder," Star guessed.

"Think carefully, Jenny," Adam said after she was ensconced in an armchair inside the cottage.

Star had pressed a steaming mug of tea in her hand and covered her with a soft rug.

"Tell me exactly what happened."

"I don't know. We were standing on the sidewalk, waiting to cross the road. I must have lost my balance."

"Or someone pushed you," Jason said bluntly.

"Where was Wayne Newman when this happened?" Adam asked grimly.

"He was right behind me."

Chapter 22

Jenny's bridesmaid's dress fit her properly this time. The blue sling on her arm matched her dress.

Star got all choked up as she looked at her. She had come to drop Jenny off at the country club.

"You look beautiful, sweetie."

Jenny held up her arm.

"I'm going to be an eyesore. They will probably keep me out of the wedding photos."

Star gave Jenny a meaningful look.

"Are you sure you want to go to this shindig? We can just turn around and drive home, you know."

"I need to be there," Jenny stressed. "This is my last chance to get a close look at these people. I'm sure one of them is the murderer."

"You'll be careful, won't you?" Star frowned.

"Don't worry about me, Auntie."

Star looked down at her paint spattered smock. She would have crashed the wedding party if she was wearing something decent.

"Jason's going to meet you here?"

"Yes, he's my date."

Star pulled up in the club's porte-cochere. Jason was waiting for them. He helped Jenny out of the car and escorted her up the steps.

Heather and Chris Williams were seated in the lounge, sipping slim flutes of champagne. Heather came around to hug Jenny.

"So what's the plan?" Jenny asked.

"The studio people are setting up on the lawn," Heather reported. "It's going to be a fairy-tale wedding, Jenny."

Jenny and Heather discussed wedding details like flowers and arches and dresses. Jason and Chris pretended they were bored. One of Crystal's posse came in and began rounding everyone up.

Jenny spotted the wedding arch from a distance. A big white tent was erected at one side for the reception. The color theme of white and yellow was reflected everywhere. A bunch of ushers began leading people to their seats. Jason and Chris chose a couple of chairs in the back row.

A lot of studio staff was milling around, dressed in black. A man sat in a crane forty feet high, fiddling with a large camera. The crane swept across the landscape, recording the activities of the guests.

A couple of tight lipped men wearing tuxedos stood at one side, observing everything with eagle-like precision.

"They are the big bosses," Heather whispered. "The show's producers."

The bridesmaids huddled together in a group, dressed in blue like Heather and Jenny. One of the girls came over and told Jenny the studio wanted her to stand aside.

"It's your sling," she said apologetically. "It won't look good on film."

"No problem," Jenny shrugged.

"Where's the groom?" Jenny mumbled to herself.

A whir sounded just then and a plane came into view.

"Are you kidding me?" Jenny burst out.

All the assembled guests trained their eyes toward the plane. Some of them were clutching each other's hands. A body dropped from the plane followed by another. The two bodies plummeted to the ground, gaining speed rapidly until their fall was thwarted mid-air. A canopy unfurled over each body and they began drifting to the ground.

Jenny heard the crane whir as the camera captured the spectacle.

A cheer went up through the crowd as the two bodies landed on the ground with a soft thud. Wayne stood up first and pulled off his parachute. He was dressed in a tuxedo, wearing a white rose in his lapel. He turned around and helped Crystal out of her chute.

"Wasn't Crystal deathly afraid of heights?" Jenny asked Heather urgently. "She said she wouldn't jump from a plane for all the money in the world."

One of the studio execs overheard them. He leaned toward Jenny with a smirk on his face.

"All the money in the world turned out to be a million dollars in this case. They all have their price."

"I just hope she's worth it," the other guy in the suit said.

The first studio exec looked up toward the guy on the crane. He gave them a thumbs up sign.

"After that dive, I say she's worth every penny."

"Aren't you glad we sent her for that certification course?"

"What course?" Jenny asked urgently, grabbing one of the men by his arm.

"The sky diving certification of course!" he said, raising an eyebrow at her arm.

"So Crystal has knowledge of sky diving?"

"How do you think she did a solo dive?" one of the studio execs asked. "She can't do that without being a certified diver."

"She must know all about parachutes and stuff."

The other studio exec butted in.

"I'm a C level diver. Even the most basic level requires you to know all about your equipment."

"You're sure about all this, right?" Jenny asked.

"Of course we are," the guys chorused. "We are very particular about licensing requirements. There's no way we will let an actor do something without the proper permissions."

The strains of the wedding march sounded. Kathy Mars stood ready to walk Crystal down the aisle. Wayne stood at the other end, an inscrutable expression on his face. One of the studio minions held up a big sign saying 'smile' and waved it in front of Wayne. Wayne's lips stretched in a ghastly smile. Then his eyes crinkled at the edges and the smile almost looked real.

"Stop!" Jenny roared. "Stop this wedding."

Everyone stared at her as if she was a mad woman.

"Stop this wedding now, Wayne, or you will regret it."

Jenny elbowed Crystal and walked down the aisle toward Wayne. She whispered something in his ear. Wayne pulled a phone out of his pocket and pressed some buttons.

"What is this crap?" one of the studio execs thundered. "Who is that woman?"

Sirens split the sky as the crowd began to murmur.

Crystal flung her bouquet aside with a cry and plowed into Jenny. Before she realized what was happening, Jenny found herself flat on the ground with Crystal sitting on top of her.

"You couldn't heed my warning, could you?"

Several pairs of hands rushed to pull her off Jenny. Jenny doubled up in pain as Crystal punched her ailing shoulder.

A couple of cars with lights flashing drove up on the grass and stopped right next to Crystal. Adam Hopkins leapt out of one of them.

"Stop running, Crystal," Jenny said, struggling to get up from the floor. "We know you did it. You killed Bella and Rainbow."

Crystal let out an inhuman shriek.

"Yes!" she screamed. "I killed them both. And I almost got away with it too."

"Are you getting this?" one of the studio execs whispered in a walkie-talkie.

"Why did you do it, Crystal?" Wayne asked. "Do you know you killed my baby too?"

"That's why she had to go, of course," Crystal said, laughing hysterically. "I didn't want to be saddled with someone else's brat."

"Bella and Ray were going to raise the child as their own."

"You expect me to believe that?" Crystal leered. "You were seeing Bella behind my back. You think I didn't know, did you? Everyone knew, Wayne. The whole world knew. You made a laughing stock out of me."

"You didn't have to marry him," Jenny pointed out.

"Of course I had to marry him," Crystal cried. "I had to marry some idiot. He was as good as any other."

"How did you do it, Crystal?" Adam asked. "Did you slash Bella's parachute yourself?"

"It was all meticulously planned," Crystal boasted. "My mother paid Rainbow to get Bella thrown off the set. I knew Rainbow felt guilty about it. I told her the show was doing a special segment. Two brides would turn up for Wayne Newman's wedding. But he would choose just one of them. I told her the studio wanted to bring Bella back on the show. And this was going to be her entry vehicle."

"Rainbow bought that?"

"She bought it hook, line and sinker," Crystal laughed. "Rainbow took details of my wedding dress and ordered the exact same one. It was going to be Bella's 'something borrowed' item. The sapphire was her 'something blue'."

"What about the parachute?" Jenny asked. "Bella was an experienced diver. How did she go up without checking her rig?"

"I told them it was specially provided by the studio. It had the show's name painted on it. Or some such crap. They swallowed it without question."

"So Bella went up wearing that chute, thinking she was doing it for the cameras?"

Crystal nodded. "Imagine the look on her face when the chute didn't open!"

"Didn't Rainbow suspect you after Bella died?" Jenny asked.

"I threatened to have her fired. What would happen to her poor kid then?"

"Did Rainbow try to blackmail you later?"

"If only… I could have thrown some money at her. But she developed a conscience. I followed her out to the airfield, saw her talking to that pilot. That's when I knew she had to go."

"How did you kill Rainbow?" Adam asked her.

"I knew she carried that metal water bottle everywhere she went. Some crap about saving the environment…I ground some of her sleeping pills and my mom's anxiety pills and put them in the steel bottle."

"Did you ask her to drink that water?"

Crystal laughed again.

"I gave her some pain pills when she complained about a headache. Told her to wash them down with plenty of water. She drank the whole bottle. Said she was thirsty from being out in the sun."

"Why did you do it, Crystal?" Jenny asked. "You were already the star of the show. What did Bella ever do to you?"

"She was going to steal Wayne away from me," Crystal howled. "I couldn't let that happen."

She looked at Kathy Mars, a bewildered expression on her face.

"Could I, Mom?"

"If Wayne was cheating on you, wouldn't it have been easier to just dump him and find a new guy?"

"I'm going to be Mrs. Wayne Newman," Crystal whined. "It's already scripted."

Adam and his officers took Crystal away. Jason and Chris whisked Jenny and Heather away from the club as soon as possible.

"Are you feeling alright?" Heather asked her worriedly. "We need to take you to the doctor again."

"I'm fine. I just need to ask Wayne something."

Wayne came over when Jenny beckoned him.

"Did you really not know Bella was on that plane with you?"

"I swear, Jenny, I had no idea. I was thinking about our baby. I was hoping Ray and Bella would let me see him now and then."

Jason's eyes gleamed as he stared at Jenny.

"You did it again! You're one amazing woman, Jenny King."

Epilogue

The Boardwalk Café looked brand spanking new. The contractors had finished the renovations in record time. Other Main Street businesses had done their bit and Mandy James had accomplished the job she had been hired for.

Small blue plaques proclaiming Pelican Cove to be the Prettiest Town in America hung over every lamp post on Main Street. Flowers bloomed in window boxes and small flower beds. Colorful bikes were lined up against the café, inviting locals and tourists alike to pedal down the boardwalk and enjoy the beauty.

The Magnolias were assembled on the deck of the café. Petunia had graciously invited Barb and Mandy too. The other café regulars were all present. Jason, Adam, Chris and Captain Charlie sipped sweet tea from tall glasses and talked about some football game. Jimmy Parsons walked up the steps shyly, looking freshly showered, wearing a clean shirt.

Jenny greeted him warmly and led him toward the guys. Jenny's son Nick chatted with Adam's twin girls. They were spending the rest of the summer in Pelican Cove.

Mandy was leaving town in a few days so everyone was gathered for an informal farewell party for her.

"Let's eat," Jenny announced, bringing out a big tray loaded with plates and bowls brimming with food.

Heather and Molly followed with another tray.

"This barbecue sauce is super, Mom," Nick declared, licking his fingers as he bit into some juicy chicken.

"You're a good cook, Petunia," Captain Charlie winked, "but Jenny here has you beat. Got any more specials coming up?"

"Something with blueberries, maybe?" Jenny grinned. "Wait and see."

The party proceeded merrily and everyone declared they had eaten too much.

"Asher Cohen's centennial is coming up," Betty Sue Morse reminded the group. "Too bad you won't be here to plan it, Mandy. We could have used your help."

After the town won the award, Betty Sue had decided Mandy was the best thing that ever happened to Pelican Cove.

"There's a 100 year old man in Pelican Cove?" Mandy asked, wide eyed.

"Sure is," Petunia nodded. "We are planning a big party for him. Star is in charge of the Centennial Committee."

"You should bake a special cake for the occasion, Jenny," Betty Sue declared.

Adam sidled close to Jenny and pulled her aside.

"What are you doing tomorrow night?"

"Let me check my calendar," Jenny joked.

Her eyes twinkled as she looked up at Adam.

"Were you thinking of asking me out, Sheriff?"

The twins and Nick stole glances at them, giggling at some secret joke.

"Yes, Jenny King. I am asking you out on a date. A proper date."

Jenny placed a hand on Adam's arm and leaned forward to whisper in his ear.

"I thought you'd never ask."

THE END

Sprinkles and Skeletons – Pelican Cove Cozy Mystery Series Book 4

By Leena Clover

Chapter 1

Jenny King dipped a warm donut in strawberry glaze and swirled it around. She placed it on a wire rack and smiled to herself, thinking about her new home.

"Don't forget the sprinkles," Heather Morse, Jenny's friend, reminded her as she entered the kitchen.

At forty four, Jenny had completely reinvented herself. Dumped by her husband of twenty years, she had grabbed her aunt's invitation to come visit her like a lifeline. She had arrived in the small seaside town of Pelican Cove to lick her wounds. After letting her wallow for a few days, her aunt had coaxed her into helping out at the local café, just to keep busy. The rest, as they said, was history.

The Boardwalk Café had always been a landmark in Pelican Cove. Jenny's presence added a Midas touch and kicked it up a few notches. Thanks to the Internet and social media, her fame had spread quickly. People were coming from far and wide to sample her food. Jenny didn't disappoint them, churning out tasty recipes that used the abundant local seafood and fresh produce.

The strawberry glazed donuts were her latest creation and people couldn't stop ordering them.

"You're early," Jenny said lightly.

"Grandma's feeling a bit poorly," Heather explained. "She's staying home with Tootsie."

Tootsie was Heather's black poodle, adorable but totally spoilt.

"What's wrong with Betty Sue?" Jenny's brows furrowed in concern.

Betty Sue Morse, Heather's grandmother, was the fourth generation descendant of James Morse, the first owner and inhabitant of the island. It had been called Morse Isle then.

James Morse of New England travelled south with his wife Caroline and his three children in 1837. He bought the island for $125 and named it Morse Isle. He built a house for his family on a large tract of land. Fishing provided him with a livelihood, so did floating wrecks. He sent for a friend or two from up north. They came and settled on the island with their families. They in turn invited their friends. Morse Isle soon became a thriving community.

Being a barrier island, it took a battering in the great storm of 1962. Half the island was submerged forever. Most of that land had belonged to the Morse family. A new town emerged in the aftermath of the storm and it was named Pelican Cove.

Betty Sue was a force to reckon with in Pelican Cove. Well into her eighties, she ran the Bayview Inn and the whole town with a vigor that would shame someone half her age.

"It's the weather," Heather shrugged. "She's coming down with a cold, I guess."

October in the coastal Virginia town was milder than in the north. But the temperatures had dropped suddenly. Islanders could be seen wearing an extra layer. Jenny herself didn't feel the cold in the warm kitchen.

"I'm making pumpkin soup today. I'll save some for Betty Sue."

"You'll have to bring it to her yourself," Heather told her. "I have a date."

Jenny refused to comment.

Heather was a recent convert to online dating. She had finally confided in her grandmother about it. It hadn't gone down well.

"Who are you seeing this time?" Jenny piped up.

"It's a first date," Heather admitted.

"How many first dates have you been on in the last few weeks?" Jenny asked.

Petunia Clark, the owner of the Boardwalk Café, breezed in and started a fresh pot of coffee.

"They are here," she told the girls.

A group of women met for coffee around ten each morning at the Boardwalk Café. They called themselves the Magnolias. Petunia Clark, Betty Sue Morse and Jenny's aunt Star were the older generation. Jenny, Heather and their friend Molly completed the group. Jenny treasured their friendship and would do anything for this group of women.

Jenny carried a tray of donuts out to the deck overlooking the Atlantic Ocean.

"Have you moved all your stuff in?" Molly Henderson asked, biting into a warm strawberry glazed donut.

"Nick's bringing some of my things over from the city," Jenny told the ladies.

Jenny's son Nick was a college freshman. Luckily, he had been over eighteen when Jenny separated from her husband. He visited Jenny regularly and spent a lot of time in Pelican Cove.

"Your husband agreed to it?" Molly asked.

"What's he going to do with my clothes?" Jenny asked. "Nick's also getting some mementos, old photos and some of his trophies from school. They will look fine on the mantel at Seaview."

Seaview was an imposing three storey house facing the ocean. It was right next to her aunt Star's cottage. Jenny had fallen in love with the old house and bought it with her divorce settlement. Seaview had been lying abandoned for over twenty five years. Everyone had been surprised when they learned Jenny was planning to make it her home.

"I wish you weren't moving out," Star muttered.

She had grown used to Jenny in the past few months.

"I'm not moving out alone," Jenny reminded her. "We are both moving out."

Jenny had invited Star to come live with her at Seaview. The house was big enough. Star was a local artist who painted landscapes and seascapes of the surrounding region. Her work was popular among the tourists who thronged to the island every year. She had her own art gallery in town and it did brisk business. Jenny had turned part of the third floor into a studio for Star. With tall glass windows and multiple skylights, it had plenty of natural light. The view of the ocean it offered was priceless.

Star was a bit reluctant to give up her cottage though. Jenny had suggested renting it out. It would provide an extra stream of income for Star.

"You will have your own room," Jenny said subtly. "And all the privacy you want."

Star blushed and the ladies laughed. Star had been getting close to a local man. Jimmy Parsons was better known as the town drunk. He had a soft spot for Star. Earlier that summer, he had decided to turn sober. Star had been a good friend to him, providing him the support and understanding he needed. They were not officially dating yet but Jenny knew that day was coming soon.

"The house looks beautiful," Star admitted. "I'm tempted."

"Don't think too much about it," Jenny pleaded. "Nicky won't be here all the time. I need you there."

"You're scared of being there alone, aren't you?" Heather asked, getting up to leave. "I'm off. See you later."

"Why would I be scared?" Jenny asked with a smile.

Heather left without answering her. Molly and Petunia looked uncomfortable.

Star rolled her eyes. "You don't believe in those old rumors, do you?"

"Please!" Jenny groaned. "You too, Molly? You don't really believe the house is haunted?"

"I saw a light flickering there on Halloween when I was 11," Molly said hoarsely. "It was on the top floor."

"Bunch of kids up to no good, I bet," Star said.

She caught Molly's eye and shook her head. Jenny saw the exchange.

"You don't think those old stories are going to spook me, are you?" Jenny asked. "Any abandoned house is bait for this kind of talk. I don't believe any of it."

"Believe what?" an attractive man asked as he came up the steps of the Boardwalk Café.

The cool breeze coming off the ocean ruffled his brown hair. His almond shaped eyes crinkled at the corners as he gave Jenny a wide smile.

Jason Stone was handsome, intelligent and well off. He was the only lawyer in Pelican Cove. He was one of two local men who had a crush on Jenny. Jason had a cheerful, magnanimous personality. He made no secret of the fact that he wanted to date Jenny.

"Have a donut," Jenny offered, hugging him back.

"I'll have two," Jason said, taking a big bite. "So are you ready for the party this weekend?"

"I can't wait," Jenny said eagerly. "Star and I planned the menu."

"You should just order some pizza from Mama Rosa's," Jason told her. "It's your big day. We don't want you slaving in the kitchen."

"Try telling her that!" Star exclaimed.

"What's a party without crab puffs?" Jenny asked. "I have it all under control. And we'll have pizza too, don't worry."

"Will you let me bring the wine?" Jason pleaded. "I did some work for this local winery and they give me a big discount."

"Thanks Jason," Jenny smiled. "I won't worry about the wine then."

Three days later, Jenny's housewarming party was in full swing. Seaview was lit up like a Christmas tree. The contractors had done a great job with the renovation. Jenny loved how they had modernized everything while preserving the best of the original features.

Jenny had decorated the massive great room in a nautical theme.

"The place looks beautiful, Jenny," Adam Hopkins whispered in her ear.

Jenny's heart sped up as she looked at Adam. His blue shirt was the exact shade of his eyes. He seemed relaxed as he leaned on his cane. Adam was a war veteran with a bum leg but he hadn't let it pull him down. He was the sheriff of Pelican Cove, a job which had frequently pitted him against Jenny. Neither could deny the attraction they felt for each other. They had been out on a few dates since summer.

"Mom's done a great job with Seaview, hasn't she?" her son Nick crowed, putting an arm around Jenny's shoulders.

Adam's twin girls handed Jenny a gift wrapped package. They pulled at Nick's arm and were soon out of sight.

"Going after the booze, I bet," Adam snorted.

Luke Stone tipped his glass at Jenny and complimented her. He had been the main force behind the renovation.

"Are you happy with our work, Jenny?"

"Of course!" Jenny nodded. "Cohen Construction has done a fabulous job with the remodel. When am I getting my garden back though?"

Seaview was set on a large ten acre tract. The house itself was surrounded by towering pine trees. It boasted a sprawling garden which had run wild over the years. Gardenias and honeysuckle dotted the grounds and blue wisteria sprawled over the wraparound porch and gazebo. Climbing roses spanned windows and side walls, their heady perfume mingling with the scent of the other blooms.

When Jenny first arrived in Pelican Cove, she had been mesmerized by the roses and the gardenias. It was one of the things that had drawn her to Seaview.

Jenny had been tempted to let the garden run wild. Luke Stone had talked her out of it. He had brought in a landscaper who assured Jenny they would preserve most of the old bushes and trees. There was only one patch of land that needed to be cleared to put in a water feature.

"They are almost done," Luke assured her. "They are working late tonight so they can install that stone fountain tomorrow."

Jason appeared behind Jenny and planted a kiss on her head.

"Congratulations Jenny. May you be happy here for the rest of your days."

Jenny felt a warm glow inside her. Jason always made her feel relaxed.

"Do we have more crab puffs?"

Jenny smiled all the way to the kitchen. Heather was pulling out a tray of warm crab puffs from the oven.

"These are yum!" she exclaimed. "I don't know what I like more, the puffs or that tomato dip."

Molly entered the kitchen, beaming all over.

"Chris likes my dress."

"He's just being kind," Heather dismissed.

"Don't be nasty, Heather," Jenny snapped. She smiled at Molly. "You look pretty tonight."

Molly Henderson was tall and scrawny, with eyes that seemed to pop out of the Coke-bottle glasses covering them. She had begun dating Chris Williams, a local guy who had been Heather's beau until recently.

Adam Hopkins hobbled in just then, wearing a grim expression.

Jenny had a sudden feeling of déjà vu.

"What now?" she whispered.

"It's Luke's men," Adam said curtly. "The ones working in the garden…"

Jenny's eyebrows shot up as she waited for more.

"They found something. I don't know how to say this, Jenny …" Adam hesitated just for a second. "There's a skeleton in your back yard!"

Chapter 2

Jenny stifled a yawn as she mixed muffin batter for breakfast. Her regular customers would be lining up soon to get their morning fix.

The housewarming party had gone downhill after the startling discovery. Adam had taken over in his role as sheriff. Law enforcement had swooped in with their forensic team and secured the area. Jenny and her guests had been asked to leave the premises.

None of her guests had been ready to go home, of course. They had just moved the party next door to Star's cottage. The food and wine had continued to flow as everyone talked about the discovery of the skeleton.

"Why does this always happen to you?" Star had moaned. "I don't want you getting involved in this, Jenny."

"It's my house. I'm already involved."

"You know what I mean?"

Jenny's reputation for amateur sleuthing preceded her. Star had been unjustly accused of a murder a few months ago. Jenny had stepped in to clear her name. Since then, she had been instrumental in solving a few murders in town.

"What's wrong with Pelican Cove?" Heather cried. "The bodies just keep dropping."

"This one dropped a long time ago," Jason commented.

"Did you see it?" Jenny asked eagerly. "Tell us something about it."

Jason had barely noticed the tattered remains of some clothes on the skeleton. He tried to steer Jenny away from the gruesome topic.

"That house has been sitting empty for twenty five years," Betty Sue proclaimed. "Anyone could have been squatting there."

"So you think this was a tramp?" Jenny asked eagerly.

"We won't know more until the police tell us something," Star quipped.

"Adam's not going to tell us much," Jenny said flatly.

Adam Hopkins was never forthcoming with information related to crimes. Jenny had been at loggerheads with him about it several times.

"Good Morning, young lady!" Captain Charlie's voice boomed, snapping Jenny out of her reverie.

Jenny looked up at her favorite customer. Captain Charlie was always the first in line when the Boardwalk Café opened at 6 AM.

"Your usual?" she asked him, pouring coffee and placing a warm muffin on a small plate.

News traveled fast in Pelican Cove.

"What's this I hear?" Captain Charlie asked. "You're like a magnet for dead bodies."

He guffawed at his own joke, then turned serious.

"You be careful now, you hear? Take care of yourself."

"There's nothing to be afraid of, Captain Charlie. Whoever it was died a long time ago."

"This is going to stir up a storm. Mark my words."

Captain Charlie's warning barely registered as locals and tourists thronged the café. Jenny eagerly waited for a chance to take a break.

Betty Sue swooped in a few hours later, her hands busy knitting something purple. Heather followed close behind.

Jenny went out to the deck, carrying an assortment of baked goodies and fresh coffee. Her aunt was already there, talking softly to Petunia.

Molly was engrossed in a book as usual.

"I guess you won't be moving in to your new home now," Betty Sue clucked.

"It might take a couple of days," Jenny agreed. "I'm thinking I will let Luke's men finish the landscaping first."

"But you're still moving in?" Molly asked, looking up from her book.

"Of course I am. What do you mean?"

"You aren't spooked by Mr. Bones?" Heather laughed.

"How do you know it's not Mrs. Bones?" Jenny asked.

The girls found it funny and broke into a giggling fit.

"Stop kidding around, girls," Star grumbled. "This is serious."

"What do you expect me to do?" Jenny demanded. "Shut up Seaview again?"

"Nothing good ever came from living there," Betty Sue warned "That place is jinxed."

"Don't you mean haunted?" Jenny asked.

"That too," Betty Sue huffed.

"That's it!" Jenny said, banging a fist on the table. "I have had enough of these insinuations. I want to know everything about Seaview. Right now."

"What's the point of that now?" Star asked.

"I am the new owner of Seaview, for better or for worse. I want to know the history of my house."

Star looked at Betty Sue and gave a slight nod. Betty Sue put her knitting down with a sigh and sat back in her chair. She folded her hands and got ready to tell a story.

"Why don't you pour us all a fresh cup of coffee?" Betty Sue asked. "You are going to need it."

Molly bit into her second donut and everyone hunkered down with their food and their drinks.

"You have heard about the Pioneers," Betty Sue began.

The town of Pelican Cove had a peculiar hierarchy. People who had originally moved to Morse Isle with James Morse were called the Pioneers. There were five such families and they considered themselves special. Betty Sue belonged to this coveted group.

"You mean the five Pioneer families?" Jenny nodded.

"Once there were six," Betty Sue explained. "John Davis was the first man to come join my ancestor here on the island. The Davis family flourished on the island. One of their descendants built Seaview."

"I think that name sounds familiar," Jenny agreed. She remembered seeing the name on some legal papers related to Seaview. "So the Davis family lived at Seaview? When was that?"

"The house was built in the 1950s. The family moved in toward the end of that decade."

"You must have been really young then, huh, Grandma?" Heather asked.

"I was a young woman in my teens," Betty Sue dismissed.

"How many people were there in this family?" Jenny asked eagerly.

"Old man Davis and his wife Mary and their two children," Betty Sue told them. "Their daughter Lily was my best friend."

"You had a best friend?" Heather asked, surprised. "But you never talk about her!"

Betty Sue ignored Heather's outburst.

"Their son Roy lived with them. He had a wife and two sons. Alan was four and Ricky was just a baby."

Betty Sue paused and took a deep breath. Her eyes were moist and she had a faraway look in her eyes.

"They were such a happy family," Betty Sue whispered. "A pretty family."

"What happened?" Jenny prompted gently.

"The great storm of 1962," Betty Sue said heavily. "Half the island was washed away. People scrambled for their lives. Some managed to evacuate in time. Some didn't."

"Seaview must have been hit hard, being on the beach," Jenny spoke.

"Old man Davis thought he was invincible," Betty Sue said angrily. "He thought his new house was strong enough to withstand any storm. His overconfidence cost him his life."

There were gasps and exclamations around the table.

"The waves hit strong and hard. Half the house was submerged. The old couple was swept away. Roy died saving little Alan. Roy's wife took the baby up to the third floor. She and Lily watched their family drown in the sea."

"That's horrible," Molly said.

"Didn't anyone try to save them?" Jenny questioned.

She was so engrossed in the story she could almost hear the waves roar.

"There wasn't anyone around to help," Betty Sue explained. "Everyone was trying to save their own lives and their families."

"So your friend lost most of her family in a single day," Petunia clucked.

"Lily was devastated," Betty Sue nodded. "She came to stay with us for a while. I remember she cried for hours, calling for her mother."

"Those poor women!" Star gushed. "What did they do?"

"Roy's wife Ann shut the house up. She was from somewhere in the mountains of North Carolina. She took Lily and the baby with her."

"And Seaview has been abandoned since then?" Jenny asked.

"Do I look like I am done yet?" Betty Sue snapped.

She cleared her throat and tapped her empty cup. Jenny went inside to get a fresh pot of coffee.

"It was the summer of 1989," Betty Sue continued after taking a bracing sip. "Heather was three or four. Her parents were letting her spend the summer with me."

"I vaguely remember going to visit someone," Heather said. "It was in a big house by the sea."

"Lily came back to Pelican Cove that summer," Betty Sue told them. "She was married, with a family of her own. Her son was in college and her daughter had just started high school."

"Why did Lily come back?" Molly asked Betty Sue.

"She said she missed town. Her husband got a job in Virginia Beach. Her kids had grown up hearing about Pelican Cove and Seaview. The kids had never seen the ocean. They were eager to live in a beach community."

"They sound like a normal family," Jenny said.

"They were normal alright," Betty Sue sighed wistfully. "Laughter rang through the halls of Seaview. Lily was the perfect mom, baking cookies for her daughter's friends, volunteering in school activities. Then disaster struck."

"What now?" Jenny cried.

"Lily's daughter died."

"What?" Heather burst out. "You never told me any of this, Grandma."

"What's to tell? You were just a child then. You wouldn't have remembered any of them."

"What happened to the girl?" Jenny interrupted.

"It was some kind of tropical virus. Nobody knew where she got it. Her fever soared overnight. She was gone within hours."

"Poor Lily," Jenny mumbled.

As a mother, she couldn't imagine anything happening to her son. Losing a child was any parent's worst nightmare.

"Lily was devastated," Betty Sue said grimly. "Grief must have turned her head."

"Why? What did she do?"

"Lily ran away."

"What?" Jenny cried out.

"She must have been seeing someone on the sly," Betty Sue reasoned.

"Did you know anything about it, Grandma?" Heather asked. "Wasn't she your best friend?"

Betty Sue looked sad.

"We had grown apart by then. I tried to reach out to her after her baby girl died. But Lily locked herself in that house. Her husband was at work most of the time. Her son was in college. She barely left the house. I took some food to her a few times. After a while, I just gave up."

"And all this time she was having an affair?" Molly mused.

"We'll never know that," Betty Sue pursed her lips. "Rumor has it, she got into a car one dark night and ran out of town."

"How did her husband take it?"

"He closed up the house and went away. The son never came back either."

"When was this, Betty Sue?" Jenny asked.

"Fall of 1991."

"And you never heard from any of them again?" Heather asked.

Betty Sue shook her head.

"I will never understand why Lily abandoned her family. The Davis name has never been spoken of again in town. Most of the people who settled here after the big storm have never heard of them."

"Now you know why that house is jinxed?" Betty Sue thundered. "None of the locals like to talk about it."

"Why didn't you tell me all this before I bought the house?" Jenny asked curiously.

"You didn't ask," Betty Sue shrugged. "You just announced one fine day that you bought Seaview. I didn't see a point in saying anything after that."

"Say what you will," Jenny said firmly. "I don't believe in superstition. I know the Davises had a string of bad luck. But that's not going to happen to me."

Jenny forced herself to ignore the obvious – the skeleton the men had found in her backyard.

"Hello ladies!" a cheery voice startled them out of their misery. "It's a beautiful day, isn't it?"

Jenny rushed into Jason Stone's arms and hugged him tightly. He made her believe everything was going to be alright.

Chapter 3

Jenny ladled thick pumpkin soup into a bowl and garnished it with toasted pumpkin seeds. She sprinkled a bit of Old Bay seasoning on top. People on the Eastern Shore loved to add it to their food.

Molly buttered the thick crusty bread Jenny had set before her.

"You are in early," Jenny remarked as she served Molly's lunch.

"The library board is meeting today," Molly explained. "It's all hush-hush. The staff was asked to leave the building."

"This gives us a chance to catch up," Jenny smiled. "How's it going with Chris?"

Chris Williams, a thirty something young man, came from a local Pioneer family. He had always been tight with Heather. Their families had been sure they would get engaged soon. Heather had shocked everyone that summer with a different kind of announcement. She wanted to date other people. Chris had matched her step for step by putting up his own profile on the online dating sites. Molly had expressed an interest in going out with Chris.

"We went out a couple of times," Molly said shyly. "Just as friends."

"You think he's just waiting for Heather to go back to him?"

"I don't know, Jenny," Molly muttered.

Molly really liked Chris. She had confessed as much to Jenny. Jenny was afraid Heather and Chris were just playing some kind of game. Molly was going to end up getting hurt.

"Don't get too attached," Jenny warned. She tried to change the subject. "How do you like the soup?"

"It's delicious!" Molly exclaimed. "The tourists are going to love it."

"Petunia says we have more tourists this fall," Jenny said, "thanks to Instagram. They just won't stop coming."

"Good for business, right?" Molly said. "I just wish there was a way tourists could come to the library. We can use the business."

A short, middle aged man entered the café. Jenny guessed he was around fifty. She had never seen him before. His clothes were rumpled and had seen better days. The man came up to the counter.

"Hello!" Jenny greeted the stranger. "Here for some lunch?"

The man looked at the floor and mumbled something.

"How about some pumpkin soup?" Jenny suggested, trying to guess what he had said. "I just made a batch of chicken salad sandwiches."

The man nodded but didn't look up. Jenny brought his order out and pointed to a table near the window.

"How do you do it?" Molly asked, biting into her sandwich. "You are so good with people."

"It's just instinct," Jenny shrugged.

She placed a slice of chocolate cake before Molly and took one to the stranger.

"Care for some dessert?" she asked. "It's on the house."

"Have you moved into your house?" the stranger asked suddenly.

Jenny was speechless. She stared at the man, unable to think of a reply.

"You are the new owner of Seaview, aren't you?" the man asked.

He looked directly at Jenny, his light brown eyes boring into hers.

"Who told you that?"

"It's all over town," the man laughed. "You can't keep a secret in a small town like this."

"Do you live in Pelican Cove?" Jenny asked.

"Oh no! I'm just visiting."

Jenny held out her hand and introduced herself.

"My name is Jenny King. I moved here a few months ago."

"I know who you are," the man nodded, taking a bite of his cake. "Yes Sir!"

"What is your name?" Jenny asked him directly.

"Keith Bennet," the man said softly. "You can call me Keith."

"Nice to meet you, Keith," Jenny said lightly. "So where are you from?"

"Here and there," the man answered evasively.

He shoved another bite of cake into his mouth and spoke with his mouth open.

"Did you know about the skeleton in your backyard?"

"I did not."

"Gave you a shock, I suppose."

"I guess you can say that."

"Are you selling the house? Good luck with that. It's falling apart."

"No it's not," Jenny argued. "I did some extensive renovations. Seaview is ready to be lived in."

"How did you buy the place anyway?" Keith asked. "Didn't anyone tell you the place is jinxed?"

"I don't believe in such nonsense."

"You will," Keith nodded. "Wait and watch."

"Excuse me, are you threatening me?" Jenny cried.

"Nope," Keith said, getting up. "Just telling it like it is. If I were you, I would get rid of it as soon as possible."

"Thanks," Jenny snorted. "I'll think about it."

"What was all that about?" Molly asked. "He sounded like a nutcase."

"He knew a lot about what's happening in town."

"Be careful, Jenny," Molly urged. "Don't talk to strangers."

Jenny put her hands on her hips and glared at Molly.

"What am I, eight? I run a café, Molly. Half the people walking in are strangers. How can I not talk to them?"

"Just be careful then," Molly repeated as she rushed out.

Jenny walked to the police station after the café closed. Nora, the desk clerk, waved her through.

"He's not in a good mood," she warned.

Adam Hopkins had a mercurial temper. His mood swings were frequently brought on by his injured leg. Jenny found him struggling with a bottle of pain pills. She took the bottle from him and unscrewed the top. Adam popped a couple of pills and washed them down with water.

"What do you want, Jenny?" he snapped.

"Thanks for the nice welcome," Jenny smiled back.

"I'm busy."

"Just tell me when I can move into my home."

"It's going to take a while," Adam grunted.

"How long is a while?" Jenny pushed. "A week? Two weeks? A month?"

"I really can't say at this time."

"You know I moved most of my stuff into Seaview. I barely have a few clothes at Star's cottage."

"I can send a deputy with you to the house. Take what you need."

"What I really want is to start living there."

"I know that, but my hands are tied. This is an ongoing investigation."

"What is the urgency? Whoever it was, obviously died a long time ago."

"I'm waiting for the autopsy results."

Jenny sighed and sat back in her chair.

"Do you think the house is jinxed, Adam? That's what everyone is saying."

"Have you lost your mind, Jenny?"

"A guy came in to the café asking all kinds of questions about the house. He even knew about the skeleton."

"Every kid in town knows about it," Adam smirked. "It's front page news in the Pelican Cove Chronicle."

"He seemed suspicious."

"I'm sure," Adam muttered, flicking the pages of a thick file.

"He gave me all kinds of warnings about the house."

Adam looked up and sighed.

"People are talking about Seaview up and down the coast. I'm sure each one of them is going to have some advice for you. Are you going to listen to all of them?"

"You're right," Jenny said, getting up. "Am I seeing you later?"

Adam and Jenny had an unofficial standing date every evening. Jenny loved going for a walk on the beach after dinner. Adam went there with his dog Tank. After running into each other a few times, they began looking forward to it.

"I have an appointment in the city," Adam told her. "I might be late getting in."

Jenny walked out, wondering why Adam made her heart flutter. He was in a grumpy mood most of the time.

Star was sitting on the porch of her cottage. Jimmy Parsons sat with his arm around her. Jenny greeted them when she got home. Her son Nick had gone back to college. She rubbed the tiny gold heart that hung on a chain around her neck. Nick had gifted her a gold charm every Mother's Day since he was eight. Jenny wore all the charms on a chain. They stayed close to her heart, giving her a tangible connection to her only child.

"I am heating some leftovers," Star called out. "Come out when you are ready."

They dined on an assortment of dips and crackers and leftover pizza.

"You'll have to tolerate me some more, Auntie," Jenny joked. "They aren't allowing me to move in yet."

"Don't be silly, child. I never reckoned you were going to buy that mansion next door. You can stay here as long as you want. We are getting along fine, aren't we?"

Jenny stole a glance at Jimmy.

"I don't want to be in the way."

"You're not in the way, Jenny," Jimmy assured her. "And your aunt and I, we're not…" His face turned red as he trailed off.

A car drove up outside.

"That must be Jason," Jenny said, springing up.

Jason Stone did not come bearing good news.

"You will have to be patient, Jenny," he told her. "They won't be letting you in yet."

Jenny fixed a plate for Jason and they sat out on the porch.

"I'm tired of people telling me the place is jinxed," Jenny grumbled. "I want to move in as soon as possible and prove them wrong."

"All in good time," Jason said. "So you're not scared of going to live there?"

"I'm tougher than that," Jenny said firmly.

She felt a frisson of uncertainty in her heart but she ignored it. She was a strong, modern woman and she needed to prove her mettle.

"I know," Jason said, tucking a strand of hair behind her ear. "That's the girl I'm crazy about."

"Are you trying to butter me up?" Jenny asked slyly. "What do you want, Jason?"

"A date."

"We talked about this," Jenny protested.

Jenny had resigned herself to the lonely life of a divorced woman after moving to Pelican Cove. She had never imagined that not one but two handsome men would be pursuing her. All the Magnolias teased her relentlessly about it. They were making bets on who Jenny would ultimately choose. After going on a few dates with Adam, Jenny was clearly leaning toward him.

"It's a law society dinner in the city," Jason pleaded. "And I want a smart, sophisticated, intelligent woman to be my date."

"You forgot beautiful," Jenny teased.

"So you'll come?" Jason asked hopefully.

"Just this once," Jenny said reluctantly.

Jason was so nice it was hard to disappoint him.

"I feel bad about this whole Seaview business," Jason apologized. "I never told you the whole story."

"I didn't give you a chance," Jenny argued.

"Yes, but I could have been more upfront about the Davis family."

"Did you know there was a skeleton buried in the garden?" Jenny asked.

"Of course not!"

"Then I don't see what you could have done. I knew how old the property was. Any house that ancient has some rumors attached to it."

"So you aren't repenting you bought the place?"

Jenny paused to consider.

"Not yet. I want to tackle this situation with a positive attitude."

"That's admirable," Jason said. "I'm here to help any way I can."

"I know that, Jason," Jenny smiled. "You're the one person in this town I rely on completely."

Jenny wondered why she couldn't fall in love with Jason. He made her feel safe and protected. She could talk to him about any topic on earth. He was handsome, successful and sensitive. But he didn't make her heart beat wildly. He was the safe harbor she could come home to but he wasn't the storm that would sweep her off her feet.

Jenny walked on the beach, eager to run into Adam. She turned back after a while. The motion detectors set off the lights at Seaview. Jenny smelled the roses and the gardenias and looked up at the imposing mansion. Was she going to be happy there?

Chapter 4

Jenny was surprised to see Adam in the café.

"You're up early," she observed.

"Shift starts at 8. I thought I would get your special omelet for breakfast today. Dinner wasn't great."

"Western omelets on the menu today," Jenny nodded. "With ham and peppers."

Jenny curbed herself until Adam finished eating. She topped up his coffee and looked at him speculatively.

"Any news?"

"I suppose you are referring to the thing we found in your backyard?"

"Heather and Molly are calling it Mr. Bones," she laughed. "Or Mrs. Bones. Can't you tell me anything about it?"

"You wear me down, Jenny," Adam sighed. "I don't want to argue with you this early in the day."

"Then don't," Jenny winked. "Just throw me some scraps."

"It's female," Adam said. "That's all I can tell you for now."

Jenny sucked in a breath.

"Poor woman," she muttered.

"I have to get going," Adam said. "See you later."

"That's all Adam told you?" Molly asked as she sipped her coffee.

Betty Sue was busy knitting something with bright orange yarn. She grunted without looking up.

"What else?" Star asked.

"Nothing," Jenny wailed. "Who was this woman? Where did she come from? What was she doing here? I have no idea."

"Let the police investigate," Petunia remarked. "It's their job. Although I assume it's going to be very difficult to find out anything."

"We need to do some research."

"We?" Star's eyebrows shot up. "You're not getting involved in this mess, are you?"

"I'm already involved."

"Not really," Star argued. "Whatever it was, happened before you got here. You should stay away from this, Jenny."

"That's no reason to let a murderer roam free."

"How do you know it was a murder?" Heather asked.

"Why else would someone bury a body in my garden?" Jenny demanded. "Do you really believe that poor woman died naturally?"

The women paused to think and shook their heads.

"You have no leads at all," Molly said. "Where will you begin?"

Jenny looked at Betty Sue.

"Where I always do. By talking to people who were in the area."

Betty Sue looked up and twirled a thread of wool over her needles.

"Why are you staring at me like that, girl?"

"You are always my best source of information, Betty Sue," Jenny smiled. "You have been around for so long, you know almost everything that happened in this region."

"Are you saying I'm old?" Betty Sue roared.

Jenny struggled to find the right words. Betty Sue laughed at her discomfort.

"I'm just yanking your chain. What do you want to know?"

"Do you remember any missing women?"

Betty Sue shook her head.

"Not in Pelican Cove."

"Do we know how old the skeleton is?" Molly asked.

"Adam didn't say. I'm not sure he knows."

"What's your next step?" Molly wanted to know.

"I'm going to look up some old newspapers," Jenny said. "I'll see you at the library later, Molly."

Jenny walked to the library after the café closed. She settled down in a small cubicle and began looking at old newspapers. She decided to go back ten years at a time. Small town news covered missing cats and local festivals. Jenny saw no mention of any missing persons.

Jenny skipped through the current decade and focused on the first ten years of the Millennium. Her search didn't return anything. She started on the 1990s after that.

"I can't find anything for 1995-1998," she told the girl at the desk.

The girl looked through her records and shook her head.

"Looks like they were misplaced."

"How is that possible?" Jenny asked sharply.

The girl shrank back in fright.

"I don't know. I wasn't working here at that time."

"How can I find out anything for that period?"

"You can try the newspaper offices," the girl suggested. "They have an archives section too."

"How can a library lose stuff?" Jenny complained. "Aren't you supposed to keep everything safe?"

"We moved here from the old building twelve years ago," the girl told her. "They might have been lost at that time."

"You didn't try to replace what you lost?" Jenny grumbled.

"You're the only one who's asked for those records," the girl said. "It's not a priority, I guess."

Jenny gave up arguing with the librarian. She wondered why Molly wasn't at her desk.

Adam Hopkins leaned back in his chair when Jenny swarmed into his office.

"How can I help you?" he asked with a smile.

Adam was in a rare good mood.

"I need to see the missing person records from 1995 to 1998."

"What's so special about them?"

"I'm doing some research on missing women," Jenny explained. "I went to the library and looked at their archives. They have lost all the data from those three years. I can go to the newspaper offices but it will be better if I can directly look at your records."

"There you go again, Jenny," Adam sighed. "Why are you doing all this?"

"I want to find out who Mrs. Bones is."

"That's my job, not yours."

"Are you going to let me see your files?"

"They must be down in the archives section. I'll have Nora pull them up for you."

"Thanks," Jenny smiled.

"Do you want to grab some dinner at Ethan's?" Adam asked. "He just got a fresh batch of oysters."

"Oyster season is just starting, isn't it?" Jenny asked. "I'm thinking of adding them to the café menu."

"Are we having dinner or not?" Adam asked impatiently.

"I want to go home and change."

"I'll pick you up in an hour," Adam nodded.

Jenny had a smile on her face as she sailed out of the police station. Molly was sitting out on the porch when Jenny got home. She looked worried.

"Molly!" Jenny exclaimed. "What's the matter? Did you have a fight with Chris?"

Molly shook her head.

"Worse. I'm about to be fired."

"Fired from the library?" Jenny exclaimed. "Aren't you the top librarian there? What about that award you won last year?"

"Most Popular Librarian," Molly grimaced. "Yeah. That's not going to help me."

"Tell me the whole story," Jenny said, sitting down next to Molly.

She placed an arm around Molly's shoulders. Star came out with tall, frosty glasses of sweet tea.

"Start with this. We can move to something stronger after that."

"The library is out of funds," Molly began. "They are cutting jobs."

"Are you sure about that?" Star asked.

"They are being quiet about it. But I know a girl who took the minutes at the library board meeting."

"Don't they get rid of the nonperforming people first?"

Molly nodded.

"That won't be enough. They are going to cut all the jobs that were added in the last five years. That includes me."

"Will they give you a reference?" Jenny asked.

Jenny didn't have a lot of experience when it came to jobs. She had been a housewife all her life. She had recently started helping out at the Boardwalk Café. Although she was fully committed to the café, it wasn't her livelihood.

"I'm not worried about references, Jenny," Molly sighed. "Where will I go?"

"I'm sure there must be plenty of opportunities for someone with your skills and experience."

"Sure," Molly nodded. She had studied library science in college and was very good at what she did. "But all those jobs are in the city. I'm very happy living in Pelican Cove."

"Oh!" Jenny exclaimed. "What about the other towns along the shore?"

"Most libraries are already staffed. Librarians generally don't go job hopping. Once a position is filled, it's for life."

"We'll think of something," Jenny consoled her. "I want you to stop worrying first."

Molly drank her tea and sobbed silently.

"All's not lost yet, sweetie," Star said. "And you're not alone. We are all going to help you through this."

A car drove up to the cottage and honked. Jenny had completely forgotten about her dinner date.

"I'm going to have dinner at Ethan's," she told Molly. "Why don't you come with me?"

Molly glanced at Adam and shook her head.

"I didn't know you had a date, Jenny. I'm so sorry for holding you up."

"No need to apologize," Jenny said. "The more the merrier. Let's go in and clean up."

Molly texted Chris to come meet them at Ethan's Crab Shack. He was already seated at a table by the water when they got there. He sprang up and hugged Molly.

"Don't worry, Molls. We're going to take care of you."

"The library has never cut jobs before," Adam reasoned. "They must be in really bad shape if they are thinking about it."

"Funding's been reduced thrice in the past year," Molly explained.

"Why don't we forget about that for now?" Jenny asked. "Let's eat."

Ethan came over with platters heaped high with crisp, fried oysters, fat coconut shrimp and beer battered fish.

Adam ordered some raw oysters on the shell. Jenny had never tried them before. Adam sprinkled some hot sauce on an oyster, squeezed some lemon juice on it and coaxed Jenny into tasting it.

"You can't live on the Eastern Shore and not like oysters, Jenny," Chris laughed. "They are going to be your next favorite thing after the soft shell crabs."

Chris offered to drive Molly home. Adam drove Jenny to a small, secluded beach a few miles out of town. Moonlight shimmered over the water and big, frothy waves of an incoming high tide battered the shore.

"You don't mind I brought Molly along?" Jenny asked Adam.

"She's lucky to have you," Adam said gently. "So am I. You're a good friend, Jenny."

"I thought we were more than friends," Jenny said boldly.

"I might need some proof of that," Adam whispered in her ear.

Jenny shivered in the crisp fall air and snuggled close to Adam. Adam pulled up outside Star's cottage an hour later. He picked up a file from the back seat and handed it to Jenny.

"This is a surprise," Jenny said as she saw '1995' printed in bold letters on the file.

"Just this once," Adam said. "I'm not sure what you are going to find in there though."

"You might be surprised, Adam."

Jenny thought of what she had already discovered in the course of her research. But she wasn't ready to talk about it yet.

"How far back are you going to look?" Adam asked. "The skeleton could be a hundred years old for all we know."

"Seaview was built in the 1950s," Jenny pointed out. "I don't think Mrs. Bones is older than that."

"What makes you say that?" Adam asked curiously. "Maybe she's been there for centuries."

"I don't think so," Jenny insisted. "Look, I have to assume something for the purpose of my search. I think this happened after the big storm. Most of the land was submerged at that time, right?"

"Do you think the skeleton was washed up here in the storm?" Adam asked. "It could have got buried in the debris?"

"That's possible too," Jenny agreed. "I'm going after the missing women for now."

"What missing women?" Adam asked as Jenny turned around and walked inside.

Star and Jimmy Parsons were watching an old movie.

"Do you know who owned this stretch of land, Jimmy?" she asked. "Before Seaview was built, that is?"

"That's a bit before my time," Jimmy drawled. "But my guess is the Morse family. They owned pretty much everything on the island at one point."

"Why don't you ask Betty Sue tomorrow?" Star suggested.

"I'm going to," Jenny nodded purposefully.

Was Adam right? Had Mrs. Bones been resting there for the past hundred years? Was she the wife of one of Betty Sue's ancestors? Or a concubine?

Jenny settled into a fitful sleep and dreamed of a family of skeletons living at Seaview.

Chapter 5

Betty Sue Morse wiped the sugar glaze off her mouth with a linen napkin. She picked up her knitting and debated going for a second donut.

"My doctor says I need to watch my sugar."

"We do have muffins," Jenny offered. "I use whole wheat flour and brown sugar in the recipe."

"Tell me what you found out at the library."

Molly hadn't turned up for their coffee break. Jenny decided she was afraid to leave her desk. She was torn between telling the girls about the issues in the library and what she had found out.

"I found plenty of missing women."

"What?" Heather, Betty Sue and Star chorused.

Jenny nodded.

"I went as far back as 1955. Believe it or not, plenty of women have been filed as missing from Pelican Cove."

"I assume all of these reports are from 1962 or 1963?" Betty Sue asked.

"How did you know that?"

"Have you forgotten the big storm?" Betty Sue questioned her. "Entire families were displaced. Many poor souls were literally swept away. I bet all those accounts you read about are from that period."

Jenny's shoulders slumped.

"Why did I not think of that?"

"I'm sure there was a flurry of petty crimes around that time," Betty Sue said. "I remember how it was at the time. The town set up some makeshift camps. We offered shelter to anyone who asked for it."

"And these people repaid you by robbing stuff?" Jenny asked, horrified.

"Many houses were lying abandoned. Doors and windows had been blown away. They were wide open for anyone to plunder."

"I can't believe it!" Jenny breathed. "What were the police doing?"

"There were massive rescue efforts up and down the coast. The priority was taking care of the injured and the infirm. Some people were stranded on the barrier islands. It was a hard time for the town."

"Do you think our skeleton might have been washed ashore from somewhere?"

"Wouldn't someone have spotted it?" Heather asked, barely looking up from her phone. She was engrossed in tapping some keys.

"Put that thing down," Betty Sue rasped. "Are you talking to us or what?"

"I can do both, Grandma!" Heather dismissed.

"The Davis family was grieving," Betty Sue explained. "It was just Ann and Lily and the baby. They were gone within a week."

"Could the garden just have grown over Mrs. Bones?" Jenny gasped.

"Say that's what happened," Star mused, "she has to be from around here. I think you are on the right track, Jenny. You should keep looking for missing women."

"Some of these must have been found, right?" Jenny wondered.

"Either that, or they were declared dead," Betty Sue said.

"I am going to reconcile these names against the county records," Jenny decided.

"That sounds like a lot of work," Star said. "Why don't you split it up among us?"

"I'll get Molly's help," Jenny told them. "She knows her way around the library records."

"Where is Molly, by the way?" Heather asked, looking up. "Why isn't she here today?"

Jenny told them about the problems at the library.

"I know funding has been poor," Betty Sue said. "But I had no idea it was this bad. I missed the last meeting when I had that cold."

"You're on the library board?" Jenny asked, surprised. "Why didn't I think of that? You can find out what's really happening, Betty Sue."

"They mailed me the minutes of the meeting," Betty Sue said. She turned to Heather. "Go get them for me, Heather. They are in the roll top desk where I keep my mail."

Heather stood up and started walking out, her eyes still glued to her phone.

"What's wrong with that girl?" Betty Sue cried. "She hasn't stopped looking at that phone ever since she started that Internet dating nonsense."

Petunia went in to get a fresh pot of coffee.

"Were there any refugees living at Seaview?" Jenny asked suddenly. "Surely they had plenty of room?"

"They sure did," Betty Sue nodded. "But Seaview was a house of mourning. Ann Davis was beside herself. She could barely take care of the baby. She lost her husband and young son in a single stroke. Lily was too young to take any decisions by herself. She came to live with us."

"What about after they left? It wouldn't have taken a lot of effort to break a window and get in."

"It was a sitting duck," Betty Sue said with a faraway look in her eyes. "There were so many people who needed a roof over their heads. There were a couple of break-ins. The police interfered. Then the town people kept watch over the house for a while."

"Why would they do that?"

"We take care of our own here," Betty Sue said grimly. "The Davis family was well respected in these parts. The old man was known for his generosity. He had done a lot for the town. No one thought twice about doing something for them."

"Was Ann Davis supposed to come back?"

"People assumed she would return some day. She was a chicken necker. She barely said goodbye to anyone before leaving."

Jenny recognized the term the islanders used for anyone who wasn't born there.

"Lily was your best friend, right? You must have stayed in touch with her."

"We wrote to each other for a while," Betty Sue replied. "She got married after a few years. So did I. I guess we got busy in our lives. Next thing I know, she's back here with a brood of kids."

"There were almost twenty eight years in between," Jenny calculated. "Was the house empty for all that time?"

"Sure was," Betty Sue said.

"Why didn't they rent it out?"

Betty Sue shrugged.

"There were stories. No one wanted to go near the place."

"What about tramps or other transients? No one ever entered that house?"

"I don't know about that," Betty Sue said, shaking her head. "It was the only house on that stretch of beach for years. Nobody went there after dark. Someone built a couple of cottages there in the 80s. That's when people started living on that side of town."

Heather came back, carrying her poodle Tootsie on a leash.

"Don't take her inside, please," Petunia pleaded. "Just make sure she stays on the deck."

"Don't worry, Petunia," Heather assured her. "I'll tie her to this post. She can play in the sand."

Heather handed over an envelope to Betty Sue.

"What does it say, Betty Sue?" Star pressed. "Read it quickly."

Betty Sue peered at the paper in her hand and her face fell.

"Job cuts are coming alright," she told them. "The board has voted to cull all the jobs created in the last five years."

"That affects Molly!" Jenny gasped. "Poor thing. She really wants to stay in Pelican Cove."

"We need to do something about this, Betty Sue," Star said urgently.

"I can't be directly involved, but I'm all for it. What do you have in mind?"

"We need to raise money for the library, of course," Jenny said. "We need to rally the local businesses and ask them to pitch in."

"Sounds like a drop in the ocean," Betty Sue grumbled. "There is a huge deficit. I don't know how we are ever going to fill it."

"Could you be a bit more optimistic?" Star snapped. "Jenny will think of something."

"You can have a bake sale," Heather said eagerly. "People love your food."

"I don't think a bake sale is going to cut it, Heather," Jenny said thoughtfully. "We need a big fundraiser, something on a grand scale."

"This is not the city," Petunia observed. "People don't have deep pockets."

"We just need to gather more people then," Jenny said resolutely.

"You need to set up a committee," Star said. "That's the first thing we do here when we have a problem."

"Can you make a few posters?" Jenny asked her aunt. "Ask for volunteers for the committee. I'll post them around at a few local places."

Star rummaged in a bag that lay by her feet. She pulled out a sketch pad and a few colored pens.

"I'll get right to it," she said. "Keep talking."

"Heather, why don't you run a search for library fund raising ideas on that phone of yours?"

"I'm chatting with a new guy," Heather pouted. "I need to fix a date for the weekend."

"Haven't you any shame?" Betty Sue clucked. "This is the fourth first date you are going on this month. Why don't you ever go on a second date?"

"None of them has been worth a second date," Heather sulked.

"Of course they haven't," Betty Sue cried. "You are never going to find someone as good as Chris."

"Not that again!" Heather moaned. "Chris understands why I'm doing this. He has agreed to wait for me."

"You do know Chris and Molly are seeing each other?" Jenny asked incredulously.

"Oh, that!" Heather dismissed. "They are just hanging out."

"Watch out, Heather. You might have to repent at leisure."

"Stop talking like my grandma, Jenny!" Heather complained.

"Molly's a wonderful girl," Betty Sue observed. "I wouldn't be surprised if Chris fell in love with her."

"Chris has loved only one girl since he was in third grade," Heather boasted. "That's me!"

"You are not being very nice, Heather," Petunia said softly. "Your head has turned ever since you started that online dating."

Petunia rarely said much. Everyone was taken aback by her straight talk. Heather huffed and went on tapping the keys on her phone.

"Here you go!" Star said with a flourish. "Do you like any of these?"

"Already?" Jenny exclaimed in delight.

Star had produced three different posters, each of them asking for volunteers for the library committee.

"'Save our Library' … I like that." Betty Sue bobbed her head.

They haggled over their choice and finally picked one.

"Let's get this photocopied," Jenny said, getting up. "Coming, Heather?"

"What about the lunch rush?" Star asked. "I can stay back and help Petunia."

"Soup's already on," Jenny assured her. "It's creamy chicken with peas. We are making smoked turkey and pesto sandwiches today. The pesto's already made."

"We can take care of the rest," Petunia said. "You go get those copies."

"I'll be back soon," Jenny promised. "I can put these up later this afternoon."

Jenny walked to the Rusty Anchor after the café closed. It was the local watering hole. Everyone in Pelican Cove eventually ended up there for a pint or a game of pool.

"Hey Jenny!" Eddie Cotton, the proprietor and bartender, greeted her.

"Can you put these up for me?" Jenny asked.

Eddie looked at the poster and frowned.

"What's wrong with our library?"

Jenny spotted Chris and Molly at a table. She walked over and showed Molly the poster.

"We are going to take care of this, Molly. You won't be losing your job anytime soon."

Molly seemed to cheer up a bit.

"What's the latest on Mrs. Bones?" Chris asked with a smile.

"Nothing much," Jenny told him. "None of the local women were reported missing."

"You know, Pelican Cove is pretty isolated. We sometimes forget it's an island."

"What do you mean, Chris?"

"What if someone dumped her here? We are just a dot on the map. The perfect place to hide something, or someone."

"You have given me something to think about," Jenny said.

Eddie brought over a pint and Jenny took a big gulp, her thoughts racing with numerous possibilities.

Chapter 6

The library was crowded when Jenny entered. News of the library's troubles had spread like wildfire. Someone started a rumor that the library was closing down. It seemed like everyone had turned up to check out as many books as they could. Bossy mothers pushed kids into line, clutching piles of books. Jenny tapped her foot impatiently as she waited for her turn.

She had finally squeezed time out to do some research. It had been another busy day at the café. She had fried dozens of donuts, baked several trays of muffins and assembled sandwiches until they ran out of all the food. Her feet ached from running around all day. She ignored her fatigue and settled into a small cubicle.

Widening her search to surrounding areas gave Jenny a lot of different results. Her eyes were heavy with sleep but she plodded on, starting at the year 2000 and moving backwards. She finally hit pay dirt. Jenny eagerly noted her findings in a small notebook. Now she needed to tackle Adam.

Adam Hopkins sat with his bum leg propped up on a chair.

"I'm very busy today, Jenny. I don't have time for small talk."

"This could be important," Jenny bristled. "I want information about some missing women."

"Do you think the police department is here to dance to your tune?" Adam barked. "Go away."

"Why don't you pull these files for me?" Jenny asked, writing down some names on a piece of paper.

"I'm doing no such thing," Adam snapped. "You can forget about it."

"What about Mrs. Bones?" Jenny asked, her hands on her hips. "Have you found anything new about her?"

"Your bag of bones is not a priority," Adam drawled. "Other cases have a higher preference."

"What about my house?" Jenny demanded. "If you're not really investigating, why don't you release it to me?"

"We'll be out of there in a day or two," Adam nodded. "You can move in then if you still want to."

"Of course I want to. It's my home."

"It's not your home yet, Jenny," Adam said softly. "You haven't really lived there yet. Maybe you should reconsider."

"What are you saying, Adam?" Jenny asked him.

"Why don't you talk to Chris? You know he's a part-time realtor, right? Put it on the market. You might get a good price."

Jenny's face took on a pinched expression as she listened to Adam.

"I'm not selling Seaview. I don't understand why you should even suggest such a thing."

Adam leaned back in his chair and folded his hands.

"Aren't you even a bit flustered by this skeleton? Any other woman in your position would have wanted to wash her hands off the whole thing."

"I'm not any woman, Sheriff," Jenny said stiffly. "I'm not going to worry about something that happened decades ago."

"You're one of a kind, Jenny King," Adam agreed.

His eyes glinted with admiration as he stared back at Jenny.

"Pelican Cove is my new home, and so is Seaview," Jenny emphasized. "I plan to grow old there. Anyone who wants to be my friend will have to be fine with my living there."

Jenny turned around in a huff and stomped out.

The Magnolias were all dressed warmly. It was an unusually cold fall day. Salty winds whipped across the deck of the Boardwalk Café, overturning salt shakers and displacing paper napkins. But none of the assembled women wanted to give up their priced view and go inside.

Betty Sue gave a shudder as she pulled off an intricate stitch. She clutched a ball of blue wool in her armpit. Heather was glued to her phone. Molly sat staring in the distance, lost in thought. Star and Petunia were talking about pumpkins.

"How was your trip to the library, Jenny?" Betty Sue asked. "Find anything new?"

Jenny looked pleased with herself.

"I did. Nothing much happened between 1965 and 1990. But three women went missing between 1990 and 2000. I have decided to focus on them for now."

"How will you get more information on them?" Molly asked.

"I exhausted everything I could learn from the library," Jenny told them. "I'm guessing the newspaper archives won't have much more to offer."

"What about old police records?" Molly asked.

Jenny rolled her eyes in disgust.

"That sourpuss Adam refused to help me. So I guess I'm on my own."

"We are here to help you," Star said. "Why don't you run the names by us? One of us might know something about these girls."

"I was going to do that anyway," Jenny nodded.

She pulled out a small notebook and began flipping its pages. A loud voice interrupted them and they stared at each other in dismay.

"Yooohoooo …"

A short, plump woman panted up the café stairs, followed by a well dressed man.

"Hello ladies!" Barb Norton sang out. "I knew I would find you all here."

Barb Norton was the local do-gooder. She volunteered for every town festival and local event and always wanted to take charge.

"I saw those flyers you posted all over town, Star," she began. "Why didn't you just pick up the phone and call me?"

"I thought you must be busy working for the harvest festival," Star mumbled.

"Oh, you are right, dear. The harvest festival is taking up a lot of my time at the moment. But the library!"

She took a deep breath as she said that.

"The library is one of our greatest assets. We can't let it close down."

"It's not closing down yet, Barb," Betty Sue thundered. "Not if I have anything to say about it."

"Job cuts are always the first sign," Barb continued. "What's next, eh? I just couldn't take it."

"What brings you here, Barb?" Petunia asked. "Have you tried Jenny's strawberry glazed donuts yet? They are the latest craze."

"Oh, I can't think of food at a time like this," Barb clucked. "I'm here to offer myself for the library committee."

"Thanks Barb," Jenny said earnestly.

She knew the older Magnolias were always a bit brusque with Barb Norton. But the woman meant well. And she had an endless store of energy she often channelized in altruistic tasks.

"I'll put you down as a volunteer."

Barb patted Jenny on the arm and beamed at her.

"That's not going to be enough. The town needs a strong leader to get through this crisis."

"And that's you?" Star snorted.

Barb ignored her and kept talking to Jenny.

"I'm offering my services as chairperson of the Save our Library committee. You don't need to look any further."

"You know every committee votes for the chairperson together," Betty Sue objected. "We haven't even had our first meeting yet."

"That's just a formality," Barb dismissed. "I'm the person most equipped to lead this effort."

"Aren't you always?" Star muttered.

The man who accompanied Barb Norton had been silent all this time. He cleared his throat and looked at her expectantly.

"I haven't forgotten you," she told him. "Like any strong leader, I've taken the initiative and sought expert help."

"Who's your friend, Barb?" Heather asked, looking up from her phone.

She was eyeing the tall, blue eyed stranger with interest. His brown hair was combed neatly and his khakis and button down shirt were neatly pressed. Jenny decided he was a salesman of some kind.

Heather spotted the ring on the man's finger and her mouth fell in disappointment.

"Ladies, this is Dale. He lives two towns over."

They greeted the man called Dale, waiting for Barb to list his virtues.

"Dale was dubbed Library Savior by his town newspaper," Barb beamed. "He single handedly led a massive fund raising effort to raise thousands of dollars for their library."

Molly looked at the man with interest.

"Are you a librarian?" she asked.

"Oh no," Dale said. "I work at a local car dealership. I just love books. Always have. I believe a library is the heart and soul of any community. It provides the right foundation for raising smart, well informed kids. It educates society and keeps it from stagnating."

"You got that part right," Betty Sue said grudgingly. "What is it you did for raising all that money?"

"Dale has plenty of ideas," Barb butted in. "He's agreed to sit in on our meetings so we can discuss them. When is the first meeting, Jenny?"

"It's up to you, Barb," Jenny said. She grabbed the opportunity to get something off her plate. "You have more experience about these things."

"Don't worry," Barb consoled her. "You'll be a pro at this too, once you have chaired a few committees."

"Do you have any specific ideas for the fund raiser?" Molly asked Dale.

"I do," Dale told her. "But I prefer to give everyone a chance. Let's see what the people in your town come up with first."

"Isn't that idiotic?" Molly burst out after Barb and Dale left. "If he has some suggestions, why not come out with them right now? What's the point in wasting time?"

"He's so full of himself," Heather complained.

She had lost all interest in Dale after spotting his wedding ring.

"Calm down, Molly," Jenny soothed. "He's just milking the situation. Let him. I don't mind giving him credit if he has concrete ideas."

"Forget about Barb for a moment," Heather said. "What are you going to do about those missing women?"

"I'm not sure, Heather. I'm open to ideas."

"Start with the phone book," Star advised. "It's an old fashioned way of finding someone but it still works."

"That's so quaint," Heather scoffed. "I can look them up online right now."

"Do you expect to find their social profiles?" Molly asked Heather. "They are missing, remember?"

"You both have a point," Jenny told them. "I need to determine if they are still missing. I think I am going to track down their families. Go and talk to them."

"I'm up for a road trip any time," Heather whooped. "Now I have to get going. I have a lunch date in Cape Charles."

"Who are you meeting this time?" Jenny asked.

"A gorgeous stud muffin," Heather crowed. "Here. I'll show you his picture."

"Character is more important than looks," Betty Sue preached. "You should know that by now."

"I'd rather have both," Heather said smugly.

She picked up her fancy new handbag and skipped down the café steps.

"Did she have her bag with her all this time?" Betty Sue asked the ladies, looking bewildered. "Who's going to take Tootsie for her walk?"

"I'll do it, Betty Sue," Molly offered.

"No. You get back to your desk. Don't give anyone a chance to point fingers."

"What's the use? I'm losing my job anyway."

"Don't give up yet, Molly," Star said. "Barb Norton's taken up your cause. She's sure to raise a storm and get you those donations."

Molly looked surprised.

"We might give her a hard time, Molly," Petunia spoke up. "But Barb gets the job done."

Jenny added her two cents.

"She won us that Prettiest Town award, didn't she? Save our Library is in good hands."

Jenny pushed her notebook toward Betty Sue. She didn't want to waste time looking in phone books if there was a quicker way to get that information.

Betty Sue picked up the notebook confidently. "I know the old Eastern Shore families. Some of them have been here for generations. James Morse, my ancestor, was known to be a very social man. He invited sailors like him from neighboring towns for an annual barbecue."

"So?" Jenny asked hopefully.

Betty Sue peered at the names and shook her head.

"None of these sound familiar."

"I have a stack of old phonebooks," Star told her. "I'll dig them out for you."

"You think one of these women is Mrs. Bones?" Molly asked.

"I hope not, Molly," Jenny sighed. "I hope they were all found long ago and are living happy, healthy lives with their families."

"What are the odds of that?" Molly asked.

None of the women had an answer to that question.

Chapter 7

Jenny dredged fresh slimy oysters in seasoned flour and fried them. She had already made her special tartar sauce.

"These oyster po'boys are going to be a big hit," Petunia said confidently.

"You really think so?"

"Of course. We have all tasted them. They are delicious."

The aroma of the frying oysters wafted through the café and on to the street. There was a sudden influx of customers asking about the day's specials.

Jenny got busy assembling the sandwiches and served them as quickly as she could. She spotted a familiar figure at a small window table, taking a big bite of her sandwich.

"Hello," Jenny said tentatively, going over to greet Keith. "How's it going?"

"Your food is so tasty," Keith Bennet said, giving her a thumbs up. "Almost like my mom's."

"That's the biggest compliment you could give me," Jenny beamed. "Does your mother make these a lot?"

"She used to," Keith said, sounding morose. "She left us."

"Oh," Jenny exclaimed. "I'm sorry about that."

"Why should you be sorry?" Keith laughed.

His eyes shone with a strange light and his laughter sounded a bit crazed to Jenny.

"Enjoy your meal," Jenny told him as she topped up his sweet tea.

"Have you moved into your new home?" Keith asked.

"Not yet," Jenny said.

"Good for you."

"I beg your pardon?"

"Seaview's not going to do you any favors."

Jenny ignored him and walked to the next table. There were two big groups of tourists who were tasting the local oysters for the first time. Jenny glowed as they complimented her food. She had cooked multi course gourmet meals for her husband and his rich friends, but they had never taken the time to praise her cooking. Jenny rubbed the heart shaped charm around her neck, thinking about her old life. She had come a long way from the suburban housewife who scrambled to fulfill her husband's slightest whim.

Petunia handed her a slice of carrot cake when she went back to the kitchen.

"That thug ordered this."

"Who, Keith?" Jenny asked. "He's a bit rough around the edges, huh?"

Keith was sucking his tea through a straw, making a gurgling noise.

"I hear you turned the top floor into a studio?" he called out to Jenny.

"What?"

"Those skylights are cool, aren't they? And the view from those windows is priceless."

"How do you know that?" Jenny asked in alarm.

Keith shrugged and attacked his carrot cake.

"Have you been inside Seaview?" she pressed.

"I'd say that," Keith shrugged.

"How? When?"

Jenny looked at Keith's scruffy beard and noticed the slight tremor in his hands. She pictured him sneaking into her house, touching everything.

"It was a while ago."

"How is that possible? Seaview has been locked up for several years."

Keith scratched his beard and looked a bit uncertain.

"Let's say I managed, okay?"

Jenny put her hands on her hips and glared at him.

"Did you break into Seaview, Keith?"

"Didn't need to," Keith said with a mouth full of cake.

"What does that mean?"

Keith looked over his shoulder and leaned toward Jenny. "I had a key."

"Did the realtor give you one?"

Keith shook his head.

"I used to live there."

"What?"

Jenny collapsed in a chair and stared at Keith.

"Who are you, really?"

"My grandpa planted that garden at Seaview," Keith told her. "He chose every detail, right from the wainscoting to the drapes at the windows. Didn't live to enjoy it though, poor guy."

"You are related to old man Davis?" Jenny asked, her eyes round with surprise.

"Yes Ma'am."

"You're Lily's son," Jenny said in a rush as she connected the dots.

"Guilty as charged!"

"What are you doing in Pelican Cove?"

Keith looked around the café meaningfully.

"Enjoying my summer, like everyone else."

"Do you come here often?" Jenny asked curiously.

Keith shook his head. "I've always wanted to visit. But I never made it back, until now."

"How long is your vacation?" Jenny asked.

"It's kinda open ended. I don't need to rush anywhere."

"Would you like a tour of Seaview?" Jenny asked generously. "The police should let me move in any day now."

"About that …" Keith muttered. He rubbed his eyes and frowned. "Seaview belongs to me, actually."

"You mean Seaview will always be home for you?" Jenny quizzed.

"No. I mean it's my house. I own Seaview."

Jenny laughed.

"Nice try."

"What's so funny? Seaview belongs to me."

"I bought Seaview with a big chunk of money," Jenny said gently. "My lawyer did all the paperwork. I am the legal owner of the house now."

Keith shook his head.

"That's where you are wrong. As a direct descendant of Grandpa Davis, I have an equal right to the property. I am part owner of Seaview. And I didn't give permission to sell."

"I don't know about that," Jenny said, beginning to lose her cool. "There's a piece of paper that says I am the new owner. Seaview is my home now and no one is going to take it from me."

Keith was equally agitated.

"But I didn't give permission to sell."

"Maybe you should see a lawyer," Jenny bristled.

She pulled out a small notepad from her pocket and scribbled Jason's name on it.

"Here's my lawyer's information. Feel free to discuss this with him."

Keith's face had settled into a pout.

"I didn't say they could sell," he repeated. "I'm an heir too. I have rights."

"Goodbye, Keith," Jenny said, getting up.

"I don't like lawyers," Keith mumbled, reading the piece of paper Jenny had slapped on the desk.

He struggled to his feet and shuffled out of the café. Jenny stood staring at his back until he was out of sight. She was trying hard to keep her chin up. Seaview seemed to present a new problem every day. Jenny was beginning to believe the place was jinxed.

Barb Norton came in with Dale. They ordered the oyster po'boys.

"Jenny here has put our town on the map," Barb boasted. "It's October, but the tourist season is still going strong."

Jenny blushed furiously as Dale gave her an admiring look. She sensed he was a bit of a player. He looked very handsome in a blue shirt and neatly pressed khakis. Like Heather, Jenny noticed his wedding band and sighed.

"Does your wife like to read?" she asked politely.

"Our whole family loves books," Dale gushed. "My wife and I read to our girls since they were babies. My youngest started reading at three."

"Is that why you started lobbying for the library?"

"I believe in giving back," Dale said a tad pompously. "The library has given us so much. I want every family like ours to utilize the same benefits."

"Dale and I went through some of the fund raising suggestions," Barb interrupted.

She needed to be the center of attention all the time.

"Oh yeah," Jenny said. "I'm sorry I missed the first meeting. I couldn't get away."

"If you have any input, you can give it to me now," Barb conceded. "I'll make an allowance for you this time, since you started this whole effort."

"You're the expert, Barb. I'm sure you will choose the best option. Just put me to work when the time comes."

Barb narrowed her eyes and questioned Jenny.

"What do you think about setting up a concession stand outside the library?"

"Is that going to be enough?" Jenny asked doubtfully.

"You will just be selling food to the people that come to the main event," Barb explained. "Every little bit helps."

"I need to talk to Petunia about this," Jenny considered. "But I think we can do it at cost. We will donate any profit we make to the library fund."

"That's great," Barb beamed. "Now let me taste these oysters the whole town is raving about."

She took a bite of her sandwich and moaned in delight.

"Charge double for this," she ordered. "It's for a good cause."

Petunia came out and handed her a basket.

"Delivery for the police station."

"Good," Jenny said. "I need to talk to Adam anyway."

"I packed your lunch in there too," Petunia smiled. "Don't rush back."

Adam Hopkins rummaged through the basket and pulled out two sandwiches. He offered one to Jenny.

"Care to have lunch with me?"

Jenny sat down with a sigh. Her feet ached and she had a blister which was beginning to hurt a lot.

"Delicious!" Adam pronounced as he bit into his po'boy. "This sauce is the real deal, Jenny."

"Do you know the family that lived at Seaview?"

"Barely," Adam told her. "The girl was much younger. The boy went to our high school for a semester. Didn't really hang out with him."

"He's here and he's giving me a hard time."

"Who is?" Adam asked with a frown.

He unwrapped two giant cookies and bit into one.

"Keith! Remember I told you about him?"

"You mean the guy you were complaining about two days ago?"

"He says he owns Seaview."

"That's ridiculous," Adam said. "Didn't Jason handle your deal? I'm sure he checked all the boxes."

"I have full confidence in Jason," Jenny said. "But I have a feeling Keith is going to be a nuisance."

"Maybe he just wants to see his old house."

"I offered him a tour. But I guess he wants more."

"More what? Money?"

"He looks quite uncouth," Jenny said. "You should bring him in."

"For what? He hasn't done anything wrong … yet."

"You don't agree he's suspicious?"

"Where do you meet these people, Jenny?" Adam grumbled. "I think you go looking for trouble."

"He just walked into the café one day. How am I to know he's the prodigal son?"

"You're giving him too much importance."

"He calls himself the heir of old man Davis."

"So he is."

"That doesn't mean he can threaten me."

"Has he really threatened you??" Adam asked patiently. "We might have some grounds to bring him in if he has."

"Not really," Jenny admitted. "He just keeps talking about Seaview."

"Ignore him."

"That's what I plan to do," Jenny said meekly.

Secretly, she decided to give Keith a piece of her mind. Then she realized she had no idea where he was staying.

"Did you go to the Save our Library committee meeting?" she asked Adam.

"Is that the latest of Barb's projects?" Adam laughed.

"Laugh all you want. Molly's about to lose her job."

Adam sobered at the thought.

"Those ladies are always up to something," he explained. "Sign me up as a volunteer. I will help any way I can. But no frivolous meetings."

"When can I have my house back?" Jenny asked next.

"I was saving the best for dessert," Adam smiled.

He pulled open a drawer and took a key from it. He handed it to Jenny.

"All yours, Madam. You can move in whenever you want."

"I hope you didn't mess up the place too much?"

"It could do with a cleaning," Adam grimaced. "I can pitch in."

"We need an army of people to clean a house that size," Jenny sighed.

Jenny felt exhausted just thinking about it.

"Let's meet there at six," Adam suggested.

"It's been a long day," Jenny yawned. "I guess the cleaning can wait till tomorrow."

"Weren't you badgering me all this time about getting that house back?" Adam asked. "Just meet me there at six. And don't worry about dinner."

Jenny walked back home, grumbling about how unromantic Adam was. A group of people greeted her at Star's cottage. Heather, Molly, Chris, Jason and Star stood around, armed with buckets, mops and cleaning supplies.

"Let's get this party started," Star cried.

Seaview sparkled like a jewel a few hours later. Jenny sat on the carpet in the great room downstairs, eating pizza with her friends.

"Welcome home, Jenny," Adam said softly, feeding her a slice of pizza.

He was just a different kind of romantic.

Chapter 8

"How are you settling in?" Betty Sue asked Jenny, her hands busy knitting something new.

"It's a bit different from Star's cottage," Jenny admitted, "but we're loving it."

"We sure are!" Star exclaimed.

She hadn't moved all her stuff into Seaview yet but she had been living there with Jenny.

"I might give in and rent out my cottage after all."

"No suspicious sounds at night?" Heather needled. "Weird lights?"

"None, thank you," Jenny said lightly.

"You can be honest with us," Heather persisted. "Are you saying you aren't afraid at all? Not even a tiny bit?"

Jenny rubbed the tiny horseshoe hanging around her neck.

"I've been so tired, I'm out like a light. And Star's there to keep me company."

"Is Nick coming this weekend?" Petunia asked with a smile.

She had grown fond of Jenny's son.

"Oh yes," Jenny said with a smile. "He can't wait. He's struggling through his midterms but he'll be here soon."

"Has Adam visited you there yet?" Heather asked with a wink. "What does he think of your room?"

Jenny's ears turned red.

"How's your love life, Heather?" she shot back. "Been on any dates recently"?

"I bet she's lost count," Betty Sue snapped.

Jenny heard a shout and saw Molly waving at them from the boardwalk. Heather and Jenny watched mystified as she scrambled over the café steps.

"What's the matter, Molls?" Heather asked while Molly caught her breath.

"Haven't you heard?" Molly panted. "It's all over town."

"Sit down, girl," Betty Sue ordered. "Get her some water, Jenny."

Jenny obliged and went in to get some water.

Molly's face was blotchy from the exertion. She dabbed at it with a paper napkin and drained the glass of water Jenny offered her.

"Someone died."

"Who?" all the women screamed in unison.

"Anyone we know?" Betty Sue asked with a quiver.

Molly shook her head in denial.

"Must be a tourist, I think."

"How did you find out?" Star asked. "We've been here for a while but we didn't hear anything."

"It's Mrs. Daft," Molly explained. "That nosy old lady who is my neighbor. She's been renting her spare room by the week."

"Serves her right," Betty Sue muttered. "She should have thought twice before taking a stranger into her home."

Jenny suppressed a giggle. Betty Sue ran the Bayview Inn. She took strangers into her home every day.

"No, no," Molly corrected her. "The woman is fine. And it's not a room in her house. It's a room over her garage."

"You're not making sense, Molls," Heather said, tapping some keys on her phone.

"She rented the room to a tourist," Molly began again. "Some guy. They found him dead this morning. An ambulance arrived along with some cop cars just as I was leaving for work. I know because it's right across the street."

"What happened to the poor guy?" Star asked.

Molly shrugged. "No idea."

A familiar voice called out to them from the boardwalk.

"Yooohooo …"

Barb Norton came up the steps, dragging Dale behind her.

"Good Morning," she greeted them. "I think we have it. Dale's come up with the best fund raising idea."

The Magnolias smiled at her politely. None of them mentioned the dead man.

"What about all the ideas we suggested at the committee meeting?" Star demanded. "Didn't any of them meet with your approval?"

"There were some really good ideas," Dale said. "But they are not scalable. Barb told me the amount you need to raise. It's quite a challenge."

"Are we just supposed to accept what he came up with?" Star persisted.

"We are having another meeting of the Save our Library Committee," Barb said patiently. "Dale will have a presentation ready. He's really good at those."

"The people of Pelican Cove can decide if my idea is worthy enough," Dale added.

"That's really kind of you, Dale," Jenny said with a smile.

She could see Heather shaking with laughter, her back to them.

"Dale has been a Godsend for the library in his town. They are working on an expansion plan as we speak. I'm hoping he can work the same magic for us."

"We look forward to the meeting, Barb," Star said grudgingly.

"I have to get back to work," Dale said. "I took a few hours off this morning. Guess who's working late tonight?"

The ladies held off until Barb was out of sight.

"Where does she find these people?" Heather said with a laugh.

"Forget Barb Norton," Betty Sue said impatiently. "We need to find out more about this dead man."

"How do you propose we do that, Betty Sue?" Star asked.

"Send Jenny to the police station," Betty Sue beamed. "Talk to that young man of yours, Jenny."

"Have you met Adam?" Jenny asked with a roll of her eyes. "He's not going to tell me jack. He'll puff up like a balloon and tell me to stop getting into police business."

"So what?" Heather asked impishly. "You manage to get around him every time."

Petunia cleared her throat and widened her eyes. The ladies hadn't noticed the man who was standing beside them on the deck, leaning on his cane.

"Adam!" Jenny exclaimed. "What brings you here?"

"An early lunch," he said, glowering at Heather. "I need to go into the city."

"Does it have anything to do with that dead man?" Betty Sue asked.

Adam sighed.

"Yes, Betty Sue. And I can't tell you anything else."

"Why not?" she thundered. "We have a right to know what's happening in our town."

Jenny came to Adam's rescue.

"Let's go get your lunch."

Adam followed Jenny into the café.

"What will you have?" she asked him. "Oyster po'boy or the Autumn Chicken Salad Sandwich?"

"I'll go with the chicken today," Adam told her.

His eyes had circles under their eyes. Jenny surmised he hadn't slept well. Adam didn't like being dependent on pain pills. Sometimes he chose to bear the pain. It took a visible toll on his body.

"Are you doing your exercises like the therapist told you?" Jenny asked.

"Stop treating me like a child, Jenny," he snapped.

"You know your leg starts hurting if you skip the exercises," Jenny persisted.

"Do you want to announce my private business to the whole world?" Adam yelled at her.

Jenny took a step back and held up her hands.

"No need to be nasty."

She packed Adam's sandwich in a small bag and added a large cup of coffee. She tossed in two packets of cookies and a muffin, just in case he wanted a snack later.

"Can you tell me who died?" she asked, handing over the bag.

Adam struggled with his answer.

"We haven't released any information yet. The news is already spreading through town though."

"Is it going to stop the tourists from coming here?"

"I don't think so."

"Molly said the man was a tourist. Won't it put a damper on business?"

"He wasn't your regular tourist," Adam said reluctantly. "More like a drifter."

"What's his name?" Jenny asked. "Have you seen him around?"

Adam tapped his foot impatiently and leaned forward.

"You know him," he said. "We found a wallet with his driver's license and a couple of credit cards. His name was Keith Bennet."

"Keith?" Jenny exclaimed. "What happened to him?"

"Can't say yet," Adam said, tight lipped. "You're the only person I know who talked to him."

He pulled out his phone and started tapping on it. He thrust it in Jenny's face.

"That's the guy, right?"

Jenny realized she was looking at a dead body. She shrank back involuntarily.

"That's him," she said with a gulp.

"I have to get going," Adam said. "I guess you'll be talking to the ladies about this."

"Drive safe," Jenny called out after him. "Don't forget your pills."

Jenny's feet wobbled a bit as she went out on the deck. The Magnolias were getting ready to leave.

"Hold on a minute, Betty Sue."

"What's the matter, sweetie?" Star asked with concern.

"Are you feeling alright?" Petunia clucked.

"I'm fine," Jenny assured them. "It's that dead guy. I found out who he is. Or was."

"Who?" Five voices chorused.

"Keith Bennet. He came to the café a couple of times. I talked to him."

"You poor girl," Star said, stroking Jenny's back. "Did he seem ill?"

Jenny shook her head and swallowed a lump. She looked at Betty Sue, uncertain how to break the news.

"He was Lily's son."

Betty Sue sat down with a thud.

"Lily's son? I didn't know he was in town. What was he doing here?"

"Who's Lily again?" Heather asked.

She had put her phone down on the table for once.

"Lily Davis," Molly reminded her. "Betty Sue's best friend?"

"Oh!" Heather nodded. "That dame who abandoned her kids and ran away."

"That's the one," Betty Sue said stonily.

Molly pinched Heather and shut her up before she said anything more.

"What was he doing here?" Betty Sue asked Jenny.

"He said he was taking a vacation. He always wanted to come back here."

"Why after all these years?" Molly asked.

"I think it had something to do with Seaview," Jenny confessed. "He kept asking me all kinds of questions about the house."

"He must be nostalgic," Star said.

"I offered to take him there," Jenny told them. "He warned me. He told me the place was jinxed. Nothing good would come from living there."

"That old crap?" Star asked, incensed. "How dare he!"

"He called himself the heir. Said he had a stake in Seaview."

"But you bought the place, didn't you?" Petunia asked with a frown. "Did he really own the house?"

Jenny shook her head.

"I have proof. And Jason did the paperwork. Keith was just trying to make trouble."

"He won't be doing any more of that, poor guy," Molly said.

"What about his family?" Betty Sue asked hopefully. "Did he say where he lived? Did he mention his mother?"

"He did," Jenny nodded. "He told me she was a great cook."

"Oh," Betty Sue murmured. She seemed disappointed. "Lily created magic in the kitchen. Just like you, Jenny."

"Let's go, Grandma," Heather urged. "I need to do some housekeeping before that couple checks in later today."

"Tootsie must be hungry," Betty Sue said suddenly.

She dropped her knitting in her bag and struggled to her feet. Her face had turned ashen. Jenny felt worried about her.

"How about some lemonade before you go, Betty Sue?" she asked. "Just a couple of sips?"

"I'm fine, girl!" Betty Sue's voice trembled. "I've buried more loved ones than I can remember."

Star stayed behind, assuring Jenny she wasn't busy. Jenny and Petunia worked in tandem and assembled a platter of chicken sandwiches. Jenny started frying oysters.

"The hungry hordes will be here soon," Petunia chirped. "Do we have enough cookies for dessert?"

Jenny nodded as she transferred a basket full of crispy oysters to a paper lined tray.

"What happened to that guy?" Star asked Jenny. "How did he die?"

"Adam didn't say."

"Seems kind of suspicious, huh?"

"You think so?" Jenny asked, whirling around to face her aunt. "He was about my age, I guess."

"A healthy young man," Star repeated. "Did he look ill?"

Jenny thought for a moment while she dredged a bunch of oysters.

"Not really. But he looked scruffy. He wasn't normal."

"Poor guy," Star sighed. "What else did he say to you?"

"He told me his grandpa planted our garden," Jenny said sadly.

"Luke's men are setting up the fountain today," Star reminded her. "Are you going home early?"

"I want to," Jenny said hesitantly.

"Why don't you go on then?" Star said. "Petunia and I can take care of the lunch crowd."

"Eat before you go, Jenny," Petunia told her.

Jenny sat at the small kitchen table and took a bite of her chicken sandwich. A single thought nagged her as she remembered the photo Adam had shown her. Why had Keith really come to Pelican Cove?

Chapter 9

Jason Stone sat in his office, working through a big stack of files. Jenny knocked on his door tentatively.

"Can I come in?"

Jason's face lit up.

"Jenny! Please say you are here to save me from this."

"You need to get a paralegal," Jenny told him. "Or a secretary at least."

"I want to manage on my own as much as I can," Jason explained. "Never mind that. You're a sight for sore eyes."

"This is not a social call," Jenny warned him.

"How can I help you?" Jason asked seriously.

"Did you hear about the dead man?"

"I heard some buzz," he nodded. "But I don't know much."

"Do you remember Keith? Lily's son?"

"Keith Bennet? Vaguely. Why?"

"It was him."

Jason's eyebrows shot up.

"What are you saying, Jenny? The dead guy was Keith Bennet? What was he doing here in town? And how do you know him?"

"He was here on vacation."

"Again, how do you know that?"

"He came to the café a couple of times," Jenny told him. "We talked."

"He's been absconding for a long time."

"He kept talking about Seaview and his grandpa – old man Davis. Said he was an heir and Seaview belonged to him."

"You have nothing to worry about," Jason assured her. "You own it clear. No one can ask you to leave."

"I told him that," Jenny nodded. "I even offered to let him look around."

"How did he die?"

"You'll have to ask Adam. He's not volunteering any information."

Jason opened a small refrigerator tucked in an alcove and pulled out two bottles of juice. He offered one to Jenny.

"So Keith Bennet comes back to Pelican Cove after twenty five years and now he's gone. It's almost as if he came here to die."

"I had the same thought," Jenny said glumly. "He warned me about Seaview. Said nothing good would come of living there."

"Wait. You don't seriously believe that?"

"I moved in, didn't I?"

"That doesn't answer my question."

"I don't know, Jason. A lot of bad things happened in that house."

"That was a long time ago."

"What about Keith?"

"You don't even know how he died. I think you're letting the talk get to you."

"What did you mean earlier when you said he was absconding?"

"Keith was right about being an heir," Jason sighed. "Roy and Lily were the old man's direct descendants. Their kids were next in line to inherit. That's Ricky and Keith."

"So Keith didn't know Seaview was being sold?"

"Ann Davis was listed as the sole owner. When you expressed an interest in the house, I tracked her down. She told me Keith had an equal stake in the house."

"That was nice of her."

"I thought so too," Jason agreed. "We tried to track Keith down. It seems he didn't stick around in one place for long."

"He doesn't have a family?"

"Lily's husband, his father, is still alive. He's in a senior home in Texas."

"How did you convince Ann?"

"Ricky tried to track Keith down. We even placed an ad in the paper, asking him to get in touch. But like I said, he was nowhere to be found."

"He must have got wind of it somehow."

"I guess," Jason speculated. "Ann told me she would split the money with Keith whenever he turned up."

"Maybe he didn't want to sell," Jenny mused. "It sounded like he had an emotional attachment to the house."

"He had plenty of time to come back here and live at Seaview," Jason said, shaking his head. "For whatever reason, he chose not to. You shouldn't worry about it,

Jenny."

"I need to get a dress for that law dinner," Jenny said, changing the subject.

"You look beautiful in anything," Jason said sincerely.

"I don't want people to talk behind your back. I know how those dinners work. The women gossip about who was wearing what for weeks after."

"Let them," Jason said loyally. "I care about you, sweet Jenny, not some catty women I may never meet again."

Jenny had a smile on her face as she walked to the seafood market. Jason always made her happy.

Chris Williams was stacking some cans when Jenny walked in.

"Hey Jenny," he greeted her. "Got a minute?"

"Sure, Chris. What's on your mind?"

A troubled expression flitted over his face.

"I am thinking of taking Molly to the Steakhouse."

The Steakhouse was the only formal restaurant in Pelican Cove. It was reserved for special occasions. Jenny realized Chris was taking a big step.

"Do you think she is ready?" he asked.

Molly had confessed her feelings to Jenny a few weeks ago. She had admired Chris from a distance ever since high school. She had been infatuated with him for a long time. Jenny was sure Molly was ready to date Chris seriously.

"I think so, Chris," Jenny smiled. "When are you going to ask her?"

Chris rubbed his hands and looked uncertain.

"Tonight. I hope she doesn't say no. This will be our first official date."

"What about Heather?" Jenny asked shrewdly.

"What about her?" Chris shrugged. "Heather and I will always be friends. But I need to get on with my life. Molly and I click. Who would've thunk, huh?"

"You are all dear to me, Chris," Jenny said sincerely. "All three of you. I hope you find the happiness you deserve."

Jenny grilled fish and tossed a salad for dinner. The kitchen at Seaview had been completely renovated. Jenny had double ovens and granite countertops with a large center island for doing her prep.

"Do you want to sit out on the patio?" Star asked. "It's a bit chilly out there."

Jenny opted to eat inside. The patio had a clear view of the spot where they had found Mrs. Bones. Jenny found she wasn't ready to sit out there yet.

Jenny chatted with her aunt for some time and then stepped out for her walk. She hadn't talked to Adam all day and she was hoping to run into him. She saw him in the distance, throwing a stick for his dog Tank. Tank abandoned the stick as soon as he spotted Jenny and ran toward her.

"Hello darling!" Jenny crooned as the yellow Labrador put his paws on her shoulders.

Jenny scratched Tank below his ears and waited for Adam to walk up to her.

"Hi Jenny," he greeted her. "How was dinner in your new home?"

"Different," she admitted. "The kitchen is huge! Takes some getting used to."

Adam took Jenny's hand and started walking away from Seaview. Tank walked beside them, wagging his tail.

"Why don't we go on a trip somewhere?" he asked her.

"We can go check out the fall foliage," Jenny offered. "The twins were raving about it."

"The Shenandoah Valley is a three hour drive from here. That's six hours to and fro. We might have to stay over."

"Or we can start really early and spend the whole day there," Jenny quipped.

"You don't think we are ready for an overnight trip?" Adam asked hoarsely.

Jenny's heart fluttered at the innuendo.

"Let's start small," she blushed.

"I didn't mean … that is …" Adam muttered. He was beginning to look alarmed. "There's no rush, Jenny. I don't plan to let you go anytime soon."

Jenny giggled and snuggled into Adam's arms.

The Boardwalk Café was packed to the gills the next day. Jenny had produced a few batches of pumpkin spice donuts in the spirit of the season. They had sold before the glaze dried. She hadn't been able to taste a single one.

The Magnolias breezed in at their usual time. The Eastern Shore weather often produced warm days in October. The sun shone brightly and they sat on the deck, drinking coffee and eating warm banana nut muffins with a special cream cheese spread.

"Jenny cooked her first meal at Seaview," Star told the girls. "It was delicious."

"We need a spa night," Heather declared, peering at her toes. "What do you think, Molly?"

Molly was looking quite chipper. Jenny shared a smile with her. It looked like Chris had already talked to her about their date.

"Spa night sounds great, Heather," Jenny said. "I need to glam up before this party I have to go to."

"Adam's taking you to a party?" Star asked.

"No, Jason. It's work related."

Betty Sue looked up from her knitting and narrowed her eyes.

"What's that Hopkins boy doing on the beach?"

Adam Hopkins strode across the boardwalk, flanked by two deputies. He limped up the café steps and cleared his throat.

"You need to come with me, Jenny."

Jenny stared back at the man in uniform. He looked and acted like a stranger.

"Where are we going?" she asked, bewildered.

"You are a person of interest in the murder of Keith Bennet. I am taking you in for questioning."

"What nonsense!" Star cried.

"You just had to call, Adam," Jenny said. "I would have come over myself."

"Please come with us now," Adam said firmly.

He took Jenny by the arm and pulled her to her feet.

"No need to manhandle her, boy!" Betty Sue boomed.

"Calm down, everyone," Jenny urged.

Her eyes were frantic with worry.

"Go get Jason," she told Heather.

Adam walked down the steps with Jenny in tow.

"What's wrong with that boy?" Petunia groaned. "I thought he was going out with our Jenny."

"He doesn't have his priorities right," Star spat.

"Adam's a bit of a jerk," Molly agreed. "How dare he treat Jenny like that."

Heather hung up her phone and interrupted Molly.

"Jason's in court. He won't be back until later today."

"What do we do now?" Star asked with a frown. "Is he going to lock my Jenny up?"

"Let's all go to the police station," Betty Sue said grimly. "We will wear him down."

"You don't think we are going to scare Adam, do you?" Molly asked. "What if he arrests us all."

"I want to see him try!"

"Calm down, Grandma," Heather warned Betty Sue. "You need to watch your blood pressure."

"Hush, Heather," Betty Sue shushed her.

She looked at Star and Petunia. The two older women got the signal and stood up. They hurried down the steps to the boardwalk.

"Wait!" Molly called after them. "I'm coming with you too."

Heather's phone dinged just then and she began tapping keys on her phone.

The women were panting and sweating by the time they descended on the police station. Betty Sue's face looked like a ripe tomato.

"Where is she?" Star yelled. "Where's my Jenny"?

Nora, the desk clerk, pointed at a closed door.

"With the boss. Ya'll will have to wait outside."

The women started talking at once. A door banged and Adam came out, looking furious.

"What's all this ruckus?" he demanded.

"Have you arrested my Jenny?" Star shot back. "We have come to rescue her."

"Jenny's fine," Adam sighed. "She's answering a few questions. You can wait for her here if you promise to be quiet."

"I want to see her," Star insisted.

Adam peeked into the small room and said something. Jenny came out and waved at them.

"Where's Jason?"

"Jason won't be back until later today," Molly explained. "You're on your own until then."

"I'll be fine, I guess," Jenny said uncertainly. "It's not like I killed the man."

She glared at Adam Hopkins before she went back into the room.

"You're so busted!" Molly told Adam.

Adam leaned on his stick and limped back into the room.

The ladies sat down and waited impatiently for Jenny. It took a while for the facts to sink in.

Betty Sue voiced the question everyone wanted an answer to.

"Who killed Lily's boy?"

Chapter 10

"I hope you gave that boy a piece of your mind," Betty Sue fumed.

She had still not forgiven Adam for the way he treated Jenny. Jenny herself wasn't feeling too kindly toward Adam. But she assumed he needed to do his job.

"He's very particular about his duties as the sheriff," she said diplomatically.

"Bah!" Betty Sue exclaimed. "He's too full of himself, you mean."

"Have you met Jason yet?" Heather asked.

"I'm going to," Jenny said. "In fact, I'm leaving right now."

"Jason's the better man," Star butted in. She clearly preferred Jason over Adam. "I hope you don't find that out the hard way, Jenny."

Jenny didn't take the bait. She walked to Jason's office. He had come in late the previous night. He didn't know much about the drama that had unfolded.

Unlike Adam, Jason had a quirky sense of humor. But he could be serious when needed. He cut to the chase.

"Does Adam think you are a suspect?"

"He called me a person of interest, but that's just mumbo jumbo."

"What exactly did he ask you, Jenny?"

Jenny gave an account of her conversation at the police station.

"Do you know why he thinks you are involved?"

"I talked to Keith a couple of times," Jenny shrugged. "Apparently, I'm the only person in town to do that."

"That doesn't make sense. Surely he did other stuff? He must have gone to the pub, or grabbed dinner somewhere."

"How much trouble am I in, Jason? Do I need to rustle up bail money?"

"I hope not," Jason said in a steely voice. "You know Adam. He likes to act first and think later. I'm going to talk to him."

"So looks like someone had it in for Keith," Jenny mused. "Will you contact his family?"

"I already passed on that information to the police," Jason said. "I doubt he'll be missed. His father's memory failed long ago. Ann and Ricky are his only living relatives as far as I know."

"Poor guy," Jenny breathed. "I want to find out what happened to him, Jason."

"I strongly advise against that," Jason warned. "You are already involved. Don't make things worse for yourself."

"You said it," Jenny argued. "I'm involved anyway. The only way I can clear myself is by finding the person who did it."

"Where are you going to start?" Jason asked, folding his arms and leaning back in his chair. "What do you know about Keith Bennet?"

"You are going to help me," Jenny said sweetly. "Can't you have someone run a background check?"

"You want me to hire an investigator so you can play Nancy Drew? Isn't that a bit much?"

"We just need to know about his past," Jenny said firmly. "Like where he lived before he came here. Did he work somewhere? Was he married? Stuff like that."

"And that's going to be enough for you?"

Jenny smiled coyly.

"It's a start."

Jenny picked up Heather at the Bayview Inn that evening.

"Do we have to go?" she groaned. "I just want to put my feet up and watch a movie."

"You started this whole thing," Heather teased.

"I didn't," Jenny shook her head. "I don't know where Barb got the idea."

"You took the initiative and made those posters, didn't you? Barb's your big fan now. She's going around telling everyone how you're almost a native now."

The Save our Library committee was meeting at the town hall. The older ladies had saved them some seats. Star patted an empty one beside her when she saw Jenny. Barb eyed her and lunged toward Jenny.

"Your place is right here, up on the stage."

"Oh Barb. I couldn't."

"Take credit where it's due. You're the driving force behind this effort."

Heather grinned mischievously.

"What did I tell you?" she mouthed.

Dale sat on the stage next to Jenny. He was wearing a suit and tie.

"They are going to be blown away," he told Jenny.

Clearly, he wasn't lacking in confidence.

The lights dimmed and Dale stood up to start his presentation. Jenny had to admit he did a good job. The idea he presented was new to her. She wasn't sure how well it would work.

"Sounds like tommyrot to me," Betty Sue spoke up. "So someone pays me money to read a book? Why can't they just put the money in a drop box?"

"A read-a-thon is much more than that," Dale hastened to explain. "You are achieving several objectives at once. You nurture a love for reading among your population, young or old. People donate money to encourage that and also to further your cause."

"Let the people speak for themselves, Betty Sue," Barb Norton called out. "You can cast your vote like everyone else."

"Did that stuff make any sense to you?" Star asked Jenny as they waited at Mama Rosa's for their pizza.

"A bit," Jenny said with a frown. "People will donate money for a certain number of pages read, or hours. And they will also donate in terms of effort. And the best part is they can do both."

"There's a limit to how much people will shell out. That's why we have a funding issue in the first place."

"Don't forget the tourists," Jenny reminded her aunt. "Petunia said we are having an unprecedented season this year. The hayrides and the autumn fair will draw in more people."

"Why would a tourist care about our library?"

"Why does a donor care about anything?" Jenny asked. "They are just being charitable."

"What about the prizes that Dale guy mentioned?"

"We'll find out when the time comes."

Jenny was glad for the motion detectors at Seaview. The grounds lit up before they went in. Jenny settled into her couch and took a big bite of pizza.

"Why isn't Jimmy here?" she asked her aunt.

Jimmy Parsons hadn't made an appearance since they moved into Seaview.

"He's out of town," Star told her. "Should be back tomorrow."

"What's he doing out of town?"

"No idea," Star said with a shrug.

Aunt and niece ate their dinner and talked about mundane things. Jenny tried on the new dress which had arrived by special delivery. She looked like her old self in the mirror. But she had come a long way from being a bored and ignored wife.

Jason's eyes gleamed with admiration as he held the car door open for Jenny. Jenny enjoyed the heated seats and swanky sound system in the luxury car. Jason played her favorite blues hits and Jenny forgot about Keith Bennet for a while.

Jenny was happy to see she didn't stick out like a sore thumb at the law society dinner. She struck up a conversation with an attractive young brunette in the ladies room.

"You are one lucky woman," the girl crooned. "If I had a guy like him, I would hold on to him for life."

"Jason and I aren't married," Jenny hastened to explain. "We are just friends."

"Then you don't mind if I make a move?" the girl asked brashly.

"Aren't you here with someone?"

"My douche of a date stood me up. Didn't go down well with my partners, I can tell you."

"You're a lawyer?" Jenny asked.

"I handle divorce," the girl nodded. "These dinners can get pretty boring. Your man is like a breath of fresh air."

Jenny felt uncomfortable in the brazen girl's company. She muttered goodbye and turned to leave.

"Oh by the way, I'm Kandy," the girl said. "Kandy with a K."

"Pleased to meet you," Jenny said politely.

Jason was deep in conversation with a bunch of suits. Jenny waited for him at the bar. Kandy cornered Jason the moment he started walking toward Jenny. Jason smiled politely and made small talk with the girl. Jenny knew he would never be rude.

"That is one aggressive woman," she said when Jason finally joined her.

"Kandy? She seemed sweet."

Jenny was tense as she baked a batch of muffins at the café. Adam hadn't talked to her since he had whisked her to the station. He seemed to have forgotten everything about their trip.

Molly rushed in when Jenny was chatting with Captain Charlie.

"Molly! It's barely 6 AM. What are you doing here so early?"

Molly widened her eyes and tipped her neck at Captain Charlie.

"I couldn't sleep. How about some coffee, Jenny?"

"Have a good day, ladies!" Captain Charlie smiled and walked out with his coffee and muffin.

"Wait till you hear this, Jenny. Let's go in."

Jenny took Molly out on the deck. The early morning chill made her shiver. There wasn't a single soul on the beach that morning.

"You remember Mrs. Daft?" Molly asked urgently. "My neighbor?"

"You mean the woman who rented her room to Keith?" Jenny asked.

Molly nodded eagerly.

"Look what she found!"

She pulled a chain out of her pocket and dangled it before Jenny.

"Does this belong to Keith?"

"She cleaned the room after the police handed it over to her. This was lying in a dresser drawer."

"How could the police not find it?"

"I don't know," Molly said impatiently. "Do you want to look at it or not?"

"How many people have rented that room this year, Molly?" Jenny asked with her hands on her hips.

"I don't know. Plenty, I guess."

"How do you know this belongs to Keith then? It could have been there forever if it was that well hidden."

"Or Keith hid it really well for a reason."

"Is it gold?"

"I doubt it," Molly said, eyeing the chain.

It was tarnished beyond recognition. It was hard to say if it had been gold or silver once.

"So it's not valuable?" Jenny asked with a sigh. "Looks like a piece of junk to me."

Molly's face fell.

"It might have sentimental value."

Jenny put the chain in her apron pocket.

"We can look at it later. I have to go."

The line of people waiting for coffee stretched out to the sidewalk. Jenny apologized and offered a free muffin to the first ten people in the line.

The Magnolias arrived one by one. Jenny got off her feet and dug into a muffin. She was dreaming about getting a day off.

"So?" Molly asked as she hurried up to the deck from the boardwalk. "Did you show it to them?"

"I almost forgot," Jenny said.

She pulled out the chain from her pocket and put it on the table.

"Molly's neighbor found this. We don't know if it belonged to Keith."

"Have you checked inside?" Betty Sue asked, picking up the chain.

"Huh?" Jenny asked.

Betty Sue pressed some point and the locket sprang open.

"These kind of lockets were very popular when I was a young woman," she told them.

"There are two pictures inside," Betty Sue said, squinting her eyes.

Her eyes filled up as she peered at the photos.

"This is Lily's boy alright. He was one good looking fella."

Jenny thought about how unkempt Keith Bennet had been. He had lost his looks along with his youth.

"Hand it over, Betty Sue," Star ordered. "I might remember the boy."

"There's a girl's picture here," Betty Sue said, holding on to the locket. "But she doesn't look like Lily's girl."

"She must have been his girlfriend," Heather giggled.

The locket was passed around the table. Everyone looked at the photos and made some comment. Jenny snapped a few pictures of the locket and the photos with her cell phone.

"You're sure this is Keith?" she asked Betty Sue. "This belongs with the police. I have to turn it in. You better come with me, Molly."

Chapter 11

Jenny stifled a yawn as she dipped hot donuts in glaze.

"You look worn out," Petunia said sympathetically.

"You work as much as I do," Jenny observed. "But you always look fresh as a peach."

"Go on now," Petunia blushed. "No need to flatter me. You forget I've been doing this for twenty five years. I am used to it. And you've taken most of the work off my hands."

"I can't imagine taking care of the café alone," Jenny said honestly.

"Take a day off," Petunia pressed. "Why don't you youngsters do something fun? Go on a picnic or something."

Heather and Molly wholeheartedly embraced the idea of a picnic.

"Let me call Chris," Heather said.

"He loves the idea," Molly said before Heather could place the call. "He just texted me. He knows the perfect place."

"Are you going to invite Adam?" Heather asked Jenny.

"He hasn't spoken to me in a while," Jenny said. "He might give me a wide berth until the case is solved."

"That's ridiculous," Star said. "What if the case is never solved?"

"Keith deserves better than that."

"You barely knew the guy, Jenny," Heather said with a smirk. "How do you know what he deserved?"

"Surely no one deserves to be killed in cold blood?"

"How goes the search for the missing women?" Betty Sue asked.

"I've barely had any time to work on that," Jenny admitted. "I made a few calls using the phone book. I tracked down a couple of women on the list. One of them was found dead later. It seems she took her life."

"How sad," Molly sighed.

"One of them came back a couple of years later. So she's not missing anymore."

"Where was she for a couple of years?" Heather asked.

"I didn't ask," Jenny said. "I am thinking she needed a time out."

The older women exchanged knowing looks at that.

"How many more names do you have on the list?" Star asked. "You want me to make some calls when I get home?"

"Would you?" Jenny asked. "That will be a big help."

"So you've got a long way to go before we find out who Mrs. Bones is," Heather noted.

"There's a family in the next town. Their young girl went missing some years ago. I want to go talk to them."

"Just say when," Heather said. "You know I'm your wingman."

"Wing woman," Molly corrected her. "Or wing person."

"Whatever, Molls!" Heather snapped. "Who cares!"

Jenny hoped she wasn't around when Heather found out about Molly's date at the Steakhouse.

Two days later, the girls were piling into a big SUV. Chris was at the wheel. Heather was about to climb into the front seat when Chris held her off.

"Why don't you come on front, Molls?"

Molly nudged Heather aside and sat next to Chris. Jenny placed a big wicker basket on the back seat and patted the space next to it.

"Come on Heather, we're getting late."

"I hope we have enough food," Jenny said.

"Don't worry," Chris assured her. "There's a great restaurant overlooking the beach. We are going there for lunch."

"I thought this was a picnic," Heather pouted. "Aren't we supposed to sit on blankets and eat something from that basket?"

"We'll do that too," Chris consoled her. "Okay?"

"I hope you don't feel outnumbered," Molly murmured to Chris.

"We might even out the numbers later," Chris said cryptically.

Chris drove at a leisurely pace, and they passed signs for several small towns. Chris regaled them with stories about houses he had sold in those towns. He made a turn about an hour later and drove down a single lane road. The trees grew dense and formed a canopy over their heads. They came upon a cluster of homes and Chris pulled up in front of a corner house.

"Where are we?" the girls cried. "Aren't we going to the beach?"

"Patience, ladies!" Chris smiled.

He produced a key to the house and led them inside.

"This one just came on the market. I have the owner's permission to hang out here any time I want to."

"Sounds like a generous fellow," Jenny said graciously.

Chris rushed them through a foyer and a large great room. He flung open a set of wide doors leading on to the deck.

There was a collective gasp of surprise.

The deck ended on a white sandy beach. The blue waters of the Chesapeake Bay stretched out before them, the gentle waves lapping against the shore.

Chris pointed to a building in the distance.

"That's one of the best restaurants in these parts. We can walk there through the sand."

He turned toward Heather.

"And you can have your picnic on the beach wherever you want."

Heather was going around, clicking pictures on her phone.

"Is this the best place or what?"

Jenny had collapsed into a large armchair and put her feet up on an ottoman. The blue waters filled her vision and she sighed with pleasure.

"I'm not moving from here."

Chris and Molly picked a small couch next to Jenny. They followed her example and sat down. Chris put an arm around Molly and they shared a special smile.

Heather watched them with a curious expression.

"Don't tell me Molly's getting all lovey dovey."

"You need to tell her," Molly told Chris.

"Tell me what?"

"We went to the Steakhouse a couple of nights ago."

"Why? It's not like you're serious about each other."

Molly and Chris stared back at Heather. Jenny cleared her throat. A range of emotions flitted across Heather's face as she finally caught up.

"Molly's your girlfriend now?" she asked Chris. "Your actual girlfriend?"

"I am so grateful to you, Heather," Chris said earnestly. "If you hadn't tried that online dating business, I would never have gone out with Molly. We connect on a different level."

"I thought we had a connection, Chris," Heather said.

Jenny sensed the desperation in her voice and felt sorry for her. Chris and Heather had been together since third grade after all.

"It's different with Molly. Something you and I never had."

"Really?" Heather barely whispered.

Molly's eyes were full of adoration as she stared at Chris. She was completely oblivious to Heather's shocked expression.

Heather started pulling things out of the basket. She unwrapped a muffin and bit into it. She picked up another container and spoke to them with her mouth full.

"I'm starving. I'm eating this on the beach."

She sped down the stairs to the sand and went out of their line of vision.

"That went well," Jenny drawled.

"She'll be fine," Chris said lightly. "Heather likes to make a scene."

"Should I go check on her?" Molly asked seriously.

"No need. You are not going to feel bad about this." Chris placed both hands on Molly's cheeks and stared into her eyes. "Remember what we talked about, Molls. We have done nothing wrong."

Molly nodded. The couple embraced and Jenny found herself tearing up. All the Magnolias had warned Heather against taking Chris for granted. It looked like she was going to learn a bitter lesson. Jenny felt happy for Molly though. Molly was a victim of domestic violence. Her past had made her shy and docile. Jenny believed Chris was going to be the perfect companion for her.

Footsteps sounded on the deck and Jenny felt her pulse speed up. Adam Hopkins strode up, his eyes hidden behind dark glasses.

"Adam!" Chris smiled. "You made it."

"I started my shift early. It's a beautiful day. I didn't want to miss it."

Jenny turned her back on Adam and leaned back in her chair. She slipped on her sunglasses and pretended to stare at the water.

"Hello Jenny," Adam said tentatively, taking a seat beside her. "How are you?"

"I'm good," Jenny said tersely. "I was having a great time until now."

"Do you want me to leave?"

"I don't want you to do anything, Adam."

"You're still mad at me."

"Gee Adam, why would I be mad at you? What have you done?"

"Jenny, please, don't be like this."

"Like what?"

"You know I have a job to do. I take my duties seriously."

"I can understand that," Jenny scowled. "Did I say a single word when you carried me away like a common criminal? I didn't. Because I know you were just doing your job. Of course, there's more than one way to do your job. But let's not go there. Let's consider being nasty and rude is part of your job description."

"Jeez Jenny, take a breath."

"I don't have any problems with you doing your job, Sheriff. But where have you been since then? I haven't seen a glimpse of you these last few days."

"I've been busy at work," Adam said lamely. "Can't you forgive me, Jenny?"

"I'll think about it."

Molly was looking over the stuff in the basket.

"I'm starving. Are we going to eat this or go to the restaurant?"

"Let's finish this first," Chris said. "We can have an early dinner at the restaurant."

Jenny munched a piece of fried chicken and stared moodily at the water. Adam's presence had disturbed her equilibrium. She wasn't sure if she wanted to talk to him or give him the cold shoulder.

"How are things at the library?" Adam asked Molly.

"I am expecting to get my two week notice any time now."

"Aren't they planning some kind of fund raiser?"

"It might be too little too late. But Betty Sue is trying to convince the board to hold off for a while."

"She gets her way more often than not," Adam said kindly. "We might have some staff positions coming up at the department."

"It's not what I am trained for but I will take anything at this stage," Molly said seriously. "Thanks Adam."

There was a flurry of footsteps on the deck and Jenny turned around to see who the latest arrival was.

Jason Stone strode in with his hands in his pockets. He was dressed casually in chinos and an open collared shirt. A sweater was tied loosely around his shoulders. An attractive brunette followed him on the deck and beamed at Jenny.

"Surprise!" she shrieked.

"Cindy, right?" Jenny asked.

"No. Kandy, with a K. We met at the law society dinner?"

"Oh yeah, right … what are you doing here?"

"Jason and I met in court. He told me about this picnic on the beach."

"You came at the right time," Chris told her. "We just started eating."

Heather had come up from the beach while they were talking. Kandy regaled them with her exploits in court. She had everyone in splits. Chris and Jason found some logs stacked at one side of the deck. They built a fire as the sun went down.

Jason pulled out a can of soda from a cooler and offered it to Jenny.

"Thanks for introducing me to her. She makes me feel alive, Jenny."

"You're welcome," Jenny grunted, ignoring the pang of regret she felt inside.

"Why are you digging around in Keith Bennet's background?" Adam asked Jason.

"I'm not doing anything illegal."

"You are meddling in my investigation, Jason."

"Not true," Jason said firmly. "I'm just looking out for my client."

Adam whirled toward Jenny.

"Are you getting him to do your dirty work now?"

"Someone's gotta do it," Jenny quipped.

"When are you going to leave things alone?" Adam asked, exasperated. "Did you even know the guy?"

"If you believe Jenny didn't know the guy," Jason asked, "why are you treating her like a suspect?"

"Anyone who talked to him is a suspect," Adam shot back.

"Jenny had nothing to do with Keith's death," Jason growled. "You would believe that too if you were her true friend."

"Of course I'm her friend," Adam cried.

"Prove it," Jason seethed as he turned his back on Adam.

Chapter 12

Adam planned a day trip for him and Jenny.

"How about going this Sunday?" he asked.

"I just took a day off," Jenny told him coldly. "I can't just take off again."

"The foliage cam shows peak color at this time. Pretty soon, there won't be any fall colors left to see."

"There's always next year," Jenny said with a shrug.

Adam picked up his coffee and muffin and left the café without a word. Jenny wondered if she was being too hard on him. But she couldn't forget the humiliation he had put her through.

She went to Jason's office after the café closed. Jason sat with his feet on the table, talking to someone on the phone. He pointed at the chair, inviting Jenny to sit down. He burst into laughter a couple of times before he hung up.

"That Kandy," he said with a shake of his head. "She's a hoot."

His eyes shone with admiration.

"Looks like you two hit it off."

"You know how stodgy lawyers can be, Jenny. Kandy's a breath of fresh air. She's always ready with a smile."

Jason offered a bottle of water to Jenny and took one himself. He gulped a few mouthfuls before he spoke.

"I'm glad you came. I was going to call you anyway."

"Did you find something?" Jenny asked eagerly.

"A can of worms," Jason sighed. "Keith had a long history of drug abuse. He barely kept down a job. He was supposed to be in a rehab facility a few years ago. But we don't know if he was still sober."

"How did he get here?"

"He must have felt strongly about Seaview."

"That was obvious, I guess."

"There's more," Jason said. "He had a police record."

"Surely Adam knows about this?" Jenny asked, incensed.

"He must have run a background check, just like we did," Jason nodded.

"What was his crime?"

"Possession of drugs. My guess is he was a small time drug dealer."

Jenny sucked in a breath.

"That sounds dangerous."

"He owed money to some baddies. One of them might have followed him here."

"So he was killed for money?"

"Money, drugs, revenge – it's anybody's guess."

"What do the police say about this?"

"I was about to go talk to Adam when you came in."

"I'm coming with you."

"Let's go," Jason nodded, standing up.

Jenny noticed he didn't put an arm around her shoulders like usual.

"He's in a mood," Nora, the desk clerk, warned Jenny as they knocked on Adam's door.

Adam Hopkins sat with his leg propped up on a chair.

"What do you want?" he barked at Jenny.

"We want to share some information," Jason said, following her inside.

He gave Adam a brief version of what he had told Jenny.

"Believe it or not, we are aware of all this," Adam shot back.

"Does that mean Jenny is no longer a suspect?"

"I didn't say that," Adam said sharply.

"You have plenty of suspects who had a better motive than Jenny here," Jason argued.

"But none of those people are here in town as far as we know. They didn't have the opportunity."

"And Jenny did?"

"She's the only person we know of so far who talked to the man."

"That doesn't make her a killer."

"Imagine the number of people who could have had it in for Keith," Jason exclaimed. "Fellow junkies, dealers, loan sharks … the list is endless."

"Once again, Jason, are any of them here in town?"

"I don't think anyone would follow Keith all the way to Pelican Cove just for a bit of money."

"Thank you for your input," Adam said sarcastically. "Can I get back to work now?"

"What about his family?" Jenny asked, ignoring Adam's barb. "This aunt and cousin Jason told me about? Did they get along with him?"

"Tell me you don't suspect the Davis family, Jenny?" Jason asked.

"Why not? If I can be a suspect, why not them?"

Jason didn't have an answer for that.

"Do you have the autopsy report yet?" he asked Adam. "Surely you can share it with us?"

"He died from an overdose," Adam told them.

"Could it be suicide?" Jason asked right away.

Adam didn't care to elaborate.

"You have a lot of leads to pursue," Jason hinted.

"And I can't do that until you leave," Adam said curtly.

Jenny turned around without a word and stomped out.

"What's wrong with you, man?" Jason asked as he followed her out.

Star cooked dinner for them that evening. Jimmy Parsons was back in town and he had come over.

"You have done a great job with this place, Jenny," he complimented her. "What measures are you taking for security?"

"This is Pelican Cove, Jimmy," Star reminded him. "We don't even lock our doors here."

"Motion sensing lights come on if anyone gets close," Jenny told him. "I think that's good enough."

Seaview had always had those. For the first time, Jenny wondered why.

"You're brave," Jimmy said with a shrug. "Two women on their own in this big house."

"Two poor, helpless women?" Jenny smirked. "We can take care of ourselves if needed."

Truth be told, Jenny wasn't sure what she would do if anyone attacked them.

"I have lived right next door all these years, Jimmy. All by myself. Stop trying to scare us."

Jenny stepped out for her walk an hour later. The roses and gardenias perfumed the air with their heady fragrance. Jenny stood in the garden, reveling in the salty breeze coming off the ocean.

Her feet ached but she forced herself to walk a mile. Part of her hoped she would run into Adam. She wanted to give him a piece of her mind. But Adam and Tank were nowhere to be seen.

Jenny pulled out her third batch of banana walnut muffins out of the oven. She was making mushroom soup for lunch. Heather came in to the kitchen, looking somber.

"What's on your mind, honey?" Jenny asked immediately.

There was a temporary lull in the café. Jenny made sure everyone who was seated had what they wanted. She poured fresh coffee in two mugs and placed two muffins and a crock of butter on a plate.

"Let's go sit outside."

"Take your time," Petunia whispered to her. "Something's not right with that girl. I can feel it."

Heather barely waited for Jenny to sit down.

"Did you see how they were carrying on?" she cried. "Right in front of me too."

Jenny steeled herself for a difficult conversation.

"This is too much," Heather muttered, crumbling the muffin with her fingers. "I can't take it anymore."

"Are you talking about Molly and Chris?" Jenny asked gently.

Heather's look of despair was answer enough.

"They are serious about each other," Jenny said simply. "I think they might even have a future."

"What about my future with Chris?"

"You were the one who chose to date other people."

"Are you going to rub it in? Chris has always been there for me. Always. I trusted him."

"This is a difficult situation, Heather. You created it. Please don't ask me to judge who's right or wrong. I can't."

"What am I going to do, Jenny? I love him. How can I bear seeing him with another woman, someone who is my friend, no less."

"You'll have to suck it up. I'm sorry, sweetie. Life hands us tough breaks sometimes."

"So I just put on a smile and pretend nothing has changed?"

"Something like that."

"What if I talk to Chris? Beg him to take me back?"

Jenny took Heather's hands in hers. She could feel Heather's pain.

"I think that ship has sailed," she said reluctantly. "At least for now."

"So you think they might not make it?"

"I don't think any such thing, Heather. I can't. You are all my friends and you have come to mean a lot to me. I want you all to be happy."

"What about my grandma?" Heather asked, her eyes filling with fear. "She won't take it well."

"We'll have to break it to her gently," Jenny nodded. "But I wouldn't worry about her."

"I was always supposed to marry Chris," Heather said with a faraway look in her eyes. "I dug my own grave."

Jenny sat with Heather for a long time, trying to pacify her as much as she could. Heather finally broke down. Tears streamed down her eyes and nothing Jenny said could console her.

Heather left before it was time for the Magnolias to come in.

"Where's Heather?" Molly asked.

"She's taking Tootsie for a walk," Jenny told them.

"Tootsie had her walk in the morning," Betty Sue said sharply, looking up from her knitting. "What's that girl up to now?"

"Let me guess," Molly chirped. "She's on a date."

Molly was glowing with happiness. Her bright orange tunic suited her well. Jenny thought she looked pretty.

"What's the latest on the Save our Library project?" Star asked. "Has Barb assigned tasks to the volunteers yet?"

"We need readers," Jenny told them. "People who can read fast and read a lot."

"Everyone reads. What's the big thing about it?"

"The more people read, the more money we can raise," Molly said. "Will I be allowed to volunteer?"

"I don't see why not," Betty Sue declared. "We all need to pitch in if we want to save the library. I am going to put my name in and ask the other board members to do the same."

"So the board is not against this fund raising effort?" Star asked.

"They better not be," Betty Sue grunted.

A uniformed guy walked up the steps with a big bouquet of red roses.

"Delivery for Jenny King," he said.

The women exclaimed over the flowers and peered over Jenny's shoulder as she read the attached card.

A blush stole over her face and she smiled broadly.

"They are from Adam."

"That boy has finally done something right!" Betty Sue exclaimed. "What does he say?"

"He wants to take me to dinner tonight."

"Will you go?" Molly raised an eyebrow.

"Of course I will," Jenny gurgled.

"You're too easy," Star snorted. "I would make him squirm a bit."

"He says he's sorry," Jenny reasoned. "That's good enough for me."

"We should go on a double date," Molly beamed.

Betty Sue narrowed her eyes.

"Since when do you have a young man, Molly?"

Molly reddened and looked at Jenny. Jenny gave her a shrug. Molly gulped before answering Betty Sue.

"I have an announcement. Chris and I are seeing each other."

This was news to the older ladies. Star and Petunia congratulated her warmly. Everyone waited for Betty Sue's reaction.

"You're a good girl, Molly. I know you'll treat him better than my Heather did."

"What are you doing later?" Jenny asked her aunt. "Can you make some phone calls for me?"

"Bring them on," Star said with a nod. "Jimmy and I will do it together."

"Any updates on Mrs. Bones?" Molly asked.

"The police are tight lipped as usual. I'm going to have to ramp up my own efforts."

"You're seeing Adam tonight," Star reminded her.

"That's personal," Jenny said quickly. "Adam is very particular about keeping his professional life separate from his private one."

"What a fusspot," Star grumbled.

"He's a stickler for doing the right thing," Jenny defended him. "I like that about him."

"What else do you like?" Petunia winked. "Those baby blue eyes of his?"

Jenny let them tease her. She was busy thinking about what to wear for her date. She didn't know what Adam had planned for the evening. Would he take her to the Steakhouse?

Chapter 13

Barb Norton had taken over the conversation as usual. The Magnolias were not happy. Betty Sue drained her coffee and focused on her knitting. Star doodled something on a paper napkin. Heather was engrossed in her phone and Molly sat staring at the ocean with a smile on her face.

"Are you listening to me, Jenny?" Barb asked sharply. "What do you think?"

"I agree," Jenny nodded. She forced herself to concentrate on Barb. "So you are saying we should ask people to pay for one hour segments?"

"Donate, Jenny, donate," Barb corrected her. "We need to use the right lingo."

"I still don't get it," Star grumbled. "How much will people donate for one hour?" She stressed the word donate.

"We spread the event over three days," Barb said. "We can set up a marquee in the town square. All the readers will sit there and read as much as they can. They will report every hour that is read. One of the moderators will keep track of the hours."

"Go on," Star said, waving a pencil in the air.

"The donors will give money by the hour. So for example, one man might donate money for five hours. The moderator will deduct those hours by five."

"How much will they donate?" Jenny asked.

"We are giving them three options," Barb explained. "We want to keep it simple. So we have $5, $25 or $50. This way they can choose the hourly rate and the number of hours and pay according to that."

"So a man choosing five hours at $50 per hour pays two fifty." Star did the math.

"Exactly!" Barb beamed.

"Is this really going to work?" Jenny asked. "Do you think people will donate that kind of money?"

"They will," Dale spoke up.

He had been leaning against a pillar, listening to them.

"Most people will donate both money and time. You will see."

"I need some food photos from you," Barb told Jenny. "Those donuts you are making look good. We need to put them all over that Internet."

She looked at Heather with a frown.

"Can I count on you to spread the word online?"

"Sure, Barb," Heather said without looking up.

"People will want to make a day of it," Barb said with a gleam in her eyes. "How can we make this better? Think!"

"What about offering a hayride on the beach?" Star asked. "It's the right season. Food, fun, books and a chance to do something for a good cause … sounds like a day of fun to me."

Barb didn't leave them until she had discussed the finer points of the proposed read-a-thon. Jenny was beginning to look forward to it.

Adam came to the café for lunch. Jenny had a special smile for him as she served him his tomato soup. Jenny's wish had come true. Adam had taken her to the Steakhouse and treated her like a queen. Jenny was beginning to discover a different side of Adam. She just wasn't sure when his pleasant persona would disappear and he would start berating her. It was almost as if he had two personalities.

"What are you doing later?" he asked as he took a hefty bite of his oyster po'boy.

Jenny thought of the little excursion she had planned with Heather. Adam was better off not knowing about it.

"Just some girl stuff with Heather," she smiled.

Jenny felt apprehensive as she piled into her car that afternoon.

"Did you feed the address in your phone?" she asked Heather.

"It's pretty straightforward, Jenny. Take the bridge out of town and turn right on the state road. Then you have to make a left after ten miles."

"Do you think they'll talk to us?"

Heather shrugged. "We don't even know if these are the right people. Did you just ask them about the missing girl?"

"Their daughter," Jenny supplied. "Star talked to them. I don't know how she tackled them."

"They agreed to meet you, right?" Heather reasoned. "What's the worst that could happen?"

"They'll turn us out," Jenny quipped. "You're right. I'm just a bit nervous."

"This is so not like you."

Jenny fingered the tiny gold charm around her neck as she maneuvered her car on the bridge. Built in the seventies, the two mile long bridge connected the barrier island of Pelican Cove to the mainland.

"Actually, this is very much like me. I'm famous for being low on confidence."

"Not in our world," Heather pointed out. "You're a brave woman, Jenny. One of the strongest I have ever met. I look up to you."

Jenny flashed a grateful look at the young girl sitting beside her. Heather and Molly had come to mean a lot to her. She cherished their new friendship more than the ones she had left behind. None of the women she had hobnobbed with for the past twenty years had cared to ask after her. She had become persona non grata in the suburban soccer mom club as soon as her husband traded her in for a new model. At forty four, Jenny had given up all hopes of finding any new friends again. The Magnolias had helped her believe.

"What do you think of Jason's new girl friend?" Heather asked suddenly.

"Jason has a girl friend?" Jenny asked, swerving to avoid some debris on the road.

"Kandy?" Heather reminded her. "She's so posh."

"I didn't know Jason was going out with her."

Jenny made a left to enter another small town. Heather gave her directions until she pulled up in front of a small Cape Cod tucked away in a cul de sac. Jenny needn't have worried about her reception.

A slim woman with a salt and pepper bob greeted them at the door. Her gray eyes were warm and the smile on her face seemed genuine. She offered them coffee or tea. Jenny added sugar to her coffee and stirred it as she thought of how to begin.

"Try these cookies," the woman said. "They are fresh out of the oven."

"Thank you for seeing me, Mrs. Turner," Jenny began. "I know this might be painful for you."

"Our Emily's been gone twenty six years," the woman sighed. "People around these parts barely remember her."

"So you don't mind talking to us about her?" Heather burst out.

"I'll take any chance to talk about my baby."

"It must be hard on you," Jenny sympathized.

Jenny couldn't bear the thought of losing her son Nick. She couldn't imagine how this woman had survived all these years without any news of her daughter.

"I try to keep her memory alive."

The woman pointed to an array of photographs on the mantel. Jenny guessed they all portrayed the missing girl. There were photos of her at all ages – a bonny baby, a gap toothed toddler, a girl in pig tails, and an older girl looking grownup in a sleeveless frock and a strand of pearls around her neck.

There were several photos of the grownup girl and Jenny peered at them curiously, trying to ignore a feeling of déjà vu. Goosebumps broke out on her body as she realized why the girl looked familiar.

"Are the police still looking for your girl?"

The woman dabbed a tissue at her eyes and shook her head.

"Although she's still listed as missing, they stopped looking for her long ago."

"Did she ever contact you?"

Mrs. Turner shook her head.

"Never. I would give anything to know she's okay. I just want her to be safe and happy wherever she is."

"Did she say why she was leaving?"

"She went out for a party one Saturday evening," Mrs. Turner said hoarsely. "She never came back."

"Did you have any disagreements?" Jenny asked politely. "Any reason she might have run away?"

"My Emily was a good girl. She had a 4.0 GPA. She sang in the church choir. She was all set to go to an Ivy League college."

Emily Turner sounded perfect. Jenny wondered what had made her leave home.

"Was she involved with anyone?"

"She was going out with a local boy," Mrs. Turner told them. "We knew his folks well. He knew Emily since middle school."

"Did she tell him anything?"

"The police questioned him, of course. He didn't know about that party she went to."

"Could she have been seeing someone else?"

"I wouldn't have believed that once," Mrs. Turner said sadly. "But now, who knows? I have come up with plenty of theories over the years. None of them brought my girl back."

"I'm sorry, Mrs. Turner," Jenny apologized again.

"Why are you asking about this now?" the woman asked suddenly.

"I was doing some research on missing women," Jenny said lamely. "It's a project I am working on."

"Who told you about Emily?"

"I came across some old newspaper clippings," Jenny told her honestly.

"All the local newspapers wrote about it," Mrs. Turner nodded. "We even printed a message for her in the papers, begging her to come back home."

"Did Emily ever go to Pelican Cove?" Jenny asked in a hushed voice.

"I don't think so. She didn't have a car. We were going to buy her a new one after her high school graduation."

"But she had friends who drove cars?" Jenny asked. "She went out with them?"

"She must have," Mrs. Turner sighed. "She was always home before curfew so we didn't keep tabs on her. Maybe we should have."

Jenny and Heather said their goodbyes and promised to keep in touch with Mrs. Turner. Jenny couldn't wait to get in her car.

"Something's got you hot and bothered," Heather noted as Jenny peeled out of the driveway. "Spill it."

"Those photos on the mantel … anything ring a bell?"

"I didn't really look. It was kind of sad. Why?"

"She's the girl in the locket," Jenny burst out. "I'm sure of it."

"You mean the locket you found in that dead guy's room?"

"Your grandma confirmed the boy in the photo was Keith. But she didn't know who the girl was. I am sure it was Emily."

"So Keith knew Emily?"

Jenny's head was buzzing with different scenarios.

"You don't carry just anyone's photo in a locket. Keith not only knew Emily, I'm willing to bet he was in love with her."

"But she had a boyfriend in her own town. You just heard what her mother said."

"Think like a teenager, Heather. You have a steady boyfriend but you meet some boy in another town. Wouldn't you keep him hidden?"

"I never had eyes for anyone other than Chris," Heather said sadly.

"Never mind that," Jenny dismissed. "Think hypothetically."

"Keith was a junkie, remember? Maybe that's why Emily didn't want to tell her parents about him. She wanted to maintain her goody-goody image."

"That makes perfect sense," Jenny crowed, banging her hand on the steering wheel.

"Slow down, Jenny," Heather shrieked. "Do you want a speeding ticket?"

Jenny forced herself to calm down.

"What do they say about the scene of the crime?" she said out loud. "Something about the criminal always going back."

"What are you hinting at?"

"Why did Keith come to Pelican Cove? Why now? Why after all these years?"

"My guess is he wanted to squeeze some money from you. He just wanted to score more drugs, Jenny."

"Or, he read about the skeleton they found at Seaview and couldn't stay away."

Jenny pulled up outside the Bayview Inn and placed an arm on Heather's shoulder.

"What if our Mrs. Bones is actually Miss Bones?"

Heather stared back at Jenny, her eyes growing big as saucers.

"Are you serious, Jenny?"

Jenny had to spell it out.

"What if Mrs. Bones is Emily Turner?"

Chapter 14

Jenny spent a sleepless night mulling over her theory. She wanted to run it by Jason before presenting it to Adam. She was sure Adam wouldn't be receptive to anything she put forth.

Jenny confirmed Jason was in his office before going over. She took over a box of chocolate cupcakes. Jason was a big fan of anything chocolate.

"How's my favorite client this morning?" Jason beamed.

Jason always had a pleasant countenance but his smile seemed a bit brighter than usual to Jenny.

"You look happy."

"I was thinking about last night. Kandy and I had dinner in Virginia Beach. It was magical."

Jenny feared what Heather had told her was true.

"Are you and Kandy a thing now?"

"I don't know, Jenny. Do you think she'll have me?"

"And why shouldn't she?"

"Have you looked at her? She's smart and beautiful. She has a reputation in court, I can tell you that."

"Any girl will be lucky to have you by her side."

"I wish," Jason murmured cryptically.

He bit into a cupcake and quirked an eyebrow at her.

"So? What's up?"

Jenny told him about her visit to Mrs. Turner.

"What are you getting at, Jenny?"

"What if our Mrs. Bones is Emily Turner?"

"How did she end up here?"

"That's what we have to find out. It's not impossible."

"Let's start with what she was doing in Pelican Cove."

Jenny told him about the locket then.

"Are you sure it's the same girl? How many times did you look at this locket?"

"I'm sure. We can always compare the two photos."

"So you are thinking Keith Bennet knew this girl."

"You don't just carry any random girl's photo in a locket, Jason. Keith knew her very well. I'm willing to bet they had something going."

"Let's say you're right for a moment. Are you saying Keith killed that poor girl? Why on earth would he do that?"

"It could have been an accident," Jenny mused. "She came here to meet him. They quarreled about something. He could have hit her or pushed her or something."

"And then he buried her in his own backyard?"

"Too farfetched?"

"What about his family? You think no one noticed?"

"He had none by that time. His sister was gone and Lily had already run away. His father worked out of town, remember? He might not have been at home all the time."

"Did Keith look like a killer to you?"

"He was a drug addict. He might have done it for money."

Jason stood up and began pacing the floor.

"Say you're right. Why would he carry the girl's photo on a chain all these years? He had to have some feelings for her."

"Who says he didn't?" Jenny argued. "Maybe he spent his life repenting over it."

"So why do you think he came back? When I was working on the Seaview sale, we looked really hard for him. He chose not to turn up at that time."

"All the local papers carried the story about Mrs. Bones," Jenny said. "He must have read it. He wanted to come and look for himself."

"It's not as if they have Mrs. Bones on display."

Jenny shook her head.

"I don't know why he came back. He must have missed her. Maybe he wanted to keep his ear to the ground, see what the police found out about her."

"Did you tell the girl's mother about this?"

"Of course not!" Jenny said indignantly. "I know this is just a theory."

"We still need to talk to the police about it."

"You think Adam will listen to me?"

"You need to tell them about the girl in the photo. I think it's a possible line of investigation. Let the police decide what they want to do with it. You don't want to be accused of hiding relevant information."

They crossed the street and entered the police station two doors down. Nora greeted Jenny with a smile. She pointed at Adam's door.

Adam sat with his leg propped up, immersed in a mountain of files.

"Why do we need paperwork?" he scowled at them.

Jenny and Jason sat down without waiting for an invitation. Adam gave Jenny a warm smile. A secret message passed between them. Jenny knew he wouldn't cut her any slack though.

She began her story. Adam warded her off almost immediately.

"You think this girl, Emily Turner, has been lying in your garden all these years? Isn't that a leap of faith?"

"I tracked down most of the missing women from the region," Jenny explained. "Some came back, some were found dead. There were very few who are still reported missing."

"So there are more than one?"

"What about the locket?" Jenny asked him.

"I think you are mistaken. I'm not eager to go down to these Turners and disturb them."

"I met the woman," Jenny said soberly. "She's hungry for any information about her daughter."

"She could have lied to you," Adam mused. "Maybe they knew the girl was seeing Keith. He was slightly older, right? And he was a junkie. They might not have approved of him."

"So you agree there's some connection?" Jenny asked.

"I don't know, Jenny," Adam sighed. "It's hardly relevant now. Keith is dead."

"Exactly. And we don't know how he died."

Adam cleared his throat.

"Actually, we might. We think he took his own life. It will probably be ruled as accident or suicide."

"Keith didn't seem depressed to me," Jenny objected.

"Doesn't matter what you think," Adam snapped. "The case is almost closed now."

"Does that mean Jenny is not a suspect?" Jason asked.

"Yes. That's good news for you, Jenny. You can let go of this now."

"What about Mrs. Bones? What if she is Emily Turner?"

"We are still waiting on reports."

"There are so many tests you can do now. The Turners need some closure."

"Don't tell me how to do my job, Jenny," Adam said patiently.

"Why is he never receptive to my ideas?" Jenny complained to Jason as they walked out. "You want to come eat lunch with me?"

"Sorry Jenny, I'm meeting Kandy for lunch."

"Hot date, huh?" Jenny kidded.

She couldn't explain the green eyed monster that had suddenly reared its head.

"It's a working lunch," Jason laughed. "I need some help on one of my cases. Turns out it's Kandy's area of expertise."

"That's convenient."

Jason peered at Jenny's face.

"Are you alright, Jenny? You look a bit pale."

"I'm fine," she assured Jason and headed back to the café.

Jenny thought about Keith as a boy living in Pelican Cove. He must have had some friends. Adam and Jason were both in the same age group but they didn't remember Keith. Jenny was glad to see Captain Charlie sitting at a table in the café.

"Taking a breather," he told her. "I thought I would eat my lunch here today."

Captain Charlie was one of Jenny's regulars. He ate breakfast and lunch at the café everyday but he almost always got his order to go.

Captain Charlie smacked his lips as he sprinkled some Old Bay seasoning on his sandwich.

"Can I ask you something, Captain Charlie?" Jenny asked, sitting down in front of him. "Do you remember Keith Bennet? He lived at Seaview with his family."

"Lily's son?" Captain Charlie asked. "He didn't live here more than a year. Went off to college the year after Lily moved here."

"Did he have any friends? Who did he hang out with?"

"Was a loner," Captain Charlie said, scratching his head. "Roamed around on the bluffs by himself. Took pity on him and offered him a job but he said no."

"He was a lazy bum then?"

"You could say that," Captain Charlie nodded. "That's why I was surprised when he got himself a girl."

Jenny's ears pricked up. "Girl?"

"Pretty chit too, although I'm willing to bet she was a lot younger than him. Wasn't from around here."

"Did you know her name?" Jenny asked eagerly.

Captain Charlie shook his head.

"Saw them in the dark a few times, taking a boat out or sitting on that beach in front of your house."

"Would you recognize her if I showed you a photo?"

"It was a long time ago. My memory's not what it used to be."

"Aren't you hungry yet, Jenny?" Petunia called from the kitchen. "Time to close up."

Jenny munched on chicken salad as she went over all the facts again.

"What are you frowning about?" Petunia asked.

"Nothing. Did we use up all the salad?"

Jenny trudged to the seafood market on her way home. Chris was checking out packages at a counter, dressed in a formal shirt and trousers.

"Going somewhere?"

"I had an open house this morning. It went well."

Chris seemed eager to talk to her.

"I've let my realtor business slide. I'm going to ramp it up again. Molly won't have to worry about her job if I make good money."

Jenny wondered if Chris was putting the cart before the horse but she stayed quiet.

"Money always helps," she said lamely.

"What can I get you, Jenny?" Chris asked.

Jenny asked for her usual order, a pound of shelled and deveined shrimp and rockfish steaks. She ordered three guessing Jimmy Parsons would be joining them for dinner.

"Did you talk to Heather?" Chris asked. "How is she taking this?"

"She will be fine, Chris," Jenny said diplomatically.

"I still care for her, you know," Chris said. "I want her to be happy."

"Give it time," Jenny advised. "Things will sort themselves out."

Star and Jimmy Parsons were sitting out on the patio overlooking the garden.

"Are you ready to move in permanently?" Jenny asked her aunt.

"Let's wait for a while," Star said. "I'll feel better once they get to the bottom of this mystery."

She tipped her head at the garden and Jenny understood what she was referring to. Once again, Jenny told her what she had found out.

"So that boy you met killed this young girl. But who killed him?"

"I've thought about it dozens of times. My head's pounding right now."

"You ladies need to do something fun for a change," Jimmy spoke up. "How about some board games?"

"There's just the three of us," Jenny complained.

"We can fix that," Star smiled broadly.

She went in and placed a few calls. A couple of cars drew up outside. Molly and Chris came in followed by Adam. Tank bounded in on his heels.

Jenny greeted the dog with open arms.

"Tank! You're just the tonic I needed."

Tank showed his appreciation by licking her face down.

"I took care of dinner," Adam told her. "You just relax and put your feet up. No more sleuthing tonight."

"You're not mad at me?" Jenny murmured.

"You can be a pain, Jenny," Adam said, taking his hands in hers. "But there's always some logic in what you say."

"Does that mean …"

"What did I tell you?" Adam raised his eyebrows. "You're just going to drink some wine, eat junk food and have a good time with your friends."

"Keith didn't have any friends. Captain Charlie told me he was a loner."

"You talked to Captain Charlie about Keith Bennet?" Adam shook his head in wonder. "You're a dynamo, Jenny."

The bell rang and a delivery guy from Mama Rosa's brought in big boxes of pizza and salad.

"Olives and artichokes!" Jenny exclaimed. "That's my favorite."

She looked up into Adam's eyes and smiled adoringly.

"You remembered."

"Of course I did," he said, chucking her under the chin.

Jenny took a sip of her wine and settled against Adam on her new couch. He placed his arm around her.

Seaview rang with the laughter of friends. The roses and gardenias bloomed in the garden and for a few hours, everyone forgot about the gruesome events that had taken place at that house.

Chapter 15

The Magnolias sat sipping their morning coffee on the deck of the Boardwalk Café, sampling the pumpkin bread Jenny had baked that day.

"Not too sweet," Betty Sue remarked, licking her lips. "I like that."

"It's got a kick," Molly said. "It's a bit different from the pumpkin spice I'm used to."

"I'm trying out a special blend," Jenny told them. "I'm thinking of selling this pumpkin bread during the read-a-thon."

"That glaze makes it super yum," Heather said, wiping some crumbs from her mouth.

"So are we all going to volunteer to read for this event?" Star asked. "I'm not sure what we are supposed to do exactly."

"It's not complicated," Jenny stressed. "Just go sit there, pick up your favorite book and read."

"What if Betty Sue and I want to read the same book?"

"Two people can read the same book, but you can't read the same book twice."

Star made a face.

"Don't make it more difficult."

"I'm not," Jenny laughed. "You'll catch on when the time comes. I'm hoping to put in at least a couple of hours every day. I would do more but I have to take care of the concession stand too."

"I'm reading as much as they allow me to," Molly declared.

"Me too," Betty Sue nodded. "I used to read a lot when I was a child."

Betty Sue's face changed as she thought about old times.

"Lily and I both read a lot. We swapped books all the time."

"Any news about Keith?" Heather asked Jenny.

"The police are saying he took his own life," Jenny said stonily.

"And you don't agree, I guess?" Heather quipped. "Why not?"

"It's just a hunch."

"You were wondering why he came here," Molly mused. "Maybe it was sort of like a last wish. He wanted to see his old town and his old home, a place where he must have been happy."

"That makes sense," Star agreed. "Poor guy."

"I say he wasn't in his senses," Betty Sue said hoarsely. "He was lost in some drug induced stupor. He didn't realize what he was doing."

Jason called Jenny at the café that afternoon. He had never done that before.

"Are you winding up over there?"

"I'll be done in about thirty minutes. Why?"

"Come to my office. I have some news."

Jenny rushed through her chores and walked down the street to Jason's office, taking some of her pumpkin bread for him.

She couldn't wait to learn why he had summoned her so urgently.

"Quick, tell me what's wrong."

"Nothing's wrong," Jason said. "Just some new developments."

Jenny put her hands on her hips and raised her eyebrows.

"What are you waiting for?"

"Ann Davis is in town with her son."

"Ann Davis as in the woman I bought my house from?"

"That's the one."

"Why are they here?"

"They are here for Keith. Other than his father who is in a home, they are his only surviving family."

"Okay!" Jenny quipped. "So where's the fire?"

"Why don't you sit down?" Jason motioned to a chair in front of his desk.

Jenny flopped down and clasped her hands together.

"They are not very happy about the suicide theory. They are at the police station, talking to Adam right now."

"What do they say then?"

"They believe he was killed, Jenny."

"And what do they want?"

"I believe they want justice for Keith."

"Where were they when he was roaming around the country doing drugs?"

"We don't know anything about that," Jason sighed.

"You told me yourself. You couldn't get in touch with Keith."

"I'm beginning to wonder if I didn't look hard enough," Jason said sheepishly.

"What do you mean?"

"All those ads in the paper, those attempts to contact Keith … Ricky Davis took charge of all that. Maybe he lied to me."

"We never discussed the legalities behind the Seaview deal," Jenny said. "Was Keith listed as an owner?"

"Old man Davis listed all his grandkids as owners. Rick and Keith were the only living grandchildren. Although Ann was listed as the owner after her husband died, the grandchildren had equal rights to the house."

"So you needed Keith and Ricky to sign off on the house deal. How did you do that without Keith?"

"Ricky has a power of attorney," Jason explained. "We tried hard to contact Keith but I always knew there was a way out if he didn't turn up."

"Doesn't sound like they were close though," Jenny muttered. "Why has Ann made this trip?"

"You can ask her yourself. They want to meet you."

"Why?"

"I guess we'll know soon enough," Jason said as he spotted someone out on the street.

There was a knock on the office door and an old lady tottered in, leaning on a man's arm. Her snow white hair and craggy face hinted at an advanced age. She looked so frail Jenny thought the slightest puff of wind would blow her away. The widow's peak on her forehead split it into two equal parts.

Ricky Davis was tall and hefty with bluish gray eyes that bore into hers. He settled his mother into a chair and leaned against a wall himself.

Jason made the introductions.

"You look young," Ann Davis noted. "When I heard someone was interested in that old pile of dust, I pictured someone older."

Jenny said nothing.

"You wanted to talk to me?"

"You seem to have quite a reputation in town," Ricky cut to the chase. "How about using your skills to find what happened to Keith?"

Jenny protested.

"I'm not a professional investigator. I have a lot on my plate right now."

"Jason says you met him?" Ricky pressed. "Did he look like someone who was planning to take his life?"

Jenny thought for a minute.

"I talked to him a couple of times. Honestly, I can't tell what his state of mind was. It's not like I knew him. I had never met him before."

"Did he say why he was here?"

"Not in so many words," Jenny said. "Clearly, he wasn't happy that Seaview had been sold."

She looked pointedly at Ricky.

"It seems you didn't exactly take his permission before selling me the house?"

"Keith never cared for the house all these years," Ricky said forcefully. "You think we haven't wanted to come here? I suggested we clean up the place, spend the summer here. But Keith always wanted to stay away."

"I guess he doesn't have good memories about the place."

"You don't know the half of it," Ricky said.

"Poor Keith," Ann finally spoke. "He had a troubled life."

"Did you know he was a junkie?"

"I don't like that word," Ann said softly. "Keith lost his way."

"He was an ex-addict," Ricky told them. "Keith had been sober for three years. That's why I can't believe he died of an overdose."

"The police are saying he injected himself."

"He was very serious about his sobriety," Ann said. "We sent him to a recovery center a few years ago. He did very well in the program. He turned over a new leaf after that."

"Couldn't he have had a relapse? Coming here might have rekindled the past."

"That's what you can find out for us," Ricky pleaded.

"May I ask why you are doing this?" Jenny asked. "I thought you were estranged."

"He was a bit of a drifter," Ricky admitted. "He moved from town to town whenever it pleased him. He didn't always keep in touch with us. But he was the only family I had."

"The boys were very close growing up," Ann said, dabbing her eyes with her tissue. "You know I lost one child in the storm? Keith was like my second son. Lily should have never come back here."

"We drifted apart after Keith moved here," Ricky nodded. "I spent a lot of years trying to reconnect with him like old times."

"We lost the real Keith a long time ago," Ann agreed.

"I just want to find out what happened to my brother," Ricky said emphatically. "Can you understand that?"

"I'll see what I can do," Jenny said reluctantly. "But I can't make any promises."

"We are staying at the Bayview Inn while we are in town," Ricky told her. "You can reach us there if you want to."

Ann Davis was looking exhausted.

"We have been traveling since last night," Ricky said. "It has taken a toll on my mother."

"Betty Sue and Heather will take good care of you," Jenny smiled. "We can meet again tomorrow."

Jason and Jenny both stood up as Ricky helped his mother to her feet.

"Why don't you come to Seaview for dinner?" Jenny said suddenly. "It's like a new place altogether."

Ann's face clouded over.

"I'm not sure I want to set foot in that house again," she said weakly. "Look what happened to Keith."

Jenny was speechless. She pasted a fake smile on her face while Jason ushered the Davises out.

"Do people realize I actually live there?" Jenny cried. "Why do people keep on bad mouthing my home?"

"Just ignore them."

Jason sat down and spotted the box Jenny had brought over. He took a big bite of the pumpkin bread and groaned in pleasure.

"Does this come in chocolate?"

"It's pumpkin bread, you fool," Jenny laughed. "I'll put some chocolate chips in it for you next time."

"So?" Jason asked. "What do you think of them?"

"I'm still not sure why they are here."

"I have no doubt you'll find out soon enough."

"Have you volunteered for the read-a-thon yet?"

"Kandy and I both have," Jason said eagerly. "She's invited some of her lawyer friends. They have deep pockets, Jenny, very deep pockets."

"So you told Kandy about the issues at the library?"

"There's something about her, Jenny," Jason said, his eyes full of passion. "We talk about every topic on earth. I never thought I could get along so well with anyone."

"That's good of her."

"She loves libraries," Jason said, bobbing his head. "She grew up poor and the library was the only place she could hang out at and study. She worked at a library for many years until she became a lawyer."

Jenny wondered what else the virtuous Kandy could lay claim to.

"She sounds perfect for you."

"I'm not sure if she sees me that way," Jason confessed.

"How many dates have you been on?"

"More than a few," Jason agreed.

"You need to be bolder, Jason," Jenny said lightly. "Take the plunge."

Jason had a laid back personality. He didn't believe in pressuring anyone.

"Is that where I went wrong, Jenny?" Jason asked suddenly. "I know I'm not as aggressive as Adam."

"I love you just the way you are," Jenny said, and almost bit her lip. "You know what I mean."

Jason's expression was inscrutable.

"I'm happy for you, Jason. I'll be looking out for Kandy during the read-a-thon."

"She won't miss talking to you," Jason said. "She's sponsoring a prize. Dinner for two at a big city restaurant for the first person to finish reading all Jane Austen books."

"That's a great idea! Maybe we can give out a few prizes for meals at the café. I am going to talk to Petunia about it."

Jenny pushed back her chair and stifled a yawn.

"What's going to be your first step?" Jason asked.

"I need to get some more background on Keith. I am going to talk to Ann again tomorrow."

"Any more updates from Adam?"

"Why don't you ask him, Jason? You have a better chance of getting a civil response out of him."

"So we are ruling out suicide?"

"We are. At least until I eliminate all other possible scenarios."

Chapter 16

Molly was smiling to herself as she drank her coffee.

"What are you thinking about, girl?" Star asked.

"Chris took me out in a canoe last night," Molly gushed. "It was so romantic."

"You actually convinced him to take time out from stacking shelves?" Heather sniffed. "Good for you."

Molly said nothing, wrapped up as she was in pleasant thoughts.

"Ann Davis looks old," Betty Sue remarked, setting her knitting down. "Have you seen those wrinkles on her face?"

The other women tried not to smile. Betty Sue could be vain about her looks. Jenny had to admit she was quite well preserved for someone in her eighties.

"Did she remember you?" she asked.

"Lily and I were joined at the hip. I was in and out of that house all the time. Of course she remembered me."

"Did she mention Lily?" Star asked softly.

Betty Sue's face fell.

"Not yet. What's there to talk about but old memories?"

"Did Lily ever contact her in all these years?"

"You think Ann would mention it if she had?" Betty Sue's face looked hopeful.

"What are they doing here now?" Star asked. "Mother and son?"

"They were going to walk around in town. That shouldn't take too long."

"Did Ann ever visit after Lily came back?" Jenny asked.

"I don't know. You'll have to ask her that."

"So she's been gone since 1962. That's over fifty five years."

Betty Sue stared at the ocean moodily. Jenny guessed the Davis family was going to stir up a lot of painful memories for her friend.

Heather had barely looked up from her phone all this time. She suddenly looked up with a shout.

"I have a date!"

"It's time you stopped meeting these strangers," Betty Sue said curtly. "It's not safe."

"It's not a stranger, Grandma. It's Duster."

"That guy you met in the summer?" Jenny remembered. "What's he doing here this time of the year."

Duster and his family had rented a house up the coast for the summer.

"He has a new sales job," Heather read off the screen. "He's on a tour of the area and wants to catch up."

She looked at Molly.

"His cousin's been asking about you."

"You can tell him I'm seeing someone," Molly grinned broadly.

"We all know that, Molly," Heather snapped. "No need to rub it in."

The lunch rush kept Jenny off her feet. A familiar couple walked up the steps around 1 PM. The café was almost empty.

"Are you serving lunch?" Ricky Davis asked cheerfully. "We thought we would check here before driving out of town."

"Of course," Jenny said with a smile. "Pick any table you want."

"How about out on the deck?"

"Be my guest," Jenny said, looking at Ann Davis. "It's a bit windy though."

"I'll keep my coat on. I can't get enough of the ocean."

"Do you live near the coast?" she asked politely, trying to make conversation.

"We live in the driest part of Texas," Ann grumbled. "No beaches around us for sure. That's the one thing I miss most about this place."

Jenny told them about the day's specials.

"I have mushroom and wild rice soup, autumn chicken salad or oyster po'boys. I can also rustle up a crab salad if you want."

Ricky and Ann told her what they wanted.

"Did you grow up around these parts?" Jenny asked curiously.

"My family came to this part of the world two hundred years ago," Ann nodded. "We lived in a town up north on the Maryland border. I met my Roy at a country dance. It was love at first sight for us."

"So you still have family in these parts?"

"There's an old aunt," Ann noted. "Most of the others have moved away for jobs."

Jenny went inside and started assembling their lunch. Petunia fried a basket full of oysters and handed them over to Jenny. Jenny took the soup out and set it before mother and son.

Ricky Davis looked relaxed, stretched out in his chair with his arms around his head.

"My mom never said how beautiful this place was," he sighed.

"Is this the first time you are visiting Pelican Cove?" Jenny asked.

"I came to visit Aunt Lily, but not since the family moved out."

Jenny slathered her special tartar sauce on fresh rolls from the local bakery. She piled a generous helping of fried oysters onto each roll. Ann Davis reached for the canister of Old Bay seasoning before biting into her sandwich.

"Care to join us?" Ricky asked.

"I can sit with you," Jenny agreed, pulling out a chair.

"What's going on with the library?" Ann asked. "Surely it's not closing down?"

"Not yet, I hope," Jenny smiled. "We are doing everything we can to prevent that from happening."

"My husband's grandfather was one of the founders of the Pelican Cove Library," Ann told her. "He laid the foundation stone. It's part of the family legacy, in a way."

"We are having a read-a-thon to raise funds," Jenny supplied. "Why don't you participate?"

"You can count on our support," Ann told her. She looked at her son. "Write a check for them, Ricky."

"Can I ask you something about Keith?" Jenny ventured. "It's sort of delicate."

"The boy's already gone," Ann said bitterly. "No use tiptoeing around."

Jenny clasped her hands and struggled to find the right words.

"We found an old chain in Keith's room. It was a bit tarnished. I don't think it was valuable."

"Did it have a locket?" Ricky asked.

"Yes."

"Keith's been wearing that chain since he was nineteen. He never took it off."

"About that locket …" Jenny hesitated. "There was a picture in it. Actually there were two photos. Betty Sue confirmed one of them was Keith. The other was a girl."

Ann's neck jerked up as she stared at her son.

"A young girl?" she asked softly.

"Emily," Ricky said under his breath.

"So you can confirm that was Emily Turner?" Jenny asked sharply.

"How do you know that?" Ricky asked incredulously.

"It's a long story," Jenny sighed. "Let's say I saw her photo somewhere else and it rang a bell."

"I wish Keith had never met that girl," Ann cried.

"Was she his girl friend?"

Ricky shook his head as he chewed on his sandwich.

"Keith was madly in love with her. And we thought she loved him too, until she left him."

"Left him?" Jenny questioned. "Why do you say that?"

"She was younger than him, you know," Ricky told her. "Still a junior in high school. She hitched rides to come to Pelican Cove to meet Keith."

"Wasn't that dangerous?"

"Keith told her that. He used to meet her as often as he could. They talked about eloping."

"What did her parents feel about that?"

"She hadn't told them about Keith. She had a boyfriend back home, a kid her age."

"What happened?"

"Emily didn't turn up one day," Ricky explained. "It was the summer of 1991. I was here in town. My uncle had decided to close the house and move to a place near us. Keith didn't want to leave without Emily."

"Emily is still missing," Jenny said grimly. "She left for a party one night and never went back home."

"Keith thought she ran away with someone else."

"Why would he think that?" Jenny asked. "Didn't he trust her at all?"

"It had been a hard year for Keith," Ann explained. "His sister died a few months ago. Lily ran away that spring. He was grieving over them. Meeting this girl changed him."

"It was almost as if he was ready to live again," Ricky nodded. "Everything came crashing down when Emily left."

"Why do you keep saying that?" Jenny demanded. "How do you know she left voluntarily? She could have been attacked or had an accident."

"Keith always believed she ditched him," Ricky said sadly. "Like his mother."

"Lily did a number on her family when she abandoned them," Ann quavered. "Keith was never the same again."

"It was the beginning of his downfall," Ricky agreed.

"He was in college then, wasn't he?"

"He was a freshman," Ricky nodded. "But he never went back."

"He was smart," Ann shrugged. "But he never made use of his mind. He started doing drugs. He almost died a couple of times."

"What about his father?"

"Lily's husband boarded up the house and moved to Texas. Keith came with him. His father tried to reason with him for years. Keith never held a job or met anyone else. He used to disappear for months. Then he turned up when he wanted money."

Jenny could hear the regret in Ricky's voice.

"Do you believe Emily ran away?" Jenny asked Ricky.

"I don't know," he shrugged. "I didn't know her well. Sometimes I think that's why Keith roamed around like a vagabond. He was hoping to run into her somewhere."

"What about this latest rehab Jason mentioned?"

"Three years ago, Keith came to us," Ann began. "He wanted to start over. He wanted to take a stab at living a normal life. He sounded committed. Of course we wanted the same thing for him. We put him in the finest recovery clinic in the state. He got through the program and got a job."

"He was doing fine," Ricky muttered. "Then he fell off the radar again. We had no idea he had come to Pelican Cove."

Jenny's heart was heavy. She offered to serve dessert. Ricky and Ann both declined.

"We ate your muffins for breakfast," Ann remarked. "They were delicious."

"Where are you headed now?"

"I want to see the light house," Ann said. "We used to climb up to the top, Roy and I. My Ricky was conceived there on our third anniversary."

"Mother!" Ricky Davis groaned.

"Jimmy Parsons will show you around."

"Those Parsons are still around then?" Ann looked at her son. "One of those kids used to take you up there to show you the light."

"Did Keith have any enemies?" Jenny asked suddenly.

"He was aloof. He barely talked to anyone. I don't think he knew anyone well enough to make friends or enemies."

"What about those men he bought drugs from?" Ann asked suddenly.

"That's right," Jenny said. "Drug dealers are an unsavory lot."

"Keith was pretty good about paying up. His father did very well and set up a trust fund for him. Cash was never his problem."

"He must have met someone in all these years?" Jenny persisted. "What about that rehab you sent him to? Did he make any friends there?"

"Not that I know of." Ricky shook his head.

"What about women?" Jenny mused. "Was he seeing anyone?"

"Emily was the only girl for him."

"What if he fell for someone though? Maybe he wanted to get a fresh start in life. He could have come here to say farewell. Say goodbye to the last place he met Emily."

Jenny wondered if she sounded crazy. Truth be told, she was grasping at straws.

"I wondered if there was a woman," Rick admitted. "Especially when he wanted to clean up three years ago. I didn't know what else would motivate him that much. But he never introduced us to anyone."

"Lily's family came to a sad end," Ann said grimly. "She should have never come back here."

A hundred thoughts clamored in Jenny's head as she walked home. She had come to Pelican Cove later in life, just like Lily. She had dragged her son along with her too. Jenny couldn't help but notice the similarities between her life and Lily's. Granted, Lily's husband hadn't dumped her. But they must have had their differences. Why else had Lily left her happy family behind to run away with another man? Had losing her daughter driven her off the edge? Keith had suffered a similar fate. Maybe insanity ran in the Davis family.

Chapter 17

Jenny tapped her head with a pencil, going over the menu once again. She had been discussing what they would sell at the concession stand with Petunia.

"Normally I would just do coffee and muffins," Petunia told her. "But you have made a name for yourself. I already have requests from people."

"Heather says there have been some comments on Instagram too," Jenny said shyly. "People want to taste our seafood. And they are asking for everything from soup to sandwiches to pies."

"We need to keep the menu simple," Petunia spoke from experience. "It has to be something we can make in big quantities without too much effort."

"It's getting chilly," Jenny remarked. "We definitely need soup."

"Choose any three soups – one a day." Petunia had planned menus for many events. "Pumpkin soup, chicken soup and seafood chowder."

"We can have one sandwich for every day too," Jenny said, catching on. "chicken salad, egg salad and tomato cheese."

"Now you just have to choose the desserts," Petunia smiled. "We need cookies, lots and lots of cookies."

"Have you thought of the prizes the Boardwalk Café will sponsor?"

"Lunch for two," Petunia said, "and your special chocolate cake. We can give away a couple of both of these. That's as much as we can afford."

"Whatever you say, Petunia," Jenny agreed.

Jenny knew these prizes were small fry compared to what some other people were offering. But they just wanted to pitch in and do their bit. She thought of the money Ann Davis had promised to donate. Did Ann have a private income or was her son Ricky going to shell out the money. Jenny realized she didn't know much about them at all.

"What do we know about them, really?" Jenny asked Adam as they were walking on the beach later that night.

"You don't like them, I take it?"

"It's not a question of liking or not liking anyone. We have to think about people connected to Keith. He wasn't married so there is no spouse to worry about. His father's an invalid. Ann and Ricky are his only family."

"And you suspect them of wrongdoing?" Adam asked with a smile. "You are beginning to think like a detective, Jenny."

"If that's a compliment, I will take it."

Tank walked beside them, wagging his tail. Jenny lapsed into silence, focusing on throwing a stick for Tank to fetch.

"Have you made any progress regarding Keith?" she finally asked Adam.

"I can't talk about that," Adam protested.

"So you still think it's suicide? I can't believe that."

"Why not? You know he had a history of drug abuse. He was mooning over some girl. The man was unstable, Jenny."

"What about Mrs. Bones? Any update on her?"

"She's low on the list of priorities. All I know is they are running tests."

"You don't think Keith killed Emily Turner and buried her in his backyard?"

Adam burst out laughing. Jenny turned red and glared at him but Adam couldn't stop.

"I already told you that's farfetched, Jenny."

"But why? We know Emily left home to go to some party out of town. She might have been meeting Keith."

"Why did Keith kill her?"

"They had a lover's spat. Things got out of hand. Keith hit her or maybe she fell. He might have panicked."

Adam shook his head in denial. Jenny found herself getting incensed.

"No one found a single trace of Emily. And she never got in touch with her family again. I'm willing to bet she's gone, Adam."

"You think Keith came here to look at the grave?"

"He must have read about the skeleton somewhere. He came here to see what was going on."

"If he had really buried her there, he would have run to the other end of the country."

"He felt some kind of compulsion. Isn't that how it's supposed to be?"

"So he was a crazy, psycho boyfriend who was drawn here by a bag of bones? You can believe that but you don't believe he took his own life?"

Jenny had no answer for that.

Adam walked her back to Seaview and bid her goodnight. Star was watching TV with Jimmy.

"How's the grouch today?" she asked.

"He's not that bad," Jenny protested.

"I still think you should pick Jason," Star griped. She had always been clear about who she thought Jenny should date.

"Jason's found himself a hot girlfriend."

"And whose fault is that?" her aunt called out after her.

Ricky Davis came to the café the next morning. He rubbed his eyes and yawned as Jenny poured him a fresh cup of coffee.

"They ran out of muffins at the inn. That's what I get for sleeping in."

"How's your mother?"

"She's staying in bed this morning. She's not used to all this activity, poor thing."

Jenny wrapped up a couple of muffins for Ricky.

"So what are you going to do today?"

"I'm taking a boat tour to some of the islands," Ricky told her.

"Those are popular with the tourists," Jenny agreed.

"Why are they still sticking around here?" she asked Jason later.

Jason sat in his office with his shirt sleeves rolled up and his tie loose, buried in a mound of paperwork.

"I don't know, Jenny. Maybe they are taking a vacation."

"So they are not really grieving for Keith."

"What are you getting at?"

"What do you know about their background? What does Ricky do for a living, for instance?"

"Ann Davis went back to school after she left town. Her mother took care of Ricky while Ann got her nursing degree. She worked as a nurse for several years. I think she was a private nurse for some rich guy toward the end of her career."

"What about Ricky?"

"He has a good job, enough to have a house and support a wife and kids. You'll have to ask him more about it."

Jason narrowed his eyes as he looked at Jenny.

"Why this sudden interest? What are you thinking?"

"Where have they been the past couple of weeks? Has anyone asked about their alibi?"

Jason's eyebrows shot up.

"You think they had a hand in Keith's death? You are going too far this time."

"Anything is possible," Jenny insisted. "We don't really know them."

"What possible motive could they have for harming Keith?"

"Ann said Keith's father did well for himself. He had a trust fund. Where does all that money go now?"

"The Davises aren't hurting for money as far as I know."

"Some people can never have enough. Then there's the Seaview sale. They must have pocketed all that money. Then Keith turns up. What if Keith wanted his share?"

"Legally, half of that money did belong to Keith."

Jenny went home and placed a call to the Bayview Inn. She invited Ann Davis and Ricky for dinner. Jason had given her a fancy new grill as a housewarming present. She decided to try it out that night.

Jenny thought about how she would question mother and son. Could she dare to be direct with them? She prepared a dry rub of herbs and spices and rubbed it into chicken thighs. Potatoes boiled in a big stock pot for her warm potato salad. She started chopping vegetables. It was going to be an interesting evening.

Ann Davis looked well rested as she leaned on Ricky's arm. Star and Jimmy greeted them. Jenny had urged Jason to come over. Drinks were poured and appetizers were served.

"This crab dip is delicious," Ricky complimented.

"They don't make crabs like this in Texas," Ann said, scooping some up with a cracker.

"How are you enjoying Pelican Cove?" Star asked. "Jenny told me you took a boat out."

"My Roy used to love going out to the islands," Ann said, reminiscing. "Our family owned some of them, you know. We lost them in the big storm."

"How can you lose an island?" Jenny asked naively.

"They were submerged forever," Jason explained. "Just like a large part of Morse Isle. Pelican Cove might have been three times what it is now."

"Are you enjoying your time off work?" Jenny asked Ricky.

"It's been a while since I traveled anywhere with Mom. We are having a grand time."

"And you haven't come to Pelican Cove since the 1990s?"

"Not since 1991," Ricky corrected her.

"So you weren't in the area when Keith died?"

Jason stifled a cough and cleared his throat. Ann Davis looked bewildered.

"What are you trying to say, dear?"

"She wants to know where we were when Keith died, Mother," Ricky Davis said, catching on.

His gaze had hardened as he looked at Jenny.

"It's common to ask for alibis of people connected to the victim."

"And you think we were responsible for Keith's death?" Ricky folded his arms and stared at her.

"You asked me to do a job," Jenny argued. "I can't do it well unless I consider all aspects."

"Did you invite us here to insult us, missy?" Ann croaked. "It's this house. Nothing good ever comes from it."

She struggled to her feet. Ricky sprang into action, helping his mother.

"Would you like a tour?" Jenny asked solicitously. "The contractors did a really fine job. You won't even recognize the place."

Ann ignored her and ordered her son. "Get me out of here."

Ricky started ushering his mother out of the house.

"Please stay!" Jenny urged. "Dinner is almost ready."

"You think I am going to stay here one more minute?" Ann Davis asked sharply.

"Look, I'm sorry, okay. But I had to ask."

"Jenny believes in being thorough," Jason quipped.

"Don't pay attention to my niece," Star said. "She tends to get carried away."

Ann Davis finally calmed down and sat back in her chair.

"I have two weeks off from work," Ricky said. "My wife and I are going through a trial separation. Mom always wanted to visit Pelican Cove. We decided to come here for Keith."

"When did you plan that?"

Ricky looked at Jason.

"We learned Keith had turned up here. I started making travel arrangements. We were coming here anyway. Then Keith died on us."

"So you weren't in Texas when Keith died?"

Ricky put an arm around his mother.

"We were in Northern Virginia, visiting a cousin."

Jenny did the math in her head. Ricky could easily have driven to Pelican Cove and back in a few hours. In fact, he could have come into town at night after his mother went to sleep and got back before she woke up.

She put on her best poker face and smiled.

"That seems like a different country, doesn't it?"

"You don't know how lucky you are," Ann Davis said, extending an olive branch. "We had to use a boat to get to the shore."

"I came to town after they built the bridge," Star said, embarking on one of her favorite stories. "But I never went back. I fell in love and stayed on. Pelican Cove has been my home ever since."

"Funny, isn't it?" Ann mused. "I came here to live with my husband too. But it didn't last long."

Jenny announced dinner was ready. They made small talk as they ate, and the food disappeared quickly. Jenny brought out a lemon cake and cut generous slices. Ricky grabbed her hand when she served him.

"You don't really think I hurt Keith?"

"I need to look for suspects," Jenny said. "I'm just eliminating the possibilities."

"Why would we ask you to look into this if we were guilty? You don't think we are that foolish?"

"I need to find out more about the last month or two of Keith's life. If you know anything about it, please don't keep it from me. The tiniest detail can help."

Ricky blinked as he took a bite of his cake. Jenny was sure she had struck a chord. Ricky was hiding something.

Chapter 18

"People are offering all kinds of prizes," Petunia told the women as they sipped coffee.

Jenny had made pumpkin spice lattes. Heather told her they were a seasonal favorite. Jenny wanted to start offering them at the café and at the concession stand.

"This is a bit spicy for me," Betty Sue said, tasting her coffee.

"I made the spice mix myself," Jenny said proudly. "I can use a bit less the next time."

"What kind of prizes are we talking about?" Star asked.

"The seafood market has offered two dozen oysters to the first person to read a 100 pages."

"That's great," Jenny said, clapping her hands. "That should encourage people to come in early."

"Dinner for two at Ethan's for the person reading the most number of pages in the day," Molly added. "I bet I am going to win that one."

"How many prizes are you angling for, Molly?" Heather said.

Her mouth had twisted in a grimace. It happened every time she spoke to Molly.

"Free pint at the Rusty Anchor for a whole week," Petunia said, reading from a list. "That's going to be popular."

"Barb Norton must be happy," Jenny observed. "The read-a-thon is set to be a major success."

"Have you heard what Ada Newbury promised?" Betty Sue asked. "She's going to match whatever amount we manage to collect."

A collective gasp went up through the group.

Ada Newbury was the richest woman in town. The Newburys had become rich overnight during the big storm of 1962. Rumor had it they had found gold on a nearby shipwreck. Ada liked to flaunt her wealth and was as snooty as they came.

Jenny gave credit where it was due.

"That's very generous of her."

"Showing off," Betty Sue muttered. "Someone mentioned there are going to be TV crews here to cover the event. Ada just wants to get on TV."

"Whatever her reasons, we need the money," Molly said simply. "I'm going to read like I have never read before. That's all I can do."

"The whole town is pitching in and doing something," Petunia reminded her. "We are going to make sure you keep working at that library."

Jenny crossed her fingers and hoped the café would do brisk business at the read-a-thon. They were donating half their profits to the library.

"Any updates on that incident at your house?" Betty Sue asked her, twirling red yarn around her needles.

"The police aren't giving it much importance. Maybe they think it was a stray who wandered up to Seaview."

"He didn't bury himself though, did he?" Betty Sue questioned. "That Hopkins boy needs a kick in his pants."

"I don't think Adam has control over which cases to work on," Jenny argued, coming to his defense.

The Magnolias spent several minutes rehashing the whole incident.

"How are you sleeping these days?" Heather teased. "No weird sounds in the attic? No strange lights?"

"Nothing of that sort," Jenny said good-naturedly. "I sleep like a baby."

"So do I," Star butted in. "Stop harassing my niece, Heather."

Jenny mixed crab salad for lunch and fried a fresh batch of donuts using a new recipe. She wanted to try out a pumpkin spice glaze.

"Woman out there is asking for you," Petunia said, dumping a stack of empty plates in the sink.

"Who is it?"

"Never seen her before." Petunia shrugged. "Doesn't look like a tourist though."

Jenny wiped her hands on a towel and went out. She was surprised to see the woman sitting at a corner table. Crumbling a paper napkin in her hands, she was clearly nervous about being there.

"Mrs. Turner!" Jenny exclaimed. "What brings you here?"

The woman breathed a sigh of relief.

"I thought I would find you here but I wasn't sure."

"I'll get some coffee for us," Jenny said, "or do you prefer lemonade?"

"Coffee's fine," the older woman assured her.

Jenny came out with a tray loaded with coffee and snacks.

"I just ate," Mrs. Turner said.

"These donuts are very popular this season. You have to try them."

The woman seemed to settle down after she took a few bites and sipped her coffee.

Jenny let her take her time.

"I've been thinking," Mrs. Turner finally spoke up. "Maybe we should try looking for Emily again."

"That's a great idea," Jenny said, encouraging her. "What did you have in mind?"

"I talked to my husband," the woman said. "It seems you have a reputation."

Jenny dreaded what the woman was going to say next. If the Turners asked her to look for their daughter, would she have to tell them her suspicions? Despite what Adam or Jason had said, Jenny strongly believed that Mrs. Bones was in fact Emily Turner. How could she pretend to look for Emily when her instincts told her she was lying in a police lab somewhere.

"We want you to help us find our daughter."

"Mrs. Turner …" Jenny hesitated.

"We know what the odds are." The woman rushed ahead. "We have braced ourselves for any outcome. We just want to know."

"I get that, but …"

"Please," the woman urged, tearing up. "What if it were your son or daughter? Wouldn't you want to know?"

"I would," Jenny agreed softly. "I don't know what you heard, Mrs. Turner, but I am not a trained investigator. I just talk to people."

"Just do your best. That will be enough for us."

"We might need to interface with the police," Jenny said tentatively. "Do you have a problem with that?"

"You can do whatever you think needs to be done. We have nothing to hide. If you can get the police to look into such an old case, that will be a coup."

"Technology has changed a lot in the past twenty five years," Jenny said thoughtfully. "We might have more options. I am going to think about this."

"Let us know if you need anything from us."

Jenny asked the woman to email her some photos of Emily. Her head was churning with possibilities. She had already thought of a few things she wanted to try out.

"Aren't you taking on too much?" Star asked over dinner. "When was the last time you talked to Nick?"

Jenny stared at her pan seared fish moodily. Her aunt was right. She hadn't caught up with her son in a while. She just assumed he was busy with his classes.

"Nicky doesn't want me pestering him all the time."

"Checking up on your kid once in ten days isn't pestering," Star preached.

Jenny took Star's words to heart. She took her cell phone with her when she went for her walk.

"Is that the ocean I hear?" her son asked. "Where are you, Mom?"

"Trying to walk off the half dozen donuts I ate today," Jenny groaned. "How are you, Nicky. When are you coming home?"

"Are you throwing a Halloween party?" he asked cheekily. "We have our very own skeleton to prop up in the garden."

"Don't joke about it," Jenny sighed. "But seriously, that's not keeping you away, I hope. You're not scared of coming home, sweetie?"

"Of course not, Mom! How old do you think I am? I'm up to my ears in midterms and assignments. I'm coming as soon as I turn in my last exam. Promise."

"Can you be here for the read-a-thon? We need people."

Nick knew all about the read-a-thon. He promised he would try to be there. Jenny suspected he had already discussed the event with Adam's twins.

Jenny spotted her biggest admirer in the distance. Tank leaped in the air and almost toppled Jenny, giving her his usual wet welcome.

"I missed you," Jenny said, hugging him.

"Tank doesn't know how lucky he is," Adam said drily.

He leaned on his cane and looked hungrily at Jenny. They sat in the sand, watching the waves lap against the shore.

"I feel so fortunate," Jenny sighed happily. "I never dreamed I would have a house on the beach."

"Where did you go on vacation?" Adam asked her.

Jenny didn't like to talk much about her past life.

"Here and there," she said evasively.

She had spent many summers in Europe, waiting for her husband to join her. The expensive vacations any woman would covet hadn't brought much joy to Jenny.

"The twins are up to something," Adam said. "Did Nick say anything to you?"

"My guess is they are coming here for the read-a-thon."

"Must be something more than that."

Heather ran up the café steps the next morning, tugging at Tootsie's leash. She tied her black poodle to a post. Tootsie burrowed in the sand and settled down for a nap.

"You're grinning like a Cheshire cat," Jenny commented as she gave Heather the once over.

"Oh Jenny, I'm on cloud nine."

Heather whirled around on her toes and beamed at Jenny.

"Hot date?" Star asked.

Betty Sue clacked her needles and muttered under her breath.

"Hotter than you can imagine," Heather breathed. "Wait till you hear about it."

"Watch it, girl," Betty Sue railed. "We don't want any indecent talk here."

"Oh Grandma, you'll want to hear this."

"Where did you go this time?" Molly asked with a laugh. "Delaware?"

"Hush, Molly." Heather's high watt smile hadn't dimmed at all. "I'm dating a doctor."

Betty Sue sat up when she heard that.

"Where did you find a doctor to go out with you? On that Internet?"

"Actually, yes. I did find him online. But guess where he's from?"

Five faces looked at her expectantly.

"Pelican Cove!"

Molly burst out laughing.

"You went out with old Dr. Smith? Did you take him to a game of Bingo?"

"Not Dr. Smith!" Heather pouted. "Dr. Costa. Dr. Gianni Costa. He's the new hottie in town."

"You mean that young doctor who's moved here from Mexico?" Petunia asked.

"That's the one," Heather nodded. "And he's not from Mexico. He just lived in a border town before he came here."

"Isn't he old, dear?" Petunia spoke.

"He looks young. Age is just a number, anyway."

"So you are going to date someone old enough to be your father?" Molly asked.

"He's not that old," Heather said with a huff. "You guys are just jealous. Wait till you see him."

There was a shout from the beach. A tall, dark haired man waved at Heather. Molly and Jenny craned their necks to get a good look at him.

"He's coming here," Heather said, turning a deep red.

She waved back at the man and cupped her hands over her mouth.

"Over here, Gianni!"

Betty Sue was shaking her head and staring at her granddaughter in disbelief.

The man ambled over the boardwalk and walked up the café steps. Tootsie let out a growl but he didn't stop to pat her. His coal black hair was the same color as his eyes. The diamond stud in his ear sparkled in the morning sun. He wore a light pink shirt over chinos. The top three buttons of the shirt were undone, exposing a broad chest matted with curly black hair. A thick gold chain sporting a big medallion hung around his neck.

Jenny decided Gianni looked unlike any doctor she had ever met.

"Hello ladies," the man said, flashing his pearly whites. "Heather has told me so much about you."

"How long have you known my girl?" Betty Sue asked suspiciously.

"Ah, you're Heather's grandma," Gianni said, picking up her hand. "You're the queen of this beautiful island I now call home."

He kissed Betty Sue's wrist lightly and placed a hand on his chest.

"Now I know where Heather gets her looks."

The Magnolias stared at Dr. Gianni Costa as if he was from another planet. He gestured expansively with his hands as he spoke. He had a compliment for every one of them. Then he kissed Heather's cheek and promised to see her later.

"So? What do you think?" Heather crowed as soon as he was out of sight. "Isn't he a keeper?"

Chapter 19

Jenny chatted with Captain Charlie. The breakfast rush kept her busy. She noticed Ricky Davis sitting out on the deck when she went out to get some fresh air.

"Good Morning," she greeted him. "Out of muffins again?"

Ricky pointed to his plate. Jenny saw two of the lemon blueberry muffins she had baked that morning.

"I wanted to talk to you," Ricky said, looking over his shoulder. "Is now a good time?"

Jenny went in and made sure Petunia could handle the counter. She came out with a fresh cup of coffee and sat down before Ricky.

"What's on your mind?"

Jenny could sense Ricky's nervousness across the table. A trickle of sweat ran down his forehead and he wiped it off with the back of his hand.

"You said something about the past month or two of Keith's life."

Jenny encouraged him to go on.

"Something happened. My mother doesn't know about this."

"I can keep your secret," Jenny said, "as long as it's harmless."

"Keith had been sober for the past three years. I already told you that. He had been off the radar for some time. Somehow he got wind of the fact that we sold Seaview. Either that threw him off or it was something else. He must have started using again."

"How did you find this out?" Jenny asked.

"He was arrested for drug possession," Ricky sighed. "He called me. I came and bailed him out."

"Where did this happen?"

"Up the coast in Maryland," Ricky explained. "I had to get back home immediately. Keith promised me he would come home to Texas."

"But he didn't?"

"Looks like he stayed on in the area. I guess he eventually turned up in Pelican Cove."

"Are you saying Keith might have taken the drugs himself?"

"No! He would never do that." Ricky looked at Jenny in despair. "I don't think he did that."

Jenny tried to be gentle.

"None of us want to believe he took his own life. But this changes things. Keith did have access to drugs, apparently. I think you should talk to the police about this."

Ricky looked sad and guilty.

"I should have stuck around. Or insisted he went home with me."

"You couldn't have known." Jenny knew anything she said at this point was just a platitude.

"Mother doesn't know any of this. She will be heartbroken if she finds out."

"I'm glad you came to me with this information," Jenny told Ricky. "You did the right thing."

Jenny couldn't stop thinking about Keith as she went about her work. She wasn't ready to accept he had taken his own life. Other than Ann or Ricky, there was no one she could suspect. Jenny decided she needed to find out more about Keith's time in Pelican Cove.

Mrs. Turner emailed her a bunch of Emily's photos as promised. Jenny spoke to Adam about it that night.

"Do you think she's out there, Adam?"

Adam had a suggestion for a change.

"Why don't you use one of those software programs that tell you how a person would look in a certain number of years? Then show that photo around."

"We can print an ad in local newspapers," Jenny said eagerly. "And I can post it online too. Ask people to share it."

Jenny tried to put herself in Emily's shoes. What if she had run away from home? What would she do? Her face broke into a smile as she thought of something. Chances were slim but Jenny didn't have much else to hold on to.

Heather had invited everyone to drinks at the Rusty Anchor. They hadn't gone out as a group in a long time. Jenny reluctantly agreed to go.

"You need a change of scene," Heather convinced her. "Let your hair down for a change."

Chris and Molly sat hand in hand, talking softly to each other. Jenny felt like a third wheel and wished Adam was coming. Heather arrived with her latest friend, the colorful Dr. Costa. Jenny noticed the fourth button of his shirt was undone, his nod to the evening hour.

Dr. Costa took over the conversation and soon everyone was in splits. Jenny had to admit she hadn't laughed that much in a while. Eddie Cotton came over with another round of their drinks.

"I need to go," Molly said. "I have an early day tomorrow."

"Are you taking time off for the read-a-thon?" Jenny asked curiously.

"I'm trying to make up for a day's work," Molly told her. "I'm taking two days off."

"I hear Ricky Davis is back in town," Eddie Cotton, the proprietor of the Rusty Anchor said as he wiped a glass.

"You know him?" Jenny asked sharply.

"Our families used to be tight," Eddie nodded. "My grandpa and old man Davis grew up together. He was bummed when the old man perished in the storm."

"So you knew Ricky back when he was a baby."

"Ricky's been in and out of Pelican Cove a lot," Eddie nodded.

Jenny climbed up on a bar stool and devoted her attention to Eddie.

"What are you doing there, Miss Jenny?" Gianni Costa hollered. "We need you here."

Heather was practically sitting in the good doctor's lap. Chris Williams was staring at her with his mouth open. Jenny realized Heather was getting brazen by the day. They needed an intervention. She made a mental note to plan a girls' night soon.

Jenny turned her back on the rambunctious couple and faced Eddie.

"Wait a minute … are you talking about the time Lily ran away?"

"Ricky came here at that time," Eddie nodded. "Stuck around with Lily's boy. That was back in the 90s. I'm not talking about that."

Jenny's heart skipped a beat as she urged Eddie to go on.

"Ricky was here last week. Him and Keith, just like old times. I poured them a pint myself."

"This was just before Keith died, right?"

Eddie frowned. "Yeah. A day or two before that, I guess. Must have been the last time they saw each other."

"Are you sure about this?"

"Of course I'm sure. I just serve the drinks, Jenny. I don't touch the stuff."

"That scumbag," Jenny muttered under her breath. "Any idea what they were talking about?"

"I don't know," Eddie shrugged. "They got into a row after some time. I heard your house mentioned."

"Seaview?"

Eddie's nod was answer enough.

Jenny marched into Jason's office next morning.

"Did you know about this?" she demanded, glaring at him with her hands on her hips.

"Calm down, Jenny, take a load off."

"That scoundrel Ricky, he's been lying to me all along."

Jason pulled a cold bottle of water out of his small refrigerator and put it before Jenny. Jenny ignored it.

"Eddie Cotton told me all about it. I should have gone to the Rusty Anchor sooner."

"Why don't you begin at the beginning?" Jason's calm voice finally forced Jenny to simmer down.

"How many times have we asked Ann and Ricky about their whereabouts?"

"At the beginning, Jenny!"

"Ricky was here last week. He was spotted in town a day or two before Keith died."

"What was he doing here?"

"Arguing with Keith over Seaview."

"You don't know that for sure." Jason stared at her in disbelief.

"I don't," Jenny agreed. "But those two were fighting alright and talking about Seaview."

"What was there to fight about?"

"Money!" Jenny exclaimed. "It's obvious they sold the house without his knowledge. Wanna bet they were planning to run with the loot?"

"We bought Seaview at a very reasonable price, Jenny," Jason reminded her. "Nothing exorbitant, considering how big the house and the land is."

"And your point is?"

"Ann and Ricky are very well off. So was Keith or his father. They didn't really need the money from the sale."

"I guess they would have sold the house long ago if they needed the money," Jenny thought out loud.

"Ricky told you about his separation. I think he was thinking of coming to live here. Ann was dead set against it. She thinks the house is jinxed."

"So she sold it?"

"You made the offer, remember? It came at the right time for Ann Davis. She wanted to get rid of the property before Ricky was tempted."

"And what about Keith?"

"Keith never cared for the place either. Don't know what made him come here now."

"That's another mystery we will never solve," Jenny sighed.

"What do you want to do now?" Jason asked her.

"I can confront Ricky about this, but how is it going to help?"

Jason shook his head.

"Don't do that. Let him think he got away with it."

"Got away with what?"

"We don't know that yet … don't jump to conclusions."

"Shouldn't we tell the police about this though?"

"Tell Adam. Let him decide how he wants to handle it."

Jenny picked up the bottle of water and drank from it deeply.

"You're looking exhausted, Jenny," Jason said with concern. "Is something bothering you?"

Jenny had a glimpse of the old Jason.

"I could use a vacation. I'm busy baking and prepping for the read-a-thon. Nothing's moving on the Keith front. Emily Turner's mother has asked me to find her. We still don't know anything about Mrs. Bones. Nicky hasn't been home in weeks. Heather's turning into a hussy."

"Calm down and take a breath," Jason laughed. "You're carrying too much weight on your shoulders."

"I can't get anything done, Jason," Jenny wailed. "I'm worried about the concession stand we are setting up. What if no one turns up? All that food will be wasted. Or what if we run out of food?"

"It's all going to be fine," Jason said, taking her hand and stroking it. "You're not alone, Jenny. The Magnolias are with you. So am I. And Adam, for what he's worth."

Jenny finally smiled.

"Forget all this stressful stuff. What is this I hear about Heather?"

"Have you met Dr. Costa yet?" Jenny asked with relish. "Gianni Costa?"

The two friends spent some time catching up on what was happening in town.

"How's Kandy?" Jenny asked. "Haven't seen her in a while."

"She's busy working on a big case. She'll be in town for the read-a-thon though. She's looking forward to it."

Jenny made her autumn chicken salad and made a couple of sandwiches with double scoops of salad. She added two slices of chocolate raspberry cake for dessert and put it all in a basket.

"No need to hurry back," Petunia told her. "Your aunt is coming over for lunch."

Nora, the clerk at the police station greeted Jenny like an old friend. Jenny knocked on Adam's office and went in, bracing herself for what he might say. Jenny could never predict Adam's mood. They were often controlled by how his leg was faring that day.

"You look just like the woman in my dreams," Adam said. "She brought me cake."

Jenny unpacked the basket, fighting to hide a blush.

"I need to tell you something," she began. "It's about Ricky Davis. He's been lying to us."

Adam held up a hand.

"It can wait. Let's eat first. You are wilting before my eyes."

Jenny snorted with mirth.

"Love is blind …"

She bit her tongue and turned red as a tomato. Adam stared at her, his eyes wide.

Jenny stammered to correct herself.

"I didn't mean … that is …"

"I know exactly what you mean," Adam said softly, giving her a goofy grin.

Chapter 20

Pelican Cove bore a festive look. A huge tent had been erected in the town square for the read-a-thon. Tables and chairs were set up, forming large reading areas. People had lent rugs and carpets. These formed cozy reading nooks, piled with abundant cushions. A smaller tent was set up as a food and drinks zone. Jenny had set up shop inside it.

There was a modest crowd present for the inauguration at 9 AM on the first day. Betty Sue Morse cut the shiny red ribbon pulled across the entrance to the tent and declared the festival open. The smattering of applause was drowned by the patter of feet as people rushed into the tent and took up positions. Everyone wanted to win the early bird prizes.

"We need more people," Barb Norton boomed. She stalked around like a drill sergeant, ordering the volunteers around. "Why don't you take control of the social media?" she ordered Heather. "As it is, you are glued to that phone all the time."

"I don't need my phone now," Heather giggled. "I have a boyfriend."

"Don't you mean sugar daddy?" Jenny teased. "Are you that desperate, honey?"

"Gianni's fun," Heather said lightly. "He's perfect for me."

"What about that social media?" Barb Norton reminded her.

"Okay, okay. I'll take some pictures and post them online."

"Take a picture of that hay wagon too," Barb ordered. "And tell them about the rides."

Heather scurried along, snapping pictures of people with their heads in their books. She started tapping on her phone and gave Barb a thumbs up sign.

"We have the first break in a couple of hours," Barb said, taking Jenny to task. "Have plenty of food ready and make sure the coffee's hot."

Jenny didn't need much prompting. She had her routine meticulously planned out.

Ann Davis walked up to the reading tent, leaning on Ricky's arm. They both sat down to read. A volunteer noted the time and wrote down their names.

Barb declared the early bird prizes just before lunch. A group of tourists turned up in the afternoon, intrigued by the novelty of the event.

"We already clocked five hundred hours," Barb announced with a megaphone.

A cheer went up through the assembled group.

"How are the donations going?" Jenny asked her. "I still don't understand how all this works."

"People are donating a fixed amount for every hour. They choose the number of hours they want and the rate. It's easy to calculate their total donation."

"And they do this just because they want to help?"

Barb told Jenny she was being tiresome.

The Boardwalk Café did brisk business and the concession stand was a hit. Tourists flocked to the café after they tasted the food at the concession stand. Jenny put on a second batch of chicken soup.

"What are you serving tomorrow?" a woman asked. "I hope you have a different menu for each day."

Jenny assured the woman and started listing the weekend's menu on a chalk board.

"We are spending the weekend on the shore and we want to taste the local delicacies."

The woman asked for recommendations for dinner and Jenny told her about Ethan's Crab Shack. The read-a-thon was turning out to be quite a crowd puller. It was going to be a lucrative weekend for the whole town of Pelican Cove.

"Call for you." Petunia's voice broke into Jenny's reverie.

It was Adam, wanting to know if she was free for dinner.

"I'm going to be here till eight. I don't think I will have the energy to do anything after that."

"And here I was hoping for a romantic date."

Jenny didn't want to disappoint Adam. She gave in easily and asked him to Seaview for dinner. Star came in just before she hung up.

"Jimmy and I are going out," she announced. "You have the house to yourself."

"You don't have to leave on my account."

"Actually, we need some privacy," her aunt said with a wink.

Jenny had no response for that.

Barb Norton came into the café with Dale at her heels.

"Have you thanked the man who made all this possible?" she beamed. "Dale says the read-a-thon is a success."

"You have already surpassed what we accomplished for the whole event. And the first day isn't over yet."

"You were a big help, Dale." Barb patted him on the back and looked at Jenny expectantly.

Jenny and Star hastened to compliment the man.

The read-a-thon wound down at 8 PM. Jenny directed people to the Rusty Anchor and Ethan's place for a quick bite. She thought about what she could make for dinner as she walked home. She decided on a quick shrimp pasta.

Adam lit candles in the great room at Seaview while Jenny showered upstairs. She had set the table but he wanted to do something special for her. He went out and built a quick bouquet of flowers using the roses and gardenias she loved so much.

He went inside and poured the local wine he had brought along. Jenny had liked this particular wine when they went out before. He was ready for her when she came down the wide sweeping staircase.

Jenny took a deep breath and hesitated on the final step. She clutched the banister nervously as Adam handed her the flowers with a flourish.

"Thank you," she said, taking a quick sniff.

Dinner proceeded a bit awkwardly. They hadn't spoken to each other since her giant faux pas at the police station. She wasn't sure how Adam was going to handle it.

"Are we going to talk about what happened?" Adam asked, almost reading her mind.

"I wasn't thinking," Jenny said quickly. "You don't have to feel obligated."

"I don't," he assured her, taking hold of her hand.

"You have come to mean a lot to me, Jenny," he said hoarsely. "Maybe we should wait until we start assigning labels to this."

Jenny mentally sighed with relief.

"Whatever you are comfortable with," she said, bobbing her head.

"You know I'm not good with words," Adam said. "But I can feel what we have is special. I want to keep it that way."

"There's no rush, Adam." Jenny took a big sip of wine to bolster her courage.

"You are not going anywhere, are you?" Adam smiled. "Neither am I."

"That's right," Jenny agreed. "So we'll take it slow."

That seemed to clear the air. Adam asked for a second helping of pasta and they ate voraciously, doing full justice to the fine meal.

"Do you want to sit out on the patio?" Adam asked. "It's a fine night."

They stepped out into the garden, Jenny stopping to get a wrap for herself. The contractors had finished installing all the features in the garden. They sat on a swing, watching the gurgling stone fountain, the gold and russet fallen leaves and the ocean waves crashing against the shore.

"I hear the read-a-thon is a success?" Adam spoke, twirling a strand of Jenny's hair in his fingers.

"How could it not be? It's Barb Norton's pet project."

"What about your projects? Have you done anything to find that missing girl?"

Jenny had put some things in motion. But for the first time, she didn't expect anything to materialize out of her efforts.

"I am pretty sure that girl does not exist."

"Did you tell that to her mother?"

"You think I should have? I think the woman is prepared for any outcome. She just needs closure. Maybe you can give it to her when you get an update on Mrs. Bones."

"Why are you so sure about this?"

"Keith had to be involved." Jenny shook her head. "Ann and Ricky knew about that girl. Keith was obsessed with her, madly in love."

"Why would he kill her then?"

"We're back to the same point."

"Motive is important, Jenny. If Keith was so much in love with that girl, why did he kill her?"

"I don't have an answer for that. But he came here, didn't he? He came here because of the skeleton. I am sure about it. Something spooked him."

"He might have thought like you. He thought the skeleton was his girlfriend. He came here to find out."

"Who else would have wanted her dead?"

"What about her family?" Adam asked.

"Her family knew nothing about Keith, or so they say. In their eyes, she was a good girl who sang in the choir and was going to an Ivy League college."

"Learning about her real life would have been a shock," Adam pointed out. "What if they killed her in a fit of anger?"

"And did what? Brought her here? Why? To put the blame on Keith?"

"As long as we are considering wild theories," Adam said drily, "think about this. What if they followed her here? They found her with Keith. There was some kind of fight and the girl died."

"What about Keith? Think he would have kept quiet about it all these years?"

"They could have forced him to," Adam said thoughtfully. "Maybe that's why he came here. Once they found her, there was no need for him to keep the secret."

"Keith was in deep shock after Emily went missing. Ann said he started doing drugs after that. He spent his life roaming around the country, possibly looking for his Emily."

"Poor guy," Adam sighed.

He settled into the swing and put an arm around Jenny's shoulders.

"You think love lasts a lifetime?"

Jenny thought of the twenty years she had spent worshipping her ex-husband. Her whole life had revolved around him.

"I used to," she murmured. "Now I'm not so sure."

"What about the Davises?" Adam asked after a while. "Any idea why they are sticking around in town?"

"I know, right? What are they doing here for so long? Ricky says they are taking a vacation. But why now, after all these years?"

"How is it you haven't suspected Ricky yet?" Adam asked with a smile.

"I don't trust him." Jenny decided she had to tell Adam about Ricky's alibi. "He was here in town just before Keith died."

"What are you saying?" Adam asked sharply. "Are you sure?"

"Eddie Cotton told me. Ricky was at the Rusty Anchor with Keith."

"When were you planning on telling me?"

"I was going to," Jenny apologized. "But I know you believe the suicide theory."

"I still do, but this might be worth looking into."

"I feel we don't know enough about Emily Turner."

"I thought there was plenty of information about her."

"It's not enough." Jenny believed Emily would provide the missing piece of the puzzle. "Look, we know Keith loved Emily. He carried her picture in a locket for twenty five years. But did Emily love him?"

"What are you getting at now?" Adam asked.

"What if Keith's attentions were unwanted. Emily felt trapped and ran away."

"She could just have filed a complaint for harassment," Adam said, dismissing the idea. "Or talked to her parents."

"She was sixteen, Adam. She must have been scared out of her wits."

"So what? She ran away from home? That doesn't make sense."

"Keith must have known where she lived. Wouldn't he have gone there looking for her?"

"If he did, her parents would have known about him."

Jenny thought about Mrs. Turner and the photos on her mantel. Emily had been her perfect little angel. Had the woman managed to shut out anything unpleasant about her daughter?

"How do you feel about a little road trip?" Jenny asked.

"You think a man in uniform might make them talk?" Adam asked.

Jenny smiled and hoped Adam would remember his promise the next day.

Chapter 21

Jenny and Petunia started baking at 5 AM. They had a few trays of muffins and donuts ready for the concession stand before the usual breakfast rush started.

Jason came in with Kandy. She wasn't wearing one of her power suits for a change.

"We thought we would get breakfast here. We are going to read for the rest of the day."

"How about those famous crab omelets?" Kandy asked with childlike enthusiasm. "Jason can't stop raving about them."

"Can I talk to you?" Jenny asked Jason after serving them. "It's about Keith."

"Sure." Jason sprinkled some Old Bay seasoning on his fluffy omelet and cut a piece. "What's on your mind?"

"Someone mentioned Keith had a trust fund. Who gets all that money now that he's gone?"

"It depends," Kandy spoke up. "Did he have a will?"

Jenny wasn't too pleased with the interruption. She tried to hide her displeasure.

"We don't know anything about it."

"His father's still alive, right? If Keith didn't make a will, his father gets it all as next of kin."

"But he's incapacitated," Jenny reminded Jason.

"Well, in that case, the money will eventually go to whoever the old man's heir is. He might have appointed a trustee to handle his estate."

"Someone like Ricky Davis?"

"Could be anyone," Jason shrugged.

"So Ricky could be coming into a lot of money now that Keith is dead."

"You think Ricky Davis killed Keith for his money?" Jason asked skeptically. "Sounds farfetched to me."

Jenny agreed. She was beginning to think Keith's death was going to remain a mystery. Her gut feeling told her his killer was still out there. She wasn't ready to accept he had taken his own life.

"What are you planning to read?" Jenny asked Kandy. "Not law books?"

Kandy assured her she had a list of bestsellers she needed to catch up on. Jason and Kandy walked out of the café, arm in arm. Jenny felt a tiny twinge of jealousy but she ignored it.

"Are you ready?" Petunia asked.

Petunia had hired a few people to carry the food over to the concession stand. There was a big rush for breakfast before the first reading session started. Jenny put in a few hours, reading her old favorite - Treasure Island.

Adam sauntered over just as the lunch rush was winding down.

"Someone mentioned a road trip."

"Can we grab a bite first?" Jenny's feet ached and her stomach grumbled.

"Do you want to eat at Ethan's?" Adam asked.

"Tempting, but this will be quicker. Let me make a sandwich for us."

They sat on the deck, eating the chicken salad sandwiches Jenny had quickly put together. She packed two cupcakes for the road and poured fresh coffee into travel mugs.

Adam looked at Jenny as they drove out of town.

"Have you thought about what you want to ask them?"

"I'm going to wing it. I want to make her open up. Let's hope your presence does that."

"Are you saying I am intimidating?" Adam teased. "You talk like I'm an ogre or something."

"If they are hiding something, the sight of your uniform might rattle them."

"I checked with the forensics lab. They are running tests on your Mrs. Bones. We should know something soon."

Jenny hadn't called ahead. It was all part of her plan to catch Mrs. Turner at a disadvantage. She hoped the woman would be home.

Mrs. Turner stared at them with puffy eyes when she opened the door. She shivered when she spied Adam.

"Have you found her?" she gasped. "Have you found my Emily?"

Jenny hastened to explain.

"Calm down, Mrs. Turner. We are just here to ask you some questions."

The woman stumbled as she led them inside. Jenny held her by the shoulders and led her to a chair. The woman looked like she had been crying. An empty box of Kleenex lay toppled on the coffee table. A bunch of crumpled tissues littered the carpet and the couch.

"Have we come at a bad time?" Jenny asked nervously. "I am sorry we didn't call ahead."

All her bravado had deserted Jenny. She could almost feel the pain radiating from the older woman. Jenny wasn't sure how she could console her.

"Today's her birthday," the woman broke out in a sob. "My baby's birthday. She would have been 42." She looked up at Jenny. "About your age, I think."

The woman was off by a few years but Jenny didn't correct her.

"Do you celebrate her birthday every year?" Jenny asked.

She was really curious.

"We used to, for a few years." Mrs. Turner had pulled herself together. She pulled a fresh box of tissues from under a table and dabbed at her eyes. "Now I just bake a cake. My husband finds it silly, you know."

"That sounds wonderful," Jenny said, trying to cheer her up. "Did she like cake?"

"She loved desserts," Mrs. Turner said, brightening up. "She wanted red velvet cake for her birthday every year." A fresh stream of tears rolled down the woman's eyes. "Red was her favorite color."

Adam coughed and cleared his throat. Jenny imagined he was feeling uncomfortable with this open display of grief. Jenny debated going back home without asking any of her questions. She didn't want to prey on a helpless woman. Then she told herself she had to be strong if she wanted to find out the truth.

"Can I get you something?" Jenny asked Mrs. Turner. "How about a cup of tea?"

The woman led Jenny inside. They came back a few minutes later, carrying a tray loaded with a teapot and some cups. Jenny poured the tea and handed it around. Mrs. Turner looked better after a few sips.

"I hope you will pardon me," she began. "I'm sorry you had to see all this drama."

Jenny assured her she understood.

"What brings you here?" Mrs. Turner asked. "Have you found something?"

Her eyes filled with anticipation and she leaned forward eagerly.

Jenny shook her head sadly.

"It's too soon, Mrs. Turner. I had some more questions for you. I can come back later if you don't feel up to answering them now."

"I already told you everything about Emily."

Jenny nodded at Adam. He pulled out the chain from his pocket and handed it over.

"Have you seen this before?" Jenny asked.

Mrs. Turner took the chain from Jenny and looked at it.

"Looks like some cheap trinket. What does this have to do with my Emily?"

"Why don't you open that locket?" Jenny asked.

The woman found the clasp and the locket sprang open. Her eyes popped out of their sockets as she spotted the photo inside.

"Emily!" she whispered hoarsely.

Her head sprang up and her gaze moved sharply between Adam and Jenny.

"Where did you get this?"

"Do you confirm this is your daughter, Mrs. Turner?" Adam asked.

"Yes, Yes," the woman almost screamed. "This is my daughter Emily."

"We recently had a suspicious death in Pelican Cove," Adam explained. "This chain was found in the dead man's room. We are guessing he must have known your daughter."

"Dead man?" the woman mumbled.

She looked so bewildered Jenny had to believe her surprise was real.

"His name was Keith Bennet," she said, watching Mrs. Turner keenly. "He used to live in Pelican Cove."

"Keith …" the woman muttered. "How could it be?"

"Did you know him?" Jenny asked sharply. "Did you know Keith Bennet, Mrs. Turner?"

Mrs. Turner gave a slight nod.

"We heard that he was in love with your daughter. In fact, he loved her so much that his life went awry when your daughter disappeared. He started taking drugs. He drifted around, possibly searching for her. Do you know any of this?"

"You don't have to tell us anything," Adam warned. "But we need to know the whole truth if you want us to find your daughter."

Mrs. Turner looked like she was going to lose her composure again. But she pulled herself together.

"We knew she met someone from out of town," she admitted.

"Why didn't you tell me this before?" Jenny demanded.

"My daughter was perfect. Do you blame me if I want to preserve that memory?"

"Was she really perfect," Adam drawled, "or did you just want her to be?"

"How did a sixteen year old go meet a boy in a town ten miles away?" Jenny pressed.

"She hitched rides," Mrs. Turner said under her breath. "Emily met this boy somewhere. I don't know how. But he got into her head. He was older than her, almost 19. That makes a big difference at that age."

"You didn't approve?"

"We thought he was a bad influence."

"You said she hitched rides," Adam stepped in. "Do you realize how dangerous that can be? Did you tell that to the police when your daughter went missing?"

"We didn't want to tarnish her reputation," the woman said. "Look, Emily was a good little girl all her life. She followed the rules. Then she turned sixteen and everything changed for the worse. She started staying out beyond curfew. She didn't tell us anything."

"So age was the only thing you had against Keith?" Jenny asked.

"He was madly in love with her. You could say he was obsessed. We felt Emily was too young to seriously commit to anyone."

"What did Keith want? Wasn't he in college at that time?"

"He wanted to marry her," the woman burst out. "How ridiculous was that?"

Jenny wondered if Keith had always been a bit weird. Had Lily's disappearance pushed him off the edge?

"He had suffered some personal setbacks that year," Jenny told the woman.

"We knew that. We felt sorry for the boy. But what could we do?"

"Did he ever threaten Emily?"

"Not to my knowledge," the woman said. "Do you think he hurt my baby?"

"We can only speculate."

"Did Emily bring him here to meet you?" Jenny asked.

"No, she never told us about him."

"Then how did you find out?" Adam asked.

He had been following the conversation quietly.

"We tried to keep tabs on her," Mrs. Turner said. "We had to, once we learned she was going out of town without telling us."

"Did you have her followed?" Jenny asked, trying to hide her disgust.

The woman nodded.

"She didn't like it but what were we supposed to do? We wanted her to be safe."

"But the inevitable happened anyway," Jenny murmured. "So did you ever meet Keith?"

"He came here," Mrs. Turner explained. "Three days after she went missing, he came looking for her."

Jenny and Adam sat up.

"What did he want?" Jenny asked urgently.

"She was supposed to meet him one night but she never turned up. He thought we had held her back."

"Was that the first time you saw him?"

"Yes. We were surprised he came here. He thought we had sent Emily away. He begged us to let him meet her."

"Did you believe him?" Jenny asked eagerly. "Or did you think he was putting on an act?"

"My husband and son were convinced he had hidden her somewhere. But I thought he was telling the truth."

"Did you tell the police about him?"

The woman shook her head. Jenny wondered about how much the Turners had managed to keep from the police. Then she thought of Mrs. Bones and felt her heart race. If that was Emily, they would learn her fate soon enough. But would they ever find her killer?

She looked up at the mantle crowded with photos of a beloved daughter. Her gaze fell on an old black and white photo. A young boy and girl stood arm in arm, smiling into the camera. The face struck a chord with Jenny.

"Who's that?" she asked Mrs. Turner, walking over to the mantle to point at the photo frame.

"That's my son," the woman said proudly. "He is two years older than Emily. They were like two peas in a pod."

Chapter 22

Jenny could barely sit still on the ride home. She wanted to know what Adam was thinking.

"Do you agree he must be involved?"

"Hold your horses, Jenny," Adam cautioned. "Don't jump to conclusions without any proof."

"Are we going to get that proof?"

Adam looked grim as he took his foot off the gas pedal to accommodate a slow moving car.

"Why don't you leave this to the police now? You have done enough."

"I will gladly do that. Will you promise to look into this right away?"

"I need to sit down and revisit the whole thing."

Jenny rolled her eyes and turned her head to stare out of the window. Adam could try her patience. But at least he wasn't ruling out her theory like he usually did.

"You have to agree he had a motive?" she pressed Adam. "All this time, we hardly had any suspects. It's all clear now."

"So you think he took revenge," Adam sighed. "You think he would do something so dramatic after all these years?"

"He loved his sister. He has been grieving over her for twenty five years. It's like a wound that festers."

"If you're right about this, he could be dangerous." Adam was grim as he glanced at Jenny. "I want you to promise me you will stay out of this."

"Okay, Okay. I won't go looking for him."

"Try not to be alone," Adam continued. "Stay with Molly or Heather at all times."

"Are you going to lock me in a room now?"

Adam shook his head in frustration and muttered to himself.

"I just want you to be safe, Jenny. I don't want anything to happen to you."

"I'll take care," Jenny promised reluctantly.

Although she wasn't sure what she would do if she came face to face with the killer.

The read-a-thon was in full swing when they got back to Pelican Cove. There was a line at the concession stand and Petunia looked done in. Jenny hurried to relieve her.

Molly walked up, looking for something to eat. "I put in six hours since this morning," she bragged. "I need a break."

"Remember what I said," Adam reminded Jenny as he walked off to the station.

"You're hiding something," Molly squealed, peering at Jenny through her thick Coke-bottle glasses. "Spill it."

Jenny changed the topic by asking Molly what she had read.

"I already finished Pride and Prejudice, Emma and Mansfield Park. I am reading Persuasion now."

"So you're on track to win that Austen prize," Jenny said.

Molly was excited.

"Chris and I are looking forward to a romantic dinner in the city."

Barb Norton walked up with Dale in tow.

"Hey Jenny!" she exclaimed. "Anything left for us?"

She picked up a muffin and started peeling off the paper.

"You have done an excellent job with the food. Half the people said they came here to taste your desserts."

"Thanks for setting all this up, Barb," Jenny said sincerely.

The older women Jenny called friends were not too keen on Barb Norton. But Jenny could give credit where it was due. The success of the event proved Barb deserved any praise they could heap upon her.

Barb beamed up at Dale and patted his arm.

"This is my secret weapon. Dale has helped me so much, Jenny. You know he is the mastermind behind this whole concept. We would never have come up with such an event without Dale."

Dale seemed to puff up with pleasure. He kissed Barb on the cheek and grinned widely.

"The people of Pelican Cove really came through."

The look he directed at Jenny was full of admiration. Jenny smiled back, trying to gauge the real expression behind his baby blue eyes. Was she looking into the eyes of a killer?

There was a shout for help from the tent and Dale Turner walked away to handle it.

Ricky Davis came out of the tent, holding Ann's hand. They looked like they had been having a good time. Ann's face lit up when she spotted Jenny.

"How about some hot coffee, young lady?" she asked. "And I wouldn't mind one of those cakes. Reading is hungry business."

"Are you enjoying yourself?"

"Very much," Ann said happily. "Whoever put this thing together did a very good job."

Barb Norton sprang forward and introduced herself to Ann.

"I need to bring out a fresh batch of cupcakes," Jenny said to Ricky. "Walk with me?"

If Ricky had harmed Keith, confronting him was going to be dangerous. Jenny convinced herself her promise to Adam was limited to staying away from Dale.

"You lied to me, didn't you?" Jenny asked calmly, as she pulled out a fresh tray of cupcakes out of the big refrigerator.

"Huh, what?" Ricky stammered.

His face was mottled with red spots and sweat beaded his brow.

"You were spotted arguing with Keith just one day before he died. Are you going to deny that?"

Ricky leaned against a chair and sat down with a thud.

"Look, it's not what you think."

Jenny folded her arms and raised an eyebrow.

"I'm listening."

"We were in the area, visiting a cousin near Washington DC. Keith called me. I thought he was in trouble again."

"What did he want?"

"He insisted I come to Pelican Cove to talk to him."

Jenny pulled out a chair and sat down herself.

"What was so urgent?"

"That's how Keith was," Ricky said bitterly. "He was missing from the scene most of the time, but when he did turn up, he needed constant attention. You can say he demanded it."

"Why did you humor him?"

"He was the closest thing I had to a brother," Ricky said.

Jenny sensed regret in his voice.

"I loved him, despite what he turned out to be."

Jenny gave Ricky a few moments to settle down.

"What did he want this time, Ricky?"

Ricky smiled mirthlessly.

"This concerns you in a way. He wanted us to buy back Seaview."

Jenny thought of what the place meant to her.

"I would never have done that."

"He told me he was working on you. He was very confident he would convince you to sell."

"He told me the house was jinxed and it would bring me a lot of grief."

"That was his way of trying to scare you into submission."

"So my hunch was right. You sold the house to me without Keith's permission."

"It wasn't like that. He never cared about the place. He never expressed any affection for it."

Jenny didn't think Ricky was lying this time.

"So that's what the argument was about? Seaview?"

"Keith told me about the skeleton they found in your garden," Ricky said reluctantly. "He was convinced it was Emily."

"So that's why he came here to Pelican Cove!" Jenny exclaimed. "What happened afterwards?"

"I tried to convince him to go back with me. He said he had unfinished business. I told him Emily was gone and he needed to move on. That didn't sit too well with him."

Ricky told her they parted ways after that. Ricky drove back to his cousin's home, hoping Keith would come to his senses and join them there. Two days later, Keith was dead.

Jenny was too exhausted to go out for her walk on the beach that night. The final day of the read-a-thon brought a hefty crowd of tourists to town. Jenny scurried around, working in the kitchen, dishing out food and volunteering some reading time in between.

A small stage had been set up to announce all the prizes. Betty Sue sat on the stage, next to Ada Newbury. Dale sat next to them, wearing a suit and looking important.

Barb gave away all the small prizes and announced the total numbers. A cheer went up through the crowd. Jenny spotted Adam moving through the crowd, along with two policemen. They handcuffed Dale and took him along with them.

Jenny was hopping with excitement, wondering what was going on. Adam came to talk to her. Heather, Molly and Chris stood next to Jenny, wondering what was going on.

"We did some good old fashioned police work," Adam told them. "Dale was found stalking Keith a couple of times. He was very bold. Molly's neighbor, old Mrs. Daft, spotted him going up the stairs to Keith's room."

"Do you think he will confess?" Jenny asked with concern.

She need not have worried. Faced with all the evidence against him, Dale started talking.

Adam held Jenny's hand as they walked on the beach that night. They both wore sweaters to ward off the chill.

"Why did he do it?"

"Justice for his sister," Adam said. "Just like you thought."

"So he always suspected Keith?"

"He used to follow them years ago," Adam explained. "Just to keep an eye on his sister."

"That sounds creepy."

"Emily was really young, I guess. If the twins had fixated on some older boy when they were sixteen, I might have done the same."

Jenny knew Adam was right. Parents always wanted to protect their children from wrongdoing.

"Dale read about the skeleton they dug up at your house. He had his suspicions. He came to town offering to help with the read-a-thon. He saw Keith at your café. All the memories came flooding back."

"Did he confront him?" Jenny asked. "Did he give him a chance to defend himself?"

"Dale wanted Keith to admit he killed Emily. Keith maintained he was innocent. Dale worked himself into a frenzy. He went to Keith's room. Keith was lying asleep with a syringe by his bedside. The temptation was too much for Dale."

"Does he regret it?"

"He thinks he got justice for Emily."

Jenny told Adam about the message she had received that day. She had a hunch about what was coming.

A middle aged woman walked into the Boardwalk Café two days later. Her brown hair was faded and streaked with gray. The crow's feet around her eyes made her look a lot older than she was. She sat down at a table near the window.

Jenny walked up to her with a tray of coffee and muffins.

"How was your drive?" she asked.

"Nostalgic." The woman smiled drily.

"I'm glad you decided to come here, Emily."

Emily Turner looked at Jenny with eyes as blue as her brother's.

"I think I've done enough damage. If only I had come to my senses a few weeks ago, or a few months ago."

"Are you ready to talk about it?" Jenny asked gently.

"There's not much to say." Emily's voice was heavy with sadness. "I was a headstrong sixteen year old with stars in my eyes. I was attracted by the bright lights. I wanted to be a rock star."

"Your mother knew none of this?"

"My parents thought I was their pretty little girl. They didn't want me to grow up. I was tired of living up to their expectations."

"Parents only want the best for their kids," Jenny said softly.

Emily shrugged.

"What did I know? Then there was Keith. He followed me around like a puppy. He wanted to marry me. I wasn't going to marry him at sixteen! And what, throw my life away cooking and cleaning for him?"

"So you planned it all?"

"I used to hitch rides to come to Pelican Cove," Emily told Jenny. "I met a group of musicians. They traveled around the country, playing gigs in small towns. They heard me sing and offered to take me on."

"You fell for it."

"I was so hemmed in, you know. I felt trapped between my parents and Keith. I just wanted to fly and spread my wings."

"Why didn't you ever call? Let them know you were okay? Your mom still cries for you."

"I came to my senses just weeks after I left. My life went downhill. I got pregnant and lost the baby. Then I got into drugs. I couldn't face my parents after all that."

"So the time was never right." Jenny felt sorry for the woman sitting before her.

"What's the use of coming back now?" Emily asked in an anguished voice. "I can't save Dale."

"Your mother's still waiting for you," Jenny told her. "She just wants to know you are okay."

"Were you confident I would come back?"

Jenny thought of the ads she had strategically placed in the local newspapers.

"Actually, I was convinced you were buried in my backyard."

Epilogue

The town of Pelican Cove was ablaze with the splendor of fall. The trees were painted in an array of bright colors, the reds, golds and yellows forming a sharp contrast to the blue-green ocean and the cerulean blue skies.

A party was in progress in Jenny's garden. The roses bloomed at Seaview and their scent mingled with the salty breeze coming off the ocean. The new water fountain gurgled merrily, spraying anyone who ventured close with a fine mist.

Jenny's son Nick had come home for the party. He was arguing about something with Adam's twins. Heather pouted in a corner, sulking because Jenny hadn't invited Gianni Costa to the party.

"He's a doctor!" she wailed. "Aren't you all happy I'm dating a doctor?"

"He's fifteen years older than you, girl," Betty Sue snapped. "Find someone closer to your age."

"He looks shady to me," Star added. "He wears more diamonds than I do."

The women laughed at that.

Jenny brought out a big platter of nachos. She had kept the menu simple. A taco bar had been set up with all the fixings. She was ready to put her feet up and drink fresh apple cider laced with spiced rum.

"So, you did it again, Jenny!" Jason Stone said, raising his glass at her.

Kandy was nowhere to be seen. Jenny had invited her for Jason's sake but she was busy working on a big case.

"Did Emily Turner go home?" Molly asked.

She sat next to Chris, her hand resting in his lap.

"She did," Jenny told them. "Her mother was overjoyed to see her. They are busy catching up."

"Ann was really generous, wasn't she?" Molly gushed.

Ann Davis had written a big fat check for the library. Coupled with the money raised from the read-a-thon and the amount promised by Ada Newbury, the library was now flush with funds.

"I don't have to worry about my job for at least three years," Molly said happily. "Dale Turner did something good after all."

"I don't know about that!" Jenny said uncertainly.

A phone rang somewhere. Adam walked over to a jacket lying on a chair and pulled his phone out. His face settled into a frown as he listened to the voice at the other end. He let out an expletive as he shut off the phone.

"That was my contractor," he told Jenny. "They are projecting a month to get all the work done."

Adam's roof had collapsed a couple of days ago. The twins hadn't been home and luckily, Adam himself hadn't been hurt. Jenny had invited him to stay at Seaview until he got his house back.

"I can't impose on you that long, Jenny," Adam protested.

"Why not?" Jenny asked with a smile. "There's plenty of room. And I like having you here."

"I live here too," Star said sternly. "So don't get any ideas."

She threw back her head and laughed. Jimmy Parsons laughed along with her.

"At least let me pay rent," Adam insisted.

"Now why didn't I think of that?" Jenny said mischievously. "I'll let you know how much you owe me, Adam Hopkins."

Adam looked scandalized.

"So we still don't know who Mrs. Bones is, do we?" Heather asked.

"Hush, girl. Think before you speak." Betty Sue glanced fearfully at the stone fountain.

"All we know is it was a woman around fifty years old. Right, Adam?" Star had no qualms talking about the skeleton.

"That's correct." Adam and Jenny were sitting on a wicker sofa, munching on nachos. "She's been buried for thirty years, give or take a few."

"I've been thinking about this," Jenny told the others. "It's just a hunch, but I think I'm right."

Nick and the twins stopped arguing and looked at her.

"Think about it." Jenny widened her eyes as she stared around the group of people. "A fiftyish woman who lived around here twenty five or thirty years ago? A woman who was never seen again?"

Betty Sue's face turned ashen and tiny beads of sweat appeared on her upper lip.

"You don't mean …?" she stared at Jenny helplessly.

Jenny nodded at Betty Sue, a sad expression in her eyes.

"Lily!" Betty Sue spoke under her breath.

"Lily?" Heather exclaimed indelicately. "But she ran away with her lover."

"Did she?" Jenny voiced the question running through everyone's minds.

THE END

Waffles and Weekends – Pelican Cove Cozy Mystery Series Book 5

By Leena Clover

Chapter 1

Jenny King's cheeks flamed with embarrassment as she observed her friend Heather over the rim of her wine glass.

It was Valentine's weekend and the four couples had met for dinner at The Steakhouse, Pelican Cove's only fancy restaurant. Jenny, Heather and Molly were close friends. Jenny considered Jason Stone a friend too. He was the only lawyer in Pelican Cove and was currently dating another lawyer from the city. He had pursued Jenny for a while after she came to live in Pelican Cove. But Jenny had made her choice. She looked up into the blue eyes of her date. Adam Hopkins, the sheriff of Pelican Cove smiled back at her.

Heather Morse cuddled with a man much older than herself. She had been dating Gianni Costa, Dr. Gianni Costa, for the past few months. The flamboyant fiftyish man had set up shop as soon as he moved to the small seaside town. He flirted outrageously with his patients, most of whom were older ladies who liked being flattered by the silver-tongued Casanova.

Jenny watched as Heather engaged in behavior her grandmother would not approve of. Adam nudged her and cleared his throat.

"What did you do last night?" Jenny asked her friend Molly.

"Chris and I had a romantic dinner at home. We didn't want to spend our first Valentine's Day at a restaurant."

"We went for a canoe ride after that," Chris beamed, looking lovingly at Molly. "Molly loves those."

Jason's date spoke up.

"We went to a hot new restaurant in town. I know the chef personally. He's about to get his first Michelin star."

"The weekend's going great, then," Jenny said happily. "Don't forget you are all coming to Seaview tomorrow."

"Isn't it a bit cold for a barbecue?" Kandy, the city lawyer, asked.

"We'll have a fire going in the pit," Jason assured her. "Seaview is a great place to be, any time of the year."

Jenny still couldn't believe she was the proud owner of a sea facing mansion. Dumped by her husband of twenty years, she had grabbed her aunt's invitation like a lifeline and come to visit her in the small seaside town of Pelican Cove. A barrier island off the coast of Virginia, Pelican Cove was the perfect place to lick her wounds. Jenny's aunt Star had let her wallow for a few weeks and urged her to start working at the local café. Neither of them knew she was going to be a big success.

Jenny had started baking and cooking with the local produce and turned the Boardwalk Café around. Tourists flocked to the café to taste the delectable treats Jenny created on a regular basis.

"Your parties are legendary, Jenny," Heather nodded. "Gianni and I can't wait for tomorrow."

"Have you settled in at Seaview?" Molly asked Jenny.

Jenny had been charmed by the big three story house adjoining her aunt's cottage. She had bought the house with her divorce settlement and spent a big sum of money renovating it. The discovery of a skeleton in her garden had been unexpected. But Jenny had soldiered on and moved into the house with her aunt.

"It's a great house," Jenny told her friend. "I'm loving it more each day."

"And having Adam there helps," Heather remarked with a wink.

When Jenny first came to Pelican Cove, Adam and Jason had both fallen for her. Jenny found herself pursued by two handsome, eligible men. They were as different as chalk and cheese. Jenny had chosen to date Adam, the more unpredictable of the two.

"Adam's living on the third floor," Jenny said curtly. "It's not what you think."

"Why do you protest so much?" Heather pouted. "I don't care where he lives. By the way, as far as appearances go, you two live in the same house."

Adam grew uncomfortable. He tucked a finger in his collar and tried to loosen it. His roof had fallen in a few weeks ago and he had been forced to move out. Jenny had insisted he stay at Seaview until his house was fixed. Their living arrangement had set tongues wagging. Jenny told him she didn't care what people said.

"Let's not talk about 'appearances', Heather," Jenny fumed.

"Simmer down, you two," Jason Stone said lightly. He gave Jenny a knowing look. "Are you denying you and Adam are a couple?"

"Jenny's just being a good friend," Adam protested. "I would have come and lived with you, Jason. But you didn't offer."

Dr. Gianni Costa looked bored with the conversation.

"Basta!" he exclaimed. "How about another round of drinks? They are on me."

He ordered an expensive bottle of wine for the table. Dr. Costa had plenty of money and he believed in spending it.

"I am looking forward to this party at your home," he told Jenny. "I want to see this spot where they found that skeleton."

"There's nothing to look at there," Jenny said bluntly. "We put a water fountain on the spot."

The bottle of wine arrived and Dr. Costa and Heather drank most of it. He insisted on getting the check.

"My treat," he told the others. "You can pay next time."

Heather stumbled out of the restaurant with the good doctor, both of them swaying a bit.

"I hope you're not driving," Adam said anxiously. "Can I give you a ride somewhere?"

He had opted to be the designated driver for the group.

"We want to walk home," Heather slurred. "It's such a beautiful night."

"Not more beautiful than you, my pet," Gianni Costa murmured.

He clutched Heather's hand in his and waved goodbye to the group.

"Ciao friends," he cried with a big smile on his face. "Heather and I have our own little party planned."

He took a couple of steps and stumbled. He let out a burp and Heather giggled.

"You're totally wasted, Heather," Jenny clucked, shaking her head. "Maybe we should see you home safely."

"I'm going to Gianni's," Heather whispered in her ear. "You go have fun with Adam."

There was another round of goodbyes and the group finally dispersed. Adam drove Chris and Molly home.

"You think she'll be alright?" Molly asked Jenny.

"She's thirty five, Molls, not thirteen," Jenny said with a sigh. "I think she can take care of herself."

"Heather's changed a lot, hasn't she?" Chris muttered.

Chris Williams had been in love with Heather Morse since third grade. Everyone knew they had an understanding. Heather had shocked everyone the previous summer by deciding to date other people. Chris had found himself falling for Molly, the shy, soft spoken librarian. Chris and Molly found they had a deep connection. They were very much in love.

"What does Heather see in Gianni?" Jenny wondered, her frustration evident in her voice.

Jenny and Adam watched a movie after getting home. Adam had let her pick Casablanca in honor of the special weekend.

Jenny hummed a tune as she mixed some batter for her special waffles the next morning. The café opened a bit later than usual on Sunday. Most of her regular customers turned up for breakfast, eager to indulge in whatever sinful treat Jenny dished up.

Jenny greeted Captain Charlie as she threw open the doors of the café. He was her favorite customer, always first in line when the café opened.

"Got those waffles?" he asked her. "I've been dreaming about having them for breakfast."

Jenny brought out a platter with hot waffles drizzled with a fresh berry sauce. Captain Charlie smacked his lips as he cut into his food.

"Delicious!" he pronounced after the first bite.

"Do you want chocolate sauce too?" Jenny asked him. "Or some chocolate covered strawberries? I saved some for you."

Jenny chatted with people as she offered them a choice of fresh berry sauce or melted chocolate to top their waffles. Some opted for both.

Jenny's friends began walking in around eleven. They were an odd group of women, young and old. Betty Sue Morse, Heather's grandmother, was the unopposed leader of the pack. She was a force to reckon with even in her eighties. Jenny's aunt Star and café owner Petunia Clark formed the rest of the old guard. Jenny, Molly and Heather provided the young blood, although at 45, Jenny was much older than Heather and Molly. The ladies called themselves the Magnolias and met at the café every morning.

Betty Sue was busy with her knitting as usual. All the Magnolias were dressed warmly because they wanted to sit out on the deck. The café's deck sat right on the sand, facing the Atlantic Ocean.

"How was Valentine's Day?" Betty Sue's voice boomed. "I hope you girls are behaving yourself?"

Molly blushed prettily, making Petunia and Star laugh.

"Chris and I can't wait for the barbecue at Jenny's," Molly said. "You are coming, aren't you, Betty Sue?"

"Of course I am," Betty Sue nodded. "I am looking forward to it."

"Why don't you invite John?" Star asked.

John Newbury was Betty Sue's estranged husband. Betty Sue turned red at the mention of his name.

"Why would I do that?" she sputtered.

"It is Valentine's weekend," Star teased. "Don't you want to spend some time with your honey?"

The older ladies proceeded to tease Betty Sue mercilessly. Jenny thought it was cute how Betty Sue broke out in a sweat every time her husband was mentioned.

"Where's Heather?" Molly asked innocently.

Jenny shook her head meaningfully and tried to warn Molly. But Betty Sue had already heard her.

"She's fast asleep in her bed," Betty Sue complained. "Wouldn't budge. I had to take Tootsie for her walk myself." She looked at Jenny and Molly inquiringly. "How come you two look so fresh? Didn't Heather get any sleep at all last night?"

Jenny hastily changed the subject.

"Did Chris give you a gift, Molly?"

Molly leaned forward and showed them a new pair of earrings she was wearing. The ladies exclaimed over the heart shaped jewelry.

"Did Adam get you anything?" Molly asked.

Jenny smiled and shook her head. She hadn't expected fancy jewelry but she had hoped Adam would get her a memento of some kind. He had brought her breakfast in bed, along with a posy of her favorite roses from the garden at Seaview. Jenny told herself she didn't need fancy gifts. She had received enough of those from her ex-husband. They had meant nothing in the end.

She felt her heart skip a beat and looked around. Adam strode along the beach and ran up the café steps.

"Hello ladies," he greeted them.

His eyes softened as they met Jenny's. Adam looked apologetic. Jenny knew that look. She braced herself for what Adam would say next.

"Where is Heather?" Adam asked Betty Sue.

"Don't ask!" Betty Sue said with a roll of her eyes. "She's sleeping like the dead."

"Funny you should say that," Adam said tersely.

The Magnolias were staring at him now.

"Spit it out," Star said. "You have some bad news."

"Gianni died in his sleep last night."

A collective gasp went through the group.

"Are you sure?" Molly burst out. "Maybe he's just passed out."

"I am sure, Molly," Adam said with a sigh. "I need to talk to Heather."

Jenny sat down with a thump. They had all seen Heather go home with Gianni Costa. She had probably been the last person to see him alive. One of the last people, Jenny corrected herself.

"How did he die?" she asked Adam fearfully.

Adam's brow furrowed as he answered her.

"It's too early to say, but looks like he was drugged."

Betty Sue had put her knitting down for a change. She had been trying to get a word in.

"What does Heather have to do with that flashy doctor? She barely knew him."

Chapter 2

Jenny walked to the police station with a wicker basket on her arm. The lunch rush at the café had died down and she was off to have lunch with Adam. She had packed chicken rolls and slices of carrot cake.

Adam Hopkins sat with one leg propped up on a chair. He was a veteran who had been deployed in war zones. He had been shot in the leg and still struggled with the old injury. He had a mercurial temper which flared every time his leg bothered him.

"How are you, Jenny?" He had a special smile for her.

Although Adam and Jenny lived in the same house, their work schedules were such that they barely saw each other.

"Hungry?" Jenny asked, unpacking the basket.

Adam took a big bite of the roll and gave her a thumbs up.

"Yum! What is it?"

"It's a new Asian style chicken recipe I am trying out," Jenny explained, taking a dainty bite of her own sandwich.

They made some small talk while they ate. Adam finally polished off the last bite of cake and wiped his mouth with a tissue. He gave Jenny a grave look.

"I got some news about Mrs. Bones."

'Mrs. Bones' was the nickname Jenny and the girls had assigned the skeleton that had been discovered in Jenny's backyard. For a long time, Jenny and her friends had believed that the skeleton belonged to a missing girl from the area. That theory had been shot down. Now Jenny suspected something else.

"Tell me, quick."

"It's a woman, as you already know," Adam began. "A woman about fifty years old. She's been buried for thirty some years."

"Anything else?" Jenny asked with bated breath.

"They found a broken collar bone, probably a childhood injury."

Jenny's eyes shone with excitement.

"Finally, something we can verify. Betty Sue might know about this."

"Do you really believe that's Lily?" Adam asked.

Jenny nodded sadly. The tragic history of Seaview flashed before her eyes. Seaview had been home to the Davis family, one of the pioneer families of Pelican Cove. Old man Davis had lived there with his entire family. A big storm had wiped out most of them, leaving only his daughter Lily, his son's wife and his grandson alive. Ann Davis, the son's wife, had taken her baby and Lily and moved away. Lily came back thirty years later with her husband and children. But tragedy struck again. Lily lost her daughter to a freak virus. Then Lily herself disappeared one night. The general impression in town had been that Lily abandoned her family and ran away with another man. As more information surfaced about the skeleton, Jenny was sure Lily had met an untimely end.

"She's the only fiftyish woman who went missing from these parts," Jenny reminded Adam. "And no one heard from her again."

"You know what you are implying?" Adam asked, leaning back in his chair.

He pulled a bottle of pills from a drawer and tried to unscrew the top. Jenny took the bottle and opened it for him.

"Lily was killed," Jenny said flatly. She looked impatient as Adam popped a couple of pills in his mouth and washed them down with a sip of water. "That's obvious, isn't it? She didn't bury herself in my garden."

"You may be right," Adam continued. "Someone bashed her head in."

"Poor Lily," Jenny mumbled.

"One more mystery for you to solve, huh?" Adam teased.

"Aren't you going to tell me to stay out of it?" Jenny asked with surprise.

Adam didn't like anyone meddling into police business. He and Jenny were often at odds with each other because of it.

"It's a cold case," Adam shrugged. "There's not much anyone can do."

"But Lily deserves justice!" Jenny argued.

Lily's son had died the previous year. Her husband was in a senior home in Texas. No one was going to come and ask the police to find Lily's murderer.

"Maybe you can do something about it," Adam said mildly.

"Are you actually giving me your blessing?" Jenny asked incredulously.

"Just be careful," Adam warned, "and keep me updated."

Jenny walked to the seafood market to shop for dinner. Chris Williams filled her order. They chatted for some time and Jenny walked home. Dinner was a lively affair with her aunt's special friend Jimmy Parsons joining them. Jimmy had been better known as the town drunk for several years. He had recently turned his life around and was dating her aunt. He spent a lot of his time at Seaview.

Jenny and Adam went for their usual walk on the beach after dinner. Jenny threw a ball for Tank, Adam's yellow Labrador. Tank had moved into Seaview with Adam. He adored Jenny and could be seen following her through the house, his tail wagging.

The next morning, Jenny couldn't wait to meet the Magnolias. She baked a fresh tray of banana nut muffins and had the coffee ready. Betty Sue arrived, her needles clacking with force as she took in the guests at the café. Heather followed behind, looking morose.

"How are you holding up, Heather?" Jenny asked.

Heather's eyes filled up.

"How would you be doing in my place?"

"I didn't know you were that close," Jenny sympathized. "I mean, sure, we know you had some fun with him. But did you actually care about him?"

"Of course I did," Heather cried. "Gianni made me happy."

Betty Sue refused to acknowledge Heather's connection to the dead doctor.

"Stop mooning around, girl," she ordered. "Pour me a cup of coffee."

Molly stumbled into the café, holding on to her Coke-bottle glasses. Star wasn't far behind.

"I can smell spring in the air," Star said as she doodled a drawing on a paper napkin.

Star was an artist who painted landscapes and seascapes. The tourists loved her work. She had a gallery in town and Jenny had helped her set up a website. Star worked hard in winter and spring to replenish her catalog. The tourist season would ramp up soon.

"Spring Fest is around the corner," Betty Sue reminded them. "We need to work on it."

"Barb's back early this year," Star observed.

Barb Norton was a local woman who took an active part in all the town events. She spent winter in Florida with her daughter but got back in time to organize the spring festival. The Magnolias liked to give her the cold shoulder but they had to admit she was resourceful.

"She'll be around soon enough," Petunia said softly.

"Can we talk about Mrs. Bones?" Jenny butted in. She had been trying to find the right moment to talk about Lily. "Did Lily ever have any accidents as a child, Betty Sue?"

Betty Sue paused from her knitting and narrowed her eyes.

"Lily was a hellion. My Daddy was quite strict with me but old man Davis let Lily roam around the island. She swam with the watermen's kids and could outrow them any day."

"So you two didn't play together?"

"I'm coming to it," Betty Sue said irritably. "Lily came to visit a lot. We could play in our yard but I wasn't allowed to go out with her."

Jenny wished Betty Sue would get on with her reminisces. She tried to curb her impatience.

"One afternoon, we snuck out and walked to one of the bluffs. Someone had tied a rope swing on an oak. I got sick just looking at it. Lily scrambled up and made me push the swing."

"Is this going anywhere?" Heather asked with a yawn.

Betty Sue barely heard her. She was lost in the memories of her childhood.

"Lily begged me to push harder every time. We were both yelling, Lily with abandon, me with fright. Suddenly, she flew in the air and crashed to the ground."

"She broke her collar bone, didn't she?" Jenny asked urgently.

Betty Sue's mouth dropped open.

"Don't interrupt, Jenny," Star quipped. "Let her finish."

"She's right," Betty Sue said, pointing a finger at Jenny. "I'll never forget that day. Lily had a nasty scrape on her chin and a broken bone. She was howling for hours. We were both grounded for weeks after that."

"Mrs. Bones has a fractured collar bone," Jenny said softly.

"So there's no doubt it's Lily?" Betty Sue asked sadly.

"It's beginning to look like that," Jenny said, placing her hand on Betty Sue's. "The police might run some more tests. Then we'll know for sure."

Betty Sue's face hardened as she looked at Jenny.

"I want you to clear Lily's name. They didn't just kill her. They destroyed her reputation."

"I'm going to do my best," Jenny promised her.

"What about Gianni?" Heather wailed. "Aren't you going to find out what happened to him?"

"Gianni Costa died in his sleep," Star snapped. "He had one drink too many."

Petunia seconded Star.

"What kind of doctor was he, anyway? He should have known when to stop."

"He didn't drink that much," Heather argued. "We all drank wine at the restaurant."

"What about after he got home?" Molly asked. "He must have had a few more drinks then."

Heather had no answer for that. She didn't remember much of what had happened after they reached Gianni's home. But she wasn't ready to admit that.

"You're all just bad-mouthing him," Heather insisted. "Jenny needs to find out the truth."

"Hold on, Heather," Jenny protested. "That's not my job. The police will look into it. What do you think I am? Some kind of detective?"

"It won't be the first time you solved a murder," Heather said sullenly.

"That was different," Jenny said.

"She's right," Betty Sue spoke up. "That doctor was a menace. Good riddance, I say."

"Grandma!" Heather cried. "You barely knew him."

"Jenny has her hands full with Mrs. Bones," Molly reiterated.

Heather opened her mouth to argue. A loud voice hailed them from the boardwalk.

"Yooohoooo …"

A short, plump woman scrambled up the café steps.

"Hello Barb," Star drawled. "The Spring Fest committee doesn't meet for three more days."

Barb Norton sat down next to Molly and tried to catch her breath. Jenny offered her a cup of coffee. She took a sip gratefully and looked around at the assembled women.

"Forget the Spring Fest."

"Are you stepping down as Chairperson?" Star asked eagerly. "It's my turn now, anyway."

Barb glared at Star.

"The Spring Fest will go ahead as planned. I am here on important business."

"What's got your panties in a wad?" Betty Sue thundered.

"Dire things are afoot, Betty Sue," Barb Norton said urgently. "We need to gather everyone for an emergency town meeting."

"What's the matter now?" Jenny asked.

Jenny had lived in a city most of her life. Small town politics was new to her. She was still amazed by how the people came together to discuss and dissect every small issue. There was a committee for everything, Jenny had found.

"Our very way of life is being threatened," Barb said dramatically.

She flung a finger at Betty Sue.

"Those Newburys are doing it again. And your husband is responsible."

"What is John doing now?" Betty Sue asked mildly.

"Drugs!" Barb declared, her bosom heaving. "The Newburys are getting into the drug business."

"What nonsense!" Betty Sue dismissed.

Jenny, Heather and Molly shared a swift glance. They were trying hard not to laugh. Barb Norton pounced on them.

"You find this funny?"

"Stop being fanciful, Barb," Star said curtly. "Get to the point."

"The Newburys are planting cannabis in their fields," Barb declared triumphantly. "They are going to sell it too, right here in town. John Newbury signed a lease on that empty store on the corner of Main. Eddie Cotton owns that store. He told me himself."

"Are they opening a medical marijuana dispensary?" Jenny asked.

"I don't care how they sugarcoat it," Barb sniffed. "We cannot have drugs in Pelican Cove."

Chapter 3

Jenny added a generous amount of ground cinnamon to her waffle batter. She added some orange zest to the berries bubbling away on the stove. She was fixing a special batch of her waffles based on Barb Norton's request. The Spring Fest committee had met the previous night but hadn't reached consensus on a single point. Jenny had suggested consulting Mandy. Everyone had agreed to that suggestion.

Mandy James was a consultant the town had hired before. She had helped them win the Prettiest Town in America tag. Jenny was sure she would have plenty of ideas about how to make Spring Fest bigger and better. A conference call had been set up and the ladies were going to gather in the café to talk to Mandy via video conference.

Jenny fussed over arranging the perfect plate of waffles and wished Heather would hurry. Barb wanted a picture of the waffles for the Spring Fest flyers. Jenny also wanted to post the picture on the town's Instagram page.

"Merchandise!" Mandy James said resolutely. "Anything you can think of – t-shirts, tote bags, baseball caps – something for everyone. You make money this year and get free advertising for the next. And swag! You need to give away swag."

Mandy was on a roll. The Magnolias groaned as Mandy rattled off one suggestion after another. They hadn't missed this aspect of her personality.

"Hold on, Mandy," Jenny said. "Heather's taking notes."

"Aren't you recording this?" Mandy asked.

"We prefer to take notes the old fashioned way," Barb Norton bristled. "Now tell us what this swag is."

Mandy spent a few minutes explaining how they could give away small items like pens or key chains with the town's logo on it.

"Get some big items for the raffle," Mandy ordered. "Everything should have the town's web address on it."

Jenny's mind was working furiously, thinking about ways to spread the word about the Boardwalk Café.

"Why don't we get some special tees printed?" she asked Petunia. "We can put a pretty picture on them, like these waffles, along with our name and address."

"Whatever you think is right, dear," she said uncertainly.

Jenny turned toward the screen and spoke to Mandy.

"What about having a concert on the beach? I know you shot my suggestion down last time, but the Spring Fest seems like a good time for some music."

"That's an excellent idea, Jenny," Mandy approved. "Why don't you start contacting a few bands?"

Barb started working on the waffles while the women threw ideas around.

"You don't know what you are missing," she told Mandy. "When are you coming for a visit? Jenny's come up with plenty of yummy recipes since you left."

"Let me check my calendar," Mandy said seriously. "I will try to make it there for the Spring Fest. No promises, though."

Heather sat with a camera in her lap, staring into space. Molly nudged Jenny and tipped her head at Heather.

"We need to do something," she hissed.

"Looks like she's really grieving for Gianni," Jenny shrugged. "We need to get her out of this funk."

"How about a trip to the city?" Molly asked. "Let's catch a movie and get her favorite dinner."

The girls decided to talk to Heather after the conference call ended. Barb Norton made Jenny fix a fresh plate of waffles and ordered Heather to take a few dozen photos from all angles. She went off on another mission after that. The girls finally heaved a sigh of relief.

Heather didn't want to go to the city.

"How can I enjoy a movie when my sweetie just died?" she wailed. "How heartless do you think I am?"

"How about a visit to the spa?" Jenny offered. "My treat."

"Have you been biting these?" Molly asked, picking up Heather's hand and peering at her nails.

Vanity won and Heather agreed to tag along to the spa. Molly chattered continuously as Jenny drove off the bridge that connected the island of Pelican Cove to the mainland. Heather stared out of the window, tears streaming down her cheeks. Jenny gave her a worried glance.

"You need to pull yourself together, Heather."

Heather pulled out a few tissues from a box on the dashboard. She blew her nose and nodded wordlessly.

"I didn't realize you were so attached to him," Jenny continued.

"Gianni cared about me. I might have had a future with him."

Jenny bit her lip and forced herself to stay quiet. Had Heather really been thinking about marrying a man fifteen years her senior? She thought of the flamboyant doctor with his flashy clothes and diamond earring. His shirt had been unbuttoned every time Jenny met him, exposing his hairy chest.

"You'll find someone else," Molly soothed.

Molly's comment didn't go down well. Jenny believed Heather hadn't forgiven Molly for hooking up with Chris.

"You take as much time as you need, Heather," Jenny said diplomatically. "We can put up your profile on that dating site again."

"It's a mobile app," Heather corrected her. "No one uses websites anymore."

"Why don't we take a new photo after our spa visit, hmm?" Jenny soothed.

Heather seemed to rally around a bit after that. They chose a three hour package at the spa. Jenny found herself relaxing after a long time as she let herself be scrubbed and massaged. They went to Heather's favorite restaurant overlooking the Chesapeake Bay for a late lunch.

"I'm starving," Heather said. "I'm getting the blackened sea bass."

The girls ordered different entrees and switched them around after a few bites. Jenny couldn't resist ordering the bourbon pecan pie for dessert.

"Thanks for doing this, girls," Heather said on the way back. "I almost feel human."

Jenny squeezed Heather's hand.

"We're here for you, sweetie. Just let us know what you need."

Jason was sitting out on the patio with Star when Jenny got home. She was happy to see him.

"Jason!" she exclaimed happily. "We hardly see you anymore."

Jason sprang up and hugged Jenny. "You're glowing, Jenny."

"After what I spent at that spa, I better," Jenny joked. "What brings you here?"

"Kandy's busy with a case," he told them. "And I've cleared my desk too for a change. So I thought I would enjoy an evening at Seaview."

"You're always welcome here," Star said warmly.

She had a soft corner for Jason and preferred him over Adam. She made sure she told Jenny about it plenty of times.

"Is Adam home yet?" Jenny asked.

"He just left," Star said gleefully. "He's working till midnight."

"How's Nick?" Jason asked. "Haven't seen him in a while."

Jenny's son Nick was a sophomore in college. Jenny rubbed a small gold charm that hung around her neck. Nick had gifted her a charm for Mother's Day ever since he was a kid. They hung around Jenny's neck on a chain. She had the habit of rubbing the charms whenever she missed her son.

"He should be here for Spring Fest," Jenny said. "Hopefully even before that."

"Did you hear about John Newbury's plans?" Star asked Jason. "What do you think?"

"I think he's got guts," Jason said. "But the Newburys never cared about the town folk."

"Surely they won't do anything illegal?" Jenny asked, wide eyed.

"Having the law on their side won't be enough," Jason explained. "Communities around the country have protested against these dispensaries."

"Aren't they supposed to help sick people?" Jenny asked.

Jason let out a sigh.

"The amount of people they can help is less than the ones they can harm, I guess. People are afraid of the ramifications, and rightly so."

They argued over the pros and cons of growing medical cannabis in a small town like Pelican Cove.

"You can be sure of one thing," Star said. "There will be a protest, and a big one. Those Newburys better be ready for it."

Jenny insisted on cooking Jason's favorite pan seared fish in a wine butter sauce. He had brought a bottle of local wine Jenny loved. They lingered over chocolate brownies and ice cream on the patio. Jason had built a fire in the pit. The scent of roses and gardenias perfumed the air. Water gurgled in the stone fountain.

Jenny sighed with pleasure as she looked around her. This was her home now.

The Magnolias were all fired up about the Spring Fest the next day. Star had produced some designs for the festival T-shirts. The ladies pored over them, arguing over which one best represented Pelican Cove.

"I like this one with just the crab," Molly said. "It's simple but elegant."

"I prefer this one," Heather opposed her. "Crab, oyster, sea bass in a basket and the light house and beach in the background. It's all the best of Pelican Cove."

"Did you post that photo of the waffles on Instagram?" Jenny asked, bringing out a plate of warm muffins.

"Already done, Jenny. It has some five thousand likes. Get ready to make plenty of waffles."

Adam Hopkins came in sight, flanked by two men in uniform. He was leaning on his cane heavily, wincing with every step.

"Is your leg bothering you?" Jenny asked with concern. "Have you taken any pain pills this morning?"

Adam gave her a quelling look. He didn't like being fussed over in public.

The two men accompanying Adam had gone to stand beside Heather.

"What are you doing here, boy?" Betty Sue demanded.

"You need to come with us, Heather," Adam said curtly.

Jenny put her arms on her hips and glared at Adam.

"Not again! You are making a habit of this, Adam. I think you like coming here and harassing us."

"Just doing my job," Adam muttered.

"What has my child done?" Betty Sue asked imperiously.

"Heather was seen going home with Gianni Costa the night he died. We need to question her."

"You don't think I hurt Gianni?" Heather asked fearfully. "I cared for him. Very much."

"We can discuss all that in my office," Adam told her. "Let's go."

"Jenny!" Heather's eyes filled with panic as she looked around at the group. "What am I to do?"

"You'll have to go with him," Jenny said with a sigh.

"We are right behind you," Star said, getting up.

Heather looked bewildered as she stood up and followed Adam down the café steps. She kept glancing back at her friends, looking wild eyed.

"I'm calling Jason," Jenny said, rushing inside the café.

Betty Sue Morse had dumped her knitting on the table. She looked ashen. Molly helped her up and the ladies started walking down to the police station. Jenny ran a few steps and caught up with them.

"He'll meet us there," she said breathlessly.

Jason Stone was pacing up and down the police station lobby when they got there.

"She's inside. Don't worry. They can't hold her for long."

"I thought my Heather was rid of that awful man," Betty Sue sobbed.

"Hush, Betty Sue," Jenny warned. "Be careful what you say."

"I'm not afraid of anyone," Betty Sue puffed up. "Least of all, that beau of yours."

Jenny knew Adam had a job to do. His way of carrying out his duties often rubbed her the wrong way. Jenny realized none of that mattered in the present situation. If Heather was in trouble, she would do anything to help her clear her name.

Heather came out of a tiny room an hour later, looking bewildered. The Magnolias surrounded her immediately, throwing all kinds of questions at her.

Heather gently pushed them away and stared at Jenny.

"I need your help, Jenny. Are you going to find out who killed Gianni?"

Chapter 4

Jenny thought about Heather while frosting chocolate cupcakes. Heather had come to mean a lot to her. She was like her baby sister. Jenny resolved to do whatever needed to help Heather. The first step was going to be getting some background information on Dr. Gianni Costa.

Gianni had been in town only a short time. No one knew much about his past. Jenny had looked for his profile on social media the previous night. He had posted some photos of the beaches at Pelican Cove. There were some photos with Heather plastered to his side. But all the photos only went back a few months. There was nothing about his family or his previous life. Jenny had brought her laptop to work. She was going to dig deeper as soon as she got a chance.

Jenny fired up her laptop after lunch and began looking for Gianni Costa. Jenny was surprised when an address showed up for Gianni in Delaware. It was a small town on the coast, roughly a hundred miles from Pelican Cove.

Jenny felt a surge of energy as she spotted a phone number next to the address. She fed the number in her cell phone and crossed her fingers as she hit the green icon that would dial the number.

The phone barely rang twice before it was answered. The woman sounded brusque, as if she was just stepping out of the door.

"Does this number belong to Dr. Gianni Costa?" Jenny asked.

"Who is this?" the woman shot back.

"My name is Jenny King. I live in Pelican Cove."

"Are you Gianni's harpy?"

"Excuse me?" Jenny sputtered.

"Are you that girl he's been hanging out with lately?" the woman asked patiently.

"I'm not," Jenny said firmly. "I'm her friend."

"What do you want?"

"May I know who I am talking to?"

"Gianni's wife. Mrs. Gianni Costa."

The woman's smug tone carried over the phone line. Jenny found herself speechless.

"I didn't know Gianni was married," she finally managed to blurt out.

"You and everyone else, sister!"

"I would like to talk to you about Gianni," Jenny burst out. "Do you think we can meet?"

"You have my address," the woman said in a bored voice. "Give me a call when you are in town."

Jenny hung up. She was still trying to digest the fact that Gianni was married. Had Heather known about it?

Star came into the café's kitchen and flopped down into a chair. Her face was set in a frown.

"Had a fight with Jimmy?" Jenny teased.

"How old do you think I am, girl? Sixteen?" Star was rarely short with her.

"What's wrong, then?" Jenny asked, offering her aunt a freshly frosted cupcake.

Star considered the platter before her and chose one from the center. She took a big bite and licked the frosting off her lips.

"Are you reading minds now?" she asked Jenny.

Jenny waited patiently. She knew her aunt was just trying to buy time.

"There's a new art gallery in town."

"Where?"

"It's on the other end of town," Star explained. "Near to where all the rich people live. It's the first place they see when they come down the hills."

"Who told you about it?"

"I heard someone talking about it at the market. He has a big collection all ready to go."

"Why are you worried? People love your art."

"They didn't really have a choice all this time," Star grumbled. "My gallery was the only place you could get paintings of the region."

"And now you have competition," Jenny summed up.

"More importantly, the buyers have a choice," Star said.

Her fear and uncertainty were written clearly on her face.

"What if they don't like my stuff anymore?"

"I don't think that's possible," Jenny said loyally. "How long have you been doing this? Thirty years, forty? You are a pro at this. It's evident in your work."

"Art is subjective," Star pointed out. "What if people like his work more than mine?"

"You said it yourself," Jenny smiled. "Some people might like this new guy's paintings and some will like yours. Tourist trade is picking up in Pelican Cove. And most people roam around on Main Street. Anyone walking on the boardwalk or the beach can see your art gallery. They can't help but walk in."

"You think so?" Star asked.

"I know so. And we have your website set up too. You have more orders than you can fill right now. I don't see why you are getting so worked up."

"I have always been the only artist on the island," Star muttered.

"Have you met this guy yet?" Jenny asked. "What's his name, anyway?"

"Frank something," Star said. "He's not from around here. I can't understand why he came to Pelican Cove."

"Go meet him," Jenny suggested. "Introduce yourself."

"He could be a recluse," Star mused.

"So? He'll turn you away. But you will have tried."

"I think that's a good idea. Can I take some of these cupcakes with me?"

"That's a great idea," Jenny said brightly. "He's going to like you, don't worry. Everyone does."

Star could be outspoken but she was always ready to lend a helping hand. Although she wasn't born in Pelican Cove, she had endeared herself to the locals. After forty odd years on the island, she was almost a native.

"I guess I can finally talk shop with someone," Star said eagerly.

"That's the right attitude," Jenny cheered. "You'll be fine."

Jenny pulled out one of the fancy boxes they had recently ordered. With more and more people wanting to carry Jenny's sweet treats away with them, Petunia had suggested they print some fancy boxes with the Boardwalk Café's logo on them. Jenny packed four cupcakes in the box and tied it with a satin ribbon.

"Does he have any family?" she asked. "Will these be enough?"

"I don't know," Star shrugged. "I guess I'll find out."

Star took the box and went out. Jenny hoped she would hit it off with the new artist.

The phone rang. It was Betty Sue. Jenny was almost done with her day's chores. She rushed to the Bayview Inn to see what was wrong with Heather. The next hour was spent consoling Heather and letting her cry on her shoulder. Jenny didn't think it was the right time to tell Heather about Gianni's wife.

"How long is she going to mope around like this?" Betty Sue said worriedly.

She was twisting her lace handkerchief in her hands. Her hands were never still, even when she wasn't knitting.

"We have to give her time, Betty Sue," Jenny sighed. "Grief is personal, I guess. We can't predict how long she will take to get over Gianni."

"I hate that man," Betty Sue spat. "He misled my Heather when he was alive, and now he's messing with her even after he's dead."

Jenny fully agreed with Betty Sue.

"Why don't you find some dirt on him? I'm sure he wasn't a good man."

Jenny debated how much she wanted to reveal to Betty Sue.

"I'm working on it," she nodded. "Although I'm not sure if it will make a difference. Gianni has become some kind of hero in Heather's eyes."

Betty Sue surprised Jenny by what she said next.

"Heather needs to go out on a date. Why don't you fix up something for her on that Internet?"

"She has to be ready to meet other people, Betty Sue. Don't worry, just give it some time."

"You need to get some dirt on that man, and soon," Betty Sue insisted.

"I did find out something," Jenny finally admitted. "I spoke to his wife today."

Betty Sue sucked in a breath.

"Keep digging, Jenny. Make my Heather smile again."

Jenny went to the seafood market to shop for dinner. Chris met her as soon as she entered.

"The catch just came in," he told her. "I put aside all your favorites for you."

Back home, Jenny drew a bath for herself. She lit some scented candles and poured herself some lemonade. The hot water soothed her and she dozed a bit in the big clawfoot tub. The renovators had suggested installing a jetted tub in the lavish bathroom but Jenny had opted against it.

She dressed in her favorite faded jeans and an old sweatshirt and hopped down to the kitchen. There was some warmth in the air but she craved something rich and comforting. She slid a bread pudding in the oven and made her special whiskey and butter sauce to go on top. Then she made a simple sauce with olives and cherry tomatoes to go with the fish.

Star regaled them with an account of her encounter with the new artist.

"He didn't say much, but his eyes gleamed when he saw the cupcakes."

"Nobody can resist those cupcakes," Adam said lovingly, placing his hand over Jenny's.

"You have nothing to worry about, babe," Jimmy told Star loyally.

Jenny yearned to go for a walk. Adam and Jimmy loaded the dishwasher and helped clear up. Tank came over with his leash in his mouth and dropped it at Jenny's feet.

Jenny clipped the leash on and hugged Tank.

"Are you coming?" she asked Adam.

Tank strained on his leash, almost dragging her to the door.

The salty breeze and the flowers from the garden perfumed the air with a peculiar fragrance. Jenny closed her eyes and took a deep breath. A familiar arm came around her shoulders and she snuggled close to Adam.

They walked away from the house, Jenny throwing a ball for Tank.

"The contractor called today," Adam told Jenny. "They are almost done at my house. I should be able to move back soon."

"Do you have to go?"

"I've imposed on you long enough."

"Don't say that," Jenny argued. "I've enjoyed having you here at Seaview. The house is big enough."

"So is your heart," Adam crooned in her ear.

He planted a kiss on her head and stared into her eyes.

"I enjoyed these past few months, Jenny. We have been living in a dream."

"And I don't want to wake up from it," Jenny nodded.

"There are things to consider," Adam said cryptically.

Adam's twin girls were at college. They came home periodically. Jenny had welcomed them at Seaview but she guessed they missed their own home.

"Have the twins said something?"

"The twins have said a lot," Adam smiled. "I think I agree with them."

Jenny blushed at the suggestion. They had never discussed the status of their relationship. Jenny maintained Adam was her friend and a guest in her house. And yes, they were dating. What was the next step in their relationship?

"Tank and I are going to miss you."

"You'll still come here for your walk, won't you?" Jenny asked with a pout.

Months ago, she had run into Adam and Tank while walking on the beach. They had struck up a conversation and continued meeting with tacit agreement.

"We will try, but we may not make it out here every night."

"Then stay," Jenny urged. "Don't go yet."

Adam knew he needed to move out of Seaview before he could take any next steps. He had a solid plan and he couldn't wait to put it into action.

"We've got a couple of weeks," Adam consoled her. "But I will be gone by Spring Fest."

"Is something special happening then?"

"Wait and see," Adam grinned. "Now, did someone mention dessert?"

"Don't change the subject," Jenny said, glaring at him with her hands on her hips.

They had reached the patio at the back of the house. Star and Jimmy sat outside, enjoying their bread pudding. Adam pulled out a chair for Jenny.

"Adam's moving out," Jenny told her aunt. "It's going to be just the two of us again."

Chapter 5

Jenny brewed a fresh pot of coffee and wondered how to tackle Heather. Lately, Heather had the tendency of bursting into tears at the slightest provocation. But Jenny wanted to tell Heather about Gianni's wife before she heard about it from somewhere else.

"Can you come here before the others?" Jenny asked Heather over the phone. "We need to talk."

"Whatever," Heather mumbled without an ounce of interest.

She arrived at the café half an hour later, looking like she just got out of bed. Her eyes were sunken and there were circles under her eyes.

"How are you holding up, Heather?" Jenny asked with concern.

"Never mind that," Heather snapped. "Why did you want me here?"

Jenny led Heather to a small table inside the kitchen and made her sit down. Heather declined the offer of a freshly frosted cupcake but grabbed the cup of coffee Jenny poured for her.

"I found something out yesterday," Jenny began. "It doesn't make any difference now."

"What is it?"

"Promise me you won't flip."

"Spit it out already, Jenny!"

"I was looking Gianni up on the Internet." Jenny didn't know how to break it gently. "He was married, Heather. I am so sorry."

"Not for long," Heather said coolly.

"You knew about it?" Jenny burst out. "You never mentioned it."

"It wasn't a big deal," Heather shrugged. "It was a sham of a marriage. Gianni was going to divorce her pretty soon. His lawyer was drawing up the papers."

Jenny reflected over her conversation with Tiffany, Gianni's wife. Tiffany hadn't been aware of the impending divorce.

"Why was he leaving her?"

"She cheated on him," Heather drawled. "Gianni wasn't too happy with that."

Jenny stifled a laugh. It was the pot calling the kettle black.

"Who would be?" she said lamely. "Does she know about you?"

"I don't know," Heather shrugged. "Like you said, it doesn't matter now. What's with all the questions, Jenny?"

The Magnolias came in one by one and Heather went back to sulking in a corner.

Jenny went to The Steakhouse on her way back home. She had left her scarf in the restaurant the last time she was there. The hostess had told her to come and look in their Lost and Found. It was a pricey scarf with a designer label, a remnant of Jenny's old life. She admitted she still had some pleasant memories attached to it though and she didn't want to lose it.

It was an hour before the restaurant opened for dinner. The staff was setting the tables, filling salt shakers and getting the place ready. An attractive young woman Jenny recognized led her to a small office. Jenny spotted her scarf right away.

"Oh good," she exclaimed. "I didn't want to lose it."

"Did you have a good time here?" the girl asked eagerly. "It wasn't our best night."

"I was here Valentine's weekend," Jenny said. "I loved how you decorated the place. It was romantic."

"We try to do our best," the girl said solicitously. "I was referring to that other girl from your party. The one with the older man."

"Heather?"

The girl nodded. "She got into a big fight. You didn't know?"

Jenny shook her head. She had no idea what the girl was talking about.

"There was this other woman, platinum blonde, very attractive," the girl went on. "She was obviously a tourist. She got a table behind yours."

"Go on," Jenny urged.

"Heather got into an argument with her in the restroom. The woman pushed Heather. Heather pushed her back and slapped her. The woman fell and broke a heel. There was quite a ruckus."

Jenny was staring at the girl with wide eyes.

"We didn't hear any of that!"

"Well, the music was loud, I guess," the girl mused. "And we broke up the fight. A couple of the guys helped."

"Heather was gone from the table for some time," Jenny recollected. "I do remember that now. I thought she was fixing her face."

Jenny blushed as she remembered that night. She had been busy holding hands with Adam, thinking of the surprise she had planned for him when they got home. She had barely spared a glance at Heather.

"Heather's much older than me, of course," the girl prattled on. "But I've seen her around with that cute poodle. I never thought she was capable of using her fists."

"Any idea what they were fighting about?"

The girl looked uncomfortable.

"The blonde called Heather a slut."

Jenny had a good idea who the woman must have been. She thanked the girl for the scarf and walked home, lost in thought.

Why was Heather being so secretive? She had kept things from Jenny and also lied to her blatantly. Jenny didn't recognize the person Heather was turning into.

Star was pacing the floor in the great room at Seaview, rubbing her hands.

"What's the matter?" Jenny asked.

"I did something impulsive. I asked that new artist over for dinner."

"That's wonderful," Jenny assured her. "It will give you a chance to get to know him. We can get him talking and find out what his intentions are."

"Do we have enough food?" Star asked. "We don't have fish today."

"You don't worry about a thing. Let me handle everything."

Jenny called Jason and invited him for dinner.

"I need your discerning eye," she laughed over the phone. "We have a special guest."

Jason had just finished wrapping up a case. He agreed to pick up some shrimp from the seafood market.

Jenny marinated chicken breasts in garlic and balsamic vinegar. She plucked rosemary from the garden and crushed it before adding it to the marinade. She would make her special wine sauce to go with it.

Jason arrived a few minutes before the artist. He put on an apron and started chopping salad.

"Where's that grouchy house guest of yours?" he asked with a wink.

"Adam's working late. He won't be home for dinner."

"So I'm a sit in for him?"

Jenny placed her hands on her hips and glared at Jason.

"No good deed goes unpunished, huh. Here I thought you would enjoy a home cooked meal. But I guess I was wrong."

They bantered for a while, comfortable in each other's company. Jenny asked after Kandy but she was secretly glad the slightly overbearing lawyer wasn't with them.

The doorbell rang and they heard Star welcome someone.

"Frank's here," she said as she led a short, stout man in.

Star towered over him, at least a foot taller. The man had long arms and the slender fingers of an artist. His face was pockmarked and he wore his white hair in a crew cut.

"Frank Lopez," he introduced himself.

Jimmy Parsons hovered close to Star, his eyes keenly observing the newcomer.

Jenny brought out her crab dip and Jason poured wine. Frank declined.

"I don't drink," he said, looking at Jimmy's lemonade. "I'll have the same."

"Where are you from, Frank?" Jenny asked.

"I lived in the southwest most of my life," the artist replied. "I guess I got tired of painting canyons and deserts."

There was some polite laughter at that.

"I sold my house, put all my stuff in an Airstream and set off one day."

"Doesn't get simpler than that," Star agreed.

Jenny sensed a longing in her aunt's voice. Her aunt had been a hippie in her younger days. Jenny wondered if she still dreamt of hitting the road.

"How's that working out for you?" Jason asked.

"Much better than I ever imagined," Frank said enthusiastically. "I stop where I want, set up my easel and start painting. It's been great for my art."

"What brings you to Pelican Cove?" Jimmy asked. "Very few westerners venture into our neck of the woods."

"I was in Vermont last fall," Frank explained. "I ran into a family who hailed from the Eastern Shore. They told me so much about the region. I decided I was going to spend the next summer here."

"Wasn't Maine closer to where you were?" Jimmy asked curiously. "It's not a bad spot to paint."

"I was there last summer," Frank laughed. "Painted the cliffs and the mountains ad nauseum. The beaches here are different."

"No place is quite like Pelican Cove," Star said fondly. "Most of the beauty here is untouched. We have our share of tourists, but we are not very commercialized."

"I confess I'm something of a gourmand," Frank said, piercing his fork into a plump shrimp.

Jenny had served dinner and the lively conversation had moved to the dinner table.

Frank complimented Jenny's cooking.

"I'm making it a point to taste local delicacies. The Chesapeake crabs and oysters are next on my list."

"You came to the right place for that," Jenny told him. "Wait till you taste our soft shell crabs."

"I'm also big on meditation," Frank went on. "It helps my art, you know. Peace of mind is underrated."

"I hear you are setting up a gallery?" Star asked, finally broaching the topic that was bothering her.

Frank nodded. "It's temporary. I have landscapes from all over the country. A lot of water colors."

"I mostly use oil on canvas," Star told him.

Jenny served a cheesecake for dessert. Frank went home with a big smile on his face.

"He seems okay," Jenny said. "He'll be gone before fall sets in, Star. You don't have anything to worry about."

Jimmy wasn't too taken with the newcomer.

"I don't buy it," he said. "Peace of mind, my ass."

"You promised not to swear, Jimmy," Star chided him.

Jenny went out to see Jason off. He thanked her for the lovely dinner.

"Are you Heather's lawyer?" Jenny asked him.

Jason nodded.

"So you don't have to tell me everything she tells you?"

"Anything Heather tells me is confidential, Jenny. You know that."

"She's been lying to me, Jason. She knew Gianni was married but she never told us about it."

"Maybe she didn't want you to judge her."

"I can believe that," Jenny said. "But get this. She picked a fight with Gianni's wife at The Steakhouse. What was Gianni's wife doing there? And why was Heather punching her lights out?"

"I'll talk to her about it," Jason promised.

Jenny kept thinking about Heather as she tossed and turned that night.

"What else are you hiding, Heather?" she demanded the next morning.

Heather's eyes were swollen with too much sleep.

"Get off my back, Jenny," Heather snarled.

"I know you punched Gianni's wife. That's not like you."

Heather shrugged.

"What did you do after you went home with Gianni?" Jenny pressed. "You need to come clean if you want me to help you."

"I don't need your help," Heather wailed. "I'm innocent."

"So tell me what you did."

"I must have gone home," Heather said with a frown. "I woke up in my own bed."

"When did you go home?" Jenny pressed. "And how?"

Heather clutched her forehead in her hands as she sat down.

"Leave me alone, Jenny. I don't owe you any explanations."

"You can blow me off all you want, Heather," Jenny said, shaking her head. "But you can't stop the questions. The police will keep asking them and you better have an answer for them."

"I don't remember, okay?" Heather cried. "I went home with Gianni. I think we had a drink."

"You were already drunk."

"So what?" Heather scowled. "I woke up in my own bed the next day. I don't know how I got there. You can ask me the same question a dozen times but my answer will be the same. I don't know."

Jenny balled her fists as she realized how hopeless the situation was.

"I think you're in trouble, sweetie," Jenny said softly. "God help you get out of this."

Chapter 6

"Are you sure she won't be mad at us?" Molly asked timidly.

Jenny and Molly were driving out of town in Jenny's car, headed to the small town in Delaware where Gianni's wife lived. Jenny had wisely decided against taking Heather with them. Normally, the three friends always went out of town together, but this time they had slipped out without telling Heather about their plans.

"Given the way she's acting lately, I am sure she'll throw a fit," Jenny said with a grimace. "Let her. We are doing this for her own good."

"I don't feel so good about it," Molly whined.

Heather had taken the slightest opportunity to belittle Molly since she got together with Chris. Jenny knew her concerns were justified.

"I'll handle her, don't worry."

They drove for over an hour and Jenny crossed the state border. The town they entered seemed to be smaller than Pelican Cove.

"This place looks deserted," Jenny observed. "Hard to imagine a doctor having a thriving practice here."

"Gianni set up shop in Pelican Cove," Molly reminded her. "Maybe he had a clinic in a whole bunch of small towns up and down the coast."

"Hold that thought," Jenny said as an attractive platinum blonde pulled up in a Mercedes convertible.

Jenny waited as the girl tottered on her heels and went inside the rundown diner. Her chiseled face hinted at Botox and her flawless complexion had probably seen some chemical peels. Jenny switched off her car and stepped out.

The girls followed the other woman into the diner. She had bagged one of the three booths inside. The faux red leather was peeling and there was a smell of burnt cheese in the air.

"You must be Tiffany," Jenny said, taking a seat opposite the woman. "Thanks for coming to meet us."

The girls introduced themselves. Tiffany Costa was friendly enough. She laughed openly and asked the girls how they knew her husband.

Jenny hesitated before replying.

"Gianni knew a friend of ours. Actually, he was dating her for the past few months."

"You're talking about Heather," Tiffany said, fiddling with the sugar sachets on the table.

A tired, grumpy looking waitress came and poured coffee. Jenny took one look at the murky brown liquid and pushed her mug away.

"Do you prefer tea?" the waitress asked her with a smirk. "I've got tea bags."

"You knew Heather?" Molly asked incredulously.

Jenny hadn't told her about the infamous fight at The Steakhouse.

"I saw their photos," Tiffany said wearily. "The whole world saw them, of course. He brought her home once."

Jenny wondered what kind of a cad Gianni had been.

"That must have been hard."

"Gianni had a thing for younger women," Tiffany said. "Younger, beautiful women. He dated them for a while and promised to marry them."

"And?" Molly asked, holding her breath.

"He dumped them when he found someone new."

Tiffany shrugged and took a sip of the coffee. She seemed pretty cool about the whole thing.

"You were fine with all that?" Jenny pressed.

"He always came back to me," Tiffany told them. "So when he was in the mood for these indiscretions, I just looked the other way."

"I'm guessing the lifestyle didn't hurt."

"I made my choice," Tiffany said coldly. "I'm allowed to do that."

Tiffany seemed to get a bit defensive after that.

"Can you tell us anything else about Gianni?" Molly asked.

"What do you want to know?"

"Why did you live in this town, for instance?" Jenny asked. "There must be hardly any patients here."

"This place was just right for Gianni," Tiffany said cryptically.

"How so?"

"Gianni preyed on older people," Tiffany said with a sigh. "People who were not all there," she said, tapping her forehead with a finger. "He fleeced them as much as he could."

"Are you saying he was dishonest?" Molly asked in shock.

"He was a master at duping people," Tiffany said, her eyes gleaming. "He chose small isolated towns where most of the people were senior citizens. They were alone or their kids lived in some city. Either way, they didn't have anyone looking after them."

"What was he doing in Pelican Cove?" Jenny asked, aghast.

"He was done here. Pelican Cove was next on his list. He already had a nice racket going there."

"Why didn't you live there with him?"

"I did," Tiffany said with a shrug. "Off and on."

"Funny we never ran into you," Jenny said, narrowing her eyes.

Most new people in town came to the Boardwalk Café for a meal. Jenny was sure Tiffany had never visited the café.

"That was all part of Gianni's plan," Tiffany explained. "I was keeping a low profile."

"I don't understand," Jenny said coldly.

"He was wooing Heather, right?" Tiffany said with a yawn. "According to Gianni, it was easy to befriend people as a single man. He always showered attention on one of the local girls. That allowed him to get a foot in, meet the movers and shakers in town."

"How smart of him," Jenny said sarcastically.

"He was sneaky that way," Tiffany agreed.

"I don't understand," Jenny said, sitting up. "If you already knew Heather, what was the fight about?"

"You heard about that?" Tiffany asked with a laugh. "I was just acting on Gianni's instructions."

"Kindly explain …" Jenny said with a roll of her eyes.

"Heather was getting clingy. She probably expected some kind of grand gesture for Valentine's weekend. That's why Gianni invited me there."

"What were you going to do?"

"I just had to show up at that dingy restaurant and tell Heather I was meeting Gianni later."

"I guess she didn't believe you."

Tiffany shook her head, rubbing a spot on her chin. It seemed like she was remembering the fight.

"That girl's got a mean right hook," she said with a shudder. "She told me she was the one going home with Gianni. She warned me to stay away."

"Did you?" Jenny asked.

"I was just supposed to plant a seed of doubt. I got that done."

Jenny peered at Tiffany's face, trying to gauge if she was telling the truth.

"You are sure you didn't go home and lie in wait for Gianni?"

"Gianni was a mean drunk," Tiffany said. "I didn't want to be anywhere near him that night."

"Would you say Gianni was depressed about something?" Jenny asked as a last resort.

The police hadn't mentioned the possibility of suicide but she wanted to rule it out.

"Honey, Gianni made other people cry. He was happier than a pig in mud!"

Jenny thanked Tiffany for meeting them.

"Sure. Call me anytime."

She breezed out of the diner ahead of them. Jenny belatedly realized Tiffany looked nothing like a grieving widow.

"Heather had a close call," Molly said on the way back.

"You don't believe she was okay with Gianni being married?" Jenny asked her.

"He must have convinced her he was going to leave his wife," Molly shrugged.

"Heather must have lost it when she saw Tiffany at the restaurant," Jenny observed.

Had Heather been angry enough to take revenge?

Jenny and Molly were both hungry by the time they got back in town.

"Petunia must be closing up, but I can rustle up something for us to eat," Jenny promised.

They were surprised to see a group of women arguing loudly at the café.

"We have to do something about this," Barb Norton said, slapping the table. "It's your duty to support us, Betty Sue."

"What's going on?" Jenny asked her aunt.

Petunia, Star and Betty Sue sat on one side of the table. Barb Norton sat on the other side, glaring at them like a judge. Heather was nowhere to be seen.

"Just wait and watch," Star whispered.

Jenny pulled out a bowl of chicken salad and scooped it generously over two large slices of artisan bread. She added sliced tomatoes and lettuce and squirted her honey mustard dressing on top. She cut the sandwich in two pieces and put them on a plate.

Molly and Jenny munched their sandwich as they listened to Barb and Betty Sue.

Betty Sue's needles clacked as she went on knitting, refusing to look up.

"Are you paying attention, Betty Sue?" Barb roared. "We need to go talk to those Newburys."

Betty Sue finally looked up. She had a weary look in her eyes.

"I don't like talking to John about his business."

"His business is threatening the fabric of our society," Barb said pompously. "It's everyone's business now."

"Why don't you go the usual route? Form a committee?" Betty Sue clucked. "We can then draw up some kind of proposal and take it to the Newburys."

"I am doing all that," Barb said sternly. "But we need to push things forward. I say we take a delegation up there right now."

Star giggled at the mention of a delegation. Barb breathed fire on her.

"Is this about the medical dispensary?" Jenny mumbled, chewing on her delicious sandwich.

"Don't talk with your mouth full, young lady!" Barb snapped. "We are talking about the drug farms."

"Same difference," Jenny muttered.

"Are you saying you support this heinous undertaking?" Barb scowled at her. "I was counting on you, Jenny."

"My mind's not made up either way," Jenny said, wiping her mouth with a paper napkin. "I need more information."

"I agree with Jenny," Molly said softly.

"You too?" Barb pounced on Molly. "Have you forgotten what we did to save your job?"

"I am grateful for what the town did for me, Barb," Molly spoke up. "But this is a different issue."

"Stop blabbering," Betty Sue commanded. "You are giving me a headache."

"Put that knitting down, Betty Sue, and come with me," Barb pressed. "We should all go."

"You know Ada doesn't see people without an appointment," Betty Sue pleaded.

Ada Newbury never let anyone forget that she was the richest woman in town. She looked down her nose at everyone and was a trial to be around.

Barb and Betty Sue argued a bit more and Betty Sue finally gave in. They all set off in two cars, Jenny looking forward to seeing someone take Ada down a peg or two.

The guard at the gate let them in when he spied Betty Sue in Jenny's back seat. Ada kept them waiting for half an hour before she emerged, dressed to the nines.

"Ladies," she said with her nose in the air. "Is it an emergency? I am getting late for a party."

"Sit down, Ada," Barb Norton said brusquely. "We have come to talk about this drug farm of yours."

"My husband handles the business," Ada snipped. "People generally take an appointment and meet him in his office."

"Your husband has gone too far this time," Barb quipped. "We need you to bring him to his senses."

"Be very careful what you say next, Barb," Ada said angrily. "Don't forget you are sitting in my parlor."

"We love our town, Ada," Barb said. "It's rustic but simple and we manage it as well as possible with the limited resources we have."

Ada reminded them she donated liberally to those resources.

"The town has always been grateful for your largesse," Barb said firmly. "But we cannot open our doors to a drug business."

"I think there is some misunderstanding," Ada clucked. "We are planning to open a dispensary that will treat people."

"A marijuana dispensary?" Barb said hoarsely. "Over my dead body!"

"Stop being so dramatic," Ada said in a bored voice.

The conversation derailed after that. Ada clapped her hands and a couple of maids ran into the room. She ordered them to escort the women out.

"Now what?" Jenny asked as they stood outside the Boardwalk Café.

"We march on," Barb said, plunging her fist in the air. "Say no to cannabis!" she yelled. "Say no to drugs!"

Chapter 7

Jenny sat in Jason's office, moodily sipping from a bottle of juice. Jason leaned back in his chair with his hands behind his head, staring at a corner.

"Are you sure about this, Jenny?"

"I only have Tiffany's word for it, but why would she lie?"

"I can think of a number of reasons. She says Gianni told her about the girls he dated. But we only have her word for it."

"Any other wife would have been shocked."

"We don't know if she was really okay with all this," Jason warned. "All I am saying is, take anything she says with a pinch of salt. You just met the woman."

Jenny didn't like to be called gullible. She thought she had a good eye for people.

"What about the other stuff she said?"

"That's also her word against his."

"So you don't think he was shady? Any man who can cheat on his wife and sweet talk a young girl into going around with him …"

"We all know what he did with Heather," Jason said, warding her off. "But medical fraud …"

Jason went back to staring in the distance.

"We can't just sit around talking about this," Jenny said. "Let's go out and do something."

"Like what? Raid Gianni's office?"

Jenny's eyes gleamed and a smile lit up her face.

"Who's going to stop us?"

"I'm a lawyer, Jenny. I can't just go breaking and entering."

"We may not have to," Jenny said, springing to her feet.

She almost dragged Jason along with her.

Gianni Costa lived in a ranch style house a few blocks off Main Street. There was another ranch adjoining his which had served as his clinic. The shingle hanging off a pole announced it as the family practice of Dr. Gianni Costa, MD. Jenny walked up to the door and turned the handle. The door opened easily.

"Viola!" she said to Jason. "We are not breaking any laws going through an open door."

"I guess not," Jason shrugged.

Jenny rushed through the waiting room at the front and entered a door marked 'Staff only'.

"He must have kept some records," she mumbled to herself.

Gianni turned out to be a meticulous record keeper. Jenny spotted files in a drawer and started rifling through them.

"What are you looking for, exactly?" Jason asked.

"Anything out of the ordinary," Jenny quipped. "Heather was a patient?" she murmured as she pulled out a thick file.

Her mouth was hanging open two minutes later.

"Look at what this says," she said, pulling at Jason's sleeve. "According to this, Heather was Gianni's patient and visited him every day of the week."

"She visited him alright," Jason sniggered.

"Can you be serious for a minute?" Jenny taunted. "It's all written here. Heather Morse is a patient. There are prescription records too."

Jenny slumped into a chair, looking worried.

"Is Heather sick?" she exclaimed. "Does she have some terrible illness she's hiding from everyone?"

"You're being dramatic, Jenny," Jason said lightly. "She might have had some minor complaint."

"This says she had an appointment every day. There is some kind of code under diagnosis but I don't know what that means."

"Let's go talk to Heather."

Jason sounded resigned. He knew Jenny wouldn't rest until she got to the bottom of this.

Jenny called Heather from the clinic and asked her to wait at home. She started for the Bayview Inn with Jason.

Betty Sue fussed over them when they got to the inn, plying them with hot tea and cookies.

"Why don't you take a nap, Grandma," Heather suggested. "I've got things under control here."

"You're just trying to get rid of me," Betty Sue glowered.

Jenny sighed with relief when she went up the stairs to her room.

"What have you been hiding, Heather?" she asked, turning to look at her friend. "Please tell me nothing's wrong with you."

"What do you mean, Jenny?"

Heather looked bewildered as Jenny narrated what she had seen.

"I never saw Gianni professionally," Heather said firmly. "There must be some mistake."

"As far as I know, there's only one Heather Morse in Pelican Cove," Jenny said stoutly. "Something is fishy here."

"I still go to old Dr. Smith," Heather said again. "He's treated me since I came to live with Grandma."

"So Tiffany was right," Jenny said to Jason, slapping her leg. "That Gianni was doing something illegal."

"When did you talk to Tiffany?" Heather asked, springing to her feet. "She had it in for Gianni."

"I don't care what her relationship was with Gianni," Jenny dismissed. "She told us Gianni cheated his patients. I am beginning to think she was right."

"Just because Gianni's not here to defend himself …"

Heather curled her fists and looked anguished. Her eyes filled with tears.

"Get hold of yourself, Heather," Jenny said, grabbing her by the shoulders and shaking her. "Gianni's gone, and I say you are well rid of him."

"He was a good man," Heather blubbered through her tears.

"He was a nasty crook who was just taking you for a ride," Jenny said mercilessly. "I'm going to prove it to you."

Jenny stomped out of the Bayview Inn, muttering to herself.

"Can you give me a ride home?" she requested Jason. "I have to get ready for dinner. We are going on a double date with Molly and Chris."

"We could have triple dated," Jason said in a hurt tone.

Jenny didn't think she could tolerate another evening with Kandy the lawyer.

"Some other time," she said glibly.

Jenny took a quick shower and agonized over what to wear. She tried on and discarded four dresses. Finally, she settled on a sunflower yellow dress with a cowl neck. She rubbed the heart shaped charm around her neck as she gazed at herself in the mirror. The phone rang just then and Jenny's face lit up when she saw it was her son. She pressed the video button. She needed to see her beloved Nicky.

"When are you getting home, scamp?" she asked lovingly. "A little bird told me you are spending spring break in Pelican Cove."

"No way, Mom," Nick groaned. "You know I am going to Cancun with my friends."

They chatted for a while and Nick hung up after promising to visit soon. Jenny's face lit up in a thousand watt smile. There was a knock on the door.

Adam stood outside, leaning on his cane. He looked handsome in a black silk shirt. His faded jeans hugged his lean body.

"Ready to roll, Madam?" he grinned.

"Are we picking them up?" Jenny asked Adam as she got into the car.

They were going to an Italian restaurant in a nearby town. The Eastern Shore was home to plenty of small towns like Pelican Cove. The area was paradise for foodies, with eclectic restaurants lining the shore from north to south.

"Chris mentioned some errands," Adam told her. "They will meet us at the restaurant."

"Good," Jenny smiled, placing her hand in Adam's.

Molly and Chris were sipping wine and munching on garlic bread when the hostess ushered Adam and Jenny to their table. Jenny let out a shriek merely seconds after she sat down.

"Is that a ring, Molly?"

Molly's face glowed in the candle light.

Jenny whipped her head toward Chris. He was beaming at Molly. Molly clasped his hand in hers and held it up for Jenny.

"Congratulations, man!" Adam said, slapping Chris on the back.

"It's a promise ring," Chris said, clearing his throat. "Sort of a pre-engagement ring."

"Chris surprised me with the most beautiful engagement ring." Molly sounded hushed. "But I thought we would wear a promise ring first."

"But why?" Jenny wailed. "I can't wait to plan your wedding."

"We are taking it slow," Molly said, looking lovingly at Chris. "There's no rush."

"That's just mumbo jumbo," Adam dismissed. "As far as I am concerned, congratulations are in order. We need some champagne here."

They poured the bubbly and toasted the happy couple. Molly chattered nonstop over the osso buco, a slow cooked dish of wine braised veal. They had tiramisu for dessert and Jenny ordered an espresso to round off the meal.

"Am I allowed to tell people about this?" Jenny asked Molly.

"I'll tell them tomorrow," Molly said shyly. "I'm so happy, Jenny," she said later as they waited outside for the men to bring their cars around. "I feel like I'm in a dream."

"Chris is a good guy," Jenny assured her. "You couldn't have chosen better."

"I want to be sure he loves me," Molly said with a hint of doubt in her voice. "Technically, I'm his rebound relationship."

"Is that why you went for the promise ring?" Jenny asked her.

Molly nodded. "I want him to be sure. Very sure."

"You're one brave girl, Molly. Anyone in your position would have dragged Chris to the altar."

"I've been there," Molly reminded her, referring to her previous marriage. "You understand, don't you, Jenny? When I tie the knot again, it will be for the last time."

Jenny reflected over how different Molly was from Heather. Molly was timid but level headed. Heather was headstrong and impulsive. Chris had fallen for both these women at one time or another.

Adam accompanied Chris to the other end of the parking lot. It was late and the lot had emptied while they lingered over their meal.

"So you are almost leg-shackled," Adam laughed as he patted Chris on the back. "How does it feel?"

Chris wrung a hand through his hair. The smile he had worn all evening was nowhere to be seen.

"You know what's happening with Heather?" he muttered. "I felt pressured."

"You don't love Molly?" Adam scowled. "Are you messing with her, Chris?"

"I do love her," Chris said uncertainly. "But what if Heather needs me? I promised I would always be there for her."

"Are you kidding me?" Adam snapped at Chris. "You should have thought of that before you slipped on that ring."

He put his hand on Chris's shoulder.

"I think you are getting cold feet. Happens to the best of us."

"But what about Heather?" Chris asked with a frown.

"Heather will be fine," Adam said. "She left you, Chris. You accepted that and moved on. You need to look ahead now. Molly's a good soul. She will make you happy for the rest of your days."

"I do love Molly," Chris said earnestly. "But I feel responsible for Heather."

"Heather will be fine," Adam consoled him. "She's not alone. We will all take care of her."

Adam kept quiet about his conversation with Chris. He knew Jenny would fly off the handle if she learned what was going on in Chris's mind. He said good night to Jenny outside her door and limped to his room in search of pain pills.

Jenny brushed her hair and smiled at herself in the mirror. She was happy for Molly and Chris. Chris had always impressed her as a level headed young guy. He would take care of her friend. Her brows furrowed in concern as her phone trilled suddenly. It was past midnight. Her heart thudded in her chest as she thought of her son. She hoped he was fine.

Jenny checked the caller id and crossed her fingers before answering the phone.

"Jason? Is something wrong? Why are you calling so late?"

Jason's voice was heavy with emotion.

"Kandy dumped me."

"What?" Jenny exclaimed. "When?"

"She just sent me an email," Jason said grimly. "She doesn't want to see me anymore."

Chapter 8

Jason refused to speak about Kandy the next day.

"I bet she's just pulling your leg."

"Let's not talk about this, Jenny."

Jenny didn't know what to say. Kandy hadn't seemed like the kind who would settle down, especially in a small, isolated town like Pelican Cove. She had a high flying career in the city. Jenny had been surprised she stuck to Jason all those months.

"Did she give a reason?" Jenny had asked Jason the previous night.

"None," he had lamented. "It just says our lives don't align any more. What does that even mean?"

Jason was putting on a stoic face that morning. Her anguished and hurt friend from the previous night was nowhere in evidence.

"She'll come around," Jenny said again, giving Jason a hug. "If she doesn't, it's her loss."

"What brings you here, Jenny?" Jason asked with a sigh. "Are you just here to console me or do you have something else on your mind?"

"A bit of both," Jenny said grudgingly.

"Shoot. I'm free for the next few hours."

"Do you know the other doctor in town?"

"Old Dr. Smith?" Jason asked. "Sure. I've been seeing him all my life."

"I have an idea."

Dr. Smith's clinic turned out to be a block away from Jenny's home. Jason had called ahead for an appointment. An elderly nurse hugged and kissed Jason.

"Your half yearly appointment is overdue," she scolded.

Dr. Smith was a slim, energetic man in his seventies. Jenny guessed he was a few years older than her aunt. He welcomed Jason with a hug.

"Who's your friend?" he asked with a twinkle in his eye. "Are you finally taking my advice and starting a family?"

Jenny blushed to the roots of her hair. She hastened to explain.

"Oh, you are the young lady the whole town is talking about," the doctor said. "I've tasted most of your goodies. I just haven't had a chance to come into the Boardwalk Café myself. I'm as good as chained to this place."

The small talk went on for a few minutes until Jenny cleared her throat.

Dr. Smith took the hint.

"Look at me ramble on. So what brings you young people here?"

Dr. Smith's face darkened at the mention of Gianni Costa.

"He was a bad one."

Jenny told him about the records in the doctor's office.

"Heather insists she was never his patient. Do you know why he would have a file with her name on it?"

"I can think of a reason or two," Dr. Smith said grimly.

"Would you please look at some of the papers and give them a once over?"

"I have appointments all day," Dr. Smith apologized. "Can you bring the files here?"

"I can get you a few samples," Jenny nodded.

Jason and Jenny went to Gianni's house again. The door to the clinic portion was locked this time. A fan whirred inside and the radio was playing. Jenny rapped her knuckles on the door.

A tiny, shriveled woman opened the door, her eyes full of fear.

"Do you work here?" Jenny asked.

"I was Dr. Costa's nurse," the woman said.

Jenny realized she should have guessed that from the colorful scrubs the woman was wearing.

"You do know Dr. Costa is gone?" Jason asked.

The nurse shook her head.

"I was out of town on vacation. Did he say when he will be back?"

"We are not sure," Jenny said smoothly. "We are here for some paperwork. He said you would give it to us."

Jason was staring at Jenny with his mouth agape.

The nurse led them into the office they had been in earlier. Jenny got rid of the woman by asking for a glass of water. She pulled out the topmost boxes and began taking pictures of the papers in the files.

"Do you know what you are doing?" Jason hissed.

Jenny held a finger to her lips, asking him to be quiet.

The nurse came back with the water.

"I don't think you are allowed to touch that," she said mildly. "Those records contain confidential information."

"Sorry," Jenny said sweetly. "I thought I would save you some time."

She made up a name and asked for a duplicate report. The nurse spent some time rifling through the files.

"I don't see your name here," she said with a frown.

Jenny sensed the nurse was finally beginning to get irritated.

"Why don't you keep looking for it?" she said. "I'll be back later."

Jason berated her as soon as they got into the car.

"You know what you were doing? Getting information under false pretenses. This will never stand up in a court of law."

"I'm not thinking that far ahead," Jenny dismissed. "I just want to find out what Gianni was up to."

Dr. Smith's office was closed for lunch.

"I've never seen a doctor's office close in the middle of the day," Jenny said.

"This is Pelican Cove," Jason reminded her. "And everyone has to eat."

Jenny's stomach growled just then.

"It's time for lunch," Jason said with a smile. "How about going to Ethan's Crab Shack?"

Jenny smiled approvingly.

"I'd rather not go back to the café. I know I'll put on an apron and start working as soon as I get in there."

Jenny was feeling guilty about leaving Petunia on her own for so long. But her aunt had promised to help out so she could go play detective.

Ethan Hopkins greeted them with a big smile. He was Adam's twin but he couldn't have been more different.

"I've never been here during the day," Jenny said as they found a table by the water.

"What are you in the mood for?" Jason asked. "I am going for the fish and chips."

Jenny chose the grilled seafood salad. Their food arrived in large platters.

"This salad is huge," Jenny said, picking up a fry from Jason's plate.

Jason pushed his plate away after a few bites and lapsed into silence. Jenny let him be.

They made their way back to Dr. Smith's clinic. The old doctor studied all the photos carefully.

"That man was a crook!" he exclaimed. "I want to look at the rest of his files but I am almost certain what's going on here."

"What?" Jason and Jenny asked.

"Healthcare fraud," the doctor said grimly. "I know some of the names here. As far as I know, these people don't have the conditions Costa treated them for."

"So what was he up to?" Jenny asked, fascinated.

"There are fake visits here," Dr. Smith explained. "And false diagnoses."

"Do you know what these letters mean?" Jenny asked, pointing to some gibberish under 'diagnosis'.

"They are diagnosis codes," the doctor explained. "Each group of letters means something specific. Looks like Costa was getting money from the government based on fake data."

"So Heather was never really his patient?"

"Heather and a few others," the doctor nodded. "He's charging for patient visits that never happened. Also for services or procedures I bet he has not performed."

"Could this have harmed his patients?" Jason asked, aghast.

"Hard to say based on this data," Dr. Smith shrugged. "But I wouldn't put it past him."

Jenny thanked the doctor for his time.

"What now?" Jason asked.

"I'm going to talk to Adam," Jenny said stiffly. "Can you drop me off at the police station?"

Nora, the desk clerk, greeted Jenny as soon as she stepped into the station.

"He's not in a good mood," she warned, jerking her head toward Adam's office.

"So what's new?" Jenny said with a roll of her eyes.

Adam's mood was a popular topic of discussion at his place of work. His coworkers tiptoed around him when his temper flared.

Adam sat with his leg propped up on a chair, struggling to unscrew a bottle of pills.

"What do you want?" he snapped, tossing the bottle to Jenny.

She grabbed it and opened it without much effort. She took out two pills and handed them to Adam. Adam downed them with a glass of water and sighed deeply.

"Sit down," he said in a milder tone. "What brings you here, Jenny? I hear you are painting the town red with Jason Stone."

"Hardly," Jenny said with a grimace. "I didn't know you had Ethan spying on me."

"He brought me lunch," Adam said lightly. "You know I was just kidding. So how many laws have you broken today?"

"None that I know of," Jenny said sullenly. "Wait till you hear what I found."

Jenny spoke for the next few minutes. Adam's face was inscrutable as he listened to her.

"When are you going to learn?" he whined when she stopped to take a breath. "You are meddling in police business."

"You mean I am doing their business. Shouldn't you or your men have found all this out by now?"

Adam had no answer for that.

"Have you even met Tiffany?" Jenny demanded. "I think she's a potential suspect."

"You must be right, of course," Adam said sarcastically.

"You think Heather is guilty, don't you? Why not Tiffany? She was a woman scorned. And she was right here in Pelican Cove on that night. In fact, she was at The Steakhouse."

"Are you sure about that?" Adam asked.

"Yes, I am sure," Jenny bristled. "Just talk to the staff at the restaurant."

"I have to follow certain procedures," Adam droned. "I can't just run around the place talking up anyone I meet."

"What about this healthcare fraud? Don't you think that is important?"

"That's just an allegation," Adam said. "We don't know he was doing anything wrong for sure. We will have to bring in some specialists. And if there is any connection to his old clinic in Delaware, this case is out of my hands."

"What does that mean?" Jenny asked with alarm.

She was worried about Heather.

"Based on what you told me, whatever crimes Gianni committed crossed state lines. That puts the case out of my jurisdiction."

"I have no such restrictions," Jenny said. "I just want to take care of Heather. I'm going to keep digging."

"This healthcare fraud could be dangerous, Jenny," Adam pleaded. "Who knows how many more people are involved. You need to be careful."

"Jason was with me when we went to Gianni's clinic."

"He should have known better," Adam clucked. "Has he lost his mind?"

"He's just being a good friend," Jenny bristled. "Unlike you."

"My hands are tied," Adam said, literally holding his hands up in the air. "You know I can't be partial to you. The whole town knows I'm your house guest."

Jenny tried to calm herself. Adam always got her riled up with his strait laced ideas.

"Is that all you are?" she asked coquettishly.

"Please be careful, Jenny," Adam begged. "I couldn't bear it if something happened to you."

"I can take care of myself," Jenny said, shaking her head. "Don't you think this whole scam business is important? It might lead you to other suspects."

"I never thought of that!" Adam glared at her. "Why don't you leave me alone and let me think about this?"

"I'm leaving," Jenny said, pushing her chair back.

"Want to go out for dinner?" Adam asked. "You must be tired from running around all day."

Jenny smiled reluctantly.

"I don't mind. I was craving something spicy."

Adam made plans to take her to a Mexican restaurant ten miles up the coast.

"Have a nice day, Sheriff!" Jenny said with a wave as she breezed out of Adam's office.

She had stumbled onto her next course of action while talking to Adam.

Chapter 9

Adam and Jenny sat on the patio, sipping wine. Star and Jimmy were watching a movie. It was one of their favorite things to do after dinner. Jenny had been too tired to go for a walk. They had chosen to relax in the garden instead. Tank sat at Jenny's feet, dozing with one eye closed.

Adam looked at the stone fountain in the garden and let out a sigh.

"I have some news for you, Jenny."

"I know you are eager to move back to your house, Adam, but why don't you wait a few weeks more?"

"It's not about that," Adam hesitated.

Jenny peered into his eyes, trying to guess what he was about to say.

"The DNA results are in. There is no more doubt."

"So it was Lily Davis," Jenny said softly. "Or Lily Bennet if you consider her married name."

Adam nodded in the soft moonlight.

"She was here all along, right in her own backyard."

"Do you think she's still around?" Jenny asked with a shiver.

"What nonsense!" Adam dismissed. "We talked about this, Jenny."

"I know, I know … but all those stories about mysterious lights and the house being haunted … maybe Lily was trying to get someone's attention."

"You amaze me," Adam said with a shake of his head. "You are this smart modern woman one instant and the next instant you start talking like some illiterate person."

"I'm just saying …"

"I guess you feel some kind of compulsion to get to the bottom of this," Adam smirked.

"Believe it or not, I do," Jenny said. "I'm going to do everything I can to find out who killed Lily."

"I wish you luck. We don't have too many resources to assign to a case that old, so you might be the only one fighting for Lily."

"I might need your help, Adam."

"Let me know what you need."

"You're not going to yell at me for meddling with police business?"

"Not this time," Adam promised.

Jenny thought of Lily as she baked a batch of blueberry muffins the next morning. She wasn't looking forward to telling the Magnolias about Lily.

Betty Sue came in, clutching a ball of white wool under her armpit. Her knitting needles poked out of a tote bag. Heather followed her, biting her nails, looking lost in thought.

"Is she still biting her nails?" Betty Sue asked Jenny.

Jenny followed them out to the deck with a tray loaded with coffee and snacks. Star was coming up the steps from the beach.

"Where's Molly?" Petunia wanted to know.

"I'm right here," Molly said cheerily, looking pretty in an apple green dress.

Jenny didn't waste any time bringing the women up to speed. Betty Sue crossed herself and muttered a prayer.

Lily had been her best friend since childhood.

"I never believed she abandoned her family," Betty Sue said.

"You say that now, Grandma!" Heather said with a sneer. "But you were quick to blame her, just like everyone else."

"How was I supposed to know what happened?" Betty Sue cried. "She disappeared overnight."

"You should have known," Heather stressed. "You should have trusted her."

Jenny sensed Heather wasn't just talking about Lily. Heather's recent wild streak had driven a wedge between her and Betty Sue.

Jenny called Adam from the café.

"Did anyone file a missing person report when Lily disappeared?"

"I'll have Nora look into the archives," Adam promised. "Why don't you come here in a few hours?"

"Let's meet for lunch," Jenny suggested.

Adam pointed to a thin file on his desk when Jenny entered his office with a basket on her arm. They made quick work of the crab salad sandwich she had brought. Jenny was eager to see what the file contained. She pushed the box of cupcakes she had brought toward Adam and flipped open the file.

"Three pages?" she exclaimed. "That's all?"

"There was nothing suspicious about her disappearance. I am surprised they even filed a report."

"Lily wasn't a loose character," Jenny mused. "Why did people believe she had a lover?"

"I think the general impression was that she had lost it. She had become so unpredictable that people were ready to believe anything about her."

Jenny read the reports as she discussed different scenarios with Adam.

"This is from Ann Davis," she spoke up suddenly. "Ann says she saw Lily get into a car. What was Ann doing here, Adam?"

Adam shrugged his shoulders as he licked frosting off his lips.

Jenny decided to go to the Bayview Inn to talk to Betty Sue.

"Of course! I forgot Ann was in town at that time," Betty Sue said. "She and Ricky were both here."

"What were they doing here?" Jenny asked.

"Seaview was a house of mourning, remember? When Lily lost her daughter, Ann and her son came to visit."

"Wasn't there a lot of time in between? Like months?"

"It was a different time, dear," Betty Sue said with a faraway look in her eyes. "People came for a visit and stayed on. No one was in a hurry to rush back anywhere. And Ann and her son, they were family. Seaview was as much their home as Lily's."

"Ann was the one who saw Lily get into that car," Jenny told Betty Sue. "So either Lily really got into a car and came back, or Ann is lying."

"Did I tell you Lily wanted to sell the house?" Betty Sue asked.

"What? No, you never mentioned that."

"Lily began to hate the place after her girl died. She wanted to get away from this place. She might have put an ad in the paper."

"How did Ann feel about it?"

"You will have to ask her," Betty Sue said.

"That's right," Jenny said, her eyes growing wide. "I have Ann's number. I can talk to her. Why didn't I think of that!"

Jenny hurried home later, determined to call Ann Davis. Jenny had bought her house from her. The woman was in her eighties and lived in Texas. Jenny had met her when she came to Pelican Cove a few months ago.

Ann was surprised to hear from Jenny.

"I miss the beach and your café," she told Jenny. "Ricky and I are thinking of visiting again this summer."

"This is your home," Jenny told her. "You are always welcome here."

Ann asked after all the Magnolias. Jenny finally got to the point.

"I was looking at an old police report," she began. "You told the police that you saw Lily get into a car with someone."

"That's right," Ann said in a strong voice. "Got into a dark sedan late at night and never came back. It was a new moon, and the garden was pitch dark. But I saw it all from my window."

"Did you see who was driving?" Jenny pressed. "Do you remember anything else about the car?"

"I wish I did," Ann sighed. "It might have helped the police find Lily. But I guess she never wanted to come back."

"Didn't the police call you?" Jenny asked.

She told Ann about the DNA results.

"I can't believe it," Ann said, suddenly sounding old. "Poor Lily."

"Did you hear a car again that night?" Lily asked. "Or did you hear any noise in the garden?"

She didn't want to spell out her theory. If someone had come back and dug a pit in the garden, surely Ann would have heard something?

"I had a migraine," Ann told Jenny, dashing her hopes. "I took a sleeping pill and went to bed."

"Did you notice anything odd in the garden in the next day or two?"

"I sprained my ankle on the stairs the next day," Ann told her. "I had to keep it elevated for a week."

Jenny told Ann to call her back if she remembered anything new. She hung up, feeling dejected.

She tried to clear her mind as she made dinner. She went out in the garden and stood staring at the fountain, the spot where they had dug up the skeleton. Give me a clue, Lily, she urged silently. Give me something. She plucked a bunch of dill and went inside.

Jenny poured her orange dill marinade over a pan of fish and slid it in the oven.

"Any luck?" Star asked her as they ate dinner.

Jenny shook her head.

"Everything hinges on Ann's testimony. And Ann insists she saw Lily get into that car. If she's lying, I need a way to prove it."

"Didn't we have a toll booth at the bridge in those days?" Star asked Jimmy.

"That's right," Jimmy nodded. "Kids from the high school worked there most times."

Adam slammed his fork down in his plate and swore suddenly.

"I worked there for a few weeks. How could I not remember?"

"It's okay," Jenny teased. "Memory's the first to go when you're getting old."

"You don't get it, Jenny," Adam said urgently. "The purpose behind that booth was to find out how many tourists came to Pelican Cove. The kid working the booth had to note down the tags of all the cars that came and left."

"And your point is?"

"We can check how many cars crossed the bridge to go out of town that night."

"They keep records from 1991?" Jenny asked doubtfully.

"I'm going to find out," Adam promised.

Jenny greeted Captain Charlie, her favorite customer, the next morning. He was always first in line when the Boardwalk Café opened at 6 AM.

"Here's your muffin, Captain Charlie," Jenny said, handing him a paper bag and a tall cup of coffee. "What do you think about the new dispensary that's opening up in town?"

"I already signed the paper," he told her. "I know they say those pot brownies help with aches and pains, but I ain't going against the town. No Sir."

"What paper?"

"Heather's going around town with it. She'll get around to you soon enough."

Heather came in earlier than usual, holding a clipboard.

"Barb put me to work," she told Jenny. "This is some kind of appeal. It says you're against the marijuana dispensary. Just print your name here and sign next to it."

"You really think it's that bad?"

"I don't think," Heather said, stressing the word think. "When Barb says you have to do something, people generally fall in line."

"I'm not convinced this dispensary is such a bad idea," Jenny argued. "What about all the people it's going to help?"

"Barb says it will harm more people than it will help. Anyway, you can talk about all that at the town hall meeting. Just sign here for now."

"What is Barb going to do with these signatures?"

Heather shrugged.

"I guess she's going to stop the Newburys from getting the licenses they need."

"That sounds vindictive."

"Suit yourself," Heather said. "But get ready to tackle Barb Norton."

Jenny stirred a pot of soup and motioned Heather to sit down. She slid a freshly baked cupcake with pretty pink frosting in front of Heather.

"Lemon with a raspberry filling. Try it."

"I've gained ten pounds since you came into town, Jenny."

"You look as pretty as ever, sweetie."

Jenny patted Heather on her cheek.

"Are Chris and Molly engaged?" Heather asked with a heavy voice. "Why haven't they told me?"

"They are not officially engaged," Jenny explained. "They are somewhere in between." She hesitated before saying anything more. "You know that day is coming though, Heather."

"I've been doing some thinking, Jenny. I know I acted like a jerk these past few months. No wonder Grandma's so mad at me."

"She's worried about you."

"I don't deserve Chris," Heather said, sounding like her old self. "It's my own fault I lost him, Jenny. He's never coming back to me."

Jenny hugged her friend close, feeling sorry for her. She just hoped there was something better around the corner for Heather.

Chapter 10

"I think you should seize all the records in Gianni's office," Jenny argued with Adam. "Have some other doctor study them."

"And why would I do that?"

"You will get a list of all the people he scammed. Any of those could be a suspect."

"I talked to Dr. Smith about those scams," Adam told Jenny. "Gianni was just billing the government for work he didn't do. Most of the fake records deal with treatment that was not provided to his patients. I know it was illegal but it didn't hurt his patients."

"You can't be sure about that," Jenny persisted. "Some people got a wrong diagnosis. He might have written fake prescriptions that made their way to the patient. What if someone actually took the wrong medicine?"

"I can't go running after every wild scenario."

"This is plausible. Think about it a bit and you will agree with me."

"I'll look into it," Adam said in a resigned tone.

"What about Tiffany? Have you questioned her yet?"

"She's coming to town today for an interview."

"She's a woman scorned, Adam. She had a strong motive."

"Let me do my job, Jenny," Adam pleaded. "Please."

Jenny walked out of his office in a huff. She pulled out her cell phone as soon as she stepped out of the police station and called Tiffany Costa.

"Are you coming to Pelican Cove today? Can we meet?"

Jenny gave her directions for the Boardwalk Café and set up a time to meet.

The Magnolias came in for their mid-morning coffee. Betty Sue was looking better than she had in a long time.

"You look happy," Star observed. "What are you hiding, Betty Sue?"

Betty Sue put down her knitting and leaned toward Star.

"Heather talked to me last night. I think she's going to be okay."

"She's a good kid," Star agreed. "I told you she would come around."

Molly and Heather came in together, arm in arm. Molly looked like she was bursting to tell them something.

"I am meeting the parents," she beamed. "Chris is setting it up."

"You know old Pa Williams," Star said. "You have talked to him hundreds of times."

"Not as my prospective father-in-law," Molly said shyly. "I hope he likes me."

"Ma Williams is a good woman," Betty Sue told Molly. "She's going to love you."

"I've known her since I was a kid," Heather added. "I'll put in a good word for you, Molls."

The lunch crowd kept Jenny busy. Finally, she sat down to grab a bite with Petunia.

"Do you need any help with that cake?" the old woman asked.

"I got it, don't worry."

Jenny had started baking cakes for special occasions like birthdays and anniversaries. There was no super market in Pelican Cove where you could just pick up a cake on the fly. So Jenny's little cake business had taken off.

"What is it this time?" Petunia asked as she took a bite of her fried fish sandwich.

"Lemon cake with raspberry filling," Jenny told her, "like those cupcakes I made the other day. It's for a thirteen year old girl. I hope she likes the pink frosting."

Jenny's phone buzzed just then.

"I'm waiting for you. You can come any time."

Jenny hung up the phone and made a fresh sandwich for Tiffany. She took the plate and a pitcher of sweet tea out to the deck.

Tiffany Costa came in, looking like a young Marilyn Monroe. Petunia led her out to the deck.

"Fabulous view!" Tiffany said as she sat down.

Jenny pointed to the sandwich.

"I thought you might be hungry."

"You're a doll," Tiffany squealed. "I'm starving. That grumpy cop didn't even offer me a glass of water."

Jenny was familiar with the grumpy cop's behavior so she wasn't surprised.

Tiffany drained half the glass of tea in one gulp. She attacked her sandwich as if she hadn't eaten in days. Jenny allowed her to settle down.

"The cops found out I was here at the restaurant," Tiffany said.

She narrowed her eyes and looked at Jenny.

"It's a small town. People can spot a stranger from a mile away."

"They asked me a ton of questions. I answered every one of them. I have nothing to hide."

"That's good for you, Tiffany," Jenny said encouragingly.

"What did you want to talk about?" Tiffany asked, wiping her mouth with a tissue.

"My friend Heather is a suspect in Gianni's murder," Jenny said. "Who am I kidding? The police really think she did it. I'm trying to help her out."

"Are you some kind of detective?"

"Not really," Jenny admitted. "I just talk to people and try to find out stuff."

"How can I help you?" Tiffany asked cagily. "You are not trying to incriminate me, are you?"

"I just want to find out the truth."

"I know most people point at the trophy wife," Tiffany bristled. "I'm not just a blonde bimbo, you know."

"Trust me, Tiffany," Jenny said. "You have nothing to worry about if you are innocent."

"Do you think I would be talking to you if I wasn't?" the girl asked.

Jenny decided not to answer that.

"Tell me about Gianni," Jenny urged. "Were you a patient of his? How did you two meet?"

"We met online," Tiffany said wistfully.

Her eyes had a faraway look as if she was remembering happier times.

"He was so handsome!"

"What were you doing at the time?"

"I worked as a dental hygienist in the city," Tiffany told her. "Gianni swept me off my feet. He took me to fancy restaurants, bought me pretty things. Then on Valentine's Day two years ago, he proposed."

"Were you surprised?"

"Not really," Tiffany said. "I have been chased by many men. They always propose to me. It can get really boring."

"I am guessing it was different with Gianni?" Jenny quizzed.

Tiffany smiled.

"I wanted him to take the next step. We had a court wedding but he took me to Aruba for our honeymoon."

"What about your family?" Jenny asked.

"I come from a small town in the mountains," Tiffany explained. "I was raised by an old aunt. She's in long term care now. I don't have anyone else."

"Was he living in Delaware when you got married?"

"Oh yes. I had known that when we were dating."

"When did you learn about the affairs?"

"Two months after marriage," Tiffany said with a scowl. "Gianni was quite open about it. He said it was a ruse. He snared a local girl to get his foot into a new community."

"What about the shady activities? Did he tell you about them himself?"

"I helped him with some filing a couple of times," Tiffany explained. "I had noticed some odd things. But I was quiet about it. He started bragging about it one night when he was drunk."

"And you were fine with that?"

"I had never done anything illegal," Tiffany admitted. "But he gave me a diamond bracelet two days later. I said nothing."

"So he bought your silence."

Tiffany looked uncomfortable.

"I grew up dirt poor. I never had fancy things."

Jenny didn't torment her any further.

"Can I look at the files at your place?" she asked.

"Sure! You can come and get them any time."

"How long did Gianni plan to go out with Heather?"

"Pelican Cove turned out to be smaller than he had imagined. He said he had pretty much exhausted his options here. He had already hired a moving company. He was getting out of here by the end of February."

"What are your plans now?" Jenny asked her.

"I might get my old job back," Tiffany said. "Just to stay busy."

Jenny told her she would visit soon to look at Gianni's files.

Tiffany didn't seem worried about her future. Gianni must have left her well off, Jenny mused as she walked to the seafood market. Chris greeted her with a brilliant smile.

"Hey, Jenny!"

Jenny called her aunt to ask her what she wanted for dinner.

"We have an extra guest," her aunt told her. "That's five for dinner."

Jenny picked up fresh peppers and mushrooms from the local farm. She doubled her usual order of fish and shrimp and remembered they were out of Old Bay seasoning.

"Molly's excited about meeting your parents," she told Chris.

Chris fingered his shiny new promise ring and blushed.

"She's a bit tense too. My mother scares her."

Jenny beamed as she thought of something.

"Why don't you all come to Seaview for dinner? Star will be there, and Jimmy and Adam. It will be a more casual setting."

"That's a great idea, Jenny," Chris said eagerly. "You sure you won't mind?"

"We haven't had company in a long time. Just tell me what your parents like to eat."

"They'll eat anything," he said. "Mom doesn't like spicy food though."

"I'll keep that in mind," Jenny promised. "Let me talk to my aunt and come up with a date. I'll call you."

Jenny was in for a surprise when she reached home. Star had set up an easel on the beach outside Seaview. There was another easel next to hers. Frank, the artist, was standing beside her aunt, brush in hand, talking about something.

"They are having a plain air session," Jimmy told her with a scowl. "That creep's been here since noon. And your aunt has been standing out there with him."

"You mean 'plein' air," Jenny laughed. "It's a French term for painting outdoors."

Jimmy sat in a chair on the patio, staring out at the beach. Jenny knew he wouldn't be easy to spot from the beach, but he had a clear view of Star and her companion.

"Is that the guest we are having for dinner?" Jenny asked.

"He invited himself," Jimmy grumbled. "Said he fancied a nice home cooked meal. He can cook it in his own kitchen, can't he?"

"I thought he lived in a bus."

"He travels in that bus. He's rented a house in town. The bus is parked in his yard."

"Star's just being nice," Jenny said with a smile.

She wondered what Jimmy was worried about. Although her aunt had never said it out loud, Jenny was sure she really liked Jimmy. She wasn't going to be impressed by some vagabond artist.

Adam came home and offered to help with dinner. Jenny gave him the job of chopping the vegetables. She sprinkled Old Bay on fish and drizzled it with olive oil. She set it aside, ready to go in the oven just before they sat down to eat.

"I met Tiffany today," Jenny told him. "Sounds like you were a bit harsh with her."

"I was just doing my job," Adam told her.

"Tiffany's offered to let me look at Gianni's old records."

"That's great," Adam said eagerly. "Dr. Smith is looking at the stuff we found here in

Pelican Cove. But that's all I can do for now. The other stuff is off limits for me."

"Adam Hopkins," Jenny said with her hands on her hips. "Are you actually asking for my help?"

"You might be able to go where I can't," Adam said. "Who knows what those records will yield."

"Does Tiffany come into a lot of money?" Jenny asked.

"She's the spouse," Adam shrugged. "Unless we find a will or someone turns up with one, she is his next of kin."

"So she could have killed him for his money."

"We are trying to establish her alibi. We already know she was in town that night. Unless she can prove what time she left town, she had as much opportunity as Heather."

"She also had access to Gianni's clinic and all the drugs he kept there," Jenny reminded him.

Adam agreed with Jenny for a change. Tank came in and sat down on the floor next to Jenny.

"Who's that dude out there with Star?" Adam asked. "And why is Jimmy hiding behind the rose bushes?"

Chapter 11

Adam Hopkins walked into the Boardwalk Café at noon.

"Hello Sheriff," Jenny smiled. "Taking the day off?"

"I'm here for lunch," Adam said. "Care to join me?"

Jenny ladled pea soup in two bowls and placed strawberry chicken sandwiches on a plate. She took the tray of food out to the deck. It was a sunny spring day and the fresh breeze coming off the ocean perked her up.

Adam slurped the soup and pronounced it delicious.

"I asked around," he told Jenny. "Old Asher Cohen had sponsored the toll both all those years ago. He paid the people who worked there."

Jenny's face fell.

"Asher's gone now."

"Asher may not be around but his company, Cohen Construction is," Adam reminded her. "I spoke to Luke."

Luke Stone was Jason's uncle. He ran Cohen Construction, one of the biggest employers in town.

Jenny took a bite of her sandwich and nodded for Adam to go on.

"Asher was very meticulous about keeping records. Luke is sure they have everything from back when the booth was still running."

"When can I look at them?" Jenny asked eagerly.

"Luke's having someone pull them from their records section. You can go there later this afternoon. They are expecting you."

"Sounds great," Jenny said. "You think I'll find something?"

"Whatever you find will be something we don't know now," Adam told her. "Think of it as another piece of the puzzle."

"Yes Sir!" Jenny gave him a mock salute.

Her enthusiasm waned a bit when she saw the three foot high pile of paper set aside for her at Cohen Construction. She sat down and started looking for the right year.

Apparently, the toll booth had been operational for barely a year. It had never actually collected toll. Its only purpose had been to note down the cars entering and leaving the city. Jenny noted down the relevant information and struggled to her feet. Her legs were stiff after sitting in one spot for hours. She hoped the information she had found would provide some value.

Jenny walked back home, thinking about Lily. Lily had grown up in Pelican Cove. She had left town at nineteen and come back several years later with her husband and children. Her husband worked in the city and was traveling most of the time. Her daughter died from a freak virus. Lily's son was in college at that time. According to Betty Sue, Lily had shut herself in her house after her daughter's death. It didn't seem like she had any enemies. She hardly talked to anyone. Why had someone taken her life?

Jenny walked on for a while before she found herself in front of the library. She remembered something Betty Sue had said. Molly greeted her at the desk, looking radiant.

"Chris told me you are hosting us for dinner, Jenny," she beamed. "Thank you so much. To be honest, I was a bit intimidated at the thought of going to their home for dinner. But I'll feel right at home at Seaview."

Jenny spent some time chatting with Molly about the dinner party. She went in to the reference section and began looking at newspapers from 1991. There was no news item related to Lily's disappearance. Jenny found it odd. Why hadn't the Pelican Cove Chronicle printed anything about Lily? She moved to the classifieds section next. She spotted the ad for the sale of Seaview right away. Her eyes popped open at what she saw on the page. Had grief really addled Lily's brain?"

"Not a single car went out of town that night," she told Adam later that night.

They were taking a long walk on the beach after a rich dinner of Star's special six cheese lasagna. Tank ran in circles around them, begging Jenny to throw a stick he could fetch.

"Did anyone come into town?"

Jenny shook her head. "Not after 3 PM that day."

"Did you note those numbers?"

"I did more than that," Jenny told him. "Those same cars left town around 6:30 in the morning and got back by 4 PM. I am guessing these belonged to people who commuted to the mainland."

"Good guess," Adam complimented her. "What about the days before and after Lily disappeared?"

"I didn't see any car leaving town for a day after that."

"Are you saying Lily never got into a car?"

"I'm saying she didn't go out of town for sure," Jenny said. "At least not that night. So this whole story about her running away with someone seems pretty thin now."

"She could have stayed with someone else in town for a couple of days," Adam mused.

"Betty Sue says Lily hardly spoke to anyone those days. I find it hard to believe she had a secret lover."

"So you believe Ann lied?"

"I don't know what to believe, Adam. But it's beginning to look probable. It's Ann's word against Lily's and Lily is not here to defend herself."

"Hmmm …"

Adam lapsed into silence. Tank nudged Jenny, trying to get her attention. She played with him for a while.

"And wait till you hear this," Jenny spoke up. "Lily wanted to sell Seaview. She listed it in the classifieds for twenty thousand dollars."

"What?" Adam exclaimed. "You sure you didn't miss a zero?"

Jenny shook her head.

"It was printed in words too, Adam. I know things were cheaper back then, but surely not that cheap?"

"Why would Lily do that?"

"Betty Sue said she just wanted to get away from here."

"Do you remember Ann and her son owned half the house? I'm sure they didn't go along with that."

"Lily was acting erratic, that's for sure."

Jenny couldn't wait to tell the Magnolias all she had found out. She waited impatiently for Betty Sue's arrival the next morning. Betty Sue walked in, busy knitting something pink.

"Sit down, Betty Sue. I want to ask you something."

"How about some coffee first, eh?" Betty Sue grumbled. "What's got you so twisted?"

Jenny poured out her story.

"Twenty thousand dollars!" Betty Sue exclaimed. "There was a recession around that time but Seaview was worth several times more than that."

"How come someone didn't snap up the property?" Jenny asked her.

A knowing look flashed across Betty Sue's face.

"It was the curse. People around here believed Seaview was jinxed."

"Did Ann want to sell too?"

"Ann came here and liked what she saw. She wanted to live here with Ricky."

"But they went back!"

"I never understood why," Betty Sue nodded. "You can ask Ann about it. She was as eager to stay on here as Lily was to leave."

"Did they get along?" Jenny asked.

"Lily adored Ann when we were teenagers," Betty Sue said. "She was young, sophisticated and married, everything we aspired to as girls. Ann could do no wrong in Lily's eyes."

"Didn't Lily live with Ann for a while?"

"Those two were pretty close once upon a time," Betty Sue agreed.

"But not in 1991?"

"Lily was really hard to be around that time," Betty Sue said reluctantly. "Her mood swings had become really hard to take. She would throw tantrums at the slightest provocation. She didn't talk to a single person for days together. She sat on the balcony at Seaview, staring at the sea, sobbing her heart out for her girl."

"Ann stayed here through all that?"

"She did," Betty Sue said grimly. "She held the family together."

Jenny wondered if Ann Davis had really loved Lily.

Molly and Heather came in, arm in arm.

"Are you all set for this special dinner?" Heather asked with a smile. "Let me know if you need any help. I can give you the skinny on what Chris's mother likes."

"Thanks Heather," Jenny said. "I'm almost ready, I think. Chris is coming around with the fish around four."

"That takes care of the food," Heather said. "What are you wearing, Molly?"

"That new green dress?" Molly said uncertainly.

"Mrs. Williams likes blue. Don't you have a blue dress you can wear?" Heather was trying really hard to be likable. "What about your hair?"

"It's just a dinner, Heather," Jenny rolled her eyes. "Stop scaring Molly."

"I know, but you know what they say about first impressions."

"You're making me nervous," Molly said, beginning to look green. "I tend to puke when I get nervous."

"We can't have that," Heather frowned. "Just be your usual self, Molls. You got this."

Star had set up her easel on the patio when Jenny got home. She was muttering to herself.

"What are you doing, Star?" Jenny laughed.

"I'm trying my hand at water colors," she said. "Not as easy as it looks."

"I thought you hated them."

"I never really gave them a shot. Frank says watercolor is actually the most difficult medium."

"Frank says, huh?"

"A true artist does not shy away from different techniques. Frank says I should think of adding water colors to my portfolio."

"When did you go shopping for all these new colors?"

"Frank lent them to me. He's quite generous, that one."

"Carry on then," Jenny told her aunt. "I have my work cut out for me."

"Are we having company?" Star asked. "I was thinking of asking Frank over for dinner."

"Have you forgotten Molly's dinner party?" Jenny asked her, rubbing a charm around her neck.

She had been missing Nick all day.

"Oh yeah," Star said. "That's tonight? Why didn't you say so earlier?" Star began putting away her stuff. "I'll help you in the kitchen."

Molly's party started off well. Heather had kept her word and helped Molly get ready. Molly was wearing more makeup than usual and she kept touching her face every few minutes.

"Relax," Jenny whispered in her ear.

Pa Williams, Chris's father, was an easy going man. He put an arm around Molly and welcomed her to the family. His wife didn't seem that forthcoming. Her face had a pinched expression.

"She's not a Pioneer," she said to Star. "You know how we feel about that."

A peculiar hierarchy existed on the island of Pelican Cove. A bunch of families who had been the original settlers called themselves the Pioneers. Only five or six families had this honor. The Morse family, Betty Sue and Heather's ancestors were one of them, being the original owners of the island. So were the Stone and Williams families. They had been on the island since the nineteenth century.

Molly's family came from a group called the refugees. Her family had sought shelter in Pelican Cove after the great storm of 1962, a deadly storm which had wrought massive destruction up and down the coast.

Time didn't move very fast in Pelican Cove. Family background mattered a lot.

"Your son loves this girl," Star hissed. "Can't you be happy about that?"

Star herself was a chicken necker, a term the islanders used for someone who wasn't born there. She had come to Pelican Cove in the 1970s and never gone back.

"You wouldn't understand," Mrs. Williams told Star. "And what is this love you speak of? My son was in love with Heather Morse since third grade. I don't know how this girl managed to snare him."

Molly overheard them and turned red. Her eyes filled up and threatened to spill over.

Jenny took her by the arm and led her inside.

"She doesn't like me," Molly stuttered.

A wild look had come into her eyes.

"I can't marry Chris without their blessing. What am I going to do?"

"She's in shock," Jenny soothed. "Your engagement is kind of sudden."

"We are not even engaged," Molly cried. "And now his mother doesn't approve of me."

"Chris loves you," Jenny said firmly. "He's going to stand by you no matter what, Molls."

"Do you really believe that, Jenny?"

Jenny crossed her fingers behind her back and nodded at her friend.

Chapter 12

"Jenny, it's for you," Petunia called out.

Jenny put down the piping bag she was holding and answered the phone.

"This is Dr. Smith. You gave me this number."

"How are you, Doc?" Jenny greeted him. "Any update?"

"Can you come down to my clinic?"

"Give me an hour," Jenny said and hung up.

She immediately dialed Jason's number.

"I don't know what he's come up with. Do you want to go with me?"

Jason pulled up outside the Boardwalk Café half an hour later. Jason seemed to have lost weight since the last time Jenny saw him. There were dark circles under his eyes.

"Are you ill?" she asked with concern. "What's wrong?"

"Haven't been sleeping well," Jason said with a shrug.

"When was the last time you had a proper meal?" Jenny asked suspiciously. "That's it. You're coming to Seaview for dinner tonight."

"Whatever you say, Jenny," he mumbled.

They reached Dr. Smith's clinic ten minutes later. He was waiting for them.

"I went through most of Costa's records," he said. "I found more of what we saw before."

Jenny sensed there was more coming.

"One of the names seemed familiar," Dr. Smith sighed. "Eugenie Hampton. She died recently."

"How did she die?"

"I checked her death certificate," Dr. Smith said grimly. "She died of heart failure."

"I remember reading her obit," Jason said.

"Was she your patient, Dr. Smith?" Jenny asked.

"Was is the operative word," the doctor said bitterly. "I treated Eugenie Hampton for forty years. She started seeing Costa last winter."

"Any reason why?"

"He charmed her, I guess," Dr. Smith said. "Some of my patients started seeing him recently. I couldn't stop them."

"I'm guessing most of these were women of a certain age?" Jenny asked. "Did Eugenie have any chronic conditions?"

"I'm not supposed to discuss my patients with anyone," Dr. Smith reminded them. "But I can tell you this. I saw the treatment Costa was supposedly giving her. It was all wrong for her."

"So he actually gave someone wrong medicine?" Jenny asked, aghast. "But you said he was just billing the government for this extra stuff."

"Looks like he was doing more than that," Dr. Smith said. "Or there was some error in the paperwork. She saw something she was not meant to see and filled those prescriptions. Taking those drugs might have led to her demise."

"Can you prove that?"

"It will be hard to prove without an autopsy."

"Did she have any family?" Jason asked.

"Her husband lives in town," Dr. Smith said. "He's still my patient. I can give you his address."

"Let's go talk to him," Jenny said to Jason.

Peter Hampton was home when they went to see him. He was sitting out on his porch in a rocker, staring at a bird feeder that hung from an old oak.

Jason introduced himself.

"I know who you are," he grunted. "What do you want?"

"We wanted to talk to you about your wife."

"She's dead," he said. "Are you going to let me mourn her in peace?"

"We just want a few minutes of your time," Jenny pleaded.

The man paid no attention and continued staring in the distance.

"Maybe we'll come back some other time," Jason said.

He took Jenny's arm and led her back to the car.

"You are giving up?" she protested as he started the car.

"He won't talk to us right now," Jason said.

"I want to tell Adam about this guy. Why don't you drop me off there?"

Jason pulled up outside the police station a few minutes later.

"See you at seven sharp," Jenny said primly. "Bring your appetite."

Adam was immersed in some paperwork when Jenny breezed into his office.

"You have a new suspect," she declared.

Adam looked at her irritably.

"What are you blathering about, Jenny?"

"I'm talking about Gianni's murder. I just found a new suspect for you."

"Pray tell," Adam drawled.

"A woman called Eugenie Hampton died from the wrong medicine. I just saw her husband. He refused to talk to me."

"Genie's dead?" Adam sat up, surprised. "She used to be friends with my mom."

"Her husband looks devastated. Dr. Smith says she probably died from a wrong prescription. That gives her husband a motive."

"All this makes a fine story, Jenny," Adam said patiently. "But I need proof."

"Isn't it your job to get that?" Jenny shot back.

"I don't know, Jenny. Sounds farfetched to me."

Jenny stormed out of Adam's office and started walking home. She spotted Captain Charlie coming out of The Steakhouse. He was holding a small bag of food.

"Just delivered the catch," he told her. "The chef made me dinner."

"Do you know a man called Peter Hampton?"

"Aye."

"Can you find out if he came to The Steakhouse recently?"

"What are you up to, little lady?" Captain Charlie asked.

He went inside the restaurant again. Jenny tapped her foot impatiently while she waited for him to come out.

"He was here," Captain Charlie grunted when he came out. "One of the busboys told me."

"Are they sure? Do they know who he is?"

"Pete Hampton's lived here all his life," Captain Charlie quipped. "That's seventy some years you have not been here, missy. Most people around here know him well."

"What was he doing here?"

A lad walked out just then, pulling off his apron. Captain Charlie summoned him over.

"Tell her what you saw."

"Old Pete Hampton came here for dinner for Valentine's Day. It was kinda sad. We all know his wife passed."

"Was it Valentine's Day or the day after?" Jenny asked eagerly.

The lad shrugged.

"Could have been either. It was some time that weekend." He stared at Jenny for a few seconds. "I know you. You were in here with that big group. Pete was here the same day as you."

"Did he talk to anyone?"

"He was talking to that dude with the diamond earring."

The lad looked bored. He said a hasty goodbye and walked away from them rapidly.

"Does that help?" Captain Charlie asked.

"More than you know," Jenny told him, grinning from ear to ear.

She couldn't wait to talk to Adam. Jenny hurried through her dinner prep. Star had invited her new artist friend so there were six of them for dinner. Jenny made a big pot of gumbo to go around. She hoped Frank liked spicy food.

"Pete Hampton was at The Steakhouse with us," she told Adam as soon as he came home. "He was right there."

"Gianni didn't die in the restaurant, Jenny."

"But he could have been poisoned there."

"He wasn't. Trust me on that. I can't tell you any more than that now."

Jenny tried to make Jason talk during dinner. He ate a few spoonfuls of gumbo and pushed his plate away.

Jenny tried to hide her concern.

"Will you pick me up at nine tomorrow morning?" she asked him.

"Sure," he agreed.

Frank was asking Star to dinner.

"You have made me feel so welcome. I am taking you to dinner and I won't take no for an answer."

Star tried to hide a blush.

"Your aunt is so talented," he gushed, looking at Jenny. "She just started using water colors two days ago and her work is already better than mine."

"Oh Frank, stop it!" Star said, turning red.

Jimmy Parsons stared at them with a scowl on his face. It was clear he wasn't dealing well with the interloper.

Jason arrived at the café at nine the next morning. Jenny handed him a box with a giant chocolate cupcake. Jason's face broke into a smile.

"So you can still smile," Jenny teased. "Why didn't you say you wanted cake?"

"Where to?" Jason wanted to know.

Jenny told him what she had discovered the previous day.

"We are going to see Peter Hampton again. And this time I am not going to budge until he starts talking."

Peter Hampton was sitting in the same spot on his porch, staring at the bird feeder again. His brow furrowed when he spotted them.

"Didn't I tell you to clear off?" he roared.

"We need to talk, Mr. Hampton," Jenny said with her hands on her hips. "What were you doing at The Steakhouse?"

"It's a free country," the old man sneered. "I was getting a meal."

"You were doing more than that."

Peter Hampton folded his hands and looked away.

"Look, we are sorry about your wife," Jenny began.

"We were married for fifty six years," the man said. A single tear rolled down his eye. "I was supposed to take care of her."

"You couldn't have known," Jenny said gently.

"He had all those fancy certificates," Peter said. "My Genie said Dr. Smith was getting old. This Gianni fellow had access to all the latest technology. He promised he would make her sciatica go away. She believed him."

"He was giving fake prescriptions," Jenny stated. "When did you find out?"

"Not until it was too late," Peter Hampton said bitterly. "That Costa fellow said it was my Genie's fault. She couldn't read, he said. She was never supposed to take those pills."

"You went to The Steakhouse to cause a scene, didn't you?"

Peter Hampton straightened in his chair. His eyes hardened.

"I was prepared to do more than that. I was carrying a knife under my jacket. I was going to kill that bastard in the restroom."

"What happened?" Jason asked, fascinated.

He was finally beginning to act like his old self.

"I chickened out," the man said. "I couldn't do it. I couldn't kill a man in cold blood."

"Even though he was responsible for your wife's death?" Jenny pressed.

"I failed my Genie," Peter said. Tears were flowing down his face freely now. "How am I going to face her?"

"You did the right thing," Jason said, patting the man on his back.

"Did you argue with Gianni that day?" Jenny asked.

"I let him have it," Peter nodded. "He laughed at me. Said small town folks were gullible."

"Did you follow him home?" Jenny pressed.

"No Ma'am," Peter shook his head. "I went to the Rusty Anchor to drown myself in a bottle."

"Did anyone see you there?"

"Eddie Cotton did, I guess," Peter said with a frown. "And a bunch of other people in the bar. Why?"

"Never mind," Jenny said. "Mr. Hampton, can I bring you a casserole some time?"

"You are the girl from the café, aren't you? My Genie loved your waffles."

Jenny was quiet on the way back.

"You miss her, don't you?" she asked, placing her hand on Jason's.

"What happened, Jenny?" Jason asked, his eyes full of pain. "Where did I go wrong?"

"You could never go wrong, my friend," Jenny said fiercely.

"I tried calling her a few times," Jason admitted. "She won't answer my calls."

"You know how busy Kandy is," Jenny said. "Maybe she's working on some high profile case and doesn't want to be disturbed."

Jason shook his head.

"Her email clearly said we were done."

"Coward!" Jenny spit out.

She had never been impressed with Kandy's bossy personality.

"Can't you forget her, Jason?" she asked. "There's plenty of fish in the sea."

"I didn't go looking for anyone," Jason said bitterly. "She pursued me. And now she's backing out."

"It might be for the best," Jenny said with a shrug. "If she's so flighty, it's better you found out now."

"I wasn't completely honest with her," Jason said after a while. "I think she sensed that."

"What do you mean?" Jenny asked, bewildered.

"Kandy and I, we were hanging out, Jenny," Jason stuttered. "But I was, I am, in love with someone else."

Chapter 13

Jimmy Parsons walked into the Boardwalk Café. He wasn't a café regular.

"This is a surprise," Jenny said, welcoming him. "What can I get you, Jimmy?"

"I guess I'll have a cup of coffee, with cream and sugar."

"How about some breakfast? I am making waffles."

"Why not?" Jimmy shrugged.

He seemed agitated.

"Okay, out with it," Jenny said, placing a plate of waffles drizzled with her special berry sauce before Jimmy. "What's on your mind?"

"It's your aunt," Jimmy began. "Do you think she's sweet on this new artist fellow?"

Jenny burst out laughing.

"What makes you think that?"

"He's taking her to dinner tonight, to the Steakhouse, no less."

"I think she's just being polite."

"She can't stop talking about him," Jimmy grumbled. "It's Frank this or Frank that."

"She never gets to meet any fellow artists," Jenny offered. "It's just shop talk."

"I hope that's all it is."

Jimmy gazed moodily at his waffles and took a bite. Jenny took pity on him.

"She likes you, Jimmy. I know that much for sure."

Jenny decided to talk to her aunt later. The Magnolias came in and settled at their favorite table on the deck.

"You are coming to the town meeting, aren't you?" Heather asked Jenny. "We need a good turnout."

"Are you working with Barb now?" Jenny asked.

"She needs an assistant and I am at a loose end," Heather explained. "Plus, I feel strongly about this drugs issue."

"Calling it a 'drugs issue' gives the wrong impression," Jenny said.

"Come to the town hall meeting to voice your opinion," Heather quipped. "It's an open forum. We will let everyone speak their mind."

Jenny was glad to see Heather taking an interest in something other than men.

"How was the party at your place?" Betty Sue wanted to know.

"Jenny did a great job," Molly praised. "Chris said his father likes me."

No one wanted to talk about his mother.

"I heard about your hot date," Jenny told Star. "What do you see in that guy?"

"How do you know about it?" Star asked. She looked embarrassed. "He was quite persuasive. I couldn't say no."

"Jimmy was here this morning."

"What's he doing, talking about my business?" Star asked crossly. "I need to talk to that Jimmy."

"I think he feels left out," Jenny said. "It's cute."

"Frank's just like a tourist. He'll be gone in a few months."

"As long as you don't take off with him …"

Jenny was tossing salad for lunch when the phone rang. It was Tiffany, Gianni Costa's wife.

"You said you wanted to look at Gianni's records?" she asked Jenny. "I've put everything in a few boxes and set it aside for you. You can come and get them anytime."

Jenny told her she would come by later that day. She called Jason and asked him if he was up for a road trip.

"Who's this?" Tiffany asked as she gave Jason a once over.

"Jason lives in Pelican Cove. I rode with him today."

Jason was being his old charming self. He chatted up Tiffany.

"I was planning to leave my husband," she told Jason. "He was seeing other women on the side."

"That must have been hard on you," Jason commiserated.

"I was just a poor working girl when I met Gianni. I had nowhere to go."

"You never said you wanted to leave Gianni?" Jenny asked her.

"I put on a brave front," Tiffany shrugged. "No wife can tolerate a cheating husband. I gave him an ultimatum."

"You did?" Jenny humored her.

"He had to stop seeing this Heather girl or I was walking out."

"What did Gianni say?"

"He laughed at me. Said I was free to walk out any time I wanted."

"Did you sign any prenuptial agreement?" Jason asked.

"Jason's a lawyer," Jenny added.

"I did sign something," Tiffany said with a shrug. "But I didn't understand much of it. Gianni said I would be taken care of."

"I can take a look at it if you want me to," Jason offered.

Tiffany went in and came out with a folder.

"It's all in there."

Jason didn't need a lot of time to skim through the papers. He shook his head and gave them back to Tiffany.

"According to this, you get nothing if you leave your husband."

"Even if he cheated on me?"

"If you walk out, you don't get a penny, no matter what the reason is."

"That's not fair," Jenny said.

"Gianni said this was just a formality," Tiffany said, incensed. "I was so much in love, I didn't give it a second thought."

"What did you do later that night at the Steakhouse?" Jenny asked her.

"I was starving, but I didn't want to stay in that place for one moment more than necessary. I drove back home to Delaware."

"Alone?"

"Of course! Gianni was too busy canoodling with that tart."

"You didn't talk to Gianni at all that night?"

Tiffany shook her head.

"I'm sure he saw me there."

Jenny wanted to use the restroom. Tiffany pointed down the hallway. Jenny peeped into a powder room and walked on, taking note of the other rooms. She saw a door leading down a small path through a garden. It led to a separate building that looked like a guesthouse. Jenny went inside the bathroom and flushed the toilet. She opened a faucet for a few minutes and came out, wiping her hands.

"Do you like to swim?" she asked Tiffany. "I thought I saw a pool house."

"That's not a pool house," Tiffany pouted. "That's Gianni's clinic. It's actually a guest house."

"So he could walk to and fro between his house and workplace whenever he wanted."

"So could I," Tiffany said with a nod. "It was … convenient."

"Okay," Jenny said, standing up. "We'll get these boxes out of your way."

They stopped at a small fish and chips shop on the way back. Jenny bit into hot beer battered fish and stared moodily at the water.

"You have to convince the police that Tiffany is a suspect. That might take the spotlight away from Heather."

"Give me one reason why she's a suspect," Jason said, dipping a French fry in ketchup.

"I'll give you three," Jenny said, holding up three fingers. "Never underestimate a woman scorned. Gianni cheated on her. I don't care what she says, she must have been raving mad."

"Go on," Jason said, taking a swig of his soda.

"As you said, she didn't stand to gain anything if she left Gianni. But she inherits his entire ill gotten gains as a widow."

"And you think that was the motive? Money?"

"Money or revenge," Jenny said with a shrug. "Call it what you will."

"How did she do it?" Jason asked.

"I don't know about that," Jenny said. "But she had access to Gianni's clinic. She could have ground up any combination of pills. She had plenty of opportunity."

"And how did she feed him this deadly cocktail?" Jason asked.

"I don't have all the answers," Jenny admitted. "Why not leave something for the police?"

"So she had a strong motive and she had the means," Jason summed up. "What about opportunity?"

"She was right there at the Steakhouse," Jenny cried. "She could have easily walked to Gianni's place from there."

"That does put her on the scene," Jason agreed. "Has she given any alibi to the police?"

"I don't think they ever asked her for one."

"Why is your boyfriend convinced Heather is guilty?" Jason asked. "He's known her since she was a little girl. How could he believe her capable of something so heinous?"

"You know what Adam will say," Jenny said with exasperation. "He's just doing his job."

"I'm going to talk to him about Tiffany. She can't be ruled out as a suspect."

"You're Heather's lawyer," Jenny said with a nod. "You can talk to Adam in an official capacity. He will have to listen to you."

Groups of people were walking toward the town hall when they entered Pelican Cove.

"I forgot all about the meeting tonight," Jenny said. "You are coming, right?"

She held up her hand guessing Jason was about to say no.

"It will be fun, if nothing else."

Betty Sue sat on the stage near the front of the hall. John Newbury, her estranged husband, sat next to her. Ada Newbury sat in a corner seat, glaring at the crowd. Barb Norton stood behind the podium, calling the meeting to order. Heather stood at the back with a clipboard in her hand.

The Magnolias occupied the second row. They had saved room for Jenny and Jason.

"Thank you for coming," Barb began. "We need to raise a united voice against drugs in Pelican Cove. Thank you for signing the petition. I am sure it's going to help quash this whole thing."

"Why are we here then?" someone shouted from the crowd.

"I want to make sure every opinion is heard," Barb said pompously. "Although I am acting in the interest of the town, I'm no autocrat. And we want to tell the Newburys what we are thinking and what our concerns are."

An old woman sitting in the first row struggled to her feet, leaning heavily on a walking stick.

"I hear this marivana is going to help my knees. Is that true?"

"That's right," John Newbury spoke. "Marijuana helps in pain relief. We are going to grow high grade cannabis that will be processed into pills you can take for your arthritis."

"Where are you going to sell this?" another woman asked.

"We have leased a shop on Main Street," John replied.

"Main Street is where our kids hang out," a man said. "Minor kids. This dispensary as you call it is a bad influence on them."

Another man piped up from the crowd.

"What about ground water? I hear growing marijuana can contaminate ground water resources."

People started talking among themselves. Barb Norton tried to get their attention.

"One at a time, please."

"We don't want Pelican Cove to become a drug hangout," one man roared.

"You want to teach our kids it's okay to take drugs?" another woman demanded. "What kind of example are you setting for them?"

"You are just doing this to fill your pockets," an old woman quavered.

John Newbury stood up to answer them. Someone threw a rotten tomato at him. An egg or two followed. Barb Norton tried in vain to get everyone to behave. Someone pelted her with popcorn.

The meeting pretty much derailed after that.

"What the heck was that?" Jenny asked Star on the way home. "I didn't know people here could be so violent."

"That's just your regular town hall meeting," Star laughed.

"I don't feel like cooking tonight. Let's just order in some pizza from Mama Rosa's."

"Sounds like a plan," Star said. "Will you get my favorite?"

"Chicken, jalapeno and pineapple, I know," Jenny assured her aunt. "Jimmy's started liking it too."

Star scrunched up her face at the mention of Jimmy.

"I've been thinking," she said. "I haven't spent much time with Jimmy lately."

"He's just feeling left out," Jenny said.

"Jimmy's not the kind to throw money around," Star said.

Jenny knew what she was implying. Jimmy Parsons had a bunch of cottages he rented to tourists. He didn't have any other job. Jimmy wasn't rolling in money. It hadn't mattered to Star.

"Why don't you do something simple?" Jenny suggested. "The weather's warming up. Go for a picnic on the beach. I can make up a basket for you."

"That sounds romantic," Star sighed. "You think that will make him smile?"

"You just need to convince him he's special. He's gonna love it."

"Okay then," Star said happily. "I know the perfect place for a picnic."

"Do you need any talking points?" Jenny asked saucily.

"I don't, kid," Star said, rolling her eyes. "And I won't mention Frank at the picnic."

Chapter 14

The Magnolias were all quiet for a change. Betty Sue sipped her coffee and went on knitting furiously. Molly's head was buried in a book. Heather's eyes were rimmed with red. Petunia sat staring at them, crumpling a tissue in her hands. Star walked up the café steps, holding a few canvases.

"I'm taking these to the gallery," she told Jenny. "They are from my plein air session with Frank."

Jenny tipped her head at the women and gave her aunt a pleading look.

"What's the matter, Betty Sue?" Star boomed.

"I just got back from the police station," Heather said, blowing her nose in a tissue. "They wanted to question me again."

"What?" Jenny exclaimed. "I thought they had found other suspects."

"Apparently not," Heather said. "I'm still at the top of their list."

"I need to talk to Adam," Jenny said purposefully. "I'm going over right now."

"I'm coming with you," Betty Sue declared, discarding her knitting on the table. "I need to give that Hopkins boy a piece of my mind."

"That's not necessary, Betty Sue," Jenny said, dismayed. "Let me take care of this."

"You think I'm gonna cramp your style, girl?" Betty Sue thundered.

"Of course not," Jenny hastened to calm her down. "But I have a bone to pick with Adam. It might get ugly."

"Call me if you need me," Betty Sue relented.

"Of course," Jenny assured her.

She skipped down the café steps to the boardwalk and started walking toward the police station at a brisk pace.

Nora, the desk clerk, looked up when Jenny entered the station.

"I'm the one in a bad mood today," Jenny cautioned, holding up a hand.

Nora shrugged and shook her head.

"You know where to go."

Adam was eating a late breakfast at his desk.

"Hey Jenny," he greeted her. "This quiche is delicious. Never thought of myself as a quiche man."

"When will you stop harassing Heather?" Jenny cut to the chase.

She pulled up a chair and sat down with a thud. She crossed her arms and glared at Adam.

Adam looked at her coolly.

"I'm not harassing her as you say. I'm just questioning her which is routine in an investigation."

"Didn't Jason talk to you?" Jenny pressed. "I thought we provided you with other suspects."

"I did talk to Jason. But Heather is still a suspect too."

"But why?"

"I have my reasons, Jenny. I don't need to disclose them to you."

"What about Mr. Hampton's alibi? Did you check it out?"

"I talked to Eddie Cotton," Adam sighed. "The old man was at the pub until Eddie closed it for the night. He walked him home after that. Pete Hampton wasn't feeling too good. He was sick multiple times. Eddie stayed with him. They were up almost all night. Eddie didn't go home until morning."

"That clears the old man, I guess," Jenny said reluctantly.

"I talked to him, Jenny. I know what he was planning to do that night. But it wasn't his hand that killed the doctor. I am sure of that."

"What about Tiffany? She had means, motive and opportunity."

"She also has an alibi, Jenny."

"She had access to drugs and she also had access to Gianni's house here. She could have gone there from the restaurant."

"She left The Steakhouse while we were still there. She must have reached her home in Delaware before we left the restaurant."

"How do you know that?"

"She stopped for coffee on the way. She's on camera. That's the kind of proof we cannot ignore."

"How do you know she didn't come back into Pelican Cove?"

"I don't think she did, Jenny."

"How did Gianni die?" Jenny asked Adam. "You said he was drugged but when did that happen. And how?"

"There's a reason why we haven't released that information."

"Is it because you don't have a clue yourself?"

Adam began to look frustrated.

"You're being a nuisance, Jenny. Why don't you get back to the café and let me get on with my work?"

"Heather's been crying her eyes out."

"She has nothing to worry if she's innocent."

"You've known her all your life, Adam. Do you really think she's capable of killing someone?"

"The evidence against her is pretty strong. As an officer of the law, I cannot overlook it."

"Her relationship with Gianni wasn't a secret. Tiffany admitted she knew about it too. And Heather really liked Gianni. What possible motive could she have to kill him?"

"If I had to guess, I would say revenge."

"You need to do more than guess, Adam."

"We found Heather's fingerprints on the scene, on the very glass that contained the drugs, as a matter of fact."

"Heather's been in and out of that house for the past few weeks. She must have handled many things there."

Adam rubbed his forehead with his fingers.

"She had a prescription for antidepressants."

"Haven't you listened to anything I told you?" Jenny cried. "Gianni wrote up wrong prescriptions. It was a scam he was running."

"This is a real prescription written by Dr. Smith," Adam said gravely. "Heather admitted she filled that prescription. She even has a half empty bottle with her."

"So she took the pills herself!"

"We don't know that," Adam shrugged. "Those pills match one of the drugs found in Gianni's system. Heather could have ground up those pills and added them to Gianni's drink."

Jenny sat back in shock. Adam continued his onslaught.

"Heather had free access to Gianni's clinic here. Using the argument you use against Tiffany, Heather had access to plenty of drugs."

"You honestly believe she's guilty, don't you?"

"My feelings don't matter here, Jenny. The law only looks at the evidence. Things don't look too good for Heather right now."

"My money's still on Tiffany," Jenny insisted, scrambling to her feet. "She lied multiple times. First she told me Gianni had affairs all the time and she didn't care about them. Then she said she was going to leave Gianni because he cheated on her. Based on her prenup, she wasn't going to get a penny if she walked out on him. That's why she killed him. Now she inherits his fortune. Thanks to cops like you, she's roaming free."

"Tiffany had a prenuptial agreement?" Adam asked. "I didn't know about that."

"I'm sure there is plenty more you don't know, Sheriff," Jenny said as she stomped out.

Jenny's anger subsided as soon as she stepped out of the police station. It was replaced by worry for her friend. She crossed the road and walked into Jason Stone's office.

Jason was talking to someone on the phone.

"Kandy and I were invited to a dinner party," he said stoically. "I was calling to tell them I won't be making it."

"I can go with you," Jenny offered.

"Not this time," Jason sighed. "It was for introducing Kandy to my college buddies."

"Oh."

"All well, Jenny? What brings you here at this time of the day?"

"I think Heather's in trouble," Jenny blurted out. "I just spoke to Adam."

"Did he tell you about finding her fingerprints on the scene?" Jason asked.

Jenny nodded.

"Things are not looking good, Jason. What will happen if this case goes to court?"

"I'm not a criminal lawyer, Jenny. But I can recommend one of the best persons for this job."

"Can you negotiate a lighter sentence if Heather admits she did it?"

Jason pursed his mouth.

"We should not be talking about this."

"I'm thinking of the worst case scenario here, Jason."

"I can see that. Heather's calling the shots here Jenny. She's my client, not you."

"Let me know if I can help," Jenny offered. "I'm going to keep working on this."

Jenny walked back to the café, feeling helpless. Adam had been so confident she was beginning to doubt Heather's innocence.

She spent the day feeling cranky, even snapping at a couple of tourists who wanted more salt in their soup. She had a splitting headache by the time she got home.

A couple of duffel bags lay on the front porch. Adam sat in a chair, looking at his watch and tapping his foot. Tank leapt at Jenny when he saw her, placing his paws on her shoulders.

Jenny hugged and kissed him.

"I've had a bad day, Tank," she whispered in his ear.

She finally noticed the bags.

"Do we have guests?" she questioned. "Wait a minute, has Nick turned up with some of his friends?"

Those are my bags, Jenny," Adam said calmly. "I'm going home."

"What? No!" Jenny wailed.

She stared at Adam with a wild look in her eyes.

"When did you decide that?"

"We talked about this," Adam said softly. "The contractors moved out of my house a couple of weeks ago."

"But we never talked about a date. Why today?"

"Why not?"

"You can't spring this on me, Adam. Not after the day I've had."

"I'm sorry, Jenny. The twins are coming home this weekend. I want to air the place out before that. Stock the refrigerator."

"The twins are welcome here," Jenny said in a shocked voice. "I have always loved having them here."

Adam took Jenny by the shoulders and forced her to sit down.

"This is hard for me too, Jenny. You think I want to go?"

"Then don't."

"It's not right," Adam said with a shake of his head. "I've imposed on your hospitality for too long. People are beginning to talk, and I don't like it."

"I don't care what people say."

"But I do. I feel guilty about it."

"Is this because we fought before? Is this your way of punishing me?"

"Of course not, Jenny. How can you say that?"

"Then don't go," Jenny said mulishly. "Not today."

"You are going to feel the same any time I go, Jenny. It's got to be done some time."

"I was going to arrange a farewell party for you."

"There's no need for that. I'm not going anywhere. I will probably be here for dinner very often."

Tank sensed the tension in the air. He butted Jenny in the knee, and sat down at her feet.

"Tank doesn't want to go," Jenny declared.

"He can stay here," Adam said. "I can't."

"What can I say to make you change your mind?" Jenny's eyes filled up. She was trying hard to control herself.

"Please don't be like this, Jenny. There are some things I can't do while I am still living here."

"What things?" Jenny asked, bewildered.

"You'll find out soon," Adam promised. "It's a surprise. Now dry your tears and see me off with a smile."

"You're sure you're not mad at me?" Jenny asked.

"Of course not," Adam promised. "I'll see you soon."

Adam picked up his bags and limped to his car. Tank refused to get up.

"He needs you, Tank," Jenny whispered. "Go take care of him."

Tank gave a tiny whine and followed Adam.

Jenny waved madly until Adam was out of sight. Then she felt silly. Adam was only going a couple of miles further. But she had grown used to living in the same house with him.

Star came out of the house and hugged her.

"We need a girls' night," she declared. "I'm calling the reinforcements."

Molly arrived half an hour later with Petunia in tow. Heather and Betty Sue were next.

Heather waved a bunch of DVDs in the air.

"I got all your favorites, Jenny. Start popping the corn."

"I'm making my twice baked macaroni and cheese," Star announced. "Molly's taking care of dessert."

"Banana splits with hot fudge and my special brownies," Molly promised.

"We are going to drive that Hopkins boy out of your mind, girl," Betty Sue cackled.

Jenny let her friends pamper her, trying not to think about what kind of surprise Adam had in store for her.

Chapter 15

The Magnolias were busy. Heather and Molly were assembling pimento cheese sandwiches. Star spooned crab salad on crackers and garnished them with a sprig of dill. Jenny was frosting tray after tray of cupcakes.

"I have to say, the Newburys don't do anything half-heartedly," Petunia said, bobbing her head. Her double chins wobbled as she looked around, making sure everything looked good.

"They are generous, aren't they?" Jenny said, sweeping a hand over the food. "They are paying for all this food for the whole town."

"They see it as an investment," Betty Sue snorted. "They stand to earn millions from that drug business."

There was another meeting in the town hall that evening. The Newburys had taken note of all the objections that had been raised by the people. They were going to address all those concerns.

Ada Newbury had hired the Boardwalk Café to provide refreshments for the meeting. Jenny and her friends had been busy making sure the food matched Ada's specific instructions.

The town hall was packed. People were gorging on the food. Some openly admitted coming there just for the food. A large screen had been set up. A couple of men were rigging up some kind of fancy projector. Julius Newbury, Ada's husband, stood by the side, reading from a stack of index cards.

Barb Norton called the meeting to order.

"Julius Newbury is going to answer all your questions," she said simply. "I hope you will maintain some decorum this time."

There was a smattering of applause, accompanied by a wisecrack or two from the crowd. Jenny and the Magnolias sat in the second row. Jenny had heard a lot about the uses of medical marijuana. She was eager to see what the Newburys had to say in their defense.

Lights were dimmed and the presentation started. Julius Newbury spoke well. He walked everyone through a 3D demonstration of the proposed fields and processing plant. He laid special stress on all the safety and security measures in place. A view of Main Street came up on the screen.

A murmur started going through the crowd. Julius paused the presentation and held up a hand.

"We are now going to show you the site of the dispensary itself. I know many of you have concerns about it."

The dispensary proved to be a veritable fortress. There were multiple check points to get in and get out. Employees would be scanned before they left the premises. There was no room for illicit activities.

Julius Newbury pointed to a tall, hefty man who had been standing by his side all this time. He was introduced as the security chief.

"This man has been hired to oversee the complete security of the project. Every inch of the business, whether it is the fields, the processing plant or the dispensary itself will be closely monitored by top notch security measures. The chief is here to address your concerns."

People stood up and started firing questions. The man known as 'Chief' calmly answered all of them. The crowd finally simmered down. There was a lull for a few moments. Then a woman stood up at the back.

"What about the psychological impact your drugs will have on our kids? We are teaching them it's okay to consume psychoactive drugs like cannabis? What is the message we are giving out here?"

Julius Newbury bit his lip and tried to hide his frustration.

"Your kids need to be smart enough to understand the difference. Taking a drug for a medical purpose is different from getting stoned."

"But they are too young to know the difference," another man shouted.

"That's exactly why this will never work," a voice said from the back.

"I can't discipline your kids," Julius Newbury said, turning red. "That's your job. If they are going to get into drugs, they will do it with or without my dispensary."

"What about the fields?" a woman with a baby in her arms asked. "Kids can get in there anytime."

The security chief spoke up.

"No, they can't. We have electric fences around the fields. Anyone trying to scale the fences will be electrocuted."

"You would do that to a child?" a woman asked, looking horrified.

Barb Norton stepped in before any further chaos ensued.

"We have all had our say, Julius. It's up to them now." She turned toward the crowd and pointed at Heather. "If you still want to protest this business, please sign the petition. We are going to see to it that marijuana licenses are not granted for Pelican Cove."

She looked at Julius Newbury and shrugged.

"Nothing personal, Julius."

The Magnolias helped Jenny clear up after the meeting. They took all the leftovers to Seaview for an impromptu dinner party. Jason had fired up the grill on the patio.

"The steaks are ready to go on the grill," he told Jenny.

Everyone relaxed with a drink.

"The crab salad was gone in minutes," Star said. "I'm glad we at least get to taste these pimento cheese sandwiches."

Heather's smile slipped when Adam arrived.

"Relax," he said, putting a hand on her shoulder. "I'm just here for dinner."

"It will be over soon, sweetie," Jenny promised Heather.

She wondered if she was making an empty promise. Adam stuck around after everyone had gone home. He loaded the dishwasher while Jenny put the leftovers in the fridge.

"How about a walk?" he asked.

Tank fetched a stick from the garden and dropped it at Jenny's feet.

"I guess we are going for a walk," Jenny laughed.

"What's on your mind?" Jenny asked after they had walked a quarter mile away from the house.

"More bad news," Adam said quietly. "One of Gianni's neighbors has come forward. He saw Heather leaving Gianni's house at 5 AM."

Jenny stared at Adam, her fear clearly written on her face.

"That doesn't sound good."

Adam shook his head. "It places Heather at the scene of the crime. I'm sorry, Jenny."

Jenny spent a sleepless night worrying about Heather. She was so disturbed she almost burnt a pan of muffins while making breakfast.

She finally called the Bayview Inn at 7 AM.

"I need to talk to you, Heather," she burst out. "Can you come here right now?"

Heather came in ten minutes later, looking worried.

"What's so urgent, Jenny? I was serving breakfast at the inn."

Jenny led Heather out on the deck.

"We never talked about that night," Jenny began.

"I don't remember much, Jenny. I already told you that."

"That's not going to help you, Heather. Think!"

"I remember saying goodbye to all of you at The Steakhouse. Gianni wanted a drink when we got home. I had already had too much. The next thing I remember is waking up in my own bed."

"Someone saw you walking out of Gianni's house at 5 AM."

Heather looked dismayed.

"I must have passed out."

"Was anyone else there when you reached Gianni's house?"

"I don't think so. Wait, the door was open when we got there."

"Do you mean it was unlocked?" Jenny asked. "Or was it wide open?"

"I don't know. Gianni said something about changing the locks."

Jenny thought furiously.

"Changing the locks? That means whoever opened the door had a key."

"Tiffany had a key," Heather cried. "You think she was waiting for us there?"

"Tiffany left for Delaware after her little altercation with you."

"She could have come back?" Heather said hopefully.

"Speculation is not going to help us, Heather. Did you see her there?"

"I don't remember."

"That's your answer to everything."

"I've never been so drunk in my life, Jenny. And I'm paying for it now."

"Gianni was bad for you, Heather."

"I know that now, when it's too late. I guess I just latched on to him on the rebound."

"After dating a dozen other guys?" Jenny's disdain was clear. "Why were you taking antidepressants, Heather?"

"You know about that?" Heather asked.

"The police know about it too. It's another factor against you."

"I wasn't doing well, Jenny. All those guys I dated were just a ruse. I was all torn up inside. I couldn't sleep. Old Dr. Smith prescribed those pills. They were a life saver."

"Did you ever give them to Gianni?"

"Of course not," Heather denied. "He didn't even know I was taking those pills."

"When did you really find out he had a wife?" Jenny gave Heather a stern look. "Was it really at The Steakhouse?"

Heather was quiet for a while. Unfortunately, she looked guilty.

"Gianni never told me about his wife. But I was beginning to have doubts. There were small signs – scent of perfume in the air, a lipstick in the medicine cabinet. I knew there was another woman. I just never dreamed he was a married man."

"Weren't you mad when you found out?"

"I was pretty mad," Heather said, remembering. "He had been talking about taking me to the Caribbean, having a dream wedding. He was a cheat and a liar."

"Why did you fight with Tiffany at the restaurant then? She was the wife. You were the other woman, Heather."

"I don't know what came over me," Heather confessed. "And I was drunk. Less drunk than I was later, but drunk enough."

"None of these things will work in your favor," Jenny said sadly.

"Is there no hope for me?" Heather wailed again.

"Go to some quiet place, clear your mind and try to remember anything you can about that night. Your life depends on it, sweetie."

"I need your help, Jenny. You helped catch so many murderers in the past. Can't you do the same this time?"

"I'm trying my best," Jenny assured her. "Meanwhile, you need to be brave. We will try to bail you out if they take you in."

Jenny's fears proved to be true. The Magnolias were sitting out on the deck later when Adam arrived with his deputies. He arrested Heather for the murder of Dr. Gianni Costa.

Betty Sue Morse was in shock. She fainted without a word, her face falling flat on the wooden table. Star fanned her with a paper napkin while Petunia loosened the buttons at her throat. Molly was about to leave to get the doctor when Betty Sue opened her eyes. She was inconsolable.

"You need to be strong, Betty Sue," Jenny told her firmly. "I'm going to get Jason. We will have Heather back here soon."

Jason was out of town on business and unreachable. Jenny left several messages, urging him to get back to town immediately. It was afternoon by the time he came back.

"I had an idea this was coming," he told Jenny. "Don't worry, I already have the papers ready. She should be out soon."

Adam sat in his office with an inscrutable expression on his face. Jenny pushed open the door and went in, ready to give him a piece of her mind.

"Believe it or not, I'm just doing my job," he sighed. "If I don't do it, someone else will."

Jenny's anger deflated like a balloon.

"This is hard on all of us," she told him. "Dr. Smith gave Betty Sue a sedative. Her blood pressure shot up. Star is sitting by her side, keeping her company."

"Has anyone else come forward?" Jenny asked. "What about any new evidence?"

Adam shook his head. "You were looking at Gianni's old files, weren't you?" Adam asked. "Why don't you go through them again? Your out of the box approach is

Heather's only hope now, Jenny."

"You are actually encouraging me to keep on digging?" Jenny asked wondrously. "That doesn't sound like you."

"What are you going to do next, Jenny?" Adam asked.

"I don't know. I'm plum out of ideas."

Chapter 16

Jenny was lost in thought as she mixed the batter for banana nut muffins. She remembered how Heather had appeared on the deck one day with Gianni Costa. He had already set up his clinic in Pelican Cove at that time.

"You found Gianni on that dating site, didn't you?" she asked Heather later that morning.

"Yes, I found his profile attractive. I didn't know he lived right here."

"Did he ever talk about his earlier life? Like where he went to college or medical school?"

"He had a bunch of certificates up on the wall in his office," Heather said with a shrug. "But I never paid much attention to them."

"I think we need to find out more about Gianni," Jenny declared. "What do his patients say about him, for example? Did any of them catch on to his scams?"

"Aren't there websites where people post reviews on doctors?" Molly asked. "Doctors have a score based on the ratings patients assign them."

"I generally check those scores before going to any specialist," Jenny nodded. "Looks like I have some work to do on the Internet."

Jenny went straight home after work that day and started her laptop. Her search yielded surprising results. Gianni had been popular with his patients. Most people had written glowing reviews about how gracious the doctor was, and how he actually listened to them. Some even went on to say he was the best doctor they had ever come across.

Jenny decided Gianni had paid someone to write fake reviews. Then she looked a bit closer. The reviews started two years ago. There wasn't a single review for Dr. Gianni Costa before that. It was almost as if he hadn't existed.

She dialed Tiffany's number.

"Hey Tiffany, got a few minutes?"

"What do you need?" Tiffany asked rudely.

She was in a bad mood.

"You don't sound so good."

"The authorities have frozen all of our bank accounts. I don't have five dollars for a cup of coffee."

"What? I am so sorry to hear that."

"What did you tell them, Jenny?" Tiffany shrieked over the phone. "What am I going to do now?"

Jenny was glad. It seemed that the authorities were pursuing other lines of investigation. That was good news for Heather.

"I'm sure it's just temporary," Jenny tried to placate her.

"Are you calling to gloat?"

"No, of course not! I had a few questions about Gianni. Do you know how long he had been living in Delaware when you met him?"

"Didn't he always live there?" Tiffany asked.

"Apparently not. Did he move there from some other part of the country?"

"If he did, he never told me about it."

"What about medical school?"

"What is this, an inquisition? There's a bunch of certificates hanging up on the wall in his clinic. I never really noticed them."

"Can you do me a favor?" Jenny pleaded. "Can you take some photos of all those certificates and send them to me? It might be important."

"Why should I do that?" Tiffany demanded. "The police confirmed my alibi for the night Gianni died. I'm in the clear."

"You won't have access to your money until the case is solved. You want that, don't you?"

"Whatever!" Tiffany said churlishly. "I guess I can take a few photos."

"Thank you. Thank you so much, Tiffany."

Jenny tapped her foot and stared at her phone every few seconds. She hoped Tiffany would send the photos right away. She didn't relish the thought of having to plead with the woman again. Jenny was just about to go out in the garden to get some fresh air when her phone pinged.

She connected her phone to her computer and downloaded the photos Tiffany had sent. Jenny was surprised to see Gianni had graduated from a prestigious medical school in the area. Why had he set up his clinic in small towns with a degree like that? He could have had a job at the finest city hospitals.

Jenny didn't have much luck when she called the medical school office. Any information about students was private. She could get a transcript if she was a prospective employer. Otherwise she had nothing.

Jenny sat on her patio, breathing in the scent of the roses, staring at the gurgling water fountain. She remembered all the alumni association meetings her ex-husband had gone to every year. She went in and opened her laptop again. She had some calls to make.

Adam grinned from ear to ear when he spotted Jenny on the beach that night. Tank was running in circles around her, nudging her with a stick in his mouth. Jenny took the stick and threw it in a wide arc. Tank leapt after it with a joyous bark.

"I didn't get any complaints about you today so I am guessing you are staying out of trouble."

"Not exactly," Jenny confessed.

She thought of the talking down she had received from some of the men she had called earlier. She decided to keep it to herself.

"I thought the twins were bent on giving me a hard time, but you take the cake, Jenny."

"I'm doing it for a good cause," Jenny said woodenly.

"So are you going to tell me about it?"

"I tried to reach some of Gianni's friends. I looked up his alumni association and called a few people. None of the people I talked to remember him."

"I have never spoken to a single person I went to college with," Adam grumbled. "I doubt any of them will remember me."

"I'm sure plenty of them will," Jenny argued. "You are not easily forgettable."

"That's not the point, Jenny," Adam sighed. "Not every person is a member of their alumni association."

"My ex went to every alumni function."

"You're saying Gianni didn't."

"I don't care if he was a member," Jenny said. "I'm saying no one remembered him."

"How many people did you talk to?" Adam asked.

"Plenty," Jenny said with a grimace. "All of them were from his graduating class. None of them remembered a fellow student called Gianni Costa."

Adam was quiet for a few minutes.

"You're saying Gianni put up a fake degree in his office."

Jenny shrugged.

"He could have easily forged a document."

"I think you are shooting in the dark," Adam said bluntly. "Are you saying Gianni wasn't really a doctor?"

"I don't know what to make of it," Jenny said glumly.

"You've done all you could for Heather," Adam consoled her. "I think you should let the police do their work now. I would focus on getting her a good lawyer."

"Are you saying I should just give up?" Jenny's temper flared. "Jason would never tell me that."

"I'm not Jason," Adam said haughtily. "Don't ever confuse me for him, Jenny."

"How could I? You don't have a kind bone in your body, Adam Hopkins!"

Jenny whirled around and stomped back to Seaview. Tank followed her for a while and then turned back when Adam whistled at him.

"Gianni was a doctor alright," Jason said when Jenny visited him the next morning.

She had told him about her latest theory. Jenny had been mollified when Jason didn't reject it outright.

"Think of the scam he was running," Jason mused, scratching his chin.

He had day old stubble and his eyes were red. Jenny hoped he wasn't staying awake thinking about Kandy.

"Couldn't anyone have done it?" she asked.

"We can talk to Dr. Smith about this if you want. The scam Gianni was running required advanced knowledge about medicine and the system. Only an experienced doctor could have done it."

"Why would he put up fake credentials?"

"Because he didn't want to use his real ones?" Jason guessed.

"Wait a minute, could he have lost his license?"

"That's possible," Jason nodded. "He might have practiced in some other state before he got here."

"You won't believe it, but he has some great reviews from patients. But they only go back two years."

"What?" Jason started.

He looked at Jenny with wide eyes.

"What if it's not just the wrong medical school? What if it's the wrong person?"

"What do you mean, Jason?" Jenny asked, her heart speeding up.

"Gianni Costa could be a fake identity, Jenny. We don't know how long he was running his scams. Maybe he moved from state to state and took up a different name every time."

"New name, new credentials and new women," Jenny said softly.

"Didn't you say Tiffany came from a simple background? That's why he must have chosen her. He wanted someone who would be wowed by his money and wouldn't ask too many questions. He just wanted a wife to look respectable."

"What about Heather?"

"He needed her to build some credibility in Pelican Cove."

"Why did he get greedy, opening a clinic in two states at a time?"

Jason shrugged.

"Maybe he wanted to retire early? It's also the unique position of the Shore. He could easily live in two places at once."

"Heather dodged a bullet," Jenny said.

"We don't know what he was planning for her," Jason said seriously.

"Should we tell Adam? He's going to call this farfetched."

"Let me take care of it, Jenny. We need Adam's help to investigate further."

Jenny's phone rang, interrupting them. Her face lit up when she saw who was calling.

"It's Nick," she smiled.

"When are you coming home, Nicky?" she asked.

Jason looked on indulgently while Jenny spoke to her son. In his late forties, Jason had given up any hopes of ever being a father. But he loved watching the special bond Jenny shared with her son.

"He's coming home tonight," Jenny said happily as soon as she hung up.

Then her face clouded over. "He has something to tell me."

"Relax. I am sure it's good news."

"You will come to dinner tonight, won't you?" Jenny said briskly. "I'm going to make Nick's favorites."

"I don't want to intrude."

"Of course you won't be intruding. Star and Jimmy will be there too."

"Let me bring the wine then," Jason said.

Jenny had a huge smile on her face as she worked through her chores. She rubbed the charms around her neck, thinking of her son. She fired off a quick message to him around lunch time, warning him to drive slowly.

"Why don't you go home early?" Petunia said after they had lunch. "I can wrap up around here."

"Thanks," Jenny said.

She drove to the seafood market and picked up the catch of the day. She was planning to make Nick's favorite fried potatoes with fresh rosemary from her herb garden.

She had barely finished unloading the groceries at home when Nick arrived. He gave her a bear hug and allowed her to kiss him.

"You look scruffy," she said. "You do take a shower now and then?"

"Mom!" Nick complained. "I had a paper due today. I hit the road as soon as I turned it in."

"I'm so happy to see you, Nicky."

Jenny poured fresh squeezed lemonade in two tall glasses. She had muddled some strawberries and basil into them.

Nick drained half the glass in one gulp.

"I miss your cooking, Mom."

"Stop flattering me and tell me what you wanted to talk about."

She and Nick were sitting on a couch in the family room.

"I'm going to Europe in the summer," Nick said. "It's for a class."

"That's great," Jenny exclaimed. "You were so young when we took you there the last time. Hey, maybe I can join you when you're done."

"There's more," Nick said, making a face. "Dad's meeting me there. He's planned a road trip for the two of us."

"That's good for you," Jenny said, trying to hide her disappointment. "I'm glad your dad wants to spend some time with you."

Chapter 17

The Magnolias were enjoying their usual coffee break on the deck of the Boardwalk Café.

"Do you have any new leads?" Heather asked Jenny.

"I'm working on something."

That's all Jenny would say. She didn't want to reveal too much unless she was sure it was going to work in their favor.

"How's your little project with Barb Norton coming along?"

"Almost everyone in town has signed the petition. Over 90% of the people have said no to that dispensary. I think the Newburys are going to be disappointed."

"I feel bad for the people who really need that medicine," Jenny said. "But I guess some of the concerns people raised are real too."

Jenny packed a couple of chocolate cupcakes in a box and took them over to Jason. He loved chocolate.

"How are you, Jenny?" he asked, lighting up as he opened the box she handed over.

"Have you talked to Adam yet?" Jenny asked. "What does he say about our theory?"

"You know Adam," Jason shrugged. "He said he'll work on it. We have to give him a couple of days before we press any further."

"He's had his two days," Jenny fumed. "Time's running out."

Jason licked chocolate frosting off a fork and nodded.

"What do you want to do?"

"Let's go talk to him now."

Adam frowned when Jenny entered his office.

"I'm busy now. Come back later."

"We just need a few minutes, Adam."

She sat down and Jason followed.

"Did you find out anything more about Gianni?"

"Not yet," Adam admitted. "I'm drawing a blank."

Jenny leaned forward, her eyes shining with an idea.

"What if you ran his fingerprints? Have you done that yet? He might have a criminal record."

"Let me get back to you on that," Adam promised.

He ushered them out of his office, looking irritated. Jenny walked out, feeling hopeful.

"If Gianni was going around using a false identity, we will find that out soon enough."

"Fingers crossed, Jenny," Jason said, heading back to his office.

Jenny went back to the café. She had a big order for a birthday cake. She needed to start baking if she wanted to have the cake ready on time.

Adam came to Seaview for dinner that evening. Jenny was happy to see him. She tried to forget his boorish behavior from that morning. Adam always stressed that he wanted to keep his professional life separate from his private life. Jenny decided she would try the same. She was mad at Sheriff Adam but she was happy to see her beau Adam for dinner.

"This is like an impromptu date," Adam said, handing her a bunch of roses from the garden.

Star and Jimmy had gone out for a drive.

"It's just you and me," Jenny said with a blush. "Do you want to eat out on the patio?"

"It's kind of chilly outside," Adam said, rubbing his palms together. "I can build a fire in the pit."

They finally decided to eat in the cozy breakfast nook. Jenny lit candles and served the simple pasta dinner.

Adam dunked his crusty bread in the clam sauce and stared into Jenny's eyes.

"Do you miss having me here?"

Jenny's smile was answer enough.

"Won't be for long," Adam said cryptically.

They decided to go for a walk before dessert. Jenny went upstairs to get a wrap for herself.

"I don't want to spoil the mood but I have some more news for you, Jenny. The prints came back. They belong to a man called Joe Torres."

"What else?" Jenny asked eagerly.

"I will know more tomorrow," Adam promised.

The next day, Jenny waited impatiently to hear back from Adam. She packed some lunch for the two of them and walked over to the police station.

"I'm still working on it," Adam said, chewing on his chicken salad sandwich. "I learned a few random things but I haven't pieced it together yet."

"I'll hold on a bit longer, I guess," Jenny said reluctantly.

Heather called when Jenny was about to sit down to dinner.

"Guess who just booked two rooms at the Bayview Inn?"

"Who?" Jenny played along.

"Ann Davis and her son Ricky. They are coming here in the summer."

"So Ann wasn't kidding when she said she missed the Eastern Shore."

"Apparently not," Heather agreed. "You think they are still interested in Seaview?"

"Ann is the one who sold me the house," Jenny reminded Heather. "Keith was the one who wanted to hold on to it. But he's gone now."

"Will you invite them over?"

"I don't know, Heather, we'll see."

Jenny let Heather prattle on for some time. She was pleased to see shades of the old Heather.

"Your dinner's getting cold," Star called from the table.

Jenny giggled and hung up. She loved living with her elderly aunt. It made her feel younger and reminded her of the times she had spent summers in Pelican Cove as a teen.

Jimmy regaled them with stories of some of his tenants. With tourist season coming up, he had his work cut out for him. He fixed up all the cottages, and added a fresh coat of paint.

"Sounds like you're going to be pretty busy, Jimmy," Star said, stirring a spoon in her soup.

Jenny had made pea soup with fresh peas and mint from the garden. She paired it with lemony grilled chicken breasts in a garlic butter sauce.

"This is my usual spring routine," Jimmy shrugged. "I'm used to it."

"What do you think about taking a trip?"

"Now?" Jimmy asked. "There's no way I can get away right now."

Star said nothing and took a few bites.

"Do you need to go somewhere?" Jimmy asked a few minutes later.

"Frank had this great idea," Star hesitated. "Spring time is really beautiful in the mountains."

"But your specialty is seascapes," Jimmy pointed out. "That's what the tourists buy year after year."

"I know. But a mountain landscape would be a great addition to my work. Frank says a diverse portfolio makes the artist look more experienced."

"He would know."

"Of course he does," Star said. "He's painted mountains, deserts, canyons and beaches in every possible season. I trust his opinion."

"What are you saying?" Jimmy asked quietly.

"It's a three day trip. That gives us four or five plein air sessions. I can book a room in town and drive up into the mountains in Frank's bus every day."

"Doesn't sound like you need me there," Jimmy grumbled.

Star grasped his hand.

"Of course I need you, Jimmy. It will be fun."

"You really want to do this?" Jimmy asked.

"I've been painting the ocean and the salt marshes for years. I like the thought of trying my hand at something new."

"Let me think about it," Jimmy said.

"You're going anyway, aren't you?" Jenny asked her aunt later.

"Frank's a talented artist. I can learn a lot from him."

"Is that all?" Jenny asked. "I think you have a tiny crush on him."

Star refused to comment on that. Jenny hoped her aunt would decide not to go on the trip. She wasn't too keen on sending her off with a stranger.

Jenny spent another busy day at the café, working on a few special orders. Barb Norton came in during lunch. She tasted the chicken noodle soup Jenny placed before her and pronounced it delicious.

"What brings you here, Barb?" Jenny asked, setting down a plate of crab salad with the fat free crackers Barb preferred.

"Sit down, Jenny," Barb ordered. "Spring Fest is just a few weeks away. Have you thought about it yet?"

"I guess we'll put up something just like last time."

"You haven't signed up for it yet," Barb admonished. "I need to have your final menu by the end of the week. I am going to review all of them. I might ask you to make a few changes."

Jenny mumbled something under her breath.

"We don't want everyone offering the same thing," Barb said. "If you are working on any new recipes for the festival, arrange a tasting session in the next two days."

"That's not enough time," Jenny protested.

"Serve it at the café that day," Barb ordered. "I'm sure you can do it."

Barb gave Jenny a few more pointers about the upcoming festival while she ate her lunch.

"It's hard to choose between your cupcakes or donuts," Barb said. "No waffles. We'll have funnel cakes."

Jenny finally got a chance to eat her own lunch. Jason rushed in when she had barely taken two bites.

"Adam wants us," he said.

"Can I finish eating?" Jenny asked. "I'm starving."

"Sure. I'll join you if you have another of those." Jason looked greedily at the sandwich she was eating.

They scarfed down their food in a few minutes and started walking toward the police station.

Adam was just finishing his own lunch. He tossed everything in a trash can and turned around to beam at them.

"I have some news."

Jenny's neck muscles were taut with tension.

"Good news or bad news?"

"Relax, Jenny, this will take a while."

Adam handed over a bottle of cold water. Jenny guzzled the water and looked questioningly at Adam.

"Your hunch paid off. Joe Torres, Dr. Joe Torres, lived in a small town in New Mexico. He was arrested for medical fraud."

Jenny slammed her fist on Adam's desk.

"That's more like it. What else did you find out?"

"I talked to my counterpart over there," Adam explained. "Gianni, or Joe, whatever you call him, was one of the top doctors in the town. He had been running scams for years."

"What kind of scams?" Jason asked.

"Wrong diagnoses, double billing, there's a long list. He finally got caught. One of his patients reported him and he was arrested. But they never found enough evidence to convict."

Jenny sucked in a breath.

"He must have been tipped off."

"That's what they think," Adam agreed. "The charges didn't stick so they had to let him go. His reputation suffered though and he lost his medical license."

"That must have been a big blow," Jason said. "What did he do after that?"

Adam shrugged.

"They didn't exactly keep tabs on him. There is no record of him after that."

"So Dr. Joe Torres just disappeared?" Jenny pressed.

"Something like that, Jenny. There is no address for him in that town so all we can surmise is he went somewhere else."

"He took on a new identity," Jenny said. "But the question is, how many other identities did he have before becoming Gianni Costa."

"Does that matter?" Adam asked.

"We don't know how many people he hurt," Jenny pointed out. "If we want to find these people, we need to track down everything Gianni or Joe did."

"She has a point," Jason said, backing Jenny up.

"That's like looking for a needle in a haystack," Adam sighed.

"Are you up for the challenge?" Jenny asked him.

"We can't be sure this has any relevance to the current crime," Adam said stodgily. "It's not my job to uncover the fraud he did."

"Are you going to throw Heather under the bus just because you can't do your due diligence?"

Jenny stood with her hands on her hips and glared at Adam.

"Be careful, Jenny. I don't care for your allegations."

"Neither does Heather," Jenny snapped. "Heather may not have an alibi but I know in my heart that she is innocent."

"You're talking like the amateur you are," Adam said hotly. "Feelings don't matter in an investigation. We have to deal with hard facts."

"I will find hard facts for you, Adam Hopkins," Jenny challenged. "I will find facts you cannot ignore."

Chapter 18

"I always knew that man was up to no good," Betty Sue Morse declared. The Magnolias were huddled together on the deck of the Boardwalk Café. Coffee cooled in cups as the women mulled over what Jenny had just told them.

"What did Heather see in him?" Molly wondered out loud.

Heather sat with her hands in her lap, looking suitably contrite.

"What are you going to do next?" Star asked Jenny.

"I'm going to find out everything I can about this man, Joe Torres."

"You're a whiz at Internet research now, Jenny," Heather said meekly. "Let me know if I can help."

"I have something in mind for you," Jenny said cryptically.

Molly and Heather followed Jenny into the kitchen on the pretext of getting some food.

"What's the plan?" Molly asked, looking radiant in a new peach top.

She hadn't talked about Chris in a while but Jenny guessed the new couple was doing well.

"Heather needs to remember what happened that night," Jenny said.

Heather opened her mouth to protest. Jenny held up a hand.

"I know, I know, you were drunk! So this is what I propose. We are going to get you drunk again and try to retrace your steps. That might jog your memory."

"I promised myself I would never be that intoxicated again."

"You have to make an exception this time, Heather," Jenny said smoothly. "Your life may depend on it."

"So when are we doing this? Chris and I have a hot date tonight. We are going to Virginia Beach."

"Cancel that date," Jenny ordered. "We need you with us."

Molly agreed easily.

"You really think this idea will work?" Heather asked.

"We won't know until we try."

They agreed to meet at Seaview around 5 PM.

Jenny didn't get a chance to do her Internet research until she got home later that afternoon. She fired up her laptop and started running searches on Dr. Joe Torres. He turned out to be a popular doctor. But all the records she saw were about four years old. She started checking the social sites. Joe or Gianni appeared with a woman on his arm. There were several photos of them smiling and laughing together, at parties or at the beach. The woman was labeled as Maria or Maria Torres.

Jenny guessed the woman was his wife. The woman stopped appearing in the photos about five years ago. Jenny decided to dig deeper. She looked for other news in the region for those dates. She found some news items about a missing woman, none other than Maria Torres.

Maria had been on vacation with her husband when she disappeared. Her husband, a well known local doctor, had been devastated. The news articles printed Maria's life history. Maria had been born Maria Juanita Lopez Garcia. She had been the only child of aging parents. Her mother died when she was in high school. She had been working at the local gas company when Joe Torres saw her and fell in love with her.

A massive search had been mounted for Maria but she never came back. Many theories had been proposed. One of the theories accused Joe Torres of killing his wife and disposing of her body. It had been deemed fantastic by most people. Joe Torres was so popular in his town that no one had been willing to believe a word against him. Then he was arrested for fraud. He had been released later but the damage had been done. He lost his medical license.

Jenny couldn't find any references to Joe Torres after that. She figured he had simply relocated to another state and taken on a new identity.

Molly and Heather arrived before she had time to process all the information.

"What are we drinking?" Molly asked.

"You and I need to be sober," Jenny told her. "Heather's going to get drunk."

"Come on Jenny, we can at least have a cocktail each."

Heather chose her poison. They went into the kitchen and made strawberry daiquiris.

"Do you have something to nosh on?" Heather asked.

"You're on a liquid diet tonight, babe," Jenny teased. "Forget about food."

They watched a chick flick to while away the time. When Heather finally looked ready to pass out, Jenny drove them all to The Steakhouse.

"We are going to walk to Gianni's house from here," she told Heather.

Heather stumbled a few times but they reached the doctor's house twenty minutes later. Jenny had arranged for the door to be unlocked.

"This door was slightly ajar that night," Heather slurred.

They went in and sat down in the living room.

Heather looked around with bleary eyes.

"Gianni was sitting right there," she pointed at an arm chair. "There was a bottle on the coffee table."

"What kind of bottle?" Jenny asked.

"A fancy glass bottle full of a brown liquid."

"A crystal decanter?"

Heather shrugged. Then she sat up.

"There was a big sound, like someone banging into something."

"What did you do?"

Heather rubbed her eyes and looked at Jenny. She was beginning to sober up.

"I think I saw a shadow right there." She vaguely pointed somewhere off the living room. "And I definitely heard a sound in the kitchen."

"What did you do?"

"I told Gianni but he just laughed at me. Told me I was drunk."

"What did you do then?"

"Gianni was drinking from a glass. I grabbed it and took a sip. Then I blacked out."

"Do you remember when you woke up?"

Heather shook her head.

"I don't. Now can we please go home? This place is creeping me out."

"Let's go," Jenny agreed, helping Heather up from the couch.

They walked back to Jenny's car and got in. Jenny promised Heather a fresh pot of coffee and all the spaghetti she could eat.

Heather woke up with a headache the next morning. She went to the Boardwalk Café for breakfast. Jenny had promised her a cure for her hangover.

"Here you go," Jenny said, setting a plate of home fried potatoes before her. "Tell me when you are ready for eggs."

Heather polished off the big breakfast and sat back to enjoy her third cup of coffee.

"Did you remember anything else?" Jenny asked.

"I remember waking up," Heather replied. "It was dark outside. Gianni was sprawled on the couch."

Her eyes filled with panic when she realized what she had seen.

"Was he … he must have been …" she mumbled.

"Never mind that," Jenny soothed. "What did you do?"

"I felt nauseous," Heather told her. "The house was freezing. I realized the front door was wide open. I went out and stood there for a minute. Then I started walking home."

"Did you see anyone?"

"I don't think so," Heather shrugged. "I think I puked in some bushes somewhere."

"Did you see what time it was?"

Heather shook her head.

"I collapsed on my bed when I got home. The next thing I knew, Grandma was shaking me, telling me about Gianni."

Heather went back to the inn after that, ready to take a nap. Jenny called Molly at the library.

"How about a road trip?"

Molly managed to get some time off from the library and they set off.

"Have you called ahead?" Molly asked.

"I want to surprise her."

They reached the small Delaware town where Tiffany Costa lived. Jenny hoped she hadn't moved out yet. There was a small U-Hall outside the house and Tiffany stood by as two hefty teens loaded some furniture.

Tiffany didn't look too happy to see them.

"What are you doing here?" she asked when she spotted Jenny.

"Taking off somewhere?" Jenny asked sternly.

Tiffany shook her head.

"I'm free to go where I want. The police cleared me long ago."

"Based on a false alibi?"

Jenny folded her arms and stared at Tiffany.

"I don't know what you're talking about."

"You did stop at the coffee shop on the way out of town. But then you went back, didn't you?"

"I did no such thing."

Tiffany glared at Jenny, refusing to back down.

"Heather told me the door was ajar when she and Gianni reached home that night. Other than Gianni, you were the only one who had a key."

"That doesn't prove I used it."

"You were in the kitchen," Jenny went on. "Heather saw you."

Tiffany's nostrils flared and she looked away.

"I was looking for my bracelet," she finally admitted. "I must have dropped it in that house. It was five carats. I couldn't just let it go."

"So what? You went there looking for it?" Jenny scoffed. "Did you drug Gianni while you had a chance?"

"Of course not!" Tiffany cried. "I found the bracelet near the sink in the kitchen. I had taken it off earlier when I was doing the dishes."

"What did you see?"

"Nothing much," Tiffany said with a shrug. "Gianni was drinking whiskey from a decanter. Heather was passed out on the couch. I crept out of the living room. Gianni was too drunk to notice me. My car was parked two houses down. I got into it and drove back here."

"Did you stop anywhere on your way back?"

Tiffany answered in the negative. She had just wanted to get home and call it a night.

"So you could have been there all night," Jenny pointed out.

"Look, I'm going back home to my town. I am starting a new job next week. I want to forget I ever met Gianni."

"Good luck with that, Tiffany."

Jenny couldn't decide if Tiffany was just a victim or if she was guilty of drugging Gianni.

"What did you find out online?" Molly asked her on the way back home.

Jenny gave her a brief account of what she had learnt. They agreed Heather had escaped narrowly. Jenny dropped Molly off at the library and went to see Jason. She brought him up to date with everything she had found out.

"Let's go talk to Adam," he said grimly.

Adam Hopkins was in a bad mood again. He sat with his leg propped up on a table.

"Have you been doing your exercises?" Jenny asked him. "Your therapist can only do so much, Adam. You need to put in some effort yourself."

"Are you here to lecture me, Jenny?" Adam thundered. "What are you doing here?"

"Tiffany came back to Pelican Cove that night."

Jenny told him everything Tiffany had admitted to her. Adam didn't look convinced.

"Heather may have been present at the scene of the crime," Jason spoke. "But Tiffany was there too. They are equally innocent or guilty."

"We might have to bring Tiffany in," Adam said grudgingly.

"What about Gianni's or Joe's first wife?" Jenny asked. "Do you think he made her disappear?"

"You have been reading the tabloids," Adam told her. "There was never any proof of a crime."

Jenny and Jason walked out of the police station.

"Do you think they will drop the charges against Heather now?" Jenny asked.

"The case is not solved yet, Jenny. It's hard to say."

"Have you tried to reach Kandy again?" Jenny asked softly.

"She changed her number, Jenny." Jason sounded defeated. "I think I've tried enough. I'm done."

"Let's get your profile on that dating app Heather uses. She can show you the ropes."

"Isn't that where she met Gianni?" Jason quirked an eyebrow. "I'd rather be alone."

"You are not alone, Jason. We are all here for you."

Jason put his arm around Jenny and hugged her close. He wondered if she would ever take him seriously. He had waited too long to bare his heart.

Chapter 19

"Do you trust Tiffany?" Molly asked Jenny.

"I don't know what to say, Molls." Jenny was tired.

The girls had met for dinner at Jenny's place. Jenny had been so frustrated she had declared they needed a girls' night. Star, Petunia and Betty Sue were having their own little soiree at the Bayview Inn.

"I'm glad Grandma's not here," Heather said, taking a sip of her lemonade. "We can talk freely."

"What do you want to talk about?" Jenny asked her.

"I'm worried about her. What happens if they take me away again?"

"That's not going to happen."

Jenny's frustration was written clearly on her face.

"I haven't given up yet, Heather. I'm going to keep on digging."

"I am so sorry," Heather said with tears in her eyes. "I'm being a nuisance."

"We are here to take care of you," Molly said staunchly. "What are friends for?"

Jenny absentmindedly chewed on a piece of celery. She had hit a wall.

"Why don't we talk of something else?" she suggested. "I'm sick of thinking about Gianni. I keep going around in circles. It's not helping."

They tried to gossip about the people in town. They had talked about everyone in the next fifteen minutes.

"I need some fresh air," Heather said.

The girls moved out to the patio.

Molly shivered as some spray from the water fountain hit her.

"Do you think of her?" she asked Jenny. "Lily?"

The fountain stood on the spot where they had found the old skeleton.

"Every time I sit here," Jenny admitted. "I feel like she's waiting, asking for justice."

"Ann Davis is coming here in the summer," Heather told Molly.

"Ann was the last one to see Lily alive, wasn't she?" Molly asked. "Do you trust her?"

"I don't," Jenny said. "But I have no proof. Unless she comes forward and gives a confession, we are at an impasse."

"Looks like Lily is never going to get her justice," Molly observed.

The next day brought some surprising developments.

Adam called Jenny at the café.

"Can you come down to the station now?"

Jenny hoped they hadn't found any more evidence against Heather. Adam was waiting for her impatiently.

"Sit down, Jenny."

Adam's eyes shone with excitement. He had never been that eager to tell her anything. He pulled out a plastic evidence bag from a drawer and slapped it on the table before Jenny.

"What's this?"

"Startling developments in the Lily Davis case. They found this in the ground with the skeleton."

A ruby ring sparkled in the plastic bag. It was set in gold and had tiny diamonds surrounding it.

"Is it real?" she asked.

"Doesn't matter," Adam said. "It's a clue, Jenny. It could be vital to the investigation."

"Where was it all this time?"

"Don't know," Adam shrugged. "They must have overlooked it somehow. Doesn't matter. We have it now."

"Did it belong to Lily?"

"I don't think so," Adam said. "If it was Lily's, she would have been wearing it."

Jenny finally caught on.

"You think this belongs to the person who killed Lily?"

Adam nodded vigorously.

"That's exactly what I'm thinking."

"But we don't know who this belongs to."

"Leave it to the police," Adam bragged. "Once we find out who made it, we can easily see who ordered it."

"Do you mind if I take a picture of this?"

Adam was in a benevolent mood. He told her she could take as many pictures of the ring as she wanted.

Jenny forgot all about the ring after she got back to the café. She had two birthday cakes to bake and recipes to try for the Spring Fest.

"What about the pimento cheese sandwiches you made for that meeting?" Petunia asked. "People loved those."

"We'll see what Barb thinks about them," Jenny agreed. "I still haven't decided between cupcakes and donuts. Do you think we should make a few of each?"

"That's too much work for you, Jenny." Petunia didn't talk much most of the time but Jenny valued her advice.

"Maybe we should toss a coin," she laughed nervously.

"The people are going to love either," Petunia assured her.

Jenny was in a rare mood the next morning. She made cheese and pimento muffins along with crab omelets for breakfast. She couldn't wait to hear what the Magnolias thought of the savory muffins.

"Delicious," Molly pronounced with her mouth full. "You need to take a picture of this and put it on social media, Jenny."

"Oh, that reminds me," Jenny said, slapping the table with her palm.

She pulled out her phone from her apron pocket.

"What have you got there?" Betty Sue inquired as she looked up from her knitting.

Jenny stuck her phone in Betty Sue's face.

"Does this look familiar?"

Betty Sue's face was blank for a moment. She took the phone and adjusted her glasses. She peered at the picture with a frown. A minute later, her face cleared and an expression of incredulity came over it.

"Where…where did you get this, girl?"

"Do you recognize it?" Jenny asked eagerly.

Betty Sue was the first person Jenny went to when she had a question about the town. Betty Sue had been born there and had been around the longest. There wasn't much that slipped Betty Sue's notice in the town of Pelican Cove.

"It's a family heirloom," Betty Sue rasped. "Where did you get this?"

"Whose family?" Jenny gasped.

"The Davis family," Betty Sue said, sitting up. "This ring is over two hundred years old. It has been passed down in the family from generation to generation."

"So it's Lily's ring?"

Jenny tried to hide her disappointment.

"Are you listening to me, girl?" Betty Sue thundered. "Lily may have been born a Davis, but this ring wasn't meant for her. It was handed over to a bride coming into the family."

"What if there were many brides?" Heather asked.

"Then the oldest one got it, of course," Betty Sue snapped.

Jenny was busy making some calculations in her head.

"So you're saying this ring belongs to Ann Davis?"

"Sure does, or did," Betty Sue said confidently. "Although now that I think about it, I don't think she was wearing it last summer."

"No, she wasn't," Jenny said jubilantly.

She leapt to her feet and whirled around.

"I have to go."

"Wait a minute," Betty Sue called out. "Tell me more about this."

Jenny was already down the café steps before Betty Sue could finish her sentence. She almost jogged down the boardwalk and headed to the police station. Nora, the desk clerk waved her through.

Adam was in a meeting with a bunch of other uniformed men when Jenny burst into his office.

"How about knocking before you enter?" he asked irritably.

"It's Ann. It's Ann Davis."

"What is?"

"The ring, Adam. The ring is a Davis family jewel and it belonged to Ann Davis. Betty Sue will vouch for it."

Adam's face broke into a smile.

"Leave the rest to me, Jenny."

Jenny walked back to the café slowly, wishing for a breakthrough in Gianni's case. The Magnolias were waiting with their questions.

"That ring was found in the dirt that came with the skeleton," she told them. "Or something like that."

"What was Ann's ring doing there?" Star asked.

"That's what the police will look into now," Jenny explained. "If you ask me, it puts her on the spot."

"Why would Ann harm Lily though?" Molly asked in a puzzled voice.

"She's the only one who can tell us that."

Betty Sue's eyes had filled up.

"Lily looked up to her. She was like the older sister she never had."

"An older sister who stabbed her in the back?" Heather scoffed.

"The ring doesn't prove anything. Ann can spin any story now. I don't think she will confess after all these years."

Jenny was proven wrong.

Ann Davis unraveled like a ball of string when she saw the ring.

"She said it was an accident," Adam told her as they walked on the beach. "She didn't mean to hurt Lily."

"Why did they get into a fight?" Jenny wanted to know.

"Lily had been acting crazy," Adam explained. "Those were Ann's words. She wanted to sell Seaview for a pittance. She just wanted to get away from Pelican Cove."

"Ann wasn't ready to sell?"

"She wanted Seaview for her son."

"They fought over a piece of land?"

"That wasn't all," Adam continued. "Lily barely spoke to anyone for months. She shut herself in her room, mourning her daughter. Ann got friendly with Lily's husband. They might have had an affair."

"How dare she!" Jenny cried.

Jenny's husband had dumped her after falling in love with a much younger woman. She didn't think kindly about women who wrecked other women's homes.

"Ann didn't admit to the affair," Adam said. "She just told us they had a big argument. It got a bit violent. Ann pushed her and Lily struck her head on a stone in the garden. She died instantly."

"What if Ann was mistaken?"

"She must have tried to revive her," Adam shrugged. "We will never know that."

"So Ann decided to bury her in the garden?"

"Ann says she panicked. Ricky had watched everything from an upstairs room. Lily's son was expected back home any moment. She told Ricky to start digging."

"Didn't the son or husband notice anything amiss in the garden?"

"Ann made up that story about seeing Lily get in the car with a man. Keith was devastated when he thought his mother abandoned him."

Jenny had met Lily's son when he came to Pelican Cove. She knew he had been traumatized by his mother's actions.

"So she not only killed Lily, she also maligned her character." Jenny thought of the petite old woman she had met a few months ago. She would never have guessed she was a murderer.

"What happens now?" Jenny asked.

"Ann Davis and her son will both face charges," Adam told her.

Jenny couldn't wait to meet the Magnolias the next morning.

"I knew Lily would never turn her back on her family," Betty Sue said tersely. "Lily can finally rest in peace."

Jenny sat on the patio with her aunt, staring at the water fountain.

"Do you think it's true?" she asked her aunt. "What they say about Seaview?"

Star gave her a pained look.

"You're not thinking about that nonsense again?"

"Just think about it. Lily lost her daughter at a young age, she got herself killed, then her son got into drugs and he got himself killed. Her husband is barely alive in some senior home."

"No one can predict the future, honey," Star sighed. "You have made a beautiful home here for yourself. Try to stay happy in it."

"Here's to happy memories," Jenny nodded, clinking her cup of coffee with Star's.

Star gave her a curious look.

"I don't think you will be staying here much longer, anyway."

"What do you mean, Star?" Jenny laughed. "I'm not going anywhere."

Star looked at her niece indulgently.

"I think Adam's getting ready to pop the question."

Jenny blushed furiously.

"You do love him?" Star asked.

Jenny's eyes clouded with confusion.

"Is love enough?" Jenny asked moodily. "I loved Nick's father with all I had. Look where that got me."

"It will be different this time," Star said, patting her on the back.

"Do you approve?" Jenny asked her aunt.

"You know I like Jason more," Star winked. "But I'm with you, baby. I can't imagine being alone in this big old house though."

Jenny shook her head.

"Like I said, I'm not going anywhere."

Chapter 20

Jenny sipped her coffee quietly as the Magnolias chatted around her. Heather was giving them an update on Barb Norton's latest project. The signatures she had collected from the town people had done the job. The Newburys had not been granted the approvals they needed to set up the medical dispensary.

Heather's face was animated as she narrated what had happened. She seemed to have found a new purpose while working for Barb. But the cloud of suspicion still hung over her. Was Heather guilty after all? She had been the woman scorned.

Jenny's mind wandered as she imagined what Heather must have felt when she realized Gianni was already married. She must have been ready to bash someone's head in. Jenny chided herself for thinking the worst of her friend. There had been no new developments. The police still considered Heather their top suspect.

Jenny scratched her head and wondered what more she could do. She needed to start from scratch and go over everything with a fine-tooth comb.

"Thinking about Adam?" Molly asked with a glint in her eye.

Molly and Chris were very happy together. They felt everyone around them needed to be in a relationship.

"Come with me," Jenny said suddenly. "If you can take some time off, that is."

Molly sensed the urgency in Jenny's voice.

"Sure, Jenny, let me make a call."

Jenny started walking toward Dr. Smith's clinic.

"What are we doing?" Molly wanted to know.

"You're good at research, aren't you? I need a pair of sharp eyes."

Jenny spoke to Dr. Smith and asked for the patient records from Gianni's clinic. He pointed them to a small room at the back.

"See those four boxes?" he said. "Have at it."

"We are going to go over these again," Jenny told Molly.

"But what are we looking for?"

"Anything unusual?" Jenny shrugged. "I'm not sure, Molly. We are looking for a needle in a haystack, anything that can take the limelight away from Heather."

Jenny noticed Dr. Smith had marked some of the files. He had written remarks in the margins like 'fake diagnosis', 'wrong prescription' etc.

Molly turned out to be more efficient than Jenny. She got through a box much faster than Jenny and arranged the papers in neat piles.

"I know most of these people," Molly told Jenny. "Some are friends or acquaintances, others just sound familiar. But there's a bunch of names that don't seem to be from around here."

"They might belong to his patients in Delaware," Jenny mused. "Or they might be fictitious names. Gianni billed the government for nonexistent patients."

"What do you want to do with those?"

"Keep them in a separate pile," Jenny said thoughtfully. "I want to go through them."

The piles grew as Jenny and Molly worked through the boxes. Jenny finally turned to the pile Molly had set aside as out-of-towners. She read each file carefully, paying special attention to the names. One name caught her eye right away.

"Why does this sound familiar?" she wondered out loud. "Francis Lopez."

"Never heard of him," Molly shrugged.

The girls worked diligently for a couple of hours without much success.

"I don't know about you, Jenny, but I'm starving."

"Let's go grab a bite at the café."

They weren't in the best of spirits when they went back to the café.

"No luck?" Petunia asked sympathetically.

She placed two plates of chicken salad sandwiches before them and ladled tomato soup in earthen mugs.

"Do you know someone called Francis?" Jenny asked Petunia.

"Doesn't ring a bell," the older woman said, shaking her head. "Why don't you ask Betty Sue? She's coming here for lunch today."

Betty Sue walked in with Heather following close behind. Heather was carrying their black poodle Tootsie in her arms.

"I'll tie her out on the beach," she told Petunia immediately. "She didn't want to stay back home."

Everyone moved out to a table on the deck. Betty Sue sipped her soup and looked hopefully at Jenny.

"How's it going? Any luck?"

Jenny sighed in frustration.

"I feel I'm close, Betty Sue. But I feel I'm forgetting something."

Betty Sue had never heard of Francis Lopez either. Heather had been sitting on the café steps, playing with Tootsie. She looked up sharply.

"Isn't that the artist your aunt is going around with?"

"My aunt is not going around with anyone other than Jimmy," Jenny said sharply.

"Pay attention, Jenny," Heather pressed. "Frank Lopez? He's that new artist."

Jenny felt a chill run down her spine. She looked around at her friends.

"You think Frank Lopez is Francis Lopez?"

The ladies shrugged.

"I need to talk to Adam right away," Jenny cried, springing to her feet.

She skipped down the steps and hurried down the beach to the police station. Nora, the desk clerk, waved her through.

"Have you brought my lunch, Jenny?" Adam asked with a smile.

"Frank Lopez!" she panted. "You need to bring him in."

"Stop screaming in my ear, Jenny. I haven't had lunch yet."

"Didn't you hear what I said?" Jenny asked, putting her hands on her hips.

"You're always making outlandish demands. Now sit down and tell me what's going on."

"I think Frank Lopez is our guy. You need to bring him in right away."

"Who is he?"

"He's that new artist in town. Don't you remember?"

"And why should I arrest him?" Adam asked patiently.

Jenny launched into what she had been doing all day. She reminded him about the woman who had been Gianni's wife a few years ago.

"I think this guy is related to that girl Maria. There has to be a connection."

"Sounds farfetched to me," Adam shook his head.

"What is this Frank Lopez doing in Pelican Cove, Adam? Why is he here now?"

"We have absolutely no proof he knew Gianni."

"He was Gianni's patient. That's your connection."

Adam finally decided to humor Jenny.

"I'll send a car out to bring him in."

Jenny thanked Adam and stood up. She had decided to go confront Frank herself. Adam recognized the resolve he saw in Jenny's eyes.

"Don't do anything foolish," he called out after her.

Jenny vaguely remembered Frank talking about a house he had rented in town. Her tires spun as she raced to the address. She was looking for the trailer belonging to Frank. The house looked deserted when she got there. Her phone rang just then. It was Star.

"I'm sorry I couldn't say goodbye."

"What? Where are you?" Jenny asked, dazed.

"I'm with Frank. We are going to paint the mountains, remember? We talked about this."

"But I thought you weren't going."

"I'll be away for three days," her aunt said. "Frank's trailer is just awesome, Jenny. It has a bed and a TV and a small kitchen. I'm going to have fun."

Jenny cringed as she thought of the close quarters her aunt was sharing with Frank.

"Is Frank with you?"

"Of course he is. You don't sound too good, Jenny. Are you coming down with something?"

"I just feel bad I didn't get to say bye to you," Jenny laughed nervously. "Why don't you stop at the next rest area? I'm on my way."

"Don't be silly. I'll be back before you know it."

"No, no, I insist," Jenny said in a weird voice. "It's such a beautiful day. I'm looking forward to a nice drive."

"We're twenty miles out of town," Star said. "Can you catch up with us?"

"The trailer goes slower than a car, doesn't it? I'll be there, don't worry."

"Whatever you say, my dear." Star sounded confused but Jenny was glad she was playing along.

Jenny called Adam right away.

"You need to stop them. If I'm right, Star could be in danger."

"Aren't you getting carried away?" Adam asked.

"I'm driving out to meet them," Jenny said firmly. "You can meet me there or not. I leave it up to you."

Jenny broke the speed limit trying to reach the rest area as soon as possible. Luckily, she didn't get pulled over. A car belonging to the Pelican Cove police overtook her just as she turned into the exit lane. Adam was already out of the car by the time Jenny parked next to him. A couple of deputies stood by, waiting for a signal from Adam.

Jenny spotted Star by the vending machines and ran toward her. She flung her arms around her aunt and hugged her tight.

"Thank God, you are safe."

"What's going on, Jenny?" Star asked sharply. "Are you going to tell me why you are acting like this?"

"You'll find out soon enough."

Frank walked up, holding packets of potato chips and cans of soda.

"They didn't have the diet cola so I got regular."

He smiled at Jenny.

"You can visit with your aunt as long as you want. There's no rush."

For a moment, Jenny wondered if she was wrong about Frank.

Adam had walked up to Jenny. Frank looked at the uniformed sheriff standing before him and his shoulders slumped. He dropped the food he was carrying on a bench and held up his hands.

"I'm not sorry I avenged my daughter."

Star's eyes popped open as Adam arrested Frank and took him away.

"I'm so glad you are okay, Star," Jenny said, hugging her aunt again.

The Magnolias arrived early at the Boardwalk Café the next day. Heather was grinning widely.

"Jason just called. Frank Lopez gave a full confession."

"Tell us what happened, Jenny," Betty Sue commanded. She was looking relieved, now that Heather had been vindicated of any involvement in the crime.

"I don't have all the details," Jenny began. "This is what Adam told me at a high level. Frank's daughter Maria was married to Gianni. As far as I can tell, she was his first wife. She found out about his shady business and threatened to go to the police if he didn't clean up his act."

"So he was always crooked," Molly observed.

"Gianni promised her he would do whatever she wanted. They went on a trip after that. Maria never came back. Gianni said she walked out of the hotel room. There was a big investigation but Gianni got away because there was no evidence against him."

"Are you saying he killed that poor girl?" Petunia asked with a gasp.

Jenny nodded.

"She never surfaced anywhere else. Frank believed Gianni murdered his daughter. He hired investigators and tried hard to get Gianni convicted but he didn't succeed. Then Gianni vanished."

"How could he do that?"

"He went to a different state and took on a new identity," Jenny explained. "But he didn't change his ways. He carried out the same scams. When things got too hot, he moved and changed his name again."

"So Gianni wasn't his real name?" Heather asked.

"No, sweetie," Jenny said. "Not by a long shot."

"What do you mean, Maria was his first wife?" Star asked.

"Gianni went to small towns and wooed a local girl. He chose someone who would help him build contacts and set up his clinic. He got rid of the girl when he moved."

"So he killed more than one woman?" Heather gasped.

"That's what the police think now," Jenny told them. "We will know more after a thorough investigation."

"How did Frank know Gianni was here?" Star asked.

"Frank had been looking for Gianni ever since he disappeared. He drove around the country, following Gianni's trail. He traced him to Delaware and then to Pelican Cove. He posed as a patient and made sure Gianni was the man his daughter had been married to."

"When did he decide to murder him?" Molly asked.

"Revenge was always on his mind. Once he located Gianni, it was just a matter of when and how."

"How did he do it?" Heather asked in a hushed voice.

"That shadow you thought you saw that night," Jenny said, "that was Frank. He got into Gianni's clinic and powdered a few drugs. He added them to the whiskey decanter, knowing Gianni would probably drink from it after coming home."

"What if I had drunk from it?" Heather cried.

Jenny shrugged.

"Frank was single minded in his determination. I don't think he cared about collateral damage."

"So I almost died too?" Heather gasped.

"You had a narrow escape, girl," Betty Sue's voice boomed. "That's what comes of associating with scum."

"But he was so nice to me!"

Heather looked shocked.

"What did Frank do that night?" Molly asked, prompting Jenny to go on.

"He just stood in the shadows and watched Gianni drink from the decanter. I think he was prepared to pour it down his throat if needed."

"I don't understand one thing," Heather said. "Why did he stick around in town after that? All he had to do was get in his bus and drive away."

Jenny looked at her aunt.

"We'll never know that, I guess."

Star looked around at the group of friends gathered around the table and shook her head.

"He was a really good artist."

Epilogue

The town of Pelican Cove was busy celebrating Spring Fest. People had turned up in droves. A big marquee had been erected. Food stalls lined one side. A band was setting up on a makeshift stage on the beach.

Jenny sat among her friends, finally catching her breath after a hectic day. All the food from the Boardwalk Café had been sold. Tourists had come to the festival especially to taste Jenny's cupcakes and pimento cheese sandwiches.

"I don't know how to thank you," Heather gushed. "You saved my life, Jenny."

"You were innocent all along," Jenny said lightly. "You had nothing to fear."

Adam Hopkins limped up to the group of women. He gulped as he tried to catch Jenny's eye. Jenny had been giving him the cold shoulder for a while.

"Go talk to that Hopkins boy," Betty Sue said, tipping her head at Adam.

Jenny stood up reluctantly and took a few steps toward Adam.

"What is it?"

"Can you spare a few minutes? Please?"

The sun was low on the horizon, painting the sky in shades of orange and mauve. Jenny accompanied Adam to the beach. He was quiet while they walked away from the crowd.

"Are you going to say anything?" Jenny prompted.

Adam cleared his throat.

"You know I'm not big on words, Jenny. But I hope you know how much you mean to me."

He pulled a small gift wrapped box out of his pocket and held it out to her.

"What's this?" Jenny asked suspiciously.

"Aren't you going to open it?"

Jenny pulled off the blue satin ribbon and tore the wrapping paper. Her heart thudded a bit as she lifted the lid of the small box. A shiny key lay inside.

"Err... what's this, Adam?"

"Jenny King, you already hold the key to my heart. This is the key to my house."

Jenny's brows settled into a frown.

"I want you to move in with me, Jenny."

Jenny stared into Adam's blue eyes. She was dismayed at the hope she saw there.

"I can't do that," she said under her breath. "I'm sorry, Adam."

"Why not?" Adam asked, trying to maintain his composure.

"I am just getting settled in at Seaview. I'm not leaving it now."

"Jenny, it's just a house."

"No, Adam. It's my home. It's where I am going to spend the rest of my days."

Adam took Jenny's hands in his.

"Will you at least think about it?"

Jenny stared into the sand at her feet. She gave Adam a slight nod. Then she turned around and started walking back to her friends.

THE END

Raspberry Chocolate Murder – Dolphin Bay Cozy Mystery Series Book 1

By Leena Clover

Chapter 1

Anna Butler stomped her foot and muttered a string of oaths, shaking her head in disbelief. Was it really happening?

She stared at the paper she held in her hand, the one she had eagerly pulled out of the official brown envelope she had ripped open. Her future depended on the contents of that letter. A future she felt she had earned after the trials of the past two years. But apparently, her life would never be a bed of roses.

The powers that be had just rejected her application. That meant she would not be opening her dream café any time soon. Bayside Books, the bookstore she had lovingly tended for the past twenty years would remain just that. There would be no aroma of freshly brewed coffee mingling with the musty old books. And there would be no happy customers licking the frosting off her delicious cupcakes.

In a daze, Anna turned off the stand mixer beating a gallon of butter cream frosting and stared at the mess around her. The massive granite island in her updated kitchen was covered in a fine dusting of flour. Packets of melting butter lay next to giant mixing bowls. Tiny jars of spices stood open next to a canister of powdered sugar. A dozen freshly baked cupcakes rested on a cake stand, ready to be frosted.

Anna felt her knees wobble as she pulled herself up on a bar stool. She had barely gulped down half a cup of oatmeal that morning, eager to get on with her baking. Her heart had raced as she eagerly waited for the mail to arrive. A little bird at the town hall had told her a letter had been dispatched to her. Unfortunately, it wasn't what Anna expected.

Anna had lived in the quaint seaside town of Dolphin Bay all her life. She went to college at the local university and married as soon as she got her degree. Thirty four years of wedded bliss had ended abruptly when her husband John met an unexpected demise. Anna had been fifty five, just old enough to dream about retirement, too young to be a widow. She stumbled through the next year, leading a rudderless existence. But her troubles weren't over. A nagging pain below her armpit turned out to be breast cancer.

Anna found herself thrust down a new rabbit hole. The past year had been relentless, consumed by endless visits to specialists and hospitals. There had been a brief period of uncertainty when Anna thought she was on her way to meet John, but the tide had turned in her favor. It had been a month since her last radiation treatment and Anna was recovering well. But she had promised herself she would stop taking things for granted. She would stop putting things off. She had almost tasted death. She had a lot to do before she actually met it.

Anna's eyes flickered as she gazed out of the kitchen windows. Turquoise blue water shimmered in the California sun. A trio of cabanas lay by the poolside, each shaded by a giant umbrella. A tanned, curvy body occupied one of the chairs, dressed in a bikini that could not be called modest in any universe. Anna sighed at the thought of her grown daughter wasting another day lounging by the pool. Then she decided to let it go. She needed to be more patient.

The kitchen door was flung open as a large red headed woman barged in. Her excess weight agreed with her, giving her a larger than life personality that consumed everything around her.

"What's with all this mess, Anna?" Julie Walsh demanded, looking around with her hands on her hips.

Anna stared blankly as Julie's eyebrows bunched together and her sapphire blue eyes flashed with impatience.

"Did you forget about our lunch date?" Julie asked sharply. "How could you, Anna? I stopped mid-way through a chapter to get ready and come over."

Julie Walsh was a romance author of some repute. She was always on a deadline, scrambling to get things done before the next release. Julie barely spared a minute for most people. But she never missed weekly lunch with her friends Anna and Mary.

Anna picked up the offensive letter and handed it to Julie.

"There must be some mistake," Julie said, staring at the brief communication. "You are not going to take this lying down, are you?"

Anna suddenly felt the weight of the past year on her shoulders.

"What can I do?" she asked meekly. "They have already made their decision."

"Not worth the paper it's written on," Julie blustered. "Get off your keister, Anna Butler! We are taking care of this right now."

"Is something wrong?" a soft voice asked.

Anna turned around to welcome her friend Mary. Mary was the exact opposite of Julie, and older than both women. Her green eyes were filled with trepidation as she stared at her friends.

"You are not sick again, are you, Anna?"

"I am not ill, Mary," Anna assured her.

"Take a look at this," Julie ordered, thrusting the paper in Mary's face. "We all know who's behind this."

"We do?" Anna asked, looking puzzled.

"This has Lara Crawford written all over it," Julie said sternly. "Surely you recognize that, Anna?"

Lara Crawford was the mayor of Dolphin Bay. The whole town knew she had it in for Anna Butler. Anna had learned to ignore the brash woman. It seemed to anger her even more and Anna bore the brunt of it in many different ways.

"Why would Lara be involved in this?" Anna asked.

Julie banged a fist on the kitchen island, upsetting a box of baking soda.

"She knows how much the café means to you. She will do anything to make sure you don't succeed."

Mary nodded in agreement.

"You know I don't like to malign anyone. But I agree with Julie. Lara Crawford is pure evil. You need to fight this, Anna."

Mary and Julie pulled Anna off the stool and made her fix her face. A fresh coat of lipstick later, the three women marched to the town hall, ready to beard the lioness in her den.

A mousy, bespectacled young girl outside the mayor's office tried in vain to thwart them.

"Step aside," Julie warned. "Lara's expecting us."

Anna had shrugged off her gloom on the way and summoned all her inner strength. She barged in on Julie's heels and sat down before the odious woman who was trying to steal her dream.

Lara Crawford's mouth was set in a sneer. Her crooked nose did nothing to soften her appearance. Nor did her power suit or the strand of expensive pearls she wore around her neck.

"Is it my lucky day?" she crooned. "Dolphin Bay's famous husband killer is here to see me."

"Stop that nonsense," Julie snapped. She turned to Anna and tipped her head. "Go on, Anna."

Anna placed the letter she had received before Lara.

"Why was my application rejected?"

Lara rolled her eyes.

"Vendor licensing is not in my purview."

"This is your signature, Lara," Anna pointed out. "Do you deny that?"

"I sign dozens of documents in a day," Lara drawled. "But I am not always the decision maker."

"You know what Anna has been through, Lara," Mary said softly. "Have a heart."

"You mean how she's roaming scot free after killing her husband?" Lara asked with relish. "I wouldn't know."

"You are crossing the line, Lara," Julie warned. She took Anna's hand in hers and gave it a squeeze. "The police could never establish what happened to John."

"But I know," Lara pounced, flinging a finger at Anna. "She killed him in cold blood."

Anna shrank back in her seat. She was barely keeping it together.

"That's enough," Julie chided. "Stop abusing your power, Lara. Or you won't be sitting in that chair much longer."

"I am going to prove it," Lara hissed. "That's a promise you can take to the bank."

Anna scraped her chair back and stood up.

"I am going to open my café whether you like it or not, Lara. That's my promise to you."

She walked out with her head high.

"Watch out, Lara," Julie warned and followed her friend out.

"Stop being mean, Lara," Mary said with a soft sigh.

She was the last one to leave the room.

Lara Crawford leaned back in her chair and allowed herself a malicious grin. She had won the battle. She had plenty more tricks up her sleeve to make Anna Butler suffer. She would do anything to succeed in her mission. She planned to drive the Butler women out of Dolphin Bay.

Chapter 2

Cassandra Butler gathered her waist length golden hair and tied it in a knot on the top of her head. Her wet, shapely body carried an extra ten pounds around the middle. The spring sun warmed her back, bare except for a flimsy string bikini. She had taken care to slather it with sunscreen lotion. A healthy tan was one thing, but she couldn't risk ruining her flawless complexion with freckles or sunburn.

Cassie swam a dozen leisurely laps in her mother's swimming pool, reveling in the sense of wellbeing that stole over her. Very few things made her feel content nowadays. Being one with the water was an easy way to let go of all her worries.

Life had dealt Cassie a few hard blows. She was still reeling from the last one. Her crooked manager had absconded with most of her hard earned money, leaving her with a big tax bill. The coveted golden knight otherwise called an Oscar award lay forgotten at the back of her sock drawer. When she won the award at 21, it had been her crowning glory. At 36, it looked like it was going to be her swan song. Cassie wasn't sure if she cared much either way.

She stepped out of the pool and settled into her favorite cabana, letting the sun dry her. Her phone chirped and her face lit up as her best bud's face flashed on the screen.

"It's about time," she said with a pout, activating the video feature on the phone.

A buff, bare-chested man blew a kiss at her and laughed. It was hard to tell he was ten years younger.

"Don't sulk, Cassie. It will give you wrinkles."

Cassie straightened her mouth immediately and smiled. "So when are you getting here, Bobby? I have great plans for us."

Bobby placed a proprietary hand over his six pack abs and winced.

"I don't think I can make it this weekend, sweetie. Fox booked a last minute session for tomorrow."

Bobby was in big demand in Hollywood as a personal trainer to the stars. Making celebrities sweat was his job and he was good at it.

"I thought you had a new Pilates routine for me."

"Why don't you come to La-La land instead?" Bobby asked. "I should be done by midnight tomorrow. We can party all night and go shopping on Rodeo Drive on Sunday. It's not like you have to hurry back."

Cassie's face fell.

"Rodeo Drive's off limits for me, Bobbykins. You know that."

"Don't worry about the money, babe. I'll take care of it."

Cassie felt her cheeks burn with shame. She chatted with her friend for a while, her mind wandering to a time when she could squander a few thousand on an afternoon of casual shopping. She hung up after Bobby promised to visit soon.

Cassie took a long sip of icy lemon water and contemplated her life. She had been doing it for the past several months, ever since she came back home to take care of her ailing mother. The day stretched before her, full of nothing to do. She closed her eyes and placed her arms below her head, poised to take a nap.

A hum of muffled voices woke her. She sat up and peered at the scene playing out in the kitchen. Her mother had been bustling around all morning, baking yet another batch of cupcakes. Now she had been joined by two women. Cassie spotted the large plaid covered body of Julie Walsh, her mother's bossy author friend. The mousy Mary Sullivan stood by meekly, looking like a 1950s housewife in her green floral dress.

Cassie was used to seeing the two women around the house. The Firecrackers as they called themselves had been friends since before her birth. Apparently nothing could come between them. Cassie secretly envied them their bond.

The tableau inside the house unfurled quickly with Julie getting more excited by the minute. She waved her arms around, urging Cassie's mother Anna to do something. Finally, the women seemed to make up their minds. Cassie watched anxiously as they hurried out of the house. She waited to hear a car engine come to life. Surely her mother hadn't decided to walk in the blazing sun? What was she thinking?

Cassie moved with uncharacteristic swiftness and hurried inside. The house appeared dark after the glaring sun but she didn't have time to let her eyes adjust. Cassie walked into her closet and pulled on the first pair of jeans she could lay her hands on. A white tunic followed. Combing her hair with her fingers, Cassie grabbed her Prada bag, tied an Hermes silk scarf around her neck and rushed out to her car.

The ancient Mercedes convertible roared to life after a few attempts. Cassie floored the gas pedal and took off with a screech, trying not to think of the beloved Ferrari she had sold to appease the tax man. She reached the corner of Main Street in five minutes. Pulling into the parking lot that straddled the street, Cassie sat in the car, trying to spot her mother. Cassie had no idea what she would say to her. Anna had made it clear she didn't need to be cosseted, ill or not.

Cassie slouched in her seat and fiddled with the radio to pass the time. A couple of young women walked past with toddlers in tow. People streamed in and out of the local pub, The Tipsy Whale. It was a popular spot for lunch. Cassie debated going in to get a sandwich. She thought back longingly to the organic smoothie bowls her neighborhood café in Beverly Hills was famous for. She hoped her mother would have some healthier dishes on the menu when she opened her café. She thought of the array of cakes Anna had been experimenting with and decided it wasn't likely.

Tired of toasting in the heat, Cassie got out of the car. She walked around Main Street twice, wondering where Anna was. Although her mother was fully capable of taking care of herself, Cassie remembered the oncologist's warning. Anna wasn't supposed to go out in the sun. Her skin was still raw from the radiation and she needed to protect it from more damage.

A babble of familiar voices fell upon her ears. She whirled around and saw the Firecrackers walking out of the town hall building. Anna's head was uncovered and the peasant blouse she wore over her capris laid her shoulders bare. Cassie frowned, angered by her mother's carelessness.

Anna looked quiet and thoughtful as she walked with her friends toward the pub. The three women entered the Tipsy Whale, Julie Walsh looking like she was ready to murder anyone who crossed her path.

Cassie's stomach growled and she came to a quick decision. She strode toward the pub. Her mouth watered as she thought of what she would order for lunch. Murphy, the pub owner, was famous up and down the coast for his humungous sandwiches.

Julie Walsh stood in line at the bar, waiting to order. Cassie looked around furtively and spotted her mother sitting at a window table with her friend Mary. Julie boomed a greeting when she saw her, insisting Cassie join them for lunch.

"Some other time," Cassie said smoothly. "I am expecting a call from my agent."

"Well, in that case …" Julie hesitated. "I won't keep you."

Cassie put in an order for the roast turkey on sourdough. It came with hickory smoked bacon and avocado and loads of local Monterey Jack cheese. Cassie tried to add up the calories she was about to consume, thinking of the fat grams and carbs that were taboo to her peers. Then she gave up. She would have plenty of time to shed some weight after she landed a good role. Cassie eagerly accepted her sandwich from an apron clad girl, sniffing hungrily at the delicious smells wafting through it. She turned around swiftly and landed into a solid wall.

"Hello Princess," a deep, throaty voice whispered in her ear.

Cassie felt her knee pop as she looked into a pair of brown eyes the color of creamy milk chocolate. She was a bit too familiar with who they belonged to.

"Dylan," she said in a clipped voice. "What are you doing here?"

"Getting a bite to eat," the tall, tanned man answered, rubbing his nose. "Same as you."

Cassie nodded and walked to her mother's table. Anna and her friends were devouring their lunch with relish.

"Can I give you a ride?" Cassie asked the women.

"We can walk back," Anna said primly. "Your car's too small for all of us."

Julie struck her down. "Don't be silly, Anna. We can squeeze in." She nodded at Cassie. "We are almost done here."

"I'll be waiting in the car," Cassie said. "No need to rush."

She pulled off her scarf and handed it to her mother, ignoring the stubborn expression that settled on her face. Cassie bent down and wound the scarf around her mother's neck, showing her she meant business.

She walked out of the pub without a backward glance, ready to take a hefty bite out of her sandwich.

Chapter 3

Anna rose with the sun. She walked into her kitchen and poured herself a cup of coffee. Her husband John had talked her into buying the new fangled coffee maker his last Christmas. He barely got time to enjoy it.

Anna knew Cassie wouldn't be up for hours yet. She clucked in disapproval and headed out to the patio. Anna was meticulous about her daily yoga routine. It centered her and got her ready for the day.

Cassie was sitting at the kitchen counter when Anna went back in.

"You're up early."

Cassie shrugged and added a generous amount of cream to her coffee.

"Are we out of cereal?" she grumbled.

Anna pulled out a box of 7 grain cereal from the pantry.

"Not those sticks!" Cassie complained. "They taste like dust. Where are my frosted flakes?"

"I threw them out," Anna said lightly. "All that sugar is not good for you."

"Says the woman who bakes cupcakes by the dozen," Cassie said with a roll of her eyes.

"I use raw sugar or natural sweeteners," Anna snapped. "Not the same as processed food."

Cassie sulked. She drained her coffee and jumped down from her perch, ready to head to her room. Anna had a flashback to a similar moment twenty years ago. Had her daughter changed even a little in the past two decades?

"Why don't I fix you some breakfast?" she cajoled. "Some oatmeal will go down nicely."

"Oatmeal? Yuck! You know I hate oatmeal, Mom!"

"I thought you film types ate healthy stuff. Oatmeal is healthy."

"Maybe," Cassie said. "Doesn't mean I have to like it."

"How about avocado toast then?" Anna asked. "With a poached egg on top?"

Cassie brightened.

"That sounds cool."

Fifteen minutes later, Anna dished up the tasty breakfast.

"Bobby will have a fit if he sees me eating this," Cassie said, taking a big bite of her toast.

Anna let out a snort. Bobby had come up with an age appropriate diet plan for Anna. It hadn't gone down well.

"What's your plan for the day?" she asked. "Why don't you come to the bookstore later?"

"I'm busy, Mom."

"Doing what?" Anna spoke sharply. Then she tried to soften the blow. "What's the harm in trying something new?"

"I know you're concerned, Mom. But I need more time."

Anna bit back a retort. She didn't want to start the day with yet another disagreement with her daughter.

"I'll be at the store if you need me."

"What am I, 12?" Cassie wiped her plate clean with the last piece of toast. She picked up her coffee and went out to the pool.

Anna cleared up and went into her bedroom to fix herself. She observed herself in the full length mirror. Her clothes hung loose on her short frame, making her look gaunt. She ran a quick brush through her pixie cut salt and pepper hair. It had taken a while to grow back after her treatment. She was just getting used to the short style. The grey was new. Anna wondered if it made her look older.

A light mist was clearing up when Anna stepped out of her door. She climbed her trusty bicycle and pedaled out, admiring the wisteria that bloomed over her front porch.

Anna's store Bayside Books was situated at the corner of Main Street and Ocean Avenue. It had large windows that looked out over the Coastal Walk and some rocky bluffs. The dark blue waters of the bay shimmered in the distance.

Anna rested her bike against the wall of her store and looked up at the giant magnolia tree that stood guard over the entrance. The pink and white buds were just beginning to bloom. Anna breathed in the fresh lemony scent of the flowers and went inside. She immediately found her lips stretching into a smile.

Bayside Books was a haven for all book lovers. Floor to ceiling bookshelves covered every wall, overflowing with volumes. Every available surface had a stack of books on it. Plush armchairs were strewn across the space, inviting readers to settle down and browse through their favorite book at their leisure. Reading tables were placed by the windows, providing a priceless view of the cliffs and the water.

Anna went into a small pantry tucked behind her desk. It was just big enough to hold a refrigerator and a tiny sink with barely enough counter space for a coffee machine. Anna plugged in the coffee, picked up a feather duster and started the tedious chore of dusting all the bookshelves. It was the first thing she did after she came to the store every day.

Anna fretted over the fate of her café. She had dreamed about it with her husband John. They had meticulously saved for the expansion. Maybe it was destined to be just a pipe dream.

The phone rang, snapping Anna out of her reverie. It was her old friend Vicki Bauer. They hadn't talked in years, not since John passed. Vicki had sent flowers for the funeral but she hadn't made it to the memorial service. Most people in town hadn't, thanks to the vicious rumors Lara Crawford had started. Anna remembered feeling abandoned by Vicki at that time.

"Vicki! It's good to hear the sound of your voice. It's been a while."

Vicki reciprocated by saying something similar.

"How are things?" Anna asked, meaning to get to the purpose of the call right away. "All well?"

"Everything is fine," Vicki assured her. "Oh Anna ... I was thinking ... do you remember Book Club? Didn't we have the best time with it?"

"I do remember," Anna said coldly. "We still have a Book Club in Dolphin Bay. It meets here in the bookshop every Wednesday."

Vicki cleared her throat.

"I've been meaning to come to that," she wheedled. "But you know how it is with kids. Life's a bit overwhelming right now."

"We all feel it, dear."

"I was thinking about the other book club, the Crime Solvers' Club."

"Oh!" Anna dismissed. "That was just a bit of fun, Vicki."

"Not entirely," Vicki reminded her. "We managed to solve a mystery or two."

"If you say so," Anna said moodily.

She was still not sure what Vicki wanted from her.

"Why did it fizzle out?" Vicki asked.

"Why the sudden interest in the past, Vicki?" Anna asked. "What's bothering you?"

Vicki broke down. Anna could hear her sobbing on the phone.

"Everything is not fine, Anna," she said through her tears. "I need your help."

"Go on."

"It's my son, Cody."

"I remember Cody," Anna nodded. "He must be what, 19, 20 by now? Is he in college?"

"He's a senior at Dolphin Bay University," Vicki said, her voice filling up with pride. "He's doing good there. Or he was ..."

Anna waited patiently while Vicki indulged in another round of sobbing.

"Get a hold of yourself, Vicki," she ordered. "Get to the point."

"A girl from the college was found dead. The police think my Cody killed her."

"What?"

Anna sat down in her chair. Vicki had her undivided attention now.

"Cody barely knew her. The police took him in for questioning. They are saying he is their top suspect. What am I going to do, Anna?"

"You need to get him a lawyer," Anna told her.

"I'm working on that," Vicki said. "But I need someone who can help clear my boy of blame."

"What can I do?" Anna asked.

"You are good at solving mysteries," Vicki said. "I want you to get to the bottom of this."

"Crime Solvers' Club was just for fun," Anna argued. "Your boy's life is at stake here, Vicki. Maybe you should hire a professional investigator."

"At least come and meet Cody," Vicki pleaded. "He's in shock. He won't say anything. But he might talk to you. You were his favorite out of all my friends."

"Let me think about it," Anna said grudgingly.

She hung up after promising to get in touch with Vicki soon. The next thing she did was call the Firecrackers. She didn't make big decisions without consulting them.

Julie answered her phone immediately.

"Let me patch Mary in," she said.

Anna didn't waste time in bringing them up to speed.

"Lara's already making trouble for you, Anna," Mary said quietly. "Are you sure you want to butt horns with the police?"

"I know how it feels to be condemned without trial," Anna told them. "This poor kid has his whole life ahead of him."

"What if he is guilty?" Julie cut in.

"Then I'll be the first to turn him in," Anna said resolutely.

The three friends agreed to meet at Julie's before heading out to meet Vicki and her son.

Anna hung up and called Cassie.

"What is it, Mom?" Cassie's languor traveled along the phone line.

Anna imagined her reclining in her favorite cabana by the pool.

"I need you to come watch the store, dear."

"I'm expecting a call from my agent."

"You can take the call here," Anna shot back. "Please get here soon, Cassie. I have to leave in fifteen minutes."

Anna smiled, feeling thankful for small mercies. At least Cassie would get out of the house now.

Chapter 4

Cassie lay in her favorite cabana, trying to catch some warmth from the watery sunlight. Her mother had left for the bookstore and wouldn't be back before evening.

Cassie stood up, yawned and stepped into the pool. She had given up her rigorous exercise regimen since coming back to Dolphin Bay. But she still swam twenty laps every day, regardless of the season.

She placed a call to Bobby. He sent her a text message saying he was in the middle of a training session.

The phone rang. Cassie frowned when her mother's name flashed on the screen.

"What is it, Mom?"

Anna wanted her to go and mind the store. Cassie protested for a while before giving in. Bayside Books was new to Cassie. The store had been closed for most of the time Cassie had been back home so she didn't really know her way around it.

Cassie dragged her feet getting ready. She pulled on a black shirt over faded jeans, wrapped a silk scarf around her neck, slapped her shades on and she was done. A spritz of Joy perfume and some red lipstick made her feel human. The little Mercedes spun its tires and Cassie was walking into the store five minutes later.

"Where are you off to?" she asked her mother. "Don't forget your hat."

"Stop nagging me," Anna grumbled. "I'm just going to Julie's."

"Now?" It was Cassie's turn to complain. "I thought there was some crisis here."

"There is," Anna said curtly. "We can talk about it later."

Anna gave Cassie specific instructions about how to handle the customers. Cassie nodded her head absentmindedly, busy admiring the view from the windows.

"I got it, Mom. It's not rocket science."

"You were always a quick learner."

Anna leaned forward impulsively to hug her daughter. Cassie looked surprised. "See you later," Anna said, and stepped out.

Cassie bit her tongue and berated herself as she saw her mother ride her bike away from the store.

Cassie walked around the store, looking at the overflowing shelves. She tilted her head to read the titles off the spines and found herself smiling. She had been a voracious reader as a child. But she didn't have the time once she started working. The only thing she had read plenty of in the past twenty years were scripts. Scripts and society magazines.

A young girl walked into the store with her father. She wanted to look at the Harry Potter books. There was a steady stream of people coming in after that and Cassie stayed busy helping them. Some of them seemed like regulars. They walked confidently to a shelf, pulled out a book and settled down in an armchair without a word to Cassie. Cassie decided her mother was being too lenient with the locals. No wonder the store was bleeding money.

Cassie was watching a cat video Bobby sent her when she heard the two women. She hadn't seen them come in. Cassie figured they were housewives in their late twenties. They were weighed down by bags from the local grocery store. A baguette was thrust into one while the other overflowed with asparagus stocks.

"I thought the redwood forest was safe," the woman with a shock of blonde curls gushed. "We go for a hike there every Sunday."

"No such thing as a safe place nowadays," the other said dourly.

She wore a dress a couple of sizes too large. Cassie figured she had either lost a lot of weight suddenly or she bought her clothes at the thrift store.

"But what was she doing there alone?"

"Obviously she wasn't alone," Dour Face scoffed. "There was at least one person …"

The blonde haired woman gasped.

"Oh, you mean …"

Cassie cleared her throat.

"What are you girls talking about?"

"Haven't you heard?" Both women chorused.

"It's front page news in the Dolphin Bay Chronicle, of course," the blonde headed woman forged ahead. "Anna gets the paper."

She walked to the reading table by the window and picked up a stack of newspapers.

"I'm sure you will tell it better," Cassie coaxed.

"They found a girl dead in the woods," the dour faced woman said in a hushed voice. "Rumor is she was murdered."

"No way!" Cassie exclaimed. "In this sleepy town? Nothing ever happens here."

"It does now," the blonde haired woman said bluntly. "The police already have the killer pegged down. They should be making an arrest soon."

"How do you know that?" Cassie wondered.

"Haven't you been out and about? Everyone's talking about it."

Dour Face was looking at Cassie oddly.

"Have I seen you somewhere?" she asked. "You look familiar."

Cassie assured her there was no chance of that.

"I know," the blonde haired woman exclaimed.

The other woman had been calling her Taffy or Daffy. Cassie wasn't really sure which.

"She looks like that woman who works at the car dealership out on the highway," Taffy said.

"The one who's always blowing her nose?"

"That's the one," Taffy said triumphantly. "She has a really long nose and a mustache."

The women giggled and whispered loud enough for everyone to hear. Cassie took deep breaths and counted to what felt like hundred.

The two women finally left.

Cassie picked up the newspaper and skimmed through the front page article. It was surprisingly well written although it was light on the details.

Cassie's stomach rumbled. The clock on the wall showed it was after 2 PM. No wonder she was feeling light headed. She debated leaving the store for a few minutes to go grab something to eat. Did her mother do that?

Cassie went into the pantry, hoping to find a snack in the refrigerator. She found a bunch of takeout menus on a shelf. She ordered the sandwich of the day from the Tipsy Whale. Murphy took her order but warned her it would take a while. Cassie found a pot of strawberry yogurt in the refrigerator. It wasn't her usual probiotic organic brand. Then Cassie remembered it had cost five dollars for an eight ounce container. She couldn't afford it any longer.

A bell dinged somewhere. Cassie walked out, licking the last spoonful of the surprisingly delicious yogurt. She stopped short at the sight of the imposing woman who stood tapping a bell impatiently. Her pink suit proclaimed she dressed according to season. Cassie admired the strand of pearls she wore. She should have got one of those for her mother while she still had money.

"Stop making that racket," she said. "I'm here now."

"Like mother, like daughter," the woman muttered.

"How can I help you?" Cassie asked.

"I'm here to talk about the murder case. Where's Anna?"

"My mother went out," Cassie informed her. She pointed at the front page article in the Chronicle. "Is that what you want to talk about?"

The woman snorted.

"You don't have a clue, do you?"

"About what?" Cassie folded her hands and tried not to stare at the woman's crooked nose. "I am sorry, but have we met before?"

"You don't know who I am?" the woman in the pink suit roared. "How long have you been back in town?"

"Six months," Cassie said. "I've been busy."

"I am Lara Crawford."

"Should that mean something to me?"

"I am the mayor of this town, you ignoramus!"

"Okay, Madam Mayor. Can I take a message for you?"

"Tell Anna it won't be long now. The police will be arresting her soon."

"What are you talking about?" Cassie asked, puzzled.

"You poor girl! Anna killed your father. You are living with a cold blooded murderer."

Cassie's eyes bulged. She couldn't have shown this kind of emotion after a dozen rehearsals.

"I won't let her get away with it," Lara warned and stormed out of the store.

Cassie barely tasted the sandwich the Tipsy Whale delivered. It was barbecued chicken with crunchy slaw, another of their masterpieces.

Anna came back, looking upset. Cassie sprang up, eager to get a load off her chest.

"A mad woman came in here, saying you killed Dad."

"Lara Crawford? She's a nuisance. Just ignore her."

"But this is slander," Cassie cried. "Why are you letting her get away with it?"

Anna spied the discarded sandwich wrapper next to the cash register.

"Didn't I teach you to pick up after yourself?" she asked Cassie.

Cassie defended herself.

"I just finished eating. I was ringing up a purchase."

"You are spoilt, Cassie. That's a fact."

"Maybe I am used to a better life, Mom," Cassie said stubbornly. "My housekeeper took care of this kind of stuff."

Anna rolled her eyes.

"As you can see, there is no fancy maid here. You have to pull your own weight."

Cassie picked up her shades and slammed them on her face.

"Why are you so fussy, huh?"

She strode out of the store, simmering with anger. Maybe she wasn't meant to get along with her mother.

Chapter 5

Anna bustled about in her kitchen later that evening, getting dinner ready. She was making Chicken Parmesan as a peace offering for her daughter. Maybe she had been a bit harsh with her. Chicken Parm was Cassie's favorite meal growing up. Anna hoped it would put the smile back on her daughter's face.

She stirred the sauce and slid the crispy chicken into the oven. It was smothered in mozzarella cheese, just the way Cassie liked it.

Cassie came in and peeked at the pot on the stove.

"Smells awesome, Mom," she said. "I missed your cooking."

Anna had been on a hiatus from the kitchen while she was undergoing her treatment. Cassie had insisted on that. She had put together simple meals for them through Anna's surgery and subsequent recovery.

"I am glad to be back in the kitchen," Anna nodded happily. "Why don't you pour us some wine? I just uncorked a nice Pinot Noir for us."

"Are you sure you can drink wine?" Cassie asked, her voice laced with concern.

"It's fine. I talked to the doctor."

"What if you feel queasy or something?"

"Then I will just stop," Anna assured her.

The oven dinged, indicating it was time to eat. Cassie tossed the salad while Anna dished up the spaghetti. Cassie cut into her chicken eagerly and popped a piece in her mouth. Anna was looking at her, waiting for her reaction.

Cassie moaned in delight.

"It's delicious, Mom. Just like I remember it."

Anna's spine relaxed and she finally took a bite herself.

"I'm sorry I walked out earlier," Cassie said, twirling spaghetti on her fork. "You know I have a short fuse."

"You did have a temper," Anna chuckled. "Even in kindergarten."

They reminisced a bit about Cassie's childhood. Cassie relaxed as they chatted comfortably, sipping the excellent wine.

"What was the crisis earlier, Mom? Did you take care of it?"

Anna brought her up to speed.

"One of my old friends is in trouble. Or her son is. They are saying he murdered a girl."

"Wait a minute," Cassie said. "Is this the girl they found dead in the woods?"

"That's right," Anna nodded. "Vicki's boy Cody is the top suspect. She believes he is innocent though."

"Of course she does," Cassie countered. "She's his mother."

"I am not going to protect the boy if he turns out to be guilty. I'm just after the truth."

"Why are you getting involved? And who is this Vicki? I have never heard of her."

"We used to be in a book club," Anna explained. "It was after you left home."

"I am guessing it was more than a book club," Cassie said shrewdly.

Anna laughed. "You guessed that right. We got pulled into solving a couple of cases. We called ourselves the Crime Solvers, just for fun. Then John passed. I got sick. The whole thing kind of fell apart."

"And she came running back to you, now that she's in trouble? You must be good at this thing, Mom."

Anna shrugged.

The doorbell chimed, interrupting them. Anna scrambled to her feet.

"Are you expecting a package or something?"

Cassie shook her head. She served herself a second helping of the Chicken Parm while Anna went to the front door. She came back with a tall, hefty man with a thick crop of salt and pepper hair.

Anna introduced them.

"Chief Mancini, meet my daughter Cassandra."

Cassie tried not to stare at the handsome stranger. His cognac eyes crinkled at the corners as he gave her a warm smile.

"I am not the police chief any more, Mrs. Butler. Haven't been for a while. Call me Gino."

"Then you must call me Anna."

Cassie remembered her manners and poured him a glass of wine. Gino Mancini sniffed the glass like a pro and took a small sip.

"Perfetto! 2013 was a good year for us."

"Gino is the owner of Mystic Hill winery," Anna said, nodding at the label on the wine bottle. "This is his wine."

"A policeman who is also a vintner," Cassie mused. "That's a strange combination."

Gino laughed wholeheartedly. Dimples appeared on either side of his mouth, softening his rugged looks.

"My grandpa started Mystic Hill more than fifty years ago. You can say wine runs in my blood. I took some time sowing my wild oats. Had a stint in the Air Force. A spot on the police force opened just when I wanted to come home. Now I am retired from law enforcement. I spend my days tending my grapes and making wine."

"That sounds like an interesting life," Cassie smiled, raising her glass to him.

"How about you?" Gino asked her. "Word around town is you are some kind of actress?"

"Not just any actress," Anna boasted. "My Cassie won an Oscar award when she was 21. She's very talented."

Cassie colored.

"I'm taking a break right now," she said moodily.

"There's an amateur theatre group in town," Gino said. "I am a backstage volunteer. Maybe you can come and give us some pointers?"

"I'll think about it," Cassie promised.

There was an awkward pause and they all pretended to sip the wine.

"I suppose you are here to talk about the murder?" Anna asked.

Gino turned serious.

"I am here to caution you, Anna. Lara Crawford is making a lot of noise. She might just succeed in reopening John's case."

"Where did you hear that?" Anna asked. "Did she come talk to you?"

"Not yet. But I have my sources at the police department."

"What's spurring her on?" Anna asked, concerned. "Have they found any new evidence?"

"Not to my knowledge."

Cassie was following their conversation eagerly.

"Why is this woman getting involved, Mom? Looks like she's out to get you."

Anna sighed deeply.

"Lara was your father's friend. Somehow, she latched on to this idea that I wanted to harm your father. I don't know why. She knew how much I loved him."

"You never told me about this," Cassie said, pursing her lips in disapproval.

"I didn't think it was something I could talk about over the phone," Anna explained. "I was planning to tell you at the funeral."

Cassie had never made it to her father's funeral. She had been stuck in Mexico, filming for her telenovela.

"The whole town rose against your mother at that time," Gino spoke up. "Many people didn't come for the funeral. She got the silent treatment everywhere she went, thanks to Lara Crawford and the rumors she spread."

"I didn't know any of this," Cassie said soberly. "It must have been hard on you, Mom."

"It was unexpected," Anna agreed. "Your father did so much for the needy. He deserved a good farewell."

Her eyes teared up as she thought of her husband.

"That's why I want to help Cody," Anna said with resolve. "I know how gossip can ruin a person's reputation."

"Poor kid," Gino clucked. "Did he even know that girl?"

"Apparently, they were madly in love. He wanted to ask her to marry him."

"How do you know that?" Gino asked.

"I know his mother," Anna explained. "She thinks I can find the real killer. But I barely know where to start."

"Shouldn't be hard for you," Gino said with a twinkle in his eye. "You have done this before."

"That was a long time ago," Anna said morosely. "I may have to pick your brain on this, Gino."

"You are welcome anytime. But I need to scrape some rust off my brain."

"Don't be so modest. You were the best police chief this town has had in recent history. Not sure your successor is that competent."

"I can't comment on that," Gino said slyly. "Looks like you have your plate full, Anna. Beware of Lara though. I think you should talk to your lawyer about this."

"You don't think I am guilty?" she asked him. She turned toward her daughter. "What about you, Cassie? Do you think I am capable of murdering your father?"

"Of course not," Cassie shot back loyally. "I think this woman is misusing her power. She's just being catty."

"Whatever her motivation, you will have to deal with her," Gino warned.

Anna's special meal had grown cold while they talked.

"Can I offer you some dessert?" she asked Gino. "Tiramisu. Cassie's favorite. It's my Nona's recipe."

"I didn't know you were Italian," Gino remarked.

"My mother was Italian, so I guess I'm half Italian. My grandparents came to America at the turn of the last century."

"So we have a common heritage," Gino smiled.

Anna fought a blush. She turned around to pull a pan of tiramisu from the refrigerator. Gino didn't object to the generous helping she dished out.

"You ought to open a café or something," he said, smacking his lips.

Anna thought of her rejected café license and resolved to fight for her dream.

Chapter 6

Anna Butler sat out on her patio the next morning, savoring her first cup of coffee. A riot of daffodils bloomed in a corner, their bright yellow hue making her feel optimistic about the day ahead.

She had been up early to bake a fresh batch of her raspberry chocolate cupcakes. They were cooling on a rack in her kitchen, ready to be frosted.

Gino Mancini had compelled her to think seriously about what lay around the corner. But she was determined to put her own troubles aside and make some headway in learning more about Cody Bauer's girlfriend, the young victim.

Anna went back in and started cutting avocadoes for breakfast. Her own avocado tree had died of neglect but the local farm produced a good crop. Anna squeezed a lemon over the avocado slices to keep them from going brown and mashed them up. She was sprinkling hot sauce over her toast when Cassie walked in, sleepy eyed.

Anna got a mumbled greeting before Cassie slumped into a chair and poured herself some coffee. She sipped it with her eyes half closed.

"What are you doing today?" Anna asked her, nudging a plate of avocado toast in her direction.

Cassie yawned widely.

"I don't know, Mom. My agent might call about a new role."

"That's what you said yesterday."

"So?" Cassie shrugged, draining her coffee and frowning at the empty pot.

"You need to make a fresh pot," Anna told her. "I will be at the store. There are plenty of leftovers for your lunch."

Cassie grunted and slouched in her chair, closing her eyes again.

Anna wished her daughter would take an interest in something. She went to her room and called Julie.

"We need to come up with a plan of action," she told her. "How's your calendar looking today?"

"I'm between chapters," Julie said. "I can spare a couple of hours. Shall we meet at the store?"

"Let me call Mary," Anna said.

Mary had been waiting for their call. They generally chatted in the morning to talk about their day's plans.

Julie and Mary needed half an hour to get ready. Anna dressed in a bright yellow top inspired by the daffodils and slapped a straw hat on her head. She cycled to Bayside Books, thinking about what she wanted to discuss with her friends. She decided not to mention Gino Mancini's visit.

Anna placed her bike in its usual spot and took a moment to admire Main Street. Brick fronts and striped awnings gave it a picturesque, vintage look. Oak trees lined the street on both sides, casting some welcome shade on the sidewalks. The ancient clock tower stood at the other end, next to the town hall. There was a steady stream of early shoppers visiting the grocery store. The florist was setting out pots of fresh flowers. Anna waved at a couple of people before going into her own store.

She had dusted all the shelves and made coffee by the time Julie breezed in. Julie eyed the plate of cupcakes resting on a table and made a beeline for it.

"Mmmm …" she moaned after taking a big bite. "Did you bake these today?"

Anna nodded. "I am still tweaking the recipe."

Mary came in, looking flushed.

"Sorry I am late," she apologized. "I was talking to my lodger."

"It sounds so quaint when you say that," Julie laughed. "Are you renting out rooms again?"

"Just the bedroom over the garage," Mary explained. "We have more than enough space with the kids gone. A little extra income doesn't hurt."

"I hear ya," Anna harrumphed.

"I wouldn't feel safe doing it," Julie said, embarking on her pet theme. "What do you know about these people, anyway? Do you even look at their IDs?"

"Rain's a slip of a girl," Mary laughed. "She's not going to hurt us."

"Rain?" Julie rolled her eyes. "I rest my case."

"You'll never guess what happened," Mary continued, ignoring Julie. "Someone almost ran her down the other day."

"And that's why we don't allow cars on Main Street," Anna said with a flourish.

"Come and try these cupcakes, Mary," Julie said. "They are so rich they just melt in your mouth."

"Stop thinking about food for a while, Julie," Mary admonished. "Did you girls read the Chronicle this morning?"

"Not yet," Anna said.

She picked up the local newspaper from the reading table and skimmed the front page. The local murder had once again made headlines.

"Anything worth knowing?" she asked Mary, trying to glean any pertinent information from the paper at the same time.

"The girl's name was Briana. She was a student at the university."

"I knew that but I didn't know her name. Funny that neither Vicki nor Cody mentioned it."

"What else does the paper say?" Julie asked, dabbing her lips with a tissue.

"Her family moved here recently," Mary continued. "No one seems to know much about them."

"Does that mean she lived at home?" Anna asked.

"I guess so," Mary shrugged. "The paper doesn't say anything about that."

"What difference would that make?" Julie asked.

"I don't know that yet," Anna told them. "I just wondered if she lived in a dorm on campus."

"Does Cody live on campus?" Julie asked.

"You know what? I don't know that. I'll ask him the next time I see him."

"You do that," Julie nodded. "Meanwhile, I can talk to a few people, starting with our mailman. He might tell us something interesting about Briana's family."

"That Alfie is a big gossip," Mary fussed. "And you are no better."

Old Alfie had been the Dolphin Bay mailman since as far back as the girls could remember. He showed no signs of slowing down.

"Alfie and I have an arrangement," Julie grinned. "He keeps me informed with what's happening in town and I keep him supplied with advanced copies of all my books."

"Who would've thought Old Alfie would secretly read romance books?" Anna cackled.

"He's one of my most helpful beta readers," Julie said, defending him.

"What's Cassie doing today?" Mary asked.

Anna shook her head.

"I don't know what to do with that girl."

"She's a grown woman, Anna," Julie consoled. "She's been through a lot. Give her some time to get her bearings."

"Living here must be hard on her," Mary said. "Dolphin Bay might be charming to us, but it pales before the bright lights of Hollywood."

"I didn't ask her to come here," Anna grumbled. "She should have stayed away, like she did for the past twenty years."

Julie looked frustrated.

"Anna Butler, you need to count your blessings. You have a daughter who dropped everything to come and nurse you. Cassie loves you so much. Can't you see that?"

"She didn't have much of a choice," Anna said. "That crooked manager of hers took her to the cleaners."

"She's here now," Mary said firmly. "I think she will stick around."

"She'll be gone as soon as she lands a new role," Anna said with certainty.

"So that's what's bothering you?" Julie eyed the last cupcake on the plate. "You don't want to get used to having her around."

Anna's eyes glistened.

"I'm already used to her."

"We don't have to worry about this now," Mary said hurriedly.

"Yes," Julie agreed. "We need to talk about the café, Anna. What are you going to do now?"

"I can't proceed without a license," Anna sighed. "Frankly, I'm stumped. Lara is going to have her way this time."

"We won't let her," Julie said, biting her lip. "We need to rally the troops."

"That's a great idea, Julie," Mary agreed. "What if we come up with a petition? We can collect signatures in favor of the café. Lara will have to bow down to public demand."

"Most people don't even make eye contact with me," Anna complained. "Lara's seen to that."

"I agree some of Lara's cronies give you the cold shoulder," Julie said thoughtfully. "But they are insignificant. Most businesses on Main Street and Ocean Avenue will side with you. You'll see."

"We need to plan this well," Mary told them. "This has to be a community event. Something that involves everyone, you know."

"You already thought of something, haven't you?" Julie asked shrewdly. "Come on, Mary. Out with it."

Mary blushed. She didn't like to be the center of attention.

Anna was looking at her with a hopeful expression.

"Well, we could have a potluck."

"What!" Julie guffawed. "You want to make more work for people."

"Let her speak," Anna admonished, holding up a hand. "Go on, Mary."

"Most people have a favorite dish or two they like to show off," Mary explained. "I know I do. We can fire up the grill outside."

"Anna can bake her cupcakes," Julie said thoughtfully. "And we can convince people to vote for the café over hot dogs and potato salad."

"Something like that," Mary said meekly.

Anna finally smiled.

"I think that's an excellent idea. At the very least, we can all have a good time."

"People will stand by you, Anna," Julie stressed. "I am sure of that."

Mary left to run some errands and Julie headed home. A couple of customers trickled in and Anna got busy taking care of them. She went into the pantry to make some fresh coffee and remembered Gino's advice.

Anna placed a call to her lawyer.

"But can they really reopen the case?" she asked worriedly. "What does that mean for me?"

The lawyer wanted to know if they had found any new evidence. Anna wasn't sure about that. The lawyer promised to talk to the local Dolphin Bay authorities and find out more. He would be on hand if Anna needed anything.

Anna didn't feel reassured. She just hoped the police would believe she was innocent.

Chapter 7

Anna walked to the Yellow Tulip diner. It was situated on Ocean Avenue, parallel to Main Street. Ocean and Main made a two mile stretch known as the Downtown Loop. No vehicles were allowed in this area. People either walked or cycled, and kids whizzed around on skateboards.

Anna had asked Cody Bauer to meet her for lunch. She thought he might not be very forthcoming in his mother's presence so she had convinced Vicki to let her meet him alone.

Cody greeted her with a warm hug. Anna beamed up at him. He had grown up to be a fine young man, his athletic build and cornflower blue eyes guaranteed to make the girls swoon.

"How are you, Mrs. Butler?" Cody asked.

"I'm doing good, Cody. But looks like you are not."

Cody's shoulders slumped. Anna urged him into the diner and chose a booth at the other end. She ordered cheeseburgers for the both of them. The diner had a limited menu but they made a mean burger.

Cody picked at his food, refusing to look up. Anna dipped a French fry into ketchup and chewed on it.

"No use moping, my boy," she said. "We both know why we are here."

"You believe in me, don't you Mrs. Butler?" Cody pleaded. "I would never hurt Briana. I loved her."

"It doesn't matter what I believe," Anna said dryly. "The police must have something incriminating against you."

Cody's eyes flickered and he looked away.

"My mother said you are going to help us get out of this mess."

"I am going to try," Anna nodded. "But you will have to be completely honest with me, Cody. Don't leave anything out, especially the minor details."

Cody finally took a bite of his burger and sighed.

"What do you want to know?"

"I didn't know you attended the local university. Didn't you have a fancy baseball scholarship to some college out east?"

"That fizzled out when I hurt my elbow," he told her. "There was no question of a sports scholarship after that. We couldn't afford out of state tuition so I enrolled into our local college. It's not bad."

"No, it's not," Anna agreed. "My John worked there most of his life. We had a good life."

"People still mention Professor Butler," Cody told her. "He gave a talk at our school once."

"John enjoyed being a mentor," Anna reminisced.

The waitress came over to top up their drinks. Anna got a curious look from her. The grapevine would soon start buzzing with speculation about what Anna was doing having lunch with a suspected murderer.

Anna sipped her soda and stifled a burp.

"How did you meet Briana? She was new in town, wasn't she?"

"Briana didn't grow up here," Cody nodded. "That's how we got together, I guess."

"How do you mean?"

"We ran into each other in the library," Cody explained. "She was a little spitfire. I asked her out for coffee."

"Did you share any classes?"

"She was studying English Lit," Cody said. "I am a business major."

"What happened after you met?"

"Like you said, she was new in town. I offered to show her the sights. It wasn't long before I fell in love with her."

"Did you tell her that?"

"I am sure she knew," Cody blushed.

"How did she feel about it?"

"Briana could be aloof," Cody said thoughtfully. "She didn't want to get involved at first. But she agreed to go on dates. After some time, I figured we were a couple."

"Were you seeing anyone else?" Anna asked cagily.

Cody was indignant.

"Of course not!"

"I don't know what's the latest trend among you Millennials."

"I was going to ask her to marry me," Cody said fervently. "She was the only one for me."

"So you were both what they call exclusive," Anna stressed.

Cody played with the fries on his plate, avoiding looking at Anna.

"Yes. We were exclusive, Mrs. Butler."

Anna exhausted her questions after a while. Cody agreed to get in touch with her if he had any more information to share.

Anna went back to Bayside Books. The afternoon passed slowly. A couple of regulars lounged in chairs, thumbing through their favorite books. They treated the store like a library but Anna didn't mind.

"Will you keep an eye on things, Dolly?" she asked one of the women dozing at the reading table by the window.

The woman nodded, barely opening her eyes.

Anna wheeled her cycle out on the road, trying to figure out if she could make it to the Mystic Hill winery. She debated calling Julie for a ride. But Julie or Mary didn't know about Gino Mancini's visit. In the end, she decided to brave it.

A salty breeze blew in from the bay but the afternoon sun blazed brightly. Anna was out of breath before she exited the Downtown Loop. She stuck to her plan, refusing to admit she wasn't strong enough. Her leg muscles quivered as she pedaled up the small hill leading to Gino's place. A number of frequent stops later, Anna reached the winery, soaked in sweat, her hair plastered to her skull.

She thought about turning back.

Gino spotted her in that instant. He was unloading something from the back of a pickup.

"Anna! What are you doing here? Don't tell me you pedaled up that hill?"

Anna's chest heaved as she tried to answer him.

"Where are my manners!" Gino cried. "You don't need to talk now. Let's get you out of the sun."

Gino led her into the house, a rambling ranch house that seemed far too big for one person. Anna barely had a chance to admire it. It was several degrees cooler inside. Gino led her to a comfortable couch in a sunken living room. He excused himself and went inside, returning a few minutes later with two tall glasses of lemonade.

Anna sipped the cold drink appreciatively, and accepted the tissue Gino handed her.

"I think I was a fool," she admitted. "I shouldn't have attempted the ride here."

"I'm taking you home myself," Gino told her. "No arguments."

"I'm too old and frail to refuse that offer," Anna grumbled. "So I will just say Thank You and accept."

"You don't look old to me," Gino smiled, flashing his dimples. "I bet I have a few years on you."

"I am closer to sixty than fifty," Anna snorted.

"Age is just a number," Gino said softly. He pointed to his heart. "It's what you feel in here that matters."

Anna began to feel human after she finished her lemonade. Gino offered her more.

"I should offer wine but I think you need this more now."

"I spoke to my lawyer today," Anna began, getting around to the purpose of her visit. "He wanted to know if there was any new evidence."

"Not as far as I know. Lara Crawford is implying that we botched up the investigation."

"That's a slur on your record," Anna cried. "What does she have against you?"

"Hard to say," Gino replied. "She's making this her mission. She is really convinced there was foul play."

"What do you think, Gino?"

"Honestly, I stand by what I said two years ago. The evidence was inconclusive. We didn't have enough to seriously suspect anyone. That includes you, Anna."

"What am I going to do now?"

"My advice is to sit tight," Gino said firmly. "Lara Crawford can dig all she wants but she won't find anything. That's because there is nothing to be found."

"I hope it all blows over. I don't want Cassie worrying about it."

"You faced a lot on your own. You must be a strong woman."

Anna blushed.

"I didn't have a choice."

Gino offered her a tour of the place. Anna declined politely.

"I think I will take that ride now. I'm ready to call it a day."

Gino ushered her out to his truck. He placed her bike in the back and opened the door of the cab for her.

"Would you like to come to a wine tasting event?" he asked as he drove into town. "We have one every month. The Spring event is coming up soon."

"I would love that," Anna smiled. "I already like your wines."

"We are still finalizing the dates," Gino said. "I will get you a flyer when we finish printing them."

"Say Gino," Anna asked as he came to a stop at the drop-off point on Main.

Luckily, it was just across her store and Anna didn't have far to go.

"What kind of evidence do the police have on Cody?"

"I am not plugged into the day to day activities of the police now, Anna," Gino replied. "I left that life far behind."

Anna thanked him for the ride. Gino ignored her protests and walked her to the store, wheeling her bike himself.

"Call me the next time you want to come see me," he told her. "I can come and get you myself."

Anna felt her knees go weak as he held her hands and stared into her eyes, bidding goodbye.

Chapter 8

Cassie lay sprawled on the couch, watching Casablanca. It was her favorite movie of all time. She had worked her way through a big bowl of buttered popcorn. Now she was feasting on potato chips. She ignored the slight nausea she felt from gorging on all the butter and grease.

Humphrey Bogart and Ingrid Bergman talked about Paris on the screen. Cassie was mesmerized. She wondered if she had ever known true love. She had been married twice. Both of her marriages had ended badly. She had suffered some heartbreak when her first husband ditched her for an upcoming starlet. By the time her second husband filed divorce papers, she had become cynical. She had agreed to a mutual divorce, eager to end it all with a minimum of fuss.

Anna came in and collapsed in an armchair. Cassie didn't take her eyes off the screen but she observed her mother from the corner of her eye. She was looking sweaty and exhausted. Cassie wondered what she had been up to.

"This place looks like a trash heap," Anna complained. "How can you make such a mess, Cassie?"

"I'll take care of it later," Cassie said, caught up in the last few scenes of the movie.

"Let's do it now," Anna urged, springing to her feet. "What if someone knocked on the door right now?"

"Are you expecting company?" Cassie asked, rooting around in the chip bag for the salty crumbs.

"That's beside the point," Anna said, her voice going up another octave. "This is the living room. It has to be ready for visitors at all times."

Cassie emitted a loud sigh and switched off the TV. She made no move to get up. She leaned further back in her recliner and looked at her mother.

"Why don't you relax, Mom? You seem tired."

Anna dropped back into the chair and closed her eyes.

"Can you take care of dinner?" she asked Cassie. "Please? I don't think I can lift a finger."

Cassie dragged herself to her feet and shuffled into the kitchen, muttering something under her breath. She decided to make a quick salad. She rustled up her special Green Goddess dressing.

"Let's eat, Mom," she called out twenty minutes later.

Anna sat at the table and stared at the big plate of salad in front of her.

"What's this?" she asked. "Haven't you cooked anything?"

"This is a big salad, Mom. And the dressing's quite heavy too."

"I fancied a hot meal," Anna grumbled. "Too much to ask, I guess."

"You could have said so," Cassie shot back. "Do you want me to order a pizza for you?"

Anna shuddered.

"No thanks. I'll make do with this salad."

Cassie wished her mother wasn't so hard to please.

She put her head down and focused on cutting her salad into small bits. It was her version of a Cobb salad with boiled eggs, bacon, cherry tomatoes and plenty of ripe avocadoes.

Cassie watched as Anna worked through half her salad and buttered a second piece of bread.

"This is actually not bad," Anna said grudgingly. "I like the dressing."

"A chef from a big San Francisco hotel taught me his version of Green Goddess dressing," Cassie explained. "I made some changes to it."

"We can serve this at the café," Anna said. "It's that good."

"I thought you only wanted to sell cupcakes," Cassie countered.

Anna's eyes widened.

"We can start with baked goods. Then we could add some prepackaged stuff, or maybe add a salad bar."

"I think a salad bar is a great idea," Cassie nodded. "Don't think anyone's doing that kind of food in town. The diner's just a greasy spoon. The Tipsy Whale does great food but it's mostly carbs."

"Sounds like an odd combination," Anna mused. "Salads and dessert."

Cassie was glad to see some color back in her mother's face.

"How was your day, Mom?" she asked. "Anything interesting happen at the store?"

"I met Cody for lunch," Anna told her.

"I was in town for lunch too," Cassie said. "I'm surprised we didn't run into each other."

"Did you go to the diner?" Anna wanted to know. "That's where we were."

"I was at the Tipsy Whale," Cassie told her.

"Again?" Anna frowned.

"Wait till you hear this," Cassie said, leaning forward. "You'll be glad I went there."

Anna rolled her eyes and waited for Cassie to go on.

"Everyone was talking about this guy, your friend's son."

"Cody?"

"Right," Cassie nodded. "I don't think the natives like him."

"What do you mean?"

"They all believe he is guilty, Mom. Not a single person was saying anything good about him."

"That's how gossip works," Anna said dryly. "People rarely have anything good to say about their neighbors."

"This was more than vague gossip," Cassie explained. "It seems this guy was very possessive about the dead girl."

"Maybe he was just being protective," Anna said, giving Cody the benefit of the doubt. "He was in love with her."

"I think he was smothering her. He wanted to keep her to himself."

"That doesn't bode well for the kid," Anna said worriedly. "What else did they say?"

"A couple of young girls were saying he was obsessed with the girl. He did creepy stuff, like holding her hand tightly all the time. As if she would run away if he let her loose."

"What was he so insecure about?" Anna wondered.

"What's he like?" Cassie asked. "I mean, were they well matched?"

"Cody's a good looking boy," Anna defended him. "Well behaved too. He was very popular in high school."

"So he's a jock?" Cassie countered. "Hmmm …"

"What's that for?" Anna asked.

"You met him today … what was your first impression, Mom?"

"It wasn't the first time I met him, Cassie. I've known him since he was a child."

"But you don't know the grown up version," Cassie pointed out. "Kids change, Mom. Teenaged Cody and present day Cody could be two different people."

Anna was quiet.

"I'm not talking about myself," Cassie said, reading her mother's mind. "Can we please focus on this kid?"

"He seemed sincere," Anna reflected. "He said he loved her. He even hoped to marry her. I think I can believe that."

"But?" Cassie prompted.

"He wasn't being completely honest," Anna mused. "I think he was hiding something."

"Did you call him out on it?" Cassie asked.

"Not this time," Anna said. "I didn't want to put him on his guard."

"That means you suspect him," Cassie pressed. "Do you think he is capable of hurting that girl?"

"I don't know, Cassie," Anna sighed.

"I thought you were on his side?"

"Not if he turns out to be guilty. I already told them that."

"What else do we know about this guy?"

"Vicki's very proud of him. She says he is a good student, always top of his class. She has high hopes for him."

"Like every mother on this planet," Cassie drawled.

"Vicki says he is the quiet type," Anna continued. "He's not the kind to pick a fight."

"That's completely opposite of what people were saying at the pub."

"Forget what people say," Anna snapped. "They have said plenty of unkind things about us over the years."

"Maybe we deserved them," Cassie said in a small voice.

"No one deserves being raked over the coals for the tough breaks they had in life," Anna said firmly.

Cassie stared at her empty plate, lost in thought.

"We did the best under the circumstances," Anna stressed. "Now how about some dessert? I need a sugar fix after the day I have had."

Cassie forced herself to smile.

"I ate all the tiramisu, Mom. But we have chocolate gelato."

"An Italian never says no to gelato," Anna said.

"Want to take a dip in the hot tub?" Cassie asked. "You look like you need it."

Anna thought of her aching limbs and agreed readily. Mother and daughter were soon out on the patio, relaxing in the giant jetted tub next to the swimming pool.

Cassie broached the subject of the café.

"You are not giving up yet, are you, Mom?"

"The girls and I have a plan," Anna said.

Cassie was skeptical as her mother talked about the proposed potluck.

"You think those signatures will matter?"

"Lara Crawford will have to cede to public opinion," Anna said confidently. "She can't go against the people. Not in a town like Dolphin Bay. Certainly not if she wants to be elected again."

"What of that nonsense about Daddy?" Cassie asked finally.

She had been brooding about it all day.

"We just sit tight," Anna said. "Don't worry, we'll be fine."

Cassie didn't share her mother's confidence but she smiled and said nothing.

Chapter 9

Cassie woke up feeling refreshed the next morning. She had slept well, heartened by spending some quality time with her mother. Her phone rang, signaling a video call. Cassie hit the green button when she saw it was Bobby.

"You awake, sweetie?"

"I'm just getting up, Bobby." Cassie let out a yawn. "I must look awful."

"You look beautiful 24x7," Bobby cooed. "Wait till you hear this …"

He launched into some gossip about a certain Hollywood star. She had been virtually unknown when Cassie was at the zenith of her career. But she had risen to the top fast, her ascent as meteoric as Cassie's fall had been.

"She wore that to the gala?" Cassie asked in a hushed voice. "Are you kidding me?"

"She never had your flair for fashion," Bobby dismissed. "You're still the queen, Cass. Everyone misses you. When are you coming home?"

"I am home," Cassie sighed. "The time's not right, Bobby. I need to be here to look after my Mom."

"Well, don't take too long," Bobby said, leaning closer to the screen. "You know what they say, out of sight, out of mind."

"We'll talk about it when you come here," Cassie promised.

"Why don't you get a nice workout in, now that you're up?" Bobby asked. "We can do it together."

Cassie yawned widely.

"Maybe I'll go for a run."

"Do you promise?" Bobby asked sternly. "You need to stay fit, girl. Your arms are starting to look flabby."

"I could use a new weight training routine," Cassie pouted. "You really need to get here in person, Bobby."

Bobby promised to meet her soon and rung off.

Cassie spied the sheer white curtains at her window fluttering in the breeze and walked over. The spring morning was still cool. She breathed in the lingering scent of jasmine and smiled. Maybe a run wasn't such a bad idea.

She fished around in her closet and pulled out some running clothes. She put her hair up in a hasty pony tail. Five minutes later, she breezed into the kitchen.

Anna was fiddling around with the oven, baking a fresh batch of cupcakes.

"Good Morning, Mom," Cassie greeted her, pouring herself a glass of orange juice. "I'm going for a run."

She gulped her juice while Anna fussed about breakfast.

"I can eat later," Cassie said, rushing out of the door.

She decided to head to the Coastal Walk. It was a five mile stretch that ran along the bluffs, parallel to the bay. The path alternated between stunning views of the water and dense foliage from the towering pine and eucalyptus trees. Castle Beach Resort, a luxury retreat for the rich and famous, sat at one end of the Walk along with its award winning golf course. The other end led to Sunset Beach, a beautiful white sand paradise tucked away in a gentle cove.

Cassie walked to Bayside Books and cut onto the Coastal Walk. She headed north toward the resort, jogging slowly to warm up her body. She picked up speed as her limbs loosened, enjoying the salty breeze fanning her face. Spring was a beautiful time in Dolphin Bay and the cliffs were ablaze with wild flowers. Tourists came to town to gawk at the bright orange California poppies and the vibrant yellow mustard blooms that blanketed the ground.

Forty minutes later, Cassie slowed to a walk, taking deep breaths. The exercise had put her in a good mood. She was ravenous, looking forward to the tasty breakfast she was sure her mother would put together.

A voice hailed her. Cassie looked around and spotted a short, stocky man dressed in sweats waving at her.

"Hey Cassie!" the man beamed, jogging up to her. "Didn't know you were in town."

Cassie tried to remember how she knew the man.

"I'm Teddy," the man said, shaking his head. "Teddy Fowler. Don't you remember me?"

Cassie giggled. Teddy barely looked like the boy she had known in high school.

"Of course I remember you, Teddy," Cassie smiled. "But I didn't recognize you."

"It's been what, twenty years?"

"Something like that," Cassie nodded.

"You might have forgotten me, Cass, but I've followed your career. I have all your films on DVD. We have Cassie Butler movie night once a month."

"That's nice of you," Cassie mumbled.

She was beginning to remember bits and pieces about Teddy Fowler. He had asked her out a couple of times back in the day. Cassie had been going out with someone else at that time. It didn't seem like Teddy bore a grudge.

"Do you live in Dolphin Bay?" Cassie asked him.

"Some of us never left," Teddy said. "No complaints from me. I am happy here."

"Do you go for a run here every morning?" Cassie asked, pointing to the Coastal Walk.

"Come rain or shine," Teddy bobbed his head eagerly. "I never miss a day. Gotta keep in shape, you know. The job demands it. You should know. You Hollywood types are real sticklers for fitness."

"What do you do?" Cassie asked politely.

Teddy Fowler seemed to puff up with pride.

"I'm a detective with the local police force."

"No kidding!"

"I'm working on a very important case at the moment," Teddy preened. "A college kid was found murdered in the woods. You must have heard about it."

"I read something about it in the paper," Cassie offered. "So you are in charge of this murder investigation, huh?"

"That's right," Teddy said. "It's an open and shut case. That boy's going away for a very long time."

"You solved the case already?" Cassie asked, widening her eyes in wonder.

"We have pretty strong evidence," Teddy smiled. "Feels like it's been handed to us on a platter."

Cassie leaned closer to the detective.

"Go on, give me the scoop."

"We don't really discuss ongoing cases, but I guess I can tell you."

"My lips are sealed," Cassie promised him. "Who am I going to tell anyway?"

"We found the murder weapon right next to the body," Teddy said in a rush. "And guess what, it's got the suspect's finger prints all over it."

Cassie sucked in a breath.

"That sounds damaging."

"You bet it is," Teddy laughed. "We should be making an arrest soon. You will read about it in the Chronicle."

"I gotta go," Cassie told him. "It was nice catching up with you, Teddy."

"Hey, why don't we grab a pint sometime at the Tipsy Whale?" Teddy Fowler asked eagerly. "My wife would love to meet you. I've told her so much about you over the years."

"I'll think about it," Cassie promised.

"Come on, Cass, don't be shy!" Teddy pressed. "You are home now. I bet there's a lot of people from our class who will want to meet you."

Cassie remembered something more about Teddy Fowler. He was a bit of a leech. But he was harmless.

"Pick a day," she nodded. "I'll be there. Now I really have to go."

Teddy said goodbye and started jogging down the path. Cassie heaved a sigh of relief and dragged herself home. She was starving by the time she got there.

Anna had left a note for her on the kitchen table. A covered plate sat on the counter. Cassie lifted the top off eagerly and smiled when she saw the avocado toast and poached eggs. She polished off the food and poured herself a big mug of coffee.

Teddy Fowler had got her thinking. She took a quick shower and pulled out a couple of giant shoeboxes from her closet. They contained her most valued treasures, glimpses of her life in the past twenty years.

Cassie sat in the center of her bed, pulling stuff out of the boxes one by one, smiling at the glimpses of her life. There was a faded black and white photo of her with her first roommate in L.A. Cassie pulled out newspaper clippings depicting her going to lavish parties or receiving big awards. She stared at a photo of her holding the golden knight, the most coveted of all awards in the entertainment industry. Tears flowed down her cheeks as she thought of her past glory. Was Bobby right? Had everyone in Hollywood forgotten her? Was she supposed to spend the rest of her life in a small coastal town far away from the bright lights?

Cassie dumped everything back in the box and flung it into a corner of the room. She pulled out a bottle of vodka from underneath her bed and took a few swigs. Burying her head in the pillow, Cassie broke into sobs, blaming her fate and the world.

A few minutes later, the sobs turned into snores as Cassie settled into a disturbed sleep.

Chapter 10

Anna tasted her latest batch of raspberry chocolate cupcakes. The raspberry frosting was a bit tart, just as she liked it. She looked up as Cassie bounded into the kitchen, dressed in exercise clothes.

"Going somewhere?"

"Good Morning, Mom," Cassie greeted her with a broad smile.

She gulped some orange juice and went out for a run. Anna felt a ray of hope. Was her daughter finally getting out of her funk?

She cleared away all her baking stuff and started making breakfast. Cassie would be hungry when she got home.

An hour later, Anna pedaled her bicycle to the bookstore, enjoying the blooms in her neighbors' spring gardens. She glanced up at the magnolia tree before entering the store, noting with pleasure that some of the buds had opened and were looking very pretty, juxtaposed against the bright blue sky.

Anna finished her daily chore of dusting the shelves. She put some books back in their right spots and decided to take a look at the previous week's collections. She didn't enjoy keeping the books but it was a necessary evil for a small business owner. She couldn't afford to hire a full time accountant yet.

"Hola!" a voice called out just when she was beginning to make some sense of the numbers.

A hefty, heavily muscled man with close cropped hair walked in, wearing a sleeveless shirt stretched tightly across his formidable chest.

"Hi Jose," Anna said brightly. "How are you?"

"No time for small talk, Anna," Jose Garcia said, heading toward a window table.

Jose owned the corner store next to Bayside Books. He and Anna had an agreement. She was going to buy him out, knock down a wall and open her café in the new space.

Anna dreaded what was coming. She got up from her perch behind the cash register and sat down in front of Jose.

"Care for a cup of coffee? I was just about to make a pot."

"Thanks, but I am not here for coffee."

"What's on your mind?" Anna asked, steeling herself.

"Look, Anna. We've known each other a long time. That's why I cut you some slack. But I needed the money from the sale yesterday. When are you planning to close?"

"Soon," Anna said. "Very soon."

Jose scratched his head and stared right into her eyes.

"You're not being straight with me. I know the city didn't approve your café license."

"I have a plan, Jose," Anna pleaded. "I'll get the café approved. But I can't buy the space until then. Surely you see that?"

"I have another buyer lined up," Jose admitted. "He's offering cash upfront."

"Who is it?" Anna asked. "Some chain store from the big city?"

"Doesn't matter," Jose sighed. "I'm ready to retire. My cousin got a condo in Cabo last year and there's a unit for me right next to him. But I need to put in a deposit this month."

"I don't have that kind of cash," Anna admitted honestly. "Not right now. The bookstore hardly brings in any money."

Jose looked around in disgust.

"Aren't you tired of this dump? This guy from the city is willing to buy you out. He'll pay a bonus if he can get both units."

"Hold on a minute," Anna frowned. "I never said anything about selling this store."

"Suit yourself," Jose said, getting up. "Two weeks, Anna. We need to be in escrow by then or I am going with the other guy."

"Thanks Jose!" Anna said sarcastically.

Jose shrugged. "Hey! Nothing personal." He walked out of the store without a backward glance.

Anna wasn't in the mood to do the books after that. She went into the pantry and started a fresh pot of coffee. She had just finished adding an extra squirt of half and half to her cup when Julie walked in.

"I'll have one of that," she said, settling into an overstuffed armchair.

Anna was quiet as she handed over her friend's coffee.

"What's wrong?" Julie asked, picking up on Anna's distress immediately. "Are you sick? Is Cassie okay?"

"I'm fine," Anna assured her. "So is Cassie, as far as I know."

Julie sipped her coffee and waited for Anna to continue.

"Jose's given me an ultimatum. He has another buyer."

"What?" Julie cried. "Everyone in town knows you have a verbal agreement with Jose."

"It's some rich company from the city." Anna shrugged. "Can't say I blame him. I'm just running out of time."

"Do you have to open the café right away?" Julie asked. "Why can't you just expand the store?"

"The café is supposed to bring in the money," Anna sighed.

"That's what you should be focusing on then, Anna," Julie said. "Why are you wasting time playing Miss Marple?"

"I promised Vicki," Anna reminded her. "So? Have you learned anything new?"

"A little bit," Julie nodded. "I had a talk with Old Alfie. Had to promise him hardcover copies of my next five books."

"Did he know the girl?"

"He ran into her a couple of times. Alfie says Briana was a force to reckon with. She was super aggressive, it seems. Quite a go-getter."

"She doesn't sound like the kind to succumb to anyone," Anna reasoned.

"Exactly," Julie agreed. "You can say she was an unlikely candidate for murder."

"What about her parents?" Anna asked.

"The family moved here from the city. Her father worked in some factory. He met with a bad accident at work. He's in a wheelchair now. On disability."

"Sounds like he got a raw deal," Anna sympathized. "What about her mother?"

"The mother used to be a maid. She's been looking for a permanent job here, something that pays benefits. But she hasn't found one yet. She cleans people's houses. But I don't think that's steady work."

"Maybe we should give her a shot," Anna suggested. "It's time for spring cleaning anyway."

Julie didn't think much of the idea.

"What do we know about this woman? What if she's light fingered?"

"That's unfair, Julie," Anna protested. "You know nothing about her."

Julie ignored her and changed the subject.

"Didn't you have lunch with Cody yesterday? What's your take on him?"

"He's not being completely honest," Anna told her. "He insists he loved her, of course. And he says he is innocent."

"You don't sound convinced, Anna."

"We need to find out more about him, from people he's not related to."

"People other than Vicki, you mean," Julie said. "I agree."

"We also need more details about the crime itself," Anna continued. "All we know is Briana was found in the redwood forest. But how was she killed? What kind of weapon was used? Did they find anything else at the scene of crime?"

"You sound like a proper detective," Julie smiled. "Do you think the police will share all this information with you?"

"I doubt it," Anna said. "We might have to rely on the grapevine."

"You can talk to Gino Mancini," Julie suggested slyly.

"Gino's retired," Anna dismissed.

"No harm in asking," Julie said. "Gives you a reason to go talk to him."

"I don't need to drum up a reason," Anna said.

"Oh?" Julie arched her eyebrows.

"Actually, I went to the vineyard."

"What?" Julie exploded. "Way to bury the lead, Anna. Tell me everything. And don't skip the naughty details."

"It wasn't like that," Anna said indignantly. Then she smiled. "He invited me to a wine tasting later this month."

"The Spring Wine Tasting Event at Mystic Hill?" Julie asked. "It's a big thing, Anna. People from up and down the coast come to Dolphin Bay for it."

"So a lot of people turn up for this thing?" Anna asked.

"Yeah. Are you going as a special guest?"

"He didn't say," Anna said glumly. "I'm not sure if it was just a casual invite or …"

"Or he was asking you out on a date," Julie finished for her.

"I barely know him, Julie," Anna said morosely. "I think he was just being polite."

"Do you like him, Anna?" Julie asked.

"I loved my John. I still love him. I never thought of another man since I met him."

"Relax!" Julie chided her. "No one's asking you to declare your undying love for this man. It's just a date, a glass of wine."

"I guess so," Anna said uncertainly.

"I can go with you if you want," Julie offered.

"I might take you up on it," Anna told her.

"Gotta go," Julie said. "My deadline's looming and I can tell you my editor is not happy with me."

Anna pointed to a stack of books next to the cash register.

"These are the books you wanted."

Julie picked them up, thanked Anna and went home.

Anna decided to make a list of things she needed to do next.

Chapter 11

It was a slow day at Bayside Books. Anna moped around after Julie left, ringing up purchases for a couple of customers. She picked up an old favorite, Little Women, and began reading some of her favorite passages from the book. The much thumbed copy was a clear indicator of how much Anna liked the book.

She looked up periodically as she flipped the pages, gazing out on the street. A couple of women she knew stopped on the sidewalk and peered inside the store. Anna smiled and waved at them. The women whispered something to each other and scurried off.

Anna started craving something starchy. She gathered her bag and went outside, salivating at the thought of some Lo Mein noodles from the local Chinese restaurant. Mrs. Chang, the proprietor of China Garden, greeted her with a smile.

"How are you today, Anna? You want some Kung Pao Chicken?"

"No chicken today, Mrs. Chang."

Anna made some small talk and decided to be greedy. She went for the large portion of noodles and went back to the bookstore, crumpling the fortune cookie before she attacked her food. She preferred to know what was in store before she shoveled a mound of greasy food into her stomach. Bad news gave her indigestion.

Anna couldn't make head or tail of the cryptic message. She threw it in the trash and started enjoying the hot noodles. She got engrossed in her book again and barely realized when she had worked through the entire carton.

The phone trilled just when she was nodding off. It was Mary.

"I had a busy morning," Mary explained. "Was on that video chat thingie for over an hour. Then I had to catch up with my chores."

Mary's grandchild had come down with a nasty bout of fever. She had been entertaining the toddler virtually, reading her favorite stories until she fell asleep. Mary's daughter lived in San Jose and Anna figured she would be making the 70-80 minute drive soon to go visit her.

"Mary, I've been thinking," Anna said, stifling a yawn. "Doesn't Ben know some police doctor?"

"Oh, you mean Rory?" Mary exclaimed. "Rory Cunningham. He's the one who cuts up people and conducts autopsies."

"So he's the medical examiner?"

"I guess so. Why are you suddenly asking after him?" Mary took her suspicion two steps ahead. "You're not sweet on him suddenly, are you, Anna? He's a strapping Scot. I think you'll make a great couple."

Anna let out a screech.

"You are way off track. I'm not looking for a man."

"Then why this sudden interest in Rory?" Mary demanded.

"It's for Cody, of course," Anna bristled. "Have you forgotten we are trying to save that poor boy?"

"Okay, okay," Mary soothed. "No need to get so snarky. Where does Rory Cunningham come in?"

"We don't know much about that girl," Anna started to explain. "How exactly did she die, for example? What happened to her and when? How long was she lying there?"

"You think Rory can answer all these questions?"

"That's his job, Mary. He will have some of the answers if not all."

"And why do you think he will tell us?"

"He will tell you," Anna stressed. "Because he knows you and because you will ask nicely."

Mary backtracked.

"I don't really know him that well, Anna. I mean, sure, he's Ben's poker buddy. I just ask him how he's doing. We talk about the weather or something. He asks about the grandkids. That's about it."

"That's more than enough," Anna said firmly. "Do you want to help or not, Mary?"

Mary took the bait.

"Let me give it a shot. But I don't have high hopes."

"It's been a slow day here," Anna said. "Why don't I close up early? We can meet at the Tipsy Whale in a couple of hours."

Mary sounded resigned. "Whatever you say, Anna."

"You'll be glad you helped. Trust me."

Anna hung up and walked around the store, trying to shake off her drowsiness. She tidied up the newspapers and wiped down the reading tables with disinfectant. She tackled the glass windows next.

The whitecaps rolled over the water in the distance. Wild poppies swayed in the breeze. Anna wondered what Cassie was up to. She picked up the phone and called her home phone. The answering machine kicked in after a few rings. Anna called Cassie's cell phone next but there was still no reply. Anna muttered a few choice words and berated her offspring. Then it was time to go meet Mary.

The Tipsy Whale was half full but people were streaming in steadily, eager to get their daily pint in before heading home. Murphy, the owner and bartender, greeted Anna cheerfully.

"Is that young lass of yours here to stay?" he asked.

Anna shrugged and headed toward a booth at the back. Mary was already there, sipping something dark with a straw.

"Let me guess…root beer?" Anna grinned, taking the seat before her.

"You're late," Mary noted.

"Last minute customer," Anna said lightly. "Never mind that."

Her eyes gleamed as she stared expectantly at Mary.

"So? Anything?"

"I spoke to Rory," Mary admitted. "He's a talker. Funny I never noticed that."

"Get on with it, Mary."

"I had to promise him a whole banana cream pie," Mary told Anna. "It seems he's partial to my pie. He says it's the best he's ever had. I think it's the caramel, you know. Just a tad bitter and salty is how I like it."

"Mary …" Anna seethed.

"Calm down," Mary said lightly. "He did share a few things." She slurped her root beer and set the empty glass aside. "Briana was hit on the head with a bat. She died from the blow."

"How can he be sure?"

"They found a baseball bat right next to her, that's how."

"Oh." Anna was quiet.

"Things look really bad for Cody, Anna. The police think they have sufficient evidence against him. They are ready to bring him in."

"Why Cody? Anyone can swing a bat."

"Come on, Anna," Mary argued. "You know Cody was a star baseball player in high school. He almost went pro, didn't he?"

"He had to give up the game because of an injury," Anna sighed. "But I still say the bat could have belonged to anyone."

"There's more," Mary said. "Rory's not privy to that information but he heard some buzz."

"Thanks Mary. Did he say anything about when she died?"

"It was some time in the evening," Mary replied. "They have narrowed it down to a three hour window, I think."

"Hmmm. So what was Briana doing in the redwood forest that evening?" Anna mused.

"What next?" Mary asked.

"I need to go meet Briana's family."

"That sounds like a tough one. What will you ask them?"

"I haven't thought it through," Anna told Mary. "I am going to write down everything we know until now. That will give me a better picture of what needs to happen next."

Mary suddenly slapped the table with her hand.

"I completely forgot!"

"What now?"

"You remember I told you about that girl who's renting the room over my garage?"

"The one with the odd name?"

"Yes, Rain. I think it's a pretty name."

Anna rolled her eyes impatiently.

"She got hit by a car. And you'll never guess who was driving that car."

"Who?" Anna let out a wide yawn.

"Briana! I let Rain have some old copies of the Chronicle and she saw Briana's photo in it."

"So you are saying Briana was a bad driver?"

"Well, obviously," Mary said impatiently. "But isn't it funny?"

"I'm not laughing."

"That's not what I meant, Anna. It's odd. What a coincidence."

A couple of women walked up to their table. Anna knew one of them well. She lived down the street in the cul de sac. She had recently remarried, six months after her husband passed suddenly of a heart attack. The other woman was her sister and lived in a neighboring town. But she spent a lot of time in Dolphin Bay. She was the timid sort who nodded at everything her sister said.

"Hey Agnes," Anna greeted. "Your garden's looking pretty. Your roses have a chance at winning Best in Show this year."

"Don't you try to butter me up, Anna Butler," the woman hissed.

She was shorter than Anna with a shock of brown hair that looked odd against the deep wrinkles on her face.

"I know what you did. Heck, the whole town knows."

The sister nodded, chewing a strand of hair.

"Stop blathering, Agnes!" Anna snapped.

"Don't raise your voice, you … you murderer! We don't want your kind living on our street."

"But Anna's innocent," Mary exclaimed. "You are mistaken, Agnes!"

"That's not what Lara Crawford is saying," Agnes huffed. "You think the mayor would lie about something like this?"

"Lara Crawford has some kind of vendetta against Anna," Mary told her.

"That doesn't sound like Lara," Agnes said.

Her sister crept one step closer to her and nodded.

"Why isn't Anna defending herself?" Agnes asked with a sneer. "She's ridden with guilt, that's why."

"Are you done?" Anna asked. "Now leave me alone."

"You won't get away with it, Anna! I am going to warn everyone against you."

With that parting shot, Agnes strode away from their booth, her sister in tow.

Chapter 12

Cassie woke earlier than usual, feeling refreshed. She had slept through most of the previous day, barely getting up to eat some dinner. Her mother had thankfully left her alone.

There was a slight chill in the air and Cassie shivered as she pulled on her favorite old robe. It had cost a fortune once but Cassie had barely noticed. She trooped into the kitchen and went straight to the coffee pot. She added plenty of cream and sugar and sat at the table, sipping the delicious brew with her eyes closed.

"Did you get all the coffee? Again?"

Cassie looked up bleary eyed to find her mother scowling down at her.

"How many times have I told you to make a fresh pot?"

"Okay, okay," Cassie pleaded. "I'll make the coffee. Will that make you happy?"

She went to the sink, rinsed out the coffee pot, and refilled it.

"We are out of coffee," she groaned, staring into the empty canister.

"No, we are not," Anna sighed. "I grind the beans fresh every two days. Don't you know that by now?"

Cassie shrugged.

"So what now?"

Anna sat down at the table and folded her hands.

"Get the coffee beans from the pantry. Pull out the coffee grinder from that cabinet under the island. Grind them and then add them to the coffee maker."

"That's an awful lot of work," Cassie grumbled, searching the pantry until she found a container labeled 'coffee beans'.

"It's worth the effort, sweetie, like all good things in life."

"You don't have to go all philosophical on me, Mom."

"You're right," Anna said calmly. "I should just sit back and watch you squander your life."

"What have I done now?" Cassie asked wearily.

She gave up making the fresh coffee and went back to her own cup. It was already cold. She wondered if her mother had spotted the empty bottle beneath her bed.

"What are your plans, Cassie?" Anna asked. "What do you want to do with your life?"

"I'm an actress," Cassie said. "You know that, Mom."

"When was the last time you acted in a decent movie?"

Cassie thought her mother was being unfair. Hadn't she given up her life to come back home and nurse her through her illness? Cassie chose to ignore the fact that she had been virtually homeless when she came back to Dolphin Bay.

"I know you made a big sacrifice, Cassie," Anna said heavily. "You didn't have to do it but I really appreciate it."

"Are you turning me out, Mom?" Cassie asked, aghast. "Is that what this is about?"

"Of course not," Anna dismissed. "But you need to start thinking about your future."

"I'm reading a few scripts." Cassie was defensive. "I talk to my agent almost every day. This is just how the entertainment industry works, Mom. You have to wait for the right role to come along."

"Maybe it's time you gave it up then," Anna said.

"Give up acting?" Cassie's mouth dropped open. "No way, Mom."

Anna leaned forward across the table, trying to be more persuasive.

"Why don't you go visit the university? They have plenty of professional courses nowadays."

Cassie had dropped out of high school.

"You seriously think the university is going to accept me?"

"No harm in looking," Anna wheedled. "Once you take some courses, I could get you a steady job here in town."

Cassie couldn't imagine what kind of work her mother had in mind for her. But she decided to play along.

"I might head over there later."

"That's my girl," Anna smiled approvingly. "Can you make do with cereal today? I'm running late."

Cassie assured her mother she could fix her own breakfast.

A couple of hours later, Cassie drove to the campus, feeling a bit curious. At the very least, it would be good research for some future role.

Dolphin Bay University was a private institution. Admission there came with a hefty price tag. John Butler had taught history there for thirty five years. He had been honored with an emeritus status when he retired. Cassie vaguely remembered touring the campus with her father as a child, holding on tightly to his hand.

The campus bustled with activity. Groups of students hurried from one place to another, talking at the top of their voices. Some kids sat on the emerald lawns, reading giant books or discussing something.

Cassie felt the youthful energy ripple through the air. She spotted a group being led to a small walled garden and tagged along. The kids followed instructions given by a man wearing a white apron and plucked some fresh herbs. She followed them inside the building.

The man wearing the apron started explaining what each herb was and how it was best used. A young girl in a short haircut stood at the back, watching everything with interest. Cassie smiled at her shocking blue hair. It seemed a bit out of place in Dolphin Bay.

The instructor showed them how to cook a basic pasta dish. He offered a taste to his students. Cassie turned to leave.

The blue haired girl patted her arm.

"Don't leave yet. This is the best part."

"I don't actually go here," Cassie whispered.

"Neither do I," the girl said. "They won't mind."

Cassie ate a small morsel and widened her eyes in surprise. The instructor handed her a brochure listing various classes that were coming up in the fall. Cassie promised to get in touch if she had any questions.

She walked out with the blue haired girl a few minutes later.

"Are you a student here?" she asked the girl.

"I'm just passing through."

"Where are you going? We are not exactly a crossroads town."

"I am on a tour of the west coast," the girl explained. "Someone told me about the blooms here. So I decided to make a pit stop."

"How long are you staying?"

"I don't know," the girl laughed. "I'll hop on a bus or hitch a ride when I want to leave."

"Do your parents know where you are?" Cassie asked suspiciously.

The girl was short and skinny and her fresh face was completely unlined. Cassie pegged her age at sixteen.

"I'm legal," the girl said. "I don't need their permission. But yes, they know where I am."

"You remind me of myself," Cassie said wistfully. "I was young and fearless once."

"You don't look too old to me," the girl said kindly.

"Thanks. I'm Cassie Butler."

"Rain."

"Good luck on your travels, Rain."

Cassie said goodbye and looked around for a café of sorts. The day had cooled off and she needed something hot. She spotted a coffee cart under a tree and walked toward it.

The barista took Cassie's order for a nonfat mocha with extra cream without displaying any emotion. Cassie tapped her foot impatiently as she waited for her drink. She was beginning to wish she had brought a jacket.

Two girls huddled near the cart, sipping their coffees and whispering something. Cassie's ears perked up when she heard them mention the dead girl.

"She was trailer trash," one girl was saying. "You wouldn't know that by looking at her though."

"What are you saying?" the other asked in a scandalized tone. "She was such a diva. She had the best outfits, all branded stuff. How did she afford all that?"

"Her job took care of that," the first girl said, widening her eyes meaningfully.

"You don't mean …"

"I mean exactly that. She was one of Sherrie's girls."

The other girl had never heard of Sherrie. Cassie slid closer to them so she could get the scoop on Sherrie. She didn't learn much. The girls started discussing all the nice things Briana had owned and how much they must have cost. They both agreed she had been unfriendly and obnoxious.

"She got what was coming to her," the first girl said.

"Come on," the other girl protested. "She wasn't that bad!"

"Girls like Briana always come to a bad end."

They moved on to gossiping about some guy and walked away.

Cassie jumped when the barista called out her name. She took her coffee and stood there, thinking about what she had just heard.

There was a lot they didn't know about Briana Parks.

Chapter 13

Cassie spent the whole day on campus, stopping at one of the cafeterias for lunch. The amount of food on offer amazed her. She was yawning her head off by the time she reached home. It had been a while since she had been on her feet all day.

Anna was in the kitchen, cooking.

"Something smells nice," Cassie said appreciatively. "Is that our dinner?"

"You don't mind eating early, do you?" Anna asked. "I have to go out."

"I'm starving!" Cassie exclaimed. "Let me grab a quick shower, Mom."

Anna had finished setting the table by the time Cassie came back.

"What are we having?"

"Spaghetti and meatballs," Anna announced.

"With Nona's red sauce?" Cassie smiled brightly. "Yum!"

She loaded a bowl with salad and served herself a large helping of the pasta and meatballs.

"How was your day?" Anna asked.

"Tiring," Cassie grunted. "Tiring but awesome."

"What did you do?"

"I took your advice, Mom," Cassie said cheekily. "I went to the campus."

"You spent the whole day over there?" Anna was surprised.

"Pretty much," Cassie nodded. "It's huge, Mom. I barely checked out a few of the buildings."

"Anything interesting?" Anna asked lightly.

"Plenty!" Cassie said, pausing to take a big bite. "Did you know they have a culinary school? They have all kinds of courses. Wait till you see the brochures."

"You actually went inside a cooking school?" Anna asked.

"Yup! They have a Healthy Cooking course coming up in the fall. I might enroll in that one. They will give me a certificate."

"That's great, Cassie. You can help me create a Healthy Eats menu for the café."

"Any update on that, Mom?"

"I am meeting the girls tonight," Anna told her. "Mary has a plan. We need to put it in action."

"So you're going to meet the Firecrackers! Why didn't you ask them over?"

"We need to meet Vicki," Anna explained. "It's going to be a tough visit."

"Why is that?"

"I am beginning to lose faith in her son," Anna admitted.

She told Cassie about Mary's conversation with Rory Cunningham, the medical examiner.

"They say a baseball bat was used as a weapon. Somehow, they are using it to implicate Cody because he used to play back in high school."

"That's not the only reason," Cassie said. "I forgot to tell you, Mom. I ran into Teddy Fowler from high school. He is the detective on Cody's case."

"You never mentioned that!"

"Sorry about that. But the point is, Teddy Fowler told me they found Cody's prints on the weapon."

"I don't like the sound of that, Cassie. I already told Vicki I won't defend her son if he's guilty."

"You might be hasty in judging him, Mom."

"What do you mean?"

"You know I spent the day walking around Dolphin Bay University? I heard a lot of stuff."

"What kind of stuff?" Anna asked wearily.

"Briana Parks had a lot to hide."

"Briana? You mean the dead girl?"

"Yes, Mom. She was flashy and aggressive. I don't think she had many friends."

"Julie says her family's going through a rough patch. They barely have two pennies to rub together."

"That's not what I heard," Cassie said. "Briana dressed in the latest fashion. She wore Louboutins. We know those don't come cheap. And she had a brand new car. Not just any car, a fancy convertible."

"How did she afford all that?" Anna cried.

"Funny you ask." Cassie smiled. "Do we have any dessert?"

"Chocolate cupcakes with raspberry chocolate swirl frosting. Tell me about Briana."

"Briana worked for someone called Sherrie."

"Does this Sherrie have some kind of business?"

"You could say that," Cassie chuckled. "It's the oldest business in the world."

Anna's mouth dropped open in amazement.

"Let me get this straight. You are saying Briana handed out favors in exchange for money?"

"That's one way of saying it."

"And this Sherrie got her into it?"

"That's what I heard."

"Is this girl new in town?" Anna asked. "How come I never heard of her?"

"She's a student, Mom, just like Briana or Cody. My guess is she lives on campus and keeps a low profile."

"Why does she do this kind of work?"

"Why do you think? For money, of course. College is not cheap, least of all DBU. It's one of the most expensive places in Central California."

"But it's got to be illegal!"

"I don't think the people involved care about the legalities. Who's going to tell? The girls need the money. And the creeps who hire them value their privacy."

"This changes things," Anna mused. "Briana could have gone out with any number of men."

"So Cody is not the only suspect, you mean."

"I wonder if Cody knew about this."

"You will have to ask him, Mom. But I am sure Briana was keeping it a secret."

"I don't think any young man will approve of his girl friend doing this kind of work," Anna reasoned.

"What if Cody found out and flipped?"

"It does give him a motive," Anna said, aghast.

"We know Cody was obsessed with Briana," Cassie reminded her mother. "And he's been known to be violent."

"We don't really know that," Anna protested. "What else do you know about this Sherrie?"

"Not much. But my guess is Briana wasn't the only one working for her."

"We need to find this girl," Anna said.

"Good luck with that," Cassie snorted. "How do you propose to do that? We don't know anyone who goes there."

"We know Cody," Anna reminded her. "Maybe he knows this girl."

"If you ask me, Briana would do her best to keep Cody and Sherrie apart. They represent parts of her life she would always want to keep separate."

"You may be right. But I need to know for sure."

"How do you know Cody won't lie?"

"I have to assume he's being honest with me," Anna sighed. "If he's not, we'll find out sooner or later."

"When are you going to meet Briana's family?" Cassie asked. "They might have something different to say about their daughter."

"Soon," Anna said. "I'm hoping Cody will introduce us."

"Does he know them well?"

"No idea," Anna shrugged.

She stood up and began clearing the plates.

"I'll take care of that, Mom," Cassie said.

"I'm just putting these in the dishwasher. Speaking of suspects, you know who's the most unlikely? Mary's lodger."

"What's a lodger?" Cassie asked.

Anna rolled her eyes.

"Some girl who's renting a room from Mary."

"What does this girl have to do with Briana?" Cassie asked, puzzled.

"Two days ago, Mary told me this girl had an accident. Today she tells me Briana was the one who almost ran the girl over."

"Was she hurt?"

"I think she had some minor bruises. She stumbled after trying to get out of the way."

"You think she had a grudge against Briana. So she went and killed her with a baseball bat. That's neat, Mom."

"It does sound farfetched when you put it that way," Anna said sheepishly.

"No, you're right. We need to consider every suspect. I don't know if this girl's motive is strong enough, though."

"It's strong if she's deranged."

"What do we know about her?" Cassie asked. "Where did Aunt Mary find this girl?"

Julie and Mary had been friends with Anna long before Cassie was born. They called each other soul sisters. So Cassie had called them Aunt or Auntie ever since she learned to talk.

"Mary puts up a hand written flyer at the post office or grocery store. This girl must have seen it and come knocking."

"That's not very safe," Cassie commented.

"Mary's been doing it for years. Most people coming through town are harmless."

"Can she keep an eye on this girl?"

"Mary likes to leave these people alone. She doesn't like to invade their privacy."

"We are not asking her to spy. Or maybe we are. She could pop in with some tea or cookies. Try to make the girl talk."

Anna laughed.

"I don't think Mary's cut out for something like that. Julie could do it in a heartbeat."

"You can all be present," Cassie offered. "Ask the girl over for lunch or dinner. You can size her up then, Mom."

"That's a good idea," Anna brightened. "Let me talk to Mary about it."

"How long will you be gone?" Cassie asked, yawning widely.

"I am going to be late," Anna told her. "Don't stay up, Cassie. We are planning to go play bingo after we meet Vicki."

"Have a good time, Mom. I'm going to watch some Netflix and turn in early."

Cassie went to her room to call Bobby, forgetting she had promised to clean up.

Chapter 14

Anna stared at the overcast sky outside her window as she made coffee the next morning. A light mist hung in the air, adding to the gloom.

Anna took her coffee out to the garden and thought of the day ahead of her. She had tried hard to hold herself together the past few days. But the insinuations and whispers had really rattled her. People she had known her entire life were beginning to doubt her character. If Lara Crawford continued to be on the warpath, Anna would never be able to hold her head up in town again.

Anna ignored the stab of pain she felt in her breast. She hadn't told Cassie or the Firecrackers about it, knowing they would make a fuss. Her doctor had told her it was part of the healing process.

Anna spent longer than usual talking to her plants. She looked at the pool wistfully and wished she could forget everything that ailed her and just lie in the sun like Cassie. Her stomach rumbled, signaling it was time for breakfast. Anna decided to fix some pancakes to cheer herself up.

Cassie breezed into the kitchen some time later, looking for coffee. Anna placed a stack of cinnamon blueberry pancakes before her.

"Pancakes!" Cassie squealed like a child. "Did you know I ate pancakes only once in the past twenty years? That too because it was on set. They took the plate away as soon as the shot was finalized."

"I'm running late, Cassie. We can catch up later."

"What's bothering you, Mom? You don't look so good."

"I'm fine!" Anna said sharply. "Just fine."

Anna wove a scarf around her neck and mounted her bike. She pedaled furiously toward the bookstore, feeling guilty for being short with Cassie.

Anna realized how late she was when she spotted a couple of college kids waiting on the sidewalk outside the store. They needed some textbooks urgently. It turned out to be a busy morning and a steady stream of customers kept Anna on her feet. It was an hour before she got a chance to start the coffee.

Anna sat in the small chair behind the register, sipping her coffee and brooding again.

The front door shut with a bang, startling her. She stared at the woman who had stormed in. Her eyes breathed fire and all her wrath was directed at Anna.

"Who do you think you are?" the woman demanded, her hands on her hips.

Anna gauged the woman to be in her late forties. She wore a poorly fitting dress, stretched tight across her ample chest. Her hair hadn't seen any conditioner in a while. One of the heels on her worn out shoes was broken, making her limp.

Anna pasted a smile on her face and greeted the woman.

"How can I help you? Our bestseller section is right this way."

"I am not here to buy books, you hag."

Anna ignored the woman's threatening stance.

"This *is* a bookstore," Anna soothed, waving her hands around. "Are you here to read the newspapers? A lot of our customers like to do that."

"I'm here to warn you, you murdering witch."

"I think you should leave," Anna said, barely controlling her anger.

"I won't go until I have said my piece." The woman pursed her lips and glared.

"This is private property," Anna shot back. "If you don't get out of here in the next ten seconds, I am calling the police."

"We all know you have the police in your pocket," the woman sneered. "You got away with murdering your poor husband. Now you're helping that kid do the same."

Anna picked up the receiver and started dialing.

The woman collapsed into a chair and started sobbing.

"She was my only child. Can't you at least take pity on a grieving mother?"

"Who are you?" Anna asked, putting the receiver back in the cradle. "And what do you want from me?"

"I'm Pamela Parks," the woman spoke between sobs. "I'm Briana's mother."

Anna's face cleared.

"I am so sorry for your loss," she consoled. "I didn't know Briana but I would have loved meeting her."

"She was so young," the woman said, wiping her eyes with her hands. "She didn't deserve to be killed."

"No, she didn't." Anna handed her a box of tissues.

"Why won't you let the police do their job then?"

"I'm just trying to help," Anna said meekly.

Pamela cleared her throat.

"Word around town is you are meddling with the police. You are keeping them from arresting that boy."

"You have the wrong idea," Anna hastened to explain. "My goal is to find out what happened to Briana. If Cody is guilty, I will be the first one to turn him over to the police."

"Is that true?" Pamela asked hopefully.

"Of course," Anna nodded. "Cody and his mother both know that."

Pamela had simmered down a bit.

"I'm sorry I yelled at you," she apologized. "It's just …I lost my baby girl. I've been crying so much I don't know which end is up."

Anna folded Pamela into a hug and stroked her back.

"I'm a mother too. I couldn't take it if anything happened to my daughter."

Pamela accepted the cup of coffee Anna offered.

"I'm glad you are here," Anna told her. "I wanted to ask you some questions about Briana."

Anna grilled Pamela for a few minutes, trying to get as much information as she could about Briana.

"My husband and I aren't doing too well," Pamela said hesitantly. "But we will pay you what we can. We just want justice for our daughter."

"You don't have to pay me anything," Anna assured her. "I started on this path to help Cody. I will see this through no matter what."

"I'm new in town but I have heard some pretty nasty rumors about you," Pamela said frankly. "I think someone wants to drive you out of town."

"They can try," Anna said. "I was born here and I am going to die here."

"Watch your back," Pamela warned as she said goodbye to Anna.

Anna's mood had improved considerably. She took up a feather duster and started cleaning the bookshelves. She looked forward to dozing in her chair once she was done.

The bell behind the door jangled again. Anna gaped at her next visitor with her mouth open.

A mop of golden hair topped a chiseled face with piercing blue eyes. Dressed in a three piece suit complete with pocket watch, the short man looked like he had walked out of one of Anna's books.

"Hello Anna."

"What are you doing here, Charlie?"

"Mother misplaced her copy of Pride and Prejudice. I was hoping to replace it."

"Let me check if we have it in stock," Anna said stiffly.

Charles Robinson was the owner of the luxury resort on the hill that marked one end of the Coastal Walk. Fernhill Castle had stood sentinel over Dolphin Bay for over a century. A young and ambitious Charles III or Charlie had converted it into Castle Beach Resort, a luxury destination for the rich and famous. The family had other business interests in the area and Charlie managed them all with a Midas touch. Charlie had never married and lived with his aging mother.

Anna pulled out a copy of the book from a shelf and handed it over.

"Actually, I'll take the whole set," Charlie said.

"You want the entire Austen collection?" Anna's eyebrows shot up.

"Why not?" Charlie shrugged. "It's all mother reads anyway. Most of the books are in tatters."

Anna pulled out the necessary books and placed them in a bag while she rang up the purchase.

"Why are you really here, Charlie?" she asked. "You never needed a book in the past twenty years."

Anna's husband John and Charlie Robinson had been inseparable at one time. John was appointed to the Dolphin Bay Historical Society just around the time Charlie decided to convert the castle into a hotel. He wanted to list it as a historical property. John opposed some of the proposed renovations, most notably, the grand entrance foyer that Charlie wanted for the resort. John refused to approve the new design because it required tearing down the narrow but original door.

The issue escalated and caused a rift between the two friends. John Butler died before they could ever reconcile.

"I am hearing the rumors, Anna, just like everyone else in town."

"And you believe them?"

"You have a powerful opponent, Anna," Charlie said softly. "You need powerful friends."

"What are you saying?" Anna asked.

"I should have made up with John years ago, but I can't bring back the past. I am here to support you, Anna."

"So you believe I am innocent?"

"I never doubted it for a second."

"Thanks, Charlie. That means a lot."

Charlie frowned.

"I came to warn you, Anna. Some people are starting to believe the rumors. Get ready to fight."

Chapter 15

The Firecrackers huddled together in the China Garden restaurant. Anna had called Julie and Mary the moment Charlie Robinson left.

"I'm calling an urgent meeting," she told Julie. "Get Mary and come to the Chinese restaurant. Now!"

She had locked the bookstore in the middle of the day and rushed over to the restaurant, overwhelmed by the morning's events.

"What's got you all hot and bothered, Anna?" Julie demanded as soon as she sat down.

Mary slid in next to her, giving Anna a concerned look.

"Do we need to go to the doctor?" she asked Anna.

"For the hundredth time, I'm fine!" Anna sighed in frustration. "You girls have got to stop thinking there's something wrong with me."

"But you went through a major surgery just weeks ago," Julie argued. "You're still recovering, Anna."

"We worry about you," Mary added.

"I appreciate that," Anna stressed. "I really do. But I can't be back to normal until the people around me, you girls and Cassie, stop treating me like an invalid."

"That's crap!" Julie snapped. "If we want to treat you with kid gloves, we will."

Anna's eyes narrowed and she looked like she was about to explode.

"Let's change the subject," Mary pleaded, trying to maintain the peace as usual. "Why don't we order lunch first?"

Julie wanted Sichuan Chicken, Mary went for the Beef and Broccoli and Anna grudgingly ordered the Cashew Chicken. They each ordered an egg roll as an appetizer with their meal.

Anna had simmered down by the time she took a few bites of her egg roll.

"I didn't mean to shout at you," she said.

"We worry about you because we love you," Mary said softly, tearing up.

Anna's eyes welled up too and they dabbed at their eyes with a tissue while Julie rolled her eyes. She wiped her own eyes with the collar of her plaid shirt.

"It's been a wild day," Anna told them. "First I got a visit from Briana's mom."

"What did she want?" Julie inquired.

"She warned me against aiding the guilty party. She's convinced Cody is guilty."

"Isn't everyone?" Julie shrugged. "That kid has the odds stacked against him."

"She calmed down after a while and we talked about Briana."

"Did you learn anything new?" Mary asked.

"We know a bit about Briana's life now," Anna said. "She was an English major. Her mother Pamela told me they were proud of what she had achieved. Briana was working her way through college and supporting her parents as much as she could."

"What about her relationship with Cody?" Julie asked. "Did they know about him?"

"They must have," Anna said. "Pamela told me Cody loved Briana a lot but he was clingy. He wanted to know where she was at all times."

"What's the matter with kids these days?" Mary wondered. "They are talking with each other on that video thing all the time. And they are still insecure."

"Pamela said Cody sent text messages to Briana every few minutes. Her phone would ring if she answered a few seconds late. One time she was so tired she switched her phone off. Cody was banging on their door fifteen minutes later, worried there was something wrong with her."

"That might be a bit obsessive," Julie mused. "But it also shows he was crazy about her."

"What else?" Mary asked. "Did Briana have any other friends?"

"Pamela mentioned a girl," Anna nodded. "She helped Briana get a job and introduced her to a professor in her department. He took special interest in her, acted as her mentor."

"She was doing well in every aspect of her life," Mary noted.

"That's debatable," Anna said.

She told them what Cassie had learned on her visit to the local university.

"Now we're talking," Julie said. "This is the kind of dirt we need."

Mary looked scandalized.

"Surely things weren't that bad!"

"Old Alfie told me he saw her mother at the food bank," Julie told them. "If that's true, I don't think Briana had a choice."

"Let's not be hasty in judging her," Anna protested.

"I'm not judging," Julie argued. "I'm saying they were in dire straits. Briana rose to the challenge. I actually admire her for it."

"Does her mother know what kind of job she had?" Mary asked.

"She didn't mention it," Anna said. "I don't see any point in telling her now. Why add to their misery?"

Julie and Mary both agreed.

"What does Cody feel about all this? Did he even know about her job?"

"I talked to him today," Anna said. "I warned him about the fingerprints."

"What was his bat doing at the scene of the crime?" Julie asked.

"He doesn't know. He can't remember where he saw it last."

"Do you believe him?" Mary asked.

"I'm not sure," Anna admitted. "He may be lying about the bat, but I think he didn't know about Briana's work. He said she was very secretive about it. He sounded frustrated."

"Isn't the bat the most important?" Julie quizzed. "It's the crucial piece of evidence that's going to get him arrested."

Mrs. Chang brought over their food. The girls stopped talking for a while and attacked the food. Anna came up for air after she had wolfed down half her chicken.

"Honestly, I don't know what to think any more. I can't make sense of anything."

"You're not giving up yet, Anna," Mary said. "Think of it like a jigsaw puzzle. First you need all the pieces. Then you need to assemble them to get the complete picture."

"That's just it," Anna sighed in frustration. "I'm not even sure I have all the pieces."

"We need a systematic approach," Julie lectured. "That's what I do when I am plotting a book."

"I think this is more serious," Mary argued. "A young man's life is at stake here."

"All I mean is, we need to be logical. It's not going to be easy."

"I'm going to write down everything I know when I get back to the store," Anna said. "Then I will work on filling in the blanks."

"I think the bat is important," Julie stressed. "We can't refute where it was found and we can't deny it's covered in Cody's prints."

"I'll keep that in mind," Anna promised.

"Who was your other visitor?" Julie asked. "You said Pamela Parks was the first one."

Anna skimmed over Charlie Robinson's visit.

"That sly fox!" Julie exclaimed. "What does he want now?"

"I think it was very kind of him," Mary said. "He's right, you know. He does have a lot of clout."

"Even he can't stop all the hurtful gossip," Anna murmured.

"Just let it roll off your back," Julie said grimly.

"She's right," Mary said. "Don't feed the fire. Just ignore them and walk away."

"You saw how Agnes was acting that day," Anna reminded them. "They are saying things to my face."

"Just remember you are not alone," Julie soothed. "We are going to be right beside you no matter what."

"Thanks, girls. Most of my strength comes from you."

Anna placed her hand on the table and Julie and Mary gripped it tightly.

"How's your sleuthing coming along?" Julie asked, turning around to face Mary.

Mary shuddered.

"This is the first and last time I am going snooping for you. I don't think my poor heart can take it again."

"Did you find something?" Anna asked eagerly.

"I've never violated anyone's privacy like this," Mary frowned.

"Was it worth it?" Julie asked. "Spill it, sister."

"I went in on the pretext of vacuuming the room," Mary told them. "Rain was just going out. She told me she would run the vacuum cleaner when she got back."

"Then?" Anna asked.

"I told her it was part of the rent. She believed me and left. She seems like a well brought up kid. The bed was made and there wasn't anything lying about. So I opened a few drawers."

Mary paused to take a breath.

"I found a lot of brochures, the kind they hand out to tourists at the visitor center. One of them had Briana's name written on it along with a phone number and an email address. At least, it looked like a phone number."

Julie and Anna stared at Mary, wide eyed.

"So this girl Rain or whatever her name is met Briana?" Julie asked.

"We don't know that," Anna said.

"How else did she get her number?" Julie shot back. She turned toward Mary again. "Does she know Briana's gone?"

"She does," Mary nodded. "I gave her the Chronicle, remember? She's read the news about Briana's death."

"So what is this kid doing with a dead girl's contact information?" Anna asked.

None of them had an answer for that.

Chapter 16

Anna walked back to the bookstore after lunch, determined to come up with some answers. Lara Crawford stood outside the Tipsy Whale, talking to a group of local women. One of the women glared at Anna and shook her head in disgust. Anna ignored them and went inside the store.

She made a fresh pot of coffee and pulled out a brand new writing tablet from a box at the back of the shop. She started writing down all the facts she knew about Cody and Briana. She listed out the possible motives someone may have had against Briana. She had an epiphany of sorts and wrote down possible motives against Cody. Half an hour later, she sat back with a groan and stared at the pages she had filled.

Anna felt she was still going around in circles.

The bell over the door jingled and a gray haired woman wearing thick horn rimmed glasses walked in. Anna's face lit up when she saw her.

"Hey Sally," she greeted. "Long time no see."

Sally Davis taught mathematics at Dolphin Bay High. A spinster whose life revolved around her job, she had a secret love for historical romances. Bayside Books was her favorite place to hang out when she was not at school. Anna was used to setting aside a copy of the latest releases for her.

Sally's cheerful countenance was nowhere in sight that day.

"How are you holding up, Anna?" Her voice quivered with barely controlled rage.

"I am good, Sally," Anna said, finally noticing the woman's distress. "But you don't look too good to me."

"I hope you don't think I am on her side," Sally pressed. "I never pay attention to such drivel."

"What on earth are you talking about?"

"That vile woman – Lara Crawford. I was having lunch with some ladies from the Booster Club. She just cornered us and started spouting some nonsense about you."

"I know what she's saying, Sally," Anna said grimly. "But thanks for letting me know."

"I don't believe her one bit," Sally Davis said stoutly. "I have known you and John for years. I know how devoted you were to each other. No way you harmed a hair on his head."

"It's nice to see someone believes in me," Anna said sincerely.

"Of course I believe in you," Sally said, gratefully accepting the cup of coffee Anna handed her. "And I'm not the only one. This town knows how much you have done for the less fortunate."

Anna hung her head.

"They have short memories, Sally."

"Lara Crawford may be a smooth talker, but not everyone is gullible, Anna. I am here to remind people of what you have done, all the kids you have helped. I might call in your kids if need be."

"Don't drag them into this," Anna said in alarm. "They are busy living their lives."

"Lives they would never have had without you," Sally said in earnest. "You and John did a lot for those kids. You trusted them and believed in them. Most of all, you loved them when no one else would."

Anna's cheeks turned pink.

"We did nothing great," she protested. "Cassie was gone and there was a void in our lives. We had an extra room and enough to feed an extra mouth or two."

"So do thousands of people in this country," Sally Davis argued. "But they don't choose to be foster parents."

"It's all in the past now, Sally. John's gone. I'm not sure how many Christmases I'm going to see."

"A few dozen, at least," Sally Davis clucked. "You're a survivor, Anna. This kind of pessimistic talk doesn't suit you."

"I'm tired, Sally," Anna admitted. "The café was the only thing that kept me going through my long treatment. It's been my dream for so long. But it's never happening if I can't get a license."

"Mary told me all about it," Sally said. "I am already talking to the teachers at school. We'll be here at the potluck with a pen in our hands, ready to sign that petition."

"I appreciate that. I'm going to need all the support I can get."

Sally chatted for a few more minutes while she sipped her coffee. Then she had to rush back to school.

Anna walked around the store, rearranging books and putting them back on the right shelves. She found a wine magazine on the reading table and smiled broadly. She placed a call to Cassie and called her over.

Anna put the 'Be Right Back' sign in the window and stood under the magnolia tree, hoping to flag her daughter down before she pulled into the parking lot.

"Can you give me a ride?" she asked before Cassie rolled to a stop.

"Where to?" Cassie sulked. "This better be important, Mom. I was about to call my agent."

Anna didn't understand why Cassie said that all the time. Did such a person really exist? Why did Cassie need to call him or her every day?

"I have to go to Mystic Hill," Anna told her. "Do you know the way?"

Cassie jabbed some buttons on the map in the dash and started with a lurch. Anna clutched the door with her hand as Cassie sped up the hill.

She felt a bit lightheaded when she climbed out of the car fifteen minutes later.

"Go back to the store and stay there until I get back."

Cassie gave her a mock salute and turned the car around with a screech of tires.

"Be careful on those curves," Anna called after her.

Gino Mancini had come out to welcome Anna.

"This is a nice surprise," he said.

Anna admired his dimples and decided his smile was genuine.

"I should have called ahead," she winced.

"No need," Gino said, offering his arm. "The door's always open for my friends."

Anna entered the familiar warm sitting area and let Gino lead her to a really comfy armchair. He excused himself and came back bearing a tray with two wine glasses. A plate of biscotti rested on the side.

"Isn't it a bit early for wine?" Anna murmured.

"Mystic Hill is a winery," Gino laughed. "Wine is our default drink."

Anna let him pour the golden liquid. She watched him swirl the wine around in his glass and take a sniff. She copied his actions and took a small sip.

"It's nice," she approved. "I don't know much about wine. I just can't care about the ones that taste like vinegar."

"Mystic Hill wines will never taste like that," Gino said proudly.

Anna dipped the pistachio studded biscotti into her wine and munched on it. Then she mentioned Briana's murder.

"I'm having a hard time making sense of it all," she admitted. "I really need some help."

"Have you established a timeline?" Gino asked. "Start with a few hours before the crime was committed. Try to find out where every suspect was at that time."

"You mean check on everyone's alibi?" Anna nodded.

"They can't always pinpoint the exact time," Gino told her. "You will have to start with a wide window and then try to narrow it down as much as possible."

"You make it sound so easy," Anna gushed. "I suppose that's your experience talking."

"As police officers, we are trained to work methodically," Gino agreed. "But an amateur can bring a fresh perspective."

"You mean I should keep throwing the pasta at the wall until something sticks?" Anna blushed.

"Have I offended you?" Gino asked, alarmed. "I didn't mean to mock you, Anna. I hope you believe that."

"I wouldn't blame you," Anna said. "I've got some cheek, huh? Coming here, asking you to help me."

"I'm flattered you thought of me," Gino said. "Forget all this. Why don't you stay for dinner? I'm making pot roast."

Anna knew Gino lived alone. His wife had run away with a man years ago, abandoning him and the kids.

Anna didn't hide her surprise.

"I thought a big vintner like you would have a cook."

"You're right," Gino laughed. "But I like to potter around in the kitchen every now and then. Keeps me young, you know."

"Thanks for your tempting offer," Anna said shyly. "Maybe some other time?"

"You have an open invitation," Gino murmured. "My kids rarely have time for a visit. My nephew is the only one who takes pity on me sometimes."

"I would be honored to have dinner with you, Gino," Anna said. "And it won't be a chore."

Gino offered to drive Anna back to town and she accepted. The sun was going down over the bay when Gino reached the corner of Main Street. Flames of red and orange shot up in the sky, looking like a massive work of art. People milled around on the Coastal Walk, enjoying the view.

Anna thanked Gino and stood waving until his truck was out of sight. She was in high spirits when she went inside her store. The scene that greeted her instantly spoiled her mood.

Cassie leapt up from the chair behind the cash register as soon as she saw Anna.

"I'm off, Mom," she said, slinging her bag on her shoulder. "See ya."

Anna shook her head in disbelief at the mess around her. Books lay half open, piled on corner tables and chairs. Some books lay on the floor, as if they had been thrown off the shelves. A pile of magazines sat in an untidy heap on Anna's desk.

She started tidying up, wishing she had accepted Gino's offer and stayed at the vineyard for dinner.

Chapter 17

Cassie grabbed her bag and rushed out of the bookstore as soon as she saw her mother come in. She had been tired of being cooped up inside the store. Missing her afternoon nap had made her cranky.

Cassie decided to cook something nice for dinner and headed toward Paradise Market. The only grocery store in Dolphin Bay, it stocked much more than fresh produce, aiming to pander to the quirkiest needs of its customers. Cassie wasn't a great cook but she made some things well. Her second husband had been really good at cooking Chinese food. She had learned a basic dish from him, fried rice. It was her favorite comfort food.

Picking up a basket from a pile, Cassie began loading it with fresh vegetables.

"Cassie Butler shopping for vegetables!" a loud voice exclaimed. "Now I've seen it all."

Cassie turned to see Ted Fowler grinning at her, standing behind a loaded shopping cart.

"Don't you have minions to do this kinda work?" Teddy pressed.

Cassie decided the bright wide eyed expression on Teddy's face was genuine.

"I don't have any staff here," she gave a brief but honest answer.

She didn't have any staff anywhere but Teddy didn't need to know that.

"I told my wife about you," Teddy said. "She wants to get a haircut before we meet at the pub for drinks."

He leaned forward and whispered in Cassie's ears.

"Ain't gonna make her prettier than you."

"How's work, Teddy?" Cassie asked smugly. "Made any progress?"

"We are tying up the loose ends," Teddy bragged, "prepping for a big arrest. You'll read about it in the Chronicle soon."

"That's what you said last time," Cassie needled. "I think you have the wrong guy. The police are just stalling because they are stumped."

Teddy became flustered.

"Come now, Cassie. You stay out of it."

"Have you looked into your victim, Teddy?" Cassie asked, setting her basket down.

Her arm was beginning to ache from all the weight.

"Briana Parks was hiding something."

"How dramatic," Teddy laughed. "I guess you Hollywood types are used to making a big fuss out of everything."

"I'm telling you the truth," Cassie sighed. "The police would know that if they were doing their job."

"I'm the detective on this case," Teddy said grimly. "And I've made sure we covered our bases. If you have any information for the police, you better come clean, Cassie."

"I'm not hiding any big secrets," Cassie sizzled. "You just have to ask around."

"Stop talking in riddles, Cass. If you have something to report, just do it."

"Forget I said anything," Cassie said, picking up her basket.

She turned around and started walking toward the rotisserie chicken. It was the essential ingredient in her quick and easy dish.

Cassie lugged her grocery bags across the street as she walked to the parking lot, ignoring the pain in her knee. The doctor had told her it was early onset arthritis and it would only get worse. Bobby had given her a set of exercises to strengthen the knee and warned her to do them a few times a day. Cassie wasn't sure they helped at all.

The lights blared inside Bayside Books. Cassie could see her mother walking around, straightening things, getting ready to close. She looked preoccupied. Cassie decided she would talk to her mother about it at dinner.

Cassie had the food on the table by the time Anna got home. She had even squeezed in a shower and tidied everything up.

Anna sat down with a sigh and pulled the lid off a large pan.

"What's this?" she grumbled. "Rice?"

"It's my special Chicken Fried Rice," Cassie said eagerly. "I made some teriyaki sauce to go with it."

"But I had Chinese food for lunch!"

"You could have mentioned that before!" Cassie exclaimed, feeling deflated.

"I didn't know you were cooking," Anna mumbled.

"We are having fried bananas with ice cream for dessert," Cassie cajoled. "You love them, don't you?"

"With caramel sauce?" Anna asked hopefully.

"Of course!"

"I guess I can eat fried rice."

She took a bite and beamed at Cassie.

"This is good. Nothing like what they serve at China Garden."

Cassie accepted the olive branch her mother offered and cracked a smile.

"How was your day, Mom? Find anything new?"

"Not really. But Gino gave me some excellent advice. I am putting together a timeline of what happened the day Briana died."

"But she was found a day later, right? So you are just guessing here."

"It's not all guesswork," Anna explained. "They can tell the approximate time give or take a few hours."

"A lot can happen in that time," Cassie mused. "Dolphin Bay isn't like L.A. You can drive around town multiple times in an hour."

"You're right. That's why Mary's talking to Rory Cunningham again. He's the guy who does the autopsy. She's going to ask for his best guess."

Cassie hid a smile as Anna took a third helping of rice, scraping the pan clean. She was happy to see her mother's appetite was back to normal.

Cassie stood up to fry the banana fritters. It didn't take her long. She plated their desserts and sat down again, heartened by the wide smile that lit up Anna's face. The Butlers had a big sweet tooth and they never said no to dessert.

"You need to find out more about Briana," Cassie said, taking a big bite of ice cream. "From what I heard on campus, she wasn't very popular with the other girls."

"Girls can be catty," Anna said. "I bet they were jealous of her looks and her money."

Cassie could easily relate to that.

"There was this girl I used to share an apartment with back in the day," Cassie told her mother. "I thought she was my best friend. We auditioned for the same part. She was very supportive when neither of us got the part. Then the studio called. They couldn't make it work with the girl they had chosen. I had been their second choice. You wouldn't believe the stunts my friend pulled."

"That was the part that landed you the Oscar, wasn't it?" Anna beamed.

"How did you know that?" Cassie asked, surprised.

As far as Cassie knew, her parents had never been keen about her film career.

"I kept track of you, sweetie," Anna said. "The tabloids made a big deal of your falling out with this girl."

"I was devastated," Cassie confessed. "I never thought she would betray me like that."

They talked about the hard lessons life had taught Cassie after she left home.

"My point is," Anna stressed. "Everyone's jealous of the popular girl. Those girls might have gossiped about Briana or spread nasty rumors about her. But that doesn't mean they would actually harm her."

"What about that girl Briana was working for?" Cassie asked suddenly.

"You mean the girl who was sending her on those assignments?" Anna cringed. "I forgot all about her. What was her name?"

"Cherry," Cassie said. "No. Sherrie. Something like that."

"This girl must have taken some kind of commission. She was making money off Briana."

"What if they had a falling out?" Cassie asked. "Or what if Briana got big ideas? She might have wanted to cut this girl out of the equation."

"So what? She bumped her off?"

"We thought she managed a bunch of girls, not just Briana. She might have wanted to make an example out of her."

"You make her sound like a gangster," Anna scoffed. "Isn't she a student at DBU?"

"That's my guess. I don't know for sure."

"We need to track this girl down," Anna said thoughtfully. "She might be able to set some things straight."

"Have you talked to Cody?" Cassie asked. "How's he holding up?"

Anna shrugged.

"He's not doing good according to Vicki. But it could all be an act."

"So you think he did it?" Cassie asked, astounded. "Looks like you have made up your mind, Mom."

"I haven't," Anna insisted. "But I don't blindly believe in Cody anymore."

"What's your next move going to be?"

"Honestly, I don't want to think about this now. I think I might turn in early."

"I'll bring you some warm milk later," Cassie promised. "With nutmeg. It will help you sleep."

"What did I tell you about coddling me?"

"I'm not," Cassie said casually. "Bobby told me about this warm turmeric milk with nutmeg. They call it golden milk. It's the latest fad in Hollywood. It's great for your immunity and your skin. It's also supposed to cure a sore throat. And it's, err, it's supposed to kill cancer cells."

"Imagine that!" Anna smirked. "If only I had drunk this magic milk two years ago. I would never have had cancer!"

Cassie smiled indulgently as her mother went to her room. She had forgotten what a spitfire her mother was. The past couple of years had dampened her spirits but Cassie was glad to see Anna getting some of her spunk back.

Chapter 18

Anna woke up refreshed after a good night's sleep. She would never admit it to Cassie, but the warm milk had worked liked a charm. Anna sat out on the patio, drinking her coffee and admiring the flowers in her garden. It had been her husband John's pride and joy. She had employed a gardener for the past couple of years and tried to keep the garden flourishing just as it had in John's day.

An hour later, Anna was pedaling her bike to Bayside Books. Main Street was bustling with shoppers. Anna went in and started her daily chores. A few of the Main Street shoppers came in to browse. A couple of new bestsellers were making waves and everyone wanted a copy.

Anna was just sitting down with a cup of coffee when Julie breezed in.

"You're taking me out to lunch," she announced.

"Is it that time yet?"

"It will be, by the time I have finished telling you my story."

"What have you done now, Julie? I thought you had a class today?"

Julie taught a basic creative writing seminar at Dolphin Bay University. She wasn't very keen on it but the college had begged and pleaded until she said yes.

"That's where I am coming from," Julie said eagerly. "And you'll never guess what happened."

"What?" Anna asked wearily.

"I was going through the list of students who take my class…" Julie shook her head the moment Anna opened her mouth. "No, there are over fifty students in the class and I don't know all their names."

"Go on."

"Who do you think I found on that list? Briana. Briana Parks."

"Didn't someone say she was an English major? I suppose it's natural she might want to take a creative writing class."

"I must have seen her in class sometime," Julie mused. "But of course I didn't know who she was then. Nor did I know what was gonna happen to her."

"Are you leading up to something, Julie?"

Julie bobbed her head eagerly.

"I talked about what had happened to her and asked the kids if they wanted to say something. You know, like a eulogy."

"That was nice of you. Did anyone come forward?"

Julie shook her head.

"Not immediately. But get this. One of the kids came over to talk to me after class."

"What did he want?"

"I think he just wanted to gossip. He started talking about Briana. How she was always well groomed, her shiny new car…"

"We know all that," Anna said impatiently. "Did he actually say anything new?"

Julie smiled coyly.

"This kid said Briana got along really well with the professors. You can say she was their pet."

"Every teacher has some protégé. My John was always impressed by the brightest students in the class."

"The way this kid was talking, Briana wasn't just a protégé."

"Oh?" Anna quirked an eyebrow in question.

"Briana openly flirted with the teachers. This kid said she would do anything to get a good grade."

"That sounds a bit mean," Anna said. "How well do you know this kid anyway? Why is he badmouthing a dead girl?"

"I never noticed him before," Julie admitted.

"He could be after a good grade himself," Anna remarked.

"So you think he was saying all this just to get my attention?"

Julie sat down, looking like a deflated balloon.

"Maybe he wasn't lying outright," Anna suggested kindly. "He could have been stretching the truth."

"I think we know Briana was ambitious to a fault. She was prepared to do anything to get ahead in life."

Anna bunched her eyebrows together.

"Was Cody aware of this side of her personality?"

"She might have acted all sweet and coy with him," Julie said. "The real Briana wasn't the person he fell in love with."

"You understand we are just speculating here?" Anna said. "We need to talk to more people who knew Briana."

Julie shook her head.

"I have had enough for one day. I'm starving. Let's head out to lunch."

Anna went to the window and flipped the 'Open' sign to 'Closed'.

"Why don't you call Cassie over?" Julie asked. "We can grab a sandwich for her on our way back."

"I'd rather not," Anna dismissed. "You wouldn't believe the mess she made the last time she was here."

"Cut her some slack, Anna. So she's not a neat freak like you. She's here, isn't she?"

"Why is she here exactly?" Anna asked. "Shouldn't she be back there in Los Angeles, looking for work?"

"You know she came here to take care of you."

"She can go back now," Anna grumbled.

"You know what I think about that," Julie said. "You are getting used to having her around."

Anna's mouth settled into a pout. She slung her handbag on her shoulder and started walking toward the door.

"You are afraid she will leave again," Julie continued. "Am I right, or am I right?"

"Where do you want to eat?" Anna asked, refusing to take the bait. "I fancy a nice juicy burger."

Julie followed Anna out of the door, muttering to herself. They walked around Bayside Books to Ocean Avenue toward the Yellow Tulip Diner.

"Slow down, Anna," Julie called. "I can't keep up with you."

Anna turned around to glare at Julie and almost walked into someone.

"Oops!" she exclaimed, staring at the golden haired man smiling back at her.

Anna jumped as his arms came around to steady her.

"Are you okay, Anna?" Charlie Robinson asked.

He was wearing a golf outfit complete with a jaunty flat cap. His icy blue eyes narrowed as he nodded at Julie. There was no love lost between them.

"I'm sorry," Anna apologized. "I guess I wasn't watching my step."

"No harm done," Charlie smiled. "Can I escort you ladies somewhere?"

"Oh no," Anna burst out. "We were just going to grab a bite."

"Thanks for the kind offer," Julie said stiffly.

"I'm heading back home myself," Charlie offered. "Why don't you come to the resort for lunch? My treat. I am trying out a new chef and I would love to get your opinion, Anna."

"We are in a hurry," Julie interrupted. "And we are meeting someone else."

Anna nodded vigorously.

"Thanks for the offer though, Charlie. I read about your new menu in the Chronicle. I would love to visit sometime."

"I'll hold you to it, Anna," Charlie Robinson warned. "You ladies have a nice day."

Charlie set off on the Coastal Walk toward the resort. Julie waited until he had put a good distance between them before exploding in anger.

"He's got some gall."

"I thought he was just being polite," Anna said, bewildered.

"Charlie Robinson is a crook," Julie declared. "You better stay away from him, Anna."

"What are you talking about?"

"Don't you know his family's reputation? Smugglers, the lot of them."

"You are being ridiculous!" Anna snapped as they entered the diner. "The locals have always been unkind to the Robinsons."

"There's a reason for that!" Julie cried.

"That's enough," Anna said, holding up a hand. "Weren't you starving?"

"Why don't you order for us?" Julie huffed, folding her hands across her chest.

Anna decided to splurge and ordered root beer floats to go with their double cheeseburgers and fries.

"Do you want your fries crinkle cut?" the waitress asked.

"Of course," Anna nodded.

The crinkle cut fries at the Yellow Tulip were a legend. They were cut by hand and made fresh every day, served with a generous sprinkling of seasoned salt.

"Are you going to stop sulking?" Anna asked Julie after the waitress had left.

"You know Charlie Robinson was flirting with you?"

"You are imagining things, Julie."

"I don't care for that weasel," Julie said unkindly, "But I do think you should start dating. John's been gone for a while."

Anna's eyes welled up.

"I still reach for him in my sleep."

"We know how much you loved him," Julie said softly, patting Anna's hand. "But life has to go on, sweetie. You've still got a couple of decades ahead of you."

"John was looking forward to retirement," Anna shared. "We made big plans. We were going on a Caribbean cruise to celebrate our anniversary. John said it was a dry run for later. He wanted us to go on a world cruise."

Anna swallowed a lump and gave a watery smile when their food arrived. She had suddenly lost her appetite.

"I've spoiled your lunch, haven't I? I'm sorry, Anna."

Anna squirted ketchup over her fries and shook her head.

"I'm always thinking of John, Julie. The truth is, I'm not ready to let him go."

Julie looked contrite as she picked up her burger.

"You know who else was in my class today?"

"Cody," Anna guessed shrewdly.

"How did you know that?" Julie cried. "I was expecting him to come forward and say something about Briana. But he walked out without a word."

"Poor kid," Anna sympathized. "I think he's running scared."

Chapter 19

Anna's mood improved as she gorged on the crispy fries. She decided to snap out of her melancholy mood and focus on the excellent food. Julie kept spouting theories about how someone might be trying to frame Cody.

"Ready for pie?" the waitress came by to ask them.

They agreed to split a slice.

The waitress put in their order for a berry pie and came back to chat with them.

"I heard you talking about that kid Cody," she confessed.

"Do you know him?" Anna asked quickly.

"I sure do," the waitress sighed. "I think he did it. He killed that girl."

"Why do you say that?" Anna cried.

"He's got a short fuse, that one," the waitress said. "He's like a pit bull when he gets angry. And he does that a lot."

"Does he come here?" Julie asked.

"Very often," the waitress nodded. "He came here with that girl. They made a cute couple."

"You think they loved each other?" Anna asked.

"Oh yes," the waitress nodded. "There was no doubt about that. They held hands and whispered to each other, shared their food … they did all the lovey dovey stuff you would expect from a new couple."

"That's a good thing, right?" Anna said. "So there's no doubt Cody loved Briana."

"She seemed more sensible than him," the waitress offered. "This kid used to go off for no reason. She used to talk him down."

"Why was he so angry?" Julie asked.

"I don't know," the waitress shrugged. "It was something different every time."

"What about the girl?" Anna asked. "Did she do anything to set him off?"

"She was a wily one," the waitress said. "Came here with an older man once."

"Would you recognize the man if you saw him again?" Anna asked eagerly.

The waitress shrugged.

"He wasn't a regular. They sat here for a long time, long after I cleared their dinner."

"I'm surprised you remember so much," Julie said. "You must have known the girl well."

"It was because of what happened later," the waitress explained. "I don't know how or why but that kid Cody turned up here. He was fit to be tied."

"You think someone tattled on the girl?" Anna guessed.

"Maybe. The kid grabbed that old man by the collar and lifted him out of that booth like he weighed nothing. He threw him out of the diner and landed a few punches. The older guy's nose was bleeding by the time some people pulled the kid off him."

"That doesn't sound like Cody," Anna muttered.

"You don't believe me?" the waitress challenged. "Ask anyone. A big crowd had gathered outside. People love this kind of drama."

Anna thanked the waitress and asked for their check. She cautioned Julie to stay quiet until they stepped out of the diner.

Her head was whirling with different scenarios on the way back to the store.

Anna and Julie dragged their feet across Ocean Avenue, full from their fast food binge.

"I need a nap," Julie groaned, as they started turning the corner to go over to Main Street.

"Yo Anna!" a voice hailed them.

Jose Garcia waved at them from the other side of a glass window.

"I can't handle this now," Anna muttered, pasting a smile on her face.

Jose beckoned them inside. Anna had no choice but to go in. Julie followed her, looking curious.

"How are you, Jose?" Anna asked wearily.

She looked around her at the cavernous space. It was perfect for her café. The store was empty except for a small folding trestle table at one end and a camp chair. Jose picked up a bunch of photographs that were lying on the table and began showing them to Anna.

"My cousin sent these from Cabo," he said proudly. "This is the pool at his condo, this is the view from the balcony and this is the beach that is a two minute walk away from the condo building. Look at the color of the water, Anna. Look at the bright sunlight. That's where I'm going, Anna."

Anna flipped through the photos and made some appropriate comments. She knew what was coming next.

"You know I can't pass this up, right, Anna?" Jose groveled. "It's my dream retirement."

"You gave me two weeks, Jose," Anna reminded him. "I've still got time."

Jose gave a shrug.

"One week, two weeks, what difference does it make, eh, Anna? You are not getting your license in two weeks."

Julie had finally caught on to what was going on.

"Plenty of people are looking forward to Anna's café," she said. "Anna has a lot of support."

Jose's smile didn't reach his eyes.

"Once you buy the place, you can do what you want with it. Open a café, don't open a café. I'll be soaking up the sun in Cabo."

"He just wants his money, Julie," Anna sighed. "Can't say I blame him."

"That city developer's offer is still open," Jose coaxed. "We both get a big bonus if he can get our two stores. Think about it, Anna. You can get a big payday."

"I'm not selling, Jose," Anna said firmly.

Jose's smile hardened.

"Suit yourself. But your time is running out. I am going to sign the papers as soon as the two weeks are up."

Julie grabbed Anna's arm and stalked out of the store. Anna's hand shook as she tried to insert the key in the lock at the bookstore.

"What's this deadline Jose is talking about?" Julie demanded. "Why haven't you told us about this, Anna?"

"Hey Mom!"

Anna whirled around to see Cassie walking toward the store, holding a paper bag from the Tipsy Whale.

"What are you doing here, child?"

"I came to get some lunch," Cassie said cheerfully. "I got a sandwich for you."

Cassie handed over the bag to her mother.

"We already ate, sweetie," Julie told her. "Why don't you take this home with you?"

Cassie was staring at Anna's face.

"Is something wrong, Mom? You don't look too good."

"I'm fine," Anna snapped. "Just go home, Cassie."

Cassie looked at Julie and raised her eyebrows in question.

"Go on home," Julie said gently. "Your mother just needs a minute."

Cassie looked uncertain as she started walking toward the parking lot. She turned around twice to look at her mother. Anna had finally managed to unlock the door.

Julie sat down on one of the couches with a thud and Anna followed.

Anna looked sad as she talked about the café.

"It was always a pipe dream."

Julie got the story out of Anna.

"Don't worry, Anna," she consoled. "Something will work out."

"What do you think Briana was doing with that older man?" Anna asked suddenly. "Do you think he was one of her clients?"

Julie thought for a few seconds before shaking her head.

"Remember what we said about those clients? They would want to value their privacy. I don't think one of those creeps would accompany Briana to a public place like that."

"He could have been an uncle," Anna continued. "Or a friend or acquaintance. Why would Cody attack him? You think he suspected Briana of having an affair?"

"Why does everything always come back to Cody?" Julie asked. "You gotta admit, Anna. This kid is either guilty as sin or someone is framing him."

"I'm calling Vicki right now," Anna said. "I want to talk to Cody in her presence. She should be able to spot if he's lying."

"Let's say he is. You think she's going to call him out?"

"If Vicki believes in her son's innocence, she needs to be upfront with us. Cody could be lying for any number of reasons. He could be trying to protect someone. Or he's just afraid."

"You don't want him to be guilty."

"Of course I don't. I've known him since he was a sweet gap toothed kid."

"He's not sweet anymore, judging by what that waitress told us," Julie sighed.

"She made it very clear she doesn't like him," Anna said thoughtfully.

Julie sat up with a jerk, her mouth hanging open.

"I totally forgot something that kid said earlier today."

"You mean that kid from your class?"

Julie nodded urgently.

"Briana got into a fight with another girl."

"When were you planning on telling me that?" Anna exclaimed.

"I barely heard him," Julie admitted grudgingly. "He had been talking for a while and my mind drifted. I just wanted to get out of there and get some coffee."

"Did he say who it was?" Anna asked eagerly.

"He might have, but I don't remember."

"We need to find out who this girl is," Anna said resolutely. "She might tell us more about Briana."

Chapter 20

Cassie sat at the kitchen counter the next morning, drinking her coffee. She had been awake for hours, lying in bed, browsing the tabloids and talking with Bobby on the phone. Her knee was bothering her again and her legs were stiff. Bobby taught her some stretches she could do in bed and talked her into doing them. All Cassie wanted now was to go out to the pool and get some sun.

Anna came out of the room, ready to leave for the store. She looked at Cassie apologetically.

"You'll have to take care of breakfast today, Cassie. I made oatmeal but you don't like it."

Cassie told her not to worry.

"Where are you off to, all dressed up?"

Anna's shoulders slumped.

"Are you going to meet Gino?" Cassie smiled innocently and widened her eyes.

"Now why would I do that?" Anna was indignant.

"Because he's your boyfriend."

"Don't be silly, Cassie. What makes you say that?"

"You like him, don't you? And I'm sure he likes you. He made that very obvious."

"Gino was just being polite," Anna dismissed. "Nothing's going on between us."

Cassie rove her eyes over her mother.

"Isn't that a new top? It's just the right shade of blue. And you're wearing makeup. You haven't done that in months."

"I wanted to look good for a change. Is that a crime?"

"Of course not," Cassie sighed. "I'm happy you are getting back to your old self."

"Can I go now?" Anna scowled.

"Have a nice day, Mom!" Cassie sang. "That scarf's looking awesome, by the way."

Cassie got up to get the box of frosted flakes out of the pantry. She poured a generous helping in a big bowl and added milk. The label on the milk carton announced it was organically produced at the local Daisy Hollow Farm. That made her think of her run-in with Dylan Woods. He had grown into a fine man. She wondered why he wasn't married yet.

Cassie flicked the channels on the TV for some time, stopping when she came across a rival actress on a talk show. It had been a while since Cassie had been on any shows. She made some choice comments at the screen and then tossed the remote over a chair.

A nap seemed appealing and Cassie dozed off with the TV blaring in the background. She woke up an hour later, itching to do something. The brochures from Dolphin Bay University lay scattered on the coffee table. Cassie decided to go enroll in a class.

Dolphin Bay University was a hive of activity. The admissions office was housed in a separate building next to the library. The lady in charge frowned when she learnt Cassie hadn't finished high school.

"We don't have many options for dropouts," she grimaced. "You at least need a GED."

Cassie didn't take it to heart. She knew some of her achievements were much bigger than a college degree.

"I just want to occupy myself," she told the woman. "What about the courses at the culinary school?"

"You will get a certificate," the woman informed her. "But no college credits, okay? If you want to do a degree at some later point, you will have to start from scratch."

Cassie took a stack of application forms and walked out, promising to turn them in before the end of the week. A cluster of students was gathered outside the library. Cassie recognized the girl in the big blown up photo. Flowers and candles were placed below it, along with teddy bears and cards. It was a memorial for Briana Parks.

Cassie went and stood there with the students, trying to listen in on what they were saying. The crowd dwindled until only one girl remained. She sat cross legged on the floor, clutching a bunch of wildflowers. Tears streamed down her cheeks and fell on her T-shirt.

Cassie didn't hesitate. She sat on the ground next to the girl and placed a hand on her back.

"Did you know her well?"

"Briana was my friend," the girl said miserably. "I can't believe she's gone."

That brought a fresh onslaught of tears.

"I'm Cassie."

"Sherrie," the girl mumbled through her tears.

"Looks like she was very popular around here."

"Briana was so smart," the girl called Sherrie said. "Everyone envied her."

"I heard some girls talking about her," Cassie admitted. "I think they were just being catty."

"Briana was super ambitious," Sherrie disclosed. "That didn't go down too well with some of the kids."

"What's wrong with being ambitious?" Cassie wondered. "Isn't that why kids come to college? To build a good future?"

"You would think so," the girl sighed. "Most kids are just interested in going to parties and getting drunk."

"So Briana wasn't a party girl?"

Sherrie shook her head.

"She just liked to show off. She acted like she came from a rich family so the kids expected her to throw some money around."

"And she didn't do that."

"No," Sherrie said. "Briana could barely pay the fees when she first got here."

She hesitated.

"Go on," Cassie said encouragingly. "Did she hit the lottery or something?"

"Briana got a job," Sherri said. "It paid well. She had something left over after paying the fees. She started spending it on herself. Bought new clothes. Then she got that new car."

"What did she do?" Cassie asked, wide eyed. "Sell an arm and a leg?"

Sherrie dried her eyes with her shirt. She looked over her shoulder and sidled closer to Cassie.

"It was a bit unconventional."

Cassie summoned all her acting skills and maintained a poker face.

"I don't believe in judging people. I've had to do some twisted things to get ahead in life."

Sherrie leaned toward Cassie and gushed.

"Briana worked as a hired date."

"You mean like an escort?"

"Not really. More of a stand-in. It was all above board, you know. No hanky panky. Most of the guys she went out with were older men. They just needed the company."

"How did she get into all this? Was it through some website?"

"It's mostly word of mouth," Sherrie said. "These men value their privacy. They are not ready to post their profiles online."

"You seem to know a lot about it."

Sherrie looked over her shoulder again.

"Actually, it's kind of my thing. I found a need and decided to fill it. I vet all the girls and fix the appointments. There are strict rules. They can't tell anyone about it, not even their boyfriends. And pictures are forbidden. They can't post photos on social."

"How do you get paid?" Cassie asked.

"I take a percentage off the top. Payments are in cash only. Everyone is happy."

"Have you been on one of these dates?" Cassie was curious.

Sherrie pointed at her thick horn rimmed glasses and skinny five foot frame.

"Me?" she laughed. "My girls are hot! Who's going to pay to take a plain girl out on a date?"

"What if someone misbehaves?"

"Then the girls are on their own," Sherrie shrugged. "They know there's an element of risk here. They do it for the money."

"Did Briana have a problem with any of her clients?"

"Not as far as I know. Why?"

"What if she got into a fight with her date? You think that man might have harmed her?"

"I don't think so," Sherrie said stoutly. "Briana's boyfriend is the guilty one. I hear the police have clear evidence against him."

"How can you say for sure? She might have been on a date on the night she died."

Sherrie nodded.

"I completely forgot about that. I think she was supposed to go out that night."

"Do you know who with?"

Sherrie pulled out a small diary from her messenger bag and flipped through the pages. She jabbed her finger at an entry.

"It's right here. She was meeting Doug Crane. He's a Silicon Valley geek. There was a big technology conference here that day and he needed a plus one."

"Did Briana keep her appointment?"

"I don't know," Sherrie said. "I don't keep tabs on them. Briana usually got back to me in a day or two with my commission. But she was gone by that time."

A fresh burst of tears spilled from Sherrie's eyes. Cassie took her arm in hers and tried to pacify the girl.

"I don't trust that Cody at all," Sherrie cried suddenly. "I'm pretty sure he did it."

Cassie bit back a groan and started talking to the girl about Cody.

Chapter 21

A bank of clouds had crept up over the bay by the time Cassie got home. She had accompanied Sherrie to the university cafeteria for lunch. Cassie had been dismayed when Sherrie thanked her for lending a kind ear.

"Just like my Mom! I miss her a lot, you know. But my family's back east and I rarely get to see them."

Cassie wondered if she was looking that frumpy. Since a spa wasn't a part of Cassie's budget, she decided to do some DIY. She slathered a mask on her face and neck, placed cucumber slices on her eyes and went to sleep.

The sky had darkened when Cassie woke up from her nap. She admired the riot of colors the setting sun had painted on the horizon. Her stomach rumbled, signaling it was time to make dinner.

Cassie had very few dishes in her repertoire. Chicken Fried Rice and Cobb Salad with the Goddess dressing were her specialty. She chose the salad and hoped her mother wouldn't make a fuss.

"Salad again?" Anna grumbled when they sat down for dinner. "You need to learn how to cook a proper meal."

"This salad has all the food groups, Mom," Cassie said patiently. "And I made my special dressing."

"I do love that Goddess dressing," Anna said, slightly mollified.

She took a big bite of the salad and smiled appreciatively.

"Watch any new movies?" she asked Cassie.

"I don't sit around watching TV all day, Mom," Cassie said drily. "I went to the college and spoke to the admissions coordinator."

"Really?" Anna asked. "Are you signing up for that health food course then?"

Cassie told her about the admission forms. Anna offered to help fill them out.

"Did anyone talk about John?"

"I don't think they knew I was his daughter, Mom."

"Your father loved teaching," Anna reminisced. "They made him an Emeritus professor, you know. He was so proud about it."

"Dad died too soon," Cassie said, swallowing a lump in her throat. "I never thought I wouldn't get to spend time with him again."

"Life's fickle, kiddo. Remember that. You never know what's around the next corner."

"Speaking of …" Cassie began. "There was some kind of shrine for Briana at the college."

"Was Cody there?"

"No, he wasn't. But I met Sherrie."

"Sherrie? You mean the girl who Briana was working for?" Anna asked excitedly.

"The very same," Cassie told her. "We got talking."

"Did you learn anything new?"

"Did I?" Cassie laughed. "Sherrie's a young slip of a girl. Wears thick glasses. You would never know how enterprising she was by looking at her."

Cassie told Anna about Sherrie's business model.

"She didn't think it was immoral?"

"I don't think so. As far as she is concerned, the girls were just going out on a date."

Anna grunted in disapproval.

"Sherrie believes Cody is guilty."

"What's he done to her?"

"He did plenty to Briana, according to Sherrie. Briana was sick of him. She wanted to break up. But Cody wouldn't let her go."

"Go on."

"They got into a big fight. I think Cody must have threatened Briana or attacked her. Sherrie's not sure exactly what happened. But Briana called the police."

"Did the police arrest Cody?" Anna asked, alert. "Why has no one mentioned this before?"

"Apparently, the police just counseled them. They let Cody go with a warning. No complaint was registered."

"Even if there is no record of this incident, the policemen involved will remember," Anna mused. "And they talk amongst each other, just like anyone else."

"Do you think that's the reason the police have been set against Cody since the beginning?" Cassie wondered. "He's already proved he can be violent."

"I think the fingerprints are more damning than this incident. But something like this can just add fuel to the fire."

Cassie got up to clear the plates.

"We are skipping dessert today, Mom."

"No way," Anna said, scandalized. "There's a pint of chocolate gelato in the freezer."

"No, there isn't. I ate it."

"Julie always stocks plenty of ice cream. I'm going to call her."

Cassie burst out laughing.

"Relax, Mom. I got a pie from the market earlier. And vanilla ice cream."

Anna glared at her daughter.

"I don't see what's funny."

Cassie took the pie out of the refrigerator and cut two generous slices. She warmed them up in the microwave and scooped some vanilla ice cream on top of each slice.

"Oh, I almost forgot. Sherrie had an appointment diary. Briana was supposed to meet a guy that day."

"Does she know this guy?" Anna asked sharply.

"She had a name. She wasn't sure if Briana actually kept the appointment."

"We need to track this guy down, Cassie. He can tell us about the last day of Briana's life."

"He might have been the last person to see her alive, Mom."

"Last, or last but one."

"I wonder if the police know about this guy. He seems like a suspect to me."

"You think he could have hurt Briana?" Anna asked.

"What do we really know about him, Mom? Sherrie said he's some techie from the Valley. He could be a psycho for all we know."

"That's farfetched."

"If he actually met Briana, it's not," Cassie argued.

"What about that girl you met? Sherrie? How do you know she didn't have it in for Briana?"

"Sherrie seemed like a nice girl."

"Appearances are deceptive, Cassie. I don't understand one thing. How come she let you ask so many questions?"

"Sherrie was very distressed when I ran into her. I think she just needed a shoulder to cry on."

"Looks like she trusted you."

Cassie rolled her eyes.

"She thought I was some kind of mother figure. Do I look that old?"

"I'm not answering that question. But you are old enough to be her mother."

"I'm going to go online and try to get some info on Doug Crane."

"Is that the techie guy?"

Cassie nodded.

"I need a favor," Anna said. "Can you open the bookstore tomorrow morning? I have to go meet Vicki Bauer."

"I was planning to sleep in tomorrow," Cassie groaned. "I've had a hectic day today, Mom."

"Never mind," Anna muttered. "I shouldn't have asked."

"What if we open a couple of hours late?" Cassie asked.

"I've been running Bayside Books for twenty years, Cassie. I always open at a certain time. People expect it."

"Okay, okay," Cassie sighed. "I'll do it."

"Try not to make a mess like you did last time," Anna warned. "Once you open the store, you need to dust all the shelves."

Cassie listened glumly as her mother outlined a bunch of chores she needed to do.

"Did you meet that girl who's living at Aunt Mary's?" Cassie asked.

Anna slapped her forehead. "I forgot all about her."

"You don't seriously suspect her, do you?"

"I don't know if I told you," Anna said. "Mary found Briana's contact information in her things."

"You should ask Cody about her."

"Good idea," Anna said. "I'll make a note of that."

"Do you know anything about the Castle Beach Resort, Mom?"

"Funny you should ask. I ran into Charlie Robinson earlier today. He wanted me to try out the food at his restaurant."

"You don't mean Dad's old friend? I remember he used to get candy for me every time he came home to see Dad."

"The same," Anna nodded. "Although he and your Dad weren't talking to each other."

"Why is he asking you to lunch?" Cassie asked slyly. "Don't tell me you have one more admirer."

Anna turned red.

"Don't be ridiculous. I've barely said a word to him in the past decade."

"What about this resort, though? Bobby's thinking of getting a room there when he comes to visit."

"It's very expensive."

"That won't matter to Bobby. He's loaded."

"Why does he want to go to a hotel? I thought you knew him well."

"He's my bestie," Cassie nodded. "Bobby's stuck with me through a lot of bad times."

"Then why aren't you inviting him here? We have a couple of spare rooms."

"Are you serious, Mom?" Cassie's eyes lit up.

"We are not as fancy as the resort …"

"That's awesome, Mom!" Cassie cried, leaping across the table to give Anna a hug. "Bobby asked to come stay here but I wasn't sure."

"Why not? This is your home, sweetie, such as it is. You don't need my permission to invite anyone."

Cassie's eyes were moist with tears as she gazed lovingly at her mother.

"Thanks for making me feel so welcome, Mom."

Chapter 22

Anna fixed herself an extra cup of coffee the next morning. She wanted to be alert when she met Vicki and Cody. She knocked on Cassie's door to wake her up.

There was a muffled groan from the other side.

Anna fixed avocado toast for the both of them and rushed through her own breakfast. She was relieved to see Cassie enter the kitchen, all showered and dressed.

"Good Morning, Mom." Cassie yawned. "When are you meeting your friend?"

"As soon as I get there," Anna quipped.

"Do you need a ride?"

Anna hesitated.

Vicki Bauer lived about a mile away on top of a small hill. Anna remembered how her legs had protested when she went to the winery.

"Don't bother. I think I can manage it."

"You can always call Gino to pick you up," Cassie joked.

Anna ignored her and wound a scarf around her shoulders. She wore a broad hat that would protect her from the sun. She straddled her bike and started pedaling toward Vicki's house.

Vicki opened the door, looking red and blotchy.

"Have you been crying?" Anna asked with concern.

"We just heard from the lawyer. The police might be making an arrest today."

Anna bit back her response. She was surprised the police had held off for so long. They must be waiting on some reports.

"Everything will be fine, Vicki," she consoled, stepping inside the house. "Why don't you sit down and take a breath? Let me get you some tea."

Anna rooted around in the kitchen cabinets and found a pack of chamomile. She brewed the tea, added some honey and urged Vicki to drink it.

"This will calm you down."

"Have you made any progress, Anna?" Vicki asked earnestly. "Do you think you can help Cody?"

Anna considered a diplomatic reply.

"Give it to me straight," Vicki sighed. "We will have to face the truth some time."

"Things don't look good for Cody," Anna admitted. "Almost every person I talked to thinks he is guilty. His temper is infamous, Vicki. People have seen him getting into fights. That doesn't look good."

"Cody used to be so easy-going," Vicki reminisced. "He changed when he injured that elbow. He lost his scholarship and his dreams shattered overnight."

"That was a while ago," Anna reasoned. "It's no excuse for flinging his fists around now."

"I don't know how to handle him," Vicki sobbed. "He's staying out late at night. I think he's been drinking."

"Cody hasn't been completely honest with me. I think he's hiding something."

Vicki's expression hardened. She got up and went inside. Anna heard her banging on a door. Anna remembered Vicki couldn't afford college housing so Cody still lived at home.

Anna heard a muted conversation and Vicki came back.

"He'll be out in a minute."

Cody stepped into the living room right after, wearing a crumpled shirt that looked like it came out of the laundry basket. His eyes were bloodshot and the expression on his face was grumpy.

"Anna has some questions for you, Cody. Make sure you tell her everything. Don't leave anything out."

Anna observed Cody from the corner of her eye. She decided he was definitely hung over. She wasn't impressed.

Cody let out a wide yawn.

"I stand by what I said, Mrs. Butler. I was in love with Briana. I would never hurt her."

"That's not going to be good enough, Cody," Anna told him. "We need to prove you did not hurt that girl. Now try to answer my questions as honestly and completely as you can. Don't leave anything out. The smallest detail might be important."

Cody sat forward in his chair and gave Anna a nod.

"Based on the autopsy report, Briana died sometime between 4 PM and 7 PM. Where were you at that time?"

"I was driving to the college to pick Briana up," Cody said. "We had a date that night."

"So you met her?" Anna asked with bated breath.

"No," Cody shook his head. "She wasn't where she was supposed to be. I waited for almost half an hour, hoping she would turn up. Then I got mad and drove off."

"What about the baseball bat? How does it have your prints on it?"

Cody looked flustered.

"It does belong to me," he admitted.

"What?" Vicki cried. "You never told me that."

"I didn't want to worry you, Mom," Cody explained. He looked at Anna. "I lent it to Briana. Their class had a student versus teachers game coming up."

"Did you tell this to the police?" Anna asked.

"They just wanted to know if the bat belonged to me."

"You are being too casual about this," Anna grumbled. "No wonder people think you did it."

Cody excused himself for a minute and went inside. He came back with a glass of orange juice.

"What was this scuffle you got into with Briana?" Anna inquired. "Did you hit her or not?"

Vicki let out another cry.

"Did you hit a woman, Cody? Surely I raised you better than that?"

Cody looked guilty.

"I didn't beat her, Mom. But I came close. Look, I am ashamed of it, okay?"

"Tell us what happened," Anna prompted.

"We had a big argument. I don't remember much of it. I must have threatened Briana. She called the cops."

"I heard they didn't register a complaint against you?" Anna asked. "What did the cops say?"

"Actually, I lost all my bluster as soon as the police arrived. I couldn't believe Briana called them. They talked to us for a while. I assured them I had no intention of harming my girl. They must have believed me because they left soon after."

Anna observed Cody as he sat there, wringing his hands in despair. She wasn't convinced of his innocence.

"What about Briana's friends?" Anna asked. "Can you think of anyone who might have wanted to harm her?"

Cody's face darkened. He cleared his throat and hesitated.

"Don't keep anything back, Cody," Anna urged. "Your future is on the line here."

"Are you trying to protect someone?" Vicki wailed.

Cody expelled a breath and nodded at his mother.

"Briana was having an affair."

"What!" Anna and Vicki exclaimed at the same time.

"She was cheating on me, Mom!" Cody sounded anguished. "I called her out on it but she wouldn't admit it. We argued about it a lot."

"What made you suspect her?" Anna asked.

"I don't know," Cody shrugged. "Call it gut instinct. I tried to find proof. I went through her stuff, checked her emails and texts. But I couldn't find anything."

"You mean you spied on her?" Anna asked.

No wonder Briana wanted to break up, Anna thought. But she didn't say anything out loud.

"I had no choice," Cody said, looking miserable. "I'm sure it was someone at the college. But Briana wouldn't own up to it. I told her I was ready to forgive her. She just needed to tell me the truth."

"I don't think this girl was good for you," Vicki said, sounding like a protective mother hen.

"That's a moot point now, Vicki," Anna reminded her.

She turned toward Cody and chose her words carefully.

"There is something you don't know."

She told him about the work Briana did as a stand-in. Vicki was aghast. Cody looked surprised.

"So she just had to go out on a date, right? She didn't need to get involved with these people."

Anna nodded. "It was just part of her job. I'm sure she didn't actually care for these people."

Cody didn't look convinced.

"She was seeing someone apart from these people then. I'm sure of it."

"It doesn't make sense at the moment," Anna shared. "But I will look into this. I promise."

"How can I thank you enough, Anna?" Vicki sobbed, dabbing her eyes with a tissue.

"Come to book club," Anna joked.

"When are you opening that café, Anna?" Vicki asked.

"I hit a snag. Doesn't look like I am going to open that café."

"You're a strong woman, Anna. Don't give up so soon."

Anna squared her shoulders and gave Vicki a wan smile.

"Some obstacles are insurmountable."

"I heard the rumors that are flying around," Vicki said softly. "I don't believe them one bit."

Anna shrugged and said nothing.

"You've got a lot of people rooting for you, Anna."

"Thank you, Vicki. Mary's got some kind of petition going. Why don't you check it out?"

Vicki promised to get in touch with Mary. Anna said goodbye to mother and son and started cycling to the bookstore. She thought over the new information she had learned. If Cody was right about Briana's affair, he had one more reason to harm her.

Was Briana really in love with someone else?

Chapter 23

The spring day was bright and sunny and Anna decided to take the scenic route back to the store. She rode over to her favorite bench on the Coastal Walk. It offered a great view of the cliffs and the sea. Poppies nodded in the breeze, carpeting the bluffs in a blaze of orange. A couple of dolphins frolicked in the water in the distance.

People were out for a walk, enjoying the fine day. Some of them waved at Anna. Some went out of their way to avoid her. Anna squared her shoulders and stood up to leave.

Bayside Books was doing brisk business when Anna went back. She sat in an armchair and played the part of a silent observer. Cassie was chatting with the customers gaily, urging them to come back soon. The store emptied after a while. Cassie's phone rang and she paced the floor, talking to someone earnestly about a role.

Anna hailed her daughter after she hung up.

"Mom! When did you get back?"

"A few minutes ago," Anna replied. "Was that your agent?"

Cassie nodded.

"Did you just turn down an offer for work?"

"It was just a cameo, Mom. Not the kind of comeback I am looking for."

"I don't understand you, Cassie. I thought you needed the money."

"It's complicated, okay? You won't understand, Mom."

Anna went into the pantry, deep in thought. She hoped Cassie wasn't throwing away a good opportunity just to stay in Dolphin Bay and look after her.

"I am recovering well, Cassie," she said. "I'm strong enough to take care of myself."

"Of course you are. How did it go with Cody?"

Anna gave Cassie a brief account of what she had learnt.

"This is the first we are hearing of Briana's affair. Do you think it was one of her clients?"

"I don't know. I am going to meet the Firecrackers for lunch. Do you have any plans?"

"I thought I would go and turn in those admission forms."

Anna told Cassie to grab an early lunch. She forced herself to do some paperwork for the next hour, waiting for the town clock to signal it was noon. Flipping the door sign to Closed, Anna locked up the store and walked to the Tipsy Whale.

Julie and Mary had already grabbed a booth.

"We are ordering today's special," Julie informed Anna. "Pulled pork sandwiches with a side of fries. Shall I get the same for you?"

Anna's mouth watered.

"Sounds yum. But I'll take onion rings instead of the fries."

Anna admired some pictures of Mary's grandkids while Julie ordered their food. The waitress brought over tall glasses of sweet tea.

"How was your meeting with Vicki and that kid?" Mary asked.

Anna voiced her concerns.

"He's taking it hard, poor boy. But I still can't say I trust him completely."

"Wait till you hear what I found," Julie stepped in.

Anna waited impatiently while she took a deep sip of her drink.

"Briana was having an affair."

She sat back with a knowing smile and twitched her eyebrows at Anna.

"That's what Cody thought!" Anna exclaimed. "How did you find out, Julie?"

"I have a new neighbor," Julie began. "I knew someone had moved into the little house next door but I wasn't really paying attention. The owner rents it out over the Internet, I think. There's always someone moving in or moving out."

"Julie! Get to the point."

"You remember how Charlie Robinson wanted you to taste the new menu at his restaurant?"

"What does that have to do with anything?" Anna asked, bewildered.

"My new neighbor is the celebrated chef he was talking about."

"Your neighbor is the new fancy chef at the Castle Beach Resort?" Mary prompted. "Make nice with him, Julie. He might let us taste his food."

"Anna's already making nice with Charlie Robinson," Julie chortled. "We have an open invitation to the restaurant."

"Girls!" Anna cried. "Stop straying from the topic. Tell me what he said, Julie."

"Briana visited the resort restaurant often, with an older man."

"How does this chef know Briana?" Anna asked.

"He saw her picture in the Chronicle."

"Why hasn't he come forward with this information?"

"No one asked him, I guess. It's not against the law to have dinner with someone."

"Why did he tell you all this?" Mary wondered.

"He's a big gossip, that's why," Julie smirked.

Anna reminded them about the work Briana did for Sherrie.

"How do we know this old man wasn't just one of her clients?" Anna mused.

"That's hard to say," Julie agreed. "Do you think Briana might have confided in someone about this man?"

"Cody guessed Briana was seeing someone else. She denied it."

"Could this man have hurt Briana?" Mary asked timidly.

"We do have one more potential suspect," Julie agreed. "This is good for Cody."

"Is it?" Anna asked. "What if he was mad at Briana for cheating on him?"

"Well, if you put it that way…" Julie shrugged.

Their food arrived and they shifted their attention to the steaming sandwiches.

"Murphy makes the best barbecue sauce," Julie said, licking her fingers. "I've been trying to convince him to bottle it."

"He can sell some at the farmer's market," Mary said.

"We need to find out more about this older man," Anna said, picking up a fry from Mary's plate. "He might tell us more about Briana."

"Not if their affair was supposed to be secret. He'll try to deny any involvement with Briana."

The group dispersed after lunch. Mary had to rush to a dentist's appointment. Julie walked back to the store with Anna.

"How's your latest book coming?" Anna asked her.

"I'm half way through. But I'm stuck. I need to clear my mind completely."

"You can help me catalog all these new books," Anna said, pointing to a big box of books that had been delivered that morning.

"I didn't say I want to be put to work," Julie pouted.

The doorbell jangled just then and a young dark haired man came in. He was dressed casually in a polo shirt and chinos. He pulled a slip of paper out of his pocket and headed straight toward Anna.

"I'm looking for a book," he mumbled.

"Why don't you give me that?" Anna held out her hand for the piece of paper.

She read the title and looked apologetic.

"We don't stock a lot of technical books. But let me check my catalog, just in case."

She tapped a few keys on the computer and searched her inventory.

"Sorry. We don't have it."

The man didn't leave right away. His face had reddened a bit.

"Can I help you with something else?" Anna asked kindly.

Julie watched the man with narrowed eyes.

"Are you Cassie?" he asked.

Anna's face cleared.

"Cassie's my daughter," she replied. "She's not here right now."

"I can wait," the man said meekly.

"I'm not sure if she's coming back to the store today," Anna supplied. "Do you know her from L.A.?"

"I don't know her at all," the man said.

Anna stared at him blankly. She had no idea what was going on.

"My name is Doug Crane."

"Where have I heard that name recently?"

"You're not from around here, are you?" Julie asked.

"I live in Silicon Valley."

"Now I remember!" Anna opened her mouth and paused. "You are one of Sherrie's guys, aren't you?"

The man nodded miserably.

"I don't know how your daughter got my number. I have a very small digital presence. I pay people big money to keep my contact information private."

Anna knew her daughter was no techno geek.

"Does Sherrie have your number?" she asked.

"I guess so."

"That's how Cassie tracked you down."

"Can someone tell me what's going on?" Julie demanded. "Who is this guy?"

"You know the dating business Sherrie runs? Doug here was supposed to go out with Briana the day she died."

Julie's eyes widened as she gave the young man a once over.

"Why does a young man like you need a hired date? Can't you get a girl on your own?"

Doug looked embarrassed.

"I was here for a big tech conference. They changed the invitations after I got here. Where was I supposed to get a plus one at the last minute?"

"Never mind all that," Anna soothed. She gave Julie a warning look. "Did you meet Briana that evening?"

Doug nodded.

"I picked her up at the given address."

"How long was she with you?" Anna asked with bated breath.

"Barely ten minutes," Doug Crane replied. "She was very distracted when I picked her up. We were on our way to the conference when she suddenly demanded I stop the car."

"Do you remember where that was?"

"Not really. I am new to this area."

"Was it somewhere near the redwood forest?" Anna asked.

"The whole area we were driving through seemed wooded."

"What did you do then?"

"I pulled over," Doug said. "She got out and started walking away without a backward glance."

"Did she say where she was going, or why?"

"No explanations," Doug said with a shake of his head. "I waited for a few minutes, thinking she might come back. Then I had to drive off."

"How do we know you are telling the truth?" Anna asked.

"Dozens of people saw me at that conference," Doug Crane told them. "Why would I want to hurt her? I barely knew her."

"Thanks for coming here, Doug. If you are really innocent, you won't mind repeating all this to the police?"

"That's where I am going next."

Chapter 24

Cassie had taken Anna's advice. She stood in line at the Tipsy Whale, salivating at the sweet, smoky aromas that swirled around her.

"One Special of the Day with extra coleslaw," she told Murphy. "My Mom's coming here too. She'll be here soon."

Murphy grunted and rang up her purchase. Cassie was in a chatty mood. She asked Murphy if he posted his menu online. Murphy told her he didn't have a website. He wasn't going to have one. He had been writing the day's special on a chalkboard out on the sidewalk for thirty five years. He would continue doing so as long as he ran the pub.

"Your city ways won't fly here," a deep voice said.

Cassie whirled around to stare at the tall, brown eyed man standing in line behind her.

"Dylan."

"Cassie. Are you done? Some of us have work to get back to."

Cassie moved aside from the counter. She opened her mouth to say something smart and acerbic but nothing came to mind.

"We get your milk," she said instead. "I saw your name on the carton."

"Anna was one of the first to try our organic line. She's always been a strong advocate of Daisy Hollow Farms."

Dylan placed his order and leaned against the wooden counter, his hands in his pockets.

"It's a beautiful day," Cassie noted. "Nice day to sit on a park bench and enjoy lunch."

"I have to get back to the farm, Cassie."

Cassie turned red.

"I wasn't ... I didn't mean ..."

Dylan Woods flashed a cocky grin as he picked up his sandwich bag.

"I know!"

Cassie watched his back as he breezed out of the door, feeling like a fool. She crept out with her cheeks flaming, hoping no one had heard her talking to Dylan. There was a small park a few doors down from the pub, right in the middle of Main Street. It housed a gazebo which was the pride of downtown Dolphin Bay. Smarting from Dylan's snub, Cassie decided she was going to enjoy her pulled pork sandwich at the gazebo. She admired the pink and purple wisteria hanging down the gazebo. Climbing roses wound around the pillars, perfuming the air with their heady scent.

Cassie's mood improved by the time she finished her lunch. A nap was calling her name but she persevered. Deciding it was now or never, she walked to the parking lot and got into her car, determined to turn in the admission forms.

Dolphin Bay University was the usual beehive of activity. The woman at the admissions office greeted her like an old friend.

"You made a good choice," she said. "If you get your GED, these health food courses can count toward a nutrition degree."

"Thanks. But I'm not sure I'm cut out for that."

The woman looked disappointed. Cassie wondered if she got a commission for getting students to enroll in certain courses. She walked out of the building, wondering where she could find Sherrie. Was she also an English major like Briana?

A lot of students were outdoors, taking advantage of the fine day. Some reclined under trees with their nose in a book. Others sat around in groups, engrossed in lively discussions. Cassie decided to tackle the library first. She spotted an empty bench outside and sat down, observing the kids as they streamed in or out. Her patience was rewarded some time later.

Sherrie walked out of the library, a heavy satchel slung over her shoulders. She was typing something on her phone with her head down, eyes glued to the screen. She didn't see Cassie waving at her.

"Sherrie. Over here. Sherrie!"

Sherrie finally looked up. Her face broke into a smile. She rushed to envelop Cassie in a hug.

"This is a surprise."

"I had to submit some documents," Cassie explained. "I was hoping to run into you."

Sherrie's face fell.

"Has your mother made any progress?"

"This might not be news to you. Briana was cheating on Cody."

Sherrie's shoulders slumped.

"It was bound to come out sooner or later."

"You knew?" Cassie's eyes widened.

"I had a hunch. Briana had a huge crush on this guy. She used to get all worked up when she was going to meet him. I called her out on it but she denied it."

"Who was he?"

Sherrie leaned forward and dropped her voice a notch.

"Her English professor. He was kind of a mentor to her in the beginning. He took her under his wing, gave her special attention."

"Is he just out of college himself?"

"Oh no. He's much older, old enough to be her father."

"Was he forcing her, do you think? Misusing his power?"

Sherrie was thoughtful.

"I'm not sure. Far as I can tell, Briana hero worshipped him. She just couldn't stop talking about how smart he was."

"How did she meet him?"

"He's one of the top professors in the department. His class is really hard to get into and harder to pass. But once you get in, you learn a lot."

"Did you take that class too?"

"Last semester," Sherrie sighed. "I was the one who pushed Briana into taking that class. She dreamed of being a news anchor one day. This class would help get her there."

"So this professor guy … does he prey on the girls a lot? I mean, is he a habitual offender?"

Sherrie denied hearing any such rumors about the man.

"Do you think the professor might have hurt Briana?" Sherrie asked, her eyes filling with horror.

"I don't know, Sherrie. I'm just learning about him."

"It's all my fault. I pushed Briana toward him."

Sherrie's eyes filled with tears.

"You are not to blame," Cassie said firmly. "You couldn't know she would fall for this granddad."

Sherrie remembered she had a class to go to. She wiped her eyes, thanked Cassie and walked away. Cassie's knees creaked as she stood up to leave. She decided to stretch her legs a bit before heading home.

Cassie spotted the coffee cart just when she was beginning to long for a hot drink. She ordered a nonfat mocha with extra whipped cream and waited for the barista to fill her order. A head of bright blue grabbed her attention and Cassie smiled when she recognized the petite figure striding toward her.

"Hello! You're still here."

"Yes, I am," the girl laughed. "Sat through a drama class today. It was fun."

"They let you do that?"

"Most of them don't mind. Some don't even realize I am an outsider."

"So you like our little town, huh?"

"I really do. It's pretty out here. And quiet. I could get used to it."

"Are you still living at Aunt Mary's?"

The girl called Rain pursed her lips.

"I don't know how much longer I can afford it, though. I need to find a job."

"What kind of job?"

"I'm not picky. Anything that pays the bills."

"Why don't you come and work for my mother?"

Rain's eyes lit up.

"Is she hiring?"

"We can always use some help. It's a bookstore. Bayside Books. On the corner of Main and Ocean."

"I know where it is."

"Fantastic!"

"Thank you so much," Rain gushed. "You have saved me a lot of trouble."

"I'm just doing myself a favor. My Mom won't keep flooding me with chores if she has some help."

"I won't let you down. I promise."

"You know, I was a lot like you when I was younger."

Rain's interest was genuine.

"Did you also travel across the country?"

"Hardly," Cassie laughed. "I went south and stopped in Los Angeles. But that's exactly where I wanted to be."

"What's special about Los Angeles?" Rain asked innocently.

"Hollywood, of course. I dreamed of being in the movies ever since I was a little girl. I wanted to be a famous actress, like Meg Ryan."

"Isn't she old?"

"This was twenty years ago. Meg Ryan was a top star at that time."

"Did you do it?" Rain asked curiously. "Did you become famous?"

"I guess I did," Cassie sighed. "I have a star on the Hollywood Walk of Fame."

Rain had never heard of it.

"I won an Oscar at 21."

Rain had heard of the Oscar award. She was suitably impressed.

"You must be smart!"

Cassie had a faraway look in her eyes.

"I had ambition. Plenty of it. I worked hard and I was fortunate to get the right breaks."

"Doesn't hurt that you look gorgeous."

"It came with a price, of course. I made big sacrifices."

"I'm not ambitious at all," Rain said lightly. "I take life one day at a time."

"You are fearless," Cassie noted. "You meet life head on. Mark my words, sweetie. It will take you far."

A light blush spread across the girl's cheeks.

"I have to go now. It's been nice talking to you."

Cassie sipped her coffee and stared at Rain's retreating back. She wondered why she felt so drawn to her.

Chapter 25

The sun had set by the time Cassie woke from her nap. She had been exhausted by all the walking she had done on the campus. An aroma of roasted garlic filled the house. Cassie dragged herself into the kitchen and pulled up a chair.

"Something smells good. What are you cooking, Mom?"

Anna picked up the mound of fresh cut vegetables and added them to a pot.

"Pasta Prima Vera. I got some nice fresh asparagus and peas at the farm."

"Sounds great. I'm starving."

Anna pulled out a pan of crostini from the oven. She spooned different toppings on them and offered them to Cassie.

"We can start with the bruschetta. Why don't you pour the wine?"

"I had the best day," Cassie enthused. "Time goes by really fast at the university."

Anna hummed a tune as she whisked a creamy sauce. She added a few handfuls of shredded cheese from the piles she had ready on a cutting board. Cassie was glad to see her in a good mood.

"Looks like you had a great day too, Mom."

"I had a busy day. I am happy when I am working."

Cassie gobbled the bruschetta and waited eagerly for Anna to finish tossing the pasta together. Anna served the pasta in bright blue stoneware bowls, topped them with extra virgin olive oil and grated parmesan cheese and placed one before Cassie.

"I ran into Sherrie again," Cassie said, scooping up a big forkful of the rich, creamy pasta. "She told me Briana was mad about one of her professors."

"Was he an older guy?" Anna asked.

"How did you know?" Cassie's mouth dropped open in amazement.

"We need to swap notes. Julie got talking to one of her neighbors. It seems Briana visited Castle Beach Resort very often. She has been seen with an older man."

"Sherrie wasn't sure if Briana was just throwing herself on him. But looks like he was involved too."

"How do we know it wasn't platonic? Maybe he was just being kind to her."

"Or he was taking unfair advantage of his position," Cassie pointed out.

"Poor Cody. Looks like he might have been right about Briana."

Cassie took a second helping of the pasta and offered the rest to her mother.

"We need to find out more about this professor."

"Your father would have known," Anna said. "He had a wide social circle."

"Can't you ask Aunt Julie?" Cassie prompted. "She might have some contacts in the English department."

"Wonderful idea. I will call her as soon as we finish eating."

"Are we having tiramisu for dessert?" Cassie asked.

"Not tonight. I made some amaretto cookies. We can have them with lemon gelato."

"I met that girl who's living at Aunt Mary's."

Anna's eyes widened.

"I forgot all about her. She's a suspect too. She had Briana's contact info among her things."

"I don't think Rain had anything to do with Briana. She's a sweet kid."

"You barely know her."

"I offered her a job at the store, Mom."

"What!" Anna exclaimed. "We can't afford to hire anyone. The store barely breaks even."

"You can use the help," Cassie argued. "You have to stop climbing up on that ladder, anyway. She can do the heavy lifting."

"You should have asked me first, Cassie."

"You won't have to close the store when you step out for lunch," Cassie pointed out. "And you won't have to call me over."

"What brought this on?"

"She needs rent money," Cassie explained. "She said she was willing to do any job."

"I'll try her out for a couple of weeks."

"She can help you with the petition," Cassie said suddenly. "She can go door to door and get signatures for us."

"I don't think the good people of Dolphin Bay will pay any heed to a stranger."

Cassie's shoulders slumped.

"I just thought we could help her out a bit. She's a nomad. She'll be gone in a few days."

"Alright," Anna said grudgingly. "We'll take her on. But ask me first next time."

The phone rang, interrupting them. Vicki Bauer was on the other side and she was hysterical.

"Calm down, Vicki," Anna commanded. "I can't make head or tail of what you are saying."

Cassie stood up and started clearing the table, listening to her mother's one sided conversation. She had finished loading the dishwasher by the time Anna hung up.

"Cody's in trouble," Anna declared.

"I gathered that much," Cassie said. "What happened, Mom?"

"The police just arrested Cody." Anna ignored Cassie's gasp and continued. "Apparently, he was going out of town with some friends. The police thought he was making a run for it. They brought him in."

"What was he doing?" Cassie asked.

"He was going south for some music festival. He insists he had no intention of fleeing town."

"That's kinda hard to believe, Mom. Surely the police warned him against leaving town? Every movie old or new has a scene where the sheriff tells the suspect not to skip town."

"What's done is done. We need to think about how to get him out now."

"I can call Teddy Fowler. He's the detective on the case."

"I think we should go there in person," Anna said. "That might make a difference."

"Where's your friend Vicki?"

"She's still at home, poor thing."

"We can pick her up on the way over," Cassie said. "Grab your purse, Mom."

Cassie's temperamental car refused to start after three tries.

"Let's just walk there," Anna said.

Cassie told her mother to be patient and tried again. The car obliged and Cassie set off with the usual screech of tires. They made a brief stop to get Vicki and pulled up in front of the police station fifteen minutes later.

"Where is he? Where's my son?" Vicki asked loudly as soon as they went in.

The clerk at the desk told them to sit down and be quiet. Cassie spotted Teddy Fowler and made a beeline for him.

"Hey Teddy!" she greeted him brightly.

Teddy was happy to see her.

"Cassie? What are you doing here?"

Cassie nodded toward Vicki and her mother.

"I'm with them. Did you really just arrest Cody Bauer?"

"We had no choice, Cassie. He was fleeing town."

"From what I heard, he was just heading to a music festival."

"That's what he says, of course. I'm not naïve enough to believe him."

"But he's innocent, Teddy. There are so many other suspects."

"Yeah? Like who? I'm sorry, Cassie. We were going to bring him in today anyway. He sealed his own fate by trying to escape."

Cassie went over to talk to Anna.

"Teddy won't budge."

"Do you know anyone who works here?" Anna asked Vicki. "Someone who can talk to the detective on your behalf?"

Vicki shook her head.

"Let me make a call," Anna said.

Cassie had a hunch about what her mother was up to. Anna came back a few minutes later and confirmed it.

"I talked to Gino. He wants to talk about this in person. He's waiting for us at Mystic Hill."

Cassie's car started at the first try this time. Vicki sat mutely in the back seat, dabbing her eyes with a tissue.

"You need to keep it together for Cody," Anna told her. "He's depending on you."

Gino was waiting outside in the portico when they reached the winery. He ushered them in.

Cassie looked on as Anna gave him a brief account of what had happened.

"The police have some solid evidence against your son," Gino told Vicki. "I think they have plenty of ground to detain him today."

"But he's innocent," Vicki wailed. "I know my boy. He may be hot headed but he would never harm anyone, least of all, a girl he loved."

"I have been retired for a while," Gino said. "I don't have any control over what the police do. I can just try to learn what they are thinking."

"Teddy Fowler is handling Cody's case," Cassie told him.

Gino stepped away from the ladies and placed a call. He was on the phone for a while. He didn't look optimistic when he hung up.

"I am sorry. They are holding Cody for tonight. They will charge him tomorrow."

"What about all the other suspects?" Cassie asked. She whirled around and looked at Anna. "Tell him about the old guy, Mom."

"We think Briana was having an affair with her professor," Anna told Gino. "He might have wanted her out of the way."

"The evidence of the fingerprints is too strong," Gino explained. "I suggest you find out more about this professor. What was his relationship with Briana? Did he even have a motive to kill her?"

Chapter 26

Anna slept in late the next day. All the running around the previous night had wiped her out. She and Cassie had stayed with Vicki until she calmed down a bit. Anna herself had felt overwhelmed by the stressful situation.

Cassie sat in the kitchen, nursing a cup of coffee. She poured Anna a cup.

"I didn't realize how late it was," she said. "Why didn't you wake me up?"

"You needed the rest, Mom."

Cassie suggested they go to the diner for breakfast. Anna agreed reluctantly. They were ready to leave half an hour later. Cassie insisted Anna ride with her in the car.

"You never know. We might have to go somewhere later."

Anna had talked to Julie about the professor the previous night. Julie was going to tap her network of friends and try to get some information. Until Julie actually found something, it was a waiting game.

The town was buzzing with the news of Cody's arrest.

"About time the police did something," one righteous voice said.

Lara Crawford was sitting at a booth with a couple of women from her staff. She smiled maliciously when she saw Anna.

"Well, well, look who's decided to show her face. You are shameless, aren't you?"

"You leave my mother alone," Cassie roared. "We can sue you for harassment, you know."

"Honey, I am the mayor of this town. No judge is going to rule against me."

"Don't get cocky, Lara," Anna warned.

"On the contrary, you're the one who's strutting around when you should be locked up. You know what happened to your friend's son, don't you? You are next."

"Cody's innocent," Anna stressed, even though she wasn't so sure of it herself. "I'm going to prove it."

Cassie pulled Anna away from Lara's table and led her to a booth at the back. She ordered the breakfast special for both of them.

"I want to get out of here as soon as possible," Anna whispered. "But I'm ravenous."

"Take your time and enjoy your meal, Mom. You can't let that vile woman run you out of here."

Their food arrived quickly and the waitress didn't linger to gossip after Anna glared at her. Neither of them talked much as they focused on eating. Anna placed a twenty on the table and motioned Cassie to get up as soon as they were done.

The sky was overcast and a heavy wall of mist hung over the bay. Anna felt the whole atmosphere was rife with anticipation. A few magnolia blossoms lay on the sidewalk in front of the bookstore. Anna absentmindedly picked one up and breathed in its fragrance.

Cassie hesitated outside the door.

"Do you mind keeping me company today?" Anna asked her.

Cassie smiled eagerly and followed her inside.

Anna started dusting the shelves but her mind was preoccupied. She jumped when the phone rang. It was just a customer who wanted to know if they had the latest bestseller in stock.

"I wonder what's keeping her," Anna mumbled as she went into the pantry to make coffee.

"Why don't you call her, Mom?"

"She'll be here when she's ready."

The bell behind the door jingled just then and Julie obliged them by sweeping in.

"I called Mary. She should be here soon."

"Tell me what you found," Anna said anxiously. "We can fill Mary in later."

The door opened again and Mary arrived, looking a bit harried.

"What is it? What's happened?"

Julie flipped the sign on the door to 'Closed' and told everyone to settle down.

"You owe me big time, Anna."

Anna's impatience was written clearly on her face. Julie took notice and forged ahead.

"I made some calls. A lot of calls. The professor in question is Gordon Hunt. He's a senior professor in the English department. A bit whimsical but quite popular."

"Is he a short man who wears tweed suits all the time?" Anna asked. "I think I remember John talking about him."

"I don't know," Julie shrugged. "I have never come across him myself."

"Go on," Anna urged.

"Well, once I found out who he was, it was easier to find out more. One of my friends is in the local knitting club. Gordon's wife is in this club, apparently."

"Weren't you in the knitting club, Mary?" Anna asked.

"I stopped going a year ago. I haven't had the time since the latest grandchild."

"What did your friend say?" Cassie prompted, steering them back on track.

"Gordon's wife is sure he's having an affair. She talked to my friend about it."

"His wife knew?" Anna asked incredulously. "She could have gone after Briana."

"The wife doesn't know who Gordon was having an affair with. My friend is sure about it."

"The wife could be lying," Cassie pointed out.

"That's right," Anna said. "Why would she advertize the fact that she knew her husband's mistress?"

"All valid points," Julie agreed. "But they don't fly here. The wife has an airtight alibi."

A collective groan filled the room.

"The knitting club meet at each other's homes one by one. They were at Gordon Hunt's house the day Briana died."

"What time was this meeting?" Anna asked urgently.

"They met around 3:30. Tea and snacks were served. They did whatever they do at these meetings. Then the wine started flowing. It's their usual jam, it seems. They get drunk on wine, order pizza or Chinese food and crib about their husbands."

"Was Gordon Hunt's wife present all the time?" Anna asked.

"My friend said she was. She said all the other ladies present will confirm it."

"So the wife's no use to us," Cassie said, her voice laden with disappointment.

"I'm not done yet," Julie said. "You know who was Not present in the house during the meeting? Gordon Hunt!"

"That's very typical," Mary said. "Men don't want to be around a flock of twittering women. And the women don't like to have a man underfoot."

"That's fine, Mary," Anna said. She looked at Julie. "I don't see how that helps us."

Julie gave a secretive smile.

"Gordon came in just as the group was breaking up. My friend said he looked disheveled. His clothes were muddy. There was a tear in his jacket and he was all fidgety."

"Did he have some kind of accident?" Cassie asked.

"That's what his wife thought. She wanted to take him to the hospital. Gordon waved her off. Said he was playing golf at the resort and had a small mishap. He slipped and fell in a pond. He had a slight sprain in his ankle but he was fine otherwise."

"What else did your friend say?" Anna asked.

"She didn't stick around after that," Julie told them.

The bell over the door dinged again.

"We are closed," Anna said automatically. Then her mouth hung open as she stared at the slight blue haired girl standing before her.

"It's okay, Mom," Cassie said. "This is Rain, the girl I told you about."

"What are you doing here, sweetie?" Mary asked kindly. "Did you want to talk to me?"

"I'm here to work," the girl spoke up. "This lady here offered me a job."

"There's not a lot to do here, I'm afraid," Anna said. "Why don't we take it one week at a time?"

"Okay," the girl said with a shrug.

"We need to clear something up first," Anna said grimly. "Mary told me about your little accident. Did you know Briana?"

"No Ma'am."

"Then what were you doing with her phone number?"

Rain looked at Mary but didn't say anything. Mary turned red as she tried to think of a response.

"I was cleaning," she said lamely. "There were a bunch of brochures lying around. I wanted to tidy them up."

"It's your house," Rain said with a shrug. She stared into Anna's eyes. "This girl, Briana, she promised to pay me something. But she never got back. I got her phone number off the college website."

"See?" Mary gushed. "She had nothing to do with Briana."

Anna told Rain to come back the next day.

"What's next, Mom?" Cassie asked. "Shall we go talk to Teddy?"

"You don't have any proof against Gordon Hunt," Julie said. "What are you going to tell the police?"

"I'm going to talk to Gino about this," Anna said. "I think he will give us the right advice."

"Teddy might be more inclined to listen to him," Cassie added.

"Not unless he has something better to say," Julie argued. "If Gino had that kind of pull, Cody would never have been arrested."

Anna uttered a cry of exclamation.

"I have a hunch. Let's go to the diner first."

Anna refused to say any more about it. Cassie and the Firecrackers waited on the sidewalk while Anna locked the bookstore. They trooped after her as she walked purposefully toward the Yellow Tulip Diner.

Twenty minutes later, they were all piling into Julie's big SUV, headed for the Mystic Hill Winery.

Anna felt confused by all the new facts that had surfaced that morning. She hoped Gino Mancini would help her make some sense out of it.

Chapter 27

"I am so sorry to bother you again," Anna told Gino as she scrambled out of the car. "This is becoming a habit."

"A habit you will keep up, I hope," Gino Mancini said suavely.

Anna blushed but she found herself drawn to Gino's dimples.

"Let's go in," Gino said, ushering everyone in. "It's past noon so I arranged a light lunch for you ladies. I am sure you can use some refreshment."

"That sounds lovely," Mary said.

Cassie and Julie gave their approval.

"We don't want to impose," Anna said, sounding embarrassed.

"Please … it was no trouble. My housekeeper rarely gets a chance to impress guests."

Gino waited until everyone had filled their plates from the tiny buffet. The ladies had a choice of smoked salmon and cheese on crackers, tiny cheese quesadillas with fresh guacamole and grilled chicken on skewers with a sweet chili sauce. There was a big bowl of fresh fruit salad to round everything up.

Anna tasted everything just to be polite. Gino noticed her anxiety and nodded at her.

"Tell me what you have been up to, Anna."

"We tracked down the man Briana was having an affair with. Now we need your help in convincing the police to bring him in."

"The police won't move without any actual proof."

Anna repeated everything they had learned about Gordon Hunt.

"He went to the diner with Briana. The girl at the diner recognized him."

"He wasn't breaking any laws though, was he?" Gino asked.

"I am sure it's against the rules to have an affair with your student," Anna said. "It's definitely not ethical. Gordon's wife is sure he was having an affair. And we can place him and Briana together in multiple places."

"But they were never seen arguing, were they?" Gino asked.

Anna felt helpless.

"Is there nothing you can do?" she asked Gino.

"Hold on a second, Mom," Cassie said, tapping some keys on her phone. "I called Sherrie when you were talking to that waitress at the diner. Sherrie had Briana's laptop. She found some old emails between Gordon and Briana."

"What do they say?" Anna cried.

"There are a lot of them. She says they start off as love letters and get more intense. Briana wanted Gordon to marry her."

Anna stared at Gino.

"Does that help?"

"You have convinced me, Anna," Gino sighed. "Let me talk to Teddy Fowler."

Gino went inside his den to make the call. The women noshed on the food while they waited for him to come back. Gino came back some time later.

"Teddy agreed to bring the professor in for questioning."

The ladies cheered and clapped their hands.

"Now what?" Anna asked.

"Now we wait," Gino said. "This could take a while."

Anna thanked him profusely. She hovered around him while he fixed a plate for himself.

"Why don't you invite Gino for dinner at our place, Mom?" Cassie asked, widening her eyes suggestively.

"Great idea," Anna said, turning red. "What do you like to eat, Gino?"

"I'm not picky," Gino said. "Surprise me!"

They chatted for a while until Gino put his plate down.

"I need to get back to the store," Anna said reluctantly. "I hope we get some good news soon."

"We are having a big potluck at the bookstore," Mary told Gino. "Everyone in town is invited. We are hoping to get some signatures in favor of Anna's café."

"Anna told me about the petition," Gino told her. "Count me in."

Julie drove them back to the bookstore. The group dispersed soon after that. Mary needed to go home and start getting dinner ready. Julie had to get back to her writing. Cassie wanted to talk to Bobby and take a nap.

Anna went about her daily chores, wondering what was happening at the police station.

Vicki Bauer burst into the store as the sky darkened, Cody in tow. Anna had just started to close up.

"You did it, Anna, you did it!" Vicki yelled. "How can I ever thank you?"

Cody stood by quietly, looking dazed. Anna pulled him into a hug.

"Thank you for believing in me, Mrs. Butler," he mumbled.

"Is it over?" Anna asked Vicki.

"We don't know much yet," Vicki replied. "I'm just happy they let him go."

"Go home and relax now. I think the worst is behind us."

Anna went home as soon as Vicki left with her son.

Cassie was watching Casablanca in the living room, a big tub of popcorn in her lap.

"How many times are you going to watch that movie?" Anna grumbled goodnaturedly.

"What's for dinner, Mom?" Cassie asked, ignoring her. "I know you hate salad so I didn't make anything."

"How about Chicken Piccata?" Anna asked. "Or Ravioli Lasagna?"

Cassie chose the lasagna.

Anna pulled out a big bag of her homemade cheese ravioli from the freezer along with a carton of her red sauce. Now she just needed to grate some cheese and assemble the casserole.

Cassie had made a salad and set the table by the time Anna came out of her shower. They had barely taken a bite of their dinner when the doorbell rang.

Anna opened the door to find Gino Mancini at the doorstep.

"Come in, come in," she said. "This is like déjà vu."

"Am I interrupting your dinner again?" Gino asked.

"Why don't you join us?" Anna asked. "It's just a simple lasagna though. Very last minute."

Gino had come bearing news.

"Gordon confessed," he said. "He was a hard nut to crack though."

Anna and Cassie listened with their mouths hanging open as Gino narrated the sordid tale.

"At first, he denied any attachment to Briana. Then he admitted he hired her as a stand-in."

"Why did he need a date?" Anna asked. "He has a wife, doesn't he?"

"That part is not clear. Gordon was used to girl students fawning over him. He said it wasn't his fault Briana fell in love with him."

"What about all those times they met at the resort?" Anna asked. "He can't deny that, surely?"

"And what about the emails on Briana's laptop?" Cassie asked.

Gino took a big bite of his lasagna and nodded.

"He denied everything until the police presented the evidence to him one by one. They were testing his fingerprints while he was being questioned. Turns out his prints too were found on that bat."

Anna and Cassie both sucked in a breath.

"Briana dreamed of marrying him but Gordon had no intention of leaving his wife. Briana gave him an ultimatum. That's when he planned to kill her."

"He must have been thrilled when the police arrested Cody."

"That was his plan all along," Gino said. "Gordon talked Briana into borrowing the baseball bat, knowing it would have Cody's prints on it. Then he took Briana out to the diner and made sure Cody would see them there. He picked a fight with Cody so people would remember how Cody had lost his temper and got violent."

"I guess Briana played into his hands by calling the police on Cody," Anna mused.

"He couldn't have planned it better," Gino explained. "He made up some excuse and asked Briana to meet him in the redwood forest urgently. He knew she was supposed to meet Cody at that time."

"Poor Briana," Cassie sighed. "She never suspected him?"

"She fell for his charms. He has done this a lot, it seems. He has affairs with the young girls and dumps them when they try to get serious."

"That sounds unreal," Anna said. "None of the girls ever came forward?"

"He controlled their grades and their future. That's exactly how rascals like him get away."

"I hope they put him away for a long time," Cassie said.

"What about Cody?" Anna asked.

"Cody's free." Gino scraped his plate clean and took a second helping. "He could never have done it, you know. He doesn't have enough strength in his elbow to really swing a bat."

"His old elbow injury!" Anna exclaimed. "How did I miss that!"

"Everyone missed it, apparently," Gino said. "Teddy Fowler stumbled on it while he was interviewing Cody."

Gino stuck around for a while after dinner.

"The wine tasting event is coming up," he said when Anna saw him off at the door. "I hope you will come as my guest."

Anna grinned and nodded. "I am looking forward to it."

"Can I call him your boyfriend now, Mom?" Cassie asked with a wink as soon as Anna shut the door.

"It's your turn to do the dishes," Anna reminded her before heading to her room.

Epilogue

The party was in full swing. Bayside Books was overflowing with people enjoying a glass of wine, chatting with their friends and having a good time. A row of grills had been set up outside the store, facing the Coastal Walk and the bay. Mary's husband Ben and his buddy Rory Cunningham had volunteered to work them. Burgers and franks flamed on the grill and there was a lively discussion about whose technique was best.

Anna stood near the entrance, welcoming the steady stream of guests. Two long tables groaned with the weight of dishes overflowing with a variety of food. Julie had made her famous baked beans. Mary brought two kinds of pasta salad along with a pecan pie. There were five kinds of potato salad, roasted corn on the cob and fried chicken and biscuits.

Everyone had brought a dish and the potluck was a roaring success.

Gino Mancini had donated the wine for the event. Anna had protested at the extravagance but he hadn't taken no for an answer. Cassie had teased her mercilessly about it. Gino stood behind another table, pouring wine for the good people of Dolphin Bay. He was inviting everyone to the wine festival at Mystic Hill.

Cassie was in charge of the most important task of the day. She stood behind a big hardcover notebook, urging people to sign the petition for Anna's café. She had dialed up the charm, raving about the delicious treats the town could expect from the café. A platter of Anna's delicious cupcakes stood next to the book, a reward for anyone who showed their support.

Julie and Mary mingled with the guests, making sure they each had a drink or a plate full of food. Most of the people knew each other well. A few tourists had also walked in, lured by the quaint small town event.

Cassie was talking to a couple of ladies she didn't recognize when she felt a frisson of excitement. Dylan Woods gave her a nod and picked up a pen to sign his name.

"Anna's looking good," he said. "It's nice to see her recovering so well."

Cassie felt her mind going blank.

"She's got spunk," she croaked. "I mean, yeah, thanks."

Dylan flashed a cheeky smile and took a big bite of his hot dog.

"Great party."

Cassie nodded mutely as he walked to the food table to fix himself a fresh plate.

Jose Garcia arrived, dressed in a Hawaiian shirt, grinning from ear to ear.

"I'm off to Cabo tomorrow," he beamed.

Anna's face fell.

"You promised to wait, Jose," she said under her breath.

"You will love the new owner," Jose winked. "I am sure you can work out a long term lease."

"Huh?" Anna was confused.

Julie walked over to them and glared at Jose.

"Have you let the cat out of the bag?"

"Not yet, but you better hurry. I came to say goodbye to everyone."

"What's going on, Julie?" Anna asked.

"Hold your breath," Julie said, her eyes shining. "I bought the store next door, Anna."

Anna almost screamed in surprise.

"But why? And how?"

Julie shrugged. "Let's just say I was looking to invest. I got a big advance for my next book."

Mary had heard them talking and walked over. She called her two friends in for a group hug.

"This is a day for surprises," Anna said, wiping her tears. "Agnes and her sister came in to sign the petition. She said she wasn't convinced I was innocent but the town could use a new café. She ate two cupcakes."

"We have enough signatures to sway the licensing board," Mary said. "You better get ready to bake, Anna."

Rain was going around the room, collecting trash and cleaning up where needed. Her hair was magenta now. Anna had reluctantly admitted she was happy with the extra help.

Vicki arrived with Cody in tow. A quiet murmur rippled through the room as people recognized Cody. Anna hugged them and Julie fixed them a plate. Things returned to normal.

A sudden hush fell over the room as a surprise guest arrived. No one had invited her. Lara Crawford stood at the door, her mouth set in a superior smirk.

"Live it up while you can, Anna."

"You need to leave, Lara," Anna said calmly. "You are not welcome here."

"I wanted to give you the news myself," Lara smiled. "The police have reopened John's case. You will be hearing from them soon."

Julie, Mary and Cassie had gathered around Anna.

"You can go now," Julie glared. "This is a private event."

Lara gave a malicious grin and spun around on her heel. She had accomplished her purpose.

Anna's face had clouded over. Cassie held her shaking hand in a tight grip and urged her to calm down.

Gino had joined the group.

"We are going to face this together, Anna. This is a slur on my reputation too."

Anna smiled her way through the next two hours. Finally, all the food had been eaten and the guests went home. Julie, Mary and Anna sat huddled in an alcove, sipping a celebratory glass of wine.

Rain and Cassie were dismantling the tables and putting the room back to order. Rain held a stack of utensils in her arms, barely able to see where she was going. Cassie backed into her with a jug of iced tea. The dishes fell to the ground with a clatter. Cassie's knee popped and she was about to go down too when Rain grabbed her and pulled her up. A wallet fell out of the girl's clothes and burst open on the floor.

Rain scrambled to pick up everything and stuff it back in the purse. Cassie picked up a laminated card that had fallen a few inches away from the other stuff.

"You missed this …" she began saying.

Rain pulled at the card in Cassie's hand just when she began exclaiming over it.

"Is that your license picture? I take the most horrible license pictures."

Cassie won the tussle and brought the card closer to her face, eager to stare at the picture. Her smile froze on her face, her excitement changing into shock and horror in the fraction of a second.

The card slipped from her hand and fell to the ground.

The Firecrackers had come over to help the girls up.

"Cassie?" Anna asked sharply. "You turned white as a sheet. What's the matter?"

Mary picked up the piece of plastic and started reading what was written on it.

"Meg Butler!" she exclaimed.

She stared in disbelief at the slight girl with the shock of magenta hair. The girl stared back.

"But you said your name is Rain," Mary said hoarsely.

Rain shrugged but said nothing.

"Is it true?" Anna asked, her face a kaleidoscope of emotions. "Don't be afraid, sweetie."

Rain nodded once.

The tears began streaming down Anna's face.

"I have been looking for you."

***

A Pocket Full of Pie - A Meera Patel Mystery

By Leena Clover

Cast of Characters

MEERA PATEL – Twenty three year old graduate school dropout. Resident of Swan Creek, Oklahoma, a small university town home to Pioneer Polytechnic. She hasn't lived up to the great expectations her immigrant Indian family has of her.

ANAND PATEL – Meera's father, professor and head of electrical engineering at Pioneer Polytechnic.

MOTEE BA – Hansa or Honey Patel, or Meera's grandmother. The lady of the house and mother figure to the Patel kids.

PAPPA – Meera's irascible 80 something year old grandfather.

JEET PATEL – Meera's teen aged brother and wannabe Ivy League graduate.

TONY SINCLAIR – Gas station guy, Meera's childhood friend and one time crush. Fiercely protective, he doesn't mind being Meera's sidekick in her harebrained schemes.

BECKY – Meera's best friend since elementary school, she is the third member of the hell raising trio.

JON AND SYLVIE DAVIS – Local diner owners, staunch friends of the Patels.

STAN MILLER – Newly minted cop who acts first and thinks later.

JORDAN HARRIS – Up and coming rancher who ate too much pie and met a sticky end.

JESSICA – Ambitious young researcher at Pioneer Poly – she spent the night of her engagement at the lab.

CAMERON HARRIS – War veteran and Jordan's brother – the prodigal son who isn't sure of his welcome home.

NANCY ROBINSON – Owner of the new fancy diner in Swan Creek

And many more …

Chapter 1

The gentle waves of the lake lapped against the shore. I huffed and puffed, trying to catch my breath.

"Maybe this wasn't a good idea," I complained.

Becky turned around and jogged back to me. She made it look so easy.

"Come on, Meera! We've hardly come two hundred meters."

She jogged in place, annoying me with the hint of laughter in her voice.

"I'm not fit for this," I let out, and sprawled on the tiny jogging path.

"Which is why you need to do this," Becky taunted me with a matter of fact voice.

The mid November morning was cool with temperatures in the mid 50s. My friend Becky had dragged me out to Lake Willow Springs and the 3 mile walking cum jogging track that went around it.

"The fresh air will do you good," Motee Ba, my grandma, had nodded eagerly.

Her eyes had met Becky's and a silent message passed through them. I was in a sort of funk, feeling sorry for myself, and people were plotting to get me out of it. I love these people, don't get me wrong, but I was in a weird frame of mind.

My name is Meera Patel, and I'm a 20 something grad school dropout who shelves books for a living. I live in a small college town in central Oklahoma. My dad Anand Patel is the head of the electrical engineering department at Pioneer Polytechnic, the local university. I put in some time at the local diner because I love to feed people and experiment with recipes. I live in a big ranch style house on the outskirts of town with my brother and my grandparents. I met Becky in third grade and we've been inseparable ever since.

"Meera! You need to get fit!" Becky protested, trying to lift me off the ground.

The concrete path was cold and I could feel the chill through my thick sweats. My cheeks felt pink and my nose was cold.

"Do I have to?" I grumbled. "We stay on our feet long enough at the diner."

"That's different," Becky shook her head. "You need to get your heart rate up. Stop cribbing and look around. It's such a beautiful morning."

She gave me one last look and started running away.

"Wait," I called out, extending a hand. "At least help me get up."

Becky laughed and ran on.

I scrambled to get up, feeling my knees scrape against the rough path. I puffed again as I pulled myself up. My chest heaved with the effort and I decided to walk rather than jog. Some exercise was better than nothing, right? I promised myself my special French toast for breakfast. That put a spring in my step.

I trudged around the corner, trying to spot Becky in the distance. I took deep breaths, enjoying the misty morning, letting myself relax. I told myself I needed to get in shape. Then I spotted a welcome sight. A park bench!

It was a classic bench, painted green, set on a patch of grass a few feet off the walking track. It looked out on the water and another bench that graced the walking track on the opposite shore of the lake.

I collapsed on the bench and leaned back, taking in the area with my eyes half closed. It was a better way to enjoy the scenery, surely. Someone else had the same thoughts as me. A guy was lounging on the other corner of the bench, a hat pulled low over his eyes.

"What's up?" I said politely and closed my eyes.

Becky would be back any second to pull me off the bench.

A couple of minutes passed. I opened my eyes and glanced sideways. The guy was too well dressed to be homeless. A red and blue plaid shirt was tucked into well pressed khakis. A wedge of berry pie peeped out of his jacket. Crumbs of pie crust littered the bench and the ground by his feet.

He still hadn't returned my greeting. But I didn't take it to heart. The dead don't talk back, after all.

Some unknown reserve of energy I didn't know I had propelled me up.

"Becky," I roared, and ran flat out toward her.

A man dressed in nylon shorts and a half shirt ran toward me from the opposite direction. I waved him down.

"Something wrong?" he asked, not happy about having to break stride.

I pointed to the bench and poured out everything. Actually, I just blabbered gibberish. A bunch of drool rolled out of the side of my mouth and I wiped it away. The man jogged back to the bench and jabbed the man in the shoulder, something I hadn't dared to do.

The jogger looked at me and his eyes confirmed my suspicion. He pulled a cell phone out of his pocket and dialed 911. Becky had finally turned around and was coming toward me. Her mock anger changed to concern the moment she saw the look on my face.

"What's the matter, Meera?"

My finger shook as I pointed toward the bench. Flashing red and blue lights filled the park and three police cars converged on the road that led to the walking track.

A familiar stocky figure ambled down, looking important.

"Did you call the cops, Meera?" he demanded as soon as he saw me.

"No, I did," the other runner explained.

There wasn't much to say. The cops took in the scene and cordoned off the area.

"Is he …?" I asked slowly.

Stan looked me over and nodded.

"He's gone, Meera. It's been a while. What are you doing here anyway?"

I told him about our morning sojourn.

"Nothing wrong with trying to get fit," Stan Miller said. "I run five miles a day and do weights. I circle the lake on the weekends. But it's too much for me on a work day."

I mentally curled my fists. I really needed to shape up if Stan Miller was daring to give me fitness advice.

Becky was still in shock, and I hadn't heard a word out of her.

"You ready to go home?" I asked gently.

She barely nodded, staring in fascination at the man on the bench.

"Can we go now, Stan?" I asked, not sure of the response.

Stan gave a curt nod. "I know where to find y'all."

The truce with Stan Miller hadn't come easy. He had put me through the wringer the last few months. I had been the top suspect in the murder of Stan's girlfriend. Although his allegations didn't hold water, it had prompted me to do some leg work and actually prove myself innocent. Stan had apologized for his boorish behavior, and we had called a truce.

The truce was still in place, judging by his current conduct, but I had a feeling it was about to expire soon.

I turned the key of my Camry, uttering a silent prayer. The car started after a couple of tries and I heaved a sigh of relief. I didn't fancy asking Stan Miller for a ride.

Becky was quiet as I eased out of Willow Springs Lake Park onto Willow Drive. I swung a right onto Cedar and stopped at a traffic light.

"What are you thinking?" I asked Becky.

"I know that man," she said quietly.

"What?" I cried, as the light turned green and I took my foot off the brake. "Why didn't you say so?"

"I don't exactly know him, know him," she corrected herself. "I've seen him before."

I caught a green light at the highway intersection and turned right, speeding past Sylvie's Café & Diner and my pal Tony's gas station. I took a left onto Goat Farm Lane.

"Where?" I asked, slowing down.

The only houses on this road were ours and the Miller farm next door, which belonged to Stan Miller's uncle.

"Last night, at Sylvie's."

Becky works at Sylvie's Café. She is their full time cook and is good at it. I help out for a few hours every day, experimenting with recipes, adding some bold items to their menu.

"So what?" I asked. "Last night was quite busy, being a Sunday and all. Some 250-300 people must have come to the café."

Becky nodded. "I worked extra."

"What made you remember this guy then?" I asked.

"He was there with his girl friend. Sorry, fiancée. They were celebrating their recent engagement."

I pulled into our driveway and parked close to the house. We got out and trooped in through the back door.

It was barely 7 AM and my grandmother was boiling water for tea.

"Your Pappa's chai is almost done," she told me, her voice still groggy from sleep.

My grandfather is a stickler for his Masala Chai. Motee Ba wakes him every morning with a cup of his 'bed tea' and two digestive biscuits.

"I made a pot for you," Motee Ba signaled to the dripping coffee.

I thanked her and poured the steaming coffee into two large mugs. I dunked sugar and half & half into our mugs and handed one to Becky.

"Drink up," I ordered.

She took a few rapid sips and her color improved.

I was beating eggs in a bowl, adding in paprika. I dunked some thick Texas bread into the egg mixture and pulled out a container of salsa from the fridge. I had made it the previous evening.

Soon, I set two loaded plates on the kitchen island and urged Becky to eat.

"So he came to Sylvie's. So what?" I finally voiced the unspoken question.

"Did you see the pie, Meera?" Becky whispered.

I raised my eyebrows.

"That pie came from the diner. I know, because he ordered extra. That's why I remember him. They had a huge dinner, ordered pie a la mode, and then he ordered half a pie to take home with him. For the road, he said."

"We don't know what happened, Becky," I consoled her.

"I know, but I have this feeling …"

"Hey, when do you want to talk about the Thanksgiving menu?" I tried to distract her.

Becky's feeling turned out to be much more than that.

Chapter 2

I showered and got ready for work. The day passed quickly. The student body was busy with final projects and assignments. The library was packed with kids trying to cram a semester's worth of knowledge, watch class videos, and discuss coursework with their class mates.

I drove to Sylvie's, eager to hear if there was any more news about the man. A spanking new building slightly opposite Sylvie's caught my eye. The yellow paint almost seemed like an eye sore to me. To most other people in the town, it was fresh and cheerful. A large neon sign with 'Nancy's' in cursive hung in front of it. It was pink when lit up. A smaller sign proclaiming 'the fancy diner' hung below it, in case anyone had a doubt about the purpose of the building.

I shook my head and pulled up in front of Sylvie's. Swan Creek may be a small town, but we are loyal to our own. I didn't see any newcomer making it big with a diner, especially not in that spot.

Sylvie welcomed me with her signature hug as I breezed through the door. Her husband Jon called out to me from the kitchen and waved a spatula at me.

"Gumbo almost done," he called.

Sylvie and Jon Davis are as much a part of my family as Motee Ba or my Dad. They were the village that raised us motherless kids. Becky came out, trying to hide a frown.

"Meera, child, how are you?" Sylvie asked lovingly, trying to hide the concern in her voice. "Becky told me about earlier."

Jon came out and placed two plates of gumbo on a table. He motioned to Becky to take a break. I collapsed in a red vinyl booth and stirred my spoon through the gumbo, mixing a little rice in it. I looked out and Nancy's sat smack dab in the line of my vision.

"I suppose we have to get used to it," I groaned.

"They're a business, Meera," Sylvie reasoned. "Just like us. Can't stop anyone from earning an honest buck."

"I would like to see them do that," Becky hissed, swallowing a big spoonful of the fiery gumbo.

"None of our regulars are going there any time soon, Sylvie," I said loyally.

Honestly, I wasn't too sure.

The grapevine had been buzzing with all kinds of tidbits. Some said they had snow white table cloths on each table. Others said they had fresh flowers. French food was talked about, and artisan bread. We were all a bit nervous about the impact it would have on Sylvie's but no one wanted to voice their fears.

The small TV set over the counter was on and the news had come on. I saw a view of our local lake and some police tape.

"Turn that up, please," I urged Sylvie.

We listened agog as the announcer talked about the man who had been found on the bench by the lake.

"Police are looking into the cause of death of young Jordan Harris," the news anchor said.

"The 27 year old was in Swan Creek to celebrate his engagement with a Pioneer Poly student. Police have been tight lipped but our reporter couldn't help but notice the pie crumbs that littered the park bench where he was found. We all know there's only one place in Swan Creek that people go to for their pie fix. Does the pie figure in the cause of death of young Harris? Stay tuned for our updates…"

Sylvie turned the TV down, looking worried. The unspoken question was topmost in our minds.

"Becky says he was here yesterday," I spoke up. "Do you remember him too?"

Sylvie nodded.

"Jordan's been coming here for years. They made a cute couple. I gave them the best table. He was with that blue eyed blonde girl that comes around here often."

"Jessica," Becky supplied.

"Yes, her!" Sylvie nodded. "The one that talks a lot. Always has a word for Jon or me."

The Davises saw a wide variety of people at the diner. Some were barely civil to them, just tossing money their way for a meal. Some were polite but distant. Very few people actually took the time to show genuine interest in the people there.

Sylvie turned to Becky.

"Are you sure it was our pie? Couldn't it have been something else from the super market maybe?"

Becky's gaze said it all.

"I wrapped it myself, I remember. And I saw our logo on it. Tell her, Meera."

I backed Becky up.

"There's no doubt, Sylvie. I saw it too. But I don't see what the problem is."

"You know them cops," Jon said, coming out of the kitchen. "They tend to pick at the most obvious. What if they say our pie killed that boy?"

"Oh Jon, why would anyone say that?" I laughed.

The other three faces remained serious.

"We'll know soon enough," I muttered.

Becky tipped her head out of the window. There were lights inside Nancy's and a battered old wagon had drawn up. A couple of women got out. One of them was older, wearing a navy polka dot dress that stopped just above her knees. Her chin length bob was slightly retro. She was wearing sturdy shoes and stockings. The other woman looked thirtyish and frumpy next to the older one. They turned around and looked at Sylvie's, and caught us standing together, staring at them.

Sylvie waved and smiled, motioning them to come meet us. Five minutes later, the two women were inside Sylvie's.

"Hello, I'm Nancy," the older woman said, offering her hand. "Nancy Robinson. And this is my girl Nellie."

We shook hands all around and Sylvie offered them coffee and pie.

"Thank you for your kindness, but we have a lot to do before tomorrow," Nancy declined politely.

"Tomorrow's our opening day," Nellie supplied.

"All the best to you," Sylvie said sincerely.

"Thanks a lot, dear," Nancy Robinson gushed. "I hope you're not worried about business?"

Sylvie just smiled and Jon grunted from inside.

"There's not much common between us, really. We serve a different clientele. The slightly posh one, you know."

I was working up to say something really nasty to the woman. I wasn't getting good vibes from her.

"My Nellie's gone to culinary school," Nancy went on. "She's a trained professional."

"Oh?" Sylvie said kindly. "We're looking forward to sampling your menu then."

Nancy took our leave and turned around. Nellie leaned forward and whispered in Sylvie's ear.

"Was that your pie they found on that park bench?"

Nancy shushed her daughter.

"What did I tell you Nellie? We don't want to smear anyone's name. The police haven't released any details yet."

The duo waved at us and walked out.

"What the …" I fumed the moment the door closed. "What were they trying to say anyway?"

Sylvie was trembling and Becky's cheeks had turned red.

"This is what I'm afraid of, child," Sylvie explained. "We saw enough of this earlier when that Miller boy hounded you about that missing girl."

"Let's hope he's a bit smarter now, Sylvie." I tried to calm everyone down.

"Imagine the nerve of that woman," Becky finally spit out. "She's already starting to spread nastiness. I bet that's exactly what their marketing plan is – smearing our name."

"Girls, girls," Sylvie called out, "don't get aggravated for no reason. How about that dinner prep?"

The diner got busy with the dinner rush and I fried batches of my special fried chicken. Becky finally calmed down as she assembled yet another Blue Plate Special with chicken kabobs on a skewer. It was a curry inspired recipe I had come up with and it had become very popular at the diner.

"When's Tony coming back?" Becky asked.

"Later tonight," I told her as I squirted some creamy yogurt and mint sauce over the kabobs.

Tony Sinclair is the third point that props up the triangle of our friendship. I had a big crush on Tony in high school, but being the jock he was, he deviated to the cheerleader types. Then we went off to college and did our thing. Our lives hadn't quite turned out as planned, and now we were both back home. Tony was mourning his ex and we had decided to be just friends for now.

After a couple of hours, I was beat. I said my goodbyes and drove home, hoping Tony would get home soon. The day had been a bit drab without him.

Motee Ba, literally 'Big Ma', was at the stove making dinner.

Motee Ba just crossed 70. Together with Pappa, my 83 year old grandpa, she is the backbone of our family. My grandparents raised my brother Jeet and I after our mother went away several years ago. I don't know what I would do without her.

"How was your day, Meera?" she asked. "Dinner in thirty minutes."

I showered and trudged into the kitchen, looking for something to munch on.

Motee Ba pointed to a platter of *samosas* on the table.

"I made these earlier for Jeet and his friends. Just a few left for you."

I grabbed the tiny *samosa* dumpling and savored the flaky pastry cover. The potatoes and peas filling was mildly spiced and I gobbled a couple rapidly.

"Did you watch the news?" I asked my grandmother.

She nodded, looking worried.

"I don't know what this means for Sylvie and Jon."

"Relax, will you?" I burst out. "I said the same thing to Sylvie. Why make trouble where there isn't any?"

"It's early yet," Motee Ba refused to back out.

The clock struck nine and Motee Ba gave me the signal. I struck the dinner gong, letting everyone know it was time for dinner. My grandparents lived in British East Africa for several years and they have some habits that are a remnant of the Raj. The dinner gong is just one of them.

My brother Jeet tumbled in and dragged out a chair noisily.

"I'm starving!" he exclaimed and made a face when I mimicked his words as he said them.

At 19, he is always starving.

A tap tap sound came closer and my grandpa hobbled in, trying to walk fast with his cane. He slumped into a chair and looked around.

"Andy!" Pappa roared, calling out to his son, my father.

My dad is always last to the table, engrossed as he is in his books and papers.

"Why don't you get started?" Motee Ba motioned to Jeet, lifting the lid off a lentil stew and stir fried green beans.

Dinner commenced noisily, and my father finally joined the milieu. We leaned back one by one, sated after a simple Gujarati dinner.

"I hear you had quite a day today," Dad looked at me.

Motee Ba had brought him up to speed, apparently.

The enormity of my experience hadn't really sunk in yet. I shrugged.

"No tomfoolery this time, girl," Pappa boomed, tapping his cane. "I'm warning you."

"Pappa," I protested. "What do you mean?"

"You know what, Meera," my Dad said calmly.

"I had no choice," I protested, referring to the time earlier in the semester when I'd had to defend myself.

"Sylvie may be in trouble," Motee Ba told everyone. "We don't know for sure yet, but you all know how harmful rumors can be."

Dad gave Motee Ba a questioning glance. I told him about the pie crumbs found at the scene.

"I think you're jumping ahead, both of you," Dad said, picking up his plate and putting it in the sink.

Jeet started rinsing the plates and loading the dishwasher.

"Say someone tries to implicate Sylvie," Motee Ba mused. "We won't just look the other way, will we?"

Pappa was silent, and Dad walked out, back to his study. I answered the question they didn't want to.

"Of course we won't, Motee Ba."

Chapter 3

I woke early the next morning and chomped through a bowl of cereal, eager to get to work. Becky hadn't turned up for our morning run and I was glad. I turned into Tony's gas station, hoping to meet him.

I leaned against the heavy glass door, and sniffed at the familiar scent of Zest soap in the air. Tony grinned at me from behind the counter, looking fresh out of the shower, his wet hair curling around his ear.

"Hey Meera!" he called out.

"Have you heard?" I asked, unable to hold back any more.

He looked up as he rang up my large mug of the special holiday blend. His eyes were full of concern.

"That must've been quite a shock!"

I had dreamed about the dead guy. I was finally beginning to get creeped out as the shock wore off.

"I actually talked to him, you know," I exclaimed. "I said, 'wasup', and I was waiting for an answer."

Tony came out from behind the counter and wrapped his arms around me. I let myself be hugged properly.

"Nice day you chose to be out of town."

We walked out to my car and stood side by side, leaning against it. I sipped the hot coffee, trying to draw some much needed energy from it.

"How are Jon and Sylvie taking it?" Tony asked.

"They're worried. What if …"

"Try to relax, Meera. We don't know enough to worry."

"But we know Stan," I told Tony.

"Let's hope he's a bit smarter now," Tony sighed.

The day passed in a blur and I was rushed off my feet. I was putting in extra hours to make up for the Thanksgiving break.

I was bone tired by the time I drove up to Sylvie's. There was a lot of activity at Nancy's. Colorful red and white balloons fluttered in the evening breeze. White fairy lights were strung across the building. The parking lot was packed and some more cars lined the curb.

I parked my car in Sylvie's lot and stood looking at what was happening. Becky came out of the diner.

"They had a big to do this afternoon. It's their opening day."

"Looks festive," I commented and went inside with Becky.

The kitchen was prepped for the dinner rush. A few pies were cooling on the counter. A half cut pecan pie lay under a glass dome.

"You girls hungry?" Sylvie asked as Becky came out with two trays.

"Grilled cheese with three slices, just the way you like it."

She placed the two trays loaded with a sandwich and bowls of tomato soup. We made quick work of the food.

"When are we talking about the Thanksgiving menus?" I asked, looking up at Sylvie and Becky.

"How 'bout tomorrow?" Sylvie asked. "You look done in today, child."

I nodded and went in as a large group of locals entered. Earlier this summer, Becky and I had convinced Jon and Sylvie to modernize their menu a bit. The diner was now becoming well known for the veggie burgers and *pakoras*, my Indian spiced fried chicken and gourmet sandwiches.

"Black bean burgers today?" I asked Becky, referring to the daily specials and she nodded.

I shaped the patties and placed them gently on the grill. I placed slices of pepperjack cheese on top of each. We served them with a chipotle sour cream and sliced avocadoes with seasoned fries. It wasn't for the faint of heart. But we love our chili over here in the South, and the burger was becoming popular once people got over the idea of going meatless.

An hour passed in a blur. Then there was a buzz outside. I looked at Becky in alarm and we rushed out. My heart sank as I spied the now familiar flashing lights of a cop car in the parking lot.

The door opened and Stan Miller walked in, flanked by two more policemen. Becky and I stood on either side of Sylvie, ready to support her if necessary.

"Jon Davis?" Stan asked.

"You know who I am, young man," Jon snorted. "Get on with it."

"We are investigating the death of Jordan Harris. You need to come with us."

My eyes widened as I put my hands on my hips.

"Wait a minute, Stan," I spit out. "What do you mean, go with you? Why?"

"I'm just doing my job, Meera," Stan looked at me reproachfully. "I need to take their statements."

"Then why didn't you just call and ask them to come over? Why all this drama?"

Stan turned red.

"We wanted to catch them before they fled."

"And where are they going to flee?" I asked gently. "Stan, these people have been living in Swan Creek since before you and I were born. This diner is their livelihood. They're not going anywhere. Why would you think so, anyway?"

"Well, there's some talk of a tainted pie …" Stan began.

"Do you have proof?" I demanded.

"It's too early for any of that, Meera," Stan admitted.

Sylvie had come out and was calmly listening to our exchange.

"We'll come over right now and give your statement. But we are coming there on our own."

Stan nodded and stepped outside reluctantly.

I called Motee Ba and Tony and brought them up to speed. Becky was asked to keep the diner going.

I was about to usher Jon and Sylvie into my car when Tony's pickup screeched to a stop. He gently helped the couple into the back seat of his cab. I rode shotgun and we headed to the local police station.

I don't know how but Motee Ba had managed to beat us there.

Stan ushered Jon and Sylvie into an empty room. He held up his hand as I was about to follow.

"Just them at this time," he warned.

I paced the lobby with Tony. Motee Ba sat still in a hard plastic chair, her back ramrod straight. I admired her tight control.

"Sit down, Meera," she ordered after I had paced the short space for the hundredth time.

After what seemed like hours but was barely forty minutes, the door opened and Sylvie and Jon came out, ushered by Stan.

"Thanks for this," Stan told them.

"We have nothing to hide," Jon said simply.

Without a word, we filed out and headed back to the diner. Becky rushed out when she saw us, and sighed in relief as she saw Sylvie get out of the car.

"How about something to drink?" she asked, and I nodded.

We soon had a hot drink in front of us. Sylvie recounted what had happened.

"That boy just stopped breathing. They think it could be some kind of reaction to what he ate."

"You mean poison?" I burst out.

Jon shrugged.

"They are not actually saying anything, because they don't know for sure themselves."

"Is it the food, or isn't it?" Motee Ba asked impatiently.

She was beginning to lose her cool.

"They just don't know," Sylvie said in a tired voice. "But they do know the boy ate dinner here. Many people saw him. And we are not denying that."

"Wait a minute, though," I interrupted as I thought of something.

"Didn't that girl eat the same thing? And hundreds of people who came to the diner that day."

Jon nodded along.

"That's what I told them. But then they found that pie. Looks like it's the last thing he ate."

"Someone called in a tip about tainted pie," Sylvie sobbed. "Imagine, my pie causing harm to someone."

"But that's a load of crap," Becky burst out. "Who would do that? And if there was something wrong with the pie, why aren't more people turning up sick?"

"Maybe they fell sick and just haven't told us yet?" Tony ventured and Becky and I both smacked him on the head.

"We're talking something more serious than a headache," Motee Ba reasoned. "I don't see anyone in this town doing this kind of thing. Calling in to the police, making mad allegations? Why, that's just plain devious. Who would do that?"

My eyes met Becky's and we both pointed out of the window. Dance music blared out of speakers mounted outside. Nancy's was lit up like a Christmas tree. Nancy Walker had hinted at a tainted pie.

"They would!" I pointed a finger out of the window.

No one said anything for a minute.

Then I narrated what had happened the earlier day when the mother-daughter duo had come in to say Hi

"That's just bad karma," Motee Ba said bitterly. "I wouldn't start a new venture by lying about the competition."

Tony stood up and walked up to the counter. He cut a wedge of pecan pie and slid it onto a plate. He came back to the table and forked a piece into his mouth.

"That's what I think of tainted pie," he said.

Jon slapped him on the back, and Sylvie pinched his cheek.

"We sell the most amount of pies around this time, what with Thanksgiving and all,"

Sylvie said. "I've got advanced orders for dozens of them pies."

"I checked the order book earlier today," Becky confirmed. "Most people will be coming to pick up their order the day before Thanksgiving. The ones who are traveling will get theirs a day or two early. And then the late orders are willing to pick up their pie as late as Thursday afternoon, just before dinner."

"That's less than a week to fill all those orders, Sylvie," Motee Ba reminded her. "I will be pitching in as usual. Let's forget all this nonsense and draw up a plan for how to cook all these pies."

Sylvie smiled.

"We plan to be open for the holiday this year. Many of our regulars have requested a Thanksgiving meal. It's going to be reservations only. We'll serve at 2 PM and close at 4. That still gives us time for our own dinner."

Tony's parents were hosting all of us for Thanksgiving this year and I was looking forward to it.

"Stan seemed slightly more reasonable today, didn't he?" I admitted grudgingly.

"But he does get carried away. Why did he have to come here with all those lights flashing?" Motee Ba complained.

We said our goodbyes as Jon and Sylvie closed up for the day. I followed Motee Ba's car as we slowly drove home.

"Things don't look good, Meera," Motee Ba said quietly as she brushed my hair later that night, tying it into two plaits.

This was a nightly ritual when I was growing up, and Motee Ba still does it any time she or I are disturbed. It's our way of letting off steam.

"Sylvie and Jon have always stood by us." I was serious as I thought of what lay ahead. "I'm going to do my best to see them through this."

Chapter 4

The next few days were busy. Becky insisted we stick to our plans and still go on that morning run.

"Think of all the extra calories we're going to consume for Thanksgiving," she warned. "You won't fit into your swimwear in the spring. And we just have to do something different this year for Spring Break. You promised!"

"That's in March!" I cried. "Why do I have to work on it now?"

Becky relented only about one thing. Instead of Willow Springs Lake Park, we went to the track at Pioneer Poly. I just couldn't bear the thought of running through that park again, wondering what lay around the corner.

The extra hours at work were hell on my feet. I was glad my sneakers went with my usual garb of jeans and long sleeved tees. In the evening, I helped Sylvie with shopping and prepping for all her pie orders and worked on a couple of new recipes for the big Thanksgiving dinner.

"Try this," I said, sticking a sauce laden spatula in front of Becky. "This is my second batch."

Becky licked the spoon and frowned for a second. Then her face broke out in a smile as she fanned her tongue.

"That's awesome. Sweet at first but then the warmth of the spices seeps through. What is it?"

"Just my spiced cranberry relish. Do you think it's good enough for the day?"

"People are gonna love it," Becky enthused. "It's sweet, tart and spicy. Different!"

I grinned with pleasure, and turned as the phone rang.

Sylvie beat me to it. She spoke for a couple of minutes and then hung up. She picked up the order book lying on the counter and wrote something in it. Mostly, she just struck out a few lines.

"Sylvie?" I raised my eyebrows, trying to stay calm.

She shook her head, looking beat.

"More cancellations. At this rate, we won't be needing too many pies this year."

"What about our regulars?" I asked. "Jon's and Pappa's friends and the ladies in your Bingo group?"

"They haven't called yet, but they will."

I tried to console Sylvie. There had been no official statement yet about the cause of death in our local crime, but the jungle patrol was in full swing. People were calling in to cancel their pie orders. A few pies wouldn't make a difference to the diner business, but it was the loss of reputation that worried Jon and Sylvie.

Tony turned up at the library the next day. We have a standing lunch date at least 2-3 times a week.

"Where do you want to eat?" he asked.

"Let's just go to the food court. The sooner I get back, the sooner I can get out of here."

We walked to the food court and I got my usual chicken sandwich. Tony had a double cheeseburger. We both got fries. I was working out, after all.

In between bites of the crispy chicken and greasy fries, I brought Tony up to speed.

"What can we do to help?" he asked, cutting to the chase.

A group of women sat down at a table next to us. They were vaguely familiar. Swan Creek is a small town. I know the handful of locals, and people I went to school with. And then there are people who work on campus. I remembered these women from the bursar's office.

"My Tommy's raising a stink," one plump woman complained to the other, dousing her salad in a creamy dressing.

"Why?" the other woman asked, shoveling a big bite of salad in her mouth.

All three women were in their fifties, wearing plain skirts and blouses, with a string of pearls at their throat and gray hair at the temples. They were slightly overweight, and all three were eating salads drenched in some creamy dressing.

"He says my pie crust is not flaky enough. And it never gets cooked. His Mama doesn't like it."

"Aren't you getting your usual order?" the third woman asked.

The other two looked at her as if she was from another planet.

"Don't be a fool, Ada! Don't you know?"

Ada continued to be clueless.

"Know what?"

An urgent whispering ensued and Ada sat back, her eyes gleaming. She was slightly out of breath.

"I had no idea," she swore.

"I cancelled our order last night. And you should do it too."

"But do we know for sure?" Ada dared to contradict them.

"Who cares?" the first woman pounced. "Are you willing to risk your life for the sake of that pie?"

Ada shook her head.

"There's got to be some truth in it," the second woman said. "No smoke without fire."

I tapped my foot in anguish as I ploughed through my sandwich, listening to this crap. Tony kept a firm hold on my hand, keeping me from getting up and giving them a piece of my mind.

"Nothing you say's going to change their minds," he stated.

Tony's ears had turned red, a sure sign he was angry. He just had a better control over his actions than I did.

"What I don't get is, where is this coming from?" I fumed.

"I saw the news last night. They were showing that segment again. They mentioned that some pie was found on the bench."

"So what? Who told them it came from Sylvie's?"

Tony shrugged.

"Chances are it did! Everyone in Swan Creek knows Sylvie's."

"I think it's those two women – Nancy and Nellie. They're the ones behind this."

"Calm down, Meera. You don't know that. And you're doing the same thing, accusing them of something without proof."

I was getting tired of the whole thing.

We walked back to the library and Tony waved goodbye. Later that day, I dragged myself to the Camry and pulled in at Sylvie's, an hour past my usual time. It was after 6 PM, and normally, I would've had to park at the back. The parking lot at Sylvie's was almost deserted. Cars lined the opposite end of the street.

I pushed the door open with a heavy heart and my eyes met Sylvie's as she stood staunchly behind the counter. A berry pie was cooling on the counter.

"How are you, dear?" Sylvie tried to be upbeat.

Becky came out of the kitchen.

"Is there some event at Pioneer tonight? Our dinner crowd hasn't come in yet."

I shook my head. The order book lay open on a table, and several rows in it were scratched out.

"The phone's been ringing off the hook," Sylvie told me just as it trilled again.

"Sylvie's Diner," Becky answered.

Her face changed and became mutinous.

"Any reason?" she asked. "Change of plans? Well, you better finalize your plans next time before making reservations. We'll be charging a fine for cancellations."

She slammed the phone down. Without a single word, she grabbed the pen on the counter and scratched through another row in the order book. She almost tore through the paper.

A lone tear appeared in Sylvie's eye.

"Calm down, child. It's just a rough patch. All a part of life."

"How many people coming for dinner now?" I asked.

Sylvie looked at the book.

"Seven."

"Less work for us," I tried to joke.

"I think I'm going to cancel the dinner. Make it easier on the remaining people."

Sylvie was thoughtful. Jon had come out, untying his apron. He hung it on a hook and placed an arm around Sylvie.

"That seems best for now, Cherie. We'll do it next year."

I thought of the elaborate menu we had come up with, the recipes we had tested.

"Meera tried out all them recipes," Sylvie groaned.

"Don't worry about me," I told her. "I can make some of my cranberry relish at Aunt Reema's."

I stopped at Tony's on the way home, hoping he was still working. He came out when he saw me pull up.

"What's up, Meera. Any news?"

I poured out everything in a rush and paced the parking lot. Tony pulled me closer and we sat on the hood of my car, oblivious to the icy wind blowing in.

"How about a dinner date?" he asked.

"Are you out of your mind?" I rolled my eyes.

Tony sometimes makes these lame attempts at humor to diffuse a stressful situation.

"I hear there's this fancy new place in town. Why don't we check it out?"

I stared at Tony, thinking he had completely lost it. Then I connected the dots.

"Would this place be called Nancy's?" I asked, putting on an impish smile.

"It might," he grinned.

"Thank you, kind sir! I would love to accept your kind invitation."

I fluttered my eyelids and fanned myself and we burst out laughing. I went home in a better mood. Dinner was almost served and Motee Ba had sounded the gong.

"I'm sorry I haven't been much help around here," I apologized to her. "It's all these extra hours at work. Next week should be better."

"At least I get to eat my wife's cooking," Pappa said happily as he came in.

"Live it up, Pappa. It's back to my one pot meals next week."

Motee Ba and I shared a smile as Pappa muttered something.

The next day flew by and I drove home to get dressed for my date. I had told Sylvie I had some work related crisis. We didn't want to tell anyone about our plans. At least not until they yielded something concrete.

I put on a frock in honor of the date. It was a burnt orange silk with simple lines. I pulled on brown boots and borrowed a pair of Motee Ba's garnet earrings. I spritzed on some Shalimar perfume and I was ready.

I heard a car pull up and I ran to the door.

"Let him come in," Motee Ba twinkled. "Make him wait a few minutes."

"It's not a real date, Motee Ba!" I burst out.

"You are sharing a meal with a handsome young man. Someone you like. Whatever your reason for going out, it's a date."

I kissed my granny and we shared a smile. The doorbell rang. Tony had chosen to enter by the front door, so maybe there was something to this dating business.

"For you, Meera," my brother Jeet yelled, pitching his voice louder than the blaring TV.

I went out with my granny.

Tony hugged and kissed her.

"Hello Granny. Don't I look good?"

He twirled and made a big show of it. Motee Ba pinched his cheek.

"Mom told me to ring the doorbell," Tony whispered in Motee Ba's ear.

Tony was wearing khakis and a snow white shirt. His sports coat made him look grown up and handsome.

"Shall we?" he asked me, extending an arm.

I held on to his arm tightly and we waved goodbye to the company assembled in the living room. Pappa tapped his cane, annoyed at the interruption. Dad was closeted in his study, as usual.

The November sky was already dark, even though it was barely 6 PM. Orange and purple streaks hugged the horizon and the clear skies promised a starry night.

We were both quiet as Tony merged onto the highway. He had brought his mother's sedan for the occasion. It was easier to get into than the pickup. This kind of thoughtfulness is typical of Tony. Plus the car made me feel special.

It took all of five minutes to reach Nancy's, and before I could pick out a CD I wanted to listen to, Tony was trying to squeeze into a parking space in the crowded parking lot.

He rushed out to open the door for me. I beamed at him and took his hand as he helped me out. We wouldn't have to pretend much to look like a couple on a date.

"There's a 30 minute wait," the hostess, a young chit who looked barely sixteen informed us saucily.

"I have a reservation. Sinclair."

Tony smiled at the girl and she blushed.

"Right this way, Sir," she almost bowed, ushering us in.

I didn't have to wonder why Nancy's was the fancy diner.

Chapter 5

Round tables filled the cavernous space and booths lined the tall glass windows. Unlike the vinyl booths at Sylvie's, these were made of real leather. The tables were of mixed sizes, some cozy enough for two. Snowy white tablecloths sparkled, and a votive candle in small hurricane glasses graced each table. A small bud vase held a fresh rose.

"This is beautiful," I exclaimed.

I believe in giving credit where it is due. Someone had done a great decorating job for Nancy's. Not to mention the amount of money they must have sunk in it. It all seemed a bit much for our small town.

The hostess ushered us to a table in the center of the room. It was set for two, but it was spacious. A server turned up and took our drink orders.

They had wine, another feather in their crown.

The dinner special was Coq Au Vin, some kind of fancy French style chicken. Tony ordered steak with herbed butter.

"Boy, they really are fancy," Tony noted.

We gobbled our salads and took our time over the entrees. I was looking out for a glimpse of Nancy or Nellie.

My eyes strayed to an elderly woman who sat alone in a booth. She was reading a book and eating soup. She had her back to me but something about her seemed familiar. Maybe someone from campus, I thought.

Nellie came out, dressed in a chef's jacket.

"Welcome to Nancy's, the fancy diner," she said. "I hope y'all are enjoying your food?"

We nodded and complimented her. I waited for a sign of recognition but Nellie moved on to another table.

Our server returned with the dessert menu, right when we were finishing our entrees.

"How about some pie?" Tony asked. "Some apple pie a la mode sounds just the thing after that steak."

"We don't serve pies," the server said.

"Not a single one?" I asked incredulously.

He shook his head.

"But why?"

"We just don't. There was an incident recently in this town. It was pie related."

He hesitated as he said 'incident'.

"Are you talking about Jordan Harris?" I questioned. "There is no definite proof that any pie was involved."

"How can you get away without serving pie, anyway?" Tony asked.

We live in pie country. We want our chicken fried steak and our barbecued ribs, but they mean nothing without pie. Apple, berry, pecan, banana cream, lemon meringue – we want them all.

The server began to look worried.

"I have a six layer chocolate cake, and a caramel swirl cheesecake. Or carrot cake."

"Why no pie?" Tony persisted.

The server leaned forward.

"Look, it's company policy. We will not be serving pie, and if anyone asks for it, we are supposed to tell them about the pie related incident."

"So you just want to turn people off pie?" I demanded.

"Just doing my job," the server shrugged.

"Let's just get dessert across the street," Tony said loudly. "At Sylvie's."

"Are you sure you want to do that?" a woman at an adjoining table hissed.

"Of course I'm sure," Tony said confidently.

The woman was shaking her head, widening her eyes at her companion. A man who sat with her spoke up.

"I wouldn't take that kind of a risk, son. Not with such a pretty young lady by my side."

He leered at me and the woman rapped him on the knuckles.

Tony asked for the check. He motioned me to stay quiet. I was boiling inside but we had got what we came for. Now we knew why people were calling in to cancel orders and reservations.

The older woman in the booth paid up before us and walked by. I felt something familiar but couldn't place it.

We walked out and got in the car. Tony crossed the road and parked in Sylvie's empty parking lot.

"You look pretty, child," Sylvie smiled as we entered. "And so do you." She smiled at Tony.

Becky came out and her eyes popped out of her head.

"Were you two on a date?"

Tony looked embarrassed.

"Sort of," I admitted. "More a covert mission."

"We don't get them fancy words, Meera," Jon teased. "Spit it out clearly."

I gave them a quick account of where we'd had dinner. And then I told them about the dessert menu at Nancy's.

"See, I was right!" Becky exclaimed. "Those two witches …"

"Becky," Sylvie warned. "We'll not be talking bad stuff about our neighbors."

"She's right though, isn't she?" I argued.

Sylvie seemed shocked. She sat down in a booth and Jon collapsed next to her.

"All these years we ran the business," Jon began. "We never pointed a finger at other restaurants."

"It's not just them, though," Tony summed up. "The locals are talking too."

"Yeah!" Becky pressed on. "So there's some really bad rumors going around. And we know who's spreading them. Now what?"

"It won't last, will it?" Sylvie's voice was hopeful. "People know us, right? They'll be back in a few days or weeks."

"But how long can we afford to take a hit, honey?" Jon asked. "All our Thanksgiving orders have been cancelled. We need to do something now!"

"We need help. Yes Sir!" Sylvie nodded. "If it was just a few less pie orders, it wasn't a big deal. But we've had almost no business for over a week. We can't stay afloat much longer if this continues."

They looked at each other, and then they looked at me.

"Will you help us, Meera?"

"Anything for you, Sylvie. But I'm not sure what I can do."

"We saw how you helped find that missing girl. And you already found out who's spreading nasty tales about my pie. Can you prove the pie had nothing to do with that poor boy's death?"

I looked at Tony and Becky, my staunch helpers.

"What do you say, guys?"

"We're with you!" Becky got excited and brandished her spatula, ready for battle.

"So you want me to find out who killed that man on the bench?" I spelled it out clearly, in case I had been mistaken.

Everyone in the room nodded.

"I can try."

I was amazed at the faith these people have in me.

Jon and Sylvie were all smiles.

"We knew we could count on you," Sylvie said, slipping behind the counter.

"Where do we start?" I asked Becky.

"How about that girl who was here with the guy? The girl friend?"

"I'm not sure I remember her," I told Becky.

"You will, once you see her. She comes around here often enough. Let's make a list of anything we can think of and we can talk about it tomorrow. I have to close up now."

I nodded as I stifled a yawn.

Tony drove me home.

"I had a good time," I said shyly. "Maybe we should do this again."

"Sure, anytime," Tony smiled, ruffling my hair, kissing me on the cheek.

He walked me to the kitchen door. Motee Ba was sipping herbal tea, waiting for us. We gave her the lowdown on what had happened. She bristled with anger when she heard about what Nancy Robinson was up to.

"You did good, kids!" she patted Tony on the back.

"What's Dad going to feel about this?" I asked.

Both Pappa and Dad had been against my trying to find Jyothi, the missing girl, earlier this year. But I had taken a stand and they had relented. At that time, my own neck was on the line. I wondered how they would feel about me taking on some amateur sleuthing for someone else. I knew they were worried about my safety. They thought it was too dangerous. Then Sylvie's kind face flashed in front of me. I tightened my resolve.

"He'll be against it," Motee Ba voiced my thoughts. "He will advise Jon to hire a lawyer."

"I have your back, Meera," Tony reassured me. "But aren't you losing sight of one thing? What about the rumors? Shouldn't someone confront that woman about this? I mean, she's causing harm without reason. It's defamation. It's against the law!"

Tony went to law school for a couple of semesters. He knows this stuff.

"Talking about it will only draw more attention. I think it's best to ignore those rumors. And deny them if anyone talks about it to us."

Motee Ba looked mutinous.

"Sylvie and I can talk to that woman. We'll put her out of business."

We talked about Thanksgiving dinner at Tony's for a while and then he bid us goodnight.

"You're taking a big step, Meera," Motee Ba said as she brushed my hair later that night. "I'm proud of you."

Chapter 6

I got out of bed with a sense of purpose the next morning. I rushed through my shower and entered the kitchen in a hurry. Motee Ba was standing over a skillet, flipping *theplas*. These unleavened flatbreads are like tortillas and they are a staple in our family.

I placed two *theplas* on a plate, slathered them with *chundo*, a type of mango chutney, and tore off a piece. I fanned my mouth as I tried to swallow the hot piece of bread. A car honked outside and someone rapped loudly on the door.

I had a sudden déjà vu moment, thinking about the time Stan Miller had come barging into our kitchen earlier in the summer. The door opened inwards and sure enough, Stan Miller sauntered in.

I stared at him like a deer caught in the headlights.

"Morning, Patels!" he called out cheerfully, and I sighed.

He came in peace, apparently.

"I have an update, Meera," he explained. "I thought it best to come report in person."

Motee Ba fixed a plate for Stan. She handed him a knife and fork and he made quick work of the thin, flaky theplas. Stan had grown up on the neighboring farm, and he had been in and out of our kitchen, just like Tony and Becky. He never misses a chance to enjoy anything Motee Ba cooks.

"Well?" I asked, gulping down some coffee, waiting for Stan to spill the beans.

Pappa came in just then, tapping his cane. He settled down in his usual chair and smacked his lips at the aroma in the kitchen. Dad and Jeet would soon be coming in.

"Don't mind them," I waved around me. "Go on."

"It's about the woman," Stan began.

A woman had been observed loitering around campus since summer. The police thought she was following me around.

Motee Ba switched off the stove and came and sat next to me, ignoring Pappa's frown.

"She's been spotted in town again. She's driving a different car this time."

I sucked in a breath.

"Is she following any of us again?"

"Not to our knowledge," Stan told me.

"What does she do all day?" I asked curiously.

"Nothing specific, I think. Drives around, walks around the campus, walks around in Wal-Mart, eats in restaurants … that's about it. Last I checked, none of that is a crime."

"Why are we worried about her then?" Motee Ba asked.

"She's a loose end," Stan explained. "A lot of things pointed to her last time, in Prue's case."

Stan reddened a bit when he mentioned Prudence, his ex. She had been found dead earlier in the summer. Her death had been linked to the disappearance of another student. I had been implicated in the case, and had been a suspect. Stan had sung a pretty different tune at the time.

"How can you be sure it's the same woman?" I asked.

"We're sort of sure. She matches the general description. Of course, we didn't have any photos then. We are going to try and get some this time. But like I said, she is not implicated in any crime. So we can't just tape her or follow her all the time."

"What do you want from me then?" I asked.

"I wanted to ask if you had noticed anyone following you again. Just keep an eye out and let us know immediately. We are prepared to take her in this time."

I promised Stan I would be circumspect.

"What about the guy on that park bench? Any more news about him?"

"I can't talk about that, Meera," Stan puffed up. "We're still working on it."

"Someone said his heart gave out," I volunteered.

"Well, that much is true," Stan admitted grudgingly. "But we don't know the cause yet. Could be caused by something he ate or drank. He was a healthy young man, you know."

"What about the pie they found on him? Do you think it had anything to do with it?"

Stan shook his head.

"Can't say. Hey, I love Sylvie's pies myself. I've been eating them for years. If the pie was tainted, it happened after the pie came out of that diner."

"I'm going to try and help Sylvie," I started, expecting Stan to strike me down.

"Be careful, Meera. You're smart. You helped us a lot in Prue's case. Personally, I will take any help I can get. This has us stumped."

He picked up his hat and stepped out of the door.

Pappa was tapping his cane impatiently.

"Hansa, where are my *theplas*? How long are you going to make me wait for them?"

He glared at me next.

"You stay out of trouble, girl! This family has had enough nonsense this year. You should be living with your husband, raising kids, not running around with this tomfoolery."

I escaped before Dad came in to add his two cents.

I met Tony and Becky at our favorite Thai restaurant for lunch. It was quieter than any place on campus.

"Have you made a list?" I asked, pulling out a piece of paper.

"We need to know where the guy was from," Becky plunged ahead. "All we know is he has a ranch or a farm somewhere down south. But exactly where? Who does he live with? Like, does he have a family?"

"I'll look that up," I promised, writing down the first item on my agenda.

"What about the girl friend?" Tony asked.

I punched him in the shoulder.

"Of course you would think about her!"

"Didn't you say her name was Jessica?" I asked Becky. "Got a last name?"

Becky didn't remember a last name. She thought the girl studied something related to food or chemistry. I added another item on my list. I could look up the current students in some of the departments.

"What about those nasty women?" Becky asked. "Why are they suddenly in Swan Creek? Where did they come from?"

"I want to know that too, Becky," I objected, "but how is that relevant to Jordan Harris?"

Becky's face fell.

"I'll write it down but let's keep it aside for now," I consoled her.

The waitress brought over our Red Curry and Pad Thai noodles. We gobbled the spicy food, sniffling and wiping the tears that rolled down our eyes. We washed it down with icy coconut water.

"That was great," Tony burped, finally pushing his plate away.

I told them about Stan's visit.

"So what is it you are supposed to do, Meera?" Becky asked.

I shrugged. "I never saw the woman. So I don't really believe in her."

I knew this would annoy Tony and he interrupted me as expected.

"That woman is real, Meera. I saw her follow us all the way to Wichita and back."

"Cool your jets, bubba!" I held up a hand. "Maybe you should be on the lookout for her, then," I said. "Since you're the only one who's at least had a glimpse of her."

"You can bet I will do that," Tony promised.

"I know there's no way there was anything wrong with the pie," I began. "But say we have to prove it. We should be prepared."

"What do you want to know?" Becky asked.

"Where does all the stuff for the pie come from?" I asked.

"It's all made in house," Becky said defensively. "The flour, butter, sugar is from our usual supplier. It's the same we use for making anything in the diner. The fruits are fresh from the market. The nuts are bought wholesale from our supplier."

"Was there anything different that day?" I asked.

Becky shook her head.

"You think I haven't gone over this in my mind? The pie we served was fresh, baked earlier that afternoon. Everything was as usual, using Sylvie's secret recipe. There was not a single ingredient that was different."

"What about any spice or any other flavoring?" I persisted. "You know, you like to experiment with the food."

"With the regular food, yes, but not the pies," Becky denied. "The pies are all Sylvie. I don't touch them at all. And I wouldn't dare to add anything to them."

Tony looked at me.

"Is that good or bad?"

"At this point, hard to say. One might say there's something toxic in Sylvie's kitchen."

I held up my hand, cutting off both Tony and Becky's protests.

"I'm just saying."

We gathered our stuff and Tony dropped me off.

I was manning the front desk at the library the rest of the afternoon. I tried some searches within the school network, in between answering students' queries and keeping an eye on the audio-video room.

A search in the student directory threw up thirty three Jessicas. Boy, sure looks like a popular name, I thought.

I decided to weed out the doctoral students first. There was one girl called Jessica in Architecture and another in Chemical Engineering. Becky had mentioned something about food or nutrition. I checked the list of master's students. There was one in Management, another in English, one in Teacher's Ed and one in Agriculture. None of these seemed right.

I decided to check out the Agriculture department. I called the general department line and asked about the girl. I was hoping someone would be ready to gossip.

"Hello," I spoke in a hushed voice.

"I'm calling for Jessica. She left a ring here for resizing. Her order is ready."

"We don't take messages for students," a voice drawled at the other end.

"Oh? But this is the number she gave us. I'm sure she must be eager to wear her engagement ring."

"Look! I can see you are calling from somewhere on campus. So quit yanking my chain, alright? The Jessica I know is nowhere near getting engaged."

Strike One! I had managed to eliminate one of the Jessicas. I was pretty sure the one studying management or English wouldn't be studying food or nutrition. And the undergraduates were too young to be getting engaged. Weren't they?

On a hunch, I walked over to the Chemistry department. I preferred to tackle this in person.

A couple of women were working at their computers outside a door labeled Director, Chemical Engineering. Another door to the right listed the Head of Department and a smaller door a few paces to the left was for the Assistant Director of Admissions. This is pretty much a common set up for every department at Pioneer. A cluster of desks seated a bunch of secretaries and coordinators. They were all busy tapping on their keyboards, staring at their computer screens. One girl looked up and smiled as I entered.

"May I help you?" she asked.

"Err, I'm looking for Jessica," I dived in.

The girl's smile froze. She leaned forward and whispered.

"She's not in. She's in deep shock. We are not supposed to give out information about her."

"I was hoping to pay my respects. We went to school together. Then we lost touch. I came as soon as I heard."

I crossed my fingers behind my back, hoping my lie would fly.

The girl grinned naughtily.

"Jessica's not from around here. She's from some place down south on the Texas border. And I know you. You work at that diner."

"Busted," I admitted, holding up my hand in a peace sign. "Look, I really do want to pay my respects."

"She's holed up at the Harris ranch," the girl said. "But don't tell anyone you heard it from me."

I thanked her and stopped at a vending machine. I treated myself to a giant cookie and a can of soda. All I had to do now was find out where the Harris family lived. I already knew they didn't live in Swan Creek.

A few dozen piles of books were waiting to be reshelved. I did that and hardly noticed when the clock crept past five. I stayed on to run another online search.

I loaded up a search engine program in my browser and looked for farms in Oklahoma. There were just too many. I entered the names for nearby counties one by one. Then I tried to find ranches. I typed in 'working ranch' to narrow down the search. I found one about sixty miles south east.

"It looks like a big thing," I told Becky and Tony at the diner later that evening.

The diner was deserted. Other than a couple of regulars, no one had come in for dinner. Sylvie and Jon were trying to be upbeat.

"How big?" Tony asked.

"Over five hundred acres. They have a big lake and cabins for rent. And they have horses."

Tony whistled.

"Who manages all that?"

"That's what we have to find out. Maybe we should just drive down there this weekend and talk to someone."

"I have a better idea," Tony winked. "Why don't we go there for the weekend? Just us kids though."

Becky's face fell.

"I have to work."

Sylvie was half listening to our conversation.

"Nothing much to do around here, kid. And you deserve a break anyway."

"I'll call and ask about reservations tomorrow."

My eyes gleamed in anticipation. Whether we found any information or not, a trip out of town sounded good to me.

Chapter 7

Jeet was thrilled when he heard about the impending trip. I told him to calm down.

"Hold your horses. I haven't called them yet."

I called and asked about their cabin rentals. They offered a cabin that had two bedrooms and slept four. I booked us in for the weekend. Next week was Thanksgiving but we would be back Sunday night.

We were packed and ready to leave Friday morning. I put in half a day at work and we finally set off. Dad had reluctantly let us have the LX.

"Isn't it too cold already?" he grunted.

"We're not going camping, Dad. The cabins are heated, with TV and stuff, in case it's too cold out."

I didn't tell him about the paddle boats or the kayaks, or the outdoor swimming pool. We planned to have a blast, without parental supervision.

Motee Ba had a knowing look in her eye. She knows us too well.

"Jeet's your responsibility," she warned. "Don't let things get out of hand."

I hugged her and laughed.

"Oh Motee Ba! Do I ever? We'll be good, don't worry."

I had been a geek growing up. So okay, I had been the snarky type, but I had never gotten myself or anyone else into big trouble.

"Don't you trust me, Granny?" Tony hugged her next. "I'll have them back safe and sound."

Pappa had come out to say goodbye and wave us off. He was tapping his cane, clearing his throat, glaring at everyone.

Dad had already gone in to his books and his study.

Motee Ba was the only one who knew about the real purpose of our trip. She urged me to be sensitive to the family.

The weather for the weekend was cold and clear. Highs in the 40s were expected and the nights in the 30s. That meant some frost in the mornings, and maybe some sleet. We wouldn't get the most bang for our buck, but maybe we could meet the family and ask them some questions. I thought of Sylvie's wan face the previous evening, and strengthened my resolve to get to the bottom of Jordan Harris's death.

The ranch website said they offered three meals a day with plenty of snacks. But we had still stocked up. Food is something I never kid about. We took local two lane roads so the going was slow. Jeet had his headphones on. Becky and Tony were bickering about some latest song. I was lost in thought and an hour flew by.

"Let's stop here for a bit," Tony nudged me and I snapped out of my reverie.

There was a country store looming up and I needed a break anyway.

We used the facilities, and Tony chatted up the guy at the counter. He came back and pointed somewhere in the distance.

"Just a couple of miles now. Turn left at the sign and we're on the road to the ranch."

We piled in and Tony slowly merged onto the road. I was letting him drive. Acres of open land surrounded us. A lot of it was still green. This place deserved a visit in the summer.

I spotted the wooden hand painted sign for the Triple H ranch. Tony turned onto an unpaved road. It was smooth and well maintained, and I hoped it wouldn't mess up the suspension.

A large iron arch hung over a wooden gate announcing the Triple H. A rearing horse was placed between the two words. The gate was wide open. They must be expecting us, I thought gladly. I always appreciate good service. Who doesn't?

Tony followed directions to a central building that was called The Lodge. There were hand painted signs at various turnoffs, showing the way to a lake, hiking trails, fishing spots and different cabins. Jeet had finally ditched his headphones and was looking around with interest.

Tony parked in front of The Lodge. A golf cart with the Triple H logo was parked in one spot. Other than that, the parking lot was empty.

We went in, looking for a front desk of sorts and came across a polished wooden counter. Keys hung on a board on the wall behind it, and a calendar had notes scribbled in. I nodded at Tony. We seemed to be in the right place.

"Hellooo," Jeet hollered, tapping an old fashioned bell.

There was no response. Jeet called out again, a bit louder this time. We heard some swearing. I noticed a small room to one side for the first time. It looked like a kind of office.

A tall, hefty man hobbled out, using a cane. Becky and I looked at each other involuntarily. He was handsome enough to make a girl swoon. His golden brown hair was cut very short. He sported a thin mustache and his blue eyes were as clear as a summer Oklahoma sky.

"We are closed!" he rasped.

I cleared my throat, but Tony beat me to it.

"We have a reservation for four. For the weekend. We are in Lake View Cottage."

The man hobbled closer and his face twisted in a sneer. Suddenly, he didn't look all that handsome.

"Didn't you hear me the first time? We are closed!"

"But we have a reservation," Becky piped up this time.

"And we got it yesterday," Tony added. "Why did you give out a reservation if you are closed?"

"Pammie!" The man roared loudly.

Loud enough for me to cover my ears with my hands.

"Damn fool woman," the man muttered, and hobbled back to his room.

We looked at each other and shrugged. I wasn't about to give up so easily. I pointed to a seating area at one side.

"Let's at least get comfortable. I'm sure someone else will turn up, other than Miss Sunshine."

I tipped my head toward the room and we giggled. Jeet and Tony grabbed a chair each and Becky and I huddled together on a sofa.

"Did you see any diner or fast food place on the way?" Jeet asked. "I'm hungry."

It was past 1 PM and we were all getting antsy. The Triple H ranch was turning out to be a Triple F, triple failure!

About ten minutes later, a door banged somewhere and we heard someone shuffle in our direction.

An older woman hurried in and went behind the desk. She glugged some water and tried to catch her breath.

She motioned me over.

"Hi! You must be Patel, party of four. Sorry but I had to step out for a few minutes. Ranch crisis, you know."

She nodded as if expecting us to understand. We nodded along.

She flipped the pages of a giant register, and asked us to fill in our details. Tony stepped forward to do the honors. Meanwhile, I gave her the once over.

The woman was in her mid thirties, dressed in a gingham dress with knee high boots. She had grayed prematurely, judging by the lines on her face. She wore a cowboy style hat. I wondered how much of her costume was for show, and whether it was really her style. She managed to look dowdy inspite of the bright red lipstick she was wearing.

"I'm Pamela Harris," she introduced herself.

A round of introductions followed as we returned the favor. She pulled a key off the board.

"Lunch is almost ready. Do y'all want to eat first or check out your cottage?"

We all wanted to eat first.

Must Love Murder

"The dining hall is around the bend. I can drive you there if you like."

We all opted for the ride. It was way past our lunch time and we were all starving. Doritos and sodas only go so far. Tony was itching to ask her about the reservation but I held him back. I wanted to get some food inside me first.

The dining room had a few round tables that seated four or six. Most of those had a 'Closed' sign over them. There was a long table that seated 10. Pamela pointed to the long table.

A young girl appeared miraculously and took our drink orders.

"We serve the same meal to everyone," Pamela explained, just as the girl came back with a tray loaded with plates. "You can let me know if you have any diet restrictions or any preferences."

Lunch was roast chicken with mashed potatoes and gravy. The girl placed bowls of steamed broccoli and corn and a big bowl of salad in the center. A tray of dinner rolls followed.

We tucked in. The food was bland but rich.

"The chicken's farm raised, of course," Pamela continued as she ate with us.

The girl brought in small bowls of ice cream. We finally leaned back. I felt my mood improve. I was ready to face anything now. If they said there was no booking, I would turn away without doing anyone much harm.

Tony coughed politely before he began.

"There was a man. He said you are closed today?"

Pamela's face darkened.

"Who said that? We took your reservation, didn't we?"

"Tall, blue eyes, walks with a cane," Becky explained.

Pamela's mouth twisted in a frown.

"Ignore him. Why don't I show you to your room, err, cottage?"

She drove us back to The Lodge. We piled into the LX and followed her as she led us to our cottage for the weekend.

The road twisted a couple of times through dense greenery. We came upon a clearing. The cottage was good sized, made with some kind of wood. It set the right rustic tone. But the cottage paled in comparison to the view. A large lake stretched before us, it's water shimmering like silver in the pale sun. A cold breeze blew over the lake, making me shiver. I zipped up my fleece jacket as I looked around. We were all speechless.

"Beautiful, isn't it?" Pamela said softly.

She sounded wistful.

"Oh, I'd give anything to live here!" Becky exclaimed. She turned around and beamed at Pamela, excited. "You live here all the time?"

Pamela smiled and nodded affirmatively.

"My Daddy owns this ranch. I grew up here. And I will probably die here."

She sobered for a second and then tried to hide it.

"Let's give you a tour of the cottage."

We followed her eagerly. Any thought of Jordan Harris or investigation was farthest from my mind.

The cottage had a wide wooden porch or verandah. A patio set offered enough seating for four. I spied a hammock tied to two trees in the back. It offered a pretty view of the lake.

Pamela opened the door with the key. We entered into a small foyer that led into a great room. Spacious chairs and sofas flanked a rustic coffee table. It had a base cut out of a tree and a glass top. The place was luxurious.

A small kitchenette and bar flanked a wall. There were two bedrooms, each with their own bath. Becky and I bagged the one with a King bed. The boys were happy with the other room with two full size beds.

Pamela showed us the coffee maker.

"The fridge is stocked with creamer. You can get more coffee sachets from the lodge if you want. Dinner's at six sharp at the same place."

She turned as if to leave.

"What kind of activities do you offer?" I asked.

Pamela pointed to a file folder lying on a counter top.

"That has all the details. There's not much to do now, compared to the summer. Most guests prefer to settle in the day they arrive."

We nodded.

"Isn't there a pool here?" Jeet wanted to know.

"There's an outdoor pool but it's not heated," Pamela apologized. "We do have a hot tub on the deck in The Lodge. You can use it any time until 9 PM."

"What about tomorrow?" I asked.

Pamela smiled.

"You have our Silver package. So you pretty much call the shots. You can go kayaking or take out the paddle boats. You can get a wagon ride or a horse ride. If you want to go on a hike, we can pack a lunch for you."

Boy, were we spoiled for choice.

"I suggest you go over this binder," she pointed to the printed material. "I'll see you at six."

She got into her golf cart and sped away.

We looked around and whooped in excitement. Our camping trip hadn't turned out well this summer. Then our foliage trip had been cancelled. It had been a while since we'd had some fun. I'd worked hard through the summer, and I had money to burn. I couldn't have spent it in any better place.

Jeet jumped on the bed in his room and began flinging off his clothes.

"Who's up for a swim in that lake?" he screamed.

"The water's at least fifty degrees, you idiot. You'll freeze to death."

"Come on, Meera! Stop being such an ass!" Jeet protested.

Tony began to sneak out.

"You better not be going toward that hammock!" I ran after him and we both dove at the same time.

Luckily we collapsed into it instead of on the ground, and the thick sturdy ropes took our weight.

Becky went and sat on a small dock that reached into the water, and began reading a book.

Jeet sulked, turning the TV on full volume.

Our weekend was on in full swing.

Chapter 8

We started getting antsy by four. I made coffee and we sat in front of the TV.

"Did you notice Pamela is a Harris?" I asked. "She must be related to the guy."

"No sign of Jessica yet," Becky pointed out the obvious. "Maybe we should go looking."

"Go where? There's like a gazillion acres in this place."

"We might see her at dinner," Tony said.

"Is she even here?" I moaned.

The whole weekend suddenly seemed silly to me. Was it just going to be a big waste of money?

"Let's say Hi to Motee Ba."

I held my hand out for Tony's cell phone. Jeet ferreted out some snacks from the LX. Motee Ba had insisted we take some munchies with us, just in case. They sure came in handy.

We cleaned up and I drove the LX to the dining hall, following the directions. There were plenty of them. Someone had planned this place with care.

Pamela welcomed us and showed us to the long table. A couple of women were sitting at one of the smaller tables near a window. An older man sat slumped at another table. He looked like a poster child for a rancher, with hair that had more salt than pepper, a thick mustache and a craggy, weather beaten face. He was on the wrong side of sixty.

He nodded at us but didn't crack a smile.

"That's my dad," Pamela swung her neck toward him. "He's a bit out of sorts."

"Come meet the new guests, Pa!" she called out.

The man struggled to his feet, although he looked fitter than us.

A round of introductions followed.

"You have a nice place here, Sir," Tony said politely.

We all nodded.

"Nice? You bet it is nice." He grumbled throatily. "My boy saw to that, didn't he?"

He glared at Pamela.

"And I'm not 'out of sorts' girl. I'm thinking about my son."

His eyes shone and he shuffled back to his seat.

I found myself at a loss for words. Becky mumbled an apology and we went back and sat at our table.

"Sorry about that," Pamela said brightly. She leaned toward us and said softly. "Pa's getting a bit senile. You guys relax. Your meal will be out shortly."

"Senile?" I hissed. "The man's just lost a child, and she's calling him senile?"

My tone had alerted the two women sitting in a corner. One of them looked at us with interest.

Tony warned me to be quiet.

Dinner was served, huge platters with chicken fried steak topped with country gravy. There were large baked potatoes loaded with plenty of sour cream, bacon, chives and orange cheddar. Another bowl overflowed with fried okra. The Triple H may be giving weird vibes, but they didn't stint on food.

A warm bread pudding with plenty of raisins followed.

The blue eyed hunk from afternoon hobbled in, leaning on his cane. His face turned red when he saw us.

He pulled Pamela roughly by the arm as she came out with a flask of coffee and dragged her back into what I presumed was the kitchen.

Angry words followed.

"I'm putting a stop to this right now. It's my ranch now."

"We worked hard on this, Jordan and I," Pamela squeaked defiantly. "Where were you all this time then?"

"This will be a serious ranch now," the guy's voice rose. "None of this frippery. No more feeding people with my food."

"Shut up, Cam, these are paying customers," Pamela hissed.

"Pammie! Cam!" the older man roared.

He leaped up and strode inside.

"Shut your traps, both of you. We got company, in case you haven't noticed. Your Ma raised you better than this."

Pamela came out and mutely poured coffee. None of us dared to say a word.

"I ain't dead yet, so I'll be making any decision regarding this ranch," the old man's voice filtered through. "Now you go get your beauty sleep cuz tomorrow morning, you're taking them folks on a ride of the ranch."

A window flew open and a cold breeze came in. I shivered at some familiar feeling. Pamela walked over and shut the window.

The two other women were walking out and soon we were scraping our chairs back, wishing Pamela good night.

"Breakfast at 7 AM," she reminded us. "Dress warmly for outdoors."

"Isn't this a working ranch?" Tony wondered. "Who works the ranch?"

Pamela laughed.

"Oh. There's plenty of ranch hands and other workers. They don't eat here. This is strictly for the resort guests. We have a bunkhouse for some of the ranch hands. There are smaller cottages for the ones with families. And we have an old fashioned chuck wagon. You'll get a taste of all that tomorrow."

"I thought ranchers had to, like, get up really early," Jeet spoke up.

"They do," Pamela smiled. "We're up at 4:30 and grub's on at 5. Everyone rides out after that."

I drove the car back to our cabin. It was pitch dark without the benefit of street lights, but it was only seven in the evening.

"What do we do now?" Jeet demanded.

"How about a movie?" I asked.

The usual fight for the right tape followed and we finally settled on a scary movie.

"That hot tub sounds good right now," Tony said after a while.

We put on our swimsuits under our clothes and drove back to the lodge. We still had about thirty minutes before the 9 PM deadline. I figured that'd be enough.

The hot tub turned out to be humungous, big enough for about ten people. Everything's bigger in Texas, as they say. Technically, we were fifty or so miles shy of the Lone Star State, but the Triple H seemed to have its heart south of the border. The hot tub was occupied, but I was already freezing in my swimsuit. We walked in and cried out at the almost boiling water.

I prayed it was the older gentleman rather than the hunk but it wasn't my lucky night. He turned and nodded at us. Then he leaned back with his arms around the edge of the pool and closed his eyes. Well, two could play the game.

I wasn't going to let a sulking sour puss spoil our fun. We yapped about stuff and played around till our skin wrinkled like a prune.

Back at the cabin, we hit our beds exhausted and were out within minutes.

A few moments later, Becky was shaking me awake.

"Meera, get up. It's time for our run."

I groaned and peered out of the window. It was dark outside.

"Let's run around the lake."

I sat up in bed, rubbing my eyes.

"Why have you turned so nasty all of a sudden?" I complained.

I dragged my feet, pulled on my sweats and did a half hearted run around the lake. Becky did three laps.

Showered and dressed, we were waiting outside the dining hall at 6:45. We were all wearing jeans, boots, sweaters and jackets, along with scarves and woolen caps. It was a cold day, and there was a forecast for flurries in the afternoon.

The ranch served a full country breakfast with bacon, cheesy eggs, biscuits, sausage gravy and fluffy buttermilk pancakes. There was steak for those that wanted it.

Pamela bustled in, looking harried. She handed me a couple of printouts.

"Here's your plan for the day," she pointed out.

"A tour of the working areas of the ranch. Coffee break. A hay wagon ride after that. Mid morning snack. Horse ride. Lunch …"

Pamela had come up with an exhausting plan for us. There didn't seem to be any time to talk to people and ask questions. I decided we would have to tag team these people, and somehow squeeze our questions in.

She walked us out just as a large truck drove up.

"You'll be riding in this. Save your fancy car."

Handsome Jerk was at the wheel. He scrambled out and smiled at us. We looked at each other. Something had changed overnight.

"Hello, I'm Cameron Harris," he introduced himself. "You can call me Cam."

We mumbled our hello, refusing to shake hands. He got the signal and withdrew his.

"I think we got off to a wrong start yesterday. It's my leg, you know. Makes me cranky."

We nodded, deciding to accept this excuse for now, although I didn't care for it much. Everyone piled into the truck and we were off.

Cam took a few turns and we came upon a hive of activity. A couple of big red barns lined the periphery. Wranglers were exercising some horses in a large corral at the center. A few other buildings were scattered around.

Cam pointed to a large whitewashed building with black shutters.

"That's the homestead. It's where we live. Pa, Pammie, Jordan and I, along with Norma, our housekeeper and cook."

"Who's Jordan?" I tried to sound disinterested.

"Err, my brother. He's not here anymore."

A couple of ranch workers tipped their hats when they saw us. We were shown the horses in their stalls. Cam pointed out the mess hall and ranch quarters, and then drove slowly through the ranch's acreage.

"This one's the easy trail," he pointed. "You can walk your horse on this in a while."

We came upon a bluff. Cam stopped the car and we got out.

"Best view on this land," he said simply.

I looked around, and wondered what it would be like to own such a vast tract of land. A couple of ponds glistened in the distance. A girl sat at the edge of a pond, throwing stones in the water. She was too far off to call out to.

Becky suddenly grabbed my hand and squeezed it dramatically. Her expression told me plenty.

"Let's see about getting you that wagon ride," Cam said and hobbled back to the car.

"Must be quite a task, maintaining all this," I began.

I had to make someone talk or the whole trip was a bust.

"Do you and Pamela do most of the work?" Tony tagged on. "Your Pa must be retired by now."

"Retired?" Cam laughed. "Anything but. No one really retires on a ranch. You work from the day you can walk until the day they bury you. It's nonstop work."

"You don't sound like you're fond of it," Becky egged.

"No. I'm not. That's why I went away. But looks like I may be destined to be a rancher after all."

"Where'd you go away?" I asked.

"I joined the Army after High School," Cam said proudly. "Sounded like the only way I could get out of shoveling manure for the rest of my life. Can't ask a man to not die for his country, you know?"

This was some twisted logic, but I guess he really hated the horses.

"I've been in the Middle East for the past few years. Then I got hit." He pointed to his leg. "My appraisal is coming up. They'll probably put me out to pasture."

"You've done your bit," Tony exclaimed. "You should be proud."

"Well, I'm barely thirty with my life stretching ahead. I don't know what I'm gonna do."

"Hey, Cowboy!" Becky snorted. "I bus tables and do dishes for a living. You are born with all this, and you're crying like a baby?"

She swung her arms around, turning in a wide circle, as if making her point.

"I know I'm luckier than most. But this was never meant to be mine."

We waited for him to continue.

"My brother Jordan, he put a lot into this ranch. This whole dude ranch thing was his idea. He wanted to do weddings, for God's sakes. And Pammie fanned the flames."

Cam was getting riled up. That was just what I wanted.

"What's wrong with the resort business? We're having a good time here."

"Too much work. And too much kissing ass. I'm not cut out for that."

"And your brother was?" I probed.

"Oh, Jordan was a ninny. He never raised his voice at anyone, never lost his temper. The ranch hands took advantage of him. So did that young chit he was going to marry. She found her meal ticket all right."

"You mean he was marrying a gold digger?" Becky asked. "Why do you rich people always think that? Maybe she was really in love."

"Has your brother gone somewhere, mister?" Jeet asked.

He could look like a cherub when he wanted to.

"Yes. Up there!" Cam pointed to the sky. "He's dead!"

We tried to act suitably surprised. We offered our apologies. And Cam drove us back for our hay wagon ride.

Chapter 9

The wagon ride was fun. It almost made me forget what we were there for. One of the wranglers gave us a brief spiel on how to handle the horses. Cam offered a ride on the gentlest mare.

"You can just ride in the corral. You don't even have to go on the walking trail. One of the men will hold the bridles and lead your horse around."

I was debating whether I wanted to risk life and limb to impress Cam. Tony and Jeet were jeering, calling me lame and some other not so nice names.

"Oh, oh!" Cam said under his breath.

We looked up to see Pamela striding toward us. She was walking fast, with a sense of purpose. Her cheeks were flaming and her mouth was set in a grim line.

"The dragon's breathing fire!" Cam warned.

Pamela pointed a finger at me, a few feet before she reached us.

"You. Meera Patel! I thought your name sounded familiar."

I acted innocent. I sensed we were about to be pushed out pretty soon.

"Hello Pamela! We're having a wonderful time." Becky gushed, trying to ease the tension.

"Yesterday, when you checked in, I was focused on getting you settled. I checked what you wrote in the book today."

"And what did they write, sister?" Cam smiled.

He had thawed a bit toward us.

"You're from Swan Creek."

She stared at us. Apparently, being from Swan Creek said it all.

"So?" Tony asked.

"Swan Creek!" Pamela said meaningfully, turning to Cameron.

He had a light bulb moment and his mouth tightened.

"And that's not all. I dug out an old newspaper. You're the one that found our Jordan."

Pamela sniffled and pointed her finger at Becky next.

"You and her! It's all in the article."

"Well, well, well …" Cam's voice had twisted in a familiar snarl.

"Thought you'd snoop some on the grieving family, eh? How much are you making out of this. A few hundred? A thousand?"

"Nobody's paying us, you idiot!" Becky burst out.

"I don't care," Pamela shrieked. "You are leaving. Now. Get your stuff and hand over your keys in the next 30 minutes."

"Wait …" I called out. "What about lunch?"

Neither of the Harris siblings gave us a ride so we walked back to The Lodge. I drove the LX to our cabin and we packed up.

"Do you think we can just not leave?" Jeet asked.

He got his answer. There was a loud knocking on the door and Pamela stood on the porch, her hands folded.

"I'll take your keys now," she thrust out her hand.

We piled into the LX and hightailed it out of the Triple H. It was 1:30 and we were starving. But none of us dared to stay behind. I had spotted the shotgun in Pamela's golf cart and no one wanted to argue with it.

"I'm starving!" Jeet complained as soon as we cleared the ranch property and merged onto the highway.

"We'll stop at the next available place," I promised.

All the activity had made us all hungry. We had healthy appetites on any day. The fresh air, the cold and the early start to the day made us all long for a hot meal.

Tony pointed to a sign for the country store we had stopped at earlier. It promised home style cooking. I pulled in and we were seated. The place was small but well kept. Wooden tables and chairs looked well worn but were gleaming with polish. Lemon polish by the scent of it.

An older woman came and asked us what we wanted.

"Will y'all have lunch, or just a snack?"

"Lunch," we choroused.

"We got through our roast," the woman apologized. "I can fix some chicken and dumplings for you."

We nodded and the woman went inside. She came back with a basket of cheddar biscuits and steaming split pea soup.

"This should get you started," she smiled.

The space was a bit drafty, without central heating. Luckily, our table was placed near a wood burning fireplace.

"What a waste!" Becky groaned. "Why couldn't that Pammie have read the register a day later?"

"I was actually enjoying myself," Tony admitted.

"We did learn something, though," I pointed out.

"Like what?" Tony and Becky asked.

"Well…we confirmed Jordan was indeed a rancher. An innovative one at that. He had many ideas and a lot to look forward to."

"He didn't poison his own pie, you mean," Jeet smirked as if pointing out the obvious.

"I don't think we ever considered suicide an option," I told him, "but you're right. We can eliminate it for sure."

"What else?" Tony asked.

"He must be well to do, with such a big ranch to his name."

"We don't know that he owned the ranch," Becky pointed out. "Just that he put in a lot of work there."

"Yeah, yeah!" I said irritably. "There were three siblings, at least three that we know of. Their father's around and seemed pretty active. Jordan built this resort from the ground up. Pamela wants the resort. Cam, for some reason, doesn't want it. We don't know what he wants to do with the land, but he doesn't like the horses."

"That's quite a bit of information, once you sum it up that way," Tony agreed.

Becky's eyes widened. "And Jessica! You remember that girl by the pond? I'm sure that was her. I wanted to tell you right then."

"How can you be so sure?" I asked.

"I've seen her many times, Meera," Becky stressed. "Trust me."

"So what's she doing on the ranch?" I mused.

"Maybe she just misses the dead guy," Jeet supplied.

We took a moment to think it over and sobered. Maybe Jessica felt closer to Jordan at the ranch.

The lady brought out our food then and we tucked in. The drive back home was quiet. Tony drove and I dozed on and off, along with Jeet.

"What are you doing back so early?" Pappa demanded as we knocked on the front door.

Motee Ba's car was missing and we figured she was out with her friends. Pappa had been taking his afternoon nap in front of the TV.

"We got bored and decided to get back," I told him.

Pappa tapped his cane, muttering to himself. I heard the words 'spoiled' and 'waste of money' but I decided to ignore him. We couldn't tell him the real reason we were back anyway.

Jeet locked himself in his room and we went into mine. Becky and I slid under the covers, trying to warm up and Tony sprawled on the chair in the corner.

"What do we do now?" I began.

"Did you find it odd that the ranch still took our reservation?" Tony asked.

I looked at him inquiringly.

"Well, it's barely a week since they lost their son. Shouldn't they be shut down? What are they doing, serving meals to people, entertaining them?"

Becky sat up straighter.

"And it wasn't just us. There were those women too. I could get it if our booking was old and they were honoring it. But we called two days ago, remember?"

"Some people prefer to stay busy," I said lamely. "Maybe that helps them deal with the grief."

"Grief?" Becky smirked. "That Pamela wasn't grieving at all. She called her father senile, remember?"

"What about that guy, huh?" Tony asked. "He was too flippant."

"Maybe they need the money. Some people don't turn away paying customers."

I tried to give them the benefit of doubt.

"A month after the fact, I can agree to all your arguments, Meera," Tony said seriously. "But not in a week."

"So do you think any of these could be involved?" I asked outright.

"My money's on that Pamela. Shriveled up old prune."

Becky had taken a dislike to the woman. That much was clear. Tony disagreed.

"I pick Cameron. He can probably use a gun, and very well. He seemed bitter."

"But Jordan was supposedly poisoned," I objected. "I don't see a soldier using that as a weapon."

"What about Jessica?" Becky reminded us. "Cameron called her a gold digger, remember?"

"What was she doing getting engaged anyway? Isn't she too young?" I mused.

"She's getting her doctorate. She's the same age as us, Meera. Maybe older. People do get married in college, you know."

There was a sudden silence as we all digested this.

Tony cleared his throat.

"It's OK!" he held up his palm. "It's bound to come up sometime or the other. You don't have to walk on eggshells around me."

Tony's marriage is a subject as painful as my mother. Probably more. These are the two things we avoid talking about at all costs.

I buried my head in my pillow. The maze was getting more twisted.

"Check this, Meera," Tony said. "We have a list of people who were closely related to Jordan Harris. There may be more but this is a beginning."

"Yeah," Becky pointed on her fingers. "Old man Harris, Pamela, Cameron and Jessica. And that Norma woman we never saw."

"Well, let's not forget the ranch hands either," I insisted. "Maybe one of them had a beef with Jordan. Maybe they argued over money, or had a falling out. There's too many people on that ranch."

"I agree," Tony said. "But let's concentrate on the people closest to him for now."

"We really need to talk to Jessica," I said.

"She may be at school tomorrow," Becky said hopefully. "Or maybe she won't be back until after the Thanksgiving break."

"I'll walk over there tomorrow and try to talk to her," I offered.

"I can fill Sylvie and Jon in on what happened," Becky added.

"Did you notice those two women?" I asked Tony.

"What women?" he spread his hands wide.

Tony hardly ever notices any girl above the age of 25.

"How old do you think Pamela must be?" Becky mused. "She looked old, didn't she?"

I shrugged.

"Old and bitter," Tony said. "I wonder if she's one of the H in Triple H. Or if there's another one."

"How do you mean?" I asked.

"Well, land generally passes to the son, or sons. It all depends on when the ranch was named."

"You're such a chauvinist," I complained.

"It is what it is," Tony said, rolling his eyes. "All I'm sayin' is, we don't know."

"Maybe Harris is her married name?" Becky speculated. "She could be a widow."

I shut my eyes and lined up all their faces in my mind. Pamela had the same sharp aquiline nose of the old man. Her blue eyes were a bit cloudy, but they were the same shade as Cam's.

"Nah!" I shook my head. "I think she's a Harris by birth."

Becky yawned and that set us all off. Tony and Becky left and I gave in to an afternoon nap.

I sat at the kitchen counter, sipping Chai with Motee Ba later that evening.

"Any progress?" she asked simply.

"Yes and no," I said. "We know more than we did before."

"That's always good," Motee Ba nodded sagely.

The phone rang and we suffered yet another setback. Sylvie was on the phone, sounding frantic. Motee Ba was trying to calm her down.

"They just sealed the diner," she told me after she hung up.

She was slightly out of breath, and a few beads of perspiration mottled her brow.

"What do you mean, sealed? Who can do that?"

"The Health Department," Motee Ba spat. "Or whatever they are called in Swan Creek."

"But why?" I cried out.

"Someone reported rats. So now they are going to search the place for rodents and for any toxins lying about."

"That's ridiculous!" I was in shock.

I knew how troubled Jon and Sylvie already were. This was going to be worse.

"You need to step up your efforts, Meera," Motee Ba pointed out the obvious.

Chapter 10

I spent most of Sunday sleeping and reading. That's pretty much all you can do after gorging on Motee Ba's mutton curry. It was the only bright spot in an otherwise dreary weekend. Motee Ba had invited Jon and Sylvie to come over, but they had opted out.

The campus was quiet, it being Thanksgiving week. Most locals head home. Others have flights out sometime in the week. The international students stay put, unless they receive an invite from some American they have befriended. Dead Week, that dreaded week before the exams was looming, and kids were huddled at tables all across the library. Last minute group study sessions, project reports and exams were being discussed.

I caught a break around 11 and walked over to the engineering building. I had done some digging around on the college network and found Jessica had office hours at this time. I located her office and knocked on the door. I half expected someone else to be subbing for her.

"Come in," a voice called out softly.

I entered and came face to face with a young girl. I had never met her before so there was no way to tell if this was indeed Jessica.

The girl was about my age. Her face was scrubbed clean, devoid of makeup. There were purple patches under her eyes, which were slightly swollen. Judging by the pile of Kleenex on her desk, she'd been indulging in a sob session.

"Are you Jessica?" I asked.

She nodded.

"You were at the ranch earlier, right?"

I was glad she got to the point. I had no idea how I was going to explain my presence in her office.

"Pamela's still fuming. Why were you there anyway?"

I sat down.

"We just wanted to meet you and offer our condolences."

"That's bull."

She was blunt even in her grief.

"It's like this. I work at Sylvie's, you know, the diner over on the highway?"

"I know the place," Jessica said simply.

"Sylvie and Jon are like family. My friend Becky works there full time. I just play around with recipes."

"What can I do for you?" Jessica asked with interest.

"People are talking. They are saying Sylvie's pie killed your boyfriend. They're losing business."

Jessica had a faraway look in her eyes. I wondered if she had tuned me out. I cleared my throat, hoping to get her attention.

"I'm listening," she said.

"I promised Sylvie I would help her."

"Are you some kind of detective?" she asked curiously.

"Not really," I blushed. "It's like this. Earlier this year, I was trying to find a missing girl. Just by chance, I also solved a murder."

Jessica sat up straighter.

"Are you the one who found Prudence Walker's killer?"

I nodded.

"Sort of."

"You must be good."

I shrugged. I didn't know what I was doing. I had stumbled upon the culprit last time while looking for a missing Indian girl. This time, I just wanted to clear Sylvie's name.

"I just want to help Sylvie. And we figure the only way to do that is find out what really killed Jordan. Or who did."

"You think the family's involved?" Jessica asked cannily.

"I don't know. I'm not saying they are. But talking to them seems like the first step."

A tear rolled down Jessica's face.

"He was a good man. My Jordan. He didn't deserve this."

I saw a window of opportunity.

"Would you be willing to help me?"

"Any way I can," Jessica said eagerly. "Ask me anything. I'll do my best to answer your questions. And I'll tell you everything there is to know about Jordan Harris."

"You realize I have to consider you a potential suspect too, right?" I asked. "It's just part of the process."

"Fire away. I have nothing to hide."

Jessica took a sip of water from a bottle on her desk. I pulled out a writing pad from my bag.

"So let's start with you," I began. "Tell me something about yourself. Where are you from? How long have you been in Swan Creek? Something of that sort."

"I'm from Texas," Jessica smiled. "Just over the Oklahoma border. My Daddy has a ranch there. A working cattle ranch with a couple of thousand acres. I always wanted to go to college. Swan Creek has great bio technology research. I am working on my doctoral thesis, hoping to finish by next year."

I nodded.

"So where'd you meet Jordan? In some ranching circles?"

Jessica looked surprised.

"Right here, in Swan Creek. He went to Pioneer."

"I didn't know Jordan was an alumnus!" I wondered how this tiny detail had never come up.

Jessica nodded.

"We met in freshman year. He finished his classes in three years. He commuted while doing his thesis. By that time, he had taken on a lot of responsibility over at the Triple H."

"Freshman year?" I was impressed. "That seems like a long time ago."

"About 7 years," Jessica said glumly. "We were both on a fast track. I stayed on to do my master's and doctoral work, of course. But we were still in touch."

"Becky said you were celebrating your engagement that day?"

Jessica looked wistful.

"He had already proposed. Down by the pond over at his ranch. It was so romantic. We just wanted to get away for a meal. Have a change of scene. He wanted to take me to some fancy restaurant in OKC, but I said Swan Creek was cool. I had to get back and put in a few hours at the lab that night."

"What happened after your dinner?"

"We went to Willow Springs, of course!"

I understood.

Willow Springs, our local lake, is one of the few attractions in our small town. It's a choice hangout spot for the college kids and for couples looking for a romantic setting.

"The moon was out, and it was too cold for the usual barbecues and parties. It was perfect!"

I waited for her to go on. Silence often spurs the other person to talk, rather than a direct question.

"We talked about our future. Jordan had big plans for the Triple H. Then I had to leave."

"Did you drive back on your own?" I couldn't imagine them going to a romantic date in two cars.

"I caught a ride," Jessica said. "Jordan wanted to sit there for a while. I had a meeting back at the lab at 8:30."

Talking about some dry research topic at 8:30 on a Sunday night? This is the kind of stuff that made me drop out of grad school. These people need to get a life.

"Did you talk to him again later?" I was getting close to the wire.

"I did. Jordan called me around 10. I was just coming out of my meeting. He said he had dozed off on the bench. But he was getting ready to go home."

"Did he, err, not stay with you?"

Jessica frowned.

"Very rarely. Jordan was very prim and proper. And he had an early start at the ranch every day. He preferred to drive home if the weather was good."

"You didn't insist he spend the night?"

I tried to imagine them. Say I had just been on a romantic date with the person I was going to spend my life with. Wouldn't I want to stay over?

"I was planning an allnighter. I have to submit a research paper for a conference. I am already behind schedule. I was going to slog all of last week and then we would have Thanksgiving Week to ourselves."

I was stumped. I thought hard about my next question.

"Did he like pie?"

Jessica's eyes filled up again.

"Yes! Especially the one at Sylvie's. He couldn't eat nuts, but he always went there for her berry pie. She always set some aside for him."

"Did he get along with his family?"

Jessica thought a bit.

"He looked up to the old man. The ranch was everything to him. It flourished under his management. He planted some crops. There were the horses and then the resort. He built that from the ground up."

"What about the siblings?"

"Pamela's a spinster. She's always lived with them. He was fine with that."

"She seemed quite efficient," I observed.

"The resort gave her new life. She loved talking to the guests, adding a woman's touch. She was totally on board with Jordan's plans for expanding the resort."

"What about that sour puss?" I crinkled my nose.

Jessica frowned.

"Cam? Now Cam's a surprise."

I looked at her inquiringly.

"He hated the ranch. Still hates it. He went away and joined the Army. Now he's back, facing a discharge."

"What did Jordan feel about the prodigal brother?"

"Nothing much to feel. He's family. It's his inheritance as much as Jordan's and Pam's."

"So Jordan was okay with Cam coming back to stay on the ranch?"

"I guess. I didn't want to interfere."

"And the old man?"

"Oh, Pa Harris? He's such a dear. He grew up on that land. He was very happy with the changes Jordan made. He as good as signed over everything to Jordan."

"I bet the other two weren't pleased?"

Jessica was quiet.

"You don't think Jordan died because of money, do you?"

"Hard to say anything at this point," I quipped. "I'm just trying to get as much information as possible."

"My Daddy's rich. Super rich." Jessica looked sad. "And I'm an only child. It will all come to me one day."

"And did Jordan know that?"

"I suppose," Jessica mused. "It was kinda obvious, although we never talked about it. Jordan was the proud sort. He wanted to make it on his own. The land wasn't his, of course. But everything else was."

"How was his state of mind last week. Was he happy, sad, troubled about something? Angry?"

"You don't think he harmed himself, do you?" Jessica demanded. "Jordan would never do that. He had big plans. We were planning our wedding for next summer, after my graduation."

"He must have been feeling something," I probed further.

Jessica was silent for a while. I rode it out.

"He was a bit worried about Cam," she finally admitted. "He didn't know what to expect from him."

"How do you mean?"

"Cam never hid the fact that he hated the ranch. One day he would talk about selling off the land. Then he would want to plant wheat on all the acres. Then he wanted to plant an organic farm."

"Did they fight over it?"

"Not in front of me," Jessica shook her head. "Cam was unpredictable. You never knew what fancy plan he might come up with next."

I had a lot to process. And I couldn't think of any more questions.

"That's all I can think of right now. But I may want to ask you more questions later."

Jessica wrote down a number on a Post-It note. She slid it over to me.

"This is my number and my email. Feel free to get in touch any time. I'll do anything to help you get to the bottom of this."

"Um, about that," I ventured. "Do you think you could get me back on the ranch? I would like to talk to the rest of the family."

"I'll see what I can do," Jessica promised.

I walked back to my desk and spent the rest of the day on my feet. I drove to the diner, knowing it was closed. There was a big fat seal across the entrance. A callous flyer informed whoever concerned that the property was closed for inspection.

Becky sat on a stoop, looking morose. She had been waiting for me.

"Where's Jon and Sylvie?" I asked.

"Haven't seen them today. I spoke to Jon on the phone. Sylvie's been crying her eyes out. They are afraid they might lose their license."

"I didn't realize it was that serious."

I was trying to figure out what was wrong.

"We work here every day, Becky. We know there's no rats in there. Or any rat poison. Maybe we shouldn't be worried."

"Reputation is everything in the food business," Becky lamented. "Even if the department clears the place, people will still remember it was shut down."

"We'll deal with that when the time comes," I sighed. "Let's go!"

Chapter 11

It was Wednesday afternoon and the campus was like a deserted town in an old Western movie. I drove straight home. Tony was busy running errands for his mom. We were all invited to Thanksgiving dinner at the Sinclairs'. We've split up holidays between us so everyone can enjoy. We do Labor Day and Diwali and Aunt Reema has us over for Thanksgiving. Her menu is always a mix of traditional Thanksgiving dishes with some of her Indian recipes.

I was making my cranberry relish. It was the only dish we were taking to the party. Sylvie was expected to bring a couple of pies, but I wasn't sure she would be up to it in her current frame of mind.

I had chosen to cook the cranberries in our guest house. This is like a spacious apartment right on our property, a few feet away from the main house. It's a great hang out spot for us when we're in a rowdy mood. I like to use the kitchen there for trying out new recipes. It's one of the few places where I can be alone and undisturbed.

I switched off the burner and lifted the pot containing the spicy berries onto a cold one. I was looking forward to a few hours of solitude.

I settled down on the deep leather couch that looked out onto the patio. I closed my eyes and took a few deep breaths, trying to clear my mind of all thought. I had put this off long enough, but it was high time I embarked on my personal project.

The last memory I have of my mother is walking back home from school, holding her hand, begging for cookies. On that fateful day, Swan Creek was struck by a freak tornado and it ripped off more than the roof of our house. My mother, Sarla Patel, was a casualty of this F-3 that wreaked havoc in our lives. She was never seen or heard of again, declared dead by the State after the required number of years.

Jeet and I were raised by Motee Ba and Pappa. Dad was more an absentee father, buried in his books and his research. Anything related to Mom has been taboo in our family. Until this summer. My search for a hapless Indian student had stirred the pot, riling us all up. I had finally dared to confront Dad and voice all my anguish related to my mother. I learned how hard they had worked to track her down. I was able to forgive my Dad a bit. But a new resolve had developed in my mind.

I vowed to try and find my Mom, dead or alive. Maybe I am being foolish. What do I know, after all? The trail was cold, seventeen years later. I was setting myself up for failure.

The first time I'd mentioned this, Tony had looked at me like I was crazy. Jeet, that stupid teen brother of mine, had been ready to burst into tears. That had only strengthened my resolve and told me one thing. I had to do this on my own.

I considered the type of investigations that had already been done. Right after the accident, police had checked the neighboring states for any casualties. Mom's photograph had probably been faxed over to surrounding police stations. I didn't know exactly what had been done. But there was a good chance some new information had surfaced in the last seventeen years.

I fired up the computer and tried to find some information online. I was trying to find out if there was some kind of database for unsolved cases. I wanted to check if Mom's name was still on there. If not, I wanted to put it there.

One of the first things anyone would need was a photograph. I imagined approaching people with a twenty year old photo. It just wouldn't fly. I needed to get a brief idea of what Mom would look like today.

I wrote my first task down. Find out what Mom would look like today. Image processing was one of my favorite subjects in college. I had played around with a lot of morphing software. Now I needed to write a program that would add age to a photo. It would take a few days but I could do it.

The hard part was getting in touch with the right authorities, asking them stuff. I wrote down the scenarios that had been already considered. Death! No body had ever turned up and this gave me hope.

Dad had told me about another scenario they had thought of. What if my mother did not want to be found? I decided to table it for the time being.

What if Mom had been hurt or injured, unable to speak or tell someone about herself? Maybe she had been held against her will? I forced myself to think about worst case situations, however dire they sounded. The alternative was my Mom didn't exist. Anything was better than that.

Contacting the authorities was going to be the next step. I needed to check if there was any active missing persons report about Mom. If not, I probably had to open one. I realized I couldn't do all this on the sly. I needed to discuss this with Dad and Motee Ba. It wasn't a conversation I was looking forward to.

Writing an aging program was something I could do without anyone's help. I got started on it right away.

Everyone woke up late on Thursday. I made pumpkin pancakes and served them with a special spiced syrup. I add ricotta to the batter and these pancakes are really heavy. So okay, we would stuff ourselves at Thanksgiving dinner but that would be much later around 3 or 4 PM. A hearty brunch was in order.

Cheesy scrambled eggs with jalapenos went great with the pancakes, topped with fresh salsa and sour cream.

I had come to a decision last night. I was going to level with Dad from the onset. I decided to confront him right after brunch.

Dad had disappeared into his study the minute he finished shoveling his breakfast. Half the time, I doubt if he even notices what he eats. I knocked on the study door, bracing myself for a tough talk.

"Come in, Meera!" he called out.

Dad can always tell who's at the door.

"That brunch was excellent," he complimented.

I smiled.

"How much trouble are you in?" he joked.

"I want to reopen Mom's case," I blurted out.

Dad's face turned a shade darker.

"How do you mean?"

"I want to look for her, Dad. I need this."

He was quiet for a minute.

"I thought you might get around to this some day."

"Look, Dad. I'm glad you told me about all your efforts. I have no doubt you did your best. The best that was possible at that time. But it's been, what, seventeen years. New information could have come to light."

"So you'll look for her now," Dad began. "And what? Look again 20 years later? Who knows how far technology will advance in the next 20 years?"

I thought that was unfair, but I stuck to my point.

"I need to do this now. Reopen the case. Talk to people."

"What do you want from me?" he asked, sounding old.

"Your blessing," I answered. "I don't want to hide anything from the family. And I need you to help me with any questions that might arise."

"Alright," Dad said. "I'm with you. But remember one thing, Meera. You'll have to face the truth, whatever it is."

I told myself I was ready for that. I went around his desk and hugged Dad.

"I'm writing a program that will show age progression," I told him.

His eyes gleamed.

"Why didn't I think of that?" he slapped his head.

"I need an old photo, or a few old photos to work with."

"By all means," Dad said cheerfully. "Use the scanner here. Scan them in."

I smiled. We were supposed to be intelligent. We could achieve a lot if we put our heads together.

Dad read my mind.

"You know what, Meera? Maybe fresh eyes on this is a good thing. And everyone might come up with something different. Something they missed at that time, either because they were too close to it, or because they were grieving. I think you should start by interviewing Pappa, Ba and me."

I was amazed. I had decided to broach this at some other time, but Dad had made it easy for me.

"And," he said, stooping down with a bunch of keys, "take this."

He unlocked a drawer and pulled out a binder that was at least 10 inches thick.

"This has all the information – reports we filed, reports sent in by the investigator I hired, missing people organizations we contacted, newspapers we put ads in. Review this first."

"Thanks Dad," I teared up. "This should be a good starting point."

"I suggest you still redo all that, since we want to start fresh. But this way you'll know what was tried last time and what wasn't."

I had gone in expecting a big argument. Instead, Dad had handed me a treasure trove of information.

"Today's Thanksgiving, isn't it?" Dad mused. "It's kind of fitting that you embark on this today."

Giving Dad one more big hug, I scrambled out. I decided to call a family meeting right then. I summoned Jeet to the living room. Motee Ba and Pappa were already there, watching the Thanksgiving Day Parade on TV.

"I have an announcement!" I plunged ahead.

I gave them the short version of what I proposed to do.

"Good luck, sweetie. I hope you succeed."

Motee Ba had teared up as expected. Jeet looked resigned.

"I'll pitch in if needed, Meera."

He had been barely two when we lost Mom. He didn't remember her at all.

Pappa tapped his cane, getting excited. I thought he would blow a fuse.

"Finally you're talking sense, girl," he sputtered. "I've been waiting for you to grow up and go look for your mother."

This was my second shock of the day.

"Why didn't you say something all this time, Pappa?" I burst out.

"Waiting for you to grow up, wasn't I?" he growled.

"Hush, Mr. Patel," Motee Ba warned, fearing an argument.

She held out her arms and I went into them, sitting on the edge of her chair. Jeet rolled his eyes, made a gagging sound and disappeared into his room.

We piled into the LX a few hours later, ready to go to Tony's for dinner. I pulled him aside as soon as Aunt Reema welcomed us into their beautiful home.

I gave Tony the lowdown, waiting for him to say something.

"I'm with you, Meera!" he said, kissing the top of my head. "I'll help in any way you want."

The doorbell rang and Sylvie and Jon came in. Sylvie was slightly out of breath, but she looked happy. I was amazed. Maybe she'd started on the wine a bit early.

"Sorry we're late," she said, handing over a couple of pies to Aunt Reema. "Last minute order for some pies."

My eyes met Tony's as we mulled over this surprising development. But the smells from the kitchen soon drew us in. After multiple servings of turkey and fixings, we went out to play football. Dad joined us for a while, then the grownups dozed in front of the TV.

Becky drove up and I filled her in again on the latest. We went in for pie and a game of Monopoly, enjoying the holiday.

Chapter 12

Dead Week arrived with its usual chaos. Kids were scrambling to send in their final projects and papers. There wasn't an inch of free space in the library. Every chair was taken and in some places, kids squatted on the carpeted floors, peering over notes and books.

I was feeling a bit nostalgic. We've all been there, haven't we? Moaning over why we wasted the entire semester partying or lazing around, promising ourselves the next time would be better. And the four years just flew by like that, at the snap of your fingers.

I dragged myself home, exhausted. I had a bit of a headache and all I wanted was some peace and quiet.

"Message for you," Motee Ba announced as soon as I entered through the kitchen. "Someone called Cam. Wants you to call him back."

"Cameron Harris?" I exclaimed. "That's the dead guy's brother. We met him at the ranch."

"Seems like a handsome brother, judging by the look on your face," Motee Ba said cagily.

I blushed.

I took the number Motee Ba offered and went into my room. I dialed the number, wondering why the sour puss was calling me.

"Hello?" A voice answered hesitantly.

I recognized Cam's voice. He sounded a bit uncertain.

"This is Meera. Meera Patel. I'm just returning your call."

"Oh, Hi!" his voice came on clear. "Yes, I did call and leave a message. How are you?"

We exchanged some pleasantries. All the time I was wondering what he wanted from me.

"Jessica mentioned you're looking into Jordan, err, Jordan's death," he said after a pause. "And that you wanted to talk to the family."

"That's right," I confirmed.

"Well, I don't know about Pa or Pammie, but I'm ready to meet with you and answer any questions you may have."

"That's great." I stopped lounging and sat up in bed. "Do you want me to come to the ranch?"

"Not necessary. I'm coming that way tomorrow. How about we meet for lunch. Or an early dinner?"

I didn't think I could get away from my desk, so I picked dinner. I suggested the Thai place and he agreed readily.

"How about 5:30 then?" I asked.

I didn't have a free moment all day the next day. Lunch was just a pre-packed salad I picked up from a campus store. I was starving by the time I entered the Thai place.

Cam was waiting, leaning on his cane. The hostess showed us to a table, greeting me with familiarity. I was on friendly ground.

There was an awkward moment as we both tried to make small talk. Then Cam shook his head and leaned closer.

"Ask anything you want. I have nothing to hide. And I want to find out what happened to my little brother."

"I'm not sure how much Jessica told you," I lead. "Sylvie and Jon are…"

Cam waved a hand as if trying to rush me.

"I know all that. No need to explain. Why don't we get on with the questions?"

I sensed the cranky sourpuss surfacing. He slumped suddenly and looked ashamed.

"Look, I'm sorry. I don't mean to be rude. It's this blasted leg, see. It starts hurting suddenly, and once that happens, I can't keep a thought straight in my head. That's why I want you to get to the point. We don't have much time."

I assured him I understood. Or did I?

"Are you older than Jordan?" I led with something simple.

Cam leaned back and a nostalgic look came over his face.

"Yes. He was the baby of the family. Pam's the oldest of course. I came by almost 10 years later. And then Jordan was born."

"You must've been close, being almost the same age."

Cam nodded.

"That we were. Didn't have much choice in playmates, did we? Growing up on the ranch? Not too many neighbors."

"Did you always dislike life at the ranch?" I asked.

"Was never too fond of it," Cam agreed readily. "I wanted to get out, see the world. I grabbed my chance soon as I graduated."

"And now you've come back."

I stated the obvious.

"At least for a while, yes. Although this whole thing with Jordan has put me in a tight spot."

"How so?" I asked.

"I came to recuperate at the ranch. Pa insisted. It's actually a bit inconvenient for me, driving over to the city all the time to get my check ups."

"So you weren't planning to stay?"

Cam shook his head.

"Didn't I say I was eager to get away? Why would I go back there? I had an apartment all picked out in Dallas. Got a couple of old Army buddies there who were going to set me up in a cushy job."

"So ranching was never your thing then?"

"No sireee, it wasn't," Cam repeated, slurping the Tom Kha soup the waitress had finally brought over.

"Jessica mentioned you wanted to start an organic farm on the ranch?"

Cam looked sheepish.

"Oh that? That was just a thought. I was having a bit of fun with Jordan."

"You mean you were purposely needling him?"

Cam shrugged.

"You like picking fights, don't you?" I didn't hide my acerbic tone.

"Hey, I was just hanging around. Nothing much to do at the ranch. Jordan and Jessica were right there, canoodling all the time, talking about their future, going on and on about their big plans. It was all a bit too much."

He made a gagging motion with his hands.

"You mean you were jealous."

"A bit," he agreed. "Mostly I was feeling sorry for myself. It's this leg, like I told you."

He pointed to his foot and pulled up his trouser leg. I got a glimpse of a prosthetic. I hadn't realized how serious his injury was earlier.

"Sometimes, the pain is so severe. I'll do anything to distract myself, keep myself from crying out."

"So you picked fights with your siblings."

Somehow, I wasn't feeling too sympathetic toward Cameron Harris. He was a lesson in how looks can be deceiving. Those baby blues of his had stopped having any effect on me.

"Do you ride?" I asked.

I was getting tired. I needed to fill time to think of some more questions.

"A couple of hours every day. I did grow up on a ranch, after all."

He smiled in what may be called an engaging manner.

"So the ranch is not all that bad, huh?"

"The place was beginning to grow on me, to be honest."

"Did you tell anyone about it?"

Cameron looked uncomfortable.

"They had this pretty life. All of them did. Pa had almost signed over the ranch to Jordan. He was getting married. Pammie was happy running that dude ranch business. They didn't really want me there."

"And now?" I asked softly.

"Now it's all up in the air. Pa's getting old. He was looking forward to taking it easy."

"So you might be able to convince him to turn the ranch into an organic farm. Or plant on all 500 acres."

"I see Jessica's been talking," he sneered.

The sourpuss was beginning to surface again.

"What changed your mind?" I asked. "About the ranch?"

"It's so peaceful," Cam's tone was wistful. "It began to grow on me. I'm a bit battle weary. I've seen too much evil to last one lifetime."

"I would think it would be perfect after the stressful life you've led."

Cam's eyes widened.

"I thought of that. It's actually great for soldiers who need an extended convalescence. We already have the infrastructure for that, with the cabins. We can build more."

I was a bit confused.

"So all your other business ideas – the organic farm, the wheat crop – they were just a fib?"

"I was trying to gauge their reaction. See if they were conducive to something I suggested. How they felt about me staying on."

"And all this time you actually wanted to turn the Triple H into a fancy spa for wounded soldiers."

"Not exactly, but in a nutshell, yes."

Cam's face had brightened, and he was staring into some future I wasn't privy to.

"Just think about what we have to offer – fresh air, farm grown fresh food, the lake, the ponds, and the horses! Think of all the therapy they can offer to trauma victims. And to folks who are disabled like me."

"Have you discussed this with anyone yet?" I asked.

Cam shook his head.

"It's too soon. The ranch isn't going anywhere."

Now that Jordan was dead, it certainly wasn't.

"Couldn't you have done both? Let Jordan operate the resort and the dude ranch, and reserved some of the space for the sick people?"

Cam shrugged.

"I guess."

I pushed aside my plate of Pad Thai noodles. I thought of all the Agatha Christie books I had read, and the cop shows Pappa continuously watched on TV.

Cam seemed to have a motive, if having the ranch to himself was one. Of course, Pamela was still around, and she probably had a share in the ranch. But maybe she would just fall in line with what her brother wanted.

Did Cam have an opportunity to harm Jordan?

"Where were you that Sunday, when Jessica and Jordan were celebrating their engagement?"

He gave me a devilish grin.

"Want to know if I did it? Why don't you just ask me outright?"

I squirmed. I guess my question had been obvious.

"I was in the city," he said. "I urged them to come with me, you know. I told Jordan he should take her to a nice steakhouse in the city. Not some old diner they could go to any time."

I opened my mouth to object. He beat me to it.

"Nothing wrong with the diner, but I'm sure it's not the place for a romantic date."

I tried to picture myself on a date. I had a sparkling diamond on my finger. I wanted to show it off. Where would I want to be? I would want flowers and candles, and table cloths. As much as I loved Sylvie's, it was too down home for such an occasion.

"I get that," I admitted. "Jessica said she had some meeting at Pioneer."

Cam rolled his eyes.

"Couldn't she have bowed out of it? How many times do you celebrate your engagement, huh?"

"So you went to the city," I steered Cam to the point. "Oklahoma City, right?"

"I had a doctor's appointment at 4. And then I had a session with my therapist. It was almost 8 PM by the time I started back. Had to grab dinner from a drive through."

Cam could have been in Swan Creek sometime around 10. Jordan was still around here at that time.

"I had no need to come into Swan Creek," he said, snapping me out of my thoughts. "Far as I knew, Jordan was already home and in his bed."

"But he wasn't," I stated the obvious. "Can you think of any reason why he may have stuck around?"

Cam looked uncomfortable.

"I don't know."

He was hiding something, but I didn't want to push him.

"When did you notice he wasn't around?"

"I don't think anyone did," he told me. "Pammie's the one who locks up at night, after dinner and stuff. I think a couple of cabins were rented out that week. Jordan gets up at 4 and has grub with all the ranch hands around 5. They would notice his absence. But most people knew about his big date. I guess they thought he overslept."

"So … no one missed him until the cops called?"

I tried to imagine Dad taking that kind of a call. Especially when he thought I was in my room sleeping.

"Must've been a shock," I said softly. "For everyone."

"Pa's the one most affected," Cam said quietly. "Although you wouldn't know it, looking at him."

"So, did he have any enemies?" I asked.

"Jordan was the sweetest guy you'd ever meet. He was kind to everyone. Never thought he'd come to a sticky end."

"What about Jessica? Did they get along well?"

"Have you been listening at all?" Cam frowned. "They just got engaged, didn't they? Why would they get hitched if they didn't get along?"

"I don't know. I'm just trying to cover all the bases."

"Shooting in the dark, hoping you'll hit some target?" Cam smirked.

I realized I was doing exactly that. Cam was rubbing his leg, getting antsy.

"You've been pretty helpful, Cam."

I thanked him and he agreed to get in touch if he thought of anything more. I watched him drive off and got into my Camry. I reached home 10 minutes later. I spotted Sylvie's car outside the guest house. I found her in the kitchen, rolling out pie dough.

The diner was out of commission and we still had plenty of leftovers from Thanksgiving. I wondered who she was cooking for.

"What's this?" I raised my eyebrows.

"We have a standing order for 10 pies every day," Sylvie beamed.

She pulled out two lattice pies from the oven and set them on the counter to cool. The cherry filling oozed out, filling the air with a heady, sweet aroma.

"Are you allowed to make these?" I asked, confused about the legalities.

"I can't use the diner kitchen. But I can cook if I want. And I can make a pie if I want to."

She sounded defiant.

"Someone from town?" I asked.

Sylvie hummed along with the radio, pouring some toasted pecans into a pie plate lined with crust. Either she didn't hear me or she didn't want to say.

I wondered about this sudden demand for Sylvie's pies in Swan Creek.

Chapter 13

The meeting with Cam left me with an uncomfortable feeling. There was something not quite right about him. Maybe it was some sixth sense, or just prejudice.

I checked out some image processing books from the library and read up on it in my spare time. I started working on my program. That was the easy part. Going through the thick binder Dad had given me was the tough one. Every time I opened the file, I got lost in some minute detail and found myself tearing up. This way, I would never make any progress. I thought of asking Tony for some help.

Finals Week started and the campus emptied a bit every day. I was on pancake duty for two nights. This is a tradition at Pioneer. The library, along with the alumni office, serves pancakes at midnight every day during the exams. Students line up for the food and a much needed break from their heavy duty studying. I suppose the sugar keeps them going until morning.

I had flipped my thousandth pancake and was ready to call it quits when I held up a plate for the next person in line. I found myself staring at Jessica.

"I'm gonna miss these pancakes when I graduate," she said wistfully. "They're tradition, you know."

I nodded.

Jessica took the plate from my hands and leaned forward to whisper softly.

"I talked to Pamela and Pa Harris. They will talk to you. You have to go to the ranch, though."

I blinked to let her know I understood. She was edged out by the next person in line.

Two days later, I was riding in Tony's truck, on the way to the Triple H. I had put in a lot of overtime and I was due half a day. We had decided to go and talk to Pamela and Mr. Harris.

"Did you talk to Stan lately?" Tony asked, cruising along at the speed limit of 50 miles per hour.

"Yeah. He came home yesterday."

"Do they have any more news about Jordan? Like his cause of death?"

"That's the curious thing."

I poured out what Stan Miller had told me the earlier day.

"So he died a natural death?" Tony asked incredulously. "Why are we going to interview his family, then?"

"They are not sure," I said uncertainly. "Stan said something about him being in shock, but there not being sufficient proof. They don't know what brought it on. And in the absence of anything definite, they just might call it an accident. Or something like that."

"And they say science has advanced!" Tony smirked.

"I guess some questions are tough to answer." I tried to be philosophical.

"So he wasn't poisoned then?"

I shook my head.

"Not by the usual means. If he was poisoned, it was something untraceable."

"Like some strange foreign virus, you mean?" Tony asked, bewildered.

"I'm as clueless as you are, Tony. But our goal is to prove it wasn't the pie. Or rather, it wasn't Sylvie's pie."

"Wasn't Sylvie's pie found on him?" Tony sounded frustrated.

"Yes, but maybe someone doctored it. Doused it with something when he wasn't looking?"

"Yeah. Yeah. When he went for a swim in that lake, I suppose."

I folded my arms and looked away. Tony could be really indelicate at times.

Some flurries started blowing and the sky darkened. I cranked up the heat in the truck. Tony drove through the arches of the Triple H and pulled up outside The Lodge. Pamela was meeting us there at 3. It was ten to.

I shivered as I rushed up the steps. Tony put his arm around me, but I gently pushed it away. I was still mad at him for the snarky comment.

Pamela Harris was standing behind the check-in desk when we entered. She ushered us to a seating area near the window. She seemed restless and I wondered if Cam had railroaded her into doing this.

"You know what the police are saying?" she burst out. "They're saying Jordan died naturally. They're just a bunch of lazy country bums."

I was surprised to see Pamela display so much emotion. Maybe she would be more forthcoming with some information.

"You don't think that's likely?" I asked, setting her off again.

"Have you looked at this place? Its over 500 acres. Jordan rode for hours every day, took care of the horses and the resort. He built all the cabins with his bare hands. He was strong as an ox, and bursting with good health."

I had to agree with most of what she said.

"How was he taking Cam's sudden arrival?"

She shrugged.

"He was going to come back some time. We all knew that."

"Did they get along, though?" I asked.

"Of course they did. They were brothers after all, weren't they?"

"I heard they fought a lot."

"What brothers don't fight? When they were small, they pushed each other in the pond. Now they argued."

"About what?"

"Didn't matter. Whatever Jordan said, Cam had to oppose it. He's always been that way. Loves playing the Devil's Advocate."

"Who, Jordan?"

"Cam! Jordan's the sweet one. Everyone loved him. They all clamored for his attention."

"By all, you mean the people who work for you?"

"Everyone!" Pam enthused. "The ranch hands, the guests who came here, Pa, the locals, the neighbors, they all wanted some attention from Jordan."

"Did he like that?" Tony asked.

Pam shrugged.

"He didn't notice it. He was Mr. Nice Guy. It was all in a day's work for him."

"Did he have any enemies?" I forged ahead.

"Everyone loved him," Pam said, tearing up. "Why would anyone want to harm him?"

I gave her a minute. She plucked off a couple of Kleenex from a side table and blew her nose.

"People never stopped loving him, even after he did."

She had a gleam in her eye. I guessed she had thought of something.

"What do you mean? Are you thinking about someone in particular?"

"His ex," Pam grimaced. "She was a wrong one."

"Were they high school sweethearts? Wasn't that a long time ago?"

I know what they say about a woman scorned. Jordan Harris had been around 27. He must have graduated high school almost eight years ago. Could someone hold a grudge for that long?

"Yes and no. They were in the same high school class and they dated briefly. But nothing happened then. This was more recent. Last year."

I was shocked.

"Err, are you sure? Jessica told me they'd been together since Freshman year of college. For 7-8 years."

Pam looked uncomfortable. I waited for her to speak.

"They did meet during Freshman year," she began. "They hit it off. They were very much in love and when Jordan graduated, he wanted to get married right away. Jessica wanted to wait until she got her doctorate."

That kind of sounded reasonable.

"Did they fight over it?"

"They had a falling out. Of sorts. Then Jordan ran into this girl from high school. She pursued him. Heavily."

"Wasn't he interested?"

"I think he was confused. He went along with it. They got engaged. She started planning the wedding."

"What happened to Jessica during this time?" Tony asked. "Did she meet Jordan?"

"Maybe once or twice," Pamela replied. "Jordan was very busy at the time. He built the resort from the ground up. He shook up the ranch. Made Pa reduce his hours a bit. He had no time to call his own."

"But he had time to date this girl?" I queried.

"She was here all the time!" Pamela exclaimed. "She lived a mile down the road, so she just walked here when it took her fancy. Or she rode over on her horse."

"Is she a rancher too?" I asked.

"Her! She hasn't done a day's work in her life. Her Pa owned the ranch next door, but he died a few years ago. They let the ranch go to seed after that."

"So Jordan was going to marry this other woman. How did he meet Jessica again?"

I was fascinated by this story. So were Jordan and Jessica destined to be together, or destined to be apart?

"He ran into her at a horse show in Texas," Pam said dreamily. "Her Pa's got a big spread south of the state border."

I nodded. I remembered Jessica telling me that.

"Jordan fell for her again. It was like they had never been apart."

I sucked in a breath. All this sounded a bit surreal.

"Did they hook up on the spot?" Tony asked suggestively, and I smacked him on his arm.

"They met a few times after that," Pamela said in a hushed voice. "He changed overnight. We could all see it, feel it. He had been dragging his feet as his wedding date drew closer, but he was a changed man once he met Jessica."

"Who did you like more – the ex lady or Jessica?" Tony asked eagerly.

"We just wanted him to be happy. Pa wasn't too happy about him going back on his word. But it was better than repenting at leisure."

"So he broke up with his ex?" I asked.

Pam nodded.

"It was ugly. One minute she was shouting and screaming at him, promising all kinds of vengeance. Then she was gone, like that. She moved away within a week. We never saw her again."

"What happened to her?" I tried to imagine this girl, dumped at the altar, all because of fate.

"Some say they put her in a special place, like a rehab type of thing. We never really knew."

"How did Jessica take it?" Tony wondered.

"I'm not sure what Jordan told her, but she never talked about it. She loved the Triple H. She fit in very well here. Pa took a shine to her, eventually."

I thought about how Jessica had conveniently lied to me about their relationship. She had neglected to mention they were apart for a few years.

"Jessica's very smart. She's working on some special foods that will fatten the cows. You know what that means for a rancher."

Pam sounded wistful. I suspected she had missed her chance at college.

"You're a lot older than the boys, aren't you?" I tipped my head toward the tiny office where we had run into Cam before. I wondered if he was sitting there, listening to us.

"I was a senior in high school when we lost our Ma," she said. "The boys were so young. They needed a guiding hand. Pa was up to his ears in ranch work. So, it all fell to me."

"I lost my mother when I was seven," I shared.

She squeezed my hand, and we shared a moment, tied together in our grief.

Pamela Harris had been more a mother than a sister to the boys. She had given up on college, and maybe a married life of her own. No wonder she looked older than her years.

"They were a joy growing up," Pam's eyes filled up again. "Who would've thought I wouldn't see him grow old."

Tony cleared his throat. I bet he was getting antsy, listening to all this emotional stuff.

"Were you on the ranch that Sunday?" I tried to disguise the question the best way I could. I wanted to know if she was anywhere near Swan Creek.

"Sundays are when my quilting group meets," Pam offered. "There's five or six of us from the county and one woman a bit more up north."

She named a place that was in between Swan Creek and the Triple H.

"So do you just sit and sew?" Tony feigned interest.

"We have tea and snacks and share patterns and stuff. Mostly we just talk."

"I loved the quilt in our room at the cabin," I praised her. "Did you make that yourself?"

Pamela's face lit up. "I did!" Then she thought back to the day without any more prompting.

"I was feeling queasy that day. I wasn't getting much done. I left around 6."

6 PM. Jordan and Jessica were still having dinner at that time.

"Did you come straight home? Cam said he was out that day too."

"He had a doctor's appointment," Pamela confirmed. "Sunday evenings belong to me. Once I get back to the ranch, it's back to the chores. They never end!"

"So … you went somewhere else?" I tried to be open.

"I drove around a bit," Pamela said glumly. "Truth be told, I was feeling sorry for myself. For no reason."

She looked apologetic.

"Sometimes I just want to tune all this out, you know. I mean, I love my life, don't get me wrong. And the resort has given me a new lease on it. But some days, you just want to give in to nostalgia."

"I understand," I tried to commiserate.

I suppose I could expect something like that when I reached her age.

She suddenly stood up.

"Where are my manners? How about some coffee?"

I welcomed a hot drink. I wanted to ask many more questions, but I sensed Pam had reached her limit for the day.

Chapter 14

I savored the delicious coffee Pamela served as Tony made small talk with her. I wondered if Cam would put in an appearance. I didn't know if I wanted him to.

"Are you ready to meet Pa?" Pamela asked after I finished my second cup of coffee.

I had devoured a muffin or two while I was at it. The large windows in the lodge provided a dreamy vista. Stark trees with some yellow or brown leaves clinging to them filled my line of vision. The flurries were still blowing, and they had dusted the ground with a fine white powder by now. I was drowsy but I shook it off. I wondered what Jordan's father would have to say about him.

Pam dropped us off at the main homestead. She begged off to check on the horses.

I knocked on the door and we entered as a gruff voice invited us in. Pa Harris seemed to have aged a bit in the last few days. He was ensconced in an old fashioned wooden rocking chair. He motioned us to a couch beside him. I sat and turned around to face him, craning my neck at the awkward angle.

"Pammie said you are trying to find out what happened to my boy," he rasped.

I gave him a short account of how Sylvie was implicated and how I was trying to clear her name.

"Fair enough. Whatever your reasons, I would be grateful if you find out who harmed my boy."

He gulped, trying to control some emotion.

"You can ask me anything you want. Don't be shy. I will try to answer as much as I can."

I instantly felt better. I was expecting some kind of resistance from the old man.

"Tell me about Jordan," I began.

"Jordan was a smart boy. He went to college, you know. He's the only one in our family who got a fancy college degree."

"Was it of any use on the ranch?" I asked.

What was the use of spending four years at school if you were going to muck stalls for the rest of your life?

"Of course it was. He always knew he would come back and work on the ranch. Even as a kid, he liked making plans for it. He got a degree in agriculture, and in business management."

"Is that where he got the idea of the resort?" I asked.

"The resort was his dream. He created a solid business plan, and built it all from the ground up."

"Pam told us," Tony supplied.

"Does Pamela like living here?" I switched the topic.

The old man frowned.

"What do you mean, little lady? This is her home, ain't it? The only one she's ever known. Now if she had gone and married and lived with her husband, that would be a different deal."

"I know she has to live here. But does she like it?" I pressed.

"I dunno," the old man looked bewildered. "What's that gotta do with my boy Jordan?"

I winced.

"Well, we heard your other boy Cam hates the ranch, so we wondered if Pam hated it too."

"Cam doesn't hate the ranch. He's happy to live here, isn't he? He just loves giving people a hard time."

"So, the Triple H, you named it after your three kids?" Tony leaned forward.

I was glad to have some time to think about my next question.

"These kids?" Pa Harris guffawed. "This ranch has been around for seventy odd years. My grandpa named it after his three sons. My uncles passed away in the wars."

He didn't specify which war, but there had been plenty in the time frame he mentioned.

"My Pa came into it, and he didn't change the name, even though I was an only child. Then when my kids came along, it all made sense again."

"No wonder Jordan wanted to hold on to it," I said.

"Far as I know, all my kids wanted to. If Pammie or Cam are talking about selling the ranch, that's news to me."

"We heard Cam wanted to turn it into an organic farm. Or plant all the acres."

"Pshaw!" the old man flung a hand in the air. "He can talk all he want."

"Were you going to sign the ranch over to Jordan?" I probed.

"I was thinking about it," the old man admitted. "Jordan worked his butt off the last few years. The ranch was bleeding money before that. He deserved it."

"What about your other kids?" I queried. "Didn't they look upon it as their inheritance?"

"I wanted them to work for it," he growled.

"I bet the other two weren't happy about it?"

He shrugged.

"Cam's got his army pension. Pammie – I was sure Jordan would take care of her. Both her brothers would."

"Is the ranch worth a lot?" Tony asked.

"The land must be worth something," the old man nodded. "But the only way to make a living off the ranch is to work it. And that's back breaking work from dawn to dusk. Jordan was doing that. And he was building up the dude ranch business."

"Your sons fought a lot, didn't they?" I questioned.

"Since the day they began to walk," Pa Harris smiled, a faraway look in his eyes. "You'll understand if you have any siblings."

Not a day goes by when Jeet and I don't come to blows. So I got what he was saying.

"Did they hate each other?" Tony asked.

"What kind of damn fool question is that?" the old man roared. "They were family, weren't they?"

I caught Tony's eye and shook my head, signaling him to drop that question.

"Did Jordan have any enemies?"

"And why would he?" the old man demanded. "He turned the ranch around, brought it into the black. He was putting food in the mouths of all the people who work here, and their families. He put a roof over their head."

You would think Jordan Harris was some kind of saint, listening to these people.

"Pam said everyone loved him," I prompted.

"Sure did. They would've done anything for him."

"Do you have any idea who might've wanted to harm him?" I asked.

"I don't. They would be facing the other end of my shotgun if I did."

I decided to ignore that, cringing at the thought of guns stashed somewhere in the old man's living room.

"What about the girl he was supposed to marry?"

"Oh, Jessica! She's a sweet kid. Comes from ranching stock, too."

The old man's face had lit up. He was obviously smitten by Jessica.

"Not her," I said gently. "The other girl Jordan was going to marry."

"Her?" the old man clammed up. "What can I say? I wasn't too happy when Jordan did that. A man's word has to mean something. But then I met Jessica."

"What if Jordan had married that girl? And then run into Jessica? Would he have divorced her to marry Jessica?"

"We'll never know that," the old man said sadly.

Jordan may have been God to these people, but he had definitely wronged this unknown woman in my book.

"You must be quite lonely here, all by yourself?" I went on. "You don't have many neighbors, do you?"

"It's the ranch life. We are used to it." Pa Harris smiled. "I go meet some old fellows at our local pub sometimes. We have a monthly poker game. It's not that bad."

"Were you here on the ranch when Jordan had his date with Jessica?" I wondered if he had somehow wandered into Swan creek too on the fateful day.

"I was right here!" Pa Harris said, and I heaved a sigh of relief.

I hadn't looked forward to treating him like a suspect.

"Must have been a quiet evening, what with Cam and Pamela also out somewhere."

"I was too busy doing Jordan's chores," Pa Harris said. "And then I turned in early, exhausted. Not as strong as I used to be."

He wouldn't have heard either Pamela or Cameron come back that night.

"So you didn't hear Pam or Cameron come in, I suppose?"

He thought a minute, and then shook his head.

"I got up around 11 to get some milk." He looked apologetic. "And some leftover cake. I have a sweet tooth."

I nodded. Raiding the fridge at midnight is something I'm very familiar with.

"I looked out the kitchen window and didn't see Pammie's car. So maybe she wasn't in yet. Although …"

He stopped, lost in thought.

"She never stays out that late. What was she doing, traipsing about at 11 PM?"

I didn't have an answer for that.

"What about Cam?" Tony nudged.

"I'm not sure about Cam. He parks at the front. He snores the house down. I remember thinking it was pretty quiet."

I was bursting with excitement. Where had Cam and Pamela been that night? I remembered what Pamela had said about Jordan's health.

"Would you say Jordan was in good health?"

"He was strong as an ox. That boy had measles when he was five and other than that, he's never been sick a single day in his life. Never had that flu, even."

I was stumped.

"Any other illnesses in the family? Anything that might cause a sudden death?"

Pa Harris reddened.

"I know what them fool police are saying about my boy. I'm ready to bet the Triple H my boy didn't die of natural causes. He was done in."

He rocked his chair faster as he got irritated. I was beginning to feel dizzy, looking at him. Plus I had a crick in my neck from talking to him at an awkward angle.

"I believe you, Mr. Harris," I tried to calm him down. "That's why I'm trying to find out more."

"So what happens to the ranch now? Is Cam going to build that farm of his?" Tony asked.

Pa Harris looked tired, all of a sudden.

"Don't know! Cam's a big talker but it's hard to say what he's really thinking. Pammie's dedicated, but she needs a guiding hand. She's a woman, after all."

I bristled at this slur to my gender. Tony placed a warning hand on my shoulder.

"Do you think they might have plotted against Jordan?" I asked slowly.

I was expecting some kind of explosive reaction from the old man. A tear rolled down his eye.

"They might have. But they didn't kill him. You write that down, and remember it, little lady. Pammie or Cam didn't harm my boy. Blood's thicker than water."

Tony and I made sympathetic comments. I wondered if I should leave Pa Harris alone in this disturbed state. Pamela solved the problem for me.

"The vet's here for his weekly visit, Pa," Pam called out from the doorway. "He wants to talk to you about that new foal."

The old man nodded and stood up. He shook hands with me and Tony.

"Come back anytime. Help me get justice for my boy."

"Don't worry, Mr. Harris," I said with a confidence that amazed me. "We'll find out what happened. Meanwhile, if you think of something, please call me. Cam has my number."

We walked out and got into Tony's truck. The sun had set while we were talking to Mr. Harris, although it was barely 5:30. I was quiet as Tony merged onto the small country road that would take us back home.

"You did good there, sweetie!" Tony answered the question topmost in my mind. "I was proud of you."

"I wasn't too rude, was I? Or abrupt?"

He shook his head. My stomach growled and I wondered if Tony would agree to stop for a snack somewhere.

Chapter 15

I was working reduced hours until a week before Christmas. Then I would be out until the first week of January. We had been so busy working on solving Jordan's death that we had neglected something important.

Pappa put his foot down Sunday morning. We had just finished a lavish breakfast of frittata and skillet potatoes with some peach turnovers Sylvie had sent over. She was used to baking several hours a day. Now she was trying to fill her time, making treats for us in her home kitchen.

"Get ready, kids, we are going out," he said, tapping his cane, his mouth set firmly.

His cheeks were red and they were a sign he was about to blow. Tony and Aunt Reema had come over too.

"What's happening?" Jeet asked, looking sleepy.

"I've left this to you kids for far too long. It's the second week of December!"

"Oops," I clamped a hand on my mouth as I realized the source of Pappa's angst. "Our tree's not up yet."

"It won't be, until we go get one," Pappa roared.

Aunt Reema and Motee Ba giggled. I realized they were in on Pappa's plans. Dad excused himself, citing some deadline.

"Get back here, Anand!" Motee Ba ordered. "You're coming with us."

"But, Ba, the grades are due tomorrow!" Dad protested.

"You can get back to them later."

Dad relented and smiled. We all looked forward to this annual tradition. We piled into the LX and Tony took his truck along. We would need it to haul the trees home. We drove to our favorite tree lot. The sky was overcast and it was dark outside, even though it was morning. The Christmas tree lot was lit up like a stage. Colorful lights were strung on trees. Christmas music played from speakers.

Many people must have had the same thoughts as us, judging by the crowds. A man signaled us and we followed him.

"I've set aside these two firs for you. Both are about 6 feet."

We stared at two beautiful trees hung with a SOLD sign.

"Thanks Bud," Dad clapped him on the back.

"We want to look around some," I said, and went deeper into the lot.

I ran into the Robinsons, Nancy and Nellie. They were trying to pick out a tree.

"Hello," I said cheerfully. "Looking forward to your first Christmas in Swan Creek?"

Nancy's lip curled.

"You bet. We already got two trees for the restaurant. We hired a decorator from the city to do them. People are loving them trees."

I promised I would come and look at them.

"We are worked off our feet, you know," Nellie gleamed. "What with being the only restaurant in town. I finally had to drag Ma here to get a tree for home."

"So your business is doing good, then?" I asked unnecessarily.

I was quite aware of what they had done to make it so.

Nellie's head bobbed up and down in excitement.

"And you didn't want to move here," she said to her mother. "I told you I would make it right. Didn't I, Ma?"

Nancy looked uncomfortable.

"Are you from around here? What made you pick Swan Creek for your diner?" I asked curiously.

"We are from down south," Nancy tried to brush me off.

"Isn't the diner business better?" Nellie squealed.

Nancy shushed her and dragged her away, frowning at me. I wondered what I had done wrong.

We loaded our trees in the back of Tony's truck and went home. Jeet was sent up into the attic to fetch the boxes of Christmas decorations. Many of these were handmade, from crafts projects at school, or stuff Motee Ba had taught me to make. There was a crochet angel my Mom had knitted when she was pregnant with Jeet.

We had fun putting the tree up. Lunch was ordered in, and we were finally ready to light the tree that evening. Everyone clapped as Pappa settled into his chair. He had enjoyed the day, tapping his cane, ordering everyone about.

I went into the guest house and started working on my program. I was close to finishing it. I had made no progress over the binder. I forced myself to bring some kind of order to all the information. I started a spreadsheet and began listing out all the organizations that had been contacted, and all the police departments that had sent over some report, or worked on Mom's case. Slowly, something began to take shape.

I realized the last inquiry about Mom had been made 15 years ago. My first order of business was going to be putting in a fresh inquiry. I needed them to make her file active.

Another thing I realized was that only the neighboring states had been contacted. This included Texas to the South, Arkansas to the East and New Mexico to the West. Kansas and Colorado had been added later.

I thought about spreading a wider net. What if Mom got on a bus that was going to Florida? The possibilities were endless, but I was determined.

I was not going to leave out any option that came to mind.

I fell into a dreamless sleep, tired out from all the physical labor.

I was munching my cereal the next morning when I remembered something. I talked to Tony on my way to work.

He rung up my usual coffee and threw in a candy bar.

"You must be looking forward to a slower day at work."

I bobbed my head. "You have no idea. Hopefully, I can just doze at my desk. How about lunch?"

"I'll pick you up."

I walked out of the library at 11:40. Tony's truck was parked in a spot close to Park Street. Most campus spots were empty and now that there were no classes, the campus cops were being a bit lenient.

I got in and directed him toward the highway.

"Are you going to cook something at home?" Tony asked.

I shook my head.

"It's been a while since we checked out the competition."

"Oh!" he nodded and smiled.

Nancy's parking lot was packed as expected. Tony did the smart thing and parked in Sylvie's lot. We crossed the street over to Nancy's Fancy Diner. Now that Jon and Sylvie's place was sealed, all the locals went to Nancy's. There weren't too many options in a town like Swan Creek.

There was a 15 minute wait and we sat on the curb, enjoying the winter sunshine. I told Tony about the spreadsheet I had started.

"Let's divvy it up. We can work on a script and then we'll say the same thing to every department we call. Don't try to do it all yourself, Meera!"

The hostess beckoned and we went in. I spotted many familiar faces. Some were older people from town, some were people I knew on campus. Office workers, professors, Bingo playing grandmas – they had all converged at Nancy's. I supposed I couldn't really blame them. People have to eat, after all.

A few people waved at us, and a few tried to dodge us, looking uncomfortable. I made it a point to call out to them and say hello.

Nancy's was on a roll. They offered Early Bird Specials for seniors. They had bottomless coffee for people who spent more than $10. They had Lunch Specials under $5. Whoever was doing this had a great business mind. I had to admit Sylvie had never thought of these things.

"Do you want the soup and sandwich special?" a young waitress in a spiffy uniform asked us.

Her sunny yellow dress matched the color the building had been painted.

"What kind of soup?" Tony asked.

The waitress pointed to a placard on the table. There were three types of soups and three types of sandwich. If you went for the special, you could choose any soup from the list, and any sandwich. You got a cup of soup and half a sandwich.

I chose the tomato soup and the chicken salad sandwich. Tony went for the French Onion soup with roast beef. Our meal appeared almost instantly. They must have the soup ladled out in bowls, ready to go.

The food was okay, but portion sizes were small. Dessert was called for.

"I don't suppose you have pie," Tony began, ready to give the girl a hard time about it.

"Apple, cherry or pecan," she quipped.

"You're serving pie?" we both burst out. "I thought you people were against pie."

The waitress shrugged. She looked harried and I decided to give her a break. We put in our order and also asked for a coffee refill. Since our check was more than 10 bucks, I suppose we qualified for the bottomless cup.

Our pies came and I plunged a fork in, not expecting much. My eyes popped as I tasted the pie. Tony was having the same reaction.

"I bet you 50 bucks this is Sylvie's pie!" I cried.

A few people turned around. Most people knew who Sylvie was. They looked interested.

"Who made this pie, huh?" I scowled at the waitress.

"It's artisanal," she said with a straight face.

"You bet it's artisanal. You put this artisan out of business. And now you're peddling the same pie in your diner? How dare you?"

My hunch was proven. I had wondered where Sylvie was sending off all those pies. Nancy's had been the most obvious, considering there weren't too many restaurant type establishments in Swan Creek.

Nancy and Nellie came rushing out. Nancy breathed fire. Nellie looked scared.

"What's the problem here?"

She spotted us and folded her arms.

"You! What are you doing here?"

"Having lunch! Just like everyone else. And what do I see? You're serving Sylvie's pie. After you put her out of business."

"What are you implying, huh? Stay out of my bidness."

Nancy was angry but she also looked guilty.

"So you agree Sylvie made this pie?" I asked.

"We source a lot of our items from artisanal suppliers. We don't give out their names. We have exclusive contracts with them."

I wonder how Nancy came up with all this mumbo jumbo.

"You should be ashamed!" I felt a vein throb in my neck.

I curled my fists, afraid I was about to dock her one. Tony put a warning hand on my arm.

"I'm running an honest business here. The artisans supply a product and I pay for it. It's a simple business transaction between two people. What is your problem?"

"That's just a lot of crap!" I snorted.

I looked around. Almost every person in Nancy's was staring at us.

"And you! Y'all should be ashamed too. Sylvie's fed you for thirty years. And you're consorting with the enemy at the first sign of trouble."

A part of me realized I was losing it. I had just accused a roomful of people of something. I just wasn't sure what.

A woman hissed at her companion.

"Didn't I tell you this tasted familiar?"

"I can spot Sylvie's pie from a mile," an oldie with a cane said with a toothless grin.

"Is it true?" A man in a suit asked Nancy.

I think he was one of the bigwigs at the graduate college at Pioneer.

"Did you put Sylvie out of business?"

Nancy squirmed, and denied it.

The crowd suddenly got bolder and began to fling questions at the mother-daughter duo. Nellie was sweating like a pig, her hair in disarray. Nancy was calmly fielding all the questions, but her ears were red, the only sign of any discomfort.

Tony tugged at me and motioned toward the door. The waitress came and slapped a bill down at our desk.

"Why have you charged us for a refill?" I demanded, spotting the double charge for coffee. "Our check is above 10 bucks."

"That's 10 bucks per person," she said glibly.

Tony slapped a 20 on the table.

"Don't keep the change!"

The girl came back with the change and we stepped out. Nancy was still dealing with the commotion but I felt her razor sharp glare on my back.

Was I going to be sorry I messed with her?

We crossed the road and I collapsed on a bench on Sylvie's porch.

"You already knew they were serving Sylvie's pies, didn't you?" Tony's eyes crinkled.

"I guessed, but I wanted to be sure. Why do you think Sylvie's dealing with them? Are things that bad?"

Tony looked uncomfortable.

"Maybe they are. It's not something we should ask them about though, Meera. Maybe Granny's a better person for it."

I nodded.

Tony drove me back to the library.

"See you in a couple of hours."

I waved goodbye to Tony and went in.

Chapter 16

We had decided to meet and discuss what we had found out about Jordan. Becky, Tony and I were already present at the guest house. Stan Miller was supposed to come by. I was looking forward to getting some more information from him, however much he was willing to disclose.

I had set out some munchies. Brainstorming is hungry work at the best of times. My black bean dip was hearty enough to stick to tortilla chips. I had arranged the dip, fresh guacamole and chipotle sour cream in small bowls. A large bowl was overflowing with tortilla chips. There were some buffalo chicken bites for a more hearty option.

"Do we have to wait for Stan?" Becky grumbled.

"I'm here," he called out from the door.

He took off his cap and placed it on a side table. I let him have a few sips of his soda and a few bites. Then I began.

"It's like this. We've met a few people over the last couple of weeks. There's a lot of information. I just want to pool it and try to make sense out of it."

I had set up a white board in one corner. Being a professor's abode, there is no lack of teaching aids in our house. I'm also a very visual person. Charts and lists are my weapon in solving any problem.

Becky picked up a marker. We decided to create small sub headings as we went along.

"So, people we have talked to …' I began and Becky started a section for people who had already been interviewed.

"Jessica, Pamela, Pa Harris and Cameron," I called out.

Stan looked impressed.

"You managed to meet them all? We've had a hard time making the old man talk."

"Jordan Harris was intelligent. He got a degree at Pioneer, and built a dude ranch from the ground up. According to his Pa, he turned the ranch around, so he was smart."

Stan nodded. Tony and Becky already knew this.

"Most people loved him. Or rather, no one hated him. Cam, Pamela, Pa Harris and Jessica have all said that. Except, he dumped a girl at the altar. And what do you bet this girl bore a grudge?"

"Who's this girl?" Stan wanted to know.

"No one mentioned her name and I didn't ask."

I mentally cursed myself for this slip.

I stood up and started an Action Items section. 'Find more about ex' went under it.

"Cameron is an unstable character," Tony stated next. "Pamela thought he wanted to start a farm on the ranch or something. He told us he wanted to start a convalescent home for veterans. Pa Harris said Cam was just bluffing."

"I think he was just sounding Jordan out. He wanted to know if he was welcome at the ranch."

"Why wouldn't he be?" Stan asked, scooping up some guacamole with a tortilla chip.

"He never liked the ranch. He went away and joined the Army. Came back recently facing a discharge. Jordan did most of the work to make the ranch profitable. He may not have wanted his brother to just come and enjoy the fruits of his labor."

"If that's true, Jordan was the goose laying the golden egg," Stan pointed out. "Why would Cam want to harm him?"

I conceded the point.

"Wait a minute. Didn't the siblings say the old man was going to sign over the ranch to Jordan? Maybe they wanted their inheritance."

"In that case, it made sense to bump the old man off," Becky said. "Pamela and Cam would get their share, and Jordan would still do all the work."

"Don't forget they fought a lot," Tony reminded me.

"I don't think that means anything," I protested. "Jeet and I are at each other's throats almost every day. But I'd lay down my life for him."

"You're forgetting one thing," Stan said complacently. "Jordan Harris died here in Swan Creek. That ranch of theirs is about 60 miles away. None of the family were in the vicinity."

"But that's just it," I cried. "They could have been in Swan Creek. Cam admitted being in the city until 8 PM. He could have driven by here. Pamela wasn't home either. She said she was just driving around, she doesn't know where. And Pa Harris said neither of them was in bed at 11 PM."

Stan leaned forward, looking dumbfounded.

"What are you saying, Meera? That's news to me."

He made a note in a small notebook.

"Don't say anything to them about this now," he warned. "Now that we know they weren't home, we can ask them for alibis. And we can ask them exactly where they were. They are obligated to answer. They may not show you the same courtesy."

I wasn't sure about that but I let it slide.

"What about Jessica?" I asked Stan. "She said she talked to him at 10. That means he was alive at that time."

Stan looked shocked again.

"She said what? She never told us that."

"Do you think she lied?" Tony asked.

"What is the estimated time of death?" I asked Stan.

"Between 9 and midnight. They can't narrow it down more than that. And it's possible he was incapacitated even before that. So he could've been on that bench but unconscious."

"Jessica's call is really important, in that case," I nodded.

"What if someone else answered Jordan's phone? She should be able to tell the difference, right?" Becky came up with a bizarre question.

I was stunned.

"Have we made any progress at all?" I wrung my hands.

"Plenty!" Stan said, getting up. "Thanks to you, we know the brother is flaky. There could be an ex. Jessica may or may not be lying."

"She lied about being engaged."

I told Stan how she had let me believe she and Jordan had been together for 7 years.

"So she lied outright," Stan mused. "Maybe she was hurt the first time they broke up, and she was just stringing him along this time? Waiting for the right opportunity to have her revenge?"

"That's cold blooded," I winced.

"If Jordan didn't die naturally, chances are he ingested some kind of toxin or poison. Who could have had access to that?"

"All his family insisted he was very healthy and strong as an ox," I repeated. "He was only 27, after all."

"Jessica works on some kind of wonder food for cows, doesn't she?" Tony asked.

I remembered and explained it to Stan.

"What does that entail, exactly? Maybe she deals with poisons every day. Maybe what's superfood for a cow is harmful to humans?" Tony was seriously considering Jessica as a suspect.

I added another line to the Action Items list – find out who had access to poison.

"We are nowhere close to solving this, are we?" I was frustrated. "Jon and Sylvie's have been closed for over a week."

"You have to be patient, Meera!" Stan consoled us. "I think you have done a pretty good job for amateurs. Let's catch up again in a week or so."

Stan stood up and scooped up one more tortilla chip. He adjusted his cap on his head and turned to leave.

"One moment, Meera."

He looked uncomfortable.

"That woman was spotted on campus again. Near the library. One of the school cops called it in. She was gone by the time we got there."

I flung my hands up in the air.

"This woman's like the bogey man. What's her interest in me? Does she really want to harm me?"

"If I had to guess, I'd say no," Stan said soothingly. "She's had plenty of chances to accost you. She hasn't made any contact yet. Maybe she's just senile, or a bit touched. Maybe you remind her of someone and she wants to look at you."

"I'm not going to worry about her," I said stoutly.

Truth be told, I was finally beginning to worry. I tried to focus on the matter at hand.

"We need to find out more about Jordan's ex. And maybe talk to someone who knows Jessica."

"What about her lab mates?" Tony asked. "Shouldn't we confirm she actually turned up for that meeting that night? Or that she was in the lab later on?"

I added two more items to the Action Items list.

We talked about various alternate scenarios, and tried to come up with a motive. Did someone hate Jordan enough to kill him? Or was it all just about money?

"That's it. I've had enough. Let's do something else."

Everyone was hungry, inspite of having grazed on the tortilla chips.

I pulled a platter of marinated chicken from the refrigerator. Tony fired up the grill. I lined some corn on the cob on one side. The chicken had absorbed all the adobo seasoning and tequila I had doused it in earlier. I placed the boneless pieces on the grill and called the main house.

"We're grilling some chicken, Motee Ba," I told her. "Are you guys ready to eat?"

Jeet was the first to come over. Pappa followed, tapping his cane. Motee Ba held a rice cooker in her hand.

"I made some rice pilaf," she called out. "I think it will go well with the chicken."

I put a plate aside for Dad, knowing he would probably be busy.

We sat on the patio, warmed by a fire Tony had built.

"Your aunt may be coming for a visit," Motee Ba announced.

"Oh, cool!" I tried to be stoic.

My aunt is a trial at the best of times. She would come armed with photos of eligible Indian boys and follow me around, extolling their virtues. She would not be pleased about what I was involved in.

I met Tony for lunch at the food court the next day. The Wok was the only place open so we got stir frys.

"Granny called me. There's a message for you from your blue eyed boy."

"What does he want now?" I asked Tony, ignoring his sarcasm.

"Why don't you call him back?" Tony shrugged his shoulders.

I borrowed Tony's cell phone and put in a call to Cam.

"Hello Meera! Got a minute?" he asked cheerfully.

"Sure. You called?"

"I have an appointment in the City today. I'll be going back around 6. Would you like to have dinner with me?"

I was amazed. Was Cam asking me out on a date? Then I remembered I needed to ferret out lots of information from him. A dinner date would be a good opportunity.

"Why not? Did you have a place in mind?"

"I don't know much about Swan Creek. Just tell me where to be and at what time."

I picked a pub I liked, counting on it being crowded even on a weekday evening. We planned to meet at 6:30.

"Will you be safe?" Tony asked as I hung up.

"Relax! That's why I chose Jimmy's. What's he gonna do in a roomful of people?"

Dinner time arrived soon enough and I waited for Cam at Jimmy's, a local bar.

He came in, looking pleased.

"I lost the cane," he announced, turning in a circle.

"Congratulations!" I was genuinely happy for him.

"We are celebrating. Dinner's on me."

He signaled the server and ordered a large beer and a platter of appetizers.

"What will you have?" he raised his eyebrows and looked at me.

"A Coke," I told the server.

"Is that all?" Cam protested. "How about something stronger?"

"Maybe later," I smiled.

He poured out the details about his doctor's appointment.

"Are you done with your therapy then?"

"No. Therapy's even more important now. I need to build my strength. Luckily, I have access to the best equine therapy in the state."

"Aren't these the same horses you hated?" I teased.

"You're right," he sobered. "Life comes full circle, huh!"

The appetizers arrived and I gave them the attention they deserved. You have to respect the fried platter at Jimmy's or he'll give you the evil eye.

"Have you thought any more about what you'll do now?" I asked after he downed his second beer.

"I have to talk to Pam," he said. "Pa's never really asked her what she wanted. She's just a woman, according to him."

"She's great at handling the guests. And she seems to love the resort."

Cam lapsed into thought.

"Were you serious about the farm? Or the convalescent home? Or going to live in Dallas?" I let him know I was on to him.

Cam was apologetic.

"OK. You got me. But I was only half kidding."

"Your Pa says you love to rile people up."

He flashed me a devilish grin. The blue of his irises deepened and his whole face creased in a smile.

"I've been accused of that before, but I wasn't lying outright."

"Oh?" I challenged.

"I do want to turn at least part of the resort into a special home for veterans. The equine therapy will be a big draw. So will the organic farm. We do grow our own vegetables now. Maybe we'll do it on a larger scale as we add more cabins. And the Dallas part? I've put some feelers out. I want to be a speaker on the Army circuit. Give motivational talks, that kind of thing."

He paused and drained his glass again.

I was impressed. The Jordan family wasn't lacking in smarts.

"All those plans depend on having access to the ranch though, right?"

Cam sobered.

"And you think I would kill my brother for that piece of land?"

I was quiet.

He leaned forward.

"Jordan was willing to hand the Triple H over to me. He told me that himself."

"How? When?" I asked. "And wouldn't he have to own the ranch to be able to do that?"

"Actually, I'm the sole heir to the Triple H according to my grandpa's will."

"But I thought your Pa was going to hand it over to Jordan."

"Yes, he was," Cam said bitterly. "He always considered Jordan to be the true heir."

"So he wouldn't actually be giving it away. You'd still own it?"

I was trying to keep track.

"On paper, yes. But what does a piece of paper matter? Jordan was the one Pa chose."

I was confused. This totally ruled out money as a motive.

"So you're saying all this talk of what each of you wanted means nothing? You'll own the ranch no matter what?"

"That's right, beautiful. The ranch is not the prize. It never was. Winning Pa's approval is."

"And now you'll never know," I said under my breath.

Cam clinked his glass with mine and gave me a thumbs up sign.

"Got that right."

I motioned to the server to bring some coffee.

"Are you sure you are okay to drive back to the ranch tonight?" I was concerned about the five beers he had guzzled in an hour.

"Don't worry," Cam held up a hand. "I can sleep it off at Jessica's. She's probably in that lab of hers anyway."

Chapter 17

My dinner with Cam – I didn't want to call it a date – had shaken me up. If the Triple H was really coming to him, it ruled out money as a motive. I couldn't shake off how casual he had sounded about staying over at Jessica's. I had a feeling he had done it before. Was he trying to steal her away from Jordan? Had the brothers fought over a girl?

Tony and I stood outside his gas station, sipping large cups of scalding hot coffee. The mid December morning was cold and bracing and I was waiting for the caffeine to kick in and jolt me awake.

"This just gets more complicated each day," Tony complained. "Any news of how the diner inspection is progressing?"

I shook my head.

"They're short staffed. With the holidays, they might not get to it until the next year."

"How's Sylvie taking it? I hope you're not giving her grief about supplying pies to Nancy's."

"Of course I'm not!"

Sometimes Tony has zero faith in me.

Something about Sylvie supplying pies to Nancy's didn't sit right with me. I thought about it but nothing obvious came to mind. Then I let it go. It was Sylvie's call, after all.

"I'm meeting Pamela at the ranch later today. How about coming with us?"

"Is Becky going?" Tony asked.

I nodded.

"In that case, I'll pull out this time. I have some inventory to catch up on."

I put in a few hours at work and was ready to drive to the Triple H. Becky and I picked up some tacos from a drive through, with a double order of locos. I steered the car with one hand, giving my taco the attention it deserved. The country roads were almost deserted but it was slow going because of the icy patches.

"What are you planning to ask her today, Meera?"

"I want to ask her where she was that day, but she might take offense and chuck us out."

"What about Jordan's ex?"

"That too," I nodded.

"Let's lead with that," Becky suggested, "and then ask about her alibi."

I pulled up outside the Lodge and went in. Pam was waiting for us at the small seating area next to the tall windows. She motioned us over with a nod and we joined her.

"I hope you're a cautious driver. These roads can get icy."

She poured coffee for everyone and we settled down.

"Have you made any progress?" she asked.

I was noncommittal.

"We're just trying to get as much background information as we can. For example, we know nothing about this woman Jordan dated for a while."

"Oh, Eleanor? What's to know about her? She was batty. They finally put her in an asylum."

"Is she still there?" Becky asked.

"I don't know," Pam said. "I suppose they would let us know if they released her?"

"And why would they do that?" I quizzed her.

"She attacked Jordan, didn't she? Almost gauged his eyes out. She agreed to go to that mental place instead of jail. Only because the local magistrate was a friend of her Pa's."

"How is it you didn't mention this to the police?" I demanded.

Pam looked bewildered.

"I never thought of it. Once Jessica came back into Jordan's life, he was so happy. And we were all happy for them. I hadn't thought of this girl in a while."

I gave her Stan's number.

"He's one of the people working on Jordan's case. I think you should tell him everything. They can check and tell us where she is right now."

Pam took the note, looking disturbed.

"You think this is important, don't you?"

"It's best to consider all possible scenarios," I tried to soothe her. "Have you remembered where you were driving around on Sunday night?"

"Why don't you ask me directly if I was in Swan Creek?" she demanded.

"I'm just trying to help."

Pam stood up, clearly signaling our meeting was done. She walked over to the check-in desk and handed me an envelope.

"Your refund. I'm sorry your visit was cut short. And now you're helping us find who harmed Jordan."

I took the envelope from her. It would come in handy in my Christmas shopping.

"How's your Pa?" I asked politely. "Please tell him I stopped by."

"You can do that yourself."

Pam's temper had cooled down a bit. She drove us to the homestead in her golf cart. Pa Harris was in the barn, rubbing down a horse.

"Hello, little lady."

His face crinkled in a smile.

We made some small talk and I fed an apple to the horse. Pam offered to drive us back to my car but we chose to walk. Becky and I huddled in our jackets, shivering but enjoying the cold. We walked faster to work up some warmth. I almost crashed into a body.

"Watch where you're going," a friendly voice called out.

I slipped the hood of my jacket down. Cam was bundled up just like us. He held a large straw basket in his arms, filled with all kinds of vegetables. His hands were muddy. He held them out.

"Sorry I can't shake hands."

"Are those your organic vegetables?" I peered at the basket with interest.

"Kale, turnips, sweet potatoes … what's that?" I pointed to some greens.

"Chard, and winter squash. And mushrooms, of course."

"Are these wild mushrooms?" Becky asked.

"Some of them are," Cam nodded. "But you've got to be careful. They taste great in soups and sauces, but they can be deadly."

Becky's eyes were as big as saucers.

I pulled her along and said goodbye to Cam. I kept a tight hold on Becky's arm, hoping she wouldn't blurt out anything until we got inside the car.

"Did you see that?" Becky asked. "Do you think …"

I shook my head. So Cam had access to poisonous mushrooms. At least he knew how to tell them apart. I had to report this to Stan right away.

"Maybe they already tested for mushrooms," I said lamely.

We were quiet as I drove under the arches of the Triple H and merged onto the country road that would take us home. We passed the sign for the country store we had stopped at earlier. I pulled into their lot on a hunch.

The hostess recognized us from our previous visit.

"Pot pies are just coming out," she beamed.

My mouth watered at the thought of buttery pastry and creamy sauce with juicy chunks of meat. Becky and I both nodded eagerly.

I put my head down and worked on my pie. I can be quite devoted that way.

Becky kicked me under the table.

"Meera," she whispered, tipping her head to one side.

I looked around. The place was empty except for a table in the corner. A lone figure wearing a long winter coat sat huddled, sipping a cup of coffee. It was hard to say if it was a man or woman from the angle.

"That woman …" Becky whispered. "I think she was in the drive through line at the taco place."

"So?" I rolled my eyes.

Becky gave me a meaningful glare. I snapped out of the pie induced stupor and turned around swiftly. Becky kicked me again. We pretended to be busy eating. The figure stood up and went out without giving us a second glance.

"See? That person didn't even give us a glance."

"I don't know, Meera," Becky was glum.

The woman came by to clear our plates.

"You want to know something funny?" she asked. "Old lady over there was here the last time you had lunch. We see very few people out here in the backwoods, and then the same people turn up twice, at the same time!"

She walked away, shaking her head.

I placed some cash on the table as the woman handed over the check.

"Have you had this store for long?"

"My family's been here for over a hundred years," the woman smiled. "My Ma started this country store and restaurant. I was her only child, so I settled down here with my family."

"You must know people from the surrounding areas, then?"

"That I do. It's a shame what happened to that Harris boy. But I say he had it coming."

"We heard he was very well loved."

I looked at her face.

"By most folks, yes."

Her face had set in a frown. Becky cut to the chase.

"Are you talking about the girl he jilted? We heard she was insane."

"She was nothing of that sort. I bounced her on my knee when she was a baby. She was such a sweet girl. Then that Harris boy went and fell for some girl at that fancy college of his. He couldn't dump our local girl quick enough."

"She took it hard?" I prodded.

"That she did. Mother and daughter both moved away."

"Really, where?" I asked urgently.

"No one knows. Now, how about some dessert?"

We shook our heads and thanked the lady. I rushed home as fast as I could. The first call I put in was for Stan.

"I say, Meera, you should join the police force. That's a lot of information to process."

I hung up, feeling pleased with myself. I called Tony next and told him everything that had happened.

"Slow down, Meera! So Pam won't tell us her alibi, Cam had access to poisonous mushrooms, Jordan's ex attacked him once … Is that all?"

I had to tell him about the woman. I could hear him almost fall out of bed.

"Do you believe me now?" he roared.

"We don't know it's the same woman. Looked like some dowdy old lady. Maybe she just stopped there for a snack like we did."

"Yeah, right!" Tony refused to believe me.

I hung up. I didn't want to listen to his tirade. I walked into the kitchen, sniffing at what was cooking.

"Hungry?" Motee Ba asked.

"Not really," I said. "What's for dinner?"

"*Khichdi*," Motee Ba smiled, knowing I wouldn't refuse.

This lentil and rice stew is a staple in any Patel household. Warm, mushy, topped with plenty of ghee with a side of fried *papads*, this is the comfort food on which I was raised.

My image processing program was almost ready to be tested. I was eager to find out how successful I was in the first round. I would need to tweak it but I was hoping I wasn't too far off mark.

I checked the special email I had set up for Mom's case. Some of the departments I had approached had responded. Some needed paperwork to make Mom's case active. Some had already done it. Most of them wanted a photograph. I sent out my specially drafted email to 10 more people in Arizona and Alabama. I was widening the net bit by bit, sending the email to a new set of departments every day. I had a long list to get through.

That night, I dreamed I was flying down an icy road. I yanked the steering with my hands but it didn't respond. A car followed me, a hooded figure at the wheel. Sleet came in through the windows, soaking me. I braked hard and the car skidded, going round in circles on the narrow road.

I woke with a start. My bedroom window was open, the flimsy sheers soaked from the rain coming in. I rushed to the window, pulling it close, trying to shut it against the icy wind and sleet. Just as the window snapped close, I spied a silhouette by the guest house. I broke out in a cold sweat, refusing to believe it.

I was just remembering the figure from my dream, wasn't I?

Chapter 18

I had a tough time getting out of my bed Monday morning. It was my last day at work and I just had to put in a few hours before the school closed for the rest of the year. I tried to clear my foggy brain as I sat in bed, unwilling to climb out of the covers.

Someone rapped loudly on my door.

"7:30!" Motee Ba called out.

I slurped the warm oatmeal she had made and got dressed.

"I had a bad dream," I told Tony when I stopped to talk to him on my way to work. "It's got me unsettled."

"Eat this," he handed me a candy bar, smiling.

I was so disturbed I said no to candy.

I manned the library desk and chatted with one or two lone wolves who were stocking up on books for the 2 week break. These were the incorrigible geeks, or kids doing some research on a deadline. Soon as I thought of research, I thought of a better way to utilize my time.

I bundled up and walked over to the Chemical Engineering building. The girl from earlier greeted me. She was wearing a red sweater with a holiday motif. She remembered me.

"Hello. You again?"

"Can you tell me where Jessica's lab is?"

"Her research group has an office in the bio technology building. That's where their lab is."

"Oh, thanks. I thought she's in your department."

"She is," the girl nodded. "Her research is cross disciplinary. Their team's made up of people from different departments."

"Gotcha," I thanked the girl and turned to go.

"Have some cake. It's our annual end of year cake. It's good!"

She pointed to a large sheet cake placed on a side table. It had been sampled generously but a good part of it was still remaining. Tiny red plates and forks were placed next to it.

"Thanks. I will."

I beamed at her. Life's too short to say no to free cake.

I cut myself a generous slice and waved good bye. I went outside and chose a spot where I could lean against the wall comfortably. I made short work of the cake, and made my way to the bio technology lab. I was freezing by the time I pulled open the heavy glass doors that flanked the department.

I walked down a flight of stairs and stood outside a door that listed Jessica's name along with a few others.

"Come on in," a voice hollered from inside in answer to my knock.

Three or four workstations lined the wall. There was a desk in the center with some fancy equipment I couldn't make much sense of.

"Err, I'm looking for Jessica," I explained.

It was obvious she wasn't there.

A moon faced man with spectacles ogled me.

"She should be here soon. What is it about?"

The man was shorter than me, and he had a rumpled look about him. If I had to guess, I'd say he had probably spent the night huddled over the computer. Yellow rings of sweat circled his underarms and a faint odor I didn't want to think about wafted my way. He was almost bald, and he was licking his lips every few seconds. But he wasn't that much older than me.

"It's sort of personal," I hedged.

"I'm Colin Stevens," he said, standing up, offering me a hand.

I shook it reluctantly. This guy gave me an unclean feeling.

"Meera Patel."

"You're welcome to wait here," he offered.

I nodded and decided to take him up on the offer.

He went back to the papers he was reading and there was a deathly silence in the room for about five minutes. He kept licking his lips all the time, reminding me of a repulsive reptile.

"Not much I don't know about Jessica, you know." He crossed his fingers and held up his hand. "We are like this!"

"She hasn't mentioned you." I feigned surprise. "But I guess that's understandable. She's going through a rough time."

It was Colin's turn to act surprised.

"Really? Why is that?"

"Haven't you heard?" I leaned forward. "Her fiancée was found dead by the lake."

Colin Stevens didn't bat an eyelid.

"Are you talking about Jordan? They were breaking up."

I hid my shock well.

"No. they were celebrating their engagement."

"That's what they told everyone! To get away from that ranch and meet somewhere they could talk in private."

The slimy snake had a triumphant look on his face.

I cleared my throat.

"And why were they breaking up?"

Colin beamed from ear to ear.

"She's with me now, of course. We've been dating a while. Ever since we started working together on this project."

"When was that?" I asked.

"About three years ago."

I was finding this hard to process. I tried a different tack.

"Are you also a chemical engineer?"

"No. I'm a doctor." Colin puffed up again. "A veterinary doctor, of course."

"I don't really know what Jessica's research is about," I admitted.

"This is a cross disciplinary group," Colin Stevens explained. "We have programmers and statistics experts. Then we have people doing simulations. Jessica and I do most of the field work."

"Like what?" I had to ask.

"Working with the heifers… injecting our test subjects with different serums, taking blood and tissue samples, evaluating and mapping their progress… Stuff like that."

"Sounds very different from chemical engineering."

Colin Stevens shrugged.

"Jessica's great at it. She grew up on a cattle ranch."

This I did know.

"Real life applications of science require a lot of knowhow from different fields. Very different from academia." Colin Stevens said pompously. "We are one of the most advanced research teams on campus."

"I heard Jessica's graduating soon."

"We need her here. She got side tracked a bit with all that Jordan Harris business. This is where her true calling is."

"So she's not graduating then?" I prompted.

"I'm the Head Researcher on the project," Colin Stevens stood up, towering over me.

"I might sign off on her PHD once she decides to stay on here."

"And has she?" I asked.

"She will. She has no more distractions with Jordan out of the way."

I was bursting with this unexpected bounty of information. Was this guy above board, or was he lying?

"So you're happy Jordan's dead?" I asked bluntly.

Colin Stevens finally began looking flustered.

"That's not what I meant."

I was quiet, hoping he would spill more. And he did.

"It's just…it's hard, watching Jessica fawn over these pups of hers. But she always comes back to me. I'm a patient man, Ms. Patel."

"You're saying Jessica's a tease?" I didn't mince words.

"Not my choice of words, but yeah, something like that. I don't blame her. A beauty like her is bound to slay hearts."

The basement room was beginning to close in on me.

The door flung open with a rush and Jessica came in, followed by a couple of other guys.

"We're here," she called out cheerfully and stopped when she saw me.

"Hi Meera!"

"Hey Jessica!" I greeted her back. "I just came back to see how you were doing?"

Colin Stevens interrupted.

"You're 5 minutes late, guys. We need to start our meeting."

I was being booted out.

"Let's catch up later," Jessica pleaded.

I stood up and clambered up the stairs, rushing out to get some fresh air. I couldn't get out of there fast enough.

An hour ago, we hadn't even known Colin Stevens existed. Now he had provided a boatload of new information. I wanted to think he was some kind of psycho, spouting off delusions about Jessica. But I couldn't ignore what he had said without checking it out.

I walked back to my desk and sat out the remaining hour, clearing up as much as I could. Finally, it was time to leave and I rushed out, driving to Tony's gas station. Two weeks of holidays lay ahead, and I couldn't suppress the smile that broke out on my face.

"Hey Babe!" Tony high fived me as I got out of my car. "Are we celebrating?"

"Of course! I'm starving, and I have quite the scoop for you guys. Where's Becky?"

We debated over going out for lunch or rustling something up at home. We chose to go home. Becky was waiting for us at the guest house, busy making lunch.

"Enchiladas!" she pointed to the oven.

The day stretched before us, and the bubbly, cheesy, casserole was perfect for the cold weather.

We loaded our plates with two enchiladas each, a side of refried beans and rice. I took double helpings of sour cream and guacamole.

We attacked the food and no one spoke for the first 2- 3 bites. Okay, maybe 10 bites.

"What's this scoop you were talking about?" Tony asked.

I narrated my encounter with Colin Stevens. Tony and Becky were struck dumb. Their eyes popped and I sat back, feeling smug.

"Is that a new development, or what?"

"Has Jessica verified any of this?" Becky asked with a frown. "Maybe this guy's just bad mouthing her."

"I didn't get a chance to talk to her. But I'm thinking, of course she'll deny all this, won't she? Even if it's true."

"Don't see her admitting she was two timing Jordan," Tony agreed.

We finished our meal and collapsed in front of the TV. Becky and I each took one end of the couch, and Tony staked claim to a deep chair. A few flurries started, and I remembered my dream.

Tony laughed out loud.

"You think I was dreaming?" I demanded.

"I don't know Meera, but now you know how I feel when you dismiss that woman."

"Why go through the farce of an engagement, if Jessica wanted to split up with Jordan?" Becky mused. "They didn't have to announce it. They could have gone on dating."

I thought about Cam. I hadn't really looked at Jordan closely, or seen any photos of his. But there was no doubt, Cam was the more handsome of the brothers. I would bet my weekly stash of candy that Cam was the most handsome in the entire county.

"The other day, when I met Cam for dinner, he mentioned he would stay over at Jessica's."

Becky picked up on my meaning.

"And according to Colin Stevens, Jessica flirted around."

"Maybe she's just the friendly sort," I held up a finger.

"Yeah maybe," Becky said. "But Jordan could've felt threatened by it."

"So he didn't trust his own brother?" Tony mused. "Boy, am I glad I don't have one?"

"What about me?" Jeet called from the doorway.

He had the kind of hurt look only a teenager can have.

"I'll trust you with my life, bro. Any day!"

Tony did some kind of weird handshake with him and Jeet settled on a bar stool at the counter, happy to see the plate I'd set aside for him.

"Say Meera," Becky plunged ahead. "So Jordan thinks something's cooking between Cam and Jessica. He ups the ante by proposing to her."

"And Jessica accepts, even though she actually wants to break up with him?" I frowned.

"Saying yes would be a good way to prove she wasn't interested in Cam," Tony pointed out.

"But if she wasn't interested in Jordan either, why say yes at all?"

"Maybe she was buying some time. Or trying to avoid conflict between the brothers."

"Girls!" Tony flung his hands in the air. "Why are they so complicated? It seems to me, she was just playing around with everyone. What do you bet, her true intentions were something else entirely."

"You mean she sweet talked Cam, Jordan and Colin into thinking she was into each of them. But she actually was into someone else?"

"Some people have a hard time saying no. They just go along with whatever the other person says."

Jessica hadn't seemed like a wimp. She seemed strong enough to get her way. Maybe she was pulling a fast one over everyone, following her own agenda. That seemed more believable to me.

"I guess we have to talk to her first," I said. "And tell Stan about this. I wonder how he's coming along with the alibis."

"What about your program, Meera? Have you made any progress?" Becky asked.

I groaned, holding my stomach.

"I'm too stuffed to think of that right now."

"Who wants ice cream?" Jeet asked, scooping chocolate chip ice cream into a bowl.

We all wanted some.

Chapter 19

I pushed myself to work on the aging program later that evening. I collected a few photos of myself from 5 years ago. I took a current photo with the Logitech camera mounted on top of my desktop. This is what my program output should look like.

I wanted to run some tests myself before I gave a demo to anyone. I was afraid of failing miserably. Dad wouldn't like that. I had tested the modules, or small chunks of code as I created them. Every function worked well. But did it all come together as a whole?

I fed my old photo to the program and asked it to show me what I would look like now. I closed my eyes for a few minutes and dared myself to open them. I stared at the photo that looked back at me from the screen.

I suppose it could be my sister, except I didn't have one. The program had changed some of my features. It hadn't necessarily aged me. I did some analysis and changed a few parameters. The next result was better. I tweaked the program a bit more every time and a couple of hours passed.

Finally, I took a break for dinner.

"How's that aging progression module coming along, Meera?" Dad asked me.

"I'm close, but not perfect," I admitted.

"Don't be too hard on yourself, Meera. And don't try to be too precise. This is going to be a projection at best. Human beings don't age according to a formula. They have age spurts. And everyone ages differently."

I agreed with Dad. I was already finding it out.

"I'm running some preliminary tests, and you're right."

"Are you adding a constant factor for every year, or something variable depending on the age?" Dad launched into more detail.

"How do you mean?"

There are advantages for having a genius for a father, and there are the disadvantages.

"Well, aging a person from 10 to 20 is different from aging him from 40 to 50."

I thought for a moment and I agreed. I had missed this.

"So I need to check the starting age first, and then have different conditions …"

"Right!" Dad said. "And some people will age more around the eyes, or around the mouth. Some will go bald, or some will have a sagging chin. Some will have age spots. Depends on genetics, or health profile."

I was stunned.

"That's a whole lot of parameters, Dad! I'll never be done this way."

"Calm down, Meera. You don't have to be perfect. Do you not see what I'm trying to get at?"

Jeet spoke up, sounding bored.

"There is no single solution, sis! That's what Dad is trying to say."

I looked from Dad to Jeet, trying to make sense of their words. Dad had a silly grin on his face.

"The 19 year old has it, Meera."

I tried to hide my frustration. I ran away from the fancy future my family had planned for me. The one where I was going to be the next Bill Gates. But I didn't like it when someone made me look dumb. Especially my kid brother.

"Maybe I'm not cut out for this."

"You're too close to the problem, Meera. Change your perspective. Zoom out of the picture, eh?"

Dad winked.

It took me back to my childhood. One of the few times I had bonded with my father was when he set a puzzle for me to solve. He would give me clues, and then ask me to 'zoom out'.

Zooming out would make the image look smaller, but that wouldn't change its features. And like that, I had my Eureka moment.

"Ohhh! You mean there is no perfect solution. There are multiple solutions."

"Now you got it," Dad said happily.

What Jeet had easily grasped was that there was more than one correct answer to the problem. So I could apply a certain set of parameters and come up with one photo that showed pronounced aging around the mouth, another would show more lines on the forehead and so on. I could vary the amount of aging for each of these, based on the correction I applied. There could be hundreds of permutations and combinations.

"I have to go!" I sped back to my computer, eager to try out my latest idea.

A few minutes later, I was staring at a dozen pictures that looked a lot like me.

I tried the whole thing with my current photo and tried to see how I would look 10 years later. The results were not good for my vanity, but they pleased me. I wanted to test the program with as many different people as possible now. Pappa, Motee Ba and Dad would be great subjects.

I called Tony at midnight, waking him up.

"What is it, Meera?" he murmured.

"I need some photographs of you at different ages."

"Okay, later," he hung up.

I looked into Dad's office and found him sitting back in his chair, enjoying a glass of brandy.

"I need some photos for testing, Dad!"

He handed me a small box. He had already gathered photos of everyone in the house. The only ones missing were those of Mom. I wasn't ready for them yet.

I forced myself to sleep, letting my brain rest for a while. I was up before dawn, scanning in all the photos Dad had provided. I compared my program output of 40 year old Dad with an actual photo. Then I projected how he would look at 60. I did the same thing for Motee Ba at various stages.

Some of the output photos were very close to the mark. I applied some more correction to my program based on these results.

My program was almost perfect. I sat back, feeling a slight tremor in my hand. My heart thudded in my chest as I thought of what it meant. I was finally going to have a 'look' at my mother. Even if it was only in a photo.

My stomach rumbled and I decided to make some breakfast. I didn't have to go in to work so the day pretty much belonged to me. My aunt was flying in to spend some time with us. I had to go pick her up at the airport. With Christmas around the corner, that meant a shopping trip.

I chopped onions and tomatoes, and minced some jalapenos. Pappa walked in just as I placed a pan full of my spicy scrambled eggs on the table. He buttered his toast lavishly, taking advantage of Motee Ba's absence. She came in and flicked it out of his hand just as he was about to put it in his mouth. I tried to hide my smile.

"Are you coming to the city, Motee Ba?" I asked her.

She hesitated.

"I want to. But it's too cold out. I think I'll just stay in and make something special for dinner."

Becky bowed out so it was going to be just Tony and me. No way I was going alone to get Aunt Anita from the airport. She's a dragon, that one.

I had just finished clearing all the breakfast dishes when the phone rang.

"For you," Motee Ba beckoned.

It turned out to be Jessica.

"Hey Jessica. How are you? I didn't know you had this number."

"I got it from Pamela," she quipped. "Can we talk, Meera?"

"Let me call you back."

I guessed it was going to be a long call. I wanted to take it in the privacy of the guest house. I hurried over and called Jessica back.

"Good Morning Jessica," I greeted her. "I suppose you're back home in Texas?"

"What? No such luck. I'm where I always am. In my lab."

"Don't you have winter break?"

"Technically, I do, but there's a lot of work to be done. Research never stops, Meera. There's always some kind of urgency."

I nodded, then realized she couldn't see me. "Yeah!"

I knew that very well thanks to Dad and some of my own not so good experiences.

"So you're still in Swan Creek, you mean?"

"Unfortunately, yes. Usually I'm home by this time, busy shopping or baking cookies with my Mom, but with Jordan gone, none of it really makes sense."

I was quiet. I wondered how to disclose I was on to her.

She made it easy for me.

"Colin said he was chatting with you for quite a while yesterday."

"Sure was!"

She sucked in a deep breath and said urgently.

"Meera, we need to talk. Can you meet me today, please? Just name the place."

I really wanted to, but I couldn't dare be late for the flight.

"Sorry, I'm going out of town today. But I can give you 15 minutes now."

"Colin … he's a bit weird," she began.

I had gathered that on my own but I wanted her to go on.

"He's had a crush on me for a long time."

I maintained my silence, hoping Jessica would give me something solid.

"He's delusional," she burst out.

"Why are you telling me this?" I asked calmly.

"Did he talk about me or Jordan?" she probed.

"Plenty!" I wasn't about to make it easy for her.

"Like what?" she said, almost hysterical.

"He told me you dated him for three years, and you were getting together with him. You didn't like Jordan at all. You flirt around with people and play with them. You were about to dump Jordan that day. You had a big fight with him …"

I paused to take a breath.

"It's not like the way you make it sound," she cried.

"Okay," I deadpanned.

"Look, I was with Colin for a few years. That part is true. That was when Jordan and I had broken up. But when I met Jordan again, we reconnected. We got back together. Colin didn't like that. He can be pretty controlling. He began to threaten me."

"What about breaking up with Jordan that day? Is that part true?"

"Sort of," Jessica admitted slowly.

"Why get engaged at all, and then break it off less than a week later?"

"I did love him, Meera. I was overjoyed when he proposed. I said yes in the heat of the moment. But I could never live on at the Triple H. And Jordan wasn't willing to move with me to Texas. That's what we were talking about that day, at Willow Lake."

"So you hung your engagement over him like bait?" I wasn't feeling the warm and fuzzies toward Jessica any more.

"Colin was giving me hell, threatening to reject all my work. I've been working hard at it for years."

"Was he blackmailing you? Is that what you're trying to say?"

Jessica let out a sigh.

"Look, it's hard to explain, but it was all overwhelming for me. I just want to get out of this town, you know. I can't do that until Colin approves my research. Once I get my PHD, I can do anything I want."

"Was Jordan in on this?"

"He wasn't. He couldn't be. He wasn't that great at hiding his emotions. Unless he stopped coming around, Colin was never going to believe I had dumped Jordan for real."

"So you were planning to dump Jordan, take up with Colin, get your degree, then dump Colin and then take up with Jordan again?"

My head was reeling.

"Yes, that's pretty much it," Jessica admitted.

I whistled.

"What about Cam?" I asked.

"What about him?" Jessica was surprised.

"You weren't, you aren't going around with him too?"

"Colin told you that, didn't he?" she asked sadly. "I think he must've said something to Jordan too."

"You think?" I asked, sarcastically.

"Do you see what I'm dealing with now? Colin Stevens is pure evil!"

Jessica sounded on the verge of tears.

"Evil enough to harm Jordan?" I dove in.

There was a stunned silence.

"You don't think …" this time I could clearly hear Jessica's sobs.

"Doesn't matter what I think. You know the guy better. Was he in town that night?"

"In town?" Jessica wailed. "Meera, he was right there, in Willow Lake Park. He came to pick me up for my meeting."

I was speechless.

"Did he talk to Jordan that night?"

"He did. But I don't know what. I went to the restroom in the park. When I got back, they were glaring at each other. Colin's glasses were lying on the ground."

"I think you need to tell all this to the cops, Jessica," I advised, rubbing my hands across my forehead. "It's a lot to process, and I really need to get going now."

Jessica whimpered, but she recovered soon and thanked me. I promised to get in touch with her later that week. I needed to bring Stan up to speed on all this.

I collapsed on the couch, staring into space. How many more ants were hiding in the woodwork?

Chapter 20

My mind was churning, trying to process too much information. I definitely needed a break from Jordan Harris. Tony agreed to come with me. I looked forward to shopping my heart out in the mall before picking up my aunt from the airport.

Tony was driving his mom's sedan and I was settled into the passenger seat in my favorite pose. The seat back was reclined as far as it would go, my feet were up on the dash and I was munching Doritos like they were the last food left on earth.

I cursed as a semi nearly cut us off.

Tony laughed at me, and his eyes crinkled. I noticed how he got crow's feet around his eyes when he smiled. He was going to age around the eyes. Yes, I had begun noticing those fine signs of age people exhibited. When I do something, I live it.

"You're getting cranky from all that salt, Meera."

Tony grabbed the box of chips from my hand and chucked it behind his seat.

"Hey!" I protested.

"What's bothering you?" he asked.

"Too much information," I said cryptically. "I don't want to talk about it now," I said before Tony could ask me to elaborate.

The barren landscape was stark but beautiful. My bottom felt toasty in the heated seats and I snoozed on and off. Soon, we were at the mall.

"We can shop together for a while, but then we need to split up."

I didn't want to miss this opportunity to get something good for Tony.

"What're you getting me this year?" Tony wiggled his eyebrows.

"You'll find out on Christmas morning, and not a day sooner."

I did my best to hide the presents but Jeet and Tony ferreted them out every year. It was like an ongoing contest.

I got cashmere sweaters for the men in the family. Dad and Jeet got V neck sweaters and Pappa got a cardigan. I got a silk scarf for Motee Ba and a pair of leather gloves. Her old ones were looking very worn. Becky got a bottle of her favorite perfume. I had a hard time choosing something for Tony.

"Hungry yet?" Tony asked.

We had split for half an hour and I tried to peek at the bag he held in his hand.

"Starving. Let's hit the food court here. We don't want to be late for the flight."

We got a mix of Chinese food, bourbon chicken, falafel, burgers and milk shakes. In short, a little bit of everything we could find there.

Aunt Anita was standing just inside the Arrivals area, one hand on her hip, her eyes hidden behind dark glasses. She had taken advantage of the full luggage allowance the airline permitted.

"About time," she said, opening her arms for a hug.

I went into them dutifully and kissed her on the cheek. Tony got a similar welcome.

My aunt is a formidable force in the family. She rules her own kids and husband, the Oklahoma Patels and Uncle Vipul and his California clan with an iron hand, all from her position of power in Edison, New Jersey. I never know what to expect from her.

She gave me a once over and nodded.

"A bit shabby but as pretty as ever."

I smiled. We got into the car and headed back to Swan Creek.

"Do you want to grab something from a drive through?" I asked solicitously.

"No need. I brought plenty of food."

She pulled out a box of *theplas*. Didn't I say they are a staple in any Gujarati household? Aunt Anita had slathered the *theplas* with *chundo*, a sweet and spicy mango relish and rolled them like cigars. She picked one up and started munching on it.

Tony and I grabbed one each.

Aunt Anita launched into a detailed report of what my cousins were up to.

"What's new with you, Meera?" she asked, finally coming up for air.

"Nothing much," I shrugged.

"Hmmm ... Ba doesn't say much on the phone. But I'll get to the bottom of things soon enough."

I had no doubt she would. Ba, her mother, is my Motee Ba or grandma. Tony took the exit for Swan Creek and we reached home a few minutes later. Motee Ba was sitting by the window. She rushed out, followed by Jeet.

"*Kem Cho, Ba?*"

Aunt Anita touched Motee Ba's feet and asked her how she was.

In Indian culture, we show our respect for parents and elders by touching their feet, or the ground they walk on.

Motee Ba and Aunt Anita laughed and cried, while happily wiping their tears. They do this every time they meet. Pappa had tottered out on his cane.

"Anita!" he bellowed.

Aunt Anita followed the same ritual again, touching Pappa's feet.

"Let's go inside. I'm freezing. Get the bags, boy!" he glared at Jeet who was engrossed in telling Tony something.

Everyone settled into the living room and I was dispatched into the kitchen to make the requisite tea, or chai.

"There's some *pakoras* I just finished frying," Motee Ba called out.

Aunt Anita squealed like a child.

They say nothing tastes as good as the food your Mom cooks. I have never eaten anything that fits this criteria, but yeah, I can vouch for anything my grandma cooks.

Dad was summoned and he came out, surprised at the sign of my aunt.

"Anita? What are you doing here?"

"Hello *Bhai*! I guess you forgot I was coming."

Aunt Anita smiled and hugged Dad.

The Christmas lights twinkled as the sun set. After a couple of rounds of tea, the ladies opted for wine and Dad poured Scotch for himself and Pappa.

I excused myself and went to the guest house. I was itching to talk to Stan. I called him up.

"Meera! Where have you been? I called earlier."

We exchanged some pleasantries and got to the point.

"I have loads of information," I told him. "So much that my head is reeling with this stuff."

"Calm down and tell me one by one," Stan soothed.

I told him about Colin Stevens. Stan hadn't heard of him until then, just as I suspected.

"How do you find these people, Meera? It's amazing."

"He was just there. And then he told me all these things."

"So Jessica and Jordan weren't really the love birds we thought they were," Stan burst out. "This puts a different spin on things. We never considered Jessica important until now."

"That's just the beginning."

I told him everything Colin Stevens had said. Then I told him what Jessica had said.

"So this piece of crap is blackmailing Jessica as we speak?" he thundered.

"Apparently, not any more. He doesn't need to, now that Jordan is out of the picture."

Stan was silent. I could imagine his frustration.

"Any luck with the alibis?" I asked him.

"Pamela Harris finally opened up," Stan laughed. "She was on a date."

"What? Then why didn't she say so?"

"It was all hush hush, it seems. She didn't want to say anything unless it was serious. But the man in question confirmed it."

"How do you know he isn't lying?" I asked.

I was curious about how the police decided who was speaking the truth and who wasn't.

"They were in a pub full of people until 11, twenty or so miles away from Swan Creek. And the guy dropped her off at the ranch around midnight. One of the ranch hands saw them."

"And Cameron?" I asked in a hushed voice.

"Unfortunately, he was spotted in Swan Creek that night. He was in a bar downtown around 9. After that, we don't know."

"What does he say about that?" I wondered how Cam would field this one.

"He admitted he stopped by for a drink. He had to. His leg was hurting so he drank a bit much. He slept it off at Jessica's and drove home around 6. He was doing his usual chores at the ranch when he heard about Jordan."

"My God, Stan! This just keeps getting better, doesn't it?"

"I know!" Stan sounded as tired as I did.

"Any more information on what caused Jordan's death?"

"Could be anything," Stan moaned. "We have come up with a questionnaire for the family. Some basic medical history and behavioral questions. The medical examiner's office hopes to get some kind of indication from it about what to test."

"Why do they need that?" I wanted to know.

"They tested for a few known poisons. Now there are hundreds of substances they could test for. But we don't have the time or money to do that. Maybe this extra information will show them the way."

"What about the diner inspection?" I asked the question I dreaded most.

"Haven't you heard from Sylvie yet?" Stan was surprised. "The food guys swept the diner. They didn't find anything suspicious. The diner's cleared. I hear they are going to open for breakfast tomorrow."

"I was in the city all day. So maybe I missed this. That's the best news you could've given me, Stan."

I was really happy for Sylvie and Jon.

"Well, yes. I plan to be there bright and early tomorrow to see everything goes well.

That, and it's been too long since I've had a taste of Sylvie's sausage gravy. I've actually lost a couple of pounds, you know."

The portly Stan Miller liked to eat.

"Don't worry. A few servings of my special fried chicken and you'll be back in the ring."

We were quiet for a moment.

"This case is turning out to be something, isn't it?" Stan muttered.

"It's all a big puzzle," I agreed. "I'm still not sure what the motive is. Money doesn't seem to be it."

I promised to keep Stan updated if I came across any more information.

Dinner time was noisy. Tony's mom had come over and we all enjoyed the special dinner that had been prepared for my Aunt.

"What's this I hear about you reopening Sarla's case, Meera?" my aunt asked me later.

Dad had gone back to his study. Pappa was dozing in his chair. He woke up suddenly when he heard my aunt's voice and snorted.

"About time!" he muttered, and nodded off again.

Motee Ba took my hand in hers, silently giving me courage.

I looked at my aunt.

"You've heard right, Aunt Anita."

"Are you prepared for what you might find?" she asked incredulously.

I didn't take her words to heart. I knew she was worried about how we would deal with the consequences.

"Well, we've lived without any news for 17 years. Maybe we'll finally get some closure."

I braced myself for a tirade. My Aunt Anita is not known to mince words.

"Are you encouraging her in this, Ba?" she accused her mother. "You should know better than that."

"Anita, we've all waited for a long time to get some kind of closure on this. I'm with Meera on this one."

My aunt glared at her father next. He ignored her. If anyone could stand up to my aunt, it was my grandpa.

"What about Andy? Does he know about this?"

"Dad's helping me a lot. He's handed over all his old files. I'm going through them now."

I was trying to be calm, but I was seething inside. My aunt always does this. She riles everyone up just a few hours after she lands.

"I'm warning you, Meera! No good can come of this."

"I know you're worried about all of us, Auntie. But you can't change my mind on this one."

She stood up, ready to storm out of the room.

"You're making a big mistake. Why don't you do something normal for a change? Like run after some boy your age?"

Motee Ba was looking tired.

"Sit down, Anita! You're too old for tantrums."

"Anything else you've been keeping from me, Ba?"

"Plenty," Motee Ba shot back. "For starters, Meera has a stalker."

Chapter 21

I banged around some pots and pans as I made breakfast. I was too mad at my aunt to make any special effort for her, but I had to be polite. I made spinach and feta omelets and made a cherry tomato sauce to go with them.

"Did you know Sylvie's is going to reopen today?" I asked Motee Ba.

She put her hand on her mouth.

"Oh my God, I forgot all about that."

She stood up and dialed the café's number from the kitchen phone. Sylvie answered and Motee Ba offered her congratulations.

"Too busy to talk right now," she told me. "There's a small number of people for breakfast, but they are prepping for a big lunch crowd."

"Maybe we should give them a helping hand," I mused.

Motee Ba was all smiles.

"See, when we went to Nancy's, we noticed all these special promos they were doing. Like free coffee refills if you spend over 10 bucks. Or soup and sandwich combos. Maybe we should do that in the beginning. Just until the old crowd gets used to going to the right diner!"

I raised my eyebrows at Motee Ba and she high fived me.

"Great idea, Meera!"

"School's out so no point posting any flyers there, but maybe we can just write these up on the chalk board?"

I was eager to get on to the diner and sound my new ideas off Sylvie.

"Go!" Motee Ba said, reading my mind.

I untied my apron and grabbed my keys. I could always have biscuits with gravy at Sylvie's.

"Where are you off to?" my aunt complained, walking into the kitchen.

I waved at her and kept going.

Sylvie's was a welcome sight. Jon was rubbing down the windows with some paper, and a big wreath hung on the door.

He grinned at me.

"Hello Meera. Thought we'd get into the holiday mood."

Becky was in the kitchen, humming to herself. She looked comfortable in her old domain. I hugged Sylvie and congratulated her.

"Guess they didn't find no rats in my kitchen," she smirked.

A few old timers were already working on their eggs and hash. They lifted their coffee cups and a cheer went up.

"I have an idea, Sylvie," I cut to the chase.

"Don't be shy, baby," she encouraged me.

"How about some special offers to get the place going again?"

I explained what I was thinking and we listed out different ideas.

"Are you still planning to supply pies to Nancy's?" I asked Sylvie.

She shook her head.

"Not anymore."

"We do need to push the pies again. How about a free coffee with every slice of pie? It can be a holiday special. I don't think anyone can resist that."

Sylvie got the idea.

"And let's offer a cup of soup with every sandwich."

"Are you planning to bankrupt me, woman?" Jon complained, but the twinkle in his eye told me he was kidding.

"I think that's enough for a start," I nodded. "We'll have to make lots more soup."

"I'm on it," Becky called out from the kitchen.

"Has Stan been here yet? He was talking about missing your sausage gravy."

"He was here minutes after we opened," Sylvie laughed. "He dug into those buttermilk biscuits like there was no tomorrow."

"Things will turn around, Sylvie," I said softly, hugging her again.

We had all been through a rough time, but Sylvie and Jon had faced the brunt of it.

"Any more ideas on what happened to that boy?" she asked.

I shook my head. I helped Becky for a few hours and headed home. I looked in on Tony on the way back.

"What's cookin', good lookin'?" he teased.

"Any guesses what Pam's alibi is?"

"Just say it," Tony said.

He doesn't like these guessing games.

"She has a beau!"

"You should've thought of that!" Tony kidded, but he was half serious.

"Want to come and check out my aging program?" I asked Tony.

"Are you ready to demo it already?" his eyes gleamed.

"As ready as I'll ever be."

We drove home and I fired up the computer in the guest house. I fed in a photo of Aunt Reema's from when Tony was born. I ran the program and it spit out 10 different photos of Aunt Reema as she should look now.

Tony was speechless.

"Why do they all look different?"

I explained how each photo was a projection of a peculiar combination of aging parameters. Two or three of the photos looked very much like Aunt Reema as she looked now. The others were a good likeness.

"It's like a portrait," Tony exclaimed. "Some artists get it exactly right, while some are almost right."

I laughed.

"Yeah, sort of. The trouble is we don't know which one is going to be right, or most right, in my Mom's case. That's why I've come up with this option of getting 10 possible results."

"You mean you want to pass around 10 photos instead of just 1," Tony summed up.

"Exactly!"

"As long as the people you give these to don't mind, that should work well."

"You think I'm ready to show this to Dad?"

Tony's response was a bone crushing hug. I took that as a yes.

The guest house soon filled up with the entire family. Aunt Anita sat in a corner chair with a frown on her face. Apparently, she still hadn't forgiven me.

"Get on with it, girl," Pappa tapped his cane.

I started with a photo of Motee Ba and fed it to the program. Everyone gasped at the 10 photos the program spit out. I followed with a photo of Dad, Jeet and Pappa. Finally, I fed a photo of my Mom.

The silence in the room was deafening. The photo was in profile so I didn't expect much from it.

"I've never tried running the program with a side shot," I mumbled.

Before I finished speaking, the screen was splashed with 10 different photos. I looked at the screen in dismay. For some reason, the software hadn't worked well in this case. Many features were distorted and I ended up with what looked like funny caricatures.

Dad looked disappointed.

"You've done an excellent job, Meera," he said kindly. "But we need a better photo. Or you need to fix the code."

My aunt spoke up.

"This is like magic. You're a genius, Meera."

No one commented on that. Being a genius isn't enough in my family.

"I think I have a front facing photo of your mother," Aunt Anita announced. "Now I just have to remember where it is, and then have someone back home scan it and send it to me."

I looked at her hungrily.

She spoke to Dad.

"You remember the photos we took at the airport when you were going to the US for the first time? Sarla's staring straight at the camera in that one."

Dad had paled a bit. He licked his lips and blinked at his sister.

Aunt Anita nodded at me.

"Don't worry, Meera. I'll get it for you."

Motee Ba was gently wiping her eyes. Even Jeet looked disturbed. Everyone had realized that we would soon be privy to what my mother might have looked like now. It was an eerie feeling. We didn't know if such a person existed or if it was a ghost.

"Hansa! It's time for my lunch!" Pappa roared, breaking the tension.

Everyone dispersed. Tony and I stayed on, along with Jeet.

"You're close, Meera," he said in a hushed voice.

"This is just a photo, Jeet!"

I was close alright. Close to tears. The phone rang and I picked it up.

"For you, Meera," Motee Ba said and hung up the extension.

"Meera, Hello, can you hear me?" Pamela Harris came on the line.

"How are you Pam?" I asked.

"The cops asked for my alibi. And I had to tell them. So I guess there's no harm in telling you now."

I felt uncomfortable.

"I sort of know, Pam!"

"Oh? I suppose you spoke to that cop friend of yours?"

Pam took my silence for a yes.

"Now you know why I didn't want to talk about it," she sighed.

"I understand. Everyone's entitled to their privacy."

"It's not just that. I'm ashamed!"

"Why?" I was curious.

"Can you imagine having a beau at my age? I'm too old. What will Pa say?"

Pam may not be too old to date, but she was certainly too old to worry about what her Pa thought. I didn't say a word.

"I used to go out with someone, back when Ma was alive. Then I got busy taking care of the boys. I never met anyone. Until now, that is."

"Relax, Pam," I crooned. "No one's judging you."

"Jordan would've been happy for me," she sniffled. "He always tried to make me go out and meet people."

"Hey, have they given you some kind of questionnaire about him?"

Pam sniffled again, taking a deep breath.

"I just spoke to that policeman. They are going to be faxing it over soon. Do you want to come over and help me go through it?"

"I'm not sure I can help. You're the one that knew him."

"Please. I'll be glad of the company."

"Let me get back to you," I promised.

I asked Tony if he was up for a ride to the Triple H. We had nothing much going on anyway. I called Pam back and told her we'd start after lunch.

Jeet wanted to tag along and I agreed reluctantly.

"Maybe I can ride a horse today. We missed doing that when they kicked us out."

"You'll do no such thing. We are going there for work, Jeet. And Pam's already refunded our money from that time."

"What?" Jeet pounced. "Where is it?"

"It's gone!" I laughed, making a face at him.

"Bet she bought some fancy gift for you with it," he accused Tony.

We piled into Tony's pickup after lunch. I wondered why Pam couldn't fill out that questionnaire on her own. I decided to take this chance to ask her about Cam and Jessica.

Jeet kept Tony busy in some guy talk all the way. I was bored to death by the time we drove through the arches of the Triple H. Pam had asked us to come to the homestead.

Pa Harris was ensconced in his rocking chair, and a fire was blazing. I was glad because the temperature was beginning to drop quite a bit. Pam poured coffee, looking excited.

The lack of any holiday decorations was obvious at the Triple H.

Pa Harris must have been thinking the same thing. He nodded toward an empty corner.

"That's where we usually put our tree. Jordan had a good lot going over at the west border of the ranch. We get at least an eight foot fir every year. One year, it was so tall, the tops brushed the rafters."

He seemed lost in some old memory, his eyes looking sunken and empty. I didn't have an appropriate response so I stayed quiet.

Pam picked up a sheaf of papers held together by a clip.

"This is what they faxed over. I hope we can answer most questions without having to go to our old family doc."

I leaned forward, reading the questions as Pam checked them off one by one.

"Heart disease, No. Hypertension – No. Jordan was very calm most of the time but his temper could flare up in an instant."

I tried to peek at the next question.

"Cholesterol? Borderline."

Pam went over questions related to almost every bodily function.

"How is any of this going to help?" she began looking frustrated.

I noticed something about the papers she was holding.

"Look, Pam, these papers are all mixed up. You need to start from Page 1 and go through them in the right order. Maybe that will make some more sense?"

"You're right, Meera!" She slammed the papers in my hand. "Can you do it, please? Then we'll take it from the top again."

Pam looked like she was about to burst into tears, or blow a gasket, so I obliged.

"Okay! Was Jordan allergic to penicillin?" I asked.

She shook her head no.

I moved to the next question.

"Was he allergic to any drugs?"

"No. But he was allergic to nuts."

Pam's response was as casual as telling me she took two sugars in her tea.

"That's the next question," I said, looking up, suddenly afraid of what was coming.

Was subject allergic to any food items, such as milk or nuts?

Pam's eyes widened and she covered her mouth with one hand.

"I never thought of that."

"What kind of Southerner doesn't eat pecan pie?" Pa Harris said mournfully. "But my Jordan could never abide by it, ever since he was a child."

"What kind of pie did they find on him?" Pam asked urgently.

"Err, I'm not sure, but I think it was a berry pie."

The image of Jordan sprawled on that bench was crystal clear in my mind. So were the pie crumbs with the reddish filling, and the wedge of pie that was falling out of his pocket.

"Do you think it's important?" Pam asked.

"Let's send in the questionnaire. We'll let the police do their job."

I was trying to be nonchalant but I was sure we'd hit upon the cause of Jordan's death.

Chapter 22

Pamela couldn't usher us out fast enough. I still wanted to ask her about Cam.

"Was Cam interested in Jessica?" I asked her point blank.

She looked shocked. I didn't think she had thought about this before.

"How do you mean? Do you mean was he romantically involved with her?"

"Un-huh," I nodded my head vigorously.

"What made you say that?"

"Look, Pam, maybe it's nothing. I may be mistaken."

She stuck to her stance.

"What made you say that, Meera?"

"Well, he mentioned staying over at her place once or twice. In fact, that's where he was the day Jordan … I mean, the day Jordan and Jessica celebrated their engagement."

Pam's face settled into a mask.

"I wouldn't know anything about that."

"Please, Pam, if you know something, you should tell me now."

Pam hesitated.

"Jessica was, is, the friendly type. She was free with her favors."

My eyebrows shot up my head.

"Do you mean to say she slept around?"

"What?" Pam's face looked stricken. "Not those kind of favors! Anything, really. She never said no to anyone. Kids at the college had keys to her apartment, to her car. They raided her fridge anytime they felt like it. And I think they also raided her wallet."

"You mean she couldn't say no to people."

Pam shrugged.

"Another way of putting it. Look, she was Daddy's girl. And Daddy's rich. Those kids knew that and they took advantage."

"What about Cam?"

"I suppose Cam did it to hassle Jordan," Pamela finally admitted.

"Isn't that taking their rivalry too far?"

"That's the way they were. Cam insisted Jessica would have chosen him if she'd seen him first."

"She could still have chosen him, don't you think?" I mused.

"But she got engaged to Jordan!" Pamela shook her head. "Why would she do that if she fell for Cam?"

"Maybe she was just buying time? Maybe she thought Cam would step up if he thought time was running out."

"I don't know, Meera," Pam was uncertain.

"Jessica wanted to move to Texas. What do you think of that?"

Pamela's face blanched.

"What? Was Jordan moving with her too? Pa would be crushed."

"I hear Jordan wasn't ready to," I eased her mind. "Do you think Cam's unwanted attentions may have made her want to flee?"

Jessica had told me they fought over leaving the Triple H, but she hadn't explained why. Maybe the thought of having Cam around her all the time made her uncomfortable.

Pamela clutched her head with her hands. I felt sorry for her. I was experiencing something similar, trying to make sense out of this.

"Meera, I think I'm going to send in the questionnaire to your police friend. And let them investigate. I just can't think any more."

I nodded. We said goodbye and Tony started driving back.

"You think I gave her a hard time?" I asked Tony.

"Let's just drive back home, okay?" he said. "No stopping for snacks anywhere."

We reached home in an hour, and of course we were starving by that time.

"I hope Granny's got something to eat," Tony said, rubbing his hands.

Jeet let out a yawn. He had napped all the way back. A car pulled into our driveway and stopped a few yards from us.

"Looks like Motee Ba's just coming in too," I observed.

We piled out, watching Motee Ba and Aunt Anita get out of their car. Their eyes were shining and they seemed about to burst. Like they wanted to use the bathroom really bad.

"Let's go inside, Meera!"

My aunt held my arm in an iron grip and almost dragged me behind her.

"Sit," she ordered, pointing to the couch.

"What's the matter?"

"Ba told me about this person that's stalking you," Aunt Anita began with relish. "I came up with an idea."

We all groaned. My aunt was never short on ideas. Most of the time, they involved gossip or snooping.

"We decided to follow you," Motee Ba gushed.

"You followed us all the way to the Triple H?" Tony exclaimed. "That's a two hour drive, Granny!"

Motee Ba cracked her knuckles. She only did that when she was agitated.

"We followed you all the way there. Then we drove on and doubled back. We stopped by the side of the road until we saw you start back. Then we followed you home."

"And?" I asked, bored.

I didn't expect much from this fool endeavor.

"You had a tail, Meera. No doubt about it."

My aunt sounded triumphant.

"Maybe that person was just driving on the same road, going somewhere else?"

Aunt Anita held up a finger.

"In that case, why would they wait for you and follow you back?"

"Wait a minute, Auntie. So there were two cars just idling at the side of the road. You must have noticed each other. And I should have noticed you."

Tony was probably mad because he hadn't spotted them. We had been too busy talking.

"Well, I drove off the shoulder a bit and …" Motee Ba stopped mid sentence.

"Did you wait in a ditch?" I asked. "Unbelievable!"

"It wasn't a ditch," she protested. "Well, not exactly. It was just a bit off the road. There were a few bushes that gave us perfect cover."

I rolled my eyes.

"And what about the other car then?" Tony demanded.

"She went into a small country store," Aunt Anita began.

"We know the place." I told her about our last visit to that store, and what the woman there had said.

"We had the perfect spot!" Motee Ba said proudly. "We spotted you come out of that turnoff that takes you to the Triple H. Then when you passed the country store, we saw this car pulling out behind you. We followed."

"What about the car?"

"That car was behind you until you turned into our lane. Then it drove past."

I felt numb.

"Was it a woman, then? Are you sure?"

Aunt Anita nodded.

"Pretty sure. And I don't see a man from these parts wearing pink."

"Can you recognize her?" Tony asked eagerly.

Both Motee Ba and Aunt Anita hung their heads.

"She had some kind of scarf wrapped around her head and face. As if she's driving in a car without heat. I couldn't even spot her hair color."

My aunt sounded beaten. Motee Ba didn't look too great either. I tried to cheer them up.

"But you spotted her!! Don't you see? All this time, we've only had suspicions. Even the cops haven't actually seen her follow me."

"You need to call Stan right now, Meera," Motee Ba said urgently.

I didn't waste any time. Stan was brought up to speed.

"Your granny did this?" Stan was incredulous. "You Patels are turning into quite the sleuths."

"What now?" I pressed.

"Nothing much," Stan said. "I don't suppose your granny got the plates on that car?"

I asked Aunt Anita and she handed me a piece of paper. I rattled it off to Stan.

"I'll get on it. My guess is this is a rental, just like the last time. But maybe we'll get some more info on it this time."

"Have you heard from Pam?"

I told him about Jordan's nut allergy and told him to expect something from Pam soon.

"Maybe this is the clue we've been missing, Meera," Stan perked up. "We can test for this now."

"We still need to find out who did it, Stan," I reminded him. "Isn't that more important?"

"That's the ultimate goal alright. But knowing the method of the crime might help us narrow it down."

I thanked Stan and hung up.

"I'm starving!" Aunt Anita said.

"Hey, that's my line," Jeet said, and we all burst out laughing.

"Let's order pizza," I suggested.

Pizza sounded great to everyone, and we put in an order for two large pies.

"Any luck finding that photo, Auntie?" I almost wanted her to say no.

"Haven't checked my email since breakfast," my aunt replied. "Let me have a bite to eat first, Meera!"

I almost sighed with relief. Dad joined us reluctantly when the pizza arrived.

"Your mother's losing her mind," Pappa roared at him. "You need to control these women better, boy."

Motee Ba tried to skim over their covert mission. Dad's mouth dropped open.

"This is exactly what you do every time you come here," Dad looked at my aunt accusingly.

Then he stared at his mother.

"But Ba! You're supposed to keep an eye on them, not join their ranks."

Motee Ba ignored him, choosing to keep her mouth shut. My Dad offered some more choice words for everyone and then dug into his pizza.

"Can I check my email on your computer, Andy?" Aunt Anita asked Dad.

He stood up and she followed him into his office. She was back a few minutes later, her face covered in smiles. She came and put a hand on my shoulder.

"Just emailed it to you, Meera."

The tension in the room went up a notch.

"Are you ready?" Motee Ba asked quietly.

I was as ready as I would ever be.

Tony and Jeet followed me to the guest house. I told the others to wait for my call.

My hands shook as I opened my aunt's email. The photo was the sort I needed, although it wasn't very sharp. I downloaded it to my hard drive and fired up my program.

I looked at Tony and Jeet and took a deep breath. None of us dared to say a word. Tony folded an arm around me, and Jeet did the same. I hit the Enter key on my keyboard and closed my eyes until Tony gently prodded me.

"It's done, Meera!"

Ten images stared back at me from the screen. If my mother were alive, she would look something like this.

I picked up the extension and called Motee Ba over. They came over, Pappa tapping his cane impatiently, leaning on Dad. I pointed to the screen unnecessarily. There was a shocked silence and tears rolled down the women's eyes.

Dad cleared his throat.

"I think you can send these on now, Meera."

"Would you pick any particular ones out of these?"

All of them pointed to the same two pictures.

"Alright then, I'll get on with this."

I wanted everyone to leave so I could launch into a full blown crying session. They all seemed to have the same idea. The group split up and only Tony stayed behind. He opened his arms wide as soon as we were alone.

"You can let go now," he said softly.

The tears began to flow, and I began sobbing my heart out. I couldn't fathom what had just happened or why it was painful. Maybe seeing how my mother would have looked now had made me feel her loss all over again.

"All this time, and it still hurts to think of her," I muttered through my sobs.

Tony heated some water for tea and dunked in a chamomile tea bag. He made me drink the tea.

"You need to be strong, Meera," he soothed. "There's nothing wrong with being emotional. But now you have to take the next step."

I put all the 10 photos into a zip folder and prepared a cover letter for them. I emailed this out to the list of people who had already replied to me. I would also include it in the new queries I sent out after this.

"What a day!" Tony exclaimed. "We may have found what killed Jordan, we know you have a stalker for sure, and now this."

"A bit too much for you?" I asked.

Sometimes I worry Tony will get tired of me and stop hanging out.

"Not yet," he teased.

Chapter 23

I spent most of the next day contacting authorities in different states. I sent out the photos to dozens of people. Most of them would be busy with the holidays, ready to take their annual time off. So there was a fat chance any of them would read my email before the New Year. But I wanted to get the photos out before I had any second thoughts.

There was a hum of activity around the house. Motee Ba and my aunt were rustling up treats in the kitchen, talking about old times, catching up on gossip from the extended family. Even as a child, I had loved sitting at the kitchen table with them, shelling peas or helping them somehow, soaking up their stories of life in India. And then there was my aunt's life in New Jersey. Sometimes, it seemed to me like she lived in a mini India in the heart of Jersey.

My Dad had finished sending out grades and seemed to have a gap in his calendar. He offered to help me with the Mom Project.

I wanted to gather Tony and Becky and go over everything we had learned so far about Jordan Harris. I was going around in circles. Nothing made much sense. Every person close to him seemed to be telling the truth. Either one of them was a seasoned liar, or there was someone who hadn't come out of the wings yet. So far, I hadn't been able to discern any motive. Far as I could tell from my vast collection of Agatha Christie books, there is always a motive for murder.

I called Jessica on a whim and asked if she could meet me. She suggested the coffee shop on campus. Fifteen minutes later, I had parked in the deserted lot outside the Student Union. Jessica was already waiting for me with two coffees and cookies.

"I got you a latte," she pointed. "Is that okay?"

"Sure!" I thanked her and picked up a cookie.

Cookies speak a language I understand. They always cry 'pick me up'.

"So what's up, Meera?" Jessica got to the point.

She looked tired. She had dropped a few pounds since the first time I met her and the circles under her eyes had darkened. Her hair was dry like it gets when you run out of conditioner. I didn't know if she was always so unkempt.

"I went to the ranch yesterday," I began.

"Pam called me last night," Jessica nodded. "And she told me about that questionnaire."

She leaned closer to me.

"Do you remember the first time we met? I had told you how Jordan always got the berry pie at Sylvie's because he couldn't eat pecans."

I shook my head.

"All this time, even Sylvie didn't mention anything about a possible allergy."

"Jordan's been eating at Sylvie's for years. I guess they knew him by face. There's no way anyone there would hand him a pie that had nuts in it."

"What are you saying, Jessica?"

"If they find nuts in Jordan's body …" she paused and held back a sob. "If they find nuts, I think we can be sure it was done on purpose. There's no way Jordan would eat nuts by accident. He was very careful about it."

I placed a hand on her shoulder.

"Let's wait until we know for sure."

"Is this what you wanted to talk about?" she asked.

"You told me you wanted to move away from the Triple H," I began. "But I don't think you mentioned why."

"I'm an only child. And my Daddy has a big spread down South. We could do our own thing there."

"But I thought the resort at Triple H was Jordan's baby. Didn't he bring the ranch up to snuff by himself?"

"Jordan put a lot of sweat into the Triple H. But he wasn't really the boss. He had to get his Pa's permission before taking any decision. And then talk to Pam and get her approval. It could get tedious."

"What about his brother?" I asked.

"He didn't chime in on day to day stuff when he was away," Jessica said, "but he was beginning to take an interest, now that he's planning to settle here."

"So that was an additional person to please," I noted.

"Yep!" Jessica pursed her lips.

"And you're saying Jordan didn't like doing that," I repeated.

Jessica frowned.

"Jordan was a ninny. A pushover. He hardly ever noticed how his family was taking advantage. He put his brains and brawn into the Triple H, and he didn't have much to show for it."

I gave her a sympathetic smile. It seemed like Jessica was the one who didn't want to have Jordan's family around her. I didn't think she'd gone to the trouble of getting a doctorate just to check in guests at a dude ranch.

"Isn't your research something to do with cows?" I asked.

She smiled brightly. "We're close to developing a supplement that will naturally hasten their growth. I'm working on a pilot with a small herd on Daddy's ranch.

We've had very good results. This will almost double our output."

"Why didn't Jordan want to move?" I asked.

Jessica twisted her mouth in a grimace.

"He didn't want to leave his family. As if we were moving across the world. My Daddy's ranch is barely a 100 miles away from the H."

"Pa Harris talked about how old their ranch is," I murmured.

Jessica got excited.

"That's just it. Jordan kept on about that all the time. And he wanted to reconnect with his brother."

"Speaking of Cameron …" I paused, knowing my next line might annoy Jessica. "Do you like him?"

"You mean like, do I want to go out with him?" Jessica asked.

I gave a slight nod.

"I'm not that kind of girl, Meera. You think I would get engaged with one brother and go out with the other?"

"Did he come on to you?" I persisted.

"Guys come on to me all the time. What can I do? With Cam, I think it was more for shock effect."

"He mentioned he has a key to your apartment."

"No he doesn't. But I do keep it under a potted plant right outside my door. Things aren't that formal on campus. I live close to the lab. So people often just crash at my place for a nap. Cam did it too a couple of times. No big deal."

"He said he was at your place the night Jordan … that night."

I raised my eyebrows at Jessica.

"Maybe he was. I was working through the night. Then I napped at my desk and got home around 7."

I didn't think I would get much more out of Jessica.

"Are you going home for Christmas?" I asked.

"I'm leaving on Christmas Eve. Trying to squeeze in as much work as possible until then."

I stood up and wished her a safe drive home. She hugged me impulsively. Then she turned and walked away.

I nursed my coffee for a while more, enjoying the solitude in a place that was usually bustling with plenty of people. I dumped my empty coffee cup into a trash can and walked out, planning to visit Sylvie's on my way home.

I almost ran into Colin Stevens. He seemed to be wearing the same clothes, and looked more unwashed than before.

"Finished your meeting?" he asked.

"What?" I burst out.

"Your meeting with Jessica? How was it?"

Colin Stevens had managed to irritate me once again. I opened my mouth to give him a piece of my mind.

"Didn't I say she tells me everything?" he sneered.

"That, or you eavesdrop on her phone calls," I said mildly.

"Who do you think she called when she wanted a ride, huh?" he asked, pushing his glasses up his nose. "Who did she turn to when that so called fiancé of hers was sulking over something stupid?"

"Are you talking about the night Jordan died?" I asked.

He puffed up, looking important.

"Do you realize you may have been the last person to see him alive?"

"Of course not!" he retorted. "I mean, of course I wasn't."

"You would say that, of course. To save your skin."

Colin Stevens laughed in my face.

"You work at the library, don't you? Been reading a lot of trashy novels? Why would I want to save my skin?"

I shook my head.

"Forget it. What do you mean you weren't the last person to talk to him?"

"We had an urgent team meeting that night. Our funding depends on delivering results at a certain pace. Every person needs to pull their weight and be present at the meetings. Jessica had promised to be there by 7. We needed to prep before our 8 PM meeting with our industry sponsor. When she wasn't in by 7:30, I called her."

"Go on," I urged.

Colin Stevens had stopped to take a breath.

"I could hear Jordan cursing in the background. Apparently, they were in the middle of an argument. Jessica asked me to come pick her up. When I reached there, they weren't talking to each other. Jessica went to use the restroom."

"Did Jordan say anything?" I asked.

"He looked pretty angry. He wasn't good to me at the best of times, so I didn't say anything. He opened his truck and took out a box or something."

My blood pressure went up a notch.

"Was it like the box they wrap pies in?" I asked with bated breath.

"How would I know?" Colin pounced. "I was reading some of our test results. We really were on a tight deadline."

"Then?"

"I heard Jordan call out to someone. Sounded like he was surprised to see that person there. I think it was his brother."

"Did you see this person?" I asked.

Colin Stevens shook his head. "I told you I was busy studying something. I thought maybe Jordan was just crying out, or was drunk. Then I saw a guy somewhere in the shadows. He beckoned to Jordan and he walked away."

"What about Jessica?"

"Jessica got into my car and we raced back to campus with 5 minutes to spare."

"Was Jessica in the lab all night then?"

"We all were," Colin smiled. "We pulled an allnighter, and then went home in the morning."

Colin had managed to add something to the story again. I wondered who it was Jordan had talked to. Was it really his brother Cameron? Or was it just some random guy in the park. Maybe it was some homeless person who wanted a bite to eat.

"Have you talked to the police yet?" I asked Colin Stevens. "I'm sure they will appreciate all the valuable information you have."

Colin Stevens whipped out a card.

"They can talk to me anytime. So can you. Let me know if you have any more questions."

I took his card and put it inside my purse.

"Say Jessica and Jordan had a falling out," I mused. "What do you think she would do?"

"The real question you want to ask is would Jessica do anything to harm Jordan, right?" Colin Stevens gave me a dark look.

I pursed my lips. I didn't want to say yes.

"I'll answer anyway. She would've dumped him some time or the other. He wasn't smart enough for her. Or ambitious enough."

Soon, Colin would be extolling his own virtues as the perfect match for Jessica. I thanked him for his patience and stepped out of the building.

The cold air felt invigorating and I took a deep breath. Once again, I was overwhelmed with the sheer amount of information floating around. Was there anyone who knew all the facts? Or anyone who could make sense out of this mess?

I got into the Camry and hit the road. I was so lost in my thoughts, I found myself in our driveway about 15 minutes later. I had completely forgotten my plan to visit Sylvie's.

The spicy notes of ginger and garlic wafted out from our kitchen, along with the scent of assorted spices. Dinner was almost ready and I was just in time for it.

Chapter 24

The next couple of days were busy sampling all the yummy food Motee Ba cooked for my aunt. It was the holidays, after all. Jeet and Pappa added in some special requests. Even my Dad wasn't immune to the delicacies that came out of the kitchen at regular intervals.

"What're we doing for Christmas dinner?" my aunt asked the room in general.

We were gathered around in the living room, playing cards. There was a roaring fire in the grate. We were well insulated against the sub zero winds blowing outside.

We were drinking mulled cider, and it warmed me inside out. I groaned mentally as I realized my aunt would be with us for Christmas day too. I love my aunt, but she can be a trial. She had already sneaked in about a dozen photos of eligible young men by me. They were all Indian and extremely well educated from Top 10 schools. Some were born and raised in America while some were still in India. Almost all of them were surgeons or doctors of some kind. The least desirable of them was a lawyer.

"You're not getting any younger, Meera. Once you cross 25, no one will look at you."

I showed the appropriate fear this statement was supposed to evoke.

"You're mocking me, aren't you?" my aunt asked suspiciously.

"No, I'm not, Aunt Anita!" I protested without much conviction.

"I like Tony too, but he hasn't pulled his life together yet," she responded.

"What does that mean?" I sighed. "Where's Tony come into all this?"

Motee Ba and my aunt exchanged a look. They didn't bother to reply.

"Anand's department buddies usually invite us for Christmas dinner," Motee Ba told my aunt. "But I don't think we have an invite yet this year."

"They had to go out of town to visit a sick relative," Dad explained. "I was supposed to tell you this."

"We've got to do something!" Motee Ba straightened in her chair, looking hopeful.

"Please, Ba! No more parties …"

Even a small party ends up being fifty people and is at least 3-4 days of work.

"Why don't we do a potluck?" I asked. "With Jon & Sylvie and Tony's people if they are free?"

"Not a bad idea!" Motee Ba leapt up and dialed Sylvie.

"We're meeting tomorrow to talk about it."

She held up a hand, warding off my Dad as he opened his mouth to speak.

"Everyone's going."

No one argued because we had all looked forward to doing something special for the holidays.

The next day, we were seated at Sylvie's, drinking coffee and eating pie.

"It's nice to see everyone here after so long," Sylvie smiled.

"Mom can make the roast," Tony volunteered, then looked at his Mom.

She nodded.

We came up with a short menu and then started splitting up the dishes amongst us.

My gaze strayed around the diner. A few tables were occupied. People were busy eating their food, talking softly amongst themselves or reading the paper. Becky was busy in the kitchen, filling orders.

A couple of cars pulled up outside. I braced myself as I realized they were police cars. Stan Miller got out of one car, and walked toward the diner door. Three other deputies flanked him. He pushed open the heavy door and strode in.

He seemed taken aback at seeing all of us.

"Hello Meera," he stuttered, looking tense.

"What's the matter?" I asked fearfully.

"It's not good," he said to me, almost under his breath.

Stan Miller turned toward Jon. Two of his henchmen had already surrounded Jon. One stood near the diner door.

"I'm sorry Jon, but you'll have to come with me."

Sylvie moved closer to Jon and took his hand in hers.

"What's going on?" she asked Stan, bewildered.

"Some more tests were done on Jordan Harris. They found nuts in his stomach, along with berries. Looks like the last thing he ate was your pie."

"But haven't you already cleared us?" Sylvie asked in a rush.

She had begun to hyperventilate.

"The food department checked the diner for chemicals or poisons. Or rat infestation. They didn't check for nuts, but I'm sure you have those around."

"We sure do, yes sir!" Sylvie was defensive. "My pecan pie is our top seller. But I didn't give that boy any. I know he never eats them nuts."

"So maybe there was some cross contamination?" Stan said reluctantly. "Look, Sylvie, I've been eating that pie for years. I know there's nothing wrong with it. But I have to take Jon with me now. I'm sorry."

"But it's two days to Christmas!" Sylvie wailed, hugging Jon tightly.

"I know. I'm sorry."

Stan looked uncomfortable.

I was impressed by Stan's behavior. The old Stan would have come in with sirens blaring, and ordered his people to take Jon away. He was really maturing a bit. That didn't make the situation any easier, though.

Dad stood up and patted Jon on the shoulder.

"I don't think you have a choice."

"So, are you arresting me?" Jon had been silent so far.

Stan Miller sighed deeply. Then he gave a slight nod.

"Jon Davis. You are under arrest for the murder of Jordan Harris. You have the right to remain silent. Anything you say …"

A gasp went around as Stan Miller read Jon his rights. We were all speechless as the deputies marched Jon out and put him in the back seat of a police cruiser. They backed out slowly and sped away.

Sylvie burst into sobs, and Motee Ba rushed to console her.

"Don't you have that lawyer's number in your phone?" Motee Ba asked Dad.

She was referring to the time earlier in the year when Stan had wanted to arrest me. My Dad had contacted a city lawyer at that time and I hoped he hadn't deleted his number.

Dad was already flicking through the address book in his phone.

He stepped away and spoke to someone for about five minutes.

"The lawyer can be here right away, but it won't help much. The courts are closed for the holidays. The earliest anything can be done is on Tuesday the 26th."

Sylvie gasped and clutched her heart. She was crying openly now.

"So my Jon's going to be in Jail over Christmas?"

Motee Ba put an arm around her and tried to placate her. Aunt Reema did the same. My Aunt Anita had a frown on her face. She can be a bit stuck up at the best of times. She doesn't get how close we are to Sylvie and Jon.

The few guests in the diner were staring at the scene openly, their food forgotten. Becky had come out of the kitchen. She tried to steer the guests to their food or urged them to leave if they were done.

Tony, Jeet and I were quiet. There wasn't much to say anyway.

Motee Ba looked up and beckoned me closer. Her mouth was set in a firm line and there was a determined glint in her eye.

"Do something, Meera. Find out who did this."

I felt the weight of responsibility settle on my shoulders. So far, I had been serious about finding out what happened to Jordan. But now the stakes had gone up. The clock was ticking and someone close to me was affected.

"I'm going to do my best," I promised, clasping Sylvie's hand in mine.

Dad and Pappa looked at each other. But they didn't say anything this time.

I was very familiar with the kitchen at Sylvie's. I generally manned the grill with Becky. There was a small room that Sylvie used exclusively for baking. She took me in there and showed me the setup again.

"Look, I have separate ovens for baking my pecan pies or any other nut based pies. There's another oven for the fruit pies. This here shelf on the right holds the fruit pies and the one on the left holds the pecan pies. All the utensils are different too."

I was impressed. I hadn't known Sylvie was this meticulous about the issue.

"Cross contamination is almost impossible here," I agreed.

"But if there's no contamination, what's the alternative?" Motee Ba wondered. "Will they say it was done on purpose?"

"We need to find out who had access to the pie," I marked, "both here in the diner and outside the diner."

"Well, he certainly had his fill here," Becky noted. "He ate a whole piece of pie with ice cream, and then he took half a pie with him."

"What time did he have dinner here?" I wanted to refresh my memory.

"Around 6-6:30," Becky confirmed.

"We know he was well until almost 8-8:30. So maybe someone doctored the pie that he took along with him."

"But who? And why?" Motee Ba pounced. "The why's not important to us. We just need to know who did it so we can exonerate Jon."

"The why is going to help us in finding out who did it," I told her.

"What's our next move, Meera?" Tony asked, looking impatient.

"I think we need to recap everything again, update our board."

I was referring to the large board I had set up in the guest house to help us work through this problem.

"Can Becky come with us?" I asked Sylvie.

She waved a hand, and gestured she didn't have a problem. She hadn't said anything at all for a while.

"Sylvie, can you please do something for me?" I asked gently. "Make a list of who else was in the diner when Jordan and Jessica were having their dinner. I know it's been a while, but anything, or anyone you remember will be helpful."

"Okay, Meera. I'll do that."

The Christmas party was forgotten and we all got up to leave. Motee Ba decided to stay back at the diner just to be with Sylvie for a while.

Sylvie had started sobbing again.

"Thirty years we've been running this diner. But my food's never made anyone sick before."

The diner had emptied again and it wouldn't take long for the gossips to spread the word about Jon's arrest.

"Don't worry, Sylvie! We all know Jon's innocent. And he'll be out soon enough. You'll see."

We all hugged her as we filed out of the diner. Dad and Aunt Anita helped Pappa into the car and they went home. I got into my Camry with Tony and the others and we followed my Dad home.

Chapter 25

Lunch hour had already come and gone and my stomach rumbled as I parked my car in front of the guest house.

"I'm starving too," Jeet spoke up after a long time.

I asked Tony to update the board with what we had found out in the last two days. I decided to make a quick batch of grilled cheese sandwiches.

Becky broke open two cans of tomato soup and heated some up on the stove. I slathered thick slices of country bread with butter and grilled them until the cheese melted and began oozing out. We made short work of the food.

I had set some coffee brewing and we finally put our thinking caps on. The food had energized me and I was ready to tackle the problem with a fresh mind.

"How do you want to do this?" Tony asked.

"Let's list the main players, go over their story, and list any motives they may have had to harm Jordan."

"Do you want Stan here?" Becky asked.

I shook my head.

"There's a lot of information in my head right now. I want to make some sense out of it before I can present it to Stan. It will help if I can present it in a coherent manner."

"So let's do that," Tony said encouragingly.

"Who are the people in Jordan's immediate circle?"

Tony listed them out one by one.

"Pa Harris, Brother Cameron, Sister Pamela, Girl friend Jessica – I think that's the lot."

"Anyone else related to Jordan?" I pressed. "Aren't you forgetting the ex?"

"What about Colin Stevens?" Tony asked.

I nodded. I drew a circle around Jordan and added the people closest to him.

"This is our first tier."

Then I added another circle and added 'Ex' whose name we didn't know. Then I also added Colin Stevens to the same circle.

"What about the people on the ranch, or anyone else he may have done business with?" Becky asked.

I drew a third circle around Jordan and added 'ranch hands', and 'business contacts' to it.

"Would Sylvie and Jon be in the third circle?" Tony mused. "They did interface with Jordan in some manner."

"Correct!" I added Jon and Sylvie's names into the third circle.

"We already know Jon and Sylvie are innocent, so let's strike their names out."

Tony's suggestion was approved and I drove a line through the Davises.

"I think we should start with the immediate family now," Becky spoke up. "Let's take Jordan's father first."

"Assuming that Jordan died from consuming nuts, I suppose everyone had the means to kill him." I looked at the others. "We can say that all of these people could easily have procured nuts. So no need to consider that point every time."

Tony and Becky nodded.

"According to Pa Harris, he was at the ranch all the time. But he was alone at the homestead. We don't know if he actually went out and came back any time."

I looked at Tony, inviting him to come up with a conflicting theory.

"Would anyone have seen him if he left the ranch?"

"I guess, but not necessary," I nodded.

I wrote 'Alibi' next to Pa Harris's name and listed it as 'Not Confirmed.'

"What would he gain by this?" Tony asked.

We had come to the all important motive. Did Pa Harris have any motive to do away with his favorite son?

"According to Pa Harris, the ranch was doing poorly until Jordan turned it around. He built the dude ranch business and made it successful. Every one of the family benefitted from this. So money certainly can't have been a motive here."

Becky spoke up.

"I can't imagine any other motive. Pa Harris seemed to be grieving for Jordan. That couldn't have been an act."

"He could've kicked Jordan out if there was any problem between them," Tony added. "No need to off him permanently."

"The only source of contention between them might have been Jordan's reconnecting with Jessica. Remember, he wasn't too pleased Jordan had broken his word to this other girl."

"So he could have lost face in the community, and blamed Jordan for it."

I looked uncertain.

"Sounds farfetched," Tony agreed, "but we are here to cover every possible angle. So write it down."

I made a note of it next to Pa's name.

"Let's move on to the next," Becky said, standing up to stretch her legs.

"Pamela Harris," I wrote on the board.

"Didn't you say she could have been here in Swan Creek?" Tony started.

"I thought so at first. But then she was apparently on a date. She was seen in some bar in another town, and then her date dropped her home. The police are convinced about her alibi."

"Could this date be lying?" Tony asked. "Maybe he had a hand in it?"

"That brings us to the motive," I frowned. "Pamela doesn't seem to be too emotional. She's never expressed any deep love for either of her brothers."

"You remember how she took our resort booking?" Tony asked. "That was barely two days after Jordan was found dead. So she was more interested in making a quick buck."

"Didn't you say she almost brought up the boys after their mother passed?" Becky spoke up.

"Right. She never went to college. Or got married. Maybe she harbors some resentment against Jordan for her lost youth."

I looked questioningly at the other two.

"That would apply to both her brothers, not just Jordan," Tony objected.

"How serious is she about this beau of hers?" Becky asked.

"We don't know that," I shrugged.

"What about money? Pam must be a co-owner of the ranch along with her brothers. With Jordan gone, anything from the ranch is split two ways instead of three."

"Jordan was the one who turned the ranch around, remember?" I put in. "Without him, it's just a piece of land. I don't think Cameron has the skills to run the whole ranching operation and keep it profitable. At least, not right away."

"They could sell it, I suppose," Tony said.

I shook my head. I had remembered my meeting with Cam.

"Pa Harris doesn't think much about women inheriting anything. He thinks Pam needs her brothers to take care of her. And Cam actually owns the ranch."

Tony and Becky stared at me.

"You never mentioned that before!"

"I just remembered," I told them, making a note of it on the board.

"That's one overwhelming thing in this whole business. There's just too much information floating around."

"So is resentment a strong enough motive?" Tony asked. "Apparently, Pam's not gaining any money out of this."

"She also seemed happy running the whole resort side of the ranch," Becky chimed in.

I wrote 'resentment' next to Pam's name as a possible motive.

"Don't they say revenge is best served cold?" I mused. "Do you think Pam's resentment could have built up over a period, up to a point where she just couldn't take it anymore?"

"Why was she hiding this beau from her family?" Becky demanded. "Maybe Jordan didn't like the guy and Pam didn't want anyone to come between her and her man."

"She could always elope, come on!" Tony rolled his eyes. "She's what, 45? She's not a child!"

"She's never really done anything on her own," I reminded Tony.

"What about Jessica? What if Pam didn't like her?" Becky asked.

"Then she would have harmed Jessica, right?" I asked. "I think hating Jordan for some unknown reason is the best we can come up with."

"Let's move on to the next one," Tony nodded.

"Cameron Harris," I wrote on the board next.

"The boys fought all the time according to Pamela," Becky reminded me.

"But Pa Harris said they've done that since they were kids. I don't think that means anything. Jeet fights with me all the time."

"Money sounds like the strongest motive," Tony said.

"I thought so too," I said to the other two. "But remember, the Triple H actually belongs to Cam. It's based on their grandfather's will. The oldest son gets it. Jordan was just working the land."

"What about the resort? Didn't Cam want to convert it into a home for wounded soldiers or something?" Tony asked me.

"He could've done it any time, since he owns the place. He did recognize the potential of the dude ranch business. He was willing to do both. Setting aside a few cabins for convalescent soldiers was good enough for him."

"Was there any other money involved?" Becky asked.

"I don't know. I guess Cam will also get some kind of pension once he retires. So he's in a good spot, as far as I know."

"Could they have fought over the girl?" Tony asked. "You did say he seemed kind of close to Jessica."

I thought for a minute.

"I talked to Jessica about that. I don't think she was interested in Cam. If you ask me, Cam was just playing around. Maybe he did flirt with her. But I don't think she reciprocated."

"So why did he do it?" Tony asked.

"I think he likes riling people up. He may have done it just to pester Jordan. The brothers could've fought over it."

"But in that case, Jordan would harm Cam, not the other way around."

Becky was right.

"What if he just couldn't stand seeing Jordan happy, for whatever reason. Could he have been jealous?" Tony asked next.

"Jealous enough to kill his own brother?" I shuddered. "I hope not."

I tried not to remember how besotted I had been by Cam's good looks.

I wrote Jealousy next to Cameron's name and placed a question mark against it.

"Have you noticed how Pa Harris lights up when he talks of Jordan?" Becky asked next. "Clearly, he was the favorite child. Maybe Cameron was angry over that."

I pointed to the board.

"That's jealousy again."

"What about Cameron's alibi?" Tony asked. "We know he was in Swan Creek. He slept over at Jessica's, didn't he?"

I nodded.

"That's not all. I think he even went to Willow Lake. Don't ask me why. But according to Colin, Jordan waved to his brother and spoke to him after Jessica left."

"So you mean Cam was present right there in the park after 8 at night?" Tony burst out. "Shouldn't you have mentioned that upfront, Meera?"

Becky joined in.

"So far, he's the only person who's actually been there on the spot. That makes him a suspect."

"I know he was on the spot," I agreed, "but what did he gain out of it? His motive doesn't seem strong enough?"

"Do you really think that, Meera?" Tony narrowed his eyes. "Or are you so smitten by that blue eyed jerk, you can't see straight?"

My mouth dropped open as I stared at Tony.

"What are you talking about? I don't care one bit about Cameron Harris. All I want to do is find the culprit, and bring Jon home by Christmas."

"Could've fooled me," Tony muttered.

Becky smacked him with a magazine.

"Enough of this nonsense. Stop acting like kids, you two."

Tony collapsed on a couch and put a cushion over his head.

"I'm taking a nap," he announced.

"I need fresh air!" I declared, ignoring him. "Wanna come walk around outside?" I asked Becky.

We bundled up, pulling on coats, gloves and scarves. We walked up to the edge of our property and into the lane. Then we turned back and went in the other direction.

"Don't you think Tony was being unfair?" I asked Becky.

She looked at me incredulously.

"You went out on a couple of dates with Cameron Harris. And you go on and on about how handsome he is. You didn't think it would affect Tony?"

"Affect him how? It's not like we are dating or anything."

"Meera, you can be so dumb," Becky shook her head. "And a wounded soldier. Who's ever measured up to that?"

I ignored Becky and took an interest in the bare branches of the trees surrounding us. Little icicles had formed, and there was a peculiar beauty in the stark landscape. I breathed in the cold air and felt myself relax.

"Ready to go back in?" Becky asked after a few minutes.

"Yes. Let's finish what we're doing."

We walked back to the guest house, waving at Pappa standing in the living room window.

Chapter 26

I stepped into the kitchen to pick up some cookies for a snack. I was hoping I wouldn't run into my aunt. Back in the guest house, Becky had put on a fresh pot of coffee.

"Are you done sulking?" I asked Tony.

He didn't respond but he got up and went to the bathroom. Becky was pouring the coffee by the time he came back, looking freshly scrubbed.

Something about the smell of coffee signals my brain to snap into gear.

"So, we covered the three Harrises," Becky gave me the cue. "Who's next?"

"Jessica."

I wrote on the board.

"Isn't she Daddy's little girl?" Tony asked. "And she's got plenty of money."

"Money dries up like that on a research project," I said, snapping my fingers. "But we've established Jordan didn't actually have any money."

"Did they truly love each other? What about the time when they broke up?" Becky reminded me.

"I think she's more focused on her research. Jordan wanted to get married years ago but Jessica said no. That's why they broke up."

"What if all this was an elaborate plan? He dumped her the first time, so she wanted revenge."

Tony put forth a revenge based idea again.

"You mean she pretended to hook up with Jordan, got engaged, all for what? Just to get closer to him and … and what?"

I shook my head.

"I can see Jessica making a fool out of Jordan just to laugh at him, or teach him a lesson. But I don't see her killing Jordan for it."

"It could have been a spur of the moment thing," Becky suggested. "Didn't they have a fight that night?"

"I talked to Jessica about it," I told them. "She wanted to move down south to her Daddy's place. Jordan didn't want to leave the Triple H."

"One of them would have needed to back down," Tony observed.

"Or break up," Becky finished.

"So once again, doesn't seem like enough of a motive to take a life."

"So we have a big fat question mark in place of motive," Tony said, frustrated.

I put the question mark in front of Jessica's name. I did that to remember we had considered the question, just hadn't found anything substantial.

"What about being in the area, or having the opportunity?" Tony asked. "Jessica looks the best for this."

"She was with him in the diner, of course," Becky counted on her fingers. "She knew he was allergic to nuts. And she was with him in the park too. She could easily have doctored the pie."

"That means nothing if she didn't have a motive," I protested.

We were quiet for a while, thinking about what we may have missed.

"Let's move on to that other guy – Colin Stevens," Tony said, rubbing his eyes.

Becky let out a yawn and that set us all off.

"We can't afford to take a break. Who knows what Jon is going through right now."

I reminded them of the gravity of the situation.

Tony and Becky tried to look alert as I wrote Colin's name on the board.

"What's the motive here, Meera?"

"Colin is clearly besotted by Jessica. They used to be engaged but Jessica dumped him when she rekindled her relationship with Connor."

"He can't have liked that," Becky bobbed her head. "Does he look like the type to bear a grudge?"

"Sure does! And he keeps bragging about how Jessica tells him everything. He knows a lot about Jessica, although I suspect most of it is because he listens in on her calls."

"What a weasel," Tony said in disgust.

"He's happy now that Jordan is out of the picture. He hasn't bothered to hide it."

I remembered how pleased Colin had been that Jordan was no longer in the picture.

"So he could have done it to get Jessica back."

I thought of how repulsive Colin was. Was that reason enough to believe he could kill someone? Then I remembered how cool he was about the whole thing. He hadn't even expressed any remorse over losing Jordan. So maybe he was capable of the crime.

I wrote Jessica next to Colin's name.

"So now we need to know if he could have done it," Becky continued.

"The answer to that is yes, I guess," Tony looked at me. "Wasn't he right there in the park?"

I nodded in agreement.

"He went to the park around 8. And he was alone with Jordan for some time. Jessica had gone to use the restroom that time. He said he saw Jordan taking the pie box out of the truck."

"So when did he poison the pie?" Becky asked. "Was he already at the truck when Jordan and Jessica got there?"

I tried to think back to our conversation.

"We only have their word about this. But according to Colin, Jordan was by his truck, and Jessica had gone to the restroom."

We were stumped again. I put a question mark next to Colin's name again.

"Seems like we are coming up with more questions than answers," I moaned.

"I think we eliminated quite a bit of scenarios, though," Becky tried to cheer me up.

"What if some of these people were acting together? That changes the picture drastically."

Tony stood up and stared at the board.

"Have you noticed one thing?" I asked Tony and Becky. "None of their alibis depend on each other. Except Colin and Jessica's of course. But they went back to her lab and were with plenty of other people."

"What about the person Colin saw Jordan talking to? His brother, supposedly?" Becky asked.

I had completely forgotten about that.

"Cam never mentioned it."

"Would you?" Becky asked.

"It makes him look guilty," I paused.

"Why don't you call and ask him?" Tony smirked. "Maybe he'll spill the beans, confess over the phone."

I ignored the sarcasm and dialed Cameron's number. He answered after a couple of rings.

"Hello Cam, how are you?" I started.

"Hey Meera!" his voice sounded perky as usual.

"They arrested one of our friends …" I began.

"We heard," Cam crowed. "Pa's happy they nailed him."

"But he's innocent!"

"Of course he will say that. Look, Meera, I know you've probably known the man for a long time. And I'm not saying he did it on purpose. But it could have been an accident."

I stayed firm.

"These people have been in the food business for decades. They wouldn't make this kind of mistake."

"Are you saying there is not even a tiny chance of error here?" Cam roared into the phone.

That made me pause. If I were being logical, I had to accept Cam's argument. I decided to steer him to the purpose of my call.

"Actually, I have a question for you."

"What is it?" he asked indulgently.

"Were you present at Willow Lake Park that night?"

There was silence at the other end.

I waited a few seconds and prompted him. "Cam?"

"Who told you that, Meera?" Cam asked flippantly.

"Someone claims to have seen you there, talking to Jordan. You didn't mention this before."

"I was there," Cam responded with a sigh.

"Why?"

"Jordan had mentioned they might be going to the lake after dinner. I had a few drinks at the bar. Then I thought I would go and talk to them."

"Even when you knew they were on a date?" I pressed. "A special date celebrating their engagement?"

Cam laughed. I could imagine a naughty, irreverent look on his face.

"That engagement was a farce, if you ask me."

"That's not the point, Cam. Did you do it just to irritate them?"

"Look, I don't know. Like I told you, I was pretty wasted. I don't remember why I did it. I was just driving around. There's nowhere much to go in that small town anyway."

I knew that part was right. Cam was still speaking.

"I walked around the lake, I think, trying to spot them. Then I saw them arguing. It was something silly like where to live after they got married. Then Jessica went off somewhere. And Jordan started talking to some other dude Jessica knows from college."

"What happened after that?"

"We talked for a while. He was pretty upset. He was shoveling pie in his mouth like he hadn't eaten in a month. That was one of the few weaknesses he had. Stress eating."

"Wait a minute. So you saw Jordan eat the pie that killed him. Why haven't you said anything about it all along?"

Cam was quiet.

"You know this doesn't put you in a favorable light," I told him.

"Why would I harm my own brother?" he asked me again.

"What happened after that?"

"He wanted to be alone. So I left and drove to Jessica's. I took the key and crashed at her place. Then I drove home in the morning."

"You need to tell all this to the police," I said urgently. "It will help them establish the time of death."

Cam was quiet.

"Do you think I was the last person to talk to Jordan?" he asked me.

"It's beginning to look that way, Cam," I said gently.

"I don't even remember much of what was said," he said, sounding bitter. "Nice big brother I have turned out to him. I was right there, but I couldn't protect him."

Nothing I said would have changed anything. I thanked Cam and hung up.

"I suppose you got all that?" I asked Tony and Becky.

"Most of it," they agreed.

"Cam's big on the theatrics. But I don't think he harmed Jordan."

I moved back to the board.

"So we were looking at this second circle," I started again.

"We know almost nothing about this woman," Becky pointed out. "But if anyone has a strong motive for revenge, it's her."

Tony and I both agreed.

"Wasn't Stan going to find out where she was?" Tony asked.

"The police are working on it, but no news on her yet. Maybe Stan's found something new today."

There was a knock on the door, and Motee Ba came in.

"You're back!"

I rushed to hug her and ushered her to a seat on the sofa.

"How's Sylvie?" I asked. "Is she feeling better now?"

"She cried her head off for hours. Reema took her home." Motee Ba looked at Tony. "I wanted to bring her here, but Anita's visiting. And I knew you kids would have turned the guest house into a war room of sorts."

She swept her arm around and noticed the giant board. She stood up and read everything we had on there.

"Good work," she said, patting me on the shoulder.

"It's all beginning to run together now," I complained. "Nothing's making a lot of sense."

"Have you looked at the time?" Becky gasped.

None of us had noticed it was beyond 8 PM.

"No wonder I'm starving," Tony smiled.

"We've got some leftovers," Motee Ba said. "Why don't you kids order something? That way, you can continue working on this."

"Call Stan, Meera," Tony reminded me. "Ask him to come over for dinner."

We put in an order for a truck load of Chinese food. Motee Ba left and we all collapsed on the couch.

Stan agreed to come by. I switched on the TV and we all agreed to suspend any talk of the case until Stan got there.

The food and Stan arrived at the same time.

"Let's eat first, please!" Tony begged.

I looked at Stan as I ladled Hunan Chicken onto my plate along with some Lo Mein. I grabbed a couple of Crab Rangoon.

Stan looked relieved.

"I'm exhausted. I need to eat first too, Meera."

Everyone loaded their plates. The next fifteen minutes were spent munching greasy Chinese food, washing it down with beer or soda.

Finally, I broke open a fortune cookie and read the cryptic message.

'We often ignore what's staring us in the face.'

"That's helpful!" I scowled, trashing the paper.

Tony loaded big bowls with ice cream and drenched it in chocolate sauce. We ate our ice cream, summoning the energy to tackle yet another big discussion.

The hour was late and the clock was ticking. We needed to pull ourselves together for Jon.

Chapter 27

"How's Jon holding up?" I asked Stan.

He shrugged, looking apologetic.

"As well as possible, under the circumstances."

"Do you think he did this on purpose?" Becky asked, sounding defensive.

"No one's saying that. We think it could be a case of negligence." He held up his hand as I opened my mouth. "It's possible, Meera. Think about it a bit. No one can be perfect."

Becky crossed her arms and looked away. Her mouth was set in a firm line. She worked at the diner so maybe she could be implicated too. I hadn't thought of that.

"Personally, I don't think anyone at the diner is responsible," Stan admitted. "But I have to do my job. The only way to get around this is to find out the real culprit."

I pointed to the board. At first glance it looked like a lot of chicken scratch on a giant white surface. You had to actually read everything to make sense of it. We were quiet as Stan went through all of it.

"Have you arrived at any conclusion yet?" he asked, looking around at each of us.

I shook my head.

"We haven't found anyone with a strong enough motive. And then, all of them seem to have good alibis. We placed Cam at the scene of the crime. But as unpredictable as he is, I don't think he did this."

"My money's on Colin Stevens," Tony told Stan.

"We haven't finished talking about the second circle yet," Becky reminded us.

"Jordan's ex. We know nothing about her." I looked at Stan hopefully. "Were you able to check on her, Stan?"

Stan smiled.

"I was coming to it. Eleanor Robinson checked herself out about six months ago."

"What do you mean, checked herself out?" I asked, shocked. "Wasn't she incarcerated in an asylum?"

"Incarcerated? No. And in an asylum? No."

Stan looked smug. I bet he was holding on to some vital information.

"What do you mean?" Becky burst out.

"We questioned a few people who lived in the area. Jordan and the girl were tight.

She'd grown up on a ranch, in a very protected environment. She couldn't take it when Jordan dumped her for Jessica."

We had heard about this already.

"They had a fight and she slapped him, maybe scratched his face." Stan paused. "The Jordans, they made it look like she was mentally unstable. I don't know how that whole insane thing came into play. A local judge convinced her to go into a sanatorium type of place."

"We've heard all that before," I said impatiently.

"The point is," Stan stressed, "there were no actual charges filed. She went there voluntarily. And so she checked herself out of there voluntarily."

"Is she back at her ranch then? Someone would have seen her by now."

Stan sighed.

"They sold the ranch long ago. It was just her mother and her, anyway. We tried to find out if she mentioned her plans to anyone over at that sanatorium."

"And?" I asked, leaning forward on the edge of my seat.

"She may have gone to Dallas, but we haven't found her exact location yet."

Tony looked interested.

"That's not very far. She could be here in a few hours, any time she wanted to."

Stan agreed to that.

"Fact is, she hasn't come across as someone who would hold a grudge. She was a simple girl. Barely graduated high school. Spent her life on a ranch in a town smaller than ours."

"Jessica's definitely the smarter one then," Becky said. "I suppose she was more appealing to Jordan."

"Hello. Have you looked at Jessica?" Tony rolled his eyes. "Beauty and brains is an irresistible combination."

I ignored Tony. He had been getting on my nerves a lot.

"Are you continuing to look for this girl?" I asked Stan.

"We are. I am beginning to think she may have changed her name. There's not much of a trail."

"Do you have a photo?" I asked.

"We are waiting on one," Stan told me.

The photo reminded me of my age progression program. I hadn't talked to Stan about it yet.

"Stan, I have decided to reopen my mother's case," I began.

Stan looked surprised.

"But I thought …"

I wrung my hands, trying to swallow the bile that rose up in my throat.

"Well, yes, but I still want to find out what happened to her. Maybe some new information came to light after all these years."

"That's been known to happen," Stan nodded. "A lot of cold cases are being solved thanks to DNA evidence, or new advances in forensics."

"Ya, well," I nodded. "I am contacting different departments and trying to increase the search area. Since this is the place from where she went missing, I thought I should let the Swan Creek department know."

"You might need to send a formal email or letter," Stan said. "I'm not sure what the exact procedure is."

"I'll do whatever's needed. But I wanted to give you these first." I handed over the set of 10 photos I had printed out. "I can email you a digital image too. I'm doing that with other people."

"What's this?" Stan asked curiously.

I told Stan about the program I had written.

"This is a projection of what she might look like."

Stan gave me an admiring look.

"That's brilliant. I will put these on file right away."

I hesitated.

"Have you been able to trace that car?" I asked Stan.

I was finally beginning to believe someone was following me.

"I was coming to that," Stan said. "We ran the tags your aunt gave us. Turns out it's a rental car like we suspected. And this time, it's from a small local place."

The excitement in the room amped up.

"So? You know who it was rented out to?" Tony rushed ahead.

Stan winced.

"Not really."

"How's that possible?" Becky groaned. "Doesn't the rental company have it on their record?"

Stan shook his head.

"It's not really a rental company. It's more of a garage. They are not very particular about their records. And they can look the other way if they get more money."

"So you mean this woman paid them to not write down her name?" I asked.

"Something of that sort," Stan shrugged. "They won't say exactly. I think someone took a cash payment, maybe a double payment, to keep this off the books."

"Now what?" Tony asked.

"We have told them to inform us whenever the car is returned. Hopefully, we will get there in time to talk to this person."

I slumped down on the couch and let out a yawn.

"We still haven't considered the third circle," Becky said in a tired voice.

"That's farfetched," Stan said, reading the board. "But it's been known to happen. It is almost impossible to find out unless someone speaks up."

We were talking about the ranch hands or any unknown person who may have wanted to harm Jordan.

"Let's call it a night," Tony said, getting up.

"I have to go now, Meera," Stan stood up to leave too. "You have done a good job here. Let me know if you think of anything else."

Stan left and Tony and Becky collapsed on a couch.

"Why don't you guys stay over?" I asked. "That way, we can get an early start in the morning."

Tony and Becky readily agreed, each staking claim to a room in the guest house. I walked over to the main house and crept into my room. A hot shower helped me calm down a bit. I fell into a deep sleep which was thankfully not interrupted by any bad dreams.

Motee Ba was stirring a big pot of oatmeal when I walked into the kitchen the next morning. Becky and Tony were already munching on toast, guzzling coffee while waiting for the oatmeal. Pappa was tapping his cane, spooning his soft boiled egg into his mouth.

My Aunt Anita was quiet for a change, pouring sugar over her grapefruit.

The phone rang. It was Sylvie on the line for Motee Ba.

"How are you Sylvie? Are you at the diner?"

The cops hadn't shut down the diner this time, but Sylvie wasn't in good enough shape to run it. Becky waved her hand, trying to get my attention.

"Becky wants to know if we should go open the diner," I told Sylvie.

"I don't know, child. Who's going to turn up, anyway?"

"It will be fine, Sylvie," I tried to soothe her.

"Honey said y'all were working on finding out who killed that boy. Why don't you keep on doing that?"

"But what about the diner?" I asked.

I thought the diner would be a good distraction for Sylvie.

"It's not like the folks need me to be open anymore," Sylvie started.

People in small towns like Swan Creek depend on certain places. The diner was one such place. There weren't too many restaurants in town. And none of them were as economical as Sylvie's, or provided a down home menu that the locals depended on. It was the place you went to for your eggs and bacon in the morning, or your soup or sandwich for lunch. And it's the place you went to for a slice of pie. I wondered what the future was for Sylvie's, if Jon was convicted. I tried to steer myself away from worst case scenarios.

Sylvie had continued talking while I was lost in thought. There was a pause, and I realized she had asked me something.

"I'm sorry Sylvie, I didn't get that last part."

Sylvie sighed.

"I know you must be exhausted, Meera. And you're supposed to be on Christmas break."

"I'm fine, Sylvie," I tried to reassure her. "We'll have Jon home for Christmas, you'll see."

Sylvie let out another sigh.

"Now what were you saying?" I reminded her.

"Don't worry about the diner. And tell Becky the same thing. We'll let those Robinsons earn a buck or two."

Bells clanged in my head as something clicked.

"Who are the Robinsons?" I was almost afraid to ask.

"It's those two women from that fancy diner place!" I could almost see Sylvie shaking her head.

"You mean Nancy's?" I asked.

I wanted to be doubly sure.

"That's the one alright," Sylvie said, suddenly sounding tired.

"Sylvie?" My heart skipped a beat. "Do you remember I asked you to make a list of all the people in the diner the day Jordan and Jessica were there?"

"I have it," Sylvie confirmed. "Maybe Becky can add something to it. My memory's not that good anymore."

I coaxed her to tell me the names she had come up with. I wrote them down on the back of an envelope I found on a side table. Finally, I hung up, forgetting that Sylvie had called to talk to Motee Ba.

"I think she called for you, Motee Ba," I apologized. "I forgot."

"I'll call her back," Motee Ba smiled. "Don't worry."

I begged Jeet to help clear the dishes. I hurried over to the guest house with Tony and Becky following me. They had picked up on my excitement.

"Spill it, Meera," Tony said, as soon as we entered the guest house. "What did you find out?"

"I don't want to jump to conclusions."

I handed over the envelope to Becky.

"These are the people that were present at Sylvie's when Jordan and Jessica were having their celebratory dinner. Can you think of anyone she might have missed?"

Becky skimmed her eyes over the paper. She checked off the names I had written down one by one.

"I don't remember some of these. But if Sylvie wrote them down, they were there."

"I know that," I cut her off. "Was there anyone she missed?"

"Well, I was in and out of the kitchen," Becky began.

Her eyes had a faraway look in them. I knew she was thinking hard. Becky handled both the cooking and the serving a lot of the time. Most customers spent at least fifteen minutes in the diner, even if they were only there for coffee. So my guess was Becky would come across every customer at least once.

"I think this accounts for most people sitting on the bar stools. But there was someone at the last table, the one close to the rest rooms. I think there were two women sitting there."

"Do you remember who they were?" I asked.

Becky shook her head.

"Maybe they weren't regulars. Generally, I remember people. Most people come in at a certain time and order the same thing."

I didn't want to prompt Becky any further. I had a hunch but I wanted Becky to confirm something on her own.

Tony got a call on his cell phone.

"Meera, I think I'll have to put in a few hours at the gas station," Tony said apologetically. "There's a big delivery coming in. It's my last one before the new year."

"Go!" I waved him off. "Nothing much happening here anyway."

"Maybe I should go be with Sylvie for a while," Becky said.

"Good idea!"

Must Love Murder

I took a deep breath after saying goodbye to Becky and Tony. I placed a call to Stan. It was time to find out if my hunch had any substance.

Chapter 28

Stan sounded tired on the phone.

"Good Morning, Meera!"

"What did you say that girl's name was? The one Jordan dumped?" I asked him.

"Eleanor Robinson?" Stan asked.

"Do you know there's a mother daughter duo by the name of Robinson in town?"

Stan listened with mounting excitement as I shared what I was thinking.

"You think that's possible?" he asked eagerly.

"Can you find out if these are the same people?" I asked.

"I'll get on it right away. Check county records etc. They must have had to provide some papers somewhere if they are living in the area."

"How long will that take?" I asked eagerly.

"Can't say. Most offices will close later today. Staff is already on vacation."

"So you're saying you may not be able to confirm her identity for a while?"

Stan was quiet. I assumed he was thinking of an alternative.

"We may be able to speed things up if someone identifies her for us."

"You think Jessica might do that?" I asked eagerly. "Or Pamela?"

"I can't promise you anything," Stan said reluctantly. "But if someone identifies this girl as Jordan's ex, we can at least keep an eye on her."

"Okay, I'll get on it." I hung up, feeling a burst of energy.

After a moment's thought, I decided to approach Pamela first. Pamela must have met the girl several times.

Pam answered the phone. I didn't want to show all my cards at once, so I asked her if she would come to Swan Creek and meet me for some coffee.

"But why? Is there a reason you want to see me? It's a long drive, you know. And we've got some guests coming in today."

"Just trust me on this one," I coaxed.

Pam reluctantly agreed to meet me at Sylvie's.

I drove to Sylvie's guessing I would find Becky there. I was right. Both Becky and Sylvie were in the kitchen, rolling some cookie dough.

"Just trying to keep busy," Sylvie said.

"That's good."

I helped them decorate the cookies, adding red and green glitter on some. Most of my help consisted of sampling the different types.

"These are delicious," I exclaimed.

I heard a car drive up and went outside. Pamela got out of a truck. She wasn't looking too pleasant.

"So why have you called me here, Meera?" she snapped.

"Let's go to that new place over there," I pointed to Nancy's. "I hear they have good coffee."

Pam muttered something but she followed me as I crossed the road. Nancy's fancy diner was almost bursting at the seams. As expected, most of the locals had given Sylvie's a wide berth once again. It looked like all of Swan Creek had congregated at Nancy's.

We got a small table for two, near swinging doors that led into the kitchen.

I asked for two cups of coffee and waited.

"Why are we here?" Pam asked.

"Just enjoy your coffee, Pam," I smiled. "And be patient. Maybe you'll meet someone you know."

Pam gave up on asking me any more questions. She read through the menu and ordered some cake.

"This is good!"

She moaned as she enjoyed her chocolate cake.

"Our chef went to culinary school," the server said. "Unlike the cooks at other places in the area."

"Can we give our compliments to the chef?" I asked politely.

"I'll let her know," the server nodded.

The chef came out a few minutes later, her face wreathed in smiles.

"You like the chocolate cake?" she beamed. "It's six layers with real chocolate ganache."

Pamela's eyes widened, and she jabbed a finger at the chef. She swallowed the large bite of cake in her mouth and gulped.

"What're you doing here?" she cried.

Nancy Robinson had come out of the kitchen. She froze when she saw Pam. She leveled a dirty look at me.

"You are not welcome here," she told Pamela in a steely voice.

"See them out!" she ordered the server who was standing at one side, looking confused.

"Nellie! What are you doing here?" Pamela finally found her voice. "Why aren't you in your mental asylum?"

She stood and looked around, as if trying to capture the crowd's attention. There was no need for that because every eye in the diner was riveted on the scene playing out.

"This woman is insane!"

"Mama!" Nellie Robinson had turned red. Snot rolled down her nose. "It's her. It's her, Mama."

Nellie sniffled and started sobbing.

"Get out!" Nancy screamed at us again.

I crossed my fingers, hoping someone had called 911 by now.

Nellie curled her fists and launched herself at Pam. Pamela's face lost its smirk. I stared at them in shock.

"Do something!" I screamed at Nancy.

Sirens blared as two police cars swung into the parking lot. Stan Miller rushed in, followed by four cops.

A couple of the diner staff had managed to pry Nellie away from Pam. She was coughing, and bruise lines were appearing on her throat where Nellie had choked her.

"Didn't I say, she's insane!" Pam croaked.

Stan's eyes met mine but he didn't say anything.

The police took Nellie away, and I took Pamela's arm. We crossed the road over to Sylvie's.

"What were you thinking, Meera?" Pam screamed. "Are you mad too?"

Pam had figured out why I took her into Nancy's.

I was shook up myself. I hadn't expected the girl to turn so violent. Then I realized how foolish I had been. I suspected the woman was a murderer. Of course she was bound to be dangerous.

"I'm so sorry," I rubbed Pam on the back. "I had no idea she would turn so violent."

Becky and Sylvie were staring at us, trying to be patient.

"We need to get you to the doctor," Becky said, handing over a glass of iced water to Pam. "You need to get that checked out."

Pamela looked at me. I owed her an explanation.

"We know Jon is innocent," I began. "We thought a lot about who might have wanted to harm Jordan. His ex was a possibility but you said she was in an asylum. Then we learnt she wasn't there anymore. I had a hunch but I needed someone to confirm it was her."

"We still don't know she did it," Pam said sadly.

"The police will make her talk," I said confidently.

"She's wily. She won't own up to it."

Becky and I took Pam to the ER. They gave her some pills and advised her to rest. I offered to drive her home to the Triple H. It was the least I could do. Becky drove my car and I drove Pam's truck. We dropped her off at the ranch and started back immediately.

Becky kept peering in the side mirror and almost opened her mouth a few times.

I held up my hand before she said a word.

"Please! I don't care if anyone is following us. I can't handle it right now."

Becky nodded, patting me on the shoulder.

"Do you think that girl did it?" she asked quietly.

"I can imagine her doing it," I shuddered. "You should've been there. One minute she was crying, and the next she just flew at Pam's throat."

We pulled into Sylvie's lot. I had a headache and it was probably from hunger. I was hoping Sylvie would have something ready for us to eat.

I parked the car near the diner door and Becky beat me to it.

"Sylvie, we're starving …" she called out and stopped in her tracks.

I almost bumped into her. Then I looked up.

Nancy Robinson was pacing the floor. Sylvie was sitting at a table, looking worried. She seemed relieved to see us.

"They're here," she said.

Nancy Robinson clasped my hands tightly.

"She didn't do anything. She's innocent."

I wasn't so sure about that.

"I saw her attack Pam myself."

"I'm not talking about that," Nancy dismissed. "I'm talking about Jordan!"

"But didn't she attack Jordan earlier too? Wasn't that why she was sent to that asylum."

"For the first and last time, my daughter wasn't in an asylum!" Nancy shrieked and I took a step back.

Nancy collapsed in a chair and tried to hold back her tears.

"My Nellie was such a sweet girl. She was deeply in love with Jordan Harris. They were supposed to get married."

I nodded. We knew all about that.

"Jordan met this other girl one time, and then he just stopped talking to Nellie."

"Weren't they going to get married?" I asked.

Nancy grimaced.

"The wedding was planned. Nellie had her dream wedding dress. The invitations were sent out. All this time, that boy was seeing this other girl, and he didn't even tell us the wedding was off."

I wondered why Jordan had behaved like that.

"Nellie saw him with the girl and asked him who she was. Then they broke up."

"Is that when your daughter attacked him?" I probed.

"It was nothing. She just lost her temper."

I had just seen a live example of Nellie's temper. I wondered if Nancy was guilty too.

Nancy spoke with a casual air.

"I promised to take her to counseling so no charges were pressed. She spent some time in that place. It was like a five star resort, with bars on the windows and locks on the doors. She did some fancy cooking diploma in Dallas. She was ready for a fresh start."

"Why did you choose Swan Creek?" I asked. "Didn't you know Jessica lived here?"

Nancy shook her head.

"Jordan got his degree a long time ago. He had been running the ranch for a few years when he was engaged to my Nellie. We knew this girl was from down South, but we didn't know anything else."

"Were you shocked when you came across Jordan here?" I asked.

Nancy was quiet.

"We spruced up the place over yonder. Nellie was excited. She had big plans for it. We had big plans. We came here for some coffee. Imagine her shock when she saw Jordan sitting there, holding hands with that girl."

"So she flipped and took her revenge," I stated bluntly.

"She did no such thing!" Nancy almost screamed in my face.

She stood up abruptly and walked out.

I looked at Becky and Sylvie. They hadn't spoken a word but their shocked expressions told me what they were thinking.

Must Love Murder

Becky spoke first.

"You remember the two women I told you about?"

I nodded. I had been waiting for Becky to connect the dots.

"I'm almost sure it was them – Nancy and her daughter."

"Were they here when Jordan got that extra pie?" I asked eagerly.

"Right there," Becky pointed to a table at the back.

"Does this mean they will let Jon go?" Sylvie asked eagerly.

"I don't know!" I tried to not raise her hopes too high. "It all depends on what Nellie admits to."

Becky was quiet.

"Do you really think she did it?"

Sylvie stood up and went into the kitchen. She shuffled out a while later with a big tray.

"Why don't you kids eat something first?" she said.

We attacked the chicken salad sandwiches Sylvie had brought out, and slurped the soup. I coaxed Sylvie to eat with us.

"What do we do now?" Sylvie asked.

I placed a call to Stan and listened for a while.

"Pam has pressed charges for assault. So they will be keeping Nellie for a while. Stan said they will try to get a confession from her."

I looked at Sylvie.

"I'm sorry Sylvie, but looks like they'll keep Jon there for a while. But he's doing well. They are taking care of him."

"Why don't we close this place up?" Becky suggested.

"Let's go watch a movie or something."

We drove to our place with Sylvie. Aunt Reema and Motee Ba came out when they heard my car in the driveway. We told them what had happened.

They all went inside. Becky and I went to the guest house. Tony and Jeet were sprawled on a couch each, watching an action movie. Becky told them the story this time and the boys high fived me.

"We don't know if she's guilty," I said glumly.

"I say she is," Tony insisted.

We all felt the same. The question was, how were the police going to prove it?

Chapter 29

We chose a Christmas movie to get into the mood. A couple of hours later, Jeet and Tony were pretending to yawn their heads off.

We were all a bit peckish, so we went into the main house to scrounge for food. Motee Ba was at the stove, frying *pakoras*. The kitchen was infused with the smell of the fritters.

"What kind are you making, Granny?" Tony asked, picking one up and popping it in his mouth.

"Onion *pakoras*!" Motee Ba announced. "And cheese if you want them."

I eagerly cut cheese into 2 inch cubes and handed it over to Motee Ba. She dipped the cubes into thick seasoned batter and dropped them in hot oil.

I took over the frying from Motee Ba and we gorged on the hot fried snacks, dunked in ketchup and washed down with hot tea.

"Where's Sylvie?" Becky asked. "Is she still here?"

"I convinced her to take a nap," Motee Ba said softly. "Any news from Stan?"

I shook my head. We went back to the guest house and slaved through one more movie, this time one chosen by the boys.

The phone rang around 9 PM. It was Motee Ba, calling us over for dinner.

We started walking out when a couple of cars pulled up in the driveway. One of them was a squad car and one was an unmarked sedan. They didn't have sirens or lights on. I crossed my fingers, hoping it was Stan with some good news.

My face lit up when I saw Jon get out of one of the cars. I ran over and threw my arms around him.

"They let you go? Thank God!"

Becky followed with a hug.

"Let's go in, Meera," Stan urged, shivering in the cold.

Everyone had rushed to the front door when they heard the cars and they were all filing out of our front door. Stan herded them in.

We sat in our living room, eager to get an update from Stan.

Sylvie sat close to Jon, her hand held tightly in his. She was looking lively for the first time since the last few days.

"Have you dropped the charges against Jon?" Dad asked Stan.

"Yes, we have, Professor."

"You should never have arrested him in the first place," Pappa put in his two cents.

"I agree," Stan said apologetically. "We needed to make an arrest at the time. And Jon and Sylvie were the obvious choice."

Jon looked around at everyone.

"I'm fine. Don't worry about me now. Listen to what he's going to say."

"Did she do it?" I burst out.

Stan's face told me the answer even before he said a word.

"Yes. She did. And she confessed to every bit of it."

"I suppose she'll get off this time too?" I said bitterly.

"It won't be that easy," Stan said. "First of all, there's nothing wrong with her mental state. The place she was in was more of a rehab place. She's just got a short temper, and she's malicious."

Stan looked uncomfortable.

"I can't reveal what went on in the interrogation. Let's say we suggested she may have been seen at the crime scene. That was enough to make her sing."

I remembered what Nancy had said earlier that afternoon.

"Was it all part of the plan then, coming to Swan Creek?"

"I don't think so," Stan said. "How much do you know so far?"

I gave everyone a quick recap of Jordan's connection to Nellie. Then I told them what Nancy had said earlier today when she came over.

Stan was thoughtful.

"I think it's possible Eleanor or Nellie remembered where Jordan used to go to college. And she may have known Jessica lived here. We'll never know for sure."

"What does she say? Was it all just a coincidence?" Tony asked impatiently.

"Nellie's story matches her mother's in this part. She spent a few months in that fancy clinic. Got her head straightened out. Then the two women went to Dallas where Nellie did some kind of food course. They wanted to move to a new place, start over. They had already sold the ranch, so they had money to invest. Swan Creek is one of the best places to live in America. They thought it would be familiar, since they were from the same state and all. Nellie said it looked like the place had potential."

"Potential to meet Jordan again, you mean," Becky smirked.

I tapped Becky on the shoulder and signaled Stan to continue.

"They found an ideal place for their restaurant, spruced up the place and were ready to go in business. They came into Sylvie's to check out the competition."

"And instead, ran into Jordan."

I tried to imagine what Nellie must have felt, how shocked she might have been to see her nemesis right in front of her, just when she thought she was making a new start.

"As luck would have it, Jordan and Jessica were celebrating their engagement. It was too much for Nellie."

"Did she ever intend to harm Jessica?" I asked. "She's the one who took Jordan away from her, so Nellie should've been mad at her too."

"We asked her that," Stan nodded. "But Nellie thought the fault lay with Jordan. He would've fallen for some other girl if not Jessica. He was the bad apple."

"Did Nancy know Nellie had spotted Jordan?" Tony asked.

I had wondered about the same thing.

"Maybe she did, but she didn't want to mention it." Stan shrugged. "It seems neither of them mentioned it to each other."

"How did she manage to mess up my pie?" Sylvie spoke up.

She had been following the conversation closely.

"Nellie heard Jordan order the extra pie. And she heard someone assure Jordan it was his special order. That's when she hatched her plan."

"Nancy said they went home afterwards."

Stan sighed.

"Nellie heard the couple mention the lake. She sneaked out and went to Willow Lake. She had crushed some pecans into a fine powder and put them in a Ziploc bag."

A hush fell over as we all realized the significance of Nellie's action.

"Nellie found Jordan's truck in the parking lot. It was open. She pulled the pie out of the box, sprinkled the powdered nuts over it and sealed it again. Then she just hid somewhere."

"She actually waited there?" I asked, aghast.

"We are hoping one of the surveillance cameras caught her."

Stan sounded as disgusted as we were feeling.

"She saw the whole thing. She saw Jessica and Jordan arguing. Then Colin came and picked up Jessica. Then Cam appeared and Jordan took the pie and followed him. She watched as he devoured the pie. Then she drove home and went to sleep."

"Did she know it was likely to be fatal?" Sylvie voiced the question at the top of everyone's minds.

"She just wanted to teach him a lesson," Stan said. "That's all she keeps saying."

We thanked Stan for bringing Jon over and bid him good night.

There was a hush over the group. Sylvie came over and hugged me.

"You said you'd have him back before Christmas and you did, Meera. How can we ever thank you enough?"

"I had a lot of help," I smiled, putting an arm around Becky and Tony.

"All that's fine, girl, but what about my dinner?" Pappa grumbled, tapping his cane. "Have you looked at the time?"

Dad poured Scotch and wine and we toasted Jon and Sylvie.

The lights on the Christmas tree twinkled and there was a festive atmosphere in the house for the first time in the season.

Tony, Becky and Jeet dragged me into my room.

"You were awesome, Meera!" Tony's eyes shone as he looked at me.

"Please, I couldn't have done it without you. I think we just stumbled onto it by luck."

"Not really," Jeet said seriously. "The police didn't even know about Jordan's first engagement until you found out about it. You explored options, examined them and eliminated them. I think you had a logical approach."

"Okay, Einstein," I ruffled his head affectionately. "You can hire me to investigate your cases when you become a hotshot lawyer."

That set off a discussion about Jeet's college admission.

I slept in the next day, exhausted by the whole episode. I sat in the kitchen, enjoying my breakfast after a long time. Motee Ba had made my favorite cheesy scrambled eggs with jalapenos. I mixed in some salsa into my eggs and scooped them up with a cheese quesadilla.

"Where's everyone else?" I asked her.

"Your aunt's gone shopping with Reema. Pappa and Dad are at the barber's. Jeet's hanging out with friends."

I wondered what Tony was up to. I thought of the gift I had got for him and wondered if it was enough.

Motee Ba smiled at me.

"He's going to love it."

I blushed.

"I don't know what you mean."

I said a quick prayer for having Motee Ba in my life. That reminded me of the other project I had taken up. The decision to look for Mom had been mine but the outcome was going to affect everyone.

Motee Ba ladled the rest of the eggs on to my plate.

"Becky said a car was following you yesterday too."

I nodded.

"She said that. But I'm not sure myself."

"Have you been in any scrapes recently?" Motee Ba asked me.

"What? Of course not!"

"Then why would someone follow you around, Meera?"

"Beats me. If they want something, they should just come forth and talk to me, right?"

The phone rang as if on cue.

"It's for you, Meera."

Motee Ba handed me the receiver. I leaned back in the kitchen chair, twisting the long telephone cord around my finger.

"What's up, Stan?" I asked, spearing another forkful of eggs and salsa.

Stan had news for me.

"The car was returned," he began. "It was a woman alright. She switched cars and drove off."

"Did you question her?" I asked eagerly.

"We missed her! We are short staffed, Meera. Today's Christmas Eve."

I sighed.

"Becky thinks she spotted a tail yesterday."

"Maybe that's why the woman switched cars," Stan said. "We have a general description, and we have the tags. We are just waiting for her to speed or run a light or something so we can pull her over. But she's very careful."

"Can't you do anything else?" I asked, frustrated.

I had been dealing with this ghost for the whole semester and I was finally beginning to lose it. I just wanted to confront whoever it was, and ask them what they wanted from me.

"Normally, a rental place copies the driver's license for records," Stan sounded as frustrated as I did. "But this place hasn't done that. I may try something different though. One of my nieces is pretty good at portraits. I am going to take her to this rental place."

"You mean get her to draw a sketch of that woman?" I was getting excited.

I was impressed with Stan Miller. The old Stan was a paper pusher who didn't think much beyond putting in his hours. But Stan was turning over a new leaf.

"Let me know if you find out something," I told him.

I went into the living room with an armful of presents. I placed them around the tree. Then I rearranged all the presents a bit so they looked pretty. Motee Ba clapped as she looked on from her favorite chair. I went and perched on the arm, placing an arm around Motee Ba.

"It's perfect, Meera," Motee Ba said softly, snuggling into my shoulder.

I remembered what Motee Ba had always taught us, growing up. Life is as perfect as you want it to be. So we had a few challenges ahead of us. But the Patels of Swan Creek, Oklahoma had a lot to be thankful for this Christmas.

***

Glossary

Desi – broadly refers to people from the Indian subcontinent

Gujarati – of the Indian state of Gujarat; pertaining to people from the western Indian state of Gujarat

Ba – Mother

Motee Ba – Grandma, literally Big Ma – pronounced with a hard T like in T-shirt

Thepla – a flatbread made with wheat flour, pan fried. Chopped fenugreek leaves are often added to the dough along with spices like turmeric and coriander.

Kem Cho - how are you; standard Gujarati greeting

Khichdi – stew made with equal quantity of rice and moong dal lentils

Kadhi – buttermilk stew thickened with gram flour, seasoned with Indian spices

Samosa – fried pastry triangles stuffed with veggies or meat

Pakora – fritters, generally vegetables dipped in batter and deep fried

RECIPE - Black Bean Burger

Ingredients

2 cans black beans

½ tsp garlic powder

½ tsp onion powder

¼ cup green peppers, diced fine

¼ cup red peppers, diced fine

¼ cup sweet corn

1 jalapeno pepper, diced

¼ cup scallions, diced fine

½ tsp Ancho chili powder

½ tsp cumin, ground

1 tsp sweet paprika

1 cup+ breadcrumbs

Method

Wash and drain the black beans until dry. Add to food processor. Add the seasonings and spices and pulse until minced.

Transfer black bean mince to a bowl.

Add the diced/ chopped peppers, scallions, chili etc.

Add salt only at the last minute before cooking the burgers.

Add in half the bread crumbs and mix. Add more breadcrumbs as needed later.

Refrigerate patty mix for half an hour or more.

Apply some water or oil to your hands and form patties.

Cook them on a hot grill, a few minutes on each side.

Add a slice of pepperjack cheese or cheese of choice on top of the patty.

To serve the burger

Squirt chipotle sour cream on one bun. Apply guacamole on the other bun.

Place patty on the bun.

Add sliced onion, tomato, lettuce etc.

Add pickled jalapenos and salsa.

Add some tortilla chips.

Place the bun with the guacamole on top.

Fiesta Black Bean Burger is ready to be served.

RECIPE - Mutton Rogan Josh Curry

Ingredients

250 g mutton cubes (lamb)

4 Tbsp ghee or clarified butter

4 pods green cardamom

4 cloves

1 inch cinnamon stick

1 tsp fennel seeds, crushed

2 bay leaf

1 Tbsp ginger, grated

1 large onion, slivered

½ cup plain yogurt

1 tsp Kashmiri chili powder or paprika

1 drop Kewra water (optional)

Salt to taste

Method

Add half the ghee to a thick bottomed pan or wok.

Fry the onions until brown. Remove with a slotted spoon and set aside.

Add the remaining ghee to the pot.

Add whole spices to the ghee and fry until aromatic and the cardamom pods split open. This can take a few seconds depending on how hot the ghee is.

Add the meat and fry for about 10 minutes until any fat is rendered.

Add the yogurt and fry until the yogurt dries up and is absorbed.

Now add onions and chili powder and fry for a minute.

Add one cup of water and the grated ginger. Add salt per taste.

Simmer on low heat for 10 minutes or more until meat is tender.

Add a drop of Kewra water or Kewra essence (optional). Be very careful with this since it is quite potent.

Serve with Naan or rice.

RECIPE – Cheesy Jalapeno eggs

Ingredients

6 large eggs

1 Tbsp sour cream

1 Tbsp butter

½ jalapeno pepper, deseeded and chopped fine

½ cup shredded cheese

Method

Crack eggs into bowl. Add a splash of water and sour cream and whisk until frothy.

Add a knob of butter to a pan.

As butter begins to melt, add in the jalapeno pepper. Fry until the pepper sizzles a bit and becomes aromatic.

Pour the whisked eggs into the pan.

Cook slowly on low heat, stirring occasionally.

Add in the cheese as eggs begin to set and switch off the heat.

Fold lightly a couple of times before serving.

RECIPE – Orange Tequila Grilled Chicken

Ingredients

4-6 boneless skinless chicken breasts

4 cloves garlic, crushed

1 cup orange juice

1 tsp orange zest

30-60 ml tequila

¼ cup olive oil

½ tsp dried oregano

½ tsp cumin, ground

½ tsp chili seasoning or

1-2 chipotles in adobo

1 Tbsp brown sugar

Salt to taste

Method

Marinate chicken breasts with all the ingredients for 4-6 hours or overnight.

Place the chicken breasts on hot grill and cook about 10-12 minutes on each side until done.

Serve with fresh lime and orange wedges and sides.

RECIPE - Cheese Pakora Fritters

Ingredients

8 ounce processed cheese/ mozzarella cheese

1 cup gram flour

¼ tsp turmeric, ground

Pinch of cayenne pepper

¼ tsp carom seeds or *Ajwain*

½ tsp baking soda

Pinch of baking powder

Salt to taste

Oil for deep frying

Method

Whisk all the flour and spices together. Add half a cup of water and more if needed to get a thick pancake like batter.

Add in the baking powder and set aside for 10 minutes. Add baking soda just before you are ready to fry the fritters.

Cube any hard cheese of choice. You can cut it in squares or sticks – any shape you want.

Heat oil in a wok for frying. When the oil is hot enough, you are ready to fry the pakora fritters.

Dip a piece of cheese in the batter, coat well and drop it in the hot oil. Fry for a few seconds until it puffs up slightly and becomes light brown. Use slotted spoon to transfer to plate.

Repeat the process for the rest of the cheese.

Serve cheese pakoras hot with ketchup or chili sauce.

Note – The batter should be thick enough to coat the cheese so that it doesn't burst open in the hot oil. The batter should not 'fall off' the cheese.

RECIPE - Anna's Avocado Toast

Anna Butler's version of avocado toast has a bit of jazz and plenty of crunch. And no, she isn't afraid of a little garlic!

Ingredients

4 bread slices

2 ripe avocadoes

2 cloves garlic

1 lime or lemon

Salt and pepper

2-4 tsp hot sauce/ pepper sauce

4 tsp+ Special Seed Mix

8-10 grape tomatoes, halved (optional)

Method

Scoop the flesh of two ripe avocadoes. Immediately squeeze lime or lemon juice over it to prevent browning. Mash with a fork and season well with salt and pepper.

Toast the bread until evenly brown and crisp.

Rub a clove of garlic over the slices of bread.

Generously spread the avocado mash on the slice of bread.

Sprinkle a spoonful of the seed mix on top.

Add a few dashes of hot sauce.

Add some grape tomatoes if you wish.

Cut in two and serve immediately.

Makes 4 avocado toasts – serves 2 or 4.

Anna's special Seed Mix

Anna makes this beforehand and stores it in an airtight container in a cool place.

Ingredients

¼ cup white sesame seeds

¼ cup black sesame seeds

¼ cup sunflower seeds

¼ cup pumpkin seeds

1 tsp vegetable oil

Method

Add a drop or two of oil in a pan. Toast the seeds one by one on a low flame until they are aromatic but not burnt.

Cool completely.

Mix well and store in an airtight container.

Sprinkle on salads, toast, noodles etc. to add some extra crunch and flavor.

Note – Anna likes to use whole grain or multigrain bread for her avocado toast.

RECIPE – Naughty Mama Cocktail

Ingredients

1/2 cup pineapple juice

1/2 cup guava juice or nectar

1/2 cup orange juice

1/2 banana

1/4 cup coconut cream

2 oz spiced rum or dark rum

2 oz white rum

2 cups ice

Method

Blend it all together and serve.

Wanna be Nice? Just leave the alcohol out!

RECIPE – Strawberry Grilled Cheese Recipe

Ingredients

4 slices bread

1 cup strawberries, sliced thick

1/4 cup balsamic vinegar

1 cup shredded mozzarella or 4-5 thick slices

1/4 cup smoked gouda

1/4 stick soft butter

1/4 cup fresh basil or arugula

balsamic reduction (optional)

Method

Core the strawberries and slice them thickly, about 4 slices per berry.

Soak in balsamic vinegar and marinate for 15-20 minutes.

Butter the bread and place slices of fresh mozzarella or a generous amount of shredded mozzarella on each slice.

Place the marinated strawberries on the cheese.

Add some fresh basil leaves or arugula leaves.

Add a layer of smoked gouda.

Cover with mozzarella cheese and the other slice of bread.

Grill on a pan or in a panini press until the cheese melts and the bread is crispy and browned to your liking.

Cut into two and serve with a drizzle of balsamic reduction.

Leena Clover

Join my Newsletter

Get access to exclusive bonus content, sneak peeks, giveaways and much more. Also get a chance to join my exclusive ARC group, the people who get first dibs on all my new books.

Sign up at the following link and join the fun.

Click here → http://www.subscribepage.com/leenaclovernl

I love to hear from my readers, so please feel free to connect with me at any of the following places.

Website – http://leenaclover.com

Facebook – http://facebook.com/leenaclovercozymysterybooks

Instagram – https://instagram.com/leenaclover

Email – leenaclover@gmail.com

Books by Leena Clover

Pelican Cove Cozy Mystery Series

Strawberries and Strangers – Pelican Cove Cozy Mystery Book 1

https://www.amazon.com/dp/B07CSW34GB/

Cupcakes and Celebrities – Pelican Cove Cozy Mystery Book 2

https://www.amazon.com/dp/B07CYX5TNR

Berries and Birthdays – Pelican Cove Cozy Mystery Book 3

https://www.amazon.com/gp/product/B07D7GG8KV

Sprinkles and Skeletons – Pelican Cove Cozy Mystery Book 4

https://www.amazon.com/dp/B07DW91NKG

Waffles and Weekends – Pelican Cove Cozy Mystery Book 5

https://www.amazon.com/dp/B07FRJ1FC1/

Muffins and Mobsters – Pelican Cove Cozy Mystery Book 6

https://www.amazon.com/dp/B07GRBCZG8/

Parfaits and Paramours – Pelican Cove Cozy Mystery Book 7

https://www.amazon.com/dp/B07K5G2DDJ

Truffles and Troubadours – Pelican Cove Cozy Mystery 8

https://www.amazon.com/dp/B07N6FQTK2/

Sundaes and Sinners

https://www.amazon.com/dp/B07PXYPNG5

Croissants and Cruises

https://www.amazon.com/dp/B082L2W6V2

Pancakes and Parrots

https://www.amazon.com/dp/B082H1DJ42

Cookies and Christmas

https://www.amazon.com/dp/B08FB1TTCJ

Dolphin Bay Cozy Mystery Series

Raspberry Chocolate Murder

Leena Clover

https://www.amazon.com/dp/B07VVQDGPN/

Orange Thyme Death

https://www.amazon.com/dp/B07W226H71

Apple Caramel Mayhem

https://www.amazon.com/dp/B07YN35K2Y

Cranberry Sage Miracle

https://www.amazon.com/dp/B08538MP3Z

Blueberry Chai Frenzy

https://www.amazon.com/dp/B08CTC9M5G

Meera Patel Cozy Mystery Series

Gone with the Wings – Meera Patel Cozy Mystery Book 1

https://www.amazon.com/dp/B071WHNM6K

A Pocket Full of Pie - Meera Patel Cozy Mystery Book 2

https://www.amazon.com/dp/B072Q7B47P/

For a Few Dumplings More - Meera Patel Cozy Mystery Book 3

https://www.amazon.com/dp/B072V3T2BV

Back to the Fajitas - Meera Patel Cozy Mystery Book 4

https://www.amazon.com/dp/B0748KPTLM

Christmas with the Franks – Meera Patel Cozy Mystery Book 5

https://www.amazon.com/gp/product/B077GXR4WS/

Printed in Great Britain
by Amazon